TALES OF MYSTER

General Editor:

AN ARSÈNE LUPIN
OMNIBUS

AN ARSÈNE LUPIN OMNIBUS

Maurice Leblanc

with an Introduction by
David Stuart Davies

WORDSWORTH EDITIONS

For my husband
Anthony John Ranson

with love from your wife, the publisher

*Eternally grateful for your unconditional
love, not just for me but for our children
Simon, Andrew and Nichola Trayler*

Customers interested in other titles from
Wordsworth Editions are invited to visit our
website at www.wordsworth-editions.com

For our latest list and a full mail order service contact
Bibliophile Books, Unit 5 Datapoint,
South Crescent, London E16 4TL
Tel: +44 020 74 74 24 74
Fax: +44 020 74 74 85 89
orders@bibliophilebooks.com

This edition published 2012 by Wordsworth Editions Limited
8B East Street, Ware, Hertfordshire SG12 9HJ

ISBN 978 1 84022 687 4

Wordsworth® is a registered trademark of
Wordsworth Editions Limited, the company
founded by Michael Trayler in 1987

Typeset in Great Britain by Roperford Editorial
Printed and bound by Clays Ltd, St Ives plc

CONTENTS

The Golden Triangle

The Eight Strokes of the Clock

INTRODUCTION

Arsène Lupin is a French character of tremendous style, dash, daring and panache, and is literature's greatest gentleman thief and detective. He was created by Maurice Leblanc (1864–1941) who was only moderately successful as a writer of short stories for various French periodicals when he published his first series of Lupin tales. In 1905 he was solicited to contribute a short story to be written in the manner of the Sherlock Holmes tales in the new periodical *Je Sais Tout* which was modelled on the *Strand* magazine, the spiritual home of Sherlock. The Holmes stories were not only popular and successful in Britain but also on the continent and Lupin was clearly encouraged to match the success of the British sleuth. Like Holmes, the roguish and glamorous Lupin was a surprise success, and fame and fortune beckoned Leblanc. In total, he went on to write twenty-one novels or collections of short stories featuring his charismatic hero.

Unlike Doyle's stories, Leblanc's are filled with spicy humour and often the plots veer towards burlesque. While there is mystery and danger running through the narratives, it would seem that Leblanc's main aim is to provide the reader with fun. Take this exchange from 'The Fair Haired Lady', the first episode in *Arsène Lupin versus Holmlock Shears*:

'Do you mean you are still a vegetarian?'
'Yes, more than ever,' said Lupin.
'From taste? Conviction? Habit?'
'For reasons of health.'
'And do you never break your rule?'
'Oh yes . . . when I go out to dinner, so as not to appear eccentric.'

Essentially Lupin is a thief, 'the Prince of Thieves' in fact, rivalling the British A. J. Raffles, E. G. Hornung's 'amateur cracksman', whose first appearance predated Lupin's by five years. But the Frenchmen is also a detective and is often involved in the solving of crimes as well as committing them, usually to prove his innocence.

Whenever he becomes involved in an intrigue, we know that some malefactor will receive his just desserts and Lupin will benefit from the affair by acquiring a precious trinket or some other financial reward. The American writer, Otto Penzler, one of the major commentators on crime fiction, summed up Lupin thus:

> A brilliant rogue, he pursues his career with carefree *élan*, mocking the law for the sheer joy of it, rather than for purely personal gain. Young, handsome, brave and quick-witted, he has a *joie de vivre* uniquely and recognisably French. His sense of humour and conceit make life difficult for the police, who attribute most of the major crimes in France to him and his gang of ruffians and urchins.

This Wordsworth collection features four of the many volumes starring this attractive, suave and charismatic anti-hero. Lupin first appeared in book form in *Arsène Lupin, Gentleman Cambrioleur* (1907), a collection of short stories originally published in *Je Sais Tout*. In one of these tales, 'Sherlock Holmes Arrives Too Late', Leblanc introduced the famous Baker Street detective into the mix. After legal objections from Conan Doyle about the use of his character, the name of the British master sleuth was changed to 'Herlock Sholmes' when the story appeared in book form. Sholmes returned in two more long stories collected in the second volume, *Arsène Lupin contre Herlock Sholmes*, which was published in the UK in 1909 under the title *Arsène Lupin versus Holmlock Shears*. This playing about with Holmes's name was fooling no one, but provided Leblanc with a loophole enabling him to carry on using the character.

Arsène Lupin versus Holmlock Shears is the first of the volumes presented to you in this collection. It features two long stories, the first of which finds Lupin in the typical situation of having perpetrated a theft but then being forced to defend himself from the charge of murder, an accusation that Holmlock Shears and his rather dull companion, Wilson, are determined to prove. The story, divided into six chapters and also known as 'The Fair-haired Lady', begins when an antique desk is stolen from a mathematics professor by Arsène Lupin. Later, both Lupin and the professor realise that a lottery ticket, left inadvertently in the desk, is the winning one and the key to a fortune. Lupin proceeds to ensure that he obtains half of the winnings while executing a near-impossible escape with the 'fair-haired lady'.

Following the theft of the famous Blue Diamond, Chief-inspector Ganimard, 'Lupin's implacable enemy', believes that Lupin and the fair-haired lady are involved in this crime also but fail to prove it. Ganimard is a wonderfully comic character. He is terminally incompetent and frustrated at every turn by the cunning Lupin. However, the policeman is so determined to catch his *bête noir* this time that he engages the services of the English detective, Holmlock Shears, the famous resident of 19 Parker Street. Inevitably Shears is more a match for Lupin than Ganimard and manages to engineer his arrest. Of course, the matter does not end there as you will discover, but throughout the author keeps the reader amused and mystified by turns. Leblanc does a brilliant job of lampooning Holmes and Watson as Shears and Wilson, a literary practice which has blossomed over the years since but was in its infancy at the time:

'Tell me, Wilson, what's your opinion: why was Lupin in the restaurant?'

Wilson, without hesitation, replied: 'To get some dinner.'

'Wilson, the longer we work together, the more clearly I perceive the constant progress you are making. Upon my word, you're becoming amazing.'

The second story in this first volume, 'The Jewish Lamp', opens with Holmlock Shears receiving a request from Baron Victor D'Imbervalle in Paris to solve the mystery of the theft of an old, apparently worthless, lamp. Indeed the lamp is worthless but it is the hiding place of a precious antique jewel. In the same post Shears is shocked to read a second letter, this time written by Lupin, warning him to 'have nothing to do with the case' because 'all your efforts would only bring about a pitiable result and you would be obliged publicly to acknowledge your defeat.' This advice is, of course, a red rag to a bull and Shears sets off for Paris immediately and thus commences another amusing and intriguing battle of wits between these two brilliant men of crime. This story is typical of the appeal of the Lupin stories, for while it moves with great pace, is witty and lively, it also has a clever page-turning mystery at the heart of the narrative. It is this, as much as the humour, which keeps the reader engrossed.

The Confessions of Arsène Lupin (1912) appears next in this collection. It is a wonderful set of ten short stories which in many ways present the real essence and appeal of Arsène Lupin. Each tale has Lupin in sparkling form: witty, brave, perceptive and always dominant. The plots are ingenious and help to show Lupin at his detective best – a real rival for Sherlock Holmes. As the man himself observes in 'The Red Silk Scarf':

Lupin juggles with inferences and deductions for all the world like a detective in a novel. My proofs are dazzling and absolutely simple.

It is true to say that in solving the crimes, he has at times remarkable prescience and knowledge which strains credulity somewhat. However that is what makes Lupin such a fantastic character in both senses of the word: slightly unbelievable but tremendous fun.

Chief Inspector Ganimard makes regular appearances in this particular set of stories and the rivalry between the two men reaches a satisfyingly comical height in 'The Red Silk Scarf'. It is in this tale that Lupin ingeniously arranges a meeting with the policeman to give him details and clues concerning a murder. Inevitably, there is a cunning purpose behind this apparent show of benevolence on Lupin's part and, equally inevitably, the Inspector is duped.

The third volume in this collection is the novel, *The Return of Arsène Lupin* (1917) (aka *The Golden Triangle*) which is a more complex and serious affair. This dramatic story chiefly concerns the mystery that surrounds the 'Little Mother Coralie', a volunteer nurse working in a military hospital in Paris, and Captain Patrice Belval, one of her patients who has lost a leg in the war. Lupin, who is believed to be dead, returns to help Belval and his beloved Coralie solve a murder, and Lupin helps them locate 300 million francs in gold that had been stolen by the cunning and evil Essarès Bey. The story is dark and very modern in tone; indeed the torture scene in Chapter Four is quite brutal and could easily feature in any current thriller.

When Lupin finally puts in an appearance – about half way through the novel – it is under the pseudonym of Don Luis Peranna – an anagram of Arsène Lupin. Lupin was a master of disguise. So much so that he actually became other characters and virtually changed identity in many of the stories. His alter-egos also include Prince Renine, Le Duc du Chamerace, Ralph de Limezy and Jim Barnett. This dazzling subterfuge not only baffles the police but the unwary reader also. In this story, as Peranna, Lupin adopts the role of avenging angel and solves the problems of Patrice and Coralie:

'There's no danger.'
'Why?'
'Because I'm here.'

Of course as events turn out, this arrogance is fully justified.

However, it is true to say that in this novel Leblanc presents the reader with a more serious Lupin, and clearly demonstrates how adept he is at creating an exciting and surprising page-turning plot. While we are waiting for the appearance of the hero, we are kept intrigued and challenged by the engaging storyline.

The fourth volume in this collection, *The Eight Strokes of the Clock* (1922), is a set of short stories which, as Leblanc tells us in his Author's Note, were related to him by Arsène Lupin himself 'as though they happened to a friend of his, Prince Renine' – although Leblanc adds, no doubt with a twinkle in the eye and tongue in cheek, 'I find it very difficult not to identify the two friends as one and the same person . . . The reader will judge for himself.' The stories, though separate, are linked by means of a clever device. In the first tale, 'On the Top of the Tower', Renine/Lupin restores a dowry fortune to young Hortense Daniel while providing her with an exciting adventure into the bargain. When she asks how she can repay him for his kindness, he comes up with a most unusual suggestion.

'Become the companion of my adventures. If anyone calls on me for help, help him with me. If chance or instinct puts me on the track of crime or the trace of a sorrow, let us both set out together. Do you consent?'

Of course she does consent – the bargain is set for three months – and the remaining seven stories recount their exploits together as a charming detective duo. Of course, the inevitable happens, as one assumes Lupin knew it would: Hortense begins to fall in love with him. It would be treacherous of me to reveal what happens at the conclusion of the final adventure. You must find out for yourself. The stories in this series are clever and beguiling, rather like a blend of the storytelling of Guy De Maupassant and Conan Doyle. Why they are not better known and respected is a shame and a mystery.

Together these four volumes demonstrate the range and scope of the Lupin stories, their brilliance in combining adventure, mystery and thrills with fun, while the quality of Leblanc's writing never falters. And although Lupin remains an elusive character to the authorities, to the reader he steps off the page as a living, breathing, vivid character with charisma and personality.

Arsène Lupin has had a varied movie career, starring in numerous silent films and a number of continental features as well as three Hollywood talkies. Most notably, John Barrymore appeared in the title role for MGM's *Arsène Lupin* (1932), with his brother Lionel playing Ganimard. The film was based on a play by Leblanc and Francis de Croisset in which Lupin announces that he will steal a famous painting from the Louvre under the nose of the police. *Arsène Lupin Returns* (1938) was another MGM movie, this time with Melvyn Douglas as the master thief. The signature of Arsène Lupin, long thought dead, is scrawled across a safe from which a precious necklace has been stolen; the real Lupin, innocent and living quietly as a country gentleman, sets out to clear his name.

Enter Arsène Lupin (Universal, 1944) moved into B movie territory with Charles Korvin as Lupin in a plot which involved the master thief stealing an emerald from a young heiress; but he returns it when he begins to suspect that the girl's aunt and uncle plan to murder her. There were several French films made for the domestic market even as late as the 1950s. Lupin's last film escapade to date was a French/German collaboration: Jean-Paul Salome's mega-budget *Arsène Lupin* (*2004*), starring Romain Duris and Kristin Scott Thomas which in the eyes of most critics was disappointing in that it failed to capture the wit and insouciance of the character. Perhaps in time some enterprising film-maker will have more success in attempting to bring the top-hatted fellow in the swirling cape, with the mischievous twinkle in his eye, back to the screen – the real Arsène Lupin, that is. While you are waiting for that moment to arrive, you have the pleasure and delight of encountering this most charming of scoundrels in your own cinema of the mind as you read and enjoy the treats in store in this volume.

DAVID STUART DAVIES

ARSÈNE LUPIN VERSUS
HOLMLOCK SHEARS

First Episode:
The Fair-Haired Lady

Chapter 1

Number 514, Series 23

On the 8th of December last, M. Gerbois, professor of mathematics at Versailles College, rummaging among the stores at a second-hand dealer's, discovered a small mahogany writing-desk, which took his fancy because of its many drawers.

'That's just what I want for Suzanne's birthday,' he thought.

M. Gerbois' means were limited and, anxious as he was to please his daughter, he felt it his duty to beat the dealer down. He ended by paying sixty-five francs. As he was writing down his address, a well-groomed and well-dressed young man, who had been hunting through the shop in every direction, caught sight of the writing-desk and asked: 'How much for this?'

'It's sold,' replied the dealer.

'Oh . . . to this gentleman?'

M. Gerbois bowed and, feeling all the happier that one of his fellow-men envied him his purchase, left the shop. But he had not taken ten steps in the street before the young man caught him up and, raising his hat, said, very politely: 'I beg a thousand pardons, sir . . . I am going to ask you an indiscreet question . . . Were you looking for this desk rather than anything else?'

'No. I went to the shop to see if I could find a cheap set of scales for my experiments.'

'Therefore, you do not want it very particularly?'

'I want it, that's all.'

'Because it's old I suppose?'

'Because it's useful.'

'In that case, would you mind exchanging it for another desk, quite as useful, but in better condition?'

'This one is in good condition and I see no point in exchanging it.'

'Still . . .'

M. Gerbois was a man easily irritated and quick to take offence. He replied, curtly: 'I must ask you to drop the subject, sir.'

The young man placed himself in front of him.

'I don't know how much you paid, sir . . . but I offer you double the price.'

'No, thank you.'

'Three times the price.'

'Oh, that will do,' exclaimed the professor, impatiently. 'The desk belongs to me and is not for sale.'

The young man stared at him, with a look that remained imprinted on M. Gerbois' memory, then turned on his heel, without a word, and walked away.

An hour later, the desk was brought to the little house on the Viroflay Road where the professor lived. He called his daughter.

'This is for you, Suzanne; that is, if you like it.'

Suzanne was a pretty creature, of a demonstrative temperament and easily pleased. She threw her arms round her father's neck and kissed him as rapturously as though he had made her a present fit for a queen.

That evening, assisted by Hortense the maid, she carried up the desk to her room, cleaned out the drawers and neatly put away her papers, her stationery, her correspondence, her picture postcards and a few secret souvenirs of her cousin Philippe.

M. Gerbois went to the college at half-past seven the next morning. At ten o'clock, Suzanne, according to her daily custom, went to meet him at the exit; and it was a great pleasure to him to see her graceful, smiling figure waiting on the pavement opposite the gate.

They walked home together.

'And how do you like the desk?'

'Oh, it's lovely! Hortense and I have polished up the brass handles till they shine like gold.'

'So you're pleased with it?'

'I should think so! I don't know how I did without it all this time.'

They walked up the front garden. The professor said: 'Let's go and look at it before lunch.'

'Yes, that's a good idea.'

She went up the stairs first, but, on reaching the door of her room, she gave a cry of dismay.

'What's the matter?' exclaimed M. Gerbois.

He followed her into the room. The writing-desk was gone.

*   *   *

What astonished the police was the wonderful simplicity of the means employed. While Suzanne was out and the maid making her purchases for the day, a ticket-porter, wearing his badge, had stopped his cart before the garden, in sight of the neighbours, and rung the bell twice. The neighbours, not knowing that the servant had left the house, suspected nothing, so that the man was able to effect his object absolutely undisturbed.

This fact must be noted: not a cupboard had been broken open, not so much as a clock displaced. Even Suzanne's purse, which she had left on the marble slab of the desk, was found on the adjacent table, with the gold which it contained. The object of the theft was clearly determined, therefore, and this made it the more difficult to understand; for, after all, why should a man run so great a risk to secure so trivial a spoil?

The only clue which the professor could supply was the incident of the day before.

'From the first, that young man displayed a keen annoyance at my refusal; and I have a positive impression that he left me under a threat.'

It was all very vague. The dealer was questioned. He knew neither of the two gentlemen. As for the desk, he had bought it for forty francs at Chevreuse, at the sale of a person deceased, and he considered that he had re-sold it at a fair price. A persistent inquiry revealed nothing further.

But M. Gerbois remained convinced that he had suffered an enormous loss. A fortune must have been concealed in some secret drawer and that was why the young man, knowing of the hiding-place, had acted with such decision.

'Poor father! What should we have done with the fortune?' Suzanne kept saying.

'What! Why, with that for your dowry, you could have made the finest match going!'

Suzanne aimed at no one higher than her cousin Philippe, who had not a penny to bless himself with, and she gave a bitter sigh. And life in the little house at Versailles went on less gaily, less carelessly than before, shadowed over as it now was with regret and disappointment.

Two months elapsed. And suddenly, one after the other, came a sequence of the most serious events, forming a surprising run of alternate luck and misfortune.

On the 1st of February, at half-past five, M. Gerbois, who had just come home, with an evening paper in his hand, sat down, put on his spectacles and began to read. The political news was uninteresting. He turned the page and a paragraph at once caught his eye, headed:

THIRD DRAWING OF THE
PRESS-ASSOCIATION
LOTTERY

First prize, 1,000,000 francs
No. 514, Series 23

The paper dropped from his hands. The walls swam before his eyes and his heart stopped beating. Number 514, series 23 was the number of his ticket! He had bought it by accident, to oblige one of his friends, for he did not believe in luck; and now he had won!

He took out his memorandum-book, quick! He was quite right: number 514, series 23 was jotted down on the fly-leaf. But where was the ticket?

He flew to his study to fetch the box of stationery in which he had put the precious ticket away; and he stopped short as he entered and staggered back, with a pain at his heart: the box was not there and – what an awful thing! – he suddenly realized that the box had not been there for weeks.

'Suzanne! Suzanne!'

She had just come in and ran up the stairs hurriedly. He stammered, in a choking voice: 'Suzanne . . . the box . . . the box of stationery . . . '

'Which one?'

'The one I bought at the Louvre . . . on a Thursday . . . it used to stand at the end of the table.'

'But don't you remember, father? . . . We put it away together . . . '

'When?'

'That evening . . . you know, the day before . . . '

'But where? . . . Quick, tell me . . . it's more than I can bear . . . '

'Where? . . . In the writing-desk.'

'In the desk that was stolen?'

'Yes.'

'In the desk that was stolen!'

He repeated the words in a whisper, with a sort of terror. Then he took her hand, and lower still: 'It contained a million, Suzanne . . . '

'Oh, father, why didn't you tell me?' she murmured innocently.

'A million!' he repeated. 'It was the winning number in the press lottery.'

The hugeness of the disaster crushed them and, for a long time, they maintained a silence which they had not the courage to break. At last, Suzanne said: 'But, father, they will pay you all the same.'

'Why? On what evidence?'

'Does it require evidence?'

'Of course!'

'And have you none?'

'Yes, I have.'

'Well?'

'It was in the box.'

'In the box that has disappeared?'

'Yes. And the other man will get the money.'

'Why, that would be outrageous! Surely, father, you can stop the payment?'

'Who knows? Who knows? That man must be extraordinarily clever! He has such wonderful resources . . . Remember . . . think how he got hold of the desk . . .'

His energy revived; he sprang up and, stamping his foot on the floor.

'No, no, no,' he shouted, 'he shan't have that million, he shan't! Why should he? After all, sharp as he may be, he can do nothing either. If he calls for the money, they'll lock him up! Ah, we shall see, my friend!'

'Have you thought of something, father?'

'I shall defend our rights to the bitter end, come what may! And we shall succeed! . . . The million belongs to me and I mean to have it!'

A few minutes later, he dispatched this telegram.

GOVERNOR, CRÉDIT FONCIER, RUE CAPUCINES, PARIS
AM OWNER NUMBER 514, SERIES 23, OPPOSE BY EVERY LEGAL
METHOD PAYMENT TO ANY OTHER PERSON.

GERBOIS

At almost the same time, the Crédit Foncier received another telegram.

NUMBER 514, SERIES 23 IS IN MY POSSESSION.

ARSÈNE LUPIN

* * *

Whenever I sit down to tell one of the numberless adventures which compose the life of Arsène Lupin, I feel a genuine embarrassment, because it is quite clear to me that even the least important of these adventures is known to every one of my readers. As a matter of fact, there is not a move on the part of 'our national thief', as he has been happily called, but has been described all over the country, not an exploit but has been studied from every point of view, not an action but has been commented upon with an abundance of detail generally reserved for stories of heroic deeds.

Who, for instance, does not know that strange case of the fair-haired lady, with the curious episodes which were reported under flaring headlines as 'NUMBER 514, SERIES 23!' . . . 'THE MURDER IN THE AVENUE HENRI-MARTIN!' . . . and 'THE BLUE DIAMOND!' . . . What an excitement there was about the intervention of Holmlock Shears, the famous English detective! What an effervescence surrounded the varying fortunes that marked the struggle between those two great artists! And what a din along the boulevards on the day when the newsboys shouted: 'Arrest of Arsène Lupin!'

My excuse is that I can supply something new: I can furnish the key to the puzzle. There is always a certain mystery about these adventures: I can dispel it. I reprint articles that have been read over and over again; I copy out old interviews: but all these things I rearrange and classify and put to the exact test of truth. My collaborator in this work is Arsène Lupin himself, whose kindness to me is inexhaustible. I am also under an occasional obligation to the unspeakable Wilson, the friend and confidant of Holmlock Shears.

My readers will remember the Homeric laughter that greeted the publication of the two telegrams. The name of Arsène Lupin alone was a guarantee of originality, a promise of amusement for the gallery. And the gallery, in this case, was the whole world.

An inquiry was immediately set on foot by the Crédit Foncier and it was ascertained that number 514, series 23 had been sold by the Versailles branch of the Crédit Lyonnais to Major Bressy of the artillery. Now the major had died of a fall from his horse; and it appeared that he told his brother officers, some time before his death, that he had been obliged to part with his ticket to a friend.

'That friend was myself,' declared M. Gerbois.

'Prove it,' objected the governor of the Crédit Foncier.

'Prove it? That's quite easy. Twenty people will tell you that I kept up constant relations with the major and that we used to meet at the café on the Place d'Armes. It was there that, one day, to oblige him in a moment of financial embarrassment, I took his ticket off him and gave him twenty francs for it.'

'Have you any witnesses to the transaction?'

'No.'

'Then upon what do you base your claim?'

'Upon the letter which he wrote me on the subject.'

'What letter?'

'A letter pinned to the ticket.'

'Produce it.'

'But it was in the stolen writing-desk!'

'Find it.'

The letter was communicated to the press by Arsène Lupin. A paragraph inserted in the *Écho de France* – which has the honour of being his official organ and in which he seems to be one of the principal shareholders – announced that he was placing in the hands of Maître Detinan, his counsel, the letter which Major Bressy had written to him, Lupin, personally.

There was a burst of delight: Arsène Lupin was represented by counsel! Arsène Lupin, respecting established customs, had appointed a member of the bar to act for him!

The reporters rushed to interview Maître Detinan, an influential radical deputy, a man endowed with the highest integrity and a mind of uncommon shrewdness, which was, at the same time, somewhat sceptical and given to paradox.

Maître Detinan was exceedingly sorry to say that he had never had the pleasure of meeting Arsène Lupin, but he had, in point of fact, received his instructions, was greatly flattered at being selected, keenly alive to the honour shown him and determined to defend his client's rights to the utmost. He opened his brief and without hesitation, showed the major's letter. It proved the sale of the ticket, but did not mention the purchaser's name. It began, 'My dear friend', simply.

' "My dear friend" means me,' added Arsène Lupin, in a note enclosing the major's letter. 'And the best proof is that I have the letter.'

The bevy of reporters at once flew off to M. Gerbois, who could do nothing but repeat: ' "My dear friend" is no one but myself. Arsène Lupin stole the major's letter with the lottery-ticket.'

'Tell him to prove it,' was Lupin's rejoinder to the journalists.

'But he stole the desk!' exclaimed M. Gerbois in front of the same journalists.

'Tell him to prove it!' retorted Lupin once again.

And a delightful entertainment was provided for the public by this duel between the two owners of number 514, series 23, by the constant coming and going of the journalists and by the coolness of Arsène Lupin as opposed to the frenzy of poor M. Gerbois.

Unhappy man! The press was full of his lamentations! He confessed the full extent of his misfortunes in a touchingly ingenuous way.

'It's Suzanne's dowry, gentlemen, that the villain has stolen! . . . For myself, personally, I don't care; but for Suzanne! Just think, a million! Ten hundred thousand francs! Ah, I always said the desk contained a treasure!'

He was told in vain that his adversary, when taking away the desk, knew nothing of the existence of a lottery-ticket and that, in any case, no one could have foreseen that this particular ticket would win the first prize. All he did was to moan: 'Don't talk to me, of course he knew! . . . If not, why should he have taken the trouble to steal that wretched desk?'

'For unknown reasons, but certainly not to get hold of a scrap of paper which, at that time, was worth the modest sum of twenty francs.'

'The sum of a million! He knew it . . . He knows everything! . . . Ah, you don't know the sort of man he is, the ruffian! . . . He hasn't defrauded you of a million, you see! . . . '

This talk could have gone on a long time yet. But, twelve days later, M. Gerbois received a letter from Arsène Lupin, marked 'Private and confidential', which worried him not a little.

DEAR SIR

The gallery is amusing itself at our expense. Do you not think that the time has come to be serious? I, for my part, have quite made up my mind.

The position is clear: I hold a ticket which I am not entitled to cash and you are entitled to cash a ticket which you do not hold. Therefore neither of us can do anything without the other.

Now you would not consent to surrender *your* rights to *me* nor I to give up *my* ticket to *you*.

What are we to do?

I see only one way out of the difficulty: let us divide. Half a million for you, half a million for me. Is not that fair? And would not this judgment of Solomon satisfy the sense of justice in each of us?

I propose this as an equitable solution, but also an immediate solution. It is not an offer which you have time to discuss, but a necessity before which circumstances compel you to bow. I give you three days for reflection. I hope that, on Friday morning, I may have the pleasure of seeing a discreet advertisement in the agony-column of the *Écho de France*, addressed to 'M. Ars. Lup.' and containing, in veiled terms, your unreserved assent to the compact which I am suggesting to you. In that event, you will at once recover possession of the ticket and receive the million, on the understanding that you will hand me five hundred thousand francs in a way which I will indicate hereafter.

Should you refuse, I have taken measures that will produce exactly the same result; but, apart from the very serious trouble which your obstinacy would bring upon you, you would be the poorer by twenty-five thousand francs, which I should have to deduct for additional expenses.

I am, dear Sir,

very respectfully yours,

ARSÈNE LUPIN

M. Gerbois, in his exasperation, was guilty of the colossal blunder of showing this letter and allowing it to be copied. His indignation drove him to every sort of folly.

'Not a penny! He shall not have a penny!' he shouted before the assembled reporters. 'Share what belongs to me? Never! Let him tear up his ticket if he likes!'

'Still, half a million francs is better than nothing.'

'It's not a question of that, but of my rights; and those rights I shall establish in a court of law.'

'Go to law with Arsène Lupin? That would be funny!'

'No, but with the Crédit Foncier. They are bound to hand me the million.'

'Against the ticket or at least against evidence that you bought it.'

'The evidence exists, seeing that Arsène Lupin admits that he stole the desk.'

'What judge is going to take Arsène Lupin's word?'

'I don't care, I shall go to law!'

The gallery was delighted. Bets were made, some people being certain that Lupin would bring M. Gerbois to terms, others that he would not go beyond threats. And people felt a sort of apprehension; for the adversaries were unevenly matched, the one being so fierce in his attacks, while the other was as frightened as a hunted deer.

On Friday, there was a rush for the *Écho de France* and the agony-column on the fifth page was scanned with feverish eyes. There was not a line addressed to 'M. Ars. Lup.' M. Gerbois had replied to Arsène Lupin's demands with silence. It was a declaration of war.

That evening, the papers contained the news that Mlle Gerbois had been kidnapped.

* * *

The most delightful factor in what I may call the Arsène Lupin entertainment is the eminently ludicrous part played by the police. Everything passes outside their knowledge. Lupin speaks, writes, warns, orders, threatens, carries out his plans, as though there were no police, no detectives, no magistrates, no impediment of any kind in existence. They seem of no account to him whatever. No obstacle enters into his calculations.

And yet the police struggle to do their best. The moment the name of Arsène Lupin is mentioned, the whole force, from top to bottom, takes fire, boils and foams with rage. He is the enemy, the enemy who mocks you, provokes you, despises you, or, even worse, ignores you. And what can one do against an enemy like that?

According to the evidence of the servant, Suzanne went out at twenty minutes to ten. At five minutes past ten, her father, on leaving the college, failed to see her on the pavement where she usually waited for him. Everything, therefore, must have taken place in the course of the short twenty minutes' walk which brought Suzanne from her door to the college, or at least quite close to the college.

Two neighbours declared that they had passed her about three hundred yards from the house. A lady had seen a girl walking along the avenue whose description corresponded with Suzanne's. After that, all was blank.

Enquiries were made on every side. The officials at the railway-stations and the customs-barriers were questioned. They had seen nothing on that day which could relate to the kidnapping of a young girl. However, a grocer at Ville-d'Avray stated that he had supplied a closed motor-car, coming from Paris, with petrol. There was a chauffeur on the front seat and a lady with fair hair – exceedingly fair hair, the witness said – inside. The car returned from Versailles an hour later. A block in the traffic compelled it to slacken speed and the grocer was able to perceive that there was now another lady seated beside the fair-haired lady whom he had seen first. This second lady was wrapped up in veils and shawls. No doubt, it was Suzanne Gerbois.

Consequently, the abduction must have taken place in broad daylight, on a busy road, in the very heart of the town! How? At what spot? Not a cry had been heard, not a suspicious movement observed.

The grocer described the car, a Peugeon limousine, 24 horse-power, with a dark-blue body. Enquiries were made, on chance, of Mme Bob-Walthour, the manageress of the Grand Garage, who used to make a speciality of motor-car elopements. She had, in fact, on Friday morning, hired out a Peugeon limousine for the day to a fair-haired lady, whom she had not seen since.

'But the driver?'

'He was a man called Ernest, whom I engaged the day before on the strength of his excellent testimonials.'

'Is he here?'

'No, he brought back the car and has not been here since.'

'Can't we get hold of him?'

'Certainly, by applying to the people who recommended him. I will give you the addresses.'

The police called on these persons. None of them knew the man called Ernest.

And every trail which they followed to find their way out of the darkness led only to greater darkness and denser fogs.

M. Gerbois was not the man to maintain a contest which had opened in so disastrous a fashion for him. Inconsolable at the disappearance of his daughter and pricked with remorse, he capitulated. An advertisement which appeared in the *Écho de France* and aroused general comment proclaimed his absolute and unreserved surrender. It was a complete defeat: the war was over in four times twenty-four hours.

Two days later, M. Gerbois walked across the court-yard of the Crédit Foncier. He was shown in to the governor and handed him number 514, series 23. The governor gave a start.

'Oh, so you have it? Did they give it back to you?'

'I mislaid it and here it is,' replied M. Gerbois.

'But you said . . . There was a question . . . '

'That's all lies and tittle-tattle.'

'But nevertheless we should require some corroborative document.'

'Will the major's letter do?'

'Certainly.'

'Here it is.'

'Very well. Please leave these papers with us. We are allowed a fortnight in which to verify them. I will let you know when you can call for the money. In the meanwhile, I think that you would be well-advised to say nothing and to complete this business in the most absolute silence.'

'That is what I intend to do.'

M. Gerbois did not speak, nor the governor either. But there are certain secrets which leak out without any indiscretion having been committed and the public suddenly learnt that Arsène Lupin had had the pluck to send number 514, series 23 back to M. Gerbois! The news was received with a sort of stupefied admiration. What a bold player he must be, to fling so important a trump as the precious ticket upon the table! True, he had parted with it wittingly, in exchange for a card which equalized the chances. But suppose the girl escaped? Suppose they succeeded in recapturing his hostage?

The police perceived the enemy's weak point and redoubled their efforts. With Arsène Lupin disarmed and despoiled by himself, caught in his own toils, receiving not a single sou of the coveted million . . . the laugh would at once be on the other side.

But the question was to find Suzanne. And they did not find her, nor did she escape!

'Very well,' people said, 'that's settled: Arsène has won the first game. But the difficult part is still to come! Mlle Gerbois is in his hands, we admit, and he will not hand her over without the five hundred thousand francs. But how and where is the exchange to take place? For the exchange to take place, there must be a meeting; and what is to prevent M. Gerbois from informing the police and thus both recovering his daughter and keeping the money?'

The professor was interviewed. Greatly cast down, longing only for silence, he remained impenetrable.

'I have nothing to say; I am waiting.'

'And Mlle Gerbois?'

'The search is being continued.'

'But Arsène Lupin has written to you?'

'No.'

'Do you swear that?'

'No.'

'That means yes. What are his instructions?'

'I have nothing to say.'

Maître Detinan was next besieged and showed the same discretion.

'M. Lupin is my client,' he replied, with an affectation of gravity. 'You will understand that I am bound to maintain the most absolute reserve.'

All these mysteries annoyed the gallery. Plots were evidently hatching in the dark. Arsène Lupin was arranging and tightening the meshes of his nets, while the police were keeping up a watch by day and night round M. Gerbois. And people discussed the only three possible endings: arrest, triumph, or grotesque and pitiful failure.

But, as it happened, public curiosity was destined to be only partially satisfied; and the exact truth is revealed for the first time in these pages.

On Thursday the 12th of March, M. Gerbois received the notice from the Crédit Foncier, in an ordinary envelope.

At one o'clock on Friday, he took the train for Paris. A thousand notes of a thousand francs each were handed to him at two.

While he was counting them over, one by one, with trembling hands – for was this money not Suzanne's ransom? – two men sat talking in a cab drawn up at a short distance from the main entrance. One of these men had grizzled hair and a powerful face, which contrasted oddly with his dress and bearing, which was that of a small clerk. It was Chief-Inspector Ganimard, old Ganimard, Lupin's implacable enemy. And Ganimard said to Detective-Sergeant Folenfant: 'The old chap won't be long . . . we shall see him come out in five minutes. Is everything ready?'

'Quite.'

'How many are we?'

'Eight, including two on bicycles.'

'And myself, who count as three. It's enough, but not too many. That Gerbois must not escape us at any price . . . if he does, we're diddled: he'll meet Lupin at the place they have agreed upon; he'll swap the young lady for the half a million; and the trick's done.'

'But why on earth won't the old chap act with us? It would be so simple! By giving us a hand in the game, he could keep the whole million.'

'Yes, but he's afraid. If he tries to jockey the other, he won't get his daughter back.'

'What other?'

'Him.'

Ganimard pronounced this word 'him' in a grave and rather awe-struck tone, as though he were speaking of a supernatural being who had already played him a nasty trick or two.

'It's very strange,' said Sergeant Folenfant, judiciously, 'that we should be reduced to protecting that gentleman against himself.'

'With Lupin, everything is upside down,' sighed Ganimard.

A minute elapsed.

'Look out!' he said.

M. Gerbois was leaving the bank. When he came to the end of the Rue des Capucines, he turned down the boulevards, keeping to the left-hand side. He walked away slowly, along the shops, and looked into the windows.

'Our friend's too quiet,' said Ganimard. 'A fellow with a million in his pocket does not keep so quiet as all that.'

'What can he do?'

'Oh, nothing, of course . . . No matter, I mistrust him. It's Lupin, Lupin . . . '

At that moment, M. Gerbois went to a kiosk, bought some newspapers, took his change, unfolded one of the sheets and, with out-stretched arms, began to read, while walking on with short steps. And, suddenly, with a bound, he jumped into a motor-cab which was waiting beside the kerb. The power must have been on, for the car drove off rapidly, turned the corner of the Madeleine and disappeared.

'By Jupiter!' cried Ganimard. 'Another of his inventions!'

He darted forward and other men, at the same time as himself, ran round the Madeleine. But he burst out laughing. The motor-car had broken down at the beginning of the Boulevard Malesherbes and M. Gerbois was getting out.

'Quick, Folenfant . . . the driver . . . perhaps it's the man called Ernest.'

Folenfant tackled the chauffeur. It was a man called Gaston, one of the motor-cab company's drivers; a gentleman had engaged him ten minutes before and had told him to wait by the newspaper kiosk, 'with steam up', until another gentleman came.

'And what address did the second fare give?' asked Folenfant.

'He gave me no address . . . "Boulevard Malesherbes . . . Avenue de Messine . . . give you an extra tip": that's all he said.'

During this time, however, M. Gerbois, without losing a minute, had sprung into the first passing cab.

'Drive to the Concorde tube-station!'

The professor left the tube at the Place du Palais-Royal, hurried into another cab and drove to the Place de la Bourse. Here he went by tube again, as far as the Avenue de Villiers, where he took a third cab.

'25, Rue Clapeyron!'

No. 25, Rue Clapeyron, is separated from the Boulevard des Batignolles by the house at the corner. The professor went up to the first-floor and rang. A gentleman opened the door.

'Does Maître Detinan live here?'

'I am Maître Detinan. M. Gerbois, I presume?'

'That's it.'

'I was expecting you. Pray come in.'

When M. Gerbois entered the lawyer's office, the clock was striking three and he at once said: 'This is the time he appointed. Isn't he here?'

'Not yet.'

M. Gerbois sat down, wiped his forehead, looked at his watch as though he did not know the time and continued, anxiously: 'Will he come?'

The lawyer replied: 'You are asking me something, sir, which I myself am most curious to know. I have never felt so impatient in my life. In any case, if he comes, he is taking a big risk, for the house has been closely watched for the past fortnight . . . They suspect me.'

'And me even more,' said the professor. 'I am not at all sure that the detectives set to watch me have been thrown off my track.'

'But then . . .'

'It would not be my fault,' cried the professor, vehemently, 'and he can have nothing to reproach me with. What did I promise to do? To obey his orders. Well, I have obeyed his orders blindly: I cashed the ticket at the time which he fixed and came on to you in the manner which he ordered. I am responsible for my daughter's misfortune and I have kept my engagements in all good faith. It is for him to keep his.' And he added, in an anxious voice, 'He will bring back my daughter, won't he?'

'I hope so.'

'Still . . . you've seen him?'

'I? No. He simply wrote asking me to receive you both, to send away my servants before three o'clock and to let no one into my flat between the time of your arrival and his departure. If I did not consent to this proposal, he begged me to let him know by means of two lines in the *Écho de France*. But I am only too pleased to do Arsène Lupin a service and I consent to everything.'

M. Gerbois moaned: 'Oh dear, how will it all end?'

He took the bank-notes from his pocket, spread them on the table and divided them into two bundles of five hundred each. Then the two men sat silent. From time to time, M. Gerbois pricked up his ears: wasn't that a ring at the door-bell? . . . His anguish increased with every minute that passed. And Maître Detinan also experienced an impression that was almost painful.

For a moment, in fact, the advocate lost all his composure. He rose abruptly from his seat.

'We shan't see him . . . How can we expect to? . . . It would be madness on his part! He trusts us, no doubt: we are honest men, incapable of betraying him. But the danger lies elsewhere.'

And M. Gerbois, shattered, with his hands on the notes, stammered: 'If he would only come, oh, if he would only come! I would give all this to have Suzanne back.'

The door opened.

'Half will do, M. Gerbois.'

Someone was standing on the threshold – a young man, fashionably dressed – and M. Gerbois at once recognized the person who had accosted him outside the curiosity-shop. He leapt towards him.

'And Suzanne? Where is my daughter?'

Arsène Lupin closed the door carefully and, quietly unbuttoning his gloves, said to the lawyer.

'My dear maître, I can never thank you sufficiently for your kindness in consenting to defend my rights. I shall not forget it.'

Maître Detinan could only murmur: 'But you never rang . . . I did not hear the door . . . '

'Bells and doors are things that have to do their work without ever being heard. I am here all the same; and that is the great thing.'

'My daughter! Suzanne! What have you done with her?' repeated the professor.

'Heavens, sir,' said Lupin, 'what a hurry you're in! Come, calm yourself; your daughter will be in your arms in a moment.'

He walked up and down the room and then, in the tone of a magnate distributing praises: 'I congratulate you, M. Gerbois, on the skilful way in which you acted just now. If the motor hadn't had that ridiculous accident, we should simply have met at the Étoile and saved Maître Detinan the annoyance of this visit . . . However, it was destined otherwise!'

He caught sight of the two bundles of bank-notes and cried: 'Ah, that's right! The million is there! . . . Let us waste no time . . . Will you allow me?'

'But,' said Maître Detinan, placing himself in front of the table, 'Mlle Gerbois is not here yet.'

'Well?'

'Well, isn't her presence indispensable?'

'I see, I see! Arsène Lupin inspires only a partial confidence. He pockets his half million, without restoring the hostage. Ah, my dear maître, I am sadly misunderstood! Because fate has obliged me to perform acts of a rather . . . special character, doubts are cast upon my good faith . . . mine! I, a man all scruples and delicacy! . . . However, my dear maître, if you're afraid, open your window and call out. There are quite a dozen detectives in the street.'

'Do you think so?'

Arsène Lupin raised the blind.

'I doubt if M. Gerbois is capable of throwing Ganimard off the scent . . . What did I tell you? There he is, the dear old chap!'

'Impossible!' cried the professor. 'I swear to you, though . . . '

'That you have not betrayed me? . . . I don't doubt it, but the fellows are clever. Look, there's Folenfant! . . . And Gréaume! . . . And Dieuzy! . . . All my best pals, what?'

Maître Detinan looked at him in surprise. What calmness! He was laughing with a happy laugh, as though he were amusing himself at some child's game, with no danger threatening him.

This carelessness did even more than the sight of the detectives to reassure the lawyer. He moved away from the table on which the banknotes lay.

Arsène Lupin took up the two bundles one after the other, counted twenty-five notes from each of them and, handing the lawyer the fifty bank-notes thus obtained, said: 'M. Gerbois' share of your fee, my dear maître, and Arsène Lupin's. We owe you that.'

'You owe me nothing,' said Maître Detinan.

'What! After all the trouble we've given you!'

'You don't forget the pleasure it has been to me to take that trouble.'

'You mean to say, my dear maître, that you refuse to accept anything from Arsène Lupin. That's the worst,' he sighed, 'of having a bad reputation.' He held out the fifty thousand francs to the professor. 'Monsieur, let me give you this in memory of our pleasant meeting: it will be my wedding-present to Mlle Gerbois.'

M. Gerbois snatched at the notes, but protested: 'My daughter is not being married.'

'She can't be married if you refuse your consent. But she is dying to be married.'

'What do you know about it?'

'I know that young ladies often cherish dreams without Papa's consent. Fortunately, there are good geniuses, called Arsène Lupin, who discover the secret of those charming souls hidden away in their writing-desks.'

'Did you discover nothing else?' asked Maître Detinan. 'I confess that I am very curious to know why that desk was the object of your attentions.'

'Historical reasons, my dear maître. Although, contrary to M. Gerbois' opinion, it contained no treasure beyond the lottery-ticket, of which I did not know, I wanted it and had been looking for it for some time. The desk, which is made of yew and mahogany, decorated with acanthus-leaf capitals, was found in Marie Walewska's discreet little house at Boulogne-sur-Seine and has an inscription on one of the drawers: *"Dedicated to Napoleon I, Emperor of the French, by his most faithful servant, Mancion"*. Underneath are these words, carved with the point of a knife: *"Thine, Marie"*. Napoleon had it copied afterwards for the Empress Josephine, so that the writing-desk which people used to admire at the Malmaison and which they still admire at the Garde-Meuble is only an imperfect copy of the one which now forms part of my collection.'

M. Gerbois sighed.

'Oh dear! If I had only known this at the shop, how willingly I would have let you have it!'

Arsène Lupin laughed.

'Yes; and you would, besides, have had the appreciable advantage of keeping the whole of number 514, series 23 for yourself.'

'And you would not have thought of kidnapping my daughter, whom all this business must needs have upset.'

'All what business?'

'The abduction . . . '

'But, my dear sir, you are quite mistaken. Mlle Gerbois was not abducted.'

'My daughter was not abducted!'

'Not at all. Kidnapping, abduction implies violence. Now Mlle Gerbois acted as a hostage of her own free will.'

'Of her own free will!' repeated the professor, in confusion.

'And almost at her own request! Why, a quickwitted young lady like Mlle Gerbois, who, moreover, harbours a secret passion at the bottom of her heart, was hardly likely to refuse the opportunity of securing her dowry. Oh, I assure you it was easy enough to make her understand that there was no other way of overcoming your resistance!'

Maître Detinan was greatly amused. He put in: 'You must have found a difficulty in coming to terms. I can't believe that Mlle Gerbois allowed you to speak to her.'

'I didn't. I have not even the honour of knowing her. A lady of my acquaintance was good enough to undertake the negotiations.'

'The fair-haired lady in the motor-car, I suppose?' said Maître Detinan.

'Just so. Everything was settled at the first interview near the college. Since then, Mlle Gerbois and her new friend have been abroad, have visited Belgium and Holland in the most agreeable and instructive manner for a young girl. However, she will tell you everything herself . . . '

The hall-door bell rang: three rings in quick succession, then a single ring, then another single ring.

'There she is,' said Lupin. 'My dear maître, if you would not mind . . . '

The lawyer ran to open the door.

Two young women entered. One of them flung herself into M. Gerbois' arms. The other went up to Lupin. She was tall and shapely, with a very pale face, and her fair hair, which glittered like gold, was parted into two loosely-waved bandeaux. Dressed in black, wearing no ornament beyond a five-fold jet necklace, she nevertheless struck a note of elegance and refinement.

Arsène Lupin spoke a few words to her and then, bowing to Mlle Gerbois, said: 'I must apologize to you, mademoiselle, for all this annoyance; but I hope, nevertheless, that you have not been too unhappy . . . '

'Unhappy! I should even have been very happy, if it had not been for my poor father.'

'Then all is for the best. Embrace him once more and take the opportunity – you will never have a better – of speaking to him about your cousin.'

'My cousin? . . . What do you mean? . . . I don't understand . . . '

'Oh, I think you understand . . . Your cousin Philippe . . . the young man whose letters you kept so preciously . . . '

Suzanne blushed, lost countenance and then, taking Lupin's advice, threw herself once more into her father's arms.

Lupin looked at them both with a melting eye.

'Ah, we are always rewarded for doing good! What a touching sight! Happy father! Happy daughter! And to think that this happiness is your work, Lupin! Those two beings will bless you later . . . Your name will be piously handed down to their children and their children's children . . . Oh, family life! . . . Family life! . . . ' He turned to the window. 'Is our dear Ganimard there still? . . . How he would love to witness this charming display of affection! . . . But no, he is not there . . . There is nobody . . . they're all gone . . . By Jove, the position is growing serious! . . . I shouldn't wonder if they were in the gateway by now . . . or by the porter's lodge . . . or even on the stairs!'

M. Gerbois made an involuntary movement. Now that his daughter was restored to him, he began to see things in their true light. The arrest of his adversary meant half a million to him. Instinctively, he took a step towards the door . . . Lupin barred his way, as though by accident.

'Where are you going, M. Gerbois? To defend me against them? You are too kind! Pray don't trouble. Besides, I assure you they are more perplexed than I.' And he continued, reflectively, 'What do they know, when all is said? That you are here . . . and, perhaps, that Mlle Gerbois is here too, for they must have seen her come with an unknown lady. But they have no idea that I am here. How could I have entered a house which they searched this morning from cellar to garret? No, in all probability they are waiting for me to catch me on the wing . . . poor fellows! . . . Unless they have guessed that the unknown lady was sent by me and presume that she has been commissioned to effect the exchange . . . In that case, they are preparing to arrest her when she leaves . . . '

The bell rang.

Lupin stopped M. Gerbois with an abrupt gesture and, in a harsh and peremptory voice, said: 'Stay where you are, sir! Think of your daughter and be reasonable; if not . . . As for you, Maître Detinan, I have your word.'

M. Gerbois stood rooted to the floor. The lawyer did not move.

Lupin took up his hat without the least show of haste. There was a little dust on it; he brushed it with the back of his coat-sleeve.

'My dear maître, if I can ever be of use to you . . . My best wishes, Mlle Suzanne, and kind regards to M. Philippe.' He took a heavy gold hunter from his pocket. 'M. Gerbois, it is now eighteen minutes to four: I authorize you to leave this room at fourteen minutes to four . . . Not a moment before fourteen minutes to four . . . Is it understood?'

'But they'll enter by force!' Maître Detinan could not help saying.

'You forget the law, my dear maître! Ganimard would never dare to violate the sanctity of a Frenchman's home. We should have time for a pleasant rubber. But forgive me, you all three seem a little upset and I would not for the world abuse . . . '

He placed the watch on the table, opened the door of the room and, addressing the fair-haired lady, said: 'Shall we go, dear?'

He stood back for her to pass, made a parting and very respectful bow to Mlle Gerbois, walked out and closed the door after him. And they heard him, in the hall, saying aloud: 'Good-afternoon, Ganimard, how are you? Remember me very kindly to Mme Ganimard . . . I must drop in on her to lunch one of these days . . . Goodbye, Ganimard!'

The bell rang again, sharply, violently, followed by repeated knocks and by the sound of voices on the landing . . .

'A quarter to four,' stammered M. Gerbois.

After a few seconds, he stepped boldly into the hall. Arsène Lupin and the fair-haired lady were not there.

'Father! . . . You mustn't! . . . Wait!' cried Suzanne.

'Wait? You're mad! . . . Show consideration to that scoundrel! . . . And what about the half a million? . . . '

He opened the door.

Ganimard rushed in.

'Where's that lady? . . . And Lupin?'

'He was there . . . he is there now.'

Ganimard gave a shout of triumph.

'We've got him! . . . The house is surrounded.'

Maître Detinan objected: 'But the servants' staircase?'

'The servants' staircase leads to the court-yard and there's only one outlet, the front door: I have ten men watching it.'

'But he did not come in by the front door . . . He won't go out that way either . . . '

'Which way then?' jeered Ganimard. 'Through the air?'

He drew back a curtain. A long passage was revealed, leading to the kitchen. Ganimard ran down it and found that the door of the servants' staircase was double-locked.

Opening the window, he called to one of the detectives.

'Seen anyone?'

'No, sir.'

'Then,' he exclaimed, 'they are in the flat! . . . They are hiding in one of the rooms! . . . It is physically impossible for them to have escaped . . . Ah, Lupin, my lad, you did me once, but I'm having my revenge this time! . . . '

* * *

At seven o'clock in the evening, astonished at receiving no news, the head of the detective-service, M. Dudouis, called at the Rue Clapeyron in person. He put a few questions to the men who were watching the house and then went up to Maître Detinan, who took him to his room. There, he saw a man, or rather a man's two legs struggling on the carpet, while the body to which they belonged was stuffed up the chimney.

'Hi! . . . Hi! . . . ' yelped a stifled voice.

And a more distant voice, from right up above, echoed: 'Hi! . . . Hi! . . . '

M. Dudouis laughed and exclaimed: 'Well, Ganimard, what are you playing sweep for?'

The inspector withdrew his body from the chimney. He was un-recognizable, with his black face, his sooty clothes and his eyes glowing with fever.

'I'm looking for him,' he growled.

'For whom?'

'Arsène Lupin . . . Arsène Lupin and his lady friend.'

'But what next? You surely don't imagine they're hiding up the chimney?'

Ganimard rose to his feet, put his five soot-covered fingers on the sleeve of his superior's coat and, in a hollow, angry voice, said: 'Where would you have them be, chief? They must be somewhere. They are beings of flesh and blood, like you and me; they can't vanish into thin air.'

'No; but they vanish for all that.'

'Where? Where? The house is surrounded! There are men on the roof!'

'What about the next house?'

'There's no communication.'

'The flats on the other floors?'

'I know all the tenants. They have seen nobody. They have heard nobody.'

'Are you sure you know them all?'

'Everyone. The porter answers for them. Besides, as an additional precaution, I have posted a man in each flat.'

'We must find them, you know.'

'That's what I say, chief, that's what I say. We must and we shall, beeause they are both here . . . they can't be anywhere else. Be easy, chief; if I don't catch them tonight, I shall tomorrow . . . I shall spend the night here! . . . I shall spend the night here! . . . '

He did, in fact, spend the night there, and the next night and the night after that. And, when three whole days and three nights had elapsed, not only had he failed to discover the elusive Lupin and his no less elusive companion, but he had not even observed the slightest clue upon which to found the slightest supposition.

And that was why he refused to budge from his first opinion: 'Once there's no trace of their flight, they must be here!'

It is possible that, in the depths of his mind, he was less firmly convinced. But he refused to admit as much to himself. No, a thousand times no: a man and a woman do not vanish into space like the wicked genii in the fairy-tales! And, without losing courage, he continued his searchings and investigations, as though he hoped to discover them hidden in some impenetrable retreat, bricked up in the walls of the house.

Chapter 2

The Blue Diamond

On the evening of the 27th of March, old General Baron d'Hautrec, who had been French Ambassador in Berlin under the Second Empire, was sleeping comfortably in an easy-chair in the house which his brother had left him six months before, at 134, Avenue Henri-Martin. His lady companion continued to read aloud to him, while Soeur Auguste warmed the bed and prepared the night-light.

As an exceptional case, the sister was returning to her convent that evening, to spend the night with the Mother Superior, and, at eleven o'clock, she said: 'I'm finished now, Mlle Antoinette, and I'm going.'

'Very well, sister.'

'And don't forget that the cook is sleeping out tonight and that you are alone in the house with the man-servant.'

'You need have no fear for monsieur le baron: I shall sleep in the next room, as arranged, and leave the door open.'

The nun went away. A minute later, Charles, the man-servant, came in for his orders. The baron had woke up. He replied himself: 'Just the same as usual, Charles. Try the electric bell, to see if it rings in your bedroom properly, and, if you hear it during the night, run down at once and go straight to the doctor.'

'Are you still anxious, general?'

'I don't feel well . . . I don't feel at all well. Come, Mlle Antoinette, where were we in your book?'

'Aren't you going to bed, monsieur le baron?'

'No, no, I don't care to go to bed till very late; besides, I can do without help.'

Twenty minutes later, the old man dozed off again and Antoinette moved away on tip-toe.

At that moment, Charles was carefully closing the shutters on the ground-floor, as usual. In the kitchen, he pushed the bolt of the door that led to the garden and, in the front-hall, he not only locked the double door, but put up the chain fastening the two leaves.

Then he went up to his attic on the third-floor, got into bed and fell asleep.

Perhaps an hour had elapsed when, suddenly, he jumped out of bed: the bell was ringing. It went on for quite a long time, seven or eight seconds perhaps, and in a steady, uninterrupted way.

'That's all right.' said Charles, recovering his wits. 'Some fresh whim of the baron's, I suppose.'

He huddled on his clothes, ran down the stairs, stopped before the door and, from habit, knocked. No answer. He entered the room.

'Hullo!' he muttered. 'No light . . . What on earth have they put the light out for?' And he called, in a whisper, 'Mademoiselle! . . . '

No reply.

'Are you there, mademoiselle? . . . What's the matter? Is monsieur le baron ill?'

The same silence continued around him, a heavy silence that ended by impressing him. He took two steps forward: his foot knocked against a chair and, on touching it, he perceived that it was overturned. And thereupon his hand came upon other objects on the floor: a small table, a fire-screen. Greatly alarmed, he went back to the wall and felt for the electric switch. He found it and turned on the light.

In the middle of the room, between the table and the looking-glass wardrobe, lay the body of his master, the Baron d'Hautrec.

'What!' he stammered. 'Is it possible?'

He did not know what to do and, without moving, with his eyes starting from his head, he stood gazing at the general disorder of the room: the chairs upset, a great crystal candle-stick smashed into a thousand pieces, the clock lying on the marble hearth-stone, all signs of a fierce and hideous struggle. The handle of a little steel dagger gleamed near the body. The blade was dripping with blood. A handkerchief stained with red marks hung down from the mattress.

Charles gave a yell of horror: the body had suddenly stretched itself in one last effort and then shrunk up again . . . Two or three convulsions; and that was all.

He stooped forward. Blood was trickling from a tiny wound in the neck and spotting the carpet with dark stains. The face still wore an expression of mad terror.

'They've killed him,' he stammered, 'they've killed him!'

And he shuddered at the thought of another probable crime: was not the companion sleeping in the next room? And would not the baron's murderer have killed her too?

He pushed open the door: the room was empty. He concluded that either Antoinette had been carried off or that she had gone before the crime.

He returned to the baron's room and, his eyes falling upon the writing-desk, he observed that it had not been broken open. More remarkable still, he saw a handful of louis d'or on the table, beside the bunch of keys and the pocket-book which the baron placed there every evening. Charles took up the pocket-book and went through it. One of the compartments contained bank-notes. He counted them: there were thirteen notes of a hundred francs each.

Then the temptation became too strong for him: instinctively, mechanically, while his thoughts did not even take part in the movement of his hand, he took the thirteen notes, hid them in his jacket, rushed down the stairs, drew the bolt, unhooked the chain, closed the door after him and fled through the garden.

*   *   *

Charles was an honest man at heart. He had no sooner pushed back the gate than, under the influence of the fresh air, with his face cooled by the rain, he stopped. The deed of which he had been guilty appeared to him in its true light and struck him with sudden horror.

A cab passed. He hailed the driver.

'Hi, mate! Go to the police-station and bring back the commissary . . . Gallop! There's murder been done!'

The driver whipped up his horse. But, when Charles tried to go in again, he could not: he had closed the gate himself and the gate could not be opened from the outside.

On the other hand, it was of no use ringing, for there was no one in the house. He therefore walked up and down along the gardens which, at the La Muette end, line the avenue with a pleasant border of trim green shrubs. And it was not until he had waited for nearly an hour that he was at last able to tell the commissary the details of the crime and hand him the thirteen bank-notes.

During this time, a locksmith was sent for who, with great difficulty, succeeded in forcing the gate of the garden and the front-door. The commissary went upstairs and, at once, at the first glance, said to the servant: 'Why, you told me that the room was in the greatest disorder!'

He turned round. Charles seemed pinned to the threshold, hypnotized: all the furniture had resumed its usual place! The little table was standing between the two windows, the chairs were on their legs and the clock in the middle of the mantelpiece. The shivers of the smashed candle-stick had disappeared.

Gaping with stupor, he articulated: 'The body . . . Monsieur le baron . . .'

'Yes,' cried the commissary, 'where is the victim?'

He walked up to the bed. Under a large sheet, which he drew aside, lay General the Baron d'Hautrec, late French Ambassador in Berlin. His body was covered with his general's cloak, decorated with the cross of the Legion of Honour. The face was calm. The eyes were closed.

The servant stammered: 'Someone must have come.'

'Which way?'

'I can't say, but someone has been here during my absence . . . Look, there was a very thin steel dagger there, on the floor . . . And then, on the table, a blood-stained handkerchief . . . That's all gone . . . They've taken everything away . . . They've arranged everything . . .'

'But who?'

'The murderer!'

'We found all the doors closed.'

'He must have remained in the house.'

'Then he would be here still, as you never left the pavement.'

The man reflected and said, slowly: 'That's so . . . that's so . . . and I did not go far from the gate either . . . Still . . .'

'Let us see, who was the last person you saw with the baron?'

'Mlle Antoinette, the companion.'

'What has become of her?'

'I should say that, as her bed was not even touched, she must have taken advantage of Soeur Auguste's absence to go out also. It would only half surprise me if she had: she is young . . . and pretty . . .'

'But how could she have got out?'

'Through the door.'

'You pushed the bolt and fastened the chain!'

'A good deal later! By that time, she must have left the house.'

'And the crime was committed, you think, after she went?'

'Of course.'

They searched the house from top to bottom, from the garrets to the cellars; but the murderer had fled. How? When? Was it he or an accomplice who had thought proper to return to the scene of the crime and do away with anything that might have betrayed him? Those were the questions that suggested themselves to the police.

* * *

The divisional surgeon came upon the scene at seven o'clock, the head of the detective-service at eight. Next came the turn of the public prosecutor and the examining magistrate. In addition, the house was filled with policemen, inspectors, journalists, Baron d'Hautrec's nephew and other members of the family.

They rummaged about, they studied the position of the body, according to Charles's recollection, they questioned Soeur Auguste the moment she arrived. They discovered nothing. At most, Soeur Auguste was surprised at the disappearance of Antoinette Bréhat. She had engaged the girl twelve days before, on the strength of excellent references, and refused to believe that she could have abandoned the sick man confided to her care, to go running about at night alone.

'All the more so,' the examining magistrate insisted, 'as, in that case, she would have been in before now. We therefore come back to the same point: what has become of her?'

'If you ask me,' said Charles, 'she has been carried off by the murderer.'

The suggestion was plausible enough and fitted in with certain details. The head of the detective-service said: 'Carried off? Upon my word, it's quite likely.'

'It's not only unlikely,' said a voice, 'but absolutely opposed to the facts, to the results of the investigation, in short, to the evidence itself.'

The voice was harsh, the accent gruff and no one was surprised to recognize Ganimard. He alone, besides, would be forgiven that rather free and easy way of expressing himself.

'Hullo, is that you, Ganimard?' cried M. Dudouis. 'I hadn't seen you.'

'I have been here for two hours.'

'So you do take an interest in something besides number 514, series 23, the Rue Clapeyron mystery, the fair-haired lady and Arsène Lupin?'

'Hee, hee!' grinned the old inspector. 'I won't go so far as to declare that Lupin has nothing to do with the case we're engaged on . . . But let us dismiss the story of the lottery-ticket from our minds, until further orders, and look into this matter.'

*　　*　　*

Ganimard is not one of those mighty detectives whose proceedings form a school, as it were, and whose names will always remain inscribed on the judicial annals of Europe. He lacks the flashes of genius that illumine a Dupin, a Lecoq or a Holmlock Shears. But he possesses first-rate average qualities: perspicacity, sagacity, perseverance and even a certain amount of intuition. His greatest merit lies in the fact that he is absolutely independent of outside influences. Short of a kind of fascination which Arsène Lupin wields over him, he works without allowing himself to be biased or disturbed.

At any rate, the part which he played that morning did not lack brilliancy and his assistance was of the sort which a magistrate is able to appreciate.

'To start with,' he began, 'I will ask Charles here to be very definite on one point: were all the objects which, on the first occasion, he saw upset or disturbed put back, on the second, exactly in their usual places?'

'Exactly.'

'It is obvious, therefore, that they can only have been put back by a person to whom the place of each of those objects was familiar.'

The remark impressed the bystanders. Ganimard resumed.

'Another question, Mr Charles . . . You were woke by a ring . . . Who was it, according to you, that called you?'

'Monsieur le baron, of course.'

'Very well. But at what moment do you take it that he rang?'

'After the struggle . . . at the moment of dying.'

'Impossible, because you found him lying, lifeless, at a spot more than four yards removed from the bell-push.'

'Then he rang during the struggle.'

'Impossible, because the bell, you told us, rang steadily, without interruption, and went on for seven or eight seconds. Do you think that his assailant would have given him time to ring like that?'

'Then it was before, at the moment when he was attacked.'

'Impossible. You told us that, between the ring of the bell and the instant when you entered the room, three minutes elapsed, at most. If, therefore, the baron had rung before, it would be necessary for the struggle, the murder, the dying agony and the flight to have taken place within that short space of three minutes. I repeat, it is impossible.'

'And yet,' said the examining magistrate, 'someone rang. If it was not the baron, who was it?'

'The murderer.'

'With what object?'

'I can't tell his object. But at least the fact that he rang proves that he must have known that the bell communicated with a servant's bedroom. Now who could have known this detail except a person belonging to the house?'

The circle of suppositions was becoming narrower. In a few quick, clear, logical sentences, Ganimard placed the question in its true light; and, as the old inspector allowed his thoughts to appear quite plainly, it seemed only natural that the examining magistrate should conclude: 'In short, in two words, you suspect Antoinette Bréhat.'

'I don't suspect her, I accuse her.'

'You accuse her of being the accomplice?'

'I accuse her of killing General Baron d'Hautrec.'

'Come, come! And what proof . . . ?'

'This handful of hair, which I found in the victim's right hand, dug into his flesh by the points of his nails.'

He showed the hair; it was hair of a brilliant fairness, gleaming like so many threads of gold; and Charles muttered: 'That is certainly Mlle Antoinette's hair. There is no mistaking it.' And he added, 'Besides . . . there's something more . . . I believe the knife . . . the one I didn't see the second time . . . belonged to her . . . She used it to cut the pages of the books.'

The silence that followed was long and painful, as though the crime increased in horror through having been committed by a woman. The examining magistrate argued: 'Let us admit, until further information is obtained, that the baron was murdered by Antoinette Bréhat. We should still have to explain what way she can have taken to go out after committing the crime, to return after Charles's departure and to go out again before the arrival of the commissary. Have you any opinion on this subject, M. Ganimard?'

'No.'

'Then . . . ?'

Ganimard wore an air of embarrassment. At last, he spoke, not without a visible effort.

'All that I can say is that I find in this the same way of setting to work as in the ticket 514–23 case, the same phenomenon which one might call the faculty of disappearance. Antoinette Bréhat appears and disappears in this house as mysteriously as Arsène Lupin made his way into Maître Detinan's and escaped from there in the company of the fair-haired lady.'

'Which means . . . ?'

'Which means that I cannot help thinking of these two coincidences, which, to say the least, are very odd: first, Antoinette Bréhat was engaged by Soeur Auguste twelve days ago, that is to say, on the day after that on which the fair-haired lady slipped through my fingers. In the second place, the hair of the fair-haired lady has precisely the same violent colouring, the metallic brilliancy with a golden sheen, which we find in this.'

'So that, according to you, Antoinette Bréhat . . . '

'Is none other than the fair-haired lady.'

'And Lupin, consequently, plotted both cases?'

'I think so.'

There was a loud burst of laughter. It was the chief of the detective-service indulging his merriment.

'Lupin! Always Lupin! Lupin is in everything, Lupin is everywhere!'

'He is just where he is,' said Ganimard, angrily.

'And then he must have his reasons for being in any particular place,' remarked M. Dudouis, 'and, in this case, his reasons seem to me obscure. The writing-desk has not been broken open nor the pocket-book stolen. There is even gold left lying on the table.'

'Yes,' cried Ganimard, 'but what about the famous diamond?'

'What diamond?'

'The blue diamond! The celebrated diamond which formed part of the royal crown of France and which was presented by the Duc d'Alais to Léonide Latouche and, on her death, was bought by Baron d'Hautrec in memory of the brilliant actress whom he had passionately loved. This is one of those recollections which an old Parisian like myself never forgets.'

'It is obvious,' said the examining magistrate, 'that, if the blue diamond is not found, the thing explains itself. But where are we to look?'

'On monsieur le baron's finger,' replied Charles. 'The blue diamond was never off his left hand.'

'I have looked at that hand,' declared Ganimard, going up to the corpse, 'and, as you can see for yourselves, there is only a plain gold ring.'

'Look inside the palm,' said the servant.

Ganimard unfolded the clenched fingers. The bezel was turned inwards and, contained within the bezel, glittered the blue diamond.

'The devil!' muttered Ganimard, absolutely nonplussed. 'This is beyond me!'

'And I hope that you will now give up suspecting that unfortunate Arsène Lupin?' said M. Dudouis, with a grin.

Ganimard took his time, reflected and retorted, in a sententious tone: 'It is just when a thing gets beyond me that I suspect Arsène Lupin most.'

These were the first discoveries effected by the police on the day following upon that strange murder, vague, inconsistent discoveries to which the subsequent inquiry imparted neither consistency nor certainty. The movements of Antoinette Bréhat remained as absolutely inexplicable as those of the fair-haired lady, nor was any light thrown upon the identity of that mysterious creature with the golden hair who had killed Baron d'Hautrec without taking from his finger the fabulous diamond from the royal crown of France.

Moreover and especially, the curiosity which it inspired raised the murder above the level of a sordid crime to that of a mighty, if heinous trespass, the mystery of which irritated the public mind.

* * *

Baron d'Hautrec's heirs were obliged to benefit by this great advertisement. They arranged an exhibition of the furniture and personal effects in the Avenue Henri-Martin, in the house itself, on the scene of the crime, prior to the sale at the Salle Drouot. The furniture was modern and in indifferent taste, the knicknacks had no artistic value . . . but, in the middle of the bedroom, on a stand covered with ruby velvet, the ring with the blue diamond sparkled under a glass shade, closely watched by two detectives.

It was a magnificent diamond of enormous size and incomparable purity and of that undefined blue which clear water takes from the sky which it reflects, the blue which we can just suspect in newly-washed linen. People admired it, went into raptures over it . . . and cast terrified glances round the victim's room, at the spot where the corpse had lain, at the floor stripped of its bloodstained carpet and especially at the walls, those solid walls through which the criminal had passed. They felt to make sure that the marble chimneypiece did not swing on a pivot, that there was no secret spring in the mouldings of the mirrors. They pictured yawning cavities, tunnels communicating with the sewers, with the catacombs . . .

The blue diamond was sold at the Hôtel Drouot on the 30th of January. The auction-room was crammed and the bidding proceeded madly.

All Paris, the Paris of the first nights and great public functions, was there, all those who buy and all those who like others to think that they are in a position to buy: stockbrokers, artists, ladies in every class of society, two members of the government, an Italian tenor, a king in exile who, in order to re-establish his credit, with great self-possession and in a resounding voice, permitted himself the luxury of running up the price to a hundred thousand francs. A hundred thousand francs! His Majesty was quite safe in making the bid. The Italian tenor was soon offering a hundred and fifty thousand, an actress at the Français a hundred and seventy-five.

At two hundred thousand francs, however, the competition became less brisk. At two hundred and fifty thousand, only two bidders remained: Herschmann, the financial magnate, known as the Gold-mine King; and a wealthy American lady, the Comtesse de Crozon, whose collection of diamonds and other precious stones enjoys a world-wide fame.

'Two hundred and sixty thousand . . . two hundred and seventy thousand . . . seventy-five . . . eighty,' said the auctioneer, with a questioning glance at either competitor in turn. 'Two hundred and eighty thousand for madame . . . No advance on two hundred and eighty thousand? . . . '

'Three hundred thousand,' muttered Herschmann.

A pause followed. All eyes were turned on the Comtesse de Crozon. Smiling, but with a pallor that betrayed her excitement, she stood leaning over the back of the chair before her. In reality, she knew and everybody present knew that there was no doubt about the finish of the duel: it was logically and fatally bound to end in favour of the financier, whose whims were served by a fortune of over five hundred millions. Nevertheless, she said: 'Three hundred and five thousand.'

There was a further pause. Every glance was now turned on the Gold-mine King, in expectation of the inevitable advance. It was sure to come, in all its brutal and crushing strength.

It did not come. Herschmann remained impassive, with his eyes fixed on a sheet of paper which he held in his right hand, while the other crumpled up the pieces of a torn envelope.

'Three hundred and five thousand,' repeated the auctioneer. 'Going . . . going . . . No further bid? . . . '

No one spoke.

'Once more: going . . . going . . . '

Herschmann did not move. A last pause. The hammer fell.

'Four hundred thousand!' shouted Herschmann, starting up, as though the tap of the hammer had roused him from his torpor.

Too late. The diamond was sold.

Herschmann's acquaintances crowded round him. What had happened? Why had he not spoken sooner?

He gave a laugh.

'What happened? Upon my word, I don't know. My thoughts wandered for a second.'

'You don't mean that!'

'Yes, someone brought me a letter.'

'And was that enough . . . ?'

'To put me off? Yes, for the moment.'

Ganimard was there. He had watched the sale of the ring. He went up to one of the porters.

'Did you hand M. Herschmann a letter?'

'Yes.'

'Who gave it you?'

'A lady.'

'Where is she?'

'Where is she? . . . Why, sir, there she is . . . the lady over there, in a thick veil.'

'Just going out?'

'Yes.'

Ganimard rushed to the door and saw the lady going down the staircase. He ran after her. A stream of people stopped him at the entrance. When he came outside, he had lost sight of her.

He went back to the room, spoke to Herschmann, introduced himself and asked him about the letter. Herschmann gave it to him. It contained the following simple words, scribbled in pencil and in a handwriting unknown to the financier.

'The blue diamond brings ill-luck. Remember Baron d'Hautrec.'

* * *

The tribulations of the blue diamond were not over. Already famous through the murder of Baron d'Hautrec and the incidents at the Hôtel Drouot, it attained the height of its celebrity six months later. In the summer, the precious jewel which the Comtesse de Crozon had been at such pains to acquire was stolen.

Let me sum up this curious case, marked by so many stirring, dramatic and exciting episodes, upon which I am at last permitted to throw some light.

On the evening of the 10th of August, M. and Madame de Crozon's guests were gathered in the drawing-room of the magnificent château overlooking the Bay of Somme There was a request for some music. The countess sat down to the piano, took off her rings, which included Baron d'Hautrec's, and laid them on a little table that stood beside the piano.

An hour later, the count went to bed, as did his two cousins, the d'Andelles, and Madame de Réal, an intimate friend of the Comtesse de Crozon, who remained behind with Herr Bleichen, the Austrian consul, and his wife.

They sat and talked and then the countess turned down the big lamp which stood on the drawingroom table. At the same moment, Herr Bleichen put out the two lamps on the piano. There was a second's darkness and groping; then the consul lit a candle and they all three went to their rooms. But, the instant the countess reached hers, she remembered her jewels and told her maid to go and fetch them. The woman returned and placed them on the mantelpiece. Madame de Crozon did not examine them; but, the next morning, she noticed that one of the rings was missing, the ring with the blue diamond.

She told her husband. Both immediately came to the same conclusion: the maid being above suspicion, the thief could be none but Herr Bleichen.

The count informed the central commissary of police at Amiens, who opened an inquiry and arranged discreetly for the house to be constantly watched, so as to prevent the Austrian consul from selling or sending away the ring. The château was surrounded by detectives night and day.

A fortnight elapsed without the least incident. Then Herr Bleichen announced his intention of leaving. On the same day, a formal accusation was laid against him. The commissary made an official visit and ordered the luggage to be examined. In a small bag of which the consul always carried the key, they found a flask containing toothpowder; and, inside the flask, the ring!

Mrs Bleichen fainted. Her husband was arrested.

My readers will remember the defence set up by the accused. He was unable, he said, to explain the presence of the ring, unless it was there as the result of an act of revenge on the part of M. de Crozon.

'The count ill-treats his wife,' he declared, 'and makes her life a misery. I had a long conversation with her and warmly urged her to sue for a divorce. The count must have heard of this and revenged himself by taking the ring and slipping it into my dressing-bag when I was about to leave.'

The count and countess persisted in their charge. It was an even choice between their explanation and the consul's: both were equally probable. No new fact came to weigh down either scale. A month of gossip, of guesswork and investigations, failed to produce a single element of certainty.

Annoyed by all this worry and unable to bring forward a definite proof of guilt to justify their accusation, M. and Madame de Crozon wrote to Paris for a detective capable of unravelling the threads of the skein. The police sent Ganimard.

For four days the old inspector rummaged and hunted about, strolled in the park, had long talks with the maids, the chauffeur, the gardeners, the people of the nearest post-offices, and examined the rooms occupied by the Bleichen couple, the d'Andelle cousins and Madame de Réal. Then, one morning, he disappeared without taking leave of his hosts.

But, a week later, they received this telegram.

PLEASE MEET ME FIVE O'CLOCK TOMORROW FRIDAY AFTER-NOON AT THÉ JAPONAIS, RUE BOISSY-D'ANGLAS.

GANIMARD

* * *

At five o'clock to the minute, on the Friday, their motor-car drew up in front of 9, Rue Boissy-d'Anglas. The old inspector was waiting for them on the pavement and, without a word of explanation, led them up to the first-floor of the Thé Japonais.

In one of the rooms they found two persons, whom Ganimard introduced to them.

'M. Gerbois, professor at Versailles College, whom, you will remember, Arsène Lupin robbed of half a million . . . M. Léonce d'Hautrec, nephew and residuary legatee of the late Baron d'Hautrec.'

The four sat down. A few minutes later, a fifth arrived. It was the chief of the detective-service.

M. Dudouis appeared to be in a rather bad temper. He bowed and said: 'Well, what is it, Ganimard? They gave me your telephone message at headquarters. Is it serious?'

'Very serious, chief. In less than an hour, the last adventures in which I have assisted will come to an issue here. I considered that your presence was indispensable.'

'And does this apply also to the presence of Dieuzy and Folenfant, whom I see below, hanging round the door?'

'Yes, chief.'

'And what for? Is somebody to be arrested? What a melodramatic display! Well, Ganimard, say what you have to say.'

Ganimard hesitated for a few moments and then, with the evident intention of impressing his hearers, said: 'First of all, I wish to state that Herr Bleichen had nothing to do with the theft of the ring.'

'Oh,' said M. Dudouis, 'that's a mere statement . . . and a serious one!'

And the count asked: 'Is this . . . discovery the only thing that has come of your exertions?'

'No, sir. Two days after the theft, three of your guests happened to be at Crécy, in the course of a motor-trip. Two of them went on to visit the famous battlefield, while the third hurried to the post-office and sent off a little parcel, packed up and sealed according to the regulations and insured to the value of one hundred francs.'

M. de Crozon objected: 'There is nothing out of the way in that.'

'Perhaps you will think it less natural when I tell you that, instead of the real name, the sender gave the name of Rousseau and that the addressee, a M. Beloux, residing in Paris, changed his lodgings on the very evening of the day on which he received the parcel, that is to say the ring.'

'Was it one of my d'Andelle cousins, by any chance?' asked the count.

'No, it was neither of those gentlemen.'

'Then it was Mme de Réal?'

'Yes.'

The countess, in amazement, exclaimed: 'Do you accuse my friend Mme de Réal?'

'A simple question, madame,' replied Ganimard. 'Was Mme de Réal present at the sale of the blue diamond?'

'Yes, but in a different part of the room. We were not together.'

'Did she advise you to buy the ring?'

The countess collected her memory.

'Yes . . . as a matter of fact . . . I think she was the first to mention it to me.'

'I note your answer, madame,' said Ganimard. 'So it is quite certain that it was Mme de Réal who first spoke to you of the ring and advised you to buy it.'

'Still . . . my friend is incapable . . . '

'I beg your pardon, I beg your pardon, Mme de Réal is only your chance acquaintance and not an intimate friend, as the newspapers stated, thus diverting suspicion from her. You have only known her since last winter. Now I can undertake to prove to you that all that she has told you about herself, her past, her connections is absolutely false; that Mme Blanche de Réal did not exist before she met you; and that she has ceased to exist at this present moment.'

'Well?' said M. Dudouis, 'What next?'

'What next?' echoed Ganimard.

'Yes, what next? . . . This is all very interesting; but what has it to do with the case? If Mme de Réal took the ring, why was it found in Herr Bleichen's tooth-powder? Come, Ganimard! A person who takes the trouble to steal the blue diamond keeps it. What have you to answer to that?'

'I, nothing. But Mme de Réal will answer.'

'Then she exists?'

'She exists . . . without existing. In a few words, here it is: three days ago, reading the paper which I read every day, I saw at the head of the list of arrivals at Trouville, "Hôtel Beaurivage, Mme de Réal", and so on . . . You can imagine that I was at Trouville that same evening, questioning the manager of the Beaurivage. According to the description and certain clues which I gathered, this Mme de Réal was indeed the person whom I was looking for, but she had gone from the hotel, leaving her address in Paris, 3, Rue du Colisée. On Wednesday, I called at that address and learnt that there was no Madame de Réal, but just a woman called Réal, who lived on the second-floor, followed the occupation of a diamond-broker and was often away. Only the day before, she had come back from a journey. Yesterday, I rang at her door and, under a false name, offered my services to Mme de Réal as an intermediary to introduce her to people who were in a position to buy valuable stones. We made an appointment to meet here today for a first transaction.'

'Oh, so you expect her?'

'At half-past five.'

'And are you sure? . . . '

'That it is Mme de Réal of the Château de Crozon? I have indisputable proofs. But . . . hark! . . . Folenfant's signal! . . . '

A whistle had sounded. Ganimard rose briskly.

'We have not a moment to lose. M. and Madame de Crozon, go into the next room, please. You too, M. d'Hautrec . . . and you also,

M. Gerbois . . . The door will remain open and, at the first sign, I will ask you to intervene. Do you stay, chief, please.'

'And, if anyone else comes in?' asked M. Dudouis.'

'No one will. This is a new establishment and the proprietor, who is a friend of mine, will not let a living soul come up the stairs . . . except the fair-haired lady.'

'The fair-haired lady? What do you mean?'

'The fair-haired lady herself, chief, the friend and accomplice of Arsène Lupin, the mysterious fair-haired lady, against whom I have positive proofs, but against whom I want, over and above those and in your presence, to collect the evidence of all the people whom she has robbed.'

He leant out of the window.

'She is coming . . . She has gone in . . . She can't escape now: Folenfant and Dieuzy are guarding the door . . . The fair-haired lady is ours, chief, we've got her!'

*   *   *

Almost at that moment, a woman appeared upon the threshold, a tall, thin woman, with a very pale face and violent golden hair.

Ganimard was stifled by such emotion that he stood dumb, incapable of articulating the least word. She was there, in front of him, at his disposal! What a victory over Arsène Lupin! And what a revenge! And, at the same time, that victory seemed to him to have been won with such ease that he wondered whether the fair-haired lady was not going to slip through his fingers thanks to one of those miracles which Lupin was in the habit of performing.

She stood waiting, meanwhile, surprised at the silence, and looked around her without disguising her uneasiness.

'She will go! She will disappear!' thought Ganimard, in dismay.

Suddenly, he placed himself between her and the door. She turned and tried to go out.

'No, no,' he said. 'Why go?'

'But, monsieur, I don't understand your ways. Let me pass . . . '

'There is no reason for you to go, madame, and every reason, on the contrary, why you should stay.'

'But . . . '

'It's no use, you are not going.'

Turning very pale, she sank into a chair and stammered: 'What do you want?'

Ganimard triumphed. He had got the fair-haired lady. Mastering

himself, he said: 'Let me introduce the friend of whom I spoke to
you, the one who would like to buy some jewels . . . especially
diamonds. Did you obtain the one you promised me?'

'No . . . no . . . I don't know . . . I forget . . .'

'Oh, yes . . . Just try . . . Someone you knew was to bring you a
coloured diamond . . . "Something like the blue diamond," I said,
laughing, and you answered, "Exactly, I may have what you want."
Do you remember?'

She was silent. A little wristbag which she was holding in her hand
fell to the ground. She picked it up quickly and pressed it to her. Her
fingers trembled a little.

'Come,' said Ganimard. 'I see that you do not trust us, Madame
de Réal. I will set you a good example and let you see what I have got
to show.'

He took a piece of paper from his pocket-book and unfolded it.

'Here, first of all, is some of the hair of Antoinette Bréhat, torn out
by the baron and found clutched in the dead man's hand. I have seen
Mlle de Gerbois: she has most positively recognized the colour of the
hair of the fair-haired lady . . . the same colour as yours, for that
matter . . . exactly the same colour.'

Mme de Réal watched him with a stupid expression, as though she
really did not grasp the sense of his words. He continued: 'And now
here are two bottles of scent. They are empty, it is true, and have no
labels; but enough of the scent still clings to them to have enabled
Mlle Gerbois, this very morning, to recognize the perfume of the
fair-haired lady who accompanied her on her fortnight's excursion.
Now one of these bottles comes from the room which Mme de Réal
occupied at the Château de Crozon and the other from the room
which you occupied at the Hôtel Beaurivage.'

'What are you talking about? . . . The fair-haired lady . . . the
Château de Crozon . . .'

The inspector, without replying, spread four sheets of paper on
the table.

'Lastly,' he said, 'here, on these four sheets, we have a specimen of
the handwriting of Antoinette Bréhat, another of the lady who sent a
note to Baron Herschmann during the sale of the blue diamond,
another of Mme de Réal, at the time of her stay at Crozon, and the
fourth . . . your own, madame . . . your name and address given by
yourself to the hall-porter of the Hôtel Beaurivage at Trouville. Now
please compare these four handwritings. They are one and the same.'

'But you are mad, sir, you are mad! What does all this mean?'

'It means, madame,' cried Ganimard, with a great outburst, 'that the fair-haired lady, the friend and accomplice of Arsène Lupin, is none other than yourself.'

He pushed open the door of the next room, rushed at M. Gerbois, shoved him along by the shoulders and, planting him in front of Mme Réal: 'M. Gerbois, do you recognize the person who took away your daughter and whom you saw at Maître Detinan's?'

'No.'

There was a commotion of which everyone felt the shock. Ganimard staggered back.

'No? . . . Is it possible? . . . Come, just think . . . '

'I have thought . . . Madame is fair, like the fair-haired lady . . . and pale, like her . . . but she doesn't resemble her in the least.'

'I can't believe it . . . a mistake like that is inconceivable . . . M. d'Hautrec, do you recognize Antoinette Bréhat?'

'I have seen Antoinette Bréhat at my uncle's . . . this is not she.'

'And madame is not Mme de Réal, either,' declared the Comte de Crozon.

This was the finishing stroke. It stunned Ganimard, who stood motionless, with hanging head and shifting eyes. Of all his contrivances, nothing remained. The whole edifice was tumbling about his shoulders.

M. Dudouis rose.

'I must beg you to forgive us, madame. There has been a regrettable confusion of identities, which I will ask you to forget. But what I cannot well understand is your agitation . . . the strangeness of your manner since you arrived . . . '

'Why, monsieur, I was frightened . . . there is over a hundred thousand francs' worth of jewels in my bag . . . and your friend's attitude was not very reassuring.'

'But your continual absences? . . . '

'Surely my occupation demands them?'

M. Dudouis had no reply to make. He turned to his subordinate.

'You have made your enquiries with a deplorable want of thoroughness, Ganimard, and your behaviour towards madame just now was most uncouth. You shall give me an explanation in my office.'

The interview was over and the chief of the detective-service was about to take his leave, when a really disconcerting thing happened. Mme Réal went up to the inspector and said: 'Do I understand your name to be M. Ganimard? . . . Did I catch the name right?'

'Yes.'

'In that case, this letter must be for you. I received it this morning, addressed as you see: "M. Justin Ganimard, care of Mme Réal". I thought it was a joke, as I did not know you under that name, but I have no doubt the writer, whoever he is, knew of your appointment.'

By a singular intuition, Justin Ganimard was very nearly seizing the letter and destroying it. He dared not do so, however, before his superior and he tore open the envelope. The letter contained the following words, which he uttered in a hardly intelligible voice.

There was once a Fair-haired Lady, a Lupin and a Ganimard. Now the naughty Ganimard wanted to harm the pretty Fair-haired Lady; and the good Lupin did not wish it. So the good Lupin, who was anxious for the Fair-haired Lady to become friends with the Comtesse de Crozon, made her take the name of Mme de Réal, which is the same – or nearly – as that of an honest tradeswoman whose hair is golden and her features pale. And the good Lupin said to himself, 'If ever the naughty Ganimard is on the track of the Fair-haired Lady, how useful it will be for me to shunt him on to the track of the honest tradeswoman!' A wise precaution, which has borne fruit. A little note sent to the naughty Ganimard's newspaper, a bottle of scent forgotten on purpose at the Hôtel Beaurivage by the real Fair-haired Lady, Mme Réal's name and address written by the real Fair-haired Lady in the visitors' book at the hotel and the trick is done. What do you say to it, Ganimard? I wanted to tell you the story in detail, knowing that, with your sense of humour, you would be the first to laugh at it. It is, indeed, a pretty story and I confess that, for my part, it has diverted me vastly.

My best thanks to you, then, my dear friend, and kind regards to that capital M. Dudouis.

ARSÈNE LUPIN

'But he knows everything!' moaned Ganimard, who did not think of laughing. 'He knows things that I have not told to a soul! How could he know that I would ask you to come, chief? How could he know that I had discovered the first scent-bottle? . . . How could he know? . . .'

He stamped about, tore his hair, a prey to the most tragic distress.

M. Dudouis took pity on him.

'Come, Ganimard, console yourself. We must try to do better next time.'

And the chief detective went away, accompanied by Mme Réal.

* * *

Ten minutes elapsed, while Ganimard read Lupin's letter over and over again and M. and Mme de Crozon, M. d'Hautrec and M. Gerbois sustained an animated conversation in a corner. At last, the count crossed over to the inspector and said: 'The upshot of all this, my dear sir, is that we are no further than we were.'

'Pardon me. My inquiry has established the fact that the fair-haired lady is the undoubted heroine of these adventures and that Lupin is directing her. That is a huge step forward.'

'And not the smallest use to us. If anything, it makes the mystery darker still. The fair-haired lady commits murder to steal the blue diamond and does not steal it. She steals it and does so to get rid of it for another's benefit.'

'What can I do?'

'Nothing, but someone else might . . . '

'What do you mean?'

The count hesitated, but the countess said, point-blank: 'There is one man, one man only, in my opinion, besides yourself, who would be capable of fighting Lupin and reducing him to cry for mercy. M. Ganimard, would you very much mind if we called in the assistance of Holmlock Shears?'

He was taken aback.

'No . . . no . . . only . . . I don't exactly understand . . . '

'Well, it's like this: all this mystery is making me quite ill. I want to know where I am. M. Gerbois and M. d'Hautrec have the same wish and we have come to an agreement to apply to the famous English detective.'

'You are right, madame,' said the inspector, with a loyalty that did him credit, 'you are right. Old Ganimard is not clever enough to fight against Arsène Lupin. The question is, will Holmlock Shears be more successful? I hope so, for I have the greatest admiration for him . . . Still . . . it's hardly likely . . . '

'It's hardly likely that he will succeed?'

'That's what I think. I consider that a duel between Holmlock Shears and Arsène Lupin can only end in one way. The Englishman will be beaten.'

'In any case, can he rely on you?'
'Certainly, madame. I will assist him to the very best of my power.'
'Do you know his address?'
'Yes, 219, Parker Street.'

That evening, the Comte and Comtesse de Crozon withdrew the charge against Herr Bleichen and a collective letter was addressed to Holmlock Shears.

Chapter 3

Holmlock Shears Opens Hostilities

'What can I get you, gentlemen?'

'Anything you please,' replied Arsène Lupin, in the voice of a man who takes no interest in his food. 'Anything you please, but no meat or wine.'

The waiter walked away, with a scornful air.

I exclaimed: 'Do you mean to say that you are still a vegetarian?'

'Yes, more than ever,' said Lupin.

'From taste? Conviction? Habit?'

'For reasons of health.'

'And do you never break your rule?'

'Oh, yes . . . when I go out to dinner, so as not to appear eccentric.'

We were dining near the Gare du Nord, inside a little restaurant where Arsène Lupin had invited me to join him. He is rather fond of telegraphing to me, occasionally, in the morning and arranging a meeting of this kind in some corner or other of Paris. He always arrives in the highest spirits, rejoicing in life, unaffectedly and good-humouredly, and always has some surprising anecdote to tell me, some memory, the story of some adventure that I have not heard before.

That evening, he seemed to me to let himself go even more than usual. He laughed and chatted with a singular animation and with that delicate irony which is all his own, an irony devoid of bitterness, light and spontaneous. It was a pleasure to see him like that and I could not help expressing my satisfaction.

'Oh, yes,' he cried, 'I have days when everything seems delightful, when life bubbles in me like an infinite treasure which I can never exhaust. And yet goodness knows that I live without counting!'

'Too much so, perhaps.'

'The treasure is infinite, I tell you! I can spend myself and squander myself, I can fling my strength and my youth to the four winds of heaven and I am only making room for greater and more youthful strength . . . And then, really, my life is so beautiful! . . . I need only have the wish – isn't it so? – to become, from one day to the next, anything: an orator, a great manufacturer, a politician . . . Well, I swear to you, the idea would never enter my head! Arsène Lupin I am, Arsène Lupin I remain. And I search history in vain for a destiny to compare with mine, fuller, more intense . . . Napoleon? Yes, perhaps . . . But then it is Napoleon at the end of his imperial career, during the campaign in France, when Europe was crushing him and when he was wondering whether each battle was not the last which he would fight.'

Was he serious? Was he jesting? The tone of his voice had grown more eager and he continued: 'Everything's there, you see: danger! The uninterrupted impression of danger! Oh, to breathe it like the air one breathes, to feel it around one, blowing, roaring, lying in wait, approaching! . . . And, in the midst of the storm, to remain calm . . . not to flinch! . . . If you do, you are lost . . . There is only one sensation to equal it, that of the chauffeur driving his car. But that drive lasts for a morning, whereas mine lasts all through life!'

'How lyrical we are!' I cried. 'And you would have me believe that you have no special reason for excitement!'

He smiled.

'You're a shrewd enough psychologist,' he replied. 'There is something more, as you say.'

He poured out a tumbler of water, drank it down and asked: 'Have you seen the *Temps* today?'

'No.'

'Holmlock Shears was to have crossed the Channel this afternoon; he arrived in Paris at six.'

'The devil he did! And why?'

'He's taking a little trip at the expense of the Crozons, Hautrec's nephew and the Gerbois fellow. They all met at the Gare du Nord and went on to see Ganimard. The six of them are in conference at this moment.'

Notwithstanding the immense curiosity with which he inspires me, I never venture to question Arsène Lupin as to the acts of his private life until he has spoken of them to me himself. It is a matter of discretion on my part, with which I never compound. Besides, at that time, his name had not yet been mentioned, at least not publicly, in connection with the blue diamond. I waited patiently, therefore. He continued: 'The *Temps* also prints an interview with that excellent Ganimard, according to which a certain fair-haired lady, said to be my friend, is supposed to have murdered Baron d'Hautrec and tried to steal his famous ring from Madame de Crozon. And it goes without saying that he accuses me of being the instigator of both these crimes.'

A slight shiver passed through me. Could it be true? Was I to believe that the habit of theft, his mode of life, the sheer logic of events had driven this man to murder? I looked at him. He seemed so calm! His eyes met mine so frankly!

I examined his hands: they were modelled with infinite daintiness, were really inoffensive hands, the hands of an artist.

'Ganimard is a lunatic,' I muttered.

He protested: 'Not a bit of it, not a bit of it! Ganimard is shrewd enough . . . sometimes he's even quick-witted.'

'Quick-witted!'

'Yes, yes. For instance, this interview is a masterstroke. First, he announces the coming of his English rival, so as to put me on my guard and make Shears's task more difficult. Secondly, he specifies the exact point to which he has carried the case, so that Shears may enjoy only the benefit of his own discoveries. That's fair fighting.'

'Still you have two adversaries to deal with now; and such adversaries!'

'Oh, one of them doesn't count.'

'And the other?'

'Shears? Oh, I admit that he's more of a match for me; but that's just what I love and why you see me in such good spirits. To begin with, there's the question of my vanity: they consider that I'm worth asking the famous Englishman to meet. Next, think of the pleasure which a fighter like myself must take in the prospect of a duel with Holmlock Shears. Well, I shall have to exert myself to the utmost. For I know the fellow: he won't retreat a step.'

'He's a clever man.'

'A very clever man. As a detective, I doubt if his equal exists, or has ever existed. Only, I have one advantage over him, which is that he's attacking, while I'm on the defensive. Mine is the easier game to play. Besides . . . ' He gave an imperceptible smile before completing his phrase. 'Besides, I know his way of fighting and he does not know mine. And I have a few sly thrusts in store for him which will give him something to think about . . . '

He tapped the table lightly with his fingers and flung out little sentences with a delighted air: 'Arsène Lupin versus Holmlock Shears! France versus England . . . Revenge for Trafalgar at last! . . .

Ah, the poor wretch . . . he little thinks that I am prepared . . . and a Lupin armed . . . '

He stopped suddenly, seized with a fit of coughing, and hid his face in his napkin, as though something had gone down the wrong way.

'What is it?' I asked. 'A crumb? . . . Why don't you take some water?'

'No, it's not that,' he gasped.

'What, then?'

'I want air.'

'Shall I open the window?'

'No, I shall go out . . . Quick, give me my hat and coat . . . I'm off!'

'But what does it all mean?'

'You see the taller of those two men who have just come in? Well, I want you to keep on my left as we go out, to prevent his seeing me.'

'The one sitting behind you? . . . '

'Yes . . . For personal reasons, I prefer . . . I'll tell you why outside . . . '

'But who is it?'

'Holmlock Shears.'

He made a violent effort to overcome his agitation, as though he felt ashamed of it, put down his napkin, drank a glass of water and then, quite recovered, said, with a smile, 'It's funny, isn't it? I'm not easily excited, but this unexpected meeting . . . '

'What are you afraid of, seeing that no one can recognize you under all your transformations? I myself, each time I see you, feel as if I were with a new person.'

'*He* will recognize me,' said Arsène Lupin. '*He* saw me only once,* but I felt that he saw me for life and that what he saw was not my appearance, which I can always alter, but the very being that I am . . . And then . . . and then . . . I wasn't prepared . . . What a curious meeting! . . . In this little restaurant! . . . '

'Well,' said I, 'shall we go?'

'No . . . no . . . '

'What do you propose to do?'

'The best thing will be to act frankly . . . to trust him.'

'You can't be serious?'

'Oh, but I am . . . Besides, it would be a good thing to question

---

* See *The Seven of Hearts*, by Maurice Leblanc. Chapter 9: Holmlock Shears Arrives Too Late.

him, to know what he knows . . . Ah, there, I feel that his eyes are fixed on my neck, on my shoulders . . . He's trying to think . . . to remember . . . '

He reflected. I noticed a mischievous smile on his lips; and then, obeying, I believe, some whim of his frivolous nature rather than the needs of the position itself, he rose abruptly, spun round on his heels and, with a bow, said, gaily: 'What a stroke of luck! Who would have thought it? . . . Allow me to introduce my friend.'

For a second or two, the Englishman was taken aback. Then he made an instinctive movement, as though he were ready to fling himself upon Arsène Lupin. Lupin shook his head.

'That would be a mistake . . . to say nothing of the bad taste of it . . . and the uselessness!'

The Englishman turned his head from side to side, as though looking for assistance.

'That's no better . . . And also, are you quite sure that you are entitled to lay hands upon me? Come, be a sportsman!'

The display of sportsmanlike qualities was not particularly tempting on this occasion. Nevertheless, it probably appeared to Shears to be the wisest course; for he half rose and coldly introduced his companion.

'Mr Wilson, my friend and assistant . . . M. Arsène Lupin.'

Wilson's stupefaction made us all laugh. His eyes and mouth, both wide open, drew two streaks across his expansive face, with its skin gleaming and tight-stretched like an apple's, while his bristly hair stood up like so many thickset, hardy blades of grass.

'Wilson, you don't seem able to conceal your bewilderment at one of the most natural incidents in the world,' grinned Holmlock Shears, with a touch of sarcasm in his voice.

Wilson stammered: 'Why . . . why don't you arrest him?'

'Don't you see, Wilson, that the gentleman is standing between the door and myself and at two steps from the door. Before I moved a finger, he would be outside.'

'Don't let that stand in your way,' said Lupin.

He walked round the table and sat down so that the Englishman was between him and the door, thus placing himself at his mercy. Wilson looked at Shears to see if he might admire this piece of pluck. Shears remained impenetrable. But, after a moment, he called: 'Waiter!'

The waiter came up.

'Four whiskeys and sodas.'

Peace was signed . . . until further orders. Soon after, seated all four round one table, we were quietly chatting.

*   *   *

Holmlock Shears is a man . . . of the sort one meets every day. He is about fifty years of age and looks like a decent City clerk who has spent his life keeping books at a desk. He has nothing to distinguish him from the ordinary respectable Londoner, with his clean-shaven face and his somewhat heavy appearance, nothing except his terribly keen, bright, penetrating eyes.

And then, of course, he is Holmlock Shears, that is to say, a sort of miracle of intuition, of insight, of perspicacity, of shrewdness. It is as though nature had amused herself by taking the two most extraordinary types of detective that fiction had invented, Poe's Dupin and Gaboriau's Lecoq, in order to build up one in her own fashion, more extraordinary yet and more unreal. And, upon my word, anyone hearing of the adventures which have made the name of Holmlock Shears famous all over the world must feel inclined to ask if he is not a legendary person, a hero who has stepped straight from the brain of some great novel-writer, of a Conan Doyle, for instance.

He at once, when Arsène Lupin asked him how long he meant to stay, led the conversation into its right channel and replied: 'That depends upon yourself, M. Lupin.'

'Oh,' exclaimed the other, laughing, 'if it depended on me, I should ask you to take tonight's boat back.'

'Tonight is rather early. But I hope in a week or ten days . . . '

'Are you in such a hurry?'

'I am very busy. There's the robbery at the Anglo-Chinese Bank; and Lady Eccleston has been kidnapped, as you know . . . Tell me, M. Lupin, do you think a week will do?'

'Amply, if you confine yourself to the two cases connected with the blue diamond. It will just give me time to take my precautions, supposing the solution of those two mysteries to give you certain advantages over me that might endanger my safety.'

'Yes,' said the Englishman, 'I expect to have gained those advantages in a week or ten days.'

'And to have me arrested on the eleventh?'

'On the tenth, at the very latest.'

Lupin reflected and, shaking his head: 'It will be difficult . . . it will be difficult . . . '

'Difficult, yes, but possible and, therefore, certain . . . '

'Absolutely certain,' said Wilson, as though he himself had clearly perceived the long series of operations which would lead his friend to the result announced.

Holmlock Shears smiled.

'Wilson, who knows what he is talking about, is there to confirm what I say.' And he went on, 'Of course, I have not all the cards in my hands, because the case is already a good many months old. I have not the factors, the clues upon which I am accustomed to base my enquiries.'

'Such as mud-stains and cigarette-ashes,' said Wilson, with an air of importance.

'But, in addition to the remarkable conclusions arrived at by M. Ganimard, I have at my service all the articles written on the subject, all the evidence collected and, consequently, a few ideas of my own regarding the mystery.'

'A few views suggested to us either by analysis or hypothesis,' added Wilson, sententiously.

'Would it be indiscreet,' said Arsène Lupin, in the deferential tone which he adopted towards Shears, 'would it be indiscreet to ask what general opinion you have been able to form?'

It was really most stimulating to see those two men seated together, with their elbows on the table, arguing solemnly and dispassionately, as though they were trying to solve a steep problem or to come to an agreement on some controversial point. And this was coupled with a very delicate irony, which both of them, as experts and artists, thoroughly enjoyed. As for Wilson, he was in the seventh heaven.

Shears slowly filled his pipe, lit it and said: 'I consider that this case is infinitely less complicated than it appears at first sight.'

'Very much less,' echoed Wilson, faithfully.

'I say the case, for, in my opinion, there is but one case. The death of Baron d'Hautrec, the story of the ring and – don't let us forget that – the mystery of number 514, series 23 are only the different aspects of what we may call the puzzle of the fair-haired lady. Now, in my opinion, what lies before me is simply to discover the link which connects these three phases of the same story, the particular fact which proves the uniformity of the three methods. Ganimard, who is a little superficial in his judgments, sees this uniformity in the faculty of disappearing, in the power of coming and going unseen. This intervention of miracles does not satisfy me.'

'Well?'

'Well, according to me,' said Shears, decidedly, 'the characteristic shared by the three incidents lies in your manifest and evident, although hitherto unperceived intention to have the affair performed on a stage which you have previously selected. This points to something more than a plan on your part: a necessity rather, a *sine quâ non* of success.'

'Could you give a few particulars?'

'Easily. For instance, from the commencement of your contest with M. Gerbois, it was *evident* that Maître Detinan's flat was the place selected by you, the inevitable place at which you were all to meet. No place seemed quite as safe to you, so much so that you made what one might almost call a public appointment there with the fair-haired lady and Mlle Gerbois.'

'The daughter of the professor,' explained Wilson.

'Let us now speak of the blue diamond. Did you try to get hold of it during all the years that Baron d'Hautrec had it in his possession? No. But the baron moves into his brother's house: six months later, Antoinette Bréhat appears upon the scene and the first attempt is made . . . You fail to secure the diamond and the sale takes place, amid great excitement, at the Hôtel Drouot. Is the sale free? Is the richest bidder sure of getting the diamond? Not at all. At the moment when Herschmann is about to become the owner, a lady has a threatening letter thrust into his hand and the diamond goes to the Comtesse de Crozon, who has been worked upon and influenced by the same lady. Does it vanish at once? No: you lack the facilities. So an interval ensues. But the countess moves to her country-house. This is what you were waiting for. The ring disappears.'

'To reappear in the tooth-powder of Bleichen, the consul,' objected Lupin. 'How odd!'

'Come, come!' said Shears, striking the table with his fist. 'Tell that to the marines. You can take in fools with that, but not an old fox like me.'

'What do you mean?'

Shears took his time, as though he wished to save up his effect. Then he said: 'The blue diamond found in the tooth-powder is an imitation diamond. The real one you kept.'

Arsène Lupin was silent for a moment and then, with his eyes fixed on the Englishman, said very simply: 'You're a great man, sir.'

'Isn't he?' said Wilson, emphatically and gaping with admiration.

'Yes,' said Lupin, 'everything becomes cleared up and appears in its true sense. Not one of the examining magistrates, not one of the special reporters who have been exciting themselves about these cases has come half as near the truth. I look upon you as a marvel of insight and logic.'

'Pooh!' said the Englishman, flattered at the compliment paid him by so great an expert. 'It only needed a little thought.'

'It needed to know how to use one's thought; and there are so few who do know. But, now that the field of surmise has been narrowed and the ground swept clear . . . '

'Well, now, all that I have to do is to discover why the three cases were enacted at 25, Rue Chapeyron, at 134, Avenue Henri-Martin and within the walls of the Château de Crozon. The whole case lies there. The rest is mere talk and child's play. Don't you agree?'

'I agree.'

'In that case, M. Lupin, am I not right in saying that I shall have finished my business in ten days?'

'In ten days, yes, the whole truth will be known.'

'And you will be arrested.'

'No.'

'No?'

'For me to be arrested there would have to be a conjunction of such unlikely circumstances, a series of such stupefying pieces of ill-luck, that I cannot admit the possibility.'

'What neither circumstances nor luck may be able to effect, M. Lupin, can be brought about by one man's will and persistence.'

'If the will and persistence of another man do not oppose an invincible obstacle to that plan, Mr Shears.'

'There is no such thing as an invincible obstacle, M. Lupin.'

The two exchanged a penetrating glance, free from provocation on either side, but calm and fearless. It was the clash of two swords about to open the combat. It sounded clear and frank.

'Joy!' cried Lupin. 'Here's a man at last! An adversary is a *rara avis* at any time; and this one is Holmlock Shears! We shall have some sport.'

'You're not afraid?' asked Wilson.

'Very nearly, Mr Wilson,' said Lupin, rising, 'and the proof is that I am going to hurry to make good my retreat . . . else I might risk being caught napping. Ten days, we said, Mr Shears?'

'Ten days. This is Sunday. It will all be over by Wednesday week.'

'And I shall be under lock and key?'

'Without the slightest doubt.'

'By Jove! And I was congratulating myself on my quiet life! No bothers, a good, steady little business, the police sent to the right about and a comforting sense of the general sympathy that surrounds me . . . We shall have to change all this! It is the reverse of the medal . . . After sunshine comes rain . . . This is no time for laughing! Goodbye.'

'Look sharp!' said Wilson, full of solicitude on behalf of a person whom Shears inspired with such obvious respect. 'Don't lose a minute.'

'Not a minute, Mr Wilson, except to tell you how pleased I have been to meet you and how I envy the leader who has an assistant so valuable as yourself.'

Courteous bows were exchanged, as between two adversaries on the fencing-ground who bear each other no hatred, but who are constrained by fate to fight to the death. And Lupin took my arm and dragged me outside.

'What do you say to that, old fellow? There's a dinner that will be worth describing in your memoirs of me!'

He closed the door of the restaurant and, stopping a little way off: 'Do you smoke?'

'No, but no more do you, surely.'

'No more do I.'

He lit a cigarette with a wax match which he waved several times to put it out. But he at once flung away the cigarette, ran across the road and joined two men who had emerged from the shadow, as though summoned by a signal. He talked to them for a few minutes on the opposite pavement and then returned to me.

'I beg your pardon; but I shall have my work cut out with that confounded Shears. I swear, however, that he has not done with Lupin yet . . . By Jupiter, I'll show the fellow the stuff I'm made of! . . . Good-night . . . The unspeakable Wilson is right: I have not a minute to lose.'

He walked rapidly away.

Thus ended that strange evening, or at least, that part of it with which I had to do. For many other incidents occurred during the hours that followed, events which the confidences of the others who were present at that dinner have fortunately enabled me to reconstruct in detail.

* * *

At the very moment when Lupin left me, Holmlock Shears took out his watch and rose in his turn.

'Twenty to nine. At nine o'clock, I am to meet the count and countess at the railway-station.'

'Let's go!' cried Wilson, tossing off two glasses of whiskey in succession.

They went out.

'Wilson, don't turn your head . . . We may be followed: if so, let us act as though we don't care whether we are or not . . . Tell me, Wilson, what's your opinion: why was Lupin in that restaurant?'

Wilson, without hesitation, replied: 'To get some dinner.'

'Wilson, the longer we work together, the more clearly I perceive the constant progress you are making. Upon my word, you're becoming amazing.'

Wilson blushed with satisfaction in the dark; and Shears resumed: 'Yes, he went to get some dinner and then, most likely, to make sure if I am really going to Crozon, as Ganimard says I am, in his interview. I shall leave, therefore, so as not to disappoint him. But, as it is a question of gaining time upon him, I shall not leave.'

'Ah!' said Wilson, nonplussed.

'I want you, old chap, to go down this street. Take a cab, take two cabs, three cabs. Come back later to fetch the bags which we left in the cloakroom and then drive as fast as you can to the Élysée-Palace.'

'And what am I to do at the Élysée-Palace?'

'Ask for a room, go to bed, sleep the sleep of the just and await my instructions.'

Wilson, proud of the important task allotted to him, went off. Holmlock Shears took his ticket at the railway-station and entered the Amiens express, in which the Comte and Comtesse de Crozon had already taken their seats.

He merely bowed to them, lit a second pipe and smoked it placidly, standing, in the corridor.

The train started. Ten minutes later, he came and sat down beside the countess and asked: 'Have you the ring on you, madame?'

'Yes.'

'Please let me look at it.'

He took it and examined it.

'As I thought: it is a faked diamond.'

'Faked?'

'Yes, by a new process which consists in subjecting diamond-dust to enormous heat, until it melts . . . whereupon it is simply reformed into a single diamond.'

'Why, but my diamond is real!'

'Yes, yours; but this is not yours.'

'Where is mine, then?'

'In the hands of Arsène Lupin.'

'And this one?'

'This one was put in its place and slipped into Herr Bleichen's tooth-powder flask, where you found it.'

'Then it's an imitation?'

'Absolutely.'

Nonplussed and overwhelmed, the countess said nothing more, while her husband, refusing to believe the statement, turned the jewel over and over in his fingers. She finished by stammering out: 'But it's impossible! Why didn't they just simply take it? And how did they get it?'

'That's just what I mean to try to discover.'

'At Crozon?'

'No, I shall get out at Creil and return to Paris. That's where the game between Arsène Lupin and myself must be played out. The tricks will count the same, wherever we make them; but it is better that Lupin should think that I am out of town.'

'Still . . .'

'What difference can it make to you, madame? The main object is your diamond, is it not?'

'Yes.'

'Well, set your mind at rest. Only a little while ago, I gave an undertaking which will be much more difficult to keep. On the word of Holmlock Shears, you shall have the real diamond back.'

The train slowed down. He put the imitation diamond in his pocket and opened the carriage-door. The count cried: 'Take care, that's the wrong side!'

'Lupin will lose my tracks this way, if he's having me shadowed. Goodbye.'

A porter protested. The Englishman made for the station-master's office. Fifty minutes later, he jumped into a train which brought him back to Paris a little before midnight.

He ran across the station into the refreshment-room, went out by the other door and sprang into a cab.

'Drive to the Rue Clapeyron.'

After making sure that he was not being followed, he stopped the cab at the commencement of the street and began to make a careful examination of the house in which Maître Detinan lived and of the two adjoining houses. He paced off certain distances and noted the measurements in his memorandum-book.

'Now drive to the Avenue Henri-Martin.'

He dismissed his cab at the corner of the avenue and the Rue de la Pompe, walked along the pavement to No. 134 and went through the same performance in front of the house which Baron d'Hautrec had occupied and the two houses by which it was hemmed in on either side, measuring the width of their respective frontages and calculating the depth of the little gardens in front of the houses.

The avenue was deserted and very dark under its four rows of trees, amid which an occasional gas-jet seemed to struggle vainly against the thickness of the gloom. One of these lamps threw a pale light upon a part of the house and Shears saw the notice 'To Let' hanging on the railings, saw the two neglected walks that encircled the miniature lawn and the great empty windows of the uninhabited house.

'That's true,' he thought. 'There has been no tenant since the baron's death . . . Ah, if I could just get in and make a preliminary visit!'

The idea no sooner passed through his mind than he wanted to put it into execution. But how to manage? The height of the gate made it impossible for him to climb it. He took an electric lantern from his pocket, as well as a skeleton-key which he always carried. To his great surprise, he found that one of the doors of the gate was standing ajar. He, therefore, slipped into the garden, taking care not to close the gate behind him. He had not gone three steps, when he stopped. A glimmer of light had passed along one of the windows on the second floor.

And the glimmer passed along a second window and a third, while he was able to see nothing but a shadow outlined against the walls of the rooms. And the glimmer descended from the second floor to the first and, for a long time, wandered from room to room.

'Who on earth can be walking about, at one in the morning, in the house where Baron d'Hautrec was murdered?' thought Shears, feeling immensely interested.

There was only one way of finding out, which was to enter the house himself. He did not hesitate. But the man must have seen him as he crossed the belt of light cast by the gas-jet and made his way to the steps, for the glimmer suddenly went out and Shears did not see it again.

He softly tried the door at the top of the steps. It was open also. Hearing no sound, he ventured to penetrate the darkness, felt for the knob of the baluster, found it and went up one floor. The same silence, the same darkness continued to reign.

On reaching the landing, he entered one of the rooms and went to the window, which showed white in the dim light of the night outside. Through the window, he caught sight of the man, who had doubtless gone down by another staircase and out by another door and was now slipping along the shrubs, on the left, that lined the wall separating the two gardens.

'Dash it!' exclaimed Shears. 'He'll escape me!'

He rushed downstairs and leapt into the garden, with a view to cutting off the man's retreat. At first, he saw no one; and it was some seconds before he distinguished, among the confused heap of shrubs, a darker form which was not quite stationary.

The Englishman paused to reflect. Why had the fellow not tried to run away when he could easily have done so? Was he staying there to spy, in his turn, upon the intruder who had disturbed him in his mysterious errand?

'In any case,' thought Shears, 'it is not Lupin. Lupin would be cleverer. It must be one of his gang.'

Long minutes passed. Shears stood motionless, with his eyes fixed upon the adversary who was watching him. But, as the adversary was motionless too and as the Englishman was not the man to hang about doing nothing, he felt to see if the cylinder of his revolver worked, loosened his dagger in its sheath and walked straight up to the enemy, with the cool daring and the contempt of danger which make him so formidable.

A sharp sound: the man was cocking his revolver. Shears rushed into the shrubbery. The other had no time to turn: the Englishman was upon him. There was a violent and desperate struggle, amid which Shears was aware that the man was making every effort to draw his knife. But Shears, stimulated by the thought of his coming victory and by the fierce longing to lay hold at once of this accomplice of Arsène Lupin's, felt an irresistible strength welling up within himself. He threw his adversary, bore upon him with all his weight and, holding him down with his five fingers clutching at his throat like so many claws, he felt for his electric lantern with the hand that was free, pressed the button and threw the light upon his prisoner's face.

'Wilson!' he shouted, in terror.

'Holmlock Shears!' gasped a hollow, stifled voice.

*   *   *

They remained long staring at each other, without exchanging a word, dumbfounded, stupefied. The air was torn by the horn of a motor-car. A breath of wind rustled through the leaves. And Shears did not stir, his fingers still fixed in Wilson's throat, which continued to emit an ever fainter rattle.

And, suddenly, Shears, overcome with rage, let go his friend, but only to seize him by the shoulders and shake him frantically.

'What are you doing here? Answer me! . . . What are you here for? . . . Who told you to hide in the shrubbery and watch me?'

'Watch you?' groaned Wilson. 'But I didn't know it was you.'

'Then what? Why are you here? I told you to go to bed.'

'I did go to bed.'

'I told you to go to sleep.'

'I did.'

'You had no business to wake up.'

'Your letter . . . '

'What letter?'

'The letter from you which a commissionaire brought me at the hotel.'

'A letter from me? You're mad!'

'I assure you.'

'Where is the letter?'

Wilson produced a sheet of note-paper and, by the light of his lantern, Shears read, in amazement.

Get up at once, Wilson, and go to the Avenue Henri-Martin as fast as you can. The house is empty. Go in, inspect it, make out an exact plan and go back to bed.

HOLMLOCK SHEARS

'I was busy measuring the rooms,' said Wilson, 'when I saw a shadow in the garden. I had only one idea . . . '

'To catch the shadow . . . The idea was excellent . . . Only, look here, Wilson,' said Shears, helping his friend up and leading him away, 'next time you get a letter from me, make sure first that it's not a forgery.'

'Then the letter was not from you?' asked Wilson, who began to have a glimmering of the truth.

'No, worse luck!'

'Who wrote it, then?'

'Arsène Lupin.'

'But with what object?'

'I don't know; and that's just what bothers me. Why the deuce should he take the trouble to disturb your night's rest? If it were myself, I could understand, but you . . . I can't see what interest . . . '

'I am anxious to get back to the hotel.'

'So am I, Wilson.'

They reached the gate. Wilson, who was in front, took hold of one of the bars and pulled it.

'Hullo!' he said. 'Did you shut it?'

'Certainly not: I left the gate ajar.'

'But . . . '

Shears pulled in his turn and then frantically flung himself upon the lock. An oath escaped him.

'Damn it all! It's locked! . . . The gate's locked!'

He shook the gate with all his might, but, soon realizing the hopelessness of his exertions, let his arms fall to his sides in discouragement and jerked out: 'I understand the whole thing now: it's his doing! He foresaw that I should get out at Creil and he laid a pretty little trap for me, in case I should come to start my inquiry tonight. In addition, he had the kindness to send you to keep me company in my captivity. All this to make me lose a day and also, no doubt, to show me that I would do much better to mind my own business . . . '

'That is to say that we are his prisoners.'

'You speak like a book. Holmlock Shears and Wilson are the prisoners of Arsène Lupin. The adventure is beginning splendidly . . . But no, no, I refuse to believe . . . '

A hand touched his shoulder. It was Wilson's hand.

'Look,' he said. 'Up there . . . a light . . . '

It was true: there was a light visible through one of the windows on the first floor.

They both raced up, each by his own staircase, and reached the door of the lighted room at the same time. A candle-end was burning in the middle of the floor. Beside it stood a basket, from which protruded the neck of a bottle, the legs of a chicken and half a loaf of bread.

Shears roared with laughter.

'Splendid! He gives us our supper. It's an enchanted palace, a regular fairy-land! Come, Wilson, throw off that dismal face. This is all very amusing.'

'Are you sure it's very amusing?' moaned Wilson, dolefully.

'Sure?' cried Shears, with a gaiety that was too boisterous to be quite natural. 'Of course I'm sure! I never saw anything more amusing in my life. It's first-rate farce . . . What a master of chaff this Arsène Lupin is! . . . He tricks you, but he does it so gracefully! . . . I wouldn't give my seat at this banquet for all the gold in the world . . . Wilson, old chap, you disappoint me. Can I have been mistaken in you? Are you really deficient in that nobility of character which makes a man bear up under misfortune? What have you to complain of? At this moment, you might be lying with my dagger in your throat . . . or I with yours in mine . . . for that was what you were trying for, you faithless friend!'

He succeeded, by dint of humour and sarcasm, in cheering up the wretched Wilson and forcing him to swallow a leg of the chicken and a glass of wine. But, when the candle had gone out and they had to stretch themselves on the floor to sleep, with the wall for a pillow, the painful and ridiculous side of the situation became apparent to them. And their slumbers were sad.

In the morning, Wilson woke aching in every bone and shivering with cold. A slight sound caught his ear: Holmlock Shears, on his knees, bent in two, was examining grains of dust through his lens and inspecting certain hardly perceptible chalk-marks, which formed figures which he put down in his note-book.

Escorted by Wilson, who seemed to take a particular interest in this work, he studied each room and found similar chalk-marks in two of the others. He also observed two circles on some oak panels, an arrow on a wainscoting and four figures on four steps of the staircase.

After an hour spent in this way, Wilson asked: 'The figures are correct, are they not?'

'I don't know if they're correct,' replied Shears, whose good temper had been restored by these discoveries, 'but, at any rate, they mean something.'

'Something very obvious,' said Wilson. 'They represent the number of planks in the floor.'

'Oh!'

'Yes. As for the two circles, they indicate that the panels sound hollow, as you can see by trying, and the arrow points to show the direction of the dinner-lift.'

Holmlock Shears looked at him in admiration.

'Why, my dear chap, how do you know all this? Your perspicacity almost makes me ashamed of myself.'

'Oh, it's very simple,' said Wilson, bursting with delight. 'I made those marks myself last night, in consequence of your instructions . . . or rather Lupin's instructions, as the letter I received from you came from him.'

I have little doubt that, at that moment, Wilson was in greater danger than during his struggle with Shears in the shrubbery. Shears felt a fierce longing to wring his neck. Mastering himself with an effort, he gave a grin that pretended to be a smile and said: 'Well done, well done, that's an excellent piece of work; most useful. Have your wonderful powers of analysis and observation been exercised in any other direction? I may as well make use of the results obtained.'

'No, that's all I did.'

'What a pity! The start was so promising! Well, as things are, there is nothing left for us to do but go.'

'Go? But how?'

'The way respectable people usually go: through the gate.'

'It's locked.'

'We must get it opened.'

'Whom by?'

'Would you mind calling those two policemen walking down the avenue?'

'But . . . '

'But what?'

'It's very humiliating . . . What will people say, when they learn that you, Holmlock Shears, and I, Wilson, have been locked up by Arsène Lupin?'

'It can't be helped, my dear fellow; they will laugh like anything,' replied Shears, angrily, with a frowning face. 'But we can't go on living here for ever, can we?'

'And you don't propose to try anything?'

'Not I!'

'Still, the man who brought the basket of provisions did not cross the garden either in coming or going. There must, therefore, be another outlet. Let us look for it, instead of troubling the police.'

'Ably argued. Only you forget that the whole police of Paris have been hunting for this outlet for the past six months and that I myself, while you were asleep, examined the house from top to bottom. Ah, my dear Wilson, Arsène Lupin is a sort of game we are not accustomed to hunt: he leaves nothing behind him, you see . . . '

*   *   *

Holmlock Shears and Wilson were let out at eleven o'clock and . . . taken to the nearest police-station, where the commissary, after cross-questioning them severely, released them with the most exasperating pretences of courtesy.

'Gentlemen, I am grieved beyond measure at your mishap. You will have a poor opinion of our French hospitality. Lord, what a night you must have spent! Upon my word, Lupin might have shown you more consideration!'

They took a cab to the Élysee-Palace. Wilson went to the office and asked for the key of his room.

The clerk looked through the visitors' book and replied, in great surprise: 'But you gave up your room this morning, sir!'

'What do you mean? How did I give up my room?'

'You sent us a letter by your friend.'

'What friend?'

'Why, the gentleman who brought us your letter . . . Here it is, with your card enclosed.'

Wilson took the letter and the enclosure. It was certainly one of his visiting-cards and the letter was in his writing.

'Good Lord!' he muttered. 'Here's another nasty trick.' And he added, anxiously, 'What about the luggage?'

'Why, your friend took it with him.'

'Oh! . . . So you gave it to him?'

'Certainly, on the authority of your card.'

'Just so . . . just so . . . '

They both went out and wandered down the Champs-Élysées, slowly and silently. A fine autumn sun filled the avenue. The air was mild and light.

At the rond-point, Shears lit his pipe and resumed his walk. Wilson cried: 'I can't understand you, Shears: you take it so calmly! The man laughs at you, plays with you as a cat plays with a mouse . . . and you don't utter a word!'

Shears stopped and said: 'I'm thinking of your visiting-card, Wilson.'

'Well?'

'Well, here is a man, who, by way of preparing for a possible struggle with us, obtains specimens of your handwriting and mine and who has one of your cards ready in his pocket-book. Have you thought of the amount of precaution, of perspicacity, of determination, of method, of organization that all this represents?'

'You mean to say . . . '

'I mean to say, Wilson, that, to fight an enemy so formidably armed, so wonderfully equipped – and to beat him – takes . . . a man like myself. And, even then, Wilson,' he added, laughing, 'one does not succeed at the first attempt, as you see!'

* * *

At six o'clock, the *Écho de France* published the following paragraph in its special edition.

> This morning, M. Thénard, the commissary of police of the 16th division, released Messrs. Holmlock Shears and Wilson, who had been confined, by order of Arsène Lupin, in the late Baron d'Hautrec's house, where they spent an excellent night.
>
> They were also relieved of their luggage and have laid an information against Arsène Lupin.
>
> Arsène Lupin has been satisfied with giving them a little lesson this time; but he earnestly begs them not to compel him to adopt more serious measures.

'Pooh!' said Holmlock Shears, crumpling up the paper. 'Schoolboy tricks! That's the only fault I have to find with Lupin . . . he's too childish, too fond of playing to the gallery . . . He's a street arab at heart!'

'So you continue to take it calmly, Shears?'

'Quite calmly,' replied Shears, in a voice shaking with rage. 'What's the use of being angry? *I am so certain of having the last word*!'

Chapter 4

A Glimmer in the Darkness

However impervious to outside influences a man's character may be – and Shears is one of those men upon whom ill-luck takes hardly any hold – there are yet circumstances in which the most undaunted feel the need to collect their forces before again facing the chances of a battle.

'I shall take a holiday today,' said Shears.

'And I?'

'You, Wilson, must go and buy clothes and shirts and things to replenish our wardrobe. During that time, I shall rest.'

'Yes, rest, Shears. I shall watch.'

Wilson uttered those three words with all the importance of a sentry placed on outpost duty and therefore exposed to the worst dangers. He threw out his chest and stiffened his muscles. With a sharp eye, he glanced round the little hotel bedroom where they had taken up their quarters.

'That's right, Wilson: watch. I shall employ the interval in pre-paring a plan of campaign better suited to the adversary whom we have to deal with. You see, Wilson, we were wrong about Lupin. We must start again from the beginning.'

'Even earlier, if we can. But have we time?'

'Nine days, old chap: five days more than we want.'

The Englishman spent the whole afternoon smoking and dozing. He did not begin operations until the following morning.

'I'm ready now, Wilson. We can go ahead.'

'Let's go ahead,' cried Wilson, full of martial ardour. 'My legs are twitching to start.'

Shears had three long interviews: first, with Maître Detinan, whose flat he inspected through and through; next, with Suzanne Gerbois, to whom he telegraphed to come and whom he ques-tioned about the fair-haired lady; lastly with Soeur Auguste, who had returned to the Visitation Convent after the murder of Baron d'Hautrec.

At each visit, Wilson waited outside and, after each visit, asked: 'Satisfied?'

'Quite.'

'I was sure of it. We're on the right track now. Let's go ahead.'

They did a great deal of going. They called at the two mansions on either side of the house in the Avenue Henri-Martin. From there they went on to the Rue Clapeyron and, while he was examining the front of No. 25, Shears continued: 'It is quite obvious that there are secret passages between all these houses . . . But what I cannot make out . . . '

For the first time and in his inmost heart, Wilson doubted the omnipotence of his talented chief. Why was he talking so much and doing so little?

'Why?' cried Shears, replying to Wilson's unspoken thoughts. 'Because, with that confounded Lupin, one has nothing to go upon, one works at random. Instead of deriving the truth from exact facts, one has to get at it by intuition and verify it afterwards to see if it fits in.'

'But the secret passages . . . ?'

'What then? Even if I knew them, if I knew the one which admitted Lupin to his lawyer's study or the one taken by the fair-haired lady after the murder of Baron d'Hautrec, how much further should I be? Would that give me a weapon to go for him with?'

'Let's go for him, in any case,' said Wilson.

He had not finished speaking, when he jumped back with a cry. Something had fallen at their feet: a bag half-filled with sand, which might have hurt them seriously.

Shears looked up: some men were working in a cradle hooked on to the balcony of the fifth floor.

'Upon my word,' he said, 'we've had a lucky escape! The clumsy beggars! Another yard and we should have caught that bag on our heads. One would really think . . . '

He stopped, darted into the house, rushed up the staircase, rang the bell on the fifth landing, burst into the flat, to the great alarm of the footman who opened the door, and went out on the balcony. There was no one there.

'Where are the workmen who were here a moment ago?' he asked the footman.

'They have just gone.'

'Which way?'

'Why, down the servants' staircase.'

Shears leant over. He saw two men leaving the house, leading their bicycles. They mounted and rode away.

'Have they been working on this cradle long?'

'No, only since this morning. They were new men.'

Shears joined Wilson down below.

They went home in a depressed mood; and this second day ended in silent gloom.

* * *

They followed a similar programme on the following day. They sat down on a bench in the Avenue Henri-Martin. Wilson, who was thoroughly bored by this interminable wait opposite the three houses, felt driven to desperation.

'What do you expect, Shears? To see Lupin come out?'

'No.'

'Or the fair-haired lady?'

'No.'

'What, then?'

'I expect some little thing to happen, some little tiny thing which I can use as a starting-point.'

'And, if nothing happens?'

'In that case, something will happen inside myself: a spark that will set us going.'

The only incident that broke the monotony of the morning was a rather disagreeable one. A gentleman was coming down the riding-path that separates the two roadways of the avenue, when his horse swerved, struck the bench on which they were sitting and backed against Shears's shoulder.

'Tut, tut!' snarled Shears. 'A shade more and I should have had my shoulder smashed.'

The rider was struggling with his horse. The Englishman drew his revolver and took aim. But Wilson seized his arm smartly.

'You're mad, Holmlock! Why . . . look here . . . you'll kill that gentleman!'

'Let go, Wilson . . . do let go!'

A wrestle ensued, during which the horseman got his mount under control and galloped away.

'Now you can fire!' exclaimed Wilson, triumphantly, when the man was at some distance.

'But, you confounded fool, don't you understand that that was a confederate of Arsène Lupin's?'

Shears was trembling with rage. Wilson stammered, piteously: 'What do you mean? That gentleman . . . ?'

'Was a confederate of Lupin's, like the workmen who flung that bag at our heads.'

'It's not credible!'

'Credible or not, there was a means handy of obtaining a proof.'

'By killing that gentleman?'

'By simply bringing down his horse. But for you, I should have got one of Lupin's pals. Do you see now what a fool you've been?'

The afternoon was passed in a very sullen fashion. Shears and Wilson did not exchange a word. At five o'clock, as they were pacing up and down the Rue Clapeyron, taking care, however, to keep away from the houses, three young working-men came along the pavement singing, arm-in-arm, knocked up against them and tried to continue their road without separating. Shears, who was in a bad temper, pushed them back. There was a short scuffle. Shears put up his fists, struck one of the men in the chest and gave another a blow in the face, whereupon the two men desisted and walked away with the third.

'Ah,' cried Shears, 'I feel all the better for that! . . . My nerves were a bit strained . . . Good business! . . . '

But he saw Wilson leaning against the wall.

'Hullo, old chap,' he said, 'what's up? You look quite pale.'

Old chap pointed to his arm, which was hanging lifeless by his side, and stammered: 'I don't know . . . my arm's hurting me . . . '

'Your arm? . . . Badly? . . . '

'Yes . . . rather . . . it's my right arm . . . '

He tried to lift it, but could not. Shears felt it, gently at first and then more roughly, 'to see exactly,' he said, 'how much it hurts.' It hurt exactly so much that Wilson, on being led to a neighbouring chemist's shop, experienced an immediate need to fall into a dead faint.

The chemist and his assistant did what they could. They discovered that the arm was broken and that it was a case for a surgeon, an operation and a hospital. Meanwhile, the patient was undressed and began to relieve his sufferings by roaring with pain.

'That's all right, that's all right,' said Shears, who was holding Wilson's arm. 'Just a little patience, old chap . . . in five or six weeks, you won't know that you've been hurt . . . But I'll make them pay for it, the scoundrels! . . . You understand . . . I mean him especially . . . for it's that wretched Lupin who's responsible for this . . . Oh, I swear to you that, if ever . . . '

He interrupted himself suddenly, dropped the arm, which gave Wilson such a shock of pain that the poor wretch fainted once more, and, striking his forehead, shouted: 'Wilson, I have an idea . . . Could it possibly . . . ?'

He stood motionless, with his eyes fixed before him, and muttered, in short sentences.

'Yes, that's it . . . It's all clear now . . . the explanation staring us in the face . . . Why, of course, I knew it only needed a little thought! . . . Ah, my dear Wilson, this will rejoice your heart!'

And, leaving old chap where he was, he rushed into the street and ran to No. 25.

One of the stones above the door, on the right, bore the inscription: '*Destange, architect*, 1875'.

The same inscription appeared on No. 23. So far, this was quite natural. But what would he find down there, in the Avenue Henri-Martin?

He hailed a passing cab.

'Drive to 134, Avenue Henri-Martin. Go as fast as you can.'

Standing up in the cab, he urged on the horse, promised the driver tip after tip.

'Faster! . . . Faster still! . . . '

He was in an agony as he turned the corner of the Rue de la Pompe. Had he caught a glimpse of the truth?

On one of the stones of the house, he read the words: '*Destange, architect*, 1874'. And he found the same inscription – '*Destange, architect*, 1874' – on each of the adjoining blocks of flats.

* * *

The reaction after this excitement was so great that he sank back into the cab for a few minutes, all trembling with delight. At last, a tiny glimmer flickered in the darkness! Amid the thousand intersecting paths in the great, gloomy forest, he had found the first sign of a trail followed by the enemy!

He entered a telephone-office and asked to be put on to the Château de Crozon. The countess herself answered.

'Hullo! . . . Is that you, madame?'

'Is that Mr Shears? How are things going?'

'Very well. But tell me, quickly . . . Hullo! Are you there? . . . '

'Yes . . . '

'When was the Château de Crozon built?'

'It was burnt down thirty years ago and rebuilt.'

'By whom? And in what year?'

'There's an inscription over the front door: "*Lucien Destange, architect*, 1877".'

'Thank you, madame. Goodbye.'

'Goodbye.'

'He went away, muttering: 'Destange . . . Lucien Destange . . . I seem to know the name . . . '

He found a public library, consulted a modern biographical dictionary and copied out the reference to 'Lucien Destange, born 1840, Grand-Prix de Rome, officer of the Legion of Honour, author of several valuable works on architecture,' etc.

He next went to the chemist's and, from there, to the hospital to which Wilson had been moved. Old chap was lying on his bed of pain, with his arm in splints, shivering with fever and slightly delirious.

'Victory! Victory!' cried Shears. 'I have one end of the clue.'

'What clue?'

'The clue that will lead me to success! I am now treading firm soil, where I shall find marks and indications . . . '

'Cigarette-ashes?' asked Wilson, whom the interest of the situation was reviving.

'And plenty of other things! Just think, Wilson, I have discovered the mysterious link that connects the three adventures of the fair-haired lady. Why were the three houses in which the three adventures took place selected by Arsène Lupin?'

'Yes, why?'

'Because those three houses, Wilson, were built by the same architect. It was easy to guess that, you say? Certainly it was . . . And that's why nobody thought of it.'

'Nobody except yourself.'

'Just so! And I now understand how the same architect, by contriving similar plans, enabled three actions to be performed which appeared to be miraculous, though they were really quite easy and simple.'

'What luck!'

'It was high time, old chap, for I was beginning to lose patience . . . This is the fourth day.'

'Out of ten.'

'Oh, but from now onwards . . . !'

He could no longer keep his seat, exulting in his gladness beyond his wont.

'Oh, when I think that, just now, in the street, those ruffians might have broken my arm as well as yours! What do you say to that, Wilson?'

Wilson simply shuddered at the horrid thought.

And Shears continued: 'Let this be a lesson to us! You see, Wilson, our great mistake has been to fight Lupin in the open and to expose ourselves, in the most obliging way, to his attacks. The thing is not as bad as it might be, because he only got at you . . . '

'And I came off with a broken arm,' moaned Wilson.

'Whereas it might have been both of us. But no more swaggering. Watched, in broad daylight, I am beaten. Working freely, in the shade, I have the advantage, whatever the enemy's strength may be.'

'Ganimard might be able to help you.'

'Never! On the day when I can say, "Arsène Lupin is there; that is his hiding-place; this is how you must set to work to catch him," I shall hunt up Ganimard at one of the two addresses he gave me, his flat in the Rue Pergolèse, or the Taverne Suisse, on the Place du Châtelet. But till then I shall act alone.'

He went up to the bed, put his hand on Wilson's shoulder – the bad shoulder, of course – and said, in a very affectionate voice: 'Take care of yourself, old chap. Your task, henceforth, will consist in keeping two or three of Lupin's men busy. They will waste their time waiting for me to come and enquire after you. It's a confidential task.'

'Thank you ever so much,' replied Wilson, gratefully. 'I shall do my best to perform it conscientiously. So you are not coming back?'

'Why should I?' asked Shears, coldly.

'No . . . you're quite right . . . you're quite right . . . I'm going on as well as can be expected. You might do one thing for me, Holmlock: give me a drink.'

'A drink?'

'Yes, I'm parched with thirst; and this fever of mine . . . '

'Why, of course! Wait a minute . . . '

He fumbled about among some bottles, came upon a packet of tobacco, filled and lit his pipe and, suddenly, as though he had not even heard his friend's request, walked away, while old chap cast longing glances at the water-bottle beyond his reach.

* * *

'Is M. Destange at home?'

The butler eyed the person to whom he had opened the door of the house – the magnificent house at the corner of the Place Malesherbes and the Rue Montchanin – and, at the sight of the little grey-haired, ill-shaven man, whose long and far from immaculate frock-coat matched the oddity of a figure to which nature had been anything but kind, replied, with due scorn: 'M. Destange may be at home or he may be out. It depends. Has monsieur a card?'

Monsieur had no card, but he carried a letter of introduction and the butler had to take it to M. Destange, whereupon M. Destange ordered the newcomer to be shown in.

He was ushered into a large circular room, which occupied one of the wings of the house and which was lined with books all round the walls.

'Are you M. Stickmann?' asked the architect.

'Yes, sir.'

'My secretary writes that he is ill and sends you to continue the general catalogue of my books, which he began under my direction, and of the German books in particular. Have you any experience of this sort of work?'

'Yes, sir, a long experience,' replied Stickmann, in a strong Teutonic accent.

In these conditions, the matter was soon settled; and M. Destange set to work with his new secretary without further delay.

Holmlock Shears had carried the citadel.

In order to escape Lupin's observation and to obtain an entrance into the house which Lucien Destange occupied with his daughter Clotilde, the illustrious detective had been obliged to take a leap in the dark, to resort to untold stratagems, to win the favour and confidence of a host of people under endless different names, in short, to lead forty-eight hours of the most complex life.

The particulars which he had gathered were these: M. Destange, who was in failing health and anxious for rest, had retired from business and was living among the architectural books which it had been his hobby to collect. He had no interest left in life beyond the handling and examining of those old dusty volumes.

As for his daughter Clotilde, she was looked upon as eccentric. She spent her days, like her father, in the house, but in another part of it, and never went out.

'This is all,' thought Shears, as he wrote down the titles of the books in his catalogue, to M. Destange's dictation, 'this is all more or less indefinite; but it is a good step forward. I am bound to discover the solution of one at least of these exciting problems: is M. Destange an accomplice of Arsène Lupin's? Does he see him now? Are there any papers relating to the building of the three houses? Will these papers supply me with the address of other properties, similarly faked, which Lupin may have reserved for his own use and that of his gang?'

M. Destange an accomplice of Arsène Lupin's! This venerable man, an officer of the Legion of Honour, working hand in hand with a burglar! The presumption was hardly tenable. Besides, supposing that they were accomplices, how did M. Destange come to provide for Arsène Lupin's various escapes thirty years before they occurred, at a time when Arsène was in his cradle?

No matter, the Englishman stuck to his guns. With his prodigious intuition, with that instinct which is all his own, he felt a mystery surrounding him. This was perceptible by small signs, which he could not have described with precision, but which impressed him from the moment when he first set foot in the house.

On the morning of the second day, he had as yet discovered nothing of interest. He first saw Clotilde Destange at two o'clock, when she came to fetch a book from the library. She was a woman of thirty, dark, with slow and silent movements; and her features bore the look of indifference of those who live much within themselves. She exchanged a few words with M. Destange and left the room without so much as glancing at Shears.

The afternoon dragged on monotonously. At five o'clock, M. Destange stated that he was going out. Shears remained alone in the circular gallery that ran round the library, half-way between floor and ceiling. It was growing dark and he was preparing to leave, in his turn, when he heard a creaking sound and, at the same time, felt that there was someone in the room. Minute followed slowly upon minute. And, suddenly, he started: a shadow had emerged from the semi-darkness, quite close to him, on the balcony. Was it credible? How long had this unseen person been keeping him company? And where did he come from?

And the man went down the steps and turned in the direction of a large oak cupboard. Crouching on his knees behind the tapestry that covered the rail of the gallery, Shears watched and saw the man rummage among the papers with which the cupboard was crammed. What was he looking for?

And, suddenly, the door opened and Mlle Destange entered quickly, saying to someone behind her: 'So you have quite changed your mind about going out, father? . . . In that case, I'll turn on the light . . . Wait a minute . . . don't move . . . '

The man closed the doors of the cupboard and hid himself in the embrasure of a broad window, drawing the curtains in front of him. How was it that Mlle Destange did not see him! How was it that she did not hear him? She calmly switched on the electric light and stood back for her father to pass.

They sat down side by side. Mlle Destange opened a book which she had brought with her and began to read.

'Has your secretary gone?' she said, presently.

'Yes . . . so it seems . . . '

'Are you still satisfied with him?' she continued, as if in ignorance of the real secretary's illness and of the arrival of Stickmann in his stead.

'Quite . . . quite . . . '

M. Destange's head dropped on his chest. He fell asleep.

A moment elapsed. The girl went on reading. But one of the window-curtains was moved aside and the man slipped along the wall, towards the door, an action which made him pass behind M. Destange, but right in front of Clotilde and in such a way that Shears was able to see him plainly. It was Arsène Lupin.

The Englishman quivered with delight. His calculations were correct, he had penetrated to the very heart of the mystery and Lupin was where he had expected to find him.

Clotilde, however, did not stir, although it was impossible that a single movement of that man had escaped her. And Lupin was close to the door and had his arm stretched towards the handle, when his clothes grazed a table and something fell to the ground. M. Destange woke with a start. In a moment, Arsène Lupin was standing before him, smiling, hat in hand.

'Maxime Bermond!' cried M. Destange, in delight. 'My dear Maxime! . . . What stroke of good luck brings you here today?'

'The wish to see you and Mlle Destange.'

'When did you come back?'

'Yesterday.'

'Are you staying to dinner?'

'Thank you, no, I am dining out with some friends.'

'Come tomorrow, then. Clotilde, make him come tomorrow. My dear Maxime! . . . I was thinking of you only the other day.'

'Really?'

'Yes, I was arranging my old papers, in that cupboard, and I came across our last account.'

'Which one?'

'The Avenue Henri-Martin account.'

'Do you mean to say you keep all that waste paper? What for? . . . '

The three moved into a little drawing-room which was connected with the round library by a wide recess.

'Is it Lupin?' thought Shears, seized with a sudden doubt.

All the evidence pointed to him, but it was another man as well; a man who resembled Arsène Lupin in certain respects and who, nevertheless, preserved his distinct individuality, his own features, look and complexion . . .

Dressed for the evening, with a white tie and a soft-fronted shirt following the lines of his body, he talked gaily, telling stories which made M. Destange laugh aloud and which brought a smile to Clotilde's lips. And each of these smiles seemed a reward which Arsène Lupin coveted and which he rejoiced at having won. His spirits and gaiety increased and, imperceptibly, at the sound of his clear and happy voice, Clotilde's face brightened up and lost the look of coldness that tended to spoil it.

'They are in love,' thought Shears. 'But what on earth can Clotilde Destange and Maxime Bermond have in common? Does she know that Maxime is Arsène Lupin?'

He listened anxiously until seven o'clock, making the most of every word spoken. Then, with infinite precautions, he came down and crossed the side of the room where there was no danger of his being seen from the drawing-room.

Once outside, after assuring himself that there was no motor-car or cab waiting, he limped away along the Boulevard Malesherbes. Then he turned down a side street, put on the overcoat which he carried over his arm, changed the shape of his hat, drew himself up and, thus transformed, returned to the square, where he waited, with his eyes fixed on the door of the Hôtel Destange.

Arsène Lupin came out almost at once and walked, down the Rue de Constantinople and the Rue de Londres, towards the centre of the town. Shears followed him at a hundred yards' distance.

It was a delicious moment for the Englishman. He sniffed the air greedily, like a good hound scenting a fresh trail. It really seemed infinitely sweet to him to be following his adversary. It was no longer he that was watched, but Arsène Lupin, the invisible Arsène Lupin. He kept him, so to speak, fastened at the end of his eyes, as though with unbreakable bonds. And he revelled in contemplating, among the other pedestrians, this prey which belonged to him.

But a curious incident soon struck him: in the centre of the space that separated Arsène Lupin and himself, other people were going in the same direction, notably two tall fellows in bowler hats on the left pavement, while two others, in caps, were following on the right pavement, smoking cigarettes as they went.

This might be only a coincidence. But Shears was more surprised when the four men stopped as Lupin entered a tobacconist's shop; and still more when they started again as he came out, but separately, each keeping to his own side of the Chaussée d'Antin.

'Confound it!' thought Shears. 'He's being shadowed!'

The idea that others were on Arsène Lupin's track, that others might rob him not of the glory – he cared little for that – but of the huge pleasure, the intense delight of conquering unaided the most formidable enemy that he had ever encountered: this idea exasperated him. And yet there was no possibility of a mistake: the men wore that look of detachment, that too-natural look which distinguishes persons who, while regulating their gait by another's, endeavour to remain unobserved.

'Does Ganimard know more than he pretends?' muttered Shears. 'Is he making game of me?'

He felt inclined to accost one of the four men, with a view to acting in concert with him. But, as they approached the boulevard, the crowd became denser: he was afraid of losing Lupin and quickened his pace. He turned into the boulevard just as Lupin had his foot on the step of the Restaurant Hongrois, at the corner of the Rue du Helder. The door was open and Shears, sitting on a bench on the boulevard, on the opposite side of the road, saw him take his seat at a table laid with the greatest luxury and decorated with flowers, where he was warmly welcomed by three men in evening clothes and two beautifully-dressed ladies who had been waiting for him.

Shears looked for the four rough fellows and saw them scattered among the groups of people who were listening to the Bohemian band of a neighbouring café. Strange to say, they appeared to be not nearly so much interested in Arsène Lupin as in the people surrounding them.

Suddenly, one of them took a cigarette from his case and addressed a gentleman in a frock-coat and tall hat. The gentleman offered a light from his cigar and Shears received the impression that they were talking at greater length than the mere lighting of a cigarette demanded. At last, the gentleman went up the steps and glanced into the restaurant. Seeing Lupin, he walked up to him, exchanged a few words with him and selected a table close at hand; and Shears realized that he was none other than the horseman of the Avenue Henri-Martin.

Now he understood. Not only was Arsène not being shadowed, but these men were members of his gang! These men were watching over his safety! They were his bodyguard, his satellites, his vigilant escort. Wherever the master ran any danger, there his accomplices were, ready to warn him, ready to defend him. The four men were accomplices! The gentleman in the frock-coat was an accomplice!

A thrill passed through the Englishman's frame. Would he ever succeed in laying hands on that inaccessible person? The power represented by an association of this kind, ruled by such a chief, seemed boundless.

He tore a leaf from his note-book, wrote a few lines in pencil, put the note in an envelope and gave it to a boy of fifteen who had lain down on the bench beside him.

'Here, my lad, take a cab and give this letter to the young lady behind the bar at the Taverne Suisse on the Place du Châtelet. Be as quick as you can.'

He handed him a five-franc piece. The boy went off.

Half an hour elapsed. The crowd had increased and Shears but occasionally caught sight of Lupin's followers. Then someone grazed against him and a voice said in his ear: 'Well, Mr Shears, what can I do for you?'

'Is that you, M. Ganimard?'

'Yes, I got your note. What is it?'

'He's there.'

'What's that you say?'

'Over there . . . inside the restaurant . . . Move a little to the right . . . Do you see him?'

'No.'

'He is filling the glass of the lady on his left.'

'But that's not Lupin.'

'Yes, it is.'

'I assure you . . . And yet . . . Well, it may be . . . Oh, the rascal, *how like himself he is!*' muttered Ganimard, innocently. 'And who are the others? Accomplices?'

'No, the lady beside him is Lady Cliveden. The other is the Duchess of Cleath; and, opposite her, is the Spanish Ambassador in London.'

Ganimard took a step towards the road. But Shears held him back.

'Don't be so reckless: you are alone.'

'So is he.'

'No, there are men on the boulevard mounting guard . . . Not to mention that gentleman inside the restaurant . . . '

'But I have only to take him by the collar and shout his name to have the whole restaurant on my side, all the waiters . . . '

'I would rather have a few detectives.'

'That would set Lupin's friends off . . . No, Mr Shears, we have no choice, you see.'

He was right and Shears felt it. It was better to make the attempt and take advantage of the exceptional circumstances. He contented himself with saying to Ganimard: 'Do your best not to be recognized before you can help it.'

He himself slipped behind a newspaper-kiosk, without losing sight of Arsène Lupin, who was leaning over Lady Cliveden, smiling.

The inspector crossed the street, looking straight before him, with his hands in his pockets. But, the moment he reached the opposite pavement, he veered briskly round and sprang up the steps.

A shrill whistle sounded . . . Ganimard knocked up against the head-waiter, who suddenly blocked the entrance and pushed him back with indignation, as he might push back any intruder whose doubtful attire would have disgraced the luxury of the establishment. Ganimard staggered. At the same moment, the gentleman in the frock-coat came out. He took the part of the inspector and began a violent discussion with the head-waiter. Both of them had hold of Ganimard, one pushing him forward, the other back, until, in spite of all his efforts and angry protests, the unhappy man was hustled to the bottom of the steps.

A crowd gathered at once. Two policemen, attracted by the excitement, tried to make their way through; but they encountered an incomprehensible resistance and were unable to get clear of the shoulders that pushed against them, the backs that barred their progress . . .

And, suddenly, as though by enchantment, the way was opened! . . . The head-waiter, realizing his mistake, made the most abject apologies; the gentleman in the frock-coat withdrew his assistance; the crowd parted, the policemen passed in; and Ganimard rushed towards the table with the six guests . . . There were only five left! He looked round: there was no way out except the door.

'Where is the person who was sitting here?' he shouted to the five bewildered guests. 'Yes, there were six of you . . . Where is the sixth?'

'M. Destro?'

'No, no: Arsène Lupin!'

A waiter stepped up.

'The gentleman has just gone up to the mezzanine floor.'

Ganimard flew upstairs. The mezzanine floor consisted of private rooms and had a separate exit to the boulevard!

'It's no use now,' groaned Ganimard. 'He's far away by this time!'

* * *

He was not so very far away, two hundred yards at most, in the omnibus running between the Bastille and the Madeleine, which lumbered peacefully along behind its three horses, crossing the Place de l'Opéra and going down the Boulevard des Capucines. Two tall fellows in bowler hats stood talking on the conductor's platform. On the top, near the steps, a little old man sat dozing: it was Holmlock Shears.

And, with his head swaying from side to side, rocked by the movement of the omnibus, the Englishman soliloquized.

'Ah, if dear old Wilson could see me now, how proud he would be of his chief! . . . Pooh, it was easy to foresee, from the moment when the whistle sounded, that the game was up and that there was nothing serious to be done, except to keep a watch around the restaurant! But that devil of a man adds a zest to life; and no mistake!'

On reaching the end of the journey, Shears leant over, saw Arsène Lupin pass out in front of his guards and heard him mutter: 'At the Étoile.'

'The Étoile, just so: an assignation. I shall be there. I'll let him go ahead in that motor-cab, while I follow his two pals in a four-wheeler.'

The two pals went off on foot, made for the Étoile and rang at the door of No. 40, Rue Chalgrin, a house with a narrow frontage. Shears found a hiding place in the shadow of a recess formed by the angle of that unfrequented little street.

One of the two windows on the ground-floor opened and a man in a bowler hat closed the shutters. The window-space above the shutters was lit up.

In ten minutes' time, a gentleman came and rang at the same door; and, immediately afterwards, another person. And, at last, a motor-cab drew up and Shears saw two people get out: Arsène Lupin and a lady wrapped in a cloak and a thick veil.

'The fair-haired lady, I presume,' thought Shears, as the cab drove away.

He waited for a moment, went up to the house, climbed on to the window-ledge and, by standing on tip-toe, succeeded in peering into the room through that part of the window which the shutters failed to cover.

Arsène Lupin was leaning against the chimney and talking in an animated fashion. The others stood round and listened attentively. Shears recognized the gentleman in the frock-coat and thought he recognized the head-waiter of the restaurant. As for the fair-haired lady, she was sitting in a chair, with her back turned towards him.

'They are holding a council,' he thought. 'This evening's occur-rences have alarmed them and they feel a need to discuss things . . . Oh, if I could only catch them all at one swoop!'

One of the accomplices moved and Shears leapt down and fell back into the shadow. The gentleman in the frock-coat and the head-waiter left the house. Then the first floor was lit up and someone closed the window-shutters. It was now dark above and below.

'He and she have remained on the ground-floor,' said Holmlock to himself. 'The two accomplices live on the first storey.'

He waited during a part of the night without stirring from his place, fearing lest Arsène Lupin should go away during his absence. At four o'clock in the morning, seeing two policemen at the end of the street, he went up to them, explained the position and left them to watch the house.

Then he went to Ganimard's flat in the Rue Pergolèse and told the servant to wake him.

'I've got him again.'

'Arsène Lupin?'

'Yes.'

'If you haven't got him any better than you did just now, I may as well go back to bed. However, let's go and see the commissary.'

They went to the Rue Mesnil and, from there, to the house of the commissary, M. Decointre. Next, accompanied by half-a-dozen men, they returned to the Rue Chalgrin.

'Any news?' asked Shears of the two policemen watching the house.

'No, sir, none.'

The daylight was beginning to show in the sky when the commissary, after disposing his men, rang and entered the lodge of the concierge. Terrified by this intrusion, the woman, all trembling, said that there was no tenant on the ground-floor.

'What do you mean, no tenant?' cried Ganimard.

'No, it's the people on the first floor, two gentlemen called Leroux . . . They have furnished the apartment below for some relations from the country . . . '

'A lady and gentleman?'

'Yes.'

'Did they come with them last night?'

'They may have . . . I was asleep . . . I don't think so, though, for here's the key . . . they didn't ask for it.'

With this key, the commissary opened the door on the other side of the passage. The ground-floor flat contained only two rooms: they were empty.

'Impossible!' said Shears. 'I saw them both here.'

The commissary grinned.

'I dare say, but they are not here now.'

'Let us go to the first floor. They must be there.'

'The first floor is occupied by two gentlemen called Leroux.'

'We will question the two gentlemen called Leroux.'

They all went upstairs and the commissary rang. At the second ring, a man, who was none other than one of the bodyguards, appeared in his shirtsleeves and, with a furious air: 'Well, what is it? What's all this noise about; what do you come waking people up for?'

But he stopped in confusion.

'Lord bless my soul! . . . Am I dreaming? Why, it's M. Decointre! . . . And you too, M. Ganimard? What can I do for you?'

There was a roar of laughter. Ganimard was splitting with a fit of merriment which doubled him up and seemed to threaten an apoplectic fit.

'It's you, Leroux!' he spluttered out. 'Oh, that's the best thing I ever heard: Leroux, Arsène Lupin's accomplice! . . . It'll be the death of me, I know it will! . . . And where's your brother, Leroux? Is he visible?'

'Are you there, Edmond? It's M. Ganimard come to pay us a visit.'

Another man came forward, at the sight of whom Ganimard's hilarity increased still further.

'Well, I never! Dear, dear me! Ah, my friends, you're in a nice pickle! . . . Who would have suspected it? It's a good thing that old Ganimard keeps his eyes open and still better that he has friends to help him . . . friends who have come all the way from England!'

And, turning to Shears, he said: 'Mr Shears, let me introduce Victor Leroux, detective-inspector, one of the best in the iron brigade . . . And Edmond Leroux, head-clerk in the Finger-print Department . . .'

Chapter 5
Kidnapped

Holmlock Shears restrained his feelings. What was the use of protesting, of accusing those two men? Short of proofs, which he did not possess and which he would not waste time in looking for, no one would take his word.

With nerves on edge and fists tight-clenched, he had but one thought, that of not betraying his rage and disappointment before the triumphant Ganimard. He bowed politely to those two mainstays of society, the brothers Leroux, and went downstairs.

In the hall, he turned towards a small, low door, which marked the entrance to the cellar, and picked up a small red stone: it was a garnet.

Outside, he looked up and read, close to the number of the house, the inscription: '*Lucien Destange, architect,* 1877.' He saw the same inscription on No. 42.

'Always that double outlet,' he thought. 'Nos. 40 and 42 communicate. Why did I not think of it before? I ought to have stayed with the policemen all night.'

And, addressing them, he said, pointing to the door of the next house: 'Did two people go out by that door while I was away?'

'Yes, sir: a lady and gentleman.'

He took the arm of the chief-inspector and led him along.

'M. Ganimard, you have enjoyed too hearty a laugh to be very angry with me for disturbing you like this . . . '

'Oh, I'm not angry with you at all.'

'That's right. But the best jokes can't go on for ever and I think we must put an end to this one.'

'I am with you.'

'This is our seventh day. It is absolutely necessary that I should be in London in three days hence.'

'I say! I say!'

'I shall be there, though, and I beg you to hold yourself in readiness on Tuesday night.'

'For an expedition of the same kind?' asked Ganimard, chaffingly.

'Yes, of the same kind.'

'And how will this one end?'

'In Lupin's capture.'

'You think so.'

'I swear it, on my honour.'

Shears took his leave and went to seek a short rest in the nearest hotel, after which, refreshed and full of confidence, he returned to the Rue Chalgrin, slipped two louis into the hand of the concierge, made sure that the brothers Leroux were out, learnt that the house belonged to a certain M. Harmingeat and, carrying a candle, found his way down to the cellar through the little door near which he had picked up the garnet.

At the foot of the stairs, he picked up another of exactly the same shape.

'I was right,' he thought. 'This forms the communication . . . Let's see if my skeleton-key opens the door of the cellar that belongs to the ground-floor tenant . . . Yes, capital . . . Now let's examine these wine-bins . . . Aha, here are places where the dust has been removed . . . and footprints on the floor! . . . '

A slight sound made him prick up his ears. He quickly closed the door, blew out his candle and hid behind a stack of empty wine-cases. After a few seconds, he noticed that one of the iron bins was turning slowly on a pivot, carrying with it the whole of the piece of wall to which it was fastened. The light of a lantern was thrown into the cellar. An arm appeared. A man entered.

He was bent in two, like a man looking for something. He fumbled in the dust with his fingertips and, several times, he straightened himself and threw something into a cardboard box which he carried in his left hand. Next, he removed the marks of his footsteps, as well as those left by Lupin and the fair-haired lady, and went back to the wine-bin.

He gave a hoarse cry and fell. Shears had leapt upon him. It was the matter of a moment and, in the simplest way possible, the man found himself stretched on the floor, with his ankles fastened together and his wrists bound.

The Englishman stooped over him.

'How much will you take to speak? . . . To tell what you know?'

The man replied with so sarcastic a smile that Shears understood the futility of his question. He contented himself with exploring his captive's pockets, but his investigations produced nothing more than a bunch of keys, a pocket-handkerchief and the little cardboard box used by the fellow and containing a dozen garnets similar to those which Shears had picked up. A poor booty!

Besides, what was he to do with the man? Wait until his friends came to his assistance and hand them all over to the police? What was the good? What advantage could he derive from it against Lupin?

He was hesitating, when a glance at the box made him come to a decision. It bore the address of Léonard, jeweller, Rue de la Paix.

He resolved simply to leave the man where he was. He pushed back the bin, shut the cellar-door and left the house. He went to a post-office and telegraphed to M. Destange that he could not come until the next day. Then he went on to the jeweller and handed him the garnets.

'Madame sent me with these stones. They came off a piece of jewellery which she bought here.'

Shears had hit the nail on the head. The jeweller replied: 'That's right . . . The lady telephoned to me. She will call here herself presently.'

It was five o'clock before Shears, standing on the pavement, saw a lady arrive, wrapped in a thick veil, whose appearance struck him as suspicious. Through the shop-window, he saw her place on the counter an old-fashioned brooch set with garnets.

She went away almost at once, did a few errands on foot, walked up towards Clichy and turned down streets which the Englishman did not know. At nightfall, he followed her, unperceived by the concierge, into a five-storeyed house built on either side of the doorway and therefore containing numberless flats. She stopped at a door on the second floor and went in.

Two minutes later, the Englishman put his luck to the test and, one after the other, carefully tried the keys on the bunch of which he had obtained possession. The fourth key fitted the lock.

Through the darkness that filled them, he saw rooms which were absolutely empty, like those of an unoccupied flat, with all the doors standing open. But the light of a lamp filtered through from the end of a passage; and, approaching on tip-toe, through the glass door that separated the drawing-room from an adjoining bedroom he saw the veiled lady take off her dress and hat, lay them on the one chair which the room contained and slip on a velvet tea-gown.

And he also saw her walk up to the chimney-piece and push an electric bell. And one half of the panel to the right of the chimney moved from its position and slipped along the wall into the thickness of the next panel. As soon as the gap was wide enough, the lady passed through . . . and disappeared, taking the lamp with her.

The system was a simple one. Shears employed it. He found himself walking in the dark, groping his way; but suddenly his face came upon something soft. By the light of a match, he saw that he was in a little closet filled with dresses and clothes hanging from metal bars. He thrust his way through and stopped before the embrasure of a door closed by a tapestry hanging or, at least, by the back of a hanging. And, his match being now burnt out, he saw light piercing through the loose and worn woof of the old stuff.

Then he looked.

The fair-haired lady was there, before his eyes, within reach of his hand.

She put out the lamp and turned on the electric switch. For the first time, Shears saw her face in the full light. He gave a start. The woman whom he had ended by overtaking after so many shifts and turns was none other than Clotilde Destange.

*   *   *

Clotilde Destange the murderess of Baron d'Hautrec and the purloiner of the blue diamond! Clotilde Destange the mysterious friend of Arsène Lupin! The fair-haired lady, in short!

'Why, of course,' he thought, 'I'm the biggest blockhead that ever lived! Just because Lupin's friend is fair and Clotilde dark, I never thought of connecting the two women! As though the fair-haired lady could afford to continue fair after the murder of the baron and the theft of the diamond!'

Shears saw part of the room, an elegant lady's boudoir, adorned with light hangings and valuable knick-knacks. A mahogany settee stood on a slightly-raised platform. Clotilde had sat down on it and remained motionless, with her head between her hands. And soon he noticed that she was crying. Great tears flowed down her pale cheeks, trickled by her mouth, fell drop by drop on the velvet of her bodice. And more tears followed indefinitely, as though springing from an inexhaustible source. And no sadder sight was ever seen than that dull and resigned despair, which expressed itself in the slow flowing of the tears.

But a door opened behind her. Arsène Lupin entered.

They looked at each other for a long time, without exchanging a word. Then he knelt down beside her, pressed his head to her breast, put his arms round her; and there was infinite tenderness and great pity in the gesture with which he embraced the girl. They did not move. A soft silence united them, and her tears flowed less abundantly.

'I so much wanted to make you happy!' he whispered.

'I am happy.'

'No, for you're crying. And your tears break my heart, Clotilde.'

Yielding, in spite of herself, to the sound of his coaxing voice, she listened, greedy of hope and happiness. A smile softened her face, but oh, so sad a smile! He entreated her: 'Don't be sad, Clotilde; you have no reason, you have no right to be sad.'

She showed him her white, delicate, lissom hands, and said, gravely: 'As long as these hands are mine, Maxime, I shall be sad.'

'But why?'

'They have taken life.'

Maxime cried: 'Hush, you must not think of that! The past is dead, the past does not count.'

And he kissed her long white hands and she looked at him with a brighter smile, as though each kiss had wiped out a little of that hideous memory.

'You must love me, Maxime, you must, because no woman will ever love you as I do. To please you, I have acted, I am still acting not only according to your orders, but according to your unspoken wishes. I do things against which all my instincts and all my conscience revolt; but I am unable to resist . . . All that I do I do mechanically, because it is of use to you and you wish it . . . and I am ready to begin again tomorrow . . . and always.'

He said, bitterly: 'Ah, Clotilde, why did I ever mix you up in my adventurous life? I ought to have remained the Maxime Bermond whom you loved five years ago and not have let you know . . . the other man that I am.'

She whispered very low: 'I love that other man too; and I regret nothing.'

'Yes, you regret your past life, your life in the light of day.'

'I regret nothing, when you are there!' she said, passionately. 'There is no such thing as guilt, no such thing as crime, when my eyes see you. What do I care if I am unhappy away from you and if I suffer and cry and loathe all that I do! Your love wipes out everything . . . I accept everything . . . But you must love me!'

'I do not love you because I must, Clotilde, but simply because I love you.'

'Are you sure?' she asked, trustingly.

'I am as sure of myself as I am of you. Only, Clotilde, my life is a violent and feverish one and I cannot always give you as much time as I should wish.'

She at once grew terrified.

'What is it? A fresh danger? Tell me, quick!'

'Oh, nothing serious as yet. Still . . . '

'Still what . . . ?'

'Well, he is on our track.'

'Shears?'

'Yes. It was he who set Ganimard at me at the Restaurant Hongrois. It was he who posted the two policemen in the Rue Chalgrin last night. The proof is that Ganimard searched the house this morning and Shears was with him. Besides . . . '

'Besides what?'

'Well, there is something more: one of our men is missing, Jeanniot.'

'The concierge?'

'Yes.'

'Why, I sent him to the Rue Chalgrin this morning to pick up some garnets which had fallen from my brooch.'

'There is no doubt about it, Shears has caught him in a trap.'

'Not at all. The garnets were brought to the jeweller in the Rue de la Paix.'

'Then what has become of Jeanniot since?'

'Oh, Maxime, I'm so frightened!'

'There's no cause for alarm. But I admit that the position is very serious. How much does he know? Where is he hiding? His strength lies in his isolation. There is nothing to betray him.'

'Then what have you decided on?'

'Extreme prudence, Clotilde. Some time ago, I made up my mind to move my things to the refuge you know of, the safe refuge. The intervention of Shears hastens the need. When a man like Shears is on a trail, we may take it that he is bound to follow that trail to the end. So I have made all my preparations. The removal will take place on the day after tomorrow, Wednesday. It will be finished by mid-day. By two o'clock, I shall be able myself to leave, after getting rid of the last vestige of our occupation, which is no small matter. Until then . . . '

'Yes . . . ?'

'We must not see each other and no one must see you, Clotilde. Don't go out. I fear nothing for myself. But I fear everything where you're concerned.'

'It is impossible for that Englishman to get at me.'

'Everything is possible to him and I am not easy in my mind. Yesterday, when I was nearly caught by your father, I had come to search the cupboard which contains M. Destange's old ledgers. There is danger there. There is danger everywhere. I feel that the enemy is prowling in the shade and drawing nearer and nearer. I know that he is watching us . . . that he is laying his nets around us. It is one of those intuitions which never fail me.'

'In that case,' said she, 'go, Maxime, and think no more about my tears. I shall be brave and I will wait until the danger is over. Goodbye, Maxime.'

She gave him a long kiss. And she herself pushed him outside. Shears heard the sound of their voices grow fainter in the distance.

Boldly, excited by the need of action, towards and against everything, which had been stimulating him since the day before, he made his way to a passage, at the end of which was a staircase. But, just as he was going down, he heard the sound of a conversation below and thought it better to follow a circular corridor which brought him to another staircase. At the foot of this staircase, he was greatly surprised to see furniture the shape and position of which he already knew. A door stood half open. He entered a large round room. It was M. Destange's library.

'Capital! Splendid!' he muttered. 'I understand everything now. The boudoir of Clotilde, that is to say, the fair-haired lady, communicates with one of the flats in the next house and the door of that house is not in the Place Malesherbes, but in an adjoining street, the Rue Montchanin, if I remember right . . . Admirable! And now I see how Clotilde Destange slips out to meet her sweetheart while keeping up the reputation of a person who never leaves the house. And I also see how Arsène Lupin popped out close to me, yesterday evening, in the gallery: there must be another communication between the flat next door and this library . . . ' And he concluded, 'Another faked house. Once again, no doubt, "Destange, architect!" And what I must now do is to take advantage of my presence here to examine the contents of the cupboard . . . and obtain all the information I can about the other faked houses.'

Shears went up to the gallery and hid behind the hangings of the rail. He stayed there till the end of the evening. A man-servant came to put out the electric lights. An hour later, the Englishman pressed the spring of his lantern and went down to the cupboard. As he knew, it contained the architect's old papers, files, plans, estimates and account-books. At the back stood a row of ledgers, arranged in chronological order.

He took down the more recent volumes one by one and at once looked through the index-pages, more particularly under the letter H. At last, finding the word 'Harmingeat' followed by the number 63, he turned up page 63 and read.

'Harmingeat, 40, Rue Chalgrin.'

There followed a detailed statement of works executed for this customer, with a view to the installation of a central heating apparatus in his property. And in the margin was this note.

'See file M.B.'

'I knew it,' muttered Shears. 'File M.B. is the one I want. When I have been through that, I shall know the whereabouts of M. Lupin's present abode.'

The small hours had struck before he found file M.B. It consisted of fifteen pages. One was a copy of the page concerning M. Harmingeat of the Rue Chalgrin. Another contained a detailed account of works executed for M. Vatinel, the owner of 25, Rue Clapeyron. A third was devoted to Baron d'Hautrec, 134, Avenue Henri-Martin; a fourth to the Château de Crozon; and the eleven others to different Paris landlords.

Shears took down the list of eleven names and addresses and then restored the papers to their place, opened a window and jumped out into the deserted square, taking care to close the shutters behind him.

On reaching his room at the hotel, he lit his pipe with the gravity which he always applied to that ceremony and, enveloped in clouds of smoke, studied the conclusions to be drawn from file M.B., or, to be more exact, the file devoted to Maxime Bermond, *alias* Arsène Lupin.

At eight o'clock, he sent Ganimard an express letter.

I shall probably call on you in the Rue Pergolèse this morning and place in your charge a person whose capture is of the highest importance. In any case, stay at home tonight and until twelve o'clock tomorrow, Wednesday, morning; and arrange to have thirty men at your disposal.

Then he went down the boulevard, picked out a motor-cab with a driver whose good-humoured but unintelligent face took his fancy and drove to the Place Malesherbes, fifty yards beyond the Hôtel Destange.

'Close the hood, my man,' he said, to the driver, 'turn up the collar of your fur, for it's a cold wind, and wait for me patiently. Start your engine in an hour and a half from now. The moment I get in again, drive straight to the Rue Pergolèse.'

With his foot on the doorstep of the house, he had a last moment of hesitation. Was it not a mistake to take so much trouble about the fair-haired lady, when Lupin was completing his preparations for departure? And would he not have done better, with the aid of his list of houses, to begin by finding out where his adversary lived?

'Pooh!' he said. 'When the fair-haired lady is my prisoner, I shall be master of the situation.'

And he rang the bell.

*   *   *

He found M. Destange waiting in the library. They worked together for a little while and Shears was seeking a pretext to go up to Clotilde's room, when the girl entered, said good-morning to her father, sat down in the little drawing-room and began to write letters.

From where he was sitting, Shears could see her as she bent over the table and, from time to time, meditated with poised pen and a thoughtful face. He waited and then, taking up a volume, said to M. Destange: 'Oh, this is the book which Mlle Destange asked me to give her when I found it.'

He went into the little room, stood in front of Clotilde, in such a way that her father could not see her, and said: 'I am M. Stickmann, M. Destange's new secretary.'

'Oh?' she said, without moving. 'Has my father changed his secretary?'

'Yes, mademoiselle, and I should like to speak to you.'

'Take a seat, monsieur: I have just finished.'

She added a few words to her letter, signed it, sealed the envelope, pushed back her papers, took up the telephone, asked to be put on to her dressmaker, begged her to hurry on a travelling-cloak which she needed urgently and then, turning to Shears: 'I am at your service, monsieur. But cannot our conversation take place before my father?'

'No, mademoiselle, and I will even entreat you not to raise your voice. It would be better that M. Destange should not hear us.'

'Better for whom?'

'For you, mademoiselle.'

'I will not permit a conversation which my father cannot hear.'

'And yet you must permit this one.'

They both rose, with their eyes fixed on each other. And she said: 'Speak, monsieur.'

Still standing, he began: 'You must forgive me if I am inaccurate in a few less important particulars. I will vouch for the general correctness of what I am going to say.'

'No speeches, I beg. Facts.'

He felt, from this abrupt interruption, that the girl was on her guard and he continued: 'Very well, I will come straight to the point. Five years ago, your father happened to meet a M. Maxime Bermond, who introduced himself as a contractor . . . or an architect, I am not sure which. In any case, M. Destange took a liking to this young man and, as the state of his health no longer allowed him to attend to his business, he entrusted to M. Bermond the execution of a few orders which he had accepted to please some old customers and which appeared to him to come within the scope of his assistant's capacity.'

Shears stopped. It seemed to him that the girl had grown paler. Still, she answered with the greatest calmness: 'I know nothing of the things about which you are talking, monsieur, and I am quite unable to see how they can interest me.'

'They interest you in so far, mademoiselle, that M. Maxime Bermond's real name, which you know as well as I do, is Arsène Lupin.'

She burst out laughing.

'Nonsense! Arsène Lupin? M. Maxime Bermond's name is Arsène Lupin?'

'As I have the honour to inform you, mademoiselle, and, since you refuse to understand me unless I speak plainly, I will add that Arsène Lupin, to accomplish his designs, has found in this house a friend, more than a friend, a blind and . . . passionately-devoted accomplice.'

She rose and, betraying no emotion or, at least, so little emotion that Shears was impressed by her extraordinary self-control, said: 'I do not know the reason for your behaviour, monsieur, and I have no wish to know it. I will ask you, therefore, not to add another word and to leave the room.'

'I had no intention, mademoiselle, of imposing my presence upon you indefinitely,' said Shears, as calmly as herself. 'Only I have resolved not to leave this house alone.'

'And who is going with you, monsieur?'

'You!'

'I?'

'Yes, mademoiselle, we shall leave this house together and you will accompany me without a word, without a protest.'

The strange feature of this scene was the absolute coolness of the two adversaries. To judge by their attitudes and the tone of their voices, it might have been a courteous discussion between two people who differ in opinion, rather than an implacable duel between two powerful wills.

Through the great open recess, M. Destange could be seen in the round library, handling his books with leisurely movements.

Clotilde sat down again with a slight shrug of the shoulders. Holmlock Shears took out his watch.

'It is now half-past ten. We will start in five minutes.'

'And, if I refuse?'

'If you refuse, I shall go to M. Destange and tell him . . . '

'What?'

'The truth. I shall describe to him the false life led by Maxime Bermond and the double life of his accomplice.'

'Of his accomplice?'

'Yes, of the one known as the fair-haired lady, the lady whose hair was once fair.'

'And what proofs will you give him?'

'I shall take him to the Rue Chalgrin and show him the passage which Arsène Lupin, when managing the works, made his men construct between Nos. 40 and 42, the passage employed by the two of you on the night before last.'

'Next?'

'Next, I shall take M. Destange to Maître Detinan's. We will go down the servants' staircase which you ran down, with Arsène Lupin, to escape Ganimard. And we will both look for the doubtless similar means of communication with the next house, which has its entrance on the Boulevard des Batignolles and not in the Rue Clapeyron.'

'Next?'

'Next, I shall take M. Destange to the Château de Crozon and it will be easy for him, who knows the nature of the works executed by Arsène Lupin at the time of the restoration of the château, to discover the secret passages which Arsène Lupin made his men construct. He will find that these passages enabled the fair-haired lady to enter Madame de Crozon's room at night and take the blue diamond from the chimney and, a fortnight later, to enter Herr Bleichen's room and hide the blue diamond at the bottom of a flask . . . a rather queer thing to do, I admit: perhaps it was a woman's petty vengeance; I do not know and it makes no difference.'

'Next?'

'Next,' said Holmlock Shears, in a more serious voice, 'I shall take M. Destange to 134, Avenue Henri-Martin and together we will try to discover how Baron d'Hautrec . . . '

'Hush, hush!' stammered the girl, in sudden dismay. 'You must not . . . ! Do you dare to say it was I . . . ? Do you accuse me . . . ?'

'I accuse you of killing Baron d'Hautrec.'

'No, no, this is monstrous!'

'You killed Baron d'Hautrec, mademoiselle. You entered his service under the name of Antoinette Bréhat, with the intention of robbing him of the blue diamond, and you killed him.'

Again she murmured, breaking down and reduced to entreaties: 'Hush, monsieur, I beg . . . As you know so much, you must also know that I did not murder the baron.'

'I did not say that you murdered him, mademoiselle. Baron d'Hautrec was subject to fits of insanity which only Soeur Auguste was able to check. She has told me this herself. He must have thrown himself upon you in her absence; and it was in the course of the ensuing struggle that you struck at him, in self-defence. Appalled by what you had done, you rang the bell and fled, without even taking from his finger the blue diamond which you had come to secure. A moment later, you returned with one of Lupin's accomplices, a man-servant in the next house, lifted the baron on to his bed and arranged the room . . . but still without daring to take the blue diamond. That is what happened. Therefore, I repeat, you did not murder the baron. And yet it was your hands that killed him.'

She was holding them clasped before her forehead, her slim, white, delicate hands, and she kept them long like that, motionless. Then, uncrossing her fingers, she showed her sorrow-stricken face and said: 'And you mean to tell all this to my father?'

'Yes; and I shall tell him that I have as witnesses Mlle Gerbois, who will recognize the fair-haired lady, Soeur Auguste, who will recognize Antoinette Bréhat, the Comtesse de Crozon, who will recognize Mme de Réal. That is what I shall tell him.'

'You will not dare!' she said, recovering her presence of mind, in the face of immediate danger.

He rose and took a step towards the library. Clotilde stopped him.

'One moment, monsieur.'

She reflected and, now fully mistress of herself, asked, very calmly: 'You are Holmlock Shears, are you not?'

'Yes.'

'What do you want with me?'

'What do I want? I have entered upon a contest with Arsène Lupin from which I must emerge the winner. Pending a result which cannot be far distant, I am of opinion that a hostage as valuable as yourself will give me a considerable advantage over my adversary. You shall go with me, therefore, mademoiselle, and I will place you under the care of a friend of mine. As soon as my object is attained, you shall be set free.'

'Is that all?'

'That is all. I do not belong to the police of your country and consequently I claim no . . . no justiciary rights.'

Her mind appeared made up. However, she asked for a moment's delay. Her eyelids closed and Shears stood watching her, suddenly grown calm, almost indifferent to the perils that threatened her.

'I wonder,' thought the Englishman, 'if she believes herself to be in danger? Probably not, with Lupin to protect her. With Lupin there, nothing can happen to her, she thinks: Lupin is omnipotent, Lupin is infallible . . . Mademoiselle,' he said aloud, 'I spoke of five minutes: it is now more than thirty.'

'May I go to my room, monsieur, and fetch my things?'

'If you like, mademoiselle, I will go and wait for you in the Rue Montchanin. I am a great friend of Jeanniot, the concierge.'

'Ah, so you know . . . !' she said, with visible dismay.

'I know a great many things.'

'Very well. Then I will ring . . . .'

The servant brought her hat and cloak and Shears said: 'You must give M. Destange some reason to explain our departure and the reason must be enough, in case of need, to explain your absence for two or three days.'

'That is unnecessary. I shall be back presently.'

Again, they exchanged a defiant glance, sceptical, both of them, and smiling.

'How you trust him!' said Shears.

'Blindly.'

'Whatever he does is right, is it not? Whatever he wishes is realized. And you approve of everything and are prepared to do everything for his sake.'

'I love him,' she said, with a tremor of passion.

'And you believe that he will save you?'

She shrugged her shoulders and, going up to her father, told him: 'I am robbing you of M. Stickmann. We are going to the National Library.'

'Will you be back to lunch?'

'Perhaps . . . or more likely not . . . but don't worry about me, in any case . . . '

And, in a firm voice, she said to Shears: 'I am ready, monsieur.'

'Without reserve?' he whispered.

'With my eyes closed.'

'If you try to escape, I shall shout and call for help, you will be arrested and it will mean prison. Don't forget that there is a warrant out against the fair-haired lady.'

'I swear to you on my honour that I will make no attempt to escape.'

'I believe you. Let us go.'

They left the house together, as he had foretold.

*   *   *

The motor-cab had turned round and was waiting in the square. They could see the driver's back and his cap, which was almost covered by the upturned collar of his fur. As they approached, Shears heard the humming of the engine. He opened the door, asked Clotilde to step in and sat down beside her.

The car started with a jerk, and soon reached the outer boulevards, the Avenue Hoche, the Avenue de la Grande-Armée.

Shears was thinking out his plans.

'Ganimard is at home . . . I shall leave the girl with him . . . Shall I tell him who she is? No, he would take her straight to the police-station, which would put everything out. As soon as I am alone, I will consult the M. B. list and set out on my chase. And, tonight, or tomorrow morning at latest, I shall go to Ganimard, as arranged, and deliver Arsène Lupin and his gang to him . . . '

He rubbed his hands, glad to feel that his object was at last within his reach and to see that there was no serious obstacle in the way. And, yielding to a need for expansion which was not in keeping with his usual nature, he said: 'Forgive me, mademoiselle, for displaying so much satisfaction. It was a difficult fight and I find my success particularly agreeable.'

'A legitimate success, monsieur, in which you have every right to rejoice.'

'Thank you. But what a funny way we are going! Didn't the man understand?'

At that moment, they were leaving Paris by the Porte de Neuilly. What on earth . . . ! After all, the Rue Pergolèse was not outside the fortifications!

Shears let down the glass.

'I say, driver, you're going wrong . . . Rue Pergolèse! . . . '

The man made no reply. Shears repeated, in a louder voice. 'I'm telling you to go to the Rue Pergolèse.'

The man took no notice.

'Look here, my man, are you deaf? Or are you doing it on purpose? . . . This isn't where I told you to go . . . Rue Pergolèse, do you hear! . . . Turn round at once and look sharp about it!'

Still no reply. The Englishman began to be alarmed. He looked at Clotilde: a queer smile was playing on the girl's lips.

'What are you laughing at?' he stormed. 'This doesn't affect . . . it has nothing to say to . . . '

'Nothing in the very least,' she replied.

Suddenly, he was taken aback by an idea. Half rising from his seat, he attentively scrutinized the man on the box. His shoulders were slimmer, his movements easier . . . A cold sweat broke out on Shears's forehead, his hands contracted, while the most hideous conviction forced itself upon his mind: the man was Arsène Lupin.

'Well, Mr Shears, what do you think of this little drive?'

'It's delightful, my dear sir, really delightful,' replied Shears.

Perhaps he had never in his life made a more tremendous effort than it cost him to utter those words without a tremor in his voice, without anything that could betray the exasperation that filled his whole being. But, the minute after, he was carried away by a sort of formidable reaction; and a torrent of rage and hatred burst its banks, overcame his will and made him suddenly draw his revolver and point it at Mlle Destange.

'Lupin, if you don't stop this minute, this second, I fire at mademoiselle!'

'I advise you to aim at the cheek if you want to hit the temple,' said Lupin, without turning his head.

Clotilde called out: 'Don't go too fast, Maxime! The pavement is very slippery and you know how timid I am!'

She was still smiling, with her eyes fixed on the cobbles with which the road bristled in front of the car.

'Stop him, tell him to stop!' shouted Shears, beside himself with fury. 'You can see for yourself that I am capable of anything!'

The muzzle of the revolver grazed her hair.

'How reckless Maxime is!' she murmured. 'We are sure to skid, at this rate.'

Shears replaced the revolver in his pocket and seized the handle of the door, preparing to jump out, in spite of the absurdity of the act.

'Take care, Mr Shears,' said Clotilde. 'There's a motor-car behind us.'

He leant out. A car was following them, an enormous car, fierce-looking, with its pointed bonnet, blood-red in colour, and the four men in furs inside it.

'Ah,' he said, 'I'm well guarded! We must have patience!'

He crossed his arms on his chest, with the proud submission of those who bow and wait when fate turns against them. And, while they crossed the Seine and tore through Suresnes, Rueil and Chatou, motionless and resigned, without anger or bitterness, he thought only of discovering by what miracle Arsène Lupin had put himself in the driver's place. That the decent fellow whom he had picked out that morning on the boulevard could be an accomplice, posted there of set purpose, he refused to admit. And yet Arsène Lupin must have received a warning and that only after the moment when he, Shears, had threatened Clotilde, for no one suspected his plan before. Now from that moment Clotilde and he had not left each other's presence.

Suddenly, he remembered the girl's telephoning to her dressmaker. And, all at once, he understood. Even before he spoke, at the very moment when he asked for an interview as M. Destange's new secretary, she had scented danger, guessed the visitor's name and object and, coolly, naturally, as though she were really doing what she appeared to do, had summoned Lupin to her aid, under the pretence of speaking to one of her tradespeople and by means of a formula known to themselves alone.

How Arsène Lupin had come, how that motorcab in waiting, with its throbbing engine, had aroused his suspicion, how he had bribed the driver: all this mattered little. What interested Shears almost to the point of calming his rage was the recollection of that moment in which a mere woman, a woman in love, it is true, mastering her nerves, suppressing her instinct, controlling the features of her face and the expression of her eyes, had humbugged old Holmlock Shears.

What was he to do against a man served by such allies, a man who, by the sheer ascendancy of his authority, inspired a woman with such a stock of daring and energy?

They re-crossed the Seine and climbed the slope of Saint-Germain; but, five hundred yards beyond the town, the cab slowed down. The other car came up with it and the two stopped alongside. There was no one about.

'Mr Shears,' said Lupin, 'may I trouble you to change cars? Ours is really so very slow! . . . '

'Certainly,' said Shears, all the more politely as he had no choice.

'Will you also permit me to lend you this fur, for we shall be going pretty fast, and to offer you a couple of sandwiches? . . . Yes, yes, take them: there's no telling when you will get any dinner.'

The four men had alighted. One of them came up and, as he had taken off the goggles which disguised him, Shears recognized the gentleman in the frock-coat whom he had seen at the Restaurant Hongrois. Lupin gave him his instructions.

'Take the cab back to the driver from whom I hired it. You will find him waiting in the first wine-shop on the right in the Rue Legendre. Pay him the second thousand francs I promised him. Oh, I was forgetting: you might give Mr Shears your goggles!'

He spoke a few words to Mlle Destange, then took his seat at the wheel and drove off, with Shears beside him and one of his men behind.

Lupin had not exaggerated when saying that they would go 'pretty fast'. They travelled at a giddy pace from the first. The horizon rushed towards them, as though attracted by a mysterious force, and disappeared at the same moment, as though swallowed up by an abyss into which other things – trees, houses, plains and forests – plunged with the tumultuous speed of a torrent rushing down to the pool below.

Shears and Lupin did not exchange a word. Above their heads, the leaves of the poplars made a great noise as of waves, punctuated by the regular spacing of the trees. And town after town vanished from sight: Mantes, Vernon, Gaillon. From hill to hill, from Bon-Secours to Canteleu, Rouen, with her suburbs, her harbour, her miles upon miles of quays, Rouen seemed no more than the high-street of a market-town. And they rushed through Duclair, through Caudebec, through the Pays de Caux, skimming over its hills and plains in their powerful flight, through Lillebonne, through Quillebeuf. And, suddenly, they were on the bank of the Seine, at the end of a small quay, alongside which lay a steam-yacht, built on sober and powerful lines, with black smoke curling up from her funnel.

The car stopped. They had covered over a hundred miles in two hours.

*   *   *

A man dressed in a blue pea-jacket came forward and touched his gold-laced cap.

'Well done, captain!' said Lupin. 'Did you get my telegram?'

'Yes, sir.'

'Is the *Hirondelle* ready?'

'Quite ready, sir.'

'In that case, Mr Shears . . . ?'

The Englishman looked around him, saw a group of people seated outside a café, another a little nearer, hesitated for a moment and then, realizing that, before anyone could interfere, he would be seized, forced on board and packed off at the bottom of the hold, he crossed the foot-plank and followed Lupin into the captain's cabin.

It was roomy, specklessly clean and shone brightly with its varnished wainscoting and gleaming brass.

Lupin closed the door and, without beating about the bush, said to Shears, almost brutally: 'Tell me exactly how much you know.'

'Everything.'

'Everything? I want details.'

His voice had lost the tone of politeness, tinged with irony, which he adopted towards the Englishman. Instead, it rang with the imperious accent of the master who is accustomed to command and accustomed to see everyone bow before his will, even though it be a Holmlock Shears.

They eyed each other now from head to foot as enemies, declared and passionate enemies.

Lupin resumed, with a touch of nervousness: 'You have crossed my path, sir, on several occasions. Each occasion has been one too many; and I am tired of wasting my time avoiding the traps you lay for me. I warn you, therefore, that my conduct towards you will depend upon your answer. How much exactly do you know?'

'Everything, I tell you.'

Arsène Lupin mastered his annoyance and jerked out: 'I will tell you what you know. You know that, under the name of Maxime Bermond, I . . . "touched up" fifteen houses built by M. Destange.'

'Yes.'

'Of those fifteen houses, you know four.'

'Yes.'

'And you have a list of the eleven others.'

'Yes.'

'You made out the list at M. Destange's, last night, no doubt.'

'Yes.'

'And, as you presume that, among those eleven properties, there must inevitably be one which I keep for my own needs and those of my friends, you have instructed Ganimard to take the field and discover my retreat.'

'No.'

'What do you mean?'

'I mean that I am acting alone and that I intended to take the field alone.'

'So I have nothing to fear, seeing that I have you in my hands.'

'You have nothing to fear so long as I *remain* in your hands.'

'You mean to say that you will not remain?'

'I do.'

Arsène Lupin went up to Holmlock Shears and placed his hand very gently on the Englishman's shoulder.

'Listen to me, sir. I am not in the mood for argument and you, unfortunately for yourself, are not in a position to check me. Let us put an end to this.'

'Yes, let us.'

'You shall give me your word of honour not to attempt to escape from this boat until she reaches English waters.'

'I give you my word of honour that I shall attempt to escape by every means in my power,' said Shears, nothing daunted.

'But, dash it all, you know I have only to speak a word to reduce you to helplessness! All these men obey me blindly. At a sign from me, they will put a chain round your neck . . . '

'Chains can be broken.'

'And throw you overboard at ten miles from the coast.'

'I can swim.'

'Well said,' cried Lupin, laughing. 'Heaven forgive me, but I lost my temper! Accept my apology, maître . . . and let us conclude. Will you allow me to seek the necessary measures for my safety and that of my friends?'

'Any measures you like. But they are useless.'

'Agreed. Still, you will not mind if I take them?'

'It's your duty.'

'To work, then.'

Lupin opened the door and called the captain and two of the crew. The latter seized the Englishman and, after searching him, bound his legs together and tied him down in the captain's berth.

'That will do,' ordered Lupin. 'Really, sir, nothing short of your obstinacy and the exceptional gravity of the circumstances would have allowed me to venture . . . '

The sailors withdrew. Lupin said to the captain: 'Captain, one of the crew must remain in the cabin to wait on Mr Shears and you yourself must keep him company as much as you can. Let him be treated with every consideration. He is not a prisoner, but a guest. What is the time by your watch, captain?'

'Five minutes past two.'

Lupin looked at his own watch and at a clock which hung on the cabin-wall.

'Five minutes past two? . . . Our watches agree. How long will it take you to reach Southampton?'

'Nine hours, without hurrying.'

'Make it eleven. You must not touch land before the departure of the steamer which leaves Southampton at midnight and is due at the Havre at eight in the morning. You understand, captain, do you not? I repeat: it would be exceedingly dangerous for us all if this gentleman returned to France by the steamer; and you must not arrive at Southampton before one o'clock in the morning.'

'Very well, sir.'

'Goodbye, maître,' said Lupin, turning to Shears. 'We shall meet next year, in this world or another.'

'Let's say tomorrow.'

A few minutes later, Shears heard the car drive away and the engines of the *Hirondelle* at once began to throb with increased force. The yacht threw off her moorings. By three o'clock, they had left the estuary of the Seine and entered the Channel. At that moment, Holmlock Shears lay sound asleep in the berth to which he was fastened down.

* * *

On the following morning, the tenth and last day of the war between the two great rivals, the *Écho de France* published this delicious paragraph.

A decree of expulsion was pronounced by Arsène Lupin yesterday against Holmlock Shears, the English detective. The decree was published at noon and executed on the same day. Shears was landed at Southampton at one o'clock this morning.

Chapter 6

The Second Arrest of Arsène Lupin

By eight o'clock on Wednesday morning, a dozen pantechnicon vans were blocking the Rue Crevaux from the Avenue du Bois de Boulogne to the Avenue Bougeaud. M. Félix Davey was leaving the flat which he occupied on the fourth floor of No. 8. And, by a sheer coincidence – for the two gentlemen were not acquainted – M. Dubreuil, the expert, who had knocked into one the fifth-floor flat of No. 8 and the fifth-floor flats of the two adjoining houses, had selected the same day on which to send off the collection of furniture and antiques which used to be visited daily by one or other of his many foreign correspondents.

A peculiarity which attracted notice in the neighbourhood, but which was not mentioned until later was that none of the twelve vans bore the name and address of the firm of removers and that none of the men in charge of them loitered in the wineshops round about. They worked to such good purpose that all was over by eleven o'clock. Nothing remained but those piles of old papers and rags which are always left behind in the corners of empty rooms.

M. Félix Davey was a young man of smart appearance, dressed in the latest fashion, but carrying a heavily-weighted cane which seemed to indicate unusual muscular strength on the part of its owner. He walked away quietly and sat down on a bench in the cross alley which intersects the Avenue du Bois, opposite the Rue Pergolèse. Beside him sat a young woman, clad in the costume of the lower middle-class and reading her paper, while a child played with its spade in the sand beside her.

Presently, Félix Davey said to the woman, without turning his head: 'Ganimard?'

'Went out at nine o'clock this morning.'

'Where to?'

'Police headquarters.'

'Alone?'

'Yes.'

'No telegram last night?'

'No.'

'Do they still trust you at the house?'

'Yes. I do odd work for Madame Ganimard and she tells me all her husband does . . . We spent the morning together.'

'Good. Continue to come here at eleven every morning, until further orders.'

He rose and walked to the Pavillon Chinois, near the Porte Dauphine, where he took a frugal meal: two eggs, some vegetables and a little fruit. Then he returned to the Rue Crevaux and said to the concierge: 'I am going to have a look round upstairs and then I'll give you the keys.'

He finished his inspection with the room which he used as a study. There he took hold of the end of a jointed gas-bracket which was fixed beside the chimney, unscrewed the brass nozzle, fitted a little funnel-shaped instrument to it and blew up the pipe.

A faint whistle sounded in reply. Putting the pipe to his mouth, he whispered: 'Anyone there, Dubreuil?'

'No.'

'Can I come up?'

'Yes.'

He replaced the bracket, saying, as he did so: 'Where will progress stop? Our age teems with little inventions that make life really charming and picturesque. And so amusing too . . . especially when a man knows the game of life as I know it!'

He touched one of the marble mouldings of the mantel-piece and made it swing round on a pivot. The marble slab itself moved and the mirror above it slid between invisible grooves, revealing a yawning gap which contained the lower steps of a stair-case built in the body of the chimney itself. It was all very clean, in carefully-polished iron and white porcelain tiles.

He climbed up to the fifth floor, which had a similar opening over the mantel-piece, and found M. Dubreuil awaiting him.

'Is everything finished here?'

'Everything.'

'All cleared up?'

'Quite.'

'The staff?'

'All gone, except the three men keeping watch.'

'Let's go up.'

They climbed by the same way to the servants' floor and emerged in a garret where they found three men, one of whom was looking out of the window.

'Any news?'

'No, governor.'

'Is the street quiet?'

'Absolutely.'

'I shall leave for good in ten minutes . . . You will go too. In the meantime, if you notice the least suspicious movement in the street, let me know.'

'I've got my finger on the alarm-bell, governor.'

'Dubreuil, did you remember to tell the removers not to touch the bell-wires?'

'Yes. They work perfectly.'

'That's all right, then.'

The two gentlemen returned to Félix Davey's flat. And Davey, after readjusting the marble moulding, exclaimed, gaily: 'Dubreuil, I should love to see the faces of those who discover all these wonderful contrivances: alarm-bells, a net-work of electric wires and speaking-tubes, invisible passages, sliding floorboards, secret staircases! . . . A regular pantomime machinery!'

'What an advertisement for Arsène Lupin!'

'We could very well have done without the advertisement. It seems a pity to leave so fine an installation. We shall have to begin all over again, Dubreuil . . . and upon a new plan, of course, for it never does to repeat oneself. Confound that Shears!'

'He's not come back, I suppose?'

'How could he? There's only one boat from Southampton, which leaves at midnight. From the Havre, there's only one train, which leaves at eight in the morning and arrives at eleven three. Once he has not taken the midnight steamer – and he has not, for my orders to the captain were formal – he can't reach France till this evening, *viâ* Newhaven and Dieppe.'

'If he comes back!'

'Shears never throws up the game. He will come back, but it will be too late. We shall be far away.'

'And Mlle Destange?'

'I am to meet her in an hour.'

'At her house?'

'No, she won't go home for a few days, until the storm has blown over . . . and I am able to look after her more thoroughly . . . But you must hurry, Dubreuil. It will take a long time to ship all the cases and you will be wanted on the wharf.'

'You're sure we are not being watched?'

'Whom by? I was never afraid of anyone but Shears.'

Dubreuil went away. Félix Davey took a last walk round the flat, picked up a torn letter or two and then, seeing a piece of chalk, he took it, drew a large circle on the dark wall-paper of the diningroom, and wrote, after the style of a commemorative tablet.

ARSÈNE LUPIN,

GENTLEMAN BURGLAR,

LIVED HERE

FOR 5 YEARS

AT THE COMMENCEMENT

OF

THE TWENTIETH CENTURY

This little joke seemed to cause him a lively satisfaction. He whistled gaily as he looked at it and cried: 'Now that I have put myself right with the historians of the future generations, let's be off! Hurry up, Maître Holmlock Shears! In three minutes, I shall have left my lair and your defeat will be absolute . . . Two minutes more! You're keeping me waiting, maître! . . . One minute more! Aren't you coming? Very well, I proclaim your downfall and my apotheosis . . . With which last words I proceed to make myself scarce. Farewell, O Kingdom of Arsène Lupin! I shall not look upon you again. Farewell, ye five-and-fifty rooms of the six flats over which I reigned! Farewell, austere and humble dwelling!'

A bell cut short his lyrical effusion, a short, shrill, strident bell, twice interrupted, twice resumed and then ceasing. It was the alarm-bell.

What could it mean? Some unexpected danger? Ganimard? Surely not . . . !

He was on the point of making for his study and escaping. But first he turned to the window. There was no one in the street. Was the enemy already in the house, then? He listened and seemed to distinguish confused sounds. Without further hesitation, he ran to his study and, as he crossed the threshold, heard the sound of a latchkey fumbling at the lock of the hall-door.

'By Jove!' he muttered. 'I have only just time. The house may be surrounded . . . No use trying the servants' staircase . . . Fortunately, the chimney . . .'

He pushed the moulding smartly: it did not move. He exerted greater force: it did not move.

At the same moment, he received the impression that the outer door was opening and that steps sounded.

'Curse it all!' he swore. 'I'm lost, if this confounded spring . . .'

His fingers clutched the moulding; he bore upon it with all his weight. Nothing moved, nothing! By some incredible bad luck, by a really bewildering piece of malice on the part of fate, the spring, which was working only a moment before, now refused to work!

He persisted madly, convulsively. The block of marble remained inert, motionless. Curse it! Was it conceivable that this stupid obstacle should bar his way? He struck the marble, struck it furious blows with his fists, hammered it, insulted it . . .

'Why, M. Lupin, is something not going as you wish?'

Lupin turned round, terror-stricken. Holmlock Shears stood before him.

* * *

Holmlock Shears! Lupin gazed at him, blinking his eyes, as though smarting under a cruel vision. Holmlock Shears in Paris! Holmlock Shears whom he had packed off to England the day before, as he might a compromising parcel, stood there before him, triumphant and free! Ah, for this impossible miracle to be performed in despite of Arsène Lupin's will there must have been a revolution of the laws of nature, a victory of all that is illogical and abnormal! Holmlock Shears standing opposite him!

And the Englishman, resorting to irony in his turn, said, with that supercilious politeness with which his adversary had so often lashed him.

'M. Lupin, believe me, from this minute I shall cease to remember the night you made me spend in Baron d'Hautrec's house, cease to remember my friend Wilson's mishaps, cease to remember how I was kidnapped by motor-car, cease to remember the sea-voyage which I have just taken, fastened down, by your orders, to an uncomfortable berth. This minute wipes out all. I forget everything. I am rewarded, amply rewarded.'

Lupin did not speak. The Englishman added: 'Don't you think so yourself?'

He appeared to be insisting, as though demanding an assent, a sort of receipt with regard to the past.

After a moment's reflection, during which the Englishman felt himself searched and fathomed to the very bottom of his soul, Lupin said: 'I presume, sir, that your present action rests upon serious motives?'

'Extremely serious motives.'

'The fact of your escaping from my captain and his crew is only a secondary incident in our struggle. But the fact of your being here, before me, alone, do you understand, *alone* in the presence of Arsène Lupin, makes me believe that your revenge is as complete as possible.'

'It is as complete as possible.'

'This house . . . ?'

'Surrounded.'

'The two next houses . . . ?'

'Surrounded.'

'The flat above this . . . ?'

'The three flats on the fifth floor which were occupied by M. Dubreuil are invested.'

'So that . . . ?'

'So that you are caught, M. Lupin, irredeemably caught.'

Lupin now experienced the same feelings that had stirred Shears during his motor-car drive: the same concentrated rage, the same rebellion; but also, when all was said and done, the same sense of loyalty which compelled him to bow before the force of circumstances. Both were equally strong: both alike were bound to accept defeat as a temporary evil, to be received with resignation.

'We are quits, sir,' he said, bluntly.

The Englishman seemed delighted at this confession. The two men were silent. Then Lupin, already master of himself, resumed, with a smile: 'And I am not sorry. It was becoming wearisome to win every thrust. I had only to put out my arm to hit you full in the chest. This time, you score one. Well hit, maître!' He laughed wholeheartedly.

'At last we shall have some fun! Lupin is caught in the trap! . . . How will he get out? . . . Caught in the trap! . . . What an adventure! . . . Ah, maître, I have to thank you for a grand emotion. This is what I call life!'

He pressed his clenched fists to his temples as though to restrain the ungovernable joy that was bubbling up within him; and he also had gestures like those of a child amusing itself beyond its power of endurance.

At last, he went up to the Englishman.

'And now, what are you here for?'

'What am I here for?'

'Yes. Ganimard is outside, with his men. Why does he not come in?'

'I asked him not to.'

'And he consented?'

'I called in his services only on the express condition that he would be led by me. Besides, he believes that M. Félix Davey is merely an accomplice of Lupin's.'

'Then I will repeat my question under another form. Why did you come in alone?'

'I wanted to speak to you first.'

'Aha! You want to speak to me!'

The idea seemed to please Lupin greatly. There are circumstances in life in which we much prefer words to deeds.

'Mr Shears, I am sorry not to have a chair to offer you. Does this broken box suit you? Or the window-ledge? I am sure a glass of beer would be acceptable . . . Do you like it light or dark? . . . But do sit down, I beg . . . '

'Never mind that: let us talk.'

'I am listening.'

'I shall not be long. The object of my stay in France was not to effect your arrest. I was obliged to pursue you, because no other means offered of attaining my real object.'

'Which was?'

'To recover the blue diamond.'

'The blue diamond!'

'Certainly; because the one discovered in Herr Bleichen's tooth-powder flask was not the real one.'

'Just so. The real one was posted by the fair-haired lady. I had an exact copy made; and as, at that time, I had designs upon the Comtesse de Crozon's other jewels and as the Austrian consul was already under suspicion, the aforesaid fair-haired lady, lest she should be suspected in her turn, slipped the imitation diamond into the aforesaid consul's luggage.'

'While you kept the real one.'

'Quite right.'

'I want that diamond.'

'Impossible. I'm sorry.'

'I have promised it to the Comtesse de Crozon. I mean to have it.'

'How can you have it, seeing that it's in my possession?'

'I mean to have it just because it is in your possession.'

'You mean that I shall give it back to you?'

'Yes.'

'Voluntarily?'

'I will buy it of you.'

Lupin had a fit of merriment.

'Anyone can tell what country *you* come from! You treat this as a matter of business.'

'It is a matter of business.'

'And what price do you offer?'

'The liberty of Mlle Destange.'

'Her liberty? But I am not aware that she is under arrest.'

'I shall give M. Ganimard the necessary information. Once deprived of your protection, she will be taken also.'

Lupin burst out laughing again.

'My dear sir, you are offering me what you do not possess. Mlle Destange is safe and fears nothing. I want something else.'

The Englishman hesitated, obviously embarrassed and flushing slightly. Then he put his hand brusquely on his adversary's shoulder.

'And, if I offered you . . .'

'My liberty?'

'No . . . but, still, I might leave the room, to arrange with M. Ganimard . . .'

'And leave me to think things over?'

'Yes.'

'Well, what on earth would be the good of that? This confounded spring won't work,' said Lupin, irritably pushing the moulding of the mantel.

He stifled an exclamation of surprise: this time, freakish chance had willed that the block of marble should move under his fingers! Safety, flight became possible. In that case, why submit to Holmlock Shears's conditions?

He walked to and fro, as though reflecting upon his answer. Then he, in his turn, put his hand on the Englishman's shoulder.

'After due consideration, Mr Shears, I prefer to settle my little affairs alone.'

'Still . . .'

'No, I don't want anybody's help.'

'When Ganimard has you, it will be up with you. They won't let you go again.'

'Who knows?'

'Come, this is madness. Every outlet is watched.'

'One remains.'

'Which one?'

'The one I shall select.'

'Words! Your arrest may be looked upon as effected.'

'It is not effected.'

'So . . . ?'

'So I shall keep the blue diamond.'

Shears took out his watch.

'It is ten minutes to three. At three o'clock, I call Ganimard.'

'That gives us ten minutes to chat in. Let us make the most of our time, Mr Shears, and tell me, to satisfy the curiosity by which I am devoured: how did you procure my address and my name of Félix Davey?'

Keeping a watchful eye on Lupin, whose good-humour made him feel uneasy, Shears gladly consented to give this little explanation, which flattered his vanity, and said: 'I had your address from the fair-haired lady.'

'Clotilde?'

'Yes. You remember . . . yesterday morning . . . when I meant to carry her off in the motor-cab, she telephoned to her dressmaker.'

'So she did.'

'Well, I understood later that the dressmaker was yourself. And, last night, in the boat, thanks to an effort of memory which is perhaps one of the things of which I am most proud, I succeeded in recollecting the last two figures of your telephone number: 73. In this way, as I possessed the list of the houses which you had "touched up", it was easy for me, on my arrival in Paris at eleven o'clock this morning, to look through the telephone directory until I discovered the name and address of M. Félix Davey. The name and address once known, I called in the aid of M. Ganimard.'

'Admirable! First-rate! I make you my bow! But what I can't quite grasp is that you took the train at the Havre. How did you manage to escape from the *Hirondelle?*'

'I did not escape.'

'But . . .'

'You gave the captain orders not to reach Southampton until one o'clock. Well, they landed me at twelve and I caught the Havre boat.'

'The captain played me false? Impossible.'

'He did not play you false.'

'What then . . . ?'

'It was his watch.'

'His watch?'

'Yes, I put his watch on an hour.'

'How?'

'The only way in which one can put a watch on, by turning the winder. We were sitting together chatting and I told him things that interested him . . . By Jove, he noticed nothing!'

'Well done, well done! It's a good trick and I must remember it. But what about the cabin clock?'

'Oh, the clock was more difficult, for my legs were bound: but the sailor who was put in charge of me whenever the captain went on deck kindly consented to give the hands a push.'

'The sailor? Nonsense! Do you mean to say, he consented . . . ?'

'Oh, he did not know the importance of what he was doing! I told him I must, at all costs, catch the first train to London and . . . he allowed himself to be persuaded . . .'

'In consideration . . .'

'In consideration of a little present . . . which the decent fellow, however, intends faithfully to send to you.'

'What present?'

'A mere nothing.'

'Well, but what?'

'The blue diamond.'

'The blue diamond!'

'Yes, the imitation one, which you substituted for the countess's diamond and which she left in my hands . . .'

Arsène Lupin gave a sudden and tumultuous burst of laughter. He seemed ready to die: his eyes were wet with tears.

'Oh, what a joke! My faked diamond handed back to the sailor! And the captain's watch! And the hands of the clock! . . .'

Never before had Holmlock Shears felt the struggle between Arsène Lupin and himself grow so intense as now. With his prodigious intuition, he guessed that, under this excessive gaiety, Lupin was concentrating his formidable mind and collecting all his faculties.

Lupin had gradually drawn closer. The Englishman stepped back and slipped his fingers, as though absent-mindedly, into his pocket.

'It's three o'clock, M. Lupin.'

'Three o'clock already? What a pity! . . . We were having such fun! . . .'

'I am waiting for your answer.'

'My answer? Goodness me, what a lot you want! So this finishes the game. With my liberty for the stakes!'

'Or the blue diamond.'

'Very well . . . It's your lead. What do you do?'

'I mark the king,' said Shears, firing a shot with his revolver.

'And here's *my hand*,' retorted Arsène, hurling his fist at the Englishman.

Shears had fired at the ceiling, to summon Ganimard, the need for whose intervention now seemed urgent. But Arsène's fist caught him full in the wind and he turned pale and staggered back. Lupin gave one bound towards the chimney and the marble slab moved . . . Too late! The door opened.

'Surrender, Lupin! If not . . .'

Ganimard, who had doubtless been posted nearer than Lupin thought, stood there, with his revolver aimed at him. And, behind Ganimard, ten men, twenty men crowded upon one another's heels, powerful, ruthless fellows, prepared to beat Lupin down like a dog at the least sign of resistance.

He made a quiet gesture.

'Hands off there! I surrender.'

And he crossed his arms over his chest.

*   *   *

A sort of stupor followed. In the room stripped of its furniture and hangings, Arsène Lupin's words seemed drawn-out like an echo.

'I surrender!'

The words sounded incredible. The others were expecting to see him vanish suddenly down a trap or a panel of the wall to fall back and once more to hide him from his assailants. And he surrendered!

Ganimard stepped forward and, greatly excited, with all the gravity that the act demanded, brought his hand slowly down upon his adversary's shoulder and enjoyed the infinite satisfaction of saying: 'Lupin, I arrest you.'

'Brrrrr!' shivered Lupin. 'You make me feel quite overcome, my dear Ganimard. What a solemn face! One would think you were making a speech over a friend's grave. Come, drop these funereal airs!'

'I arrest you.'

'You seem quite flabbergasted! In the name of the law, of which he is a faithful limb, Chief-Inspector Ganimard arrests wicked Arsène Lupin. It is an historic moment and you grasp its full importance . . . And this is the second time a similar fact occurs. Bravo, Ganimard, you will do well in your career!'

And he held out his wrists for the handcuffs . . .

They were fastened on almost solemnly. The detectives, in spite of their usual roughness and the bitterness of their resentment against Lupin, acted with reserve and discretion, astounded as they were at being allowed to touch that intangible being.

'My poor Lupin,' he sighed, 'what would your smart friends say if they saw you humbled like this!'

He separated his wrists with a growing and continuous effort of every muscle. The veins on his forehead swelled. The links of the chain dug into his skin.

'Now then!' he said.

The chain snapped and broke in two.

'Another, mates: this one's no good.'

They put two pairs on him. He approved.

'That's better. You can't be too careful.'

Then, counting the detectives, he continued: 'How many of you are there, my friends? Twenty-five? Thirty? That's a lot . . . I can't do anything against thirty. Ah, if there had been only fifteen of you!'

He really had a manner about him, the manner of a great actor playing his instinctive, spirited part impertinently and frivolously. Shears watched him as a man watches a fine sight of which he is able to appreciate every beauty and every shade. And he absolutely received the strange impression that the struggle was an equal one between those thirty men on the one hand, backed up by all the formidable machinery of the law, and that single being on the other, fettered and unarmed. The two sides were evenly matched.

'Well, maître,' said Lupin, 'this is your work. Thanks to you, Lupin is going to rot on the damp straw of the cells. Confess that your conscience is not quite easy and that you feel the pangs of remorse.'

The Englishman gave an involuntary shrug, as though to say: 'You had the chance . . . '

'Never! Never!' exclaimed Lupin. 'Give you back the blue diamond? Ah, no, it has cost me too much trouble already! I value it, you see. At the first visit I have the honour of paying you in London, next month, I dare say, I will tell you why . . . But shall you be in London next month? Would you rather I met you in Vienna? Or St Petersburg? . . . '

He started. Suddenly, an electric bell rang just below the ceiling. And, this time, it was not the alarm-bell but the bell of the telephone, which had not been removed and which stood between the two windows.

The telephone! Ah, who was going to fall into the trap laid by an odious chance? Arsène Lupin made a furious move towards the instrument, as though he would have smashed it to atoms and, in so doing, stifled the unknown voice that wished to speak to him. But Ganimard took the receiver from its hook and bent down.

'Hullo! . . . Hullo! . . . 648.73 . . . Yes, that's right . . . '

With a brisk gesture of authority, Shears pushed him aside, took the two receivers and put his handkerchief over the mouthpiece to make the sound of his voice less distinct.

At that moment, he glanced at Lupin. And the look which they exchanged showed them that the same thought had struck them both and that they both foresaw to the end the consequences of that possible, probable, almost certain supposition: it was the fair-haired lady telephoning. She thought that she was telephoning to Félix Davey, or, rather, Maxime Bermond; and she was about to confide in Holmlock Shears!

And the Englishman repeated: 'Hullo! . . . Hullo! . . . '

A pause and Shears: 'Yes, it's I, Maxime.'

The drama took shape forthwith, with tragic precision. Lupin, the mocking, indomitable Lupin, no longer even thought of concealing his anxiety and, with features pale as death, strove to hear, to guess. And Shears continued, in reply to the mysterious voice: 'Yes, yes, it's all finished and I was just getting ready to come on to you, as arranged . . . Where? Why, where you are . . . Isn't that best?'

He hesitated, seeking his words, and then stopped. It was evident that he was trying to draw out the girl without saying too much himself and that he had not the least idea where she was. Besides, Ganimard's presence seemed to hinder him . . . Oh, if some miracle could have cut the thread of that diabolical conversation! Lupin called for it with all his might, with all his strained nerves!

And Shears went on: 'Hullo! . . . Hullo! . . . Can't you hear? . . . It's very bad at this end too . . . and I can hardly make out . . . Can you hear me now? Well . . . on second thoughts . . . you had better go home . . . Oh no, there's no danger at all . . . Why, he's in England! I've had a telegram from Southampton!'

The irony of the words! Shears uttered them with an inexpressible sense of satisfaction. And he added: 'So go at once, dear, and I shall be with you soon.'

He hung up the receivers.

'M. Ganimard, I propose to borrow three of your men.'

'It's for the fair-haired lady, I suppose?'

'Yes.'

'Do you know who she is, where she is?'

'Yes.'

'By Jove! A fine capture! She and Lupin . . . that completes the day's work. Folenfant, take two men and go with Mr Shears.'

The Englishman walked away, followed by the three detectives.

The end had come. The fair-haired lady also was about to fall into Shears's hands. Thanks to his wonderful persistency, thanks to the aid of fortunate events, the battle was turning to victory for him and irreparable disaster for Lupin.

'Mr Shears!'

The Englishman stopped.

'Yes, M. Lupin?'

Lupin seemed completely crushed by this last blow. His forehead was wrinkled; he was worn out and gloomy. Yet he drew himself up, with a revival of energy; and, in spite of all, exclaimed, in a voice of glad unconcern: 'You must admit that fate is dead against me. Just now, it prevented me from escaping by the chimney and delivered me into your hands. This moment, it has made use of the telephone to make you a present of the fair-haired lady. I bow before its decrees.'

'Meaning . . . ?'

'Meaning that I am prepared to reopen negotiations.'

Shears took the inspector aside and begged permission, but in a tone that allowed of no refusal, to exchange a few words with Lupin. Then he walked across to him. The momentous conversation took place. It opened in short, nervous phrases.

'What do you want?'

'Mlle Destange's liberty.'

'You know the price?'

'Yes.'

'And you agree?'

'I agree to all your conditions.'

'Ah!' exclaimed the astonished Englishman. 'But . . . you refused just now . . . for yourself . . . '

'It was a question of myself, Mr Shears. Now it involves a woman . . . and a woman whom I love. You see, we have very peculiar ideas about these things in France. And it does not follow that, because a man's name is Lupin, he will act differently: on the contrary!'

He said this quite simply. Shears gave him an imperceptible nod and whispered: 'Where is the blue diamond?'

'Take my cane, over there, in the chimney corner. Hold the knob in one hand and turn the iron ferrule with the other.'

Shears took the cane, turned the ferrule and, as he turned it, perceived that the knob became unscrewed. Inside the knob was a ball of putty. Inside the putty a diamond.

He examined it. It was the blue diamond.

'Mlle Destange is free, M. Lupin.'

'Free in the future as in the present? She has nothing to fear from you?'

'Nor from anyone else.'

'Whatever happens?'

'Whatever happens. I have forgotten her name and where she lives.'

'Thank you. And *au revoir*. For we shall meet again, Mr Shears, shall we not?'

'I have no doubt we shall.'

A more or less heated explanation followed between the Englishman and Ganimard and was cut short by Shears with a certain roughness.

'I am very sorry, M. Ganimard, that I can't agree with you. But I have no time to persuade you now. I leave for England in an hour.'

'But . . . the fair-haired lady . . . ?'

'I know no such person.'

'Only a moment ago . . . '

'You must take it or leave it. I have already caught Lupin for you. Here is the blue diamond . . . which you may have the pleasure of handing to the countess yourself. I can't see that you have anything to complain of.'

'But the fair-haired lady?'

'Find her.'

He settled his hat on his head and walked away with a brisk step, like a gentleman who has no time to loiter once his business is done.

* * *

'Goodbye, maître!' cried Lupin. 'And a pleasant journey! I shall always remember the cordial relations between us. My kind regards to Mr Wilson!'

He received no reply and chuckled.

'That's what we call taking English leave. Ah, those worthy islanders do not possess that elegant courtesy which distinguishes us. Just think, Ganimard, of the exit which a Frenchman would have made in similar circumstances! Under what exquisite politeness would he not have concealed his triumph! . . . But, Lord bless my soul, Ganimard, what are you doing? Well, I never: a search! But there's nothing left, my poor friend, not a scrap of paper! My archives have been moved to a place of safety.'

'One can never tell.'

Lupin looked on in resignation. Held by two inspectors and surrounded by all the rest, he patiently watched the various operations. But, after twenty minutes, he sighed: 'Come along, Ganimard, you'll never be finished, at this rate.'

'Are you in a great hurry?'

'Yes, I should think I was! I have an important engagement!'

'At the police-station?'

'No, in town.'

'Tut, tut! At what time?'

'At two o'clock.'

'It's past three.'

'Exactly: I shall be late; and there's nothing I detest so much as being late.'

'Will you give me five minutes?'

'Not a minute longer.'

'You're too good . . . I'll try . . . '

'Don't talk so much . . . What, that cupboard too? Why, it's empty!'

'There are some letters, for all that.'

'Old bills.'

'No, a bundle done up in ribbon.'

'A pink ribbon, is it? Oh, Ganimard, don't untie it, for Heaven's sake!'

'Are they from a woman?'

'Yes.'

'A lady?'

'Rather!'

'What's her name?'

'Mme Ganimard.'

'Very witty! Oh, very witty!' cried the inspector, in an affected tone.

At that moment, the men returned from the other rooms and declared that their search had led to nothing. Lupin began to laugh.

'Of course not! Did you expect to find a list of my friends, or a proof of my relations with the German Emperor? What you ought to have looked for, Ganimard, is the little mysteries of this flat. For instance, that gas-pipe is a speaking-tube. The chimney contains a staircase. This wall here is hollow. And such a tangle of bell-wires! Look here, Ganimard: just press that button.'

Ganimard did as he was asked.

'Did you hear anything?'

'No.'

'Nor I. And yet you have instructed the captain of my balloon-park to get ready the airship which is soon to carry us up to the sky.'

'Come,' said Ganimard, who had finished his inspection. 'Enough of this nonsense. Let us start.'

He took a few steps, followed by his men.

Lupin did not budge a foot's breadth.

His custodians pushed him. In vain.

'Well,' said Ganimard, 'do you refuse to come?'

'Not at all.'

'Then . . .'

'It all depends.'

'Depends on what?'

'On where you're taking me.'

'To the police-station, of course.'

'Then I shan't come. I have nothing to do at the station.'

'You're mad!'

'Didn't I tell you I had an important engagement?'

'Lupin!'

'Come, Ganimard, the fair-haired lady must be getting quite anxious about me; and do you think I could have the rudeness to keep her waiting? It would not be the conduct of a gentleman!'

'Listen to me, Lupin,' said the inspector, who was beginning to lose his temper under all this chaff. 'So far, I have treated you with excessive consideration. But there are limits. Follow me.'

'Impossible. I have an engagement and that engagement I mean to keep.'

'For the last time?'

'Im-possible!'

Ganimard made a sign. Two men seized Lupin under the arms and lifted him from the floor. But they dropped him at once with howls of pain: with his two hands, Arsène Lupin had dug two long needles into their flesh.

Maddened with rage, the others rushed upon him, wreaking their hatred at last, burning to avenge their comrades and themselves for the numberless affronts put upon them, and they rained a shower of blows upon his body. One blow, more violent than the rest, struck him on the temple. He fell to the floor.

'If you hurt him,' growled Ganimard, angrily, 'you'll have me to deal with.'

He bent over Lupin, prepared to assist him. But, finding that he was breathing freely, he told the men to take Lupin by the head and feet, while he himself supported his hips.

'Slowly, now, gently! . . . Don't jolt him! . . . Why, you brutes, you might have killed him. Well, Lupin, how do you feel?'

Lupin opened his eyes and stammered: 'Not up to much, Ganimard . . . You shouldn't have let them knock me about.'

'Dash it, it's your own fault . . . with your obstinacy!' replied Ganimard, in real distress. 'But you're not hurt?'

They reached the landing. Lupin moaned: 'Ganimard . . . the lift . . . they'll break my bones . . .'

'Good idea, capital idea!' agreed the inspector. 'Besides, the stairs are so narrow . . . it would be impossible . . .'

He got the lift up. They laid Lupin on the seat with every imaginable precaution. Ganimard sat down beside him and said to his men: 'Go down the stairs at once. Wait for me by the porter's lodge. Do you understand?'

He shut the door. But it was hardly closed when shouts arose. The lift had shot up, like a balloon with its rope cut. A sardonic laugh rang out.

'Damnation!' roared Ganimard, feeling frantically in the dark for the lever. And failing to find it, he shouted, 'The fifth floor! Watch the door on the fifth floor!'

The detectives rushed upstairs, four steps at a time. But a strange thing happened: the lift seemed to shoot right through the ceiling of the top floor, disappeared before the detectives' eyes and suddenly emerged on the upper storey, where the servants' bed-rooms were, and stopped.

Three men were in waiting and opened the door. Two of them overpowered Ganimard, who, hampered in his movements and completely bewildered, hardly thought of defending himself. The third helped Lupin out.

'I told you, Ganimard! . . . Carried off by balloon . . . and thanks to you! . . . Next time, you must show less compassion. And, above all, remember that Arsène Lupin does not allow himself to be bashed and mauled about without good reasons. Goodbye . . . '

The lift-door was already closed and the lift, with Ganimard inside, sent back on its journey towards the ground-floor. And all this was done so expeditiously that the old detective caught up his subordinates at the door of the porter's lodge.

Without a word, they hurried across the courtyard and up the servants' staircase, the only means of communication with the floor by which the escape had been effected.

A long passage, with many windings, lined with small, numbered rooms, led to a door, which had been simply left ajar. Beyond this door and, consequently, in another house, was another passage, also with a number of turns and lined with similar rooms. Right at the end was a servants' staircase. Ganimard went down it, crossed a yard, a hall and rushed into a street: the Rue Picot. Then he understood: the two houses were built back to back and their fronts faced two streets, running not at right angles, but parallel, with a distance of over sixty yards between them.

He entered the porter's lodge and showed his card.

'Have four men just gone out?'

'Yes, the two servants of the fourth and fifth floors, with two friends.'

'Who lives on the fourth and fifth floors?'

'Two gentlemen of the name of Fauvel and their cousins, the Provosts . . . They moved this morning. Only the two servants remained . . . They have just gone.'

'Ah,' thought Ganimard, sinking on to a sofa in the lodge, 'what a fine stroke we have missed! The whole gang occupied this rabbit-warren! . . . '

* * *

Forty minutes later, two gentlemen drove up in a cab to the Gare du Nord and hurried towards the Calais express, followed by a porter carrying their bags.

One of them had his arm in a sling and his face was pale and drawn. The other seemed in great spirits.

'Come along, Wilson, it won't do to miss the train! . . . Oh, Wilson, I shall never forget these ten days!'

'No more shall I.'

'What a fine series of battles!'

'Magnificent!'

'A regrettable incident, here and there, but of very slight importance.'

'Very slight, as you say.'

'And, lastly, victory all along the line. Lupin arrested! The blue diamond recovered!'

'My arm broken!'

'With a success of this kind, what does a broken arm matter?'

'Especially mine.'

'Especially yours. Remember, Wilson, it was at the very moment when you were at the chemist's, suffering like a hero, that I discovered the clue that guided me through the darkness.'

'What a piece of luck!'

The doors were being locked.

'Take your seats, please. Hurry up, gentlemen!'

The porter climbed into an empty compartment and placed the bags in the rack, while Shears hoisted the unfortunate Wilson in.

'What are you doing, Wilson? Hurry up, old chap! . . . Pull yourself together, do!'

'It's not for want of pulling myself together.'

'What then?'

'I can only use one hand.'

'Well?' cried Shears, gaily. 'What a fuss you make! One would think you were the only man in your plight. What about the fellows who have really lost an arm? Well, are you settled? Thank goodness for that!'

He gave the porter a half-franc piece.

'Here, my man. That's for you.'

'Thank you, Mr Shears.'

The Englishman raised his eyes: Arsène Lupin!

'You! . . . You!' he blurted in his bewilderment.

And Wilson stammered, waving his one hand with the gestures of a man proving a fact: 'You! . . . You! . . . But you're arrested! Shears told me so. When he left you, Ganimard and his thirty detectives had you surrounded! . . . '

Lupin crossed his arms, with an air of indignation.

'So you thought I would let you go without coming to see you off? After the excellent friendly relations which we never ceased to keep up? Why, it would have been unspeakably rude. What do you take me for?'

The engine whistled.

'However, I forgive you . . . Have you all you want? Tobacco, matches? . . . That's right . . . And the evening-papers? You will find the details of my arrest in them: your last exploit, maître! And now, *au revoir*; and delighted to have made your acquaintance . . . delighted, I mean it! . . . And, if ever I can do anything for you, I shall be only too pleased . . . '

He jumped down to the platform and closed the door.

'Goodbye!' he cried again, waving his handkerchief. 'Goodbye . . . I'll write to you! . . . Mind you write too: let me know how the broken arm is, Mr Wilson! I shall expect to hear from both of you . . . Just a picture-postcard, now and again . . . "Lupin, Paris" will always find me . . . It's quite enough . . . Never mind about stamping the letters . . . Goodbye! . . . See you soon, I hope! . . . '

Second Episode:
The Jewish Lamp

Chapter 1

Holmlock Shears and Wilson were seated on either side of the fireplace in Shears's sitting-room. The great detective's pipe had gone out. He knocked the ashes into the grate, refilled his briar, lit it, gathered the skirts of his dressing-gown around his knees, puffed away and devoted all his attention to sending rings of smoke curling gracefully up to the ceiling.

Wilson watched him. He watched him as a dog, rolled up on the hearth-rug, watches its master, with wide-open eyes and unblinking lids, eyes which have no other hope than to reflect the expected movement on the master's part. Would Shears break silence? Would he reveal the secret of his present dreams and admit Wilson to the realm of meditation into which he felt that he was not allowed to enter uninvited?

Shears continued silent.

Wilson ventured upon a remark.

'Things are very quiet. There's not a single case for us to nibble at.'

Shears was more and more fiercely silent; but the rings of tobacco-smoke became more and more successful and anyone but Wilson would have observed that Shears obtained from this the profound content which we derive from the minor achievements of our vanity, at times when our brain is completely void of thought.

Disheartened, Wilson rose and walked to the window. The melancholy street lay stretched between the gloomy fronts of the houses, under a dark sky whence fell an angry and pouring rain. A cab drove past; another cab. Wilson jotted down their numbers in his note-book. One can never tell!

The postman came down the street, gave a treble knock at the door; and, presently, the servant entered with two registered letters.

'You look remarkably pleased,' said Wilson, when Shears had unsealed and glanced through the first.

'This letter contains a very attractive proposal. You were worrying about a case: here is one. Read it . . . '

Wilson took the letter and read.

18, Rue Murillo
Paris

SIR,

I am writing to ask for the benefit of your assistance and experience. I have been the victim of a serious theft and all the investigations attempted up to the present would seem to lead to nothing.

I am sending you by this post a number of newspapers which will give you all the details of the case; and, if you are inclined to take it up, I shall be pleased if you will accept the hospitality of my house and if you will fill in the enclosed signed cheque for any amount which you like to name for your expenses.

Pray telegraph to inform me if I may expect you and believe me to be, Sir,

Yours very truly,
Baron VICTOR D'IMBLEVALLE

'Well,' said Shears, 'this comes just at the right time: why shouldn't I take a little run to Paris? I haven't been there since my famous duel with Arsène Lupin and I shan't be sorry to revisit it under rather more peaceful conditions.'

He tore the cheque into four pieces and, while Wilson, whose arm had not yet recovered from the injury received in the course of the aforesaid encounter, was inveighing bitterly against Paris and all its inhabitants, he opened the second envelope.

A movement of irritation at once escaped him, he knitted his brow as he read the letter and, when he had finished, he crumpled it into a ball and threw it angrily on the floor.

'What's the matter?' exclaimed Wilson, in amazement.

He picked up the ball, unfolded it and read, with ever-increasing stupefaction.

MY DEAR MAÎTRE,

You know my admiration for you and the interest which I take in your reputation. Well, accept my advice and have nothing to do with the case in which you are asked to assist. Your interference would do a great deal of harm, all your efforts would only bring about a pitiable result and you would be obliged publicly to acknowledge your defeat.

I am exceedingly anxious to spare you this humiliation and I beg you, in the name of our mutual friendship, to remain very quietly by your fireside.

Give my kind remembrances to Dr Wilson and accept for yourself the respectful compliments of

Yours most sincerely,

ARSÈNE LUPIN

'Arsène Lupin!' repeated Wilson, in bewilderment.

Shears banged the table with his fist.

'Oh, I'm getting sick of the brute! He laughs at me as if I were a schoolboy! I am publicly to acknowledge my defeat, am I? Didn't I compel him to give up the blue diamond?'

'He's afraid of you,' suggested Wilson.

'You're talking nonsense! Arsène Lupin is never afraid; and the proof is that he challenges me.'

'But how does he come to know of Baron d'Imblevalle's letter?'

'How can I tell? You're asking silly questions, my dear fellow!'

'I thought . . . I imagined . . . '

'What? That I am a sorcerer?'

'No, but I have seen you perform such marvels!'

'No one is able to perform marvels . . . I no more than another. I make reflections, deductions, conclusions, but I don't make guesses. Only fools make guesses.'

Wilson adopted the modest attitude of a beaten dog and did his best, lest he should be a fool, not to guess why Shears was striding angrily up and down the room. But, when Shears rang for the servant and asked for his travelling-bag, Wilson thought himself entitled, since this was a material fact, to reflect, deduce and conclude that his chief was going on a journey.

The same mental operation enabled him to declare, in the tone of a man who has no fear of the possibility of a mistake, 'Holmlock, you are going to Paris.'

'Possibly.'

'And you are going to Paris even more in reply to Lupin's challenge than to oblige Baron d'Imblevalle.'

'Possibly.'

'Holmlock, I will go with you.'

'Aha, old friend!' cried Shears, interrupting his walk. 'Aren't you afraid that your left arm may share the fate of the right?'

'What can happen to me? You will be there.'

'Well said! You're a fine fellow! And we will shew this gentleman that he may have made a mistake in defying us so boldly. Quick, Wilson, and meet me at the first train.'

'Won't you wait for the newspapers the baron mentions?'

'What's the good?'

'Shall I send a telegram?'

'No. Arsène Lupin would know I was coming and I don't wish him to. This time, Wilson, we must play a cautious game.'

*   *   *

That afternoon, the two friends stepped on board the boat at Dover. They had a capital crossing. In the express from Calais to Paris, Shears indulged in three hours of the soundest sleep, while Wilson kept a good watch at the door of the compartment and meditated with a wandering eye.

Shears woke up feeling happy and well. The prospect of a new duel with Arsène Lupin delighted him; and he rubbed his hands with the contented air of a man preparing to taste untold joys.

'At last,' exclaimed Wilson, 'we shall feel that we're alive!' And he rubbed his hands with the same contented air.

At the station, Shears took the rugs and, followed by Wilson carrying the bags – each his burden! – handed the tickets to the collector and walked gaily into the street.

'A fine day, Wilson . . . Sunshine! . . . Paris is dressed in her best to receive us.'

'What a crowd!'

'So much the better, Wilson: we stand less chance of being noticed. No one will recognize us in the midst of such a multitude.'

'Mr Shears, I believe?'

He stopped, somewhat taken aback. Who on earth could be addressing him by name?

A woman was walking beside him, or rather a girl whose exceedingly simple dress accentuated her well-bred appearance. Her pretty face wore a sad and anxious expression. She repeated: 'You must be Mr Shears, surely?'

He was silent, as much from confusion as from the habit of prudence, and she asked, for the third time: 'Surely I am speaking to Mr Shears?'

'What do you want with me?' he asked, crossly, thinking this a questionable meeting.

She placed herself in front of him.

'Listen to me, Mr Shears; it is a very serious matter. I know that you are going to the Rue Murillo.'

'What's that?'

'I know . . . I know . . . Rue Murillo . . . No. 18. Well you must not . . . no, you must not go . . . I assure you you will regret it. Because I tell you this, you need not think that I am interested in any way. I have a reason, I know what I am saying.'

He tried to push her aside. She insisted: 'I entreat you, do not be obstinate . . . Oh, if I only knew how to convince you! Look into me, look into the depths of my eyes . . . they are sincere . . . they speak the truth . . . '

Desperately, she raised her eyes, a pair of beautiful grave and limpid eyes that seemed to reflect her very soul. Wilson nodded his head.

'The young lady seems quite sincere,' he said.

'Indeed I am,' she said, beseechingly, 'and you must trust me . . . '

'I do trust you, mademoiselle,' replied Wilson.

'Oh, how happy you make me! And your friend trusts me too, does he not? I feel it . . . I am sure of it! How glad I am! All will be well! . . . Oh, what a good idea I had! Listen, Mr Shears: there's a train for Calais in twenty minutes . . . Now you must take it . . . Quick, come with me: it's this way and you have not much time . . . '

She tried to drag Shears with her. He seized her by the arm and, in a voice which he strove to make as gentle as possible, said: 'Forgive me, mademoiselle, if I am not able to accede to your wish; but I never turn aside from a task which I have undertaken.'

'I entreat you . . . I entreat you . . . Oh, if you only knew!'

He passed on and walked briskly away.

Wilson lingered behind and said to the girl: 'Be of good hope . . . He will see the thing through to the end . . . He has never yet been known to fail . . . '

And he ran after Shears to catch him up.

HOLMLOCK SHEARS

VERSUS

ARSÈNE LUPIN

These words, standing out in great black letters, struck their eyes at the first steps they took. They walked up to them: a procession of sandwichmen was moving along in single file. In their hands they carried heavy ferruled canes, with which they tapped the pavement in unison as they went; and their boards bore the above legend in front and a further huge poster at the back which read:

> THE SHEARS-LUPIN CONTEST
>
> ARRIVAL OF
>
> THE ENGLISH CHAMPION
>
> THE GREAT DETECTIVE
>
> GRAPPLES WITH
>
> THE RUE MURILLO MYSTERY
>
> FULL DETAILS
>
> ÉCHO DE FRANCE

Wilson tossed his head.

'I say, Holmlock, I thought we were travelling incognito! I shouldn't be astonished to find the Republican Guard waiting for us in the Rue Murillo, with an official reception and champagne!'

'When you try to be witty, Wilson,' snarled Shears, 'you're witty enough for two!'

He strode up to one of the men with the apparent intention of taking him in his powerful hands and tearing him and his advertisement to shreds. Meanwhile, a crowd gathered round the posters, laughing and joking.

Suppressing a furious fit of passion, Shears said to the man: 'When were you hired?'

'This morning.'

'When did you start on your round?'

'An hour ago.'

'But the posters were ready?'

'Lord, yes! They were there when we came to the office this morning.'

So Arsène Lupin had foreseen that Shears would accept the battle! Nay more, the letter written by Lupin proved that he himself wished for the battle and that it formed part of his intentions to measure swords once more with his rival. Why? What possible motive could urge him to recommence the contest?

Holmlock Shears showed a momentary hesitation. Lupin must really feel very sure of victory to display such insolence; and was it not falling into a trap to hasten like that in answer to the first call? Then, summoning up all his energy: 'Come along, Wilson! Driver, 18, Rue Murillo!' he shouted.

And, with swollen veins and fists clenched as though for a boxing-match, he leapt into a cab.

*   *   *

The Rue Murillo is lined with luxurious private residences, the backs of which look out upon the Parc Monceau. No. 18 is one of the handsomest of these houses; and Baron d'Imblevalle, who occupies it with his wife and children, has furnished it in the most sumptuous style, as befits an artist and millionaire. There is a courtyard in front of the house, skirted on either side by the servants' offices. At the back, a garden mingles the branches of its trees with the trees of the park.

The two Englishmen rang the bell, crossed the courtyard and were admitted by a footman, who showed them into a small drawing-room at the other side of the house.

They sat down and took a rapid survey of the many valuable objects with which the room was filled.

'Very pretty things,' whispered Wilson. 'Taste and fancy . . . One can safely draw the deduction that people who have had the leisure to hunt out these articles are persons of a certain age . . . fifty, perhaps . . . '

He did not have time to finish. The door opened and M. d'Imblevalle entered, followed by his wife.

Contrary to Wilson's deductions, they were both young, fashionably dressed and very lively in speech and manner. Both were profuse in thanks.

'It is really too good of you! To put yourself out like this! We are almost glad of this trouble, since it procures us the pleasure . . . '

'How charming those French people are!' thought Wilson, who never shirked the opportunity of making an original observation.

'But time is money,' cried the baron. 'And yours especially, Mr Shears. Let us come to the point! What do you think of the case? Do you hope to bring it to a satisfactory result?'

'To bring the case to a satisfactory result, I must first know what the case is.'

'Don't you know?'

'No; and I will ask you to explain the matter fully, omitting nothing. What is it a case of?'

'It is a case of theft.'

'On what day did it take place?'

'On Saturday,' replied the baron. 'On Saturday night or Sunday morning.'

'Six days ago, therefore. Now pray go on.'

'I must first tell you that my wife and I, though we lead the life expected of people in our position, go out very little. The education of our children, a few receptions, the beautifying of our home: these make up our existence; and all or nearly all our evenings are spent here, in this room, which is my wife's boudoir and in which we have collected a few pretty things. Well, on Saturday last, at about eleven o'clock, I switched off the electric light and my wife and I retired, as usual, to our bedroom.'

'Where is that?'

'The next room: that door over there. On the following morning, that is to say, Sunday, I rose early. As Suzanne – my wife – was still asleep, I came into this room as gently as possible, so as not to awake her. Imagine my surprise at finding the window open, after we had left it closed the evening before!'

'A servant . . . ?'

'Nobody enters this room in the morning before we ring. Besides, I always take the precaution of bolting that other door, which leads to the hall. Therefore the window must have been opened from the outside. I had a proof of it, besides: the second pane of the right-hand casement, the one next to the latch, had been cut out.'

'And the window . . . ?'

'The window, as you perceive, opens on a little balcony surrounded by a stone balustrade. We are on the first floor here and you can see the garden at the back of the house and the railings that separate it from the Parc Monceau. It is certain, therefore, that the man came from the Parc Monceau, climbed the railings by means of a ladder and got up to the balcony.'

'It is certain, you say?'

'On either side of the railings, in the soft earth of the borders, we found holes left by the two uprights of the ladder; and there were two similar holes below the balcony. Lastly, the balustrade shows two slight scratches, evidently caused by the contact of the ladder.'

'Isn't the Parc Monceau closed at night?'

'Closed? No. But, in any case, there is a house building at No. 14. It would have been easy to effect an entrance that way.'

Holmlock Shears reflected for a few moments and resumed: 'Let us come to the theft. You say it was committed in the room where we now are?'

'Yes. Just here, between this twelfth-century Virgin and that chased-silver tabernacle, there was a little Jewish lamp. It has disappeared.'

'And is that all?'

'That is all.'

'Oh! . . . And what do you call a Jewish lamp?'

'It is one of those lamps which they used to employ in the old days, consisting of a stem and of a receiver to contain the oil. This receiver had two or more burners, which held the wicks.'

'When all is said, objects of no great value.'

'Just so. But the one in question formed a hiding-place in which we had made it a practice to keep a magnificent antique jewel, a chimera in gold, set with rubies and emeralds and worth a great deal of money.'

'What was your reason for this practice?'

'Upon my word, Mr Shears, I should find it difficult to tell you! Perhaps we just thought it amusing to have a hiding-place of this kind.'

'Did nobody know of it?'

'Nobody.'

'Except, of course, the thief,' objected Shears. 'But for that, he would not have taken the trouble to steal the Jewish lamp.'

'Obviously. But how could he know of it, seeing that it was by an accident that we discovered the secret mechanism of the lamp?'

'The same accident may have revealed it to somebody else: a servant . . . a visitor to the house . . . But let us continue: have you informed the police?'

'Certainly. The examining-magistrate has made his inquiry. The journalistic detectives attached to all the big newspapers have made theirs. But, as I wrote to you, it does not seem as though the problem had the least chance of ever being solved.'

Shears rose, went to the window, inspected the casement, the balcony, the balustrade, employed his lens to study the two scratches on the stone and asked M. d'Imblevalle to take him down to the garden.

When they were outside, Shears simply sat down in a wicker chair and contemplated the roof of the house with a dreamy eye. Then he suddenly walked towards two little wooden cases with which, in order to preserve the exact marks, they had covered the holes which the uprights of the ladder had left in the ground, below the balcony. He removed the cases, went down on his knees and, with rounded back and his nose six inches from the ground, searched and took his measurements. He went through the same performance along the railing, but more quickly.

That was all.

They both returned to the boudoir, where Madame d'Imblevalle was waiting for them.

Shears was silent for a few minutes longer and then spoke these words: 'Ever since you began your story, monsieur le baron, I was struck by the really too simple side of the offence. To apply a ladder, remove a pane of glass, pick out an object and go away: no, things don't happen so easily as that. It is all too clear, too plain.'

'You mean to say . . . ?'

'I mean to say that the theft of the Jewish lamp was committed under the direction of Arsène Lupin.'

'Arsène Lupin!' exclaimed the baron.

'But it was committed without Arsène Lupin's presence and without anybody's entering the house . . . Perhaps a servant slipped down to the balcony from his garret, along a rain-spout which I saw from the garden.'

'But what evidence have you?'

'Arsène Lupin would not have left the boudoir empty-handed.'

'Empty-handed! And what about the lamp?'

'Taking the lamp would not have prevented him from taking this snuff-box, which, I see, is studded with diamonds, or this necklace of old opals. It would require but two movements more. His only reason for not making those movements was that he was not here to make them.'

'Still, the marks of the ladder?'

'A farce! Mere stage-play to divert suspicions!'

'The scratches on the balustrade?'

'A sham! They were made with sandpaper. Look, here are a few bits of paper which I picked up.'

'The marks left by the uprights of the ladder?'

'Humbug! Examine the two rectangular holes below the balcony and the two holes near the railings. The shape is similar, but, whereas they are parallel here, they are not so over there. Measure the space that separates each hole from its neighbour: it differs in the two cases. Below the balcony, the distance is nine inches. Beside the railings, it is eleven inches.'

'What do you conclude from that?'

'I conclude, since their outline is identical, that the four holes were made with one stump of wood, cut to the right shape.'

'The best argument would be the stump of wood itself.'

'Here it is,' said Shears. 'I picked it up in the garden, behind a laurel-tub.'

The baron gave in. It was only forty minutes since the Englishman had entered by that door; and not a vestige remained of all that had been believed so far on the evidence of the apparent facts themselves. The reality, a different reality, came to light, founded upon something much more solid, the reasoning faculties of a Holmlock Shears.

'It is a very serious accusation to bring against our people, Mr Shears,' said the baroness. 'They are old family servants and not one of them is capable of deceiving us.'

'If one of them did not deceive you, how do you explain that this letter was able to reach me on the same day and by the same post as the one you sent me?'

And he handed her the letter which Arsène Lupin had written to him.

Madame d'Imblevalle was dumbfounded.

'Arsène Lupin! . . . How did he know?'

'Did you tell no one of your letter?'

'No one,' said the baron. 'The idea occurred to us the other evening, at dinner.'

'Before the servants?'

'There were only our two children. And even then . . . no, Sophie and Henriette were not at table, were they Suzanne?'

Madame d'Imblevalle reflected and declared: 'No, they had gone up to mademoiselle.'

'Mademoiselle?' asked Shears.

'The governess, Alice Demun.'

'Doesn't she have her meals with you?'

'No, she has them by herself, in her room.'

Wilson had an idea.

'The letter written to my friend Holmlock Shears was posted.'

'Naturally.'

'Who posted it?'

'Dominique, who has been with me as my own man for twenty years,' replied the baron. 'Any search in that direction would be waste of time.'

'Time employed in searching is never wasted,' stated Wilson, sententiously.

This closed the first enquiries and Shears asked leave to withdraw.

An hour later, at dinner, he saw Sophie and Henriette, the d'Imblevalles' children, two pretty little girls of eight and six respectively. The conversation languished. Shears replied to the pleasant remarks of the baron and his wife in so surly a tone that they thought it better to keep silence. Coffee was served. Shears swallowed the contents of his cup and rose from his chair.

At that moment, a servant entered with a telephone message for him. Shears opened it and read.

ACCEPT MY ENTHUSIASTIC ADMIRATION. RESULTS OBTAINED
BY YOU IN SO SHORT A TIME MAKE MY HEAD REEL. I FEEL
QUITE GIDDY.   ARSÈNE LUPIN

He could not suppress a gesture of annoyance and, showing the telegram to the baron: 'Do you begin to believe,' he said, 'that your walls have eyes and ears?'

'I can't understand it,' murmured M. d'Imblevalle, astounded.

'Nor I. But what I do understand is that not a movement takes place here unperceived by him. Not a word is spoken but he hears it.'

*   *   *

That evening, Wilson went to bed with the easy conscience of a man who has done his duty and who has no other business before him than to go to sleep. So he went to sleep very quickly and was visited by beautiful dreams, in which he was hunting down Lupin all by himself and just on the point of arresting him with his own hand; and the feeling of the pursuit was so lifelike that he woke up.

Someone was touching his bed. He seized his revolver.

'Another movement, Lupin, and I shoot!'

'Steady, old chap, steady on!'

'Hullo, is that you, Shears? Do you want me?'

'I want your eyes. Get up . . .'

He led him to the window.

'Look over there . . . beyond the railings . . .

'In the park?'

'Yes. Do you see anything?'

'No, nothing.'

'Try again, I am sure you see something.'

'Oh, so I do: a shadow . . . no, two!'

'I thought so: against the railings . . . See, they're moving . . . Let's lose no time.'

Groping and holding on to the banister, they made their way down the stairs and came to a room that opened on to the garden steps. Through the glass doors, they could see the two figures still in the same place.

'It's curious,' said Shears. 'I seem to hear noises in the house.'

'In the house? Impossible! Everybody's asleep.'

'Listen, though . . . '

At that moment, a faint whistle sounded from the railings and they perceived an undecided light that seemed to come from the house.

'The d'Imblevalles must have switched on their light,' muttered Shears. 'It's their room above us.'

'Then it's they we heard, no doubt,' said Wilson. 'Perhaps they are watching the railings.'

A second whistle, still fainter than the first.

'I can't understand, I can't understand,' said Shears, in a tone of vexation.

'No more can I,' confessed Wilson.

Shears turned the key of the door, unbolted it and softly pushed it open.

A third whistle, this time a little deeper and in a different note. And, above their heads, the noise grew louder, more hurried.

'It sounds rather as if it were on the balcony of the boudoir,' whispered Shears.

He put his head between the glass doors, but at once drew back with a stifled oath. Wilson looked out in his turn. Close to them, a ladder rose against the wall, leaning against the balustrade of the balcony.

'By Jove!' said Shears. 'There's someone in the boudoir. That's what we heard. Quick, let's take away the ladder!'

But, at that moment, a form slid from the top to the bottom, the ladder was removed and the man who carried it ran swiftly towards the railings, to the place where his accomplices were waiting. Shears and Wilson had darted out. They came up with the man as he was placing the ladder against the railings. Two shots rang out from the other side.

'Wounded?' cried Shears.

'No,' replied Wilson.

He caught the man round the body and tried to throw him. But the man turned, seized him with one hand and, with the other, plunged a knife full into his chest. Wilson gave a sigh, staggered and fell.

'Damnation!' roared Shears. 'If they've done for him, I'll do for them!'

He laid Wilson on the lawn and rushed at the ladder. Too late: the man had run up it and, in company with his accomplices, was fleeing through the shrubs.

'Wilson, Wilson, it's not serious, is it? Say it's only a scratch!'

The doors of the house opened suddenly. M. d'Imblevalle was the first to appear, followed by the men-servants carrying candles.

'What is it?' cried the baron. 'Is Mr Wilson hurt?'

'Nothing, only a scratch,' repeated Shears, endeavouring to delude himself into the belief.

Wilson was bleeding copiously and his face was deathly pale. Twenty minutes later, the doctor declared that the point of the knife had penetrated to within a quarter of an inch of the heart.

'A quarter of an inch! That Wilson was always a lucky dog!' said Shears, summing up the situation, in an envious tone.

'Lucky . . . lucky . . . ' grunted the doctor.

'Why, with his strong constitution, he'll be all right . . . '

'After six weeks in bed and two months' convalescence.'

'No longer?'

'No, unless complications ensue . . . '

'Why on earth should there be any complications?'

Fully reassured, Shears returned to M. d'Imblevalle in the boudoir. This time, the mysterious visitor had not shown the same discretion. He had laid hands without shame on the diamond-studded snuff-box, on the opal necklace and, generally, on anything that could find room in the pockets of a self-respecting burglar.

The window was still open, one of the panes had been neatly cut out and a summary inquiry held at daybreak shewed that the ladder came from the unfinished house and that the burglars must have come that way.

'In short,' said M. d'Imblevalle, with a touch of irony in his voice, 'it is an exact repetition of the theft of the Jewish lamp.'

'Yes, if we accept the first version favoured by the police.'

'Do you still refuse to adopt it? Doesn't this second theft shake your opinion as regards the first?'

'On the contrary, it confirms it.'

'It seems incredible! You have the undoubted proof that last night's burglary was committed by somebody from the outside and you still maintain that the Jewish lamp was stolen by one of our people?'

'By someone living in the house.'

'Then how do you explain . . . ?'

'I explain nothing, monsieur: I establish two facts, which resemble each other only in appearance, I weigh them separately and I am trying to find the link that connects them.'

His conviction seemed so profound, his actions based upon such powerful motives, that the baron gave way.

'Very well. Let us go and inform the commissary of police . . . '

'On no account!' exclaimed the Englishman, eagerly. 'On no account whatever! The police are people whom I apply to only when I want them.'

'Still, the shots . . . ?'

'Never mind the shots!'

'Your friend . . . '

'My friend is only wounded . . . Make the doctor hold his tongue . . . I will take all the responsibility as regards the police.'

*   *   *

Two days elapsed, devoid of all incident, during which Shears pursued his task with a minute care and a conscientiousness that was exasperated by the memory of that daring onslaught, perpetrated under his eyes, despite his presence and without his being able to prevent its success. He searched the house and garden indefatigably, talked to the servants and paid long visits to the kitchen and stables. And, though he gathered no clue that threw any light upon the subject, he did not lose courage.

'I shall find what I am looking for,' he thought, 'and I shall find it here. It is not a question now, as in the case of the fair-haired lady, of walking at hap-hazard and of reaching, by roads unknown to me, an equally unknown goal. This time, I am on the battle-field itself. The enemy is no longer the invisible, elusive Lupin, but the flesh-and-blood accomplice who moves within the four walls of this house. Give me the least little particular and I know where I stand.'

This little particular, from which he was to derive such remarkable consequences, with a skill so prodigious that the case of the Jewish lamp may be looked upon as one in which his detective genius bursts forth most triumphantly, this little particular he was to obtain by accident.

On the third day, entering the room above the boudoir, which was used as a school-room for the children, he came upon Henriette, the smaller of the two. She was looking for her scissors.

'You know,' she said to Shears, 'I make papers too, like the one you got the other evening.'

'The other evening?'

'Yes, after dinner. You got a paper with strips on it . . . you know, a telegram . . . Well, I make them too.'

She went out. To anyone else, these words would have represented only the insignificant observation of a child; and Shears himself listened without paying much attention and continued his inspection. But, suddenly, he started running after the child, whose last phrase had all at once impressed him. He caught her at the top of the staircase and said: 'So you stick strips on to paper also, do you?'

Henriette, very proudly, declared: 'Yes, I cut out words and stick them on.'

'And who taught you that pretty game?'

'Mademoiselle . . . my governess . . . I saw her do it. She takes words out of newspapers and sticks them on . . . '

'And what does she do with them?'

'Makes telegrams and letters which she sends off.'

Holmlock Shears returned to the school-room, singularly puzzled by this confidence and doing his utmost to extract from it the inferences of which it allowed.

There was a bundle of newspapers on the mantel-piece. He opened them and saw, in fact, that there were groups of words or lines missing, regularly and neatly cut out. But he had only to read the words that came before or after to ascertain that the missing words had been removed with the scissors at random, evidently by Henriette. It was possible that, in the pile of papers, there was one which mademoiselle had cut herself. But how was he to make sure?

Mechanically, Shears turned the pages of the lesson-books heaped up on the table and of some others lying on the shelves of a cupboard. And suddenly a cry of joy escaped him. In a corner of the cupboard, under a pile of old exercise-books, he had found a children's album, a sort of picture alphabet, and, in one of the pages of this album, he had seen a gap.

He examined the page. It gave the names of the days of the week: Sunday, Monday, Tuesday, and so on. The word 'Saturday' was missing. Now the Jewish lamp was stolen on a Saturday night.

Shears felt that little clutch at the heart which always told him, in the plainest manner possible, when he had hit upon the knotty point of a mystery. That grip of truth, that feeling of certainty never deceived him.

He hastened to turn over the pages of the album, feverishly and confidently. A little further on came another surprise.

It was a page consisting of capital letters followed by a row of figures.

Nine of the letters and three of the figures had been carefully removed.

Shears wrote them down in his note-book, in the order which they would have occupied, and obtained the following result.

$$C D E H N O P R Z - 237$$

'By Jove!' he muttered. 'There's not much to be made out of that, at first sight.'

Was it possible to rearrange these letters and, employing them all, to form one, two or three complete words?

Shears attempted to do so in vain.

One solution alone suggested itself, returned continually to the point of his pencil and, in the end, appeared to him the right one, because it agreed with the logic of the facts and also corresponded with the general circumstances.

Admitting that the page of the album contained each of the letters of the alphabet once and once only, it was probable, it was certain that he had to do with incomplete words and that these words had been completed with letters taken from other pages. Given these conditions, and allowing for the possibility of a mistake, the puzzle stood thus.

$$R E P O N D . Z - C H - 237$$

The first word was clear: '*Répondez*, reply.' An E was missing, because the letter E, having been once used, was no longer available.

As for the last, unfinished word, it undoubtedly formed, with the number 237, the address which the sender gave to the receiver of the letter. He was advised to fix the day for Saturday and asked to send a reply to C H 237.

Either C H 237 was the official number of a *poste restante* or else
the two letters C H formed part of an incomplete word. Shears
turned over the leaves of the album: nothing had been cut from any
of the following pages. He must, therefore, until further orders, be
content with the explanation hit upon.

'Isn't it fun?'

Henriette had returned.

He replied: 'Yes, great fun! Only, haven't you any other papers? . . .
Or else some words ready cut out, for me to stick on?'

'Papers? . . . No . . . And then mademoiselle wouldn't like it.'

'Mademoiselle?'

'Yes, mademoiselle has scolded me already.'

'Why?'

'Because I told you things . . . and she says you must never tell
things about people you are fond of.'

'You were quite right to tell me.'

Henriette seemed delighted with his approval, so much so that,
from a tiny canvas bag pinned on to her frock, she took a few strips of
stuff, three buttons, two lumps of sugar and, lastly, a square piece of
paper which she held out to Shears.

'There, I'll give it you all the same.'

It was the number of a cab, No. 8279.

'Where did you get this from?'

'It fell out of her purse.'

'When?'

'On Sunday, at mass, when she was taking out some coppers for
the collection.'

'Capital! And now I will tell you how not to get scolded. Don't tell
mademoiselle that you have seen me.'

Shears went off in search of M. d'Imblevalle and asked him straight
out about mademoiselle.

The baron gave a start.

'Alice Demun! . . . Would you think? . . . Oh, impossible! . . . '

'How long has she been in your service?'

'Only twelve months, but I know no quieter person nor any in
whom I place more confidence.'

'How is it that I have not yet seen her?'

'She was away for two days.'

'And at present?'

'Immediately on her return, she took up her position by your friend's bedside. She is a first-rate nurse ... gentle ... attentive. Mr Wilson seems delighted with her.'

'Oh!' said Shears, who had quite omitted to enquire after old chap's progress.

He thought for a moment and asked: 'And did she go out on Sunday morning?'

'The day after the robbery?'

'Yes.'

The baron called his wife and put the question to her. She replied: 'Mademoiselle took the children to the eleven o'clock mass, as usual.'

'But before that?'

'Before? No ... Or rather ... But I was so upset by the theft! ... Still, I remember that, on the evening before, she asked leave to go out on Sunday morning ... to see a cousin who was passing through Paris, I think. But surely you don't suspect her? ...'

'Certainly not. But I should like to see her.'

He went up to Wilson's room. A woman dressed like a hospital-nurse, in a long grey linen gown, was stooping over the sick man and giving him a draught. When she turned round, Shears recognized the girl who had spoken to him outside the Gare du Nord.

* * *

Not the slightest explanation passed between them. Alice Demun smiled gently, with her grave and charming eyes, without a trace of embarrassment. The Englishman wanted to speak, tried to utter a syllable or two and was silent. Then she resumed her task, moved about peacefully before Shears's astonished eyes, shifted bottles, rolled and unrolled linen bandages and again gave him her bright smile.

Shears turned on his heels, went downstairs, saw M. d'Imblevalle's motor in the court-yard, got into it and told the chauffeur to drive him to the yard at Levallois of which the address was marked on the cab-ticket given him by the child. Duprêt, the driver who had taken out No. 8279 on Sunday morning, was not there and Shears sent back the motor-car and waited until he came to change horses.

Duprêt the driver said yes, he had taken up a lady near the Parc Monceau, a young lady in black, with a big veil on her: she seemed very excited.

'Was she carrying a parcel?'

'Yes, a longish parcel.'

'And where did you drive her to?'

'Avenue des Ternes, at the corner of the Place Saint-Ferdinand. She stayed for ten minutes or so; and then we went back to the Parc Monceau.'

'Would you know the house again, in the Avenue des Ternes?'

'Rather! Shall I take you there?'

'Presently. Go first to 36, Quai des Orfèvres.'

At the police head-quarters, he had the good fortune to come upon Chief-Inspector Ganimard.

'Are you disengaged, M. Ganimard?'

'If it's about Lupin, no.'

'It is about Lupin.'

'Then I shan't stir.'

'What! You give up . . . !'

'I give up the impossible. I am tired of this unequal contest of which we are certain to have the worst. It's cowardly, it's ridiculous, it's anything you please . . . I don't care! Lupin is stronger than we are. Consequently, there's nothing to do but give in.'

'I'm not giving in!'

'He'll make you give in like the rest of us.'

'Well, it's a sight that can't fail to please you.'

'That's true enough,' said Ganimard, innocently. 'And, as you seem to want another beating, come along!'

Ganimard and Shears stepped into the cab. They told the driver to stop a little way before he came to the house and on the other side of the avenue, in front of a small café. They sat down outside it, among tubs of laurels and spindle-trees. The light was beginning to wane.

'Waiter!' said Shears. 'Pen and ink!'

He wrote a note and, calling the waiter again, said: 'Take this to the concierge of the house opposite. It's the man in the cap smoking his pipe in the gateway.'

The concierge hurried across and, after Ganimard had announced himself as a chief-inspector, Shears asked if a young lady in black had called at the house on Sunday morning.

'In black? Yes, about nine o'clock: it's the one who goes up to the second floor.'

'Do you see much of her?'

'No, but she's been oftener lately: almost every day during the past fortnight.'

'And since Sunday?'

'Only once . . . without counting today.'

'What! Has she been today?'

'She's there now.'

'She's there now?'

'Yes, she came about ten minutes ago. He cab is waiting on the Place Saint-Ferdinand, as usual. I passed her in the gateway.'

'And who is the tenant of the second floor?'

'There are two: a dressmaker, Mademoiselle Langeais, and a gentleman who hired a couple of furnished rooms, a month ago, under the name of Bresson.'

'What makes you say "under the name"?'

'I have an idea that it's an assumed name. My wife does his rooms: well, he hasn't two articles of clothing marked with the same initials.'

'How does he live?'

'Oh, he's almost always out. Sometimes, he does not come home for three days together.'

'Did he come in on Saturday night?'

'On Saturday night? . . . Wait, while I think . . . Yes, he came in on Saturday night and hasn't stirred out since.'

'And what sort of man is he?'

'Faith, I couldn't say. He changes so! He's tall, he's short, he's fat, he's thin . . . dark and fair. I don't always recognize him.'

Ganimard and Shears exchanged glances.

'It's he,' muttered Ganimard. 'It must be he.'

For a moment, the old detective experienced a real agitation, which betrayed itself by a deep breath and a clenching of the fists.

Shears too, although more master of himself, felt something clutching at his heart.

'Look out!' said the concierge. 'Here comes the young lady.'

As he spoke, mademoiselle appeared in the gateway and crossed the square.

'And here is M. Bresson.'

'M. Bresson? Which is he?'

'The gentleman with a parcel under his arm.'

'But he's taking no notice of the girl. She is going to her cab alone.'

'Oh well, I've never seen them together.'

The two detectives rose hurriedly. By the light of the street-lamps, they recognized Lupin's figure, as he walked away in the opposite direction to the square.

'Which will you follow?' asked Ganimard.

' "Him", of course. He's the big game.'

'Then I'll shadow the young lady,' suggested Ganimard.

'No, no,' said the Englishman quickly, not wishing to reveal any part of the case to Ganimard. 'I know where to find the young lady when I want her . . . Don't leave me.'

At a distance and availing themselves of the occasional shelter of the passers-by and the kiosks, Ganimard and Shears set off in pursuit of Lupin. It was an easy enough pursuit, for he did not turn round and walked quickly, with a slight lameness in the right leg, so slight that it needed the eye of a trained observer to perceive it.

'He's pretending to limp!' said Ganimard. And he continued, 'Ah, if we could only pick up two or three policemen and pounce upon the fellow! As it is, there's a chance of our losing him.'

But no policeman appeared in sight before the Porte des Ternes; and, once the fortifications were passed, they could not reckon on the least assistance.

'Let us separate,' said Shears. 'The place is deserted.'

They were on the Boulevard Victor-Hugo. They each took a different pavement and followed the line of the trees.

They walked like this for twenty minutes, until the moment when Lupin turned to the left and along the Seine. Here they saw him go down to the edge of the river. He remained there for a few seconds, during which they were unable to distinguish his movements. Then he climbed up the bank again and returned by the way he had come. They pressed back against the pillars of a gate. Lupin passed in front of them. He no longer carried a parcel.

And, as he moved away, another figure appeared from behind the corner of a house and slipped in between the trees.

Shears said, in a low voice: 'That one seems to be following him too.'

'Yes, I believe I saw him before, as we came.'

The pursuit was resumed, but was now complicated by the presence of this figure. Lupin followed the same road, passed through the Porte des Ternes again and entered the house on the Place Saint-Ferdinand.

The concierge was closing the door for the night when Ganimard came up.

'You saw him, I suppose?'

'Yes, I was turning off the gas on the stairs. He has bolted his door.'

'Is there no one with him?'

'No one: he doesn't keep a servant . . . he never has his meals here.'

'Is there no back staircase?'

'No.'

Ganimard said to Shears: 'The best thing will be for me to place myself outside Lupin's door, while you go to the Rue Demours and fetch the commissary of police. I'll give you a line for him.'

Shears objected: 'Suppose he escapes meanwhile?'

'But I shall be here! . . . '

'Single-handed, it would be an unequal contest between you and him.'

'Still, I can't break into his rooms. I'm not entitled to, especially at night.'

Shears shrugged his shoulders.

'Once you've arrested Lupin, no one will haul you over the coals for the particular manner in which you effected the arrest. Besides, we may as well ring the bell, what! Then we'll see what happens.'

They went up the stairs. There was a double door on the left of the landing. Ganimard rang the bell.

Not a sound. He rang again. No one stirred.

'Let's go in,' muttered Shears.

'Yes, come along.'

Nevertheless, they remained motionless, irresolute. Like people who hesitate before taking a decisive step, they were afraid to act; and it suddenly seemed to them impossible that Arsène Lupin should be there, so near to them, behind that frail partition, which they could smash with a blow of their fists. They both of them knew him too well, demon that he was, to admit that he would allow himself to be nabbed so stupidly. No, no, a thousand times no: he was not there. He must have escaped, by the adjoining houses, by the roofs, by some suitably-prepared outlet, and, once again, the shadow of Arsène Lupin was all that they could hope to lay hands upon.

They shuddered. An imperceptible sound, coming from the other side of the door, had as it were grazed the silence. And they received the impression, the certainty that he was there after all, separated from them by that thin wooden partition, and that he was listening to them, that he heard them.

What were they to do? It was a tragic situation. For all their coolness as old stagers of the police, they were overcome by so great an excitement that they imagined they could hear the beating of their own hearts.

Ganimard consulted Shears with a silent glance and then struck the door violently with his fist.

A sound of footsteps was now heard, a sound which there was no longer any attempt to conceal.

Ganimard shook the door. Shears gave an irresistible thrust with his shoulder and burst it open; and they both rushed in.

Then they stopped short. A shot resounded in the next room. And another, followed by the thud of a falling body . . .

When they entered, they saw the man lying with his face against the marble of the mantelpiece. He gave a convulsive movement. His revolver slipped from his hand.

Ganimard stooped and turned the dead man's head. It was covered with blood, which trickled from two large wounds in the cheek and temple.

'There's no recognizing him,' he whispered.

'One thing is certain,' said Shears. 'It's not "he".'

'How do you know? You haven't even examined him.'

The Englishman sneered: 'Do you think Arsène Lupin is the man to kill himself?'

'Still, we believed we knew him outside.'

'We believed, because we *wanted* to believe. The fellow besets our minds.'

'Then it's one of his accomplices.'

'Arsène Lupin's accomplices do not kill themselves.'

'Then who is it?'

They searched the body. In one pocket, Holmlock Shears found an empty note-case; in another, Ganimard found a few louis. There were no marks on his linen or on his clothes.

The trunks – a big box and two bags – contained nothing but personal effects. There was a bundle of newspapers on the mantelpiece. Ganimard opened them. They all spoke of the theft of the Jewish lamp.

An hour later, when Ganimard and Shears left the house, they knew no more about the strange individual whom their intervention had driven to suicide.

Who was he? Why had he taken his life? What link connected him with the disappearance of the Jewish lamp? Who was it that dogged his steps during his walk? These were all complicated questions . . . so many mysteries . . .

*   *   *

Holmlock Shears went to bed in a very bad temper. When he woke, he received an express letter couched in these words.

Arsène Lupin begs to inform you of his tragic decease in the person of one Bresson and requests the honour of your company at his funeral, which will take place, at the public expense, on Thursday the 25th of June.

Chapter 2

'You see, old chap,' said Holmlock Shears to Wilson, waving Arsène Lupin's letter in his hand, 'the worst of this business is that I feel the confounded fellow's eye constantly fixed upon me. Not one of my most secret thoughts escapes him. I am behaving like an actor, whose steps are ruled by the strictest stage-directions, who moves here or there and says this or that because a superior will has so determined it. Do you understand, Wilson?'

Wilson would no doubt have understood had he not been sleeping the sound sleep of a man whose temperature is fluctuating between 102 and 104 degrees. But whether he heard or not made no difference to Shears, who continued: 'It will need all my energy and all my re-sources not to be discouraged. Fortunately, with me, these little gibes are only so many pin-pricks which stimulate me to further exertions. Once the sting is allayed and the wound in my self-respect closed, I always end by saying, "Laugh away, my lad. Sooner or later, you will be betrayed by your own hand." For, when all is said, Wilson, wasn't it Lupin himself who, with his first telegram and the reflection which it suggested to that little Henriette, revealed to me the secret of his correspondence with Alice Demun? You forget that detail, old chap.'

He walked up and down the room, with resounding strides, at the risk of waking old chap.

'However, things might be worse; and, though the paths which I am following appear a little dark, I am beginning to see my way. To start with, I shall soon know all about Master Bresson. Ganimard and I have an appointment on the bank of the Seine, at the spot where Bresson flung his parcel, and we shall find out who he was and what he wanted. As regards the rest, it's a game to be played out between Alice Demun and me. Not a very powerful adversary, eh, Wilson? And don't you think I shall soon know the sentence in the album and what those two single letters mean, the C and the H? For the whole mystery lies in that, Wilson.'

At this moment, mademoiselle entered the room and, seeing Shears wave his arms about, said: 'Mr Shears, I shall be very angry with you if you wake my patient. It's not nice of you to disturb him. The doctor insists upon absolute calm.'

He looked at her without a word, astonished, as on the first day, at her inexplicable composure.

'Why do you look at me like that, Mr Shears? . . . You always seem to have something at the back of your mind . . . What is it? Tell me, please.'

She questioned him with all her bright face, with her guileless eyes, her smiling lips and with her attitude too, her hands joined together, her body bent slightly forward. And so great was her candour that it roused the Englishman's anger. He came up to her and said, in a low voice: 'Bresson committed suicide yesterday.'

She repeated, without appearing to understand: 'Bresson committed suicide yesterday . . . ?'

As a matter of fact, her features underwent no change whatever; nothing revealed the effort of a lie.

'You have been told,' he said, irritably. 'If not, you would at least have started . . . Ah, you are cleverer than I thought! . . . But why pretend? . . . '

He took the picture-book, which he had placed on a table close at hand, and, opening it at the cut page: 'Can you tell me,' he asked, 'in what order I am to arrange the letters missing here, so that I may understand the exact purport of the note which you sent to Bresson four days before the theft of the Jewish Lamp?'

'In what order? . . . Bresson? . . . The theft of the Jewish Lamp? . . . '

She repeated the words, slowly, as though to make out their meaning.

He insisted: 'Yes, here are the letters you used . . . on this scrap of paper. What were you saying to Bresson?'

'The letters I used . . . ? What was I saying to . . . ?'

Suddenly she burst out laughing.

'I see! I understand! I am an accomplice in the theft! There is a M. Bresson who stole the Jewish lamp and killed himself. And I am the gentleman's friend! Oh, how amusing!'

'Then whom did you go to see yesterday evening, on the second floor of a house in the Avenue des Ternes?'

'Whom? Why, my dressmaker, Mlle Langeais! Do you mean to imply that my dressmaker and my friend M. Bresson are one and the same person?'

Shears began to doubt, in spite of all. It is possible to counter-feit almost any feeling in such a way as to put another person off:

terror, joy, anxiety; but not indifference, not happy and careless laughter.

However, he said: 'One last word. Why did you accost me at the Gare du Nord the other evening? And why did you beg me to go back at once without busying myself about the robbery?'

'Oh, you're much too curious, Mr Shears,' she replied, still laughing in the most natural way. 'To punish you, I will tell you nothing and, in addition, you shall watch the patient while I go to the chemist . . . There's an urgent prescription to be made up . . . I must hurry!'

She left the room.

'I have been tricked,' muttered Shears. 'I've not only got nothing out of her, but I have given myself away.'

And he remembered the case of the blue diamond and the cross-examination to which he had subjected Clotilde Destange. Mademoiselle had encountered him with the same serenity as the fair-haired lady and he felt that he was again face to face with one of those creatures who, protected by Arsène Lupin and under the direct action of his influence, preserved the most inscrutable calmness amid the very agony of danger.

'Shears . . . Shears . . . '

It was Wilson calling him. He went to the bed and bent over him.

'What is it, old chap? Feeling bad?'

Wilson moved his lips, but was unable to speak. At last, after many efforts, he stammered out: 'No . . . Shears . . . it wasn't she . . . it can't have been . . . '

'What nonsense are you talking now? I tell you that it was she! It's only when I'm in the presence of a creature of Lupin's, trained and drilled by him, that I lose my head and behave so foolishly . . . She now knows the whole story of the album . . . I bet you that Lupin will be told in less than an hour. Less than an hour? What am I talking about? This moment, most likely! The chemist, the urgent prescription: humbug!'

Without a further thought of Wilson, he rushed from the room, went down the Avenue de Messine and saw mademoiselle enter a chemist's shop. She came out, ten minutes later, carrying two or three medicine-bottles, wrapped up in white paper. But, when she returned up the avenue, she was accosted by a man who followed her, cap in hand and with an obsequious air, as though he were begging.

She stopped, gave him an alms and then continued on her way.

'She spoke to him,' said the Englishman to himself.

It was an intuition rather than a certainty, but strong enough to induce him to alter his tactics. Leaving the girl, he set off on the track of the sham beggar.

They arrived in this way, one behind the other, on the Place Saint-Ferdinand; and the man hovered long round Bresson's house, sometimes raising his eyes to the second-floor windows and watching the people who entered the house.

At the end of an hour's time, he climbed to the top of a tram-car that was starting for Neuilly. Shears climbed up also and sat down behind the fellow, at some little distance, beside a gentleman whose features were concealed by the newspaper which he was reading. When they reached the fortifications, the newspaper was lowered, Shears recognized Ganimard and Ganimard, pointing to the fellow, said in his ear: 'It's our man of last night, the one who followed Bresson. He's been hanging round the square for an hour.'

'Nothing new about Bresson?'

'Yes, a letter arrived this morning addressed to him.'

'This morning? Then it must have been posted yesterday, before the writer knew of Bresson's death.'

'Just so. It is with the examining-magistrate, but I can tell you the exact words: "He accepts no compromise. He wants everything, the first thing as well as those of the second business. If not, he will take steps." And no signature,' added Ganimard. 'As you can see, those few lines won't be of much use to us.'

'I don't agree with you at all, M. Ganimard: on the contrary, I consider them very interesting.'

'And why, bless my soul?'

'For reasons personal to myself,' said Shears, with the absence of ceremony with which he was accustomed to treat his colleague.

The tram stopped at the terminus in the Rue du Château. The man climbed down and walked away quietly.

Shears followed so closely on his heels that Ganimard took alarm.

'If he turns round, we are done.'

'He won't turn round now.'

'What do you know about it?'

'He is an accomplice of Arsène Lupin's and the fact that an accomplice of Lupin's walks away like that, with his hands in his pockets, proves, in the first place, that he knows he's followed and, in the second, that he's not afraid.'

'Still, we're running him pretty hard!'

'No matter, he can slip through our fingers in a minute, if he wants. He's too sure of himself.'

'Come, come, you're getting at me! There are two cyclist police at the door of that café over there. If I decide to call on them and to tackle our friend, I should like to know how he's going to slip through our fingers.'

'Our friend does not seem much put out by that contingency. And he's calling on them himself!'

'By Jupiter!' said Ganimard. 'The cheek of the fellow!'

The man, in fact, had walked up to the two policemen just as these were preparing to mount their bicycles. He spoke a few words to them and then, suddenly, sprang upon a third bicycle, which was leaning against the wall of the café, and rode away quickly with the two policemen.

The Englishman burst with laughter.

'There, what did I tell you? Off before we knew where we were; and with two of your colleagues, M. Ganimard! Ah, he looks after himself, does Arsène Lupin! With cyclist policemen in his pay! Didn't I tell you our friend was a great deal too calm!'

'What then?' cried Ganimard, angrily. 'What could I do? It's very easy to laugh!'

'Come, come, don't be cross. We'll have our revenge. For the moment, what we want is reinforcements.'

'Folenfant is waiting for me at the end of the Avenue de Neuilly.'

'All right, pick him up and join me, both of you.'

Ganimard went away, while Shears followed the tracks of the bicycles, which were easily visible on the dust of the road because two of the machines were fitted with grooved tyres. And he soon saw that these tracks were leading him to the bank of the Seine and that the three men had turned in the same direction as Bresson on the previous evening. He thus came to the gate against which he himself had hidden with Ganimard and, a little farther on, he saw a tangle of grooved lines which showed that they had stopped there. Just opposite, a little neck of land jutted into the river and, at the end of it, an old boat lay fastened.

This was where Bresson must have flung his parcel or, rather, dropped it. Shears went down the incline and saw that, as the bank sloped very gently and the water was low, he would easily find the parcel . . . unless the three men had been there first.

'No, no,' he said to himself, 'they have not had time . . . a quarter of an hour at most . . . And, yet, why did they come this way?'

A man was sitting in the boat, fishing. Shears asked him: 'Have you seen three men on bicycles?'

The angler shook his head.

The Englishman insisted: 'Yes, yes . . . Three men . . . They stopped only a few yards from where you are.'

The angler put his rod under his arm, took a note-book from his pocket, wrote something on one of the pages, tore it out and handed it to Shears.

A great thrill shook the Englishman. At a glance, in the middle of the page which he held in his hand, he recognized the letters torn from the picture-book.

C D E H N O P R Z E O – 237

* * *

The sun hung heavily over the river. The angler had resumed his work, sheltered under the huge brim of his straw hat; his jacket and waistcoat lay folded by his side. He fished attentively, while the float of his line rocked idly on the current.

Quite a minute elapsed, a minute of solemn and awful silence.

'Is it he?' thought Shears, with an almost painful anxiety.

And then the truth burst upon him: 'It is he! It is he! He alone is capable of sitting like that, without a tremor of uneasiness, without the least fear as to what will happen . . . And who else could know the story of the picture-book? Alice must have told him by her messenger.'

Suddenly, the Englishman felt that his hand, that his own hand had seized the butt-end of his revolver and that his eyes were fixed on the man's back, just below the neck. One movement and the whole play was finished; a touch of the trigger and the life of the strange adventurer had come to a miserable end.

The angler did not stir.

Shears nervously gripped his weapon with a fierce longing to fire and have done with it and, at the same time, with horror of a deed against which his nature revolted. Death was certain. It would be over.

'Oh,' he thought, 'let him get up, let him defend himself . . . If not, he will have only himself to blame . . . Another second . . . and I fire . . . '

But a sound of footsteps made him turn his head and he saw Ganimard arrive, accompanied by the inspectors.

Then, changing his idea, he leapt forward, sprang at one bound into the boat, breaking the painter with the force of the jump, fell upon the man and held him in a close embrace. They both rolled to the bottom of the boat.

'Well?' cried Lupin, struggling. 'And then? What does this prove? Suppose one of us reduces the other to impotence: what will he have gained? You will not know what to do with me nor I with you. We shall stay here like a couple of fools!'

The two oars slipped into the water. The boat began to drift. Mingled exclamations resounded along the bank and Lupin continued: 'Lord, what a business! Have you lost all sense of things? . . . Fancy being so silly at your age! You great school-boy! You ought to be ashamed! . . . '

He succeeded in releasing himself.

Exasperated, resolved to stick at nothing, Shears put his hand in his pocket. An oath escaped him. Lupin had taken his revolver.

Then he threw himself on his knees and tried to catch hold of one of the oars, in order to pull to the shore, while Lupin made desperate efforts after the other, in order to pull out to mid-stream.

'Got it! . . . Missed it!' said Lupin. 'However, it makes no difference . . . If you get your oar, I'll prevent your using it . . . And you'll do as much for me . . . But there, in life, we strive to act . . . without the least reason, for it's always fate that decides . . . There, you see, fate . . . well, she's deciding for her old friend Lupin! . . . Victory! The current's favouring me!'

The boat, in fact, was drifting away.

'Look out!' cried Lupin.

Someone, on the bank, pointed a revolver. Lupin ducked his head; a shot rang out; a little water spurted up around them. He burst out laughing. 'Heaven help us, it's friend Ganimard! . . . Now that's very wrong of you, Ganimard. You have no right to fire except in self-defence . . . Does poor Arsène make you so furious that you forget your duties? . . . Hullo, he's starting again! . . . But, wretched man, be careful: you'll hit my dear maître here!'

He made a bulwark of his body for Shears and, standing up in the boat, facing Ganimard: 'There, now I don't mind! . . . Aim here, Ganimard, straight at my heart! . . . Higher . . . to the left . . . Missed again . . . you clumsy beggar! . . . Another shot? . . . But you're trembling, Ganimard! . . . At the word of command, eh? And steady now . . . one, two, three, fire! . . . Missed! Dash it all, does the government give you toys for pistols?'

He produced a long, massive, flat revolver and fired without taking aim.

The inspector lifted his hand to his hat: a bullet had made a hole through it.

'What do you say to that, Ganimard? Ah, this is a better make! Hats off, gentlemen: this is the revolver of my noble friend, Maître Holmlock Shears!'

And he tossed the weapon to the bank, right at the inspector's feet.

Shears could not help giving a smile of admiration. What superabundant life! What young and spontaneous gladness! And how he seemed to enjoy himself! It was as though the sense of danger gave him a physical delight, as though life had no other object for this extraordinary man than the search of dangers which he amused himself afterwards by averting.

Meantime, crowds had gathered on either side of the river and Ganimard and his men were following the craft, which swung down the stream, carried very slowly by the current. It meant inevitable, mathematical capture.

'Confess, maître,' cried Lupin, turning to the Englishman, 'that you would not give up your seat for all the gold in the Transvaal! You are in the first row of the stalls! But, first and before all, the prologue ... after which we will skip straight to the fifth act, the capture or the escape of Arsène Lupin. Therefore, my dear maître, I have one request to make of you and I beg you to answer yes or no, to save all ambiguity. Cease interesting yourself in this business. There is yet time and I am still able to repair the harm which you have done. Later on, I shall not be. Do you agree?'

'No.'

Lupin's features contracted. This obstinacy was causing him visible annoyance. He resumed: 'I insist. I insist even more for your sake than my own, for I am certain that you will be the first to regret your interference. Once more, yes or no?'

'No.'

Lupin squatted on his heels, shifted one of the planks at the bottom of the boat and, for a few minutes, worked at something which Shears could not see. Then he rose, sat down beside the Englishman and spoke to him in these words: 'I believe, maître, that you and I came to the river-bank with the same purpose, that of fishing up the object which Bresson got rid of, did we not? I, for my part, had made an appointment to meet a few friends and I was on the point, as my scanty costume shows, of effecting a little exploration in the depths of the Seine when my friends gave me notice of your approach. I am bound to confess that I was not surprised, having been kept informed, I venture to say, hourly, of the progress of your inquiry. It is so easy! As soon as the least thing likely to interest me occurs in the Rue Murillo, quick, they ring me up and I know all about it! You can understand that, in these conditions . . . '

He stopped. The plank which he had removed now rose a trifle and water was filtering in, all around, in driblets.

'The deuce! I don't know how I managed it, but I have every reason to think that there's a leak in this old boat. You're not afraid, maître?'

Shears shrugged his shoulders. Lupin continued: 'You can understand, therefore, that, in these conditions and knowing beforehand that you would seek the contest all the more greedily the more I strove to avoid it, I was rather pleased at the idea of playing a rubber with you the result of which is certain, seeing that I hold all the trumps. And I wished to give our meeting the greatest possible publicity, so that your defeat might be universally known and no new Comtesse de Crozon nor Baron d'Imblevalle be tempted to solicit your aid against me. And, in all this, my dear maître, you must not see . . . '

He interrupted himself again, and, using his half-closed hands as a field-glass, he watched the banks.

'By Jove! They've freighted a splendid cutter, a regular man-of-war's boat, and they're rowing like anything! In five minutes, they will board us and I shall be lost. Mr Shears, let me give you one piece of advice: throw yourself upon me, tie me hand and foot and deliver me to the law of my country . . . Does that suit you? . . . Unless we suffer shipwreck meanwhile, in which case there will be nothing for us to do but make our wills. What do you say?'

Their eyes met. This time, Shears understood Lupin's operations: he had made a hole in the bottom of the boat.

And the water was rising. It reached the soles of their boots. It covered their feet: they did not move.

It came above their ankles: the Englishman took his tobacco-pouch, rolled a cigarette and lit it.

Lupin continued.

'And, in all this, my dear maître, you must not see anything more than the humble confession of my powerlessness in face of you. It is tantamount to yielding to you, when I accept only those contests in which my victory is assured, in order to avoid those of which I shall not have selected the field. It is tantamount to recognizing that Holmlock Shears is the only enemy whom I fear and proclaiming my anxiety as long as Shears is not removed from my path. This, my dear maître, is what I wished to tell you, on this one occasion when fate has allowed me the honour of a conversation with you. I regret only one thing, which is that this conversation should take place while we are having a foot-bath . . . a position lacking in dignity, I must confess . . . And what was I saying? . . . A foot-bath! . . . A hip-bath rather!'

The water, in fact, had reached the seat on which they were sitting and the boat sank lower and lower in the water.

Shears sat imperturbable, his cigarette at his lips, apparently wrapped in contemplation of the sky. For nothing in the world, in the face of that man surrounded by dangers, hemmed in by the crowd, hunted down by a posse of police and yet always retaining his good humour, for nothing in the world would he have con-sented to display the least sign of agitation.

'What!' they both seemed to be saying. 'Do people get excited about such trifles? Is it not a daily occurrence to get drowned in a river? Is this the sort of event that deserves to be noticed?'

And the one chattered and the other mused, while both concealed under the same mask of indifference the formidable clash of their respective prides.

Another minute and they would sink.

'The essential thing,' said Lupin, 'is to know if we shall sink before or after the arrival of the champions of the law! All depends upon that. For the question of shipwreck is no longer in doubt. Maître, the solemn moment has come to make our wills. I leave all my real and personal estate to Holmlock Shears, a citizen of the British Empire . . . But, by Jove, how fast they are coming, those champions of the law! Oh, the dear people! It's a pleasure to watch them! What precision of stroke! Ah, is that you, Sergeant Folenfant? Well done! That idea of the man-of-war's cutter was capital. I shall recommend you to your superiors, Sergeant Folenfant . . . And weren't you hoping for a medal? Right you are! Consider it yours! . . . And where's your friend Dieuzy? On the left bank, I suppose, in the midst of a hundred natives . . . So that, if I escape shipwreck, I shall be picked up on the left by Dieuzy and his natives or else on the right by Ganimard and the Neuilly tribes. A nasty dilemma . . . '

There was an eddy. The boat swung round and Shears was obliged to cling to the rowlocks.

'Maître,' said Lupin, 'I beg of you to take off your jacket. You will be more comfortable for swimming. You won't? Then I shall put on mine again.'

He slipped on his jacket, buttoned it tightly like Shears's and sighed: 'What a fine fellow you are! And what a pity that you should persist in a business . . . in which you are certainly doing the very best you can, but all in vain! Really, you are throwing away your distinguished talent . . . '

'M. Lupin,' said Shears, at last abandoning his silence, 'you talk a great deal too much and you often err through excessive confidence and frivolity.'

'That's a serious reproach.'

'It was in this way that, without knowing it, you supplied me, a moment ago, with the information I wanted.'

'What! You wanted some information and you never told me!'

'I don't require you or anybody. In three hours' time, I shall hand the solution of the puzzle to M. and Mme d'Imblevalle. That is the only reply . . . '

He did not finish his sentence. The boat had suddenly foundered, dragging them both with her. She rose to the surface at once, over-turned, with her keel in the air. Loud shouts came from the two banks, followed by an anxious silence and, suddenly, fresh cries: one of the shipwrecked men had reappeared.

It was Holmlock Shears.

An excellent swimmer, he struck out boldly for Folenfant's boat.

'Cheerly, Mr Shears!' roared the detective-sergeant. 'You're all right! . . . Keep on . . . we'll see about him afterwards . . . We've got him right enough . . . one more effort, Mr Shears . . . catch hold . . . '

The Englishman seized a rope which they threw to him. But, while they were dragging him on board, a voice behind him called out: 'Yes, my dear maître, you shall have the solution. I am even surprised that you have not hit upon it already . . . And then? What use will it be to you? It's just then that you will have lost the battle . . . '

Seated comfortably astride the hulk, of which he had scaled the sides while talking, Arsène Lupin continued his speech with solemn gestures and as though he hoped to convince his hearers.

'Do understand, my dear maître, that there is nothing to be done, absolutely nothing . . . You are in the deplorable position of a gentleman who . . . '

Folenfant took aim at him. 'Lupin, surrender!'

'You're an ill-bred person, Sergeant Folenfant, you've interrupted me in the middle of a sentence. I was saying . . . '

'Lupin, surrender!'

'But, dash it all, Sergeant Folenfant, one only surrenders when in danger! Now surely you have not the face to believe that I am running the least danger!'

'For the last time, Lupin, I call on you to surrender!'

'Sergeant Folenfant, you have not the smallest intention of killing me; at the most, you mean to wound me, you're so afraid of my escaping! And supposing that, by accident, the wound should be mortal? Oh, think of your remorse, wretched man, of your blighted old age . . .'

The shot went off.

Lupin staggered, clung for a moment to the overturned boat, then let go and disappeared.

* * *

It was just three o'clock when these events happened. At six o'clock precisely, as he had declared, Holmlock Shears, clad in a pair of trou-sers too short and a jacket too tight for him, which he had borrowed from an inn-keeper at Neuilly, and wearing a cap and a flannel shirt with a silk cord and tassels, entered the boudoir in the Rue Murillo, after sending word to M. and Mme d'Imblevalle to ask for an interview.

They found him walking up and down. And he looked to them so comical in his queer costume that they had a difficulty in suppressing their inclination to laugh. With a pensive air and a bent back, he walked, like an automaton, from the window to the door and the door to the window, taking each time the same number of steps and turning each time in the same direction.

He stopped, took up a knick-knack, examined it mechanically and then resumed his walk.

At last, planting himself in front of them, he asked: 'Is mademoiselle here?'

'Yes, in the garden, with the children.'

'Monsieur le baron, as this will be our final conversation, I should like Mlle Demun to be present at it.'

'So you decidedly . . . ?'

'Have a little patience, monsieur. The truth will emerge plainly from the facts which I propose to lay before you with the greatest possible precision.'

'Very well. Suzanne, do you mind . . . ?'

Mme d'Imblevalle rose and returned almost at once, accompanied by Alice Demun. Mademoiselle, looking a little paler than usual, remained standing, leaning against a table and without even asking to know why she had been sent for.

Shears appeared not to see her and, turning abruptly towards M. d'Imblevalle, made his statement in a tone that admitted of no reply: 'After an inquiry extending over several days and although certain events for a moment altered my view, I will repeat what I said from the first, that the Jewish lamp was stolen by someone living in this house.'

'The name?'

'I know it.'

'Your evidence?'

'The evidence which I have is enough to confound the culprit.'

'It is not enough that the culprit should be confounded. He must restore . . . '

'The Jewish lamp? It is in my possession.'

'The opal necklace? The snuff-box? . . . '

'The opal necklace, the snuff-box, in short everything that was stolen on the second occasion is in my possession.'

Shears loved this dry, claptrap way of announcing his triumphs.

As a matter of fact, the baron and his wife seemed stupefied and looked at him with a silent curiosity which was, in itself, the highest praise.

He next summed up in detail all that he had done during those three days. He told how he had discovered the picture-book, wrote down on a sheet of paper the sentence formed by the letters which had been cut out, then described Bresson's expedition to the bank of the Seine and his suicide and, lastly, the struggle in which he, Shears, had just been engaged with Lupin, the wreck of the boat and Lupin's disappearance.

When he had finished, the baron said, in a low voice: 'Nothing remains but that you should reveal the name of the thief. Whom do you accuse?'

'I accuse the person who cut out the letters from this alphabet and communicated, by means of those letters, with Arsène Lupin.'

'How do you know that this person's correspondent was Arsène Lupin?'

'From Lupin himself.'

He held out a scrap of moist and crumpled paper. It was the page which Lupin had torn from his note-book, in the boat, and on which he had written the sentence.

'And observe,' said Shears, in a gratified voice, 'that there was nothing to compel him to give me this paper and thus make himself known. It was a mere school-boy prank on his part, which gave me the information I wanted.'

'What information?' asked the baron. 'I don't see . . . '

Shears copied out the letters and figures in pencil.

CDEHNOPRZEO – 237

'Well?' said M. d'Imblevalle. 'That's the formula which you have just shown us yourself.'

'No. If you had turned this formula over and over, as I have done, you would have seen at once that it contains two more letters than the first, an E and an O.'

'As a matter of fact, I did not notice . . . '

'Place these two letters beside the C and H which remained over from the word *Répondez*, and you will see that the only possible word is "ÉCHO". '

'Which means . . . ?'

'Which means the *Écho de France*, Lupin's newspaper, his own organ, the one for which he reserves his official communications. "Send reply to the *Écho de France*, agony column, No. 237." That was the key for which I had hunted so long and with which Lupin was kind enough to supply me. I have just come from the office of the *Écho de France*.'

'And what have you found?'

'I have found the whole detailed story of the relations between Arsène Lupin and . . . his accomplice.'

And Shears spread out seven newspapers, opened at the fourth page, and picked out the following lines.

1.   ARS. LUP. Lady impl. protect. 540.
2.   540. Awaiting explanations. A. L.
3.   A. L. Under dominion of enemy. Lost.
4.   540. Write address. Will make enq.
5.   A. L. Murillo.
6.   540. Park 3 p.m. Violets.
7.   237. Agreed Sat. Shall be park. Sun. morn.

'And you call that a detailed story!' exclaimed M. d'Imblevalle.

'Why, of course; and, if you will pay attention, you will think the same. First of all, a lady, signing herself 540, implores the protection of Arsène Lupin. To this Lupin replies with a request for explanations. The lady answers that she is under the dominion of an enemy, Bresson, no doubt, and that she is lost unless someone comes to her assistance. Lupin, who is suspicious and dares not yet have an interview with the stranger, asks for the address and suggests an inquiry. The lady hesitates for four days – see the dates – and, at last, under the pressure of events and the influence of Bresson's threats, gives the name of her street, the Rue Murillo. The next day, Arsène Lupin advertises that he will be in the Parc Monceau at three o'clock and asks the stranger to wear a bunch of violets as a token. Here follows an interruption of eight days in the correspondence. Arsène Lupin and the lady no longer need write through the medium of the paper: they see each other or correspond direct. The plot is contrived: to satisfy Bresson's requirements, the lady will take the Jewish lamp. It remains to fix the day. The lady, who, from motives of prudence, corresponds by means of words cut out and stuck together, decides upon Saturday and adds, "Send reply *Écho* 237". Lupin replies that it is agreed and that, moreover, he will be in the park on Sunday morning. On Sunday morning, the theft took place.'

'Yes, everything fits in,' said the baron, approvingly, 'and the story is complete.'

Shears continued: 'So the theft took place. The lady goes out on Sunday morning, tells Lupin what she has done and carries the Jewish lamp to Bresson. Things then happen as Lupin foresaw. The police, misled by an open window, four holes in the ground and two scratches on a balcony, at once accept the burglary suggestion. The lady is easy in her mind.'

'Very well,' said the baron. 'I accept this explanation as perfectly logical. But the second theft . . . '

'The second theft was provoked by the first. After the newspapers had told how the Jewish lamp had disappeared, someone thought of returning to the attack and seizing hold of everything that had not been carried away. And, this time, it was not a pretended theft, but a real theft, with a genuine burglary, ladders and so on.'

'Lupin, of course . . . ?'

'No, Lupin does not act so stupidly. Lupin does not fire at people without very good reason.'

'Then who was it?'

'Bresson, no doubt, unknown to the lady whom he had been black-mailing. It was Bresson who broke in here, whom I pursued, who wounded my poor Wilson.'

'Are you quite sure?'

'Absolutely. One of Bresson's accomplices wrote him a letter yesterday, before his suicide, which shows that this accomplice and

Lupin had entered upon a parley for the restitution of all the articles stolen from your house. Lupin demanded everything, "the first thing", that is to say, the Jewish lamp, "as well as those of the second business". Moreover, he watched Bresson. When Bresson went to the bank of the Seine yesterday evening, one of Lupin's associates was dogging him at the same time as ourselves.'

'What was Bresson doing at the bank of the Seine?'

'Warned of the progress of my inquiry . . . '

'Warned by whom?'

'By the same lady, who very rightly feared lest the discovery of the Jewish lamp should entail the discovery of her adventure . . . Bresson, therefore, warned, collected into one parcel all that might compromise him and dropped it in a place where it would be possible for him to recover it, once the danger was past. It was on his return that, hunted down by Ganimard and me and doubtless having other crimes on his conscience, he lost his head and shot himself.'

'But what did the parcel contain?'

'The Jewish lamp and your other things.'

'Then they are not in your possession?'

'Immediately after Lupin's disappearance, I took advantage of the bath which he had compelled me to take to drive to the spot chosen by Bresson; and I found your stolen property wrapped up in linen and oil-skin. Here it is, on the table.'

Without a word, the baron cut the string, tore through the pieces of wet linen, took out the lamp, turned a screw under the foot, pressed with both hands on the receiver, opened it into two equal parts and revealed the golden chimera, set with rubies and emeralds. It was untouched.

* * *

In all this scene, apparently so natural and consisting of a simple statement of facts, there was something that made it terribly tragic, which was the formal, direct, irrefutable accusation which Shears hurled at mademoiselle with every word he uttered. And there was also Alice Demun's impressive silence.

During that long, that cruel accumulation of small superadded proofs, not a muscle of her face had moved, not a gleam of rebellion or fear had disturbed the serenity of her limpid glance. What was she thinking? And, still more, what would she say at the solemn moment when she must reply, when she must defend herself and break the iron circle in which the Englishman had so cleverly imprisoned her?

The moment had struck and the girl was silent.

'Speak! speak!' cried M. d'Imblevalle.

She did not speak.

He insisted: 'One word will clear you . . . One word of protest and I will believe you.'

That word she did not utter.

The baron stepped briskly across the room, returned, went back again and then, addressing Shears: 'Well, no, sir! I refuse to believe it true! There are some crimes which are impossible! And this is opposed to all that I know, all that I have seen for a year.' He put his hand on the Englishman's shoulder. 'But are you yourself, sir, absolutely and definitely sure that you are not mistaken?'

Shears hesitated, like a man attacked unawares, who does not defend himself at once. However, he smiled and said: 'No one but the person whom I accuse could, thanks to the position which she fills in your house, know that the Jewish lamp contained that magnificent jewel.'

'I refuse to believe it,' muttered the baron.

'Ask her.'

It was, in fact, the one thing which he had not tried, in the blind confidence which he felt in the girl. But it was no longer permissible to deny the evidence.

He went up to her and, looking her straight in the eyes: 'Was it you, mademoiselle? Did you take the jewel? Did you correspond with Arsène Lupin and sham the burglary?'

She replied: 'Yes, monsieur.'

She did not lower her head. Her face expressed neither shame nor embarrassment.

'Is it possible?' stammered M. d'Imblevalle. 'I would never have believed . . . you are the last person I should have suspected . . . How did you do it, unhappy girl?'

She said: 'I did as Mr Shears has said. On Saturday night, I came down here to the boudoir, took the lamp and, in the morning, carried it . . . to that man.'

'But no,' objected the baron, 'what you say is impossible.'

'Impossible! Why?'

'Because I found the door of the boudoir locked in the morning.'

She coloured, lost countenance and looked at Shears as though to ask his advice.

The Englishman seemed struck by Alice's embarrassment even more than by the baron's objection. Had she, then, no reply to make? Did the confession that confirmed the explanation which he, Shears, had given of the theft of the Jewish lamp conceal a lie which an examination of the facts at once laid bare?

The baron continued.

'The door was locked, I repeat. I declare that I found the bolt as I left it at night. If you had come that way, as you pretend, someone must have opened the door to you from the inside, that is to say, from the boudoir or from our bedroom. Now there was no one in these two rooms . . . no one except my wife and myself.'

Shears bent down quickly and covered his face with his two hands to hide it. He had flushed scarlet. Something resembling too sudden a light had struck him and left him dazed and ill at ease. The whole stood revealed to him like a dim landscape from which the darkness was suddenly lifting.

Alice Demun was innocent.

Alice Demun was innocent. That was a certain, blinding fact and, at the same time, it explained the sort of embarrassment which he had felt since the first day at directing the terrible accusation against this young girl. He saw clearly now. He knew. It needed but a movement and, then and there, the irrefutable proof would stand forth before him.

He raised his head and, after a few seconds, as naturally as he could, turned his eyes towards Mme d'Imblevalle.

She was pale, with that unaccustomed pallor that overcomes us at the relentless hours of life. Her hands, which she strove to hide, trembled imperceptibly.

'Another second,' thought Shears, 'and she will have betrayed herself.'

He placed himself between her and her husband, with the imperious longing to ward off the terrible danger which, through his fault, threatened this man and this woman. But, at the sight of the baron, he shuddered to the very depths of his being. The same sudden revelation which had dazzled him with its brilliancy was now enlightening M. d'Imblevalle. The same thought was working in the husband's brain. He understood in his turn! He saw!

Desperately, Alice Demun strove to resist the implacable truth.

'You are right, monsieur, I made a mistake. As a matter of fact, I did not come in this way. I went through the hall and the garden and, with the help of a ladder . . . .'

It was a supreme effort of devotion . . . but a useless effort! The words did not ring true. The voice had lost its assurance and the sweet girl was no longer able to retain her limpid glance and her great air of sincerity. She hung her head, defeated.

The silence was frightful. Mme d'Imblevalle waited, her features livid and drawn with anguish and fear. The baron seemed to be still struggling, as though refusing to believe in the downfall of his happiness.

At last, he stammered: 'Speak! Explain yourself! . . . '

'I have nothing to say, my poor friend,' she said, in a very low voice, her features wrung with despair.

'Then . . . mademoiselle . . . ?'

'Mademoiselle saved me . . . through devotion . . . through affection . . . and accused herself . . . '

'Saved you from what? From whom?'

'From that man.'

'Bresson?'

'Yes, he held me by his threats . . . I met him at a friend's house . . . and I had the madness to listen to him. Oh, there was nothing that you cannot forgive! . . . But I wrote him two letters . . . you shall see them . . . I bought them back . . . you know how . . . Oh, have pity on me . . . I have been so unhappy!'

'You! You! Suzanne!'

He raised his clenched fists to her, ready to beat her, ready to kill her. But his arms fell to his sides and he murmured again: 'You, Suzanne! . . . You! . . . Is it possible? . . . '

In short, abrupt sentences, she told the heartbreaking and common-place story: her terrified awakening in the face of the man's infamy, her remorse, her madness; and she also described Alice's admirable conduct: the girl suspecting her mistress's despair, forcing a confession from her, writing to Lupin and contriving this story of a robbery to save her from Bresson's clutches.

'You, Suzanne, you!' repeated M. d'Imblevalle, bent double, overwhelmed. 'How could you . . . ?'

*   *   *

On the evening of the same day, the steamer *Ville de Londres*, from Calais to Dover, was gliding slowly over the motionless water. The night was dark and calm. Peaceful clouds were suggested rather than seen above the boat and, all around, light veils of mist separated her from the infinite space in which the moon and stars were shedding their cold, but invisible radiance.

Most of the passengers had gone to the cabins and saloons. A few of them, however, bolder than the rest, were walking up and down the deck or else dozing under thick rugs in the big rocking-chairs. Here and there the gleam showed of a cigar; and, mingling with the gentle breath of the wind, came the murmur of voices that dared not rise high in the great solemn silence.

One of the passengers, who was walking to and fro with even strides, stopped beside a person stretched out on a bench, looked at her and, when she moved slightly, said: 'I thought you were asleep, Mlle Alice.'

'No, Mr Shears, I do not feel sleepy. I was thinking.'

'What of? Is it indiscreet to ask?'

'I was thinking of Mme d'Imblevalle. How sad she must be! Her life is ruined.'

'Not at all, not at all,' he said, eagerly. 'Her fault is not one of those which can never be forgiven. M. d'Imblevalle will forget that lapse. Already, when we left, he was looking at her less harshly.'

'Perhaps . . . but it will take long to forget . . . and she is suffering.'

'Are you very fond of her?'

'Very. That gave me such strength to smile when I was trembling with fear, to look you in the face when I wanted to avoid your glance.'

'And are you unhappy at leaving her?'

'Most unhappy. I have no relations or friends . . . I had only her . . .'

'You shall have friends,' said the Englishman, whom this grief was upsetting, 'I promise you that . . . I have connections . . . I have much influence . . . I assure you that you will not regret your position . . .'

'Perhaps, but Mme d'Imblevalle will not be there . . .'

They exchanged no more words. Holmlock Shears took two or three more turns along the deck and then came back and settled down near his travelling-companion.

The misty curtain lifted and the clouds seemed to part in the sky. Stars twinkled up above.

Shears took his pipe from the pocket of his Inverness cape, filled it and struck four matches, one after the other, without succeeding in lighting it. As he had none left, he rose and said to a gentleman seated a few steps off: 'Could you oblige me with a light, please?'

The gentleman opened a box of fusees and struck one. A flame blazed up. By its light, Shears saw Arsène Lupin.

If the Englishman had not given a tiny movement, an almost imperceptible movement of recoil, Lupin might have thought that his presence on board was known to him, so great was the mastery which Shears retained over himself and so natural the ease with which he held out his hand to his adversary.

'Keeping well, M. Lupin?'

'Bravo!' exclaimed Lupin, from whom this self-command drew a cry of admiration.

'Bravo? . . . What for?'

'What for? You see me reappear before you like a ghost, after witnessing my dive into the Seine, and, from pride, from a miraculous pride which I will call essentially British, you give not a movement of astonishment, you utter not a word of surprise! Upon my word, I repeat, bravo! It's admirable!'

'There's nothing admirable about it. From the way you fell off the boat, I could see that you fell of your own accord and that you had not been struck by the sergeant's shot.'

'And you went away without knowing what became of me?'

'What became of you? I knew. Five hundred people were commanding the two banks over a distance of three-quarters of a mile. Once you escaped death, your capture was certain.'

'And yet I'm here!'

'M. Lupin, there are two men in the world of whom nothing can astonish me: myself first and you next.'

Peace was concluded.

If Shears had failed in his undertakings against Arsène Lupin, if Lupin remained the exceptional enemy whom he must definitely renounce all attempts to capture, if, in the course of the engagements, Lupin always preserved his superiority, the Englishman had, nevertheless, thanks to his formidable tenacity, recovered the Jewish lamp, just as he had recovered the blue diamond. Perhaps, this time, the result was less brilliant, especially from the point of view of the public, since Shears was obliged to suppress the circumstances in which the Jewish lamp had been discovered and to proclaim that he did not know the culprit's name. But, as between man and man, between Lupin and Shears, between burglar and detective, there was, in all fairness, neither victor nor vanquished. Each of them could lay claim to equal triumphs.

They talked, therefore, like courteous adversaries who have laid down their arms and who esteem each other at their true worth.

At Shears's request, Lupin described his escape.

'If, indeed,' he said, 'you can call it an escape. It was so simple! My friends were on the watch, since we had arranged to meet in order to fish up the Jewish lamp. And so, after remaining a good half-hour under the overturned keel of the boat, I took advantage of a moment when Folenfant and his men were looking for my corpse along the banks and I climbed on to the wreck again. My friends had only to pick me up in their motor-boat and to dash off before the astounded eyes of the five hundred sightseers, Ganimard and Folenfant.'

'Very pretty!' cried Shears. 'Most successful! And now have you business in England?'

'Yes, a few accounts to settle . . . But I was forgetting . . . M. d'Imblevalle . . . ?'

'He knows all.'

'Ah, my dear maître, what did I tell you? The harm's done now, beyond repair. Would it not have been better to let me go to work in my own way? A day or two more and I should have recovered the Jewish lamp and the other things from Bresson and sent them back to the d'Imblevalles; and those two good people would have gone on living peacefully together. Instead of which . . . '

'Instead of which,' snarled Shears, 'I have muddled everything up and brought discord into a family which you were protecting.'

'Well, yes, if you like, protecting! Is it indispensable that one should always steal, cheat and do harm?'

'So you do good also?'

'When I have time. Besides, it amuses me. I think it extremely funny that, in the present adventure, I should be the good genius who rescues and saves and you the wicked genius who brings despair and tears.'

'Tears! Tears!' protested the Englishman.

'Certainly! The d'Imblevalle home is broken up and Alice Demun is weeping.'

'She could not have remained . . . Ganimard would have ended by discovering her . . . and through her they would have worked back to Mme d'Imblevalle.'

'Quite of your opinion, maître; but whose fault was it?'

Two men passed in front of them. Shears said to Lupin, in a voice the tone of which seemed a little altered: 'Do you know who those two gentlemen are?'

'I think one was the captain of the boat.'

'And the other?'

'I don't know.'

'It is Mr Austin Gilett. And Mr Austin Gilett occupies in England a post which corresponds with that of your M. Dudouis.'

'Oh, what luck! Would you have the kindness to introduce me? M. Dudouis is a great friend of mine and I should like to be able to say as much of Mr Austin Gilett.'

The two gentlemen reappeared.

'And, suppose I were to take you at your word, M. Lupin . . . ?' said Shears, rising.

He had seized Arsène Lupin's wrist and held it in a grip of steel.

'Why grip me so hard, maître? I am quite ready to go with you.'

He allowed himself, in fact, to be dragged along, without the least resistance. The two gentlemen were walking away from them.

Shears increased his pace. His nails dug into Lupin's very flesh.

'Come along, come along!' he said, under his breath, in a sort of fevered haste to settle everything as quickly as possible. 'Come along! Quick!'

But he stopped short: Alice Demun had followed them.

'What are you doing, mademoiselle? You need not trouble to come!'

It was Lupin who replied.

'I beg you to observe, maître, that mademoiselle is not coming of her own free will. I am holding her wrist with an energy similar to that which you are applying to mine.'

'And why?'

'Why? Well, I am bent upon introducing her also. Her part in the story of the Jewish Lamp is even more important than mine. As an accomplice of Arsène Lupin and of Bresson as well, she too must tell the adventure of the Baronne d'Imblevalle . . . which is sure to interest the police immensely. And in this way you will have pushed your kind interference to its last limits, O generous Shears!'

The Englishman had released his prisoner's wrist. Lupin let go of mademoiselle's.

They stood, for a few seconds, without moving, looking at one another. Then Shears went back to his bench and sat down. Lupin and the girl resumed their places.

*   *   *

A long silence divided them. Then Lupin said: 'You see, maître, do what we may, we shall never be in the same camp. You will always be on one side of the ditch, I on the other. We can nod, shake hands, exchange a word or two; but the ditch is always there. You will always be Holmlock Shears, detective, and I Arsène Lupin, burglar. And Holmlock Shears will always, more or less spontaneously, more or less seasonably, obey his instinct as a detective, which is to hound down the burglar and "run him in" if possible. And Arsène Lupin will always be consistent with his burglar's soul in avoiding the grasp of the detective and laughing at him if he can. And, this time, he can! Ha, ha, ha!'

He burst into a cunning, cruel and detestable laugh . . . Then, suddenly becoming serious, he leant towards the girl.

'Be sure, mademoiselle, that, though reduced to the last extremity, I would not have betrayed you. Arsène Lupin never betrays, especially those whom he likes and admires. And you must permit me to say that I like and admire the dear, plucky creature that you are.'

He took a visiting-card from his pocket-book, tore it in two, gave one half to the girl and, in a touched and respectful voice: 'If Mr Shears does not succeed in his steps, mademoiselle, pray go to Lady Strongborough, whose address you can easily find out, hand her this half card and say, "Faithful memories!" Lady Strongborough will show you the devotion of a sister.'

'Thank you,' said the girl, 'I will go to her tomorrow.'

'And now, maître,' cried Lupin, in the satisfied tone of a man who has done his duty, 'let me bid you good-night. The mist has delayed us and there is still time to take forty winks.'

He stretched himself at full length and crossed his hands behind his head.

The sky had opened before the moon. She shed her radiant brightness around the stars and over the sea. It floated upon the water; and space, in which the last mists were dissolving, seemed to belong to it.

The line of the coast stood out against the dark horizon. Passengers came up on deck, which was now covered with people. Mr Austin Gilett passed in the company of two men whom Shears recognized as members of the English detective-force.

On his bench, Lupin slept . . .

THE END

THE CONFESSIONS
OF ARSÈNE LUPIN

Two Hundred Thousand Francs Reward! . . .

'Lupin,' I said, 'tell me something about yourself.'

'Why, what would you have me tell you? Everybody knows my life!' replied Lupin, who lay drowsing on the sofa in my study.

'Nobody knows it!' I protested. 'People know from your letters in the newspapers that you were mixed up in this case, that you started that case. But the part which you played in it all, the plain facts of the story, the upshot of the mystery: these are things of which they know nothing.'

'Pooh! A heap of uninteresting twaddle!'

'What! Your present of fifty thousand francs to Nicolas Dugrival's wife! Do you call that uninteresting? And what about the way in which you solved the puzzle of the three pictures?'

Lupin laughed.

'Yes, that was a queer puzzle, certainly. I can suggest a title for you if you like: what do you say to *The Sign of the Shadow*?'

'And your successes in society and with the fair sex?' I continued. 'The dashing Arsène's love-affairs! . . . And the clue to your good actions? Those chapters in your life to which you have so often alluded under the names of *The Wedding-ring*, *Shadowed by Death*, and so on! . . . Why delay these confidences and confessions, my dear Lupin? . . . Come, do what I ask you! . . . '

It was at the time when Lupin, though already famous, had not yet fought his biggest battles; the time that preceded the great adventures of *The Hollow Needle* and *813*. He had not yet dreamt of annexing the accumulated treasures of the French Royal House,[*] nor of changing the map of Europe under the Kaiser's nose;[†] he contented himself with milder surprises and humbler profits,

[*] *The Hollow Needle.* By Maurice Leblanc. Translated by Alexander Teixeira de Mattos (Eveleigh Nash).

[†] *813*. By Maurice Leblanc. Translated by Alexander Teixeira de Mattos (Mills & Boon).

making his daily effort, doing evil from day to day and doing a little good as well, naturally and for the love of the thing, like a whimsical and compassionate Don Quixote.

He was silent; and I insisted: 'Lupin, I wish you would!'

To my astonishment, he replied: 'Take a sheet of paper, old fellow, and a pencil.'

I obeyed with alacrity, delighted at the thought that he at last meant to dictate to me some of those pages which he knows how to clothe with such vigour and fancy, pages which I, unfortunately, am obliged to spoil with tedious explanations and boring developments.

'Are you ready?' he asked.

'Quite.'

'Write down, 20, 1, 11, 5, 14, 15.'

'What?'

'Write it down, I tell you.'

He was now sitting up, with his eyes turned to the open window and his fingers rolling a Turkish cigarette. He continued: 'Write down, 21, 14, 14, 5 . . .'

He stopped. Then he went on: '3, 5, 19, 19 . . .'

And, after a pause: '5, 18, 25 . . .'

Was he mad? I looked at him hard and, presently, I saw that his eyes were no longer listless, as they had been a little before, but keen and attentive and that they seemed to be watching, somewhere, in space, a sight that apparently captivated them.

Meanwhile, he dictated, with intervals between each number: '18, 9, 19, 11, 19 . . .'

There was hardly anything to be seen through the window but a patch of blue sky on the right and the front of the building opposite, an old private house, whose shutters were closed as usual. There was nothing particular about all this, no detail that struck me as new among those which I had had before my eyes for years . . .

'1, 2 . . .'

And suddenly I understood . . . or rather I thought I understood, for how could I admit that Lupin, a man so essentially level-headed under his mask of frivolity, could waste his time upon such childish nonsense? What he was counting was the intermittent flashes of a ray of sunlight playing on the dingy front of the opposite house, at the height of the second floor!

'15, 22 . . .' said Lupin.

The flash disappeared for a few seconds and then struck the house again, successively, at regular intervals, and disappeared once more.

I had instinctively counted the flashes and I said, aloud: '5 . . . '

'Caught the idea? I congratulate you!' he replied, sarcastically.

He went to the window and leant out, as though to discover the exact direction followed by the ray of light. Then he came and lay on the sofa again, saying: 'It's your turn now. Count away!'

The fellow seemed so positive that I did as he told me. Besides, I could not help confessing that there was something rather curious about the ordered frequency of those gleams on the front of the house opposite, those appearances and disappearances, turn and turn about, like so many flash signals.

They obviously came from a house on our side of the street, for the sun was entering my windows slantwise. It was as though someone were alternately opening and shutting a casement, or, more likely, amusing himself by making sunlight flashes with a pocket-mirror.

'It's a child having a game!' I cried, after a moment or two, feeling a little irritated by the trivial occupation that had been thrust upon me.

'Never mind, go on!'

And I counted away . . . And I put down rows of figures . . . And the sun continued to play in front of me, with mathematical precision.

'Well?' said Lupin, after a longer pause than usual.

'Why, it seems finished . . . There has been nothing for some minutes . . . '

We waited and, as no more light flashed through space, I said, jestingly: 'My idea is that we have been wasting our time. A few figures on paper: a poor result!'

Lupin, without stirring from his sofa, rejoined: 'Oblige me, old chap, by putting in the place of each of those numbers the corresponding letter of the alphabet. Count A as 1, B as 2 and so on. Do you follow me?'

'But it's idiotic!'

'Absolutely idiotic, but we do such a lot of idiotic things in this life . . . One more or less, you know! . . . '

I sat down to this silly work and wrote out the first letters: '*Take no . . .* '

I broke off in surprise.

'Words!' I exclaimed. 'Two English words meaning . . . '

'Go on, old chap.'

And I went on and the next letters formed two more words, which I separated as they appeared. And, to my great amazement, a complete English sentence lay before my eyes.

'Done?' asked Lupin, after a time.

'Done! . . . By the way, there are mistakes in the spelling . . . '

'Never mind those and read it out, please . . . Read slowly.'

Thereupon I read out the following unfinished communication, which I will set down as it appeared on the paper in front of me.

Take no unnecessery risks. Above all, avoid atacks, approach ennemy with great prudance and . . .

I began to laugh.

'And there you are! *Fiat lux*! We're simply dazed with light! But, after all, Lupin, confess that this advice, dribbled out by a kitchen-maid, doesn't help you much!'

Lupin rose, without breaking his contemptuous silence, and took the sheet of paper.

I remembered soon after that, at this moment, I happened to look at the clock. It was eighteen minutes past five.

Lupin was standing with the paper in his hand; and I was able at my ease to watch, on his youthful features, that extraordinary mobility of expression which baffles all observers and constitutes his great strength and his chief safeguard. By what signs can one hope to identify a face which changes at pleasure, even without the help of make-up, and whose every transient expression seems to be the final, definite expression? . . . By what signs? There was one which I knew well, an invariable sign: Two little crossed wrinkles that marked his forehead whenever he made a powerful effort of concentration. And I saw it at that moment, saw the tiny tell-tale cross, plainly and deeply scored.

He put down the sheet of paper and muttered: 'Child's play!'

The clock struck half-past five.

'What!' I cried. 'Have you succeeded? . . . In twelve minutes? . . . '

He took a few steps up and down the room, lit a cigarette and said: 'You might ring up Baron Repstein, if you don't mind, and tell him I shall be with him at ten o'clock this evening.'

'Baron Repstein?' I asked. 'The husband of the famous baroness?'

'Yes.'

'Are you serious?'

'Quite serious.'

Feeling absolutely at a loss, but incapable of resisting him, I opened the telephone-directory and unhooked the receiver. But, at that moment, Lupin stopped me with a peremptory gesture and said, with his eyes on the paper, which he had taken up again: 'No, don't say anything . . . It's no use letting him know . . . There's something more urgent . . . a queer thing that puzzles me . . . Why on earth wasn't the last sentence finished? Why is the sentence . . . '

He snatched up his hat and stick.

'Let's be off. If I'm not mistaken, this is a business that requires immediate solution; and I don't believe I *am* mistaken.'

He put his arm through mine, as we went down the stairs, and said: 'I know what everybody knows. Baron Repstein, the company-promoter and racing-man, whose colt Etna won the Derby and the Grand Prix this year, has been victimized by his wife. The wife, who was well known for her fair hair, her dress and her extravagance, ran away a fortnight ago, taking with her a sum of three million francs, stolen from her husband, and quite a collection of diamonds, pearls and jewellery which the Princesse de Berny had placed in her hands and which she was supposed to buy. For two weeks the police have been pursuing the baroness across France and the continent: an easy job, as she scatters gold and jewels wherever she goes. They think they have her every moment. Two days ago, our champion detective, the egregious Ganimard, arrested a visitor at a big hotel in Belgium, a woman against whom the most positive evidence seemed to be heaped up. On enquiry, the lady turned out to be a notorious chorus-girl called Nelly Darbal. As for the baroness, she has vanished. The baron, on his side, has offered a reward of two hundred thousand francs to whosoever finds his wife. The money is in the hands of a solicitor. Moreover, he has sold his racing-stud, his house on the Boulevard Haussmann and his country-seat of Roquencourt in one lump, so that he may indemnify the Princesse de Berny for her loss.'

'And the proceeds of the sale,' I added, 'are to be paid over at once. The papers say that the princess will have her money tomorrow. Only, frankly, I fail to see the connection between this story, which you have told very well, and the puzzling sentence . . . '

Lupin did not condescend to reply.

We had been walking down the street in which I live and had passed some four or five houses, when he stepped off the pavement and began to examine a block of flats, not of the latest construction, which looked as if it contained a large number of tenants.

'According to my calculations,' he said, 'this is where the signals came from, probably from that open window.'

'On the third floor?'

'Yes.'

He went to the portress and asked her: 'Does one of your tenants happen to be acquainted with Baron Repstein?'

'Why, of course!' replied the woman. 'We have M. Lavernoux here, such a nice gentleman; he is the baron's secretary and agent. I look after his flat.'

'And can we see him?'

'See him? . . . The poor gentleman is very ill.'

'Ill?'

'He's been ill a fortnight . . . ever since the trouble with the baroness . . . He came home the next day with a temperature and took to his bed.'

'But he gets up, surely?'

'Ah, that I can't say!'

'How do you mean, you can't say?'

'No, his doctor won't let anyone into his room. He took my key from me.'

'Who did?'

'The doctor. He comes and sees to his wants, two or three times a day. He left the house only twenty minutes ago . . . an old gentleman with a grey beard and spectacles . . . Walks quite bent . . . But where are you going sir?'

'I'm going up, show me the way,' said Lupin, with his foot on the stairs. 'It's the third floor, isn't it, on the left?'

'But I mustn't!' moaned the portress, run ning after him. 'Besides, I haven't the key . . . the doctor . . . '

They climbed the three flights, one behind the other. On the landing, Lupin took a tool from his pocket and, disregarding the woman's protests, inserted it in the lock. The door yielded almost immediately. We went in.

At the back of a small dark room we saw a streak of light filtering through a door that had been left ajar. Lupin ran across the room and, on reaching the threshold, gave a cry.

'Too late! Oh, hang it all!'

The portress fell on her knees, as though fainting.

I entered the bedroom, in my turn, and saw a man lying half-dressed on the carpet, with his legs drawn up under him, his arms contorted and his face quite white, an emaciated, fleshless face, with the eyes still staring in terror and the mouth twisted into a hideous grin.

'He's dead,' said Lupin, after a rapid examination.

'But why?' I exclaimed. 'There's not a trace of blood!'

'Yes, yes, there is,' replied Lupin, pointing to two or three drops that showed on the chest, through the open shirt. 'Look, they must have taken him by the throat with one hand and pricked him to the heart with the other. I say, "pricked", because really the wound can't be seen. It suggests a hole made by a very long needle.'

He looked on the floor, all round the corpse. There was nothing to attract his attention, except a little pocket-mirror, the little mirror with which M. Lavernoux had amused himself by making the sunbeams dance through space.

But, suddenly, as the portress was breaking into lamentations and calling for help, Lupin flung himself on her and shook her.

'Stop that! . . . Listen to me . . . you can call out later . . . Listen to me and answer me. It is most important. M. Lavernoux had a friend living in this street, had he not? On the same side, to the right? An intimate friend?'

'Yes.'

'A friend whom he used to meet at the café in the evening and with whom he exchanged the illustrated papers?'

'Yes.'

'Was the friend an Englishman?'

'Yes.'

'What's his name?'

'Mr Hargrove.'

'Where does he live?'

'At No. 92 in this street.'

'One word more: had that old doctor been attending him long?'

'No. I did not know him. He came on the evening when M. Lavernoux was taken ill.'

Without another word, Lupin dragged me away once more, ran down the stairs and, once in the street, turned to the right, which took us past my flat again. Four doors further, he stopped at No. 92, a small, low-storeyed house, of which the ground-floor was occupied by the proprietor of a dram-shop, who stood smoking in his doorway, next to the entrance-passage. Lupin asked if Mr Hargrove was at home.

'Mr Hargrove went out about half-an-hour ago,' said the publican. 'He seemed very much excited and took a taxi-cab, a thing he doesn't often do.'

'And you don't know . . . '

'Where he was going? Well, there's no secret about it He shouted it loud enough! "Prefecture of Police" is what he said to the driver . . . '

Lupin was himself just hailing a taxi, when he changed his mind; and I heard him mutter: 'What's the good? He's got too much start of us . . . '

He asked if anyone called after Mr Hargrove had gone.

'Yes, an old gentleman with a grey beard and spectacles. He went up to Mr Hargrove's, rang the bell, and went away again.'

'I am much obliged,' said Lupin, touching his hat.

He walked away slowly without speaking to me, wearing a thoughtful air. There was no doubt that the problem struck him as very difficult, and that he saw none too clearly in the darkness through which he seemed to be moving with such certainty.

He himself, for that matter, confessed to me: 'These are cases that require much more intuition than reflection. But this one, I may tell you, is well worth taking pains about.'

We had now reached the boulevards. Lupin entered a public reading-room and spent a long time consulting the last fortnight's newspapers. Now and again, he mumbled: 'Yes . . . yes . . . of course . . . it's only a guess, but it explains everything . . . Well, a guess that answers every question is not far from being the truth . . . '

It was now dark. We dined at a little restaurant and I noticed that Lupin's face became gradually more animated. His gestures were more decided. He recovered his spirits, his liveliness. When we left, during the walk which he made me take along the Boulevard Haussmann, towards Baron Repstein's house, he was the real Lupin of the great occasions, the Lupin who had made up his mind to go in and win.

We slackened our pace just short of the Rue de Courcelles. Baron Repstein lived on the left-hand side, between this street and the Faubourg Saint-Honoré, in a three-storeyed private house of which we could see the front, decorated with columns and caryatides.

'Stop!' said Lupin, suddenly.

'What is it?'

'Another proof to confirm my supposition . . . '

'What proof? I see nothing.'

'I do . . . That's enough . . . '

He turned up the collar of his coat, lowered the brim of his soft hat and said: 'By Jove, it'll be a stiff fight! Go to bed, my friend. I'll tell you about my expedition tomorrow . . . if it doesn't cost me my life.'

'What are you talking about?'

'Oh, I know what I'm saying! I'm risking a lot. First of all, getting arrested, which isn't much. Next, getting killed, which is worse. But . . . ' He gripped my shoulder. 'But there's a third thing I'm risking, which is getting hold of two millions . . . And, once I possess a capital of two millions, I'll show people what I can do!

Good-night, old chap, and, if you never see me again . . . ' He spouted Musset's lines.

> Plant a willow by my grave,
> The weeping willow that I love . . .

I walked away. Three minutes later – I am continuing the narrative as he told it to me next day – three minutes later, Lupin rang at the door of the Hôtel Repstein.

* * *

'Is monsieur le baron at home?'

'Yes,' replied the butler, examining the intruder with an air of surprise, 'but monsieur le baron does not see people as late as this.'

'Does monsieur le baron know of the murder of M. Lavernoux, his land-agent?'

'Certainly.'

'Well, please tell monsieur le baron that I have come about the murder and that there is not a moment to lose.'

A voice called from above.

'Show the gentleman up, Antoine.'

In obedience to this peremptory order, the butler led the way to the first floor. In an open doorway stood a gentleman whom Lupin recognized from his photograph in the papers as Baron Repstein, husband of the famous baroness and owner of Etna, the horse of the year.

He was an exceedingly tall, square-shouldered man. His clean-shaven face wore a pleasant, almost smiling expression, which was not affected by the sadness of his eyes. He was dressed in a well-cut morning-coat, with a tan waistcoat and a dark tie fastened with a pearl pin, the value of which struck Lupin as considerable.

He took Lupin into his study, a large, three-windowed room, lined with book-cases, sets of pigeonholes, an American desk and a safe. And he at once asked, with ill-concealed eagerness: 'Do you know anything?'

'Yes, monsieur le baron.'

'About the murder of that poor Lavernoux?'

'Yes, monsieur le baron, and about madame la baronne also.'

'Do you really mean it? Quick, I entreat you . . . '

He pushed forward a chair. Lupin sat down and began: 'Monsieur le baron, the circumstances are very serious. I will be brief.'

'Yes, do, please.'

'Well, monsieur le baron, in a few words, it amounts to this: five or six hours ago, Lavernoux, who, for the last fortnight, had been kept in a sort of enforced confinement by his doctor, Lavernoux – how shall I put it? – telegraphed certain revelations by means of signals which were partly taken down by me and which put me on the track of this case. He himself was surprised in the act of making this communication and was murdered.'

'But by whom? By whom?'

'By his doctor.'

'Who is this doctor?'

'I don't know. But one of M. Lavernoux's friends, an Englishman called Hargrove, the friend, in fact, with whom he was communicating, is bound to know and is also bound to know the exact and complete meaning of the communication, because, without waiting for the end, he jumped into a motor-cab and drove to the Prefecture of Police.'

'Why? Why? . . . And what is the result of that step?'

'The result, monsieur le baron, is that your house is surrounded. There are twelve detectives under your windows. The moment the sun rises, they will enter in the name of the law and arrest the criminal.'

'Then is Lavernoux's murderer concealed in my house? Who is he? One of the servants? But no, for you were speaking of a doctor! . . . '

'I would remark, monsieur le baron, that when this Mr Hargrove went to the police to tell them of the revelations made by his friend Lavernoux, he was not aware that his friend Lavernoux was going to be murdered. The step taken by Mr Hargrove had to do with something else . . . '

'With what?'

'With the disappearance of madame la baronne, of which he knew the secret, thanks to the communication made by Lavernoux.'

'What! They know at last! They have found the baroness! Where is she? And the jewels? And the money she robbed me of?'

Baron Repstein was talking in a great state of excitement. He rose and, almost shouting at Lupin, cried: 'Finish your story, sir! I can't endure this suspense!'

Lupin continued, in a slow and hesitating voice.

'The fact is . . . you see . . . it is rather difficult to explain . . . for you and I are looking at the thing from a totally different point of view.'

'I don't understand.'

'And yet you ought to understand, monsieur le baron . . . We begin by saying – I am quoting the newspapers – by saying, do we not, that Baroness Repstein knew all the secrets of your business and that she was able to open not only that safe over there, but also the one at the Crédit Lyonnais in which you kept your securities locked up?'

'Yes.'

'Well, one evening, a fortnight ago, while you were at your club, Baroness Repstein, who, unknown to yourself, had converted all those securities into cash, left this house with a travelling-bag, containing your money and all the Princesse de Berny's jewels?'

'Yes.'

'And, since then, she has not been seen?'

'No.'

'Well, there is an excellent reason why she has not been seen.'

'What reason?'

'This, that Baroness Repstein has been murdered . . . '

'Murdered! . . . The baroness! . . . But you're mad!'

'Murdered . . . and probably that same evening.'

'I tell you again, you are mad! How can the baroness have been murdered, when the police are following her tracks, so to speak, step by step?'

'They are following the tracks of another woman.'

'What woman?'

'The murderer's accomplice.'

'And who is the murderer?'

'The same man who, for the last fortnight, knowing that Lavernoux, through the situation which he occupied in this house, had discovered the truth, kept him imprisoned, forced him to silence, threatened him, terrorized him; the same man who, finding Lavernoux in the act of communicating with a friend, made away with him in cold blood by stabbing him to the heart.'

'The doctor, therefore?'

'Yes.'

'But who is this doctor? Who is this malevolent genius, this infernal being who appears and disappears, who slays in the dark and whom nobody suspects?'

'Can't you guess?'

'No.'

'And do you want to know?'

'Do I want to know? . . . Why, speak, man, speak! . . . You know where he is hiding?'

'Yes.'

'In this house?'

'Yes.'

'And it is he whom the police are after?'

'Yes.'

'And I know him?'

'Yes.'

'Who is it?'

'You!'

'I! . . .'

Lupin had not been more than ten minutes with the baron; and the duel was commencing. The accusation was hurled, definitely, violently, implacably.

Lupin repeated: 'You yourself, got up in a false beard and a pair of spectacles, bent in two, like an old man. In short, you, Baron Repstein; and it is you for a very good reason, of which nobody has thought, which is that, if it was not you who contrived the whole plot, the case becomes inexplicable. Whereas, taking you as the criminal, you as murdering the baroness in order to get rid of her and run through those millions with another woman, you as murdering Lavernoux, your agent, in order to suppress an unimpeachable witness, oh, then the whole case is explained! Well, is it pretty clear? And are not you yourself convinced?'

The baron, who, throughout this conversation, had stood bending over his visitor, waiting for each of his words with feverish avidity, now drew himself up and looked at Lupin as though he undoubtedly had to do with a madman. When Lupin had finished speaking, the baron stepped back two or three paces, seemed on the point of uttering words which he ended by not saying, and then, without taking his eyes from his strange visitor, went to the fireplace and rang the bell.

Lupin did not make a movement. He waited smiling.

The butler entered. His master said: 'You can go to bed, Antoine. I will let this gentleman out.'

'Shall I put out the lights, sir?'

'Leave a light in the hall.'

Antoine left the room and the baron, after taking a revolver from his desk, at once came back to Lupin, put the weapon in his pocket and said, very calmly: 'You must excuse this little precaution, sir. I am obliged to take it in case you should be mad, though that does not seem likely. No, you are not mad. But you have come here with an object which I fail to grasp; and you have sprung upon me an accusation of so astounding a character that I am curious to know the reason. I have experienced so much disappointment and undergone so much suffering that an outrage of this kind leaves me indifferent. Continue, please.'

His voice shook with emotion and his sad eyes seemed moist with tears.

Lupin shuddered. Had he made a mistake? Was the surmise which his intuition had suggested to him and which was based upon a frail groundwork of slight facts, was this surmise wrong?

His attention was caught by a detail: through the opening in the baron's waistcoat he saw the point of the pin fixed in the tie and was thus able to realize the unusual length of the pin. Moreover, the gold stem was triangular and formed a sort of miniature dagger, very thin and very delicate, yet formidable in an expert hand.

And Lupin had no doubt but that the pin attached to that magnificent pearl was the weapon which had pierced the heart of the unfortunate M. Lavernoux.

He muttered: 'You're jolly clever, monsieur le baron!'

The other, maintaining a rather scornful gravity, kept silence, as though he did not understand and as though waiting for the explanation to which he felt himself entitled. And, in spite of everything, this impassive attitude worried Arsène Lupin. Nevertheless, his conviction was so profound and, besides, he had staked so much on the adventure that he repeated: 'Yes, jolly clever, for it is evident that the baroness only obeyed your orders in realizing your securities and also in borrowing the princess's jewels on the pretence of buying them. And it is evident that the person who walked out of your house with a bag was not your wife, but an accomplice, that chorus-girl probably, and that it is your chorus-girl who is deliberately allowing herself to be chased across the continent by our worthy Ganimard. And I look upon the trick as marvellous. What does the woman risk, seeing that it is the baroness who is being looked for? And how could they look for any other woman than the baroness, seeing that you have promised a reward of two hundred thousand francs to the person who finds the baroness? . . . Oh, that two hundred thousand francs lodged with a solicitor: what a stroke of genius! It has dazzled the police! It has thrown dust in the eyes of the most clear-sighted! A gentleman who lodges two hundred thousand francs with a solicitor is a gentleman who speaks the truth . . . So they go on hunting the baroness! And they leave you quietly to settle your affairs, to sell your stud and your two houses to the highest bidder and to prepare your flight! Heavens, what a joke!'

The baron did not wince. He walked up to Lupin and asked, without abandoning his imperturbable coolness: 'Who are you?'

Lupin burst out laughing.

'What can it matter who I am? Take it that I am an emissary of fate, looming out of the darkness for your destruction!'

He sprang from his chair, seized the baron by the shoulder and jerked out: 'Yes, for your destruction, my bold baron! Listen to me! Your wife's three millions, almost all the princess's jewels, the money you received today from the sale of your stud and your real estate: it's all there, in your pocket, or in that safe. Your flight is prepared. Look, I can see the leather of your portmanteau behind that hanging. The papers on your desk are in order. This very night, you would have done a guy. This very night, disguised beyond recognition, after taking all your precautions, you would have joined your chorus-girl, the creature for whose sake you have committed murder, that same Nelly Darbal, no doubt, whom Ganimard arrested in Belgium. But for one sudden, unforeseen obstacle: the police, the twelve detectives who, thanks to Lavernoux's revelations, have been posted under your windows. They've cooked your goose, old chap! . . . Well, I'll save you. A word through the telephone; and, by three or four o'clock in the morning, twenty of my friends will have removed the obstacle, polished off the twelve detectives, and you and I will slip away quietly. My conditions? Almost nothing; a trifle to you: we share the millions and the jewels. Is it a bargain?'

He was leaning over the baron, thundering at him with irresistible energy. The baron whispered: 'I'm beginning to understand. It's blackmail . . . '

'Blackmail or not, call it what you please, my boy, but you've got to go through with it and do as I say. And don't imagine that I shall give way at the last moment. Don't say to yourself, "Here's a gentleman whom the fear of the police will cause to think twice. If I run a big risk in refusing, he also will be risking the handcuffs, the cells and the rest of it, seeing that we are both being hunted down like wild beasts." That would be a mistake, monsieur le baron. I can always get out of it. It's a question of yourself, of yourself alone . . . Your money or your life, my lord! Share and share alike . . . if not, the scaffold! Is it a bargain?'

A quick movement. The baron released himself, grasped his revolver and fired.

But Lupin was prepared for the attack, the more so as the baron's face had lost its assurance and gradually, under the slow impulse of rage and fear, acquired an expression of almost bestial ferocity that heralded the rebellion so long kept under control.

He fired twice. Lupin first flung himself to one side and then dived at the baron's knees, seized him by both legs and brought him to the ground. The baron freed himself with an effort. The two enemies rolled over in each other's grip; and a stubborn, crafty, brutal, savage struggle followed.

Suddenly, Lupin felt a pain at his chest.

'You villain!' he yelled. 'That's your Lavernoux trick; the tie-pin!'

Stiffening his muscles with a desperate effort, he overpowered the baron and clutched him by the throat, victorious at last and omnipotent.

'You ass!' he cried. 'If you hadn't shown your cards, I might have thrown up the game! You have such a look of the honest man about you! But what a biceps, my lord! . . . I thought for a moment . . . But it's all over, now! . . . Come, my friend, hand us the pin and look cheerful . . . No, that's what I call pulling a face . . . I'm holding you too tight, perhaps? My lord's at his last gasp? . . . Come, be good! . . . That's it, just a wee bit of string round the wrists; do you allow me? . . . Why, you and I are agreeing like two brothers! It's touching! . . . At heart, you know, I'm rather fond of you . . . And now, my bonnie lad, mind yourself! And a thousand apologies! . . . '

Half raising himself, with all his strength he caught the other a terrible blow in the pit of the stomach. The baron gave a gurgle and lay stunned and unconscious.

'That comes of having a deficient sense of logic, my friend,' said Lupin. 'I offered you half your money. Now I'll give you none at all . . . provided I know where to find any of it. For that's the main thing. Where has the beggar hidden his dust? In the safe? By George, it'll be a tough job! Luckily, I have all the night before me . . . '

He began to feel in the baron's pockets, came upon a bunch of keys, first made sure that the portmanteau behind the curtain held no papers or jewels, and then went to the safe.

But, at that moment, he stopped short: he heard a noise somewhere. The servants? Impossible. Their attics were on the top floor. He listened. The noise came from below. And, suddenly, he understood: the detectives, who had heard the two shots, were banging at the front door, as was their duty, without waiting for daybreak. Then an electric bell rang, which Lupin recognized as that in the hall.

'By Jupiter!' he said. 'Pretty work! Here are these jokers coming . . . and just as we were about to gather the fruits of our laborious efforts! Tut, tut, Lupin, keep cool! What's expected of you? To open a safe, of which you don't know the secret, in thirty seconds. That's a mere trifle to lose your head about! Come, all you have to do is to discover the secret! How many letters are there in the word? Four?'

He went on thinking, while talking and listening to the noise outside. He double-locked the door of the outer room and then came back to the safe.

'Four ciphers . . . Four letters . . . four letters . . . Who can lend me a hand? . . . Who can give me just a tiny hint? . . . Who? Why, Lavernoux, of course! That good Lavernoux, seeing that he took the trouble to indulge in optical telegraphy at the risk of his life . . . Lord, what a fool I am! . . . Why, of course, why, of course, that's it! . . . By Jove, this is too exciting! . . . Lupin, you must count ten and suppress that distracted beating of your heart. If not, it means bad work.'

He counted ten and, now quite calm, knelt in front of the safe. He turned the four knobs with careful attention. Next, he examined the bunch of keys, selected one of them, then another, and attempted, in vain, to insert them in the lock.

'There's luck in odd numbers,' he muttered, trying a third key. 'Victory! This is the right one! Open Sesame, good old Sesame, open!'

The lock turned. The door moved on its hinges. Lupin pulled it to him, after taking out the bunch of keys.

'The millions are ours,' he said. 'Baron, I forgive you!'

And then he gave a single bound backward, hiccoughing with fright. His legs staggered beneath him. The keys jingled together in his fevered hand with a sinister sound. And, for twenty, for thirty seconds, despite the din that was being raised and the electric bells that kept ringing through the house, he stood there, wild-eyed, gazing at the most horrible, the most abominable sight: a woman's body, half-dressed, bent in two in the safe, crammed in, like an overlarge parcel . . . and fair hair hanging down . . . and blood . . . clots of blood . . . and livid flesh, blue in places, decomposing, flaccid.

'The baroness!' he gasped. 'The baroness! . . . Oh, the monster! . . . '

He roused himself from his torpor, suddenly, to spit in the murderer's face and pound him with his heels.

'Take that, you wretch! . . . Take that, you villain! . . . And, with it, the scaffold, the bran-basket! . . . '

Meanwhile, shouts came from the upper floors in reply to the detectives' ringing. Lupin heard footsteps scurrying down the stairs. It was time to think of beating a retreat.

In reality, this did not trouble him greatly. During his conversation with the baron, the enemy's extraordinary coolness had given him the feeling that there must be a private outlet. Besides, how could the baron have begun the fight, if he were not sure of escaping the police?

Lupin went into the next room. It looked out on the garden. At the moment when the detectives were entering the house, he flung his legs over the balcony and let himself down by a rain-pipe. He walked round the building. On the opposite side was a wall lined with shrubs. He slipped in between the shrubs and the wall and at once found a little door which he easily opened with one of the keys on the bunch. All that remained for him to do was to walk across a yard and pass through the empty rooms of a lodge; and in a few moments he found himself in the Rue du Faubourg Saint-Honoré. Of course – and this he had reckoned on – the police had not provided for this secret outlet.

*　*　*

'Well, what do you think of Baron Repstein?' cried Lupin, after giving me all the details of that tragic night. 'What a dirty scoundrel! And how it teaches one to distrust appearances! I swear to you, the fellow looked a thoroughly honest man!'

'But what about the millions?' I asked. 'The princess's jewels?'

'They were in the safe. I remember seeing the parcel.'

'Well?'

'They are there still.'

'Impossible!'

'They are, upon my word! I might tell you that I was afraid of the detectives, or else plead a sudden attack of delicacy. But the truth is simpler . . . and more prosaic: the smell was too awful! . . . '

'What?'

'Yes, my dear fellow, the smell that came from that safe . . . from that coffin . . . No, I couldn't do it . . . my head swam . . . Another second and I should have been ill . . . Isn't it silly? . . . Look, this is all I got from my expedition: the tie-pin . . . The bed-rock value of the pearl is thirty thousand francs . . . But all the same, I feel jolly well annoyed. What a sell!'

'One more question,' I said. 'The word that opened the safe!'

'Well?'

'How did you guess it?'

'Oh, quite easily! In fact, I am surprised that I didn't think of it sooner.'

'Well, tell me.'

'It was contained in the revelations telegraphed by that poor Lavernoux.'

'What?'

'Just think, my dear chap, the mistakes in spelling . . .'

'The mistakes in spelling?'

'Why, of course! They were deliberate. Surely, you don't imagine that the agent, the private secretary of the baron – who was a company-promoter, mind you, and a racing-man – did not know English better than to spell "necessery" with an "e", "atack" with one "t", "ennemy" with two "n"s and "prudance" with an "a"! The thing struck me at once. I put the four letters together and got "Etna", the name of the famous horse.'

'And was that one word enough?'

'Of course! It was enough to start with, to put me on the scent of the Repstein case, of which all the papers were full, and, next, to make me guess that it was the key-word of the safe, because, on the one hand, Lavernoux knew the gruesome contents of the safe and, on the other, he was denouncing the baron. And it was in the same way that I was led to suppose that Lavernoux had a friend in the street, that they both frequented the same café, that they amused themselves by working out the problems and cryptograms in the illustrated papers and that they had contrived a way of exchanging telegrams from window to window.'

'That makes it all quite simple!' I exclaimed.

'Very simple. And the incident once more shows that, in the discovery of crimes, there is something much more valuable than the examination of facts, than observations, deductions, inferences and all that stuff and nonsense. What I mean is, as I said before, intuition . . . intuition and intelligence . . . And Arsène Lupin, without boasting, is deficient in neither one nor the other! . . .'

The Wedding-Ring

Yvonne d'Origny kissed her son and told him to be good.

'You know your grandmother d'Origny is not very fond of children. Now that she has sent for you to come and see her, you must show her what a sensible little boy you are.' And, turning to the governess, 'Don't forget, Fräulein, to bring him home immediately after dinner ... Is monsieur still in the house?'

'Yes, madame, monsieur le comte is in his study.'

As soon as she was alone, Yvonne d'Origny walked to the window to catch a glimpse of her son as he left the house. He was out in the street in a moment, raised his head and blew her a kiss, as was his custom every day. Then the governess took his hand with, as Yvonne remarked to her surprise, a movement of unusual violence. Yvonne leant further out of the window and, when the boy reached the corner of the boulevard, she suddenly saw a man step out of a motor-car and go up to him. The man, in whom she recognized Bernard, her husband's confidential servant, took the child by the arm, made both him and the governess get into the car, and ordered the chauffeur to drive off.

The whole incident did not take ten seconds.

Yvonne, in her trepidation, ran to her bedroom, seized a wrap and went to the door. The door was locked; and there was no key in the lock.

She hurried back to the boudoir. The door of the boudoir also was locked.

Then, suddenly, the image of her husband appeared before her, that gloomy face which no smile ever lit up, those pitiless eyes in which, for years, she had felt so much hatred and malice.

'It's he ... it's he!' she said to herself. 'He has taken the child ... Oh, it's horrible!'

She beat against the door with her fists, with her feet, then flew to the mantelpiece and pressed the bell fiercely.

The shrill sound rang through the house from top to bottom. The servants would be sure to come. Perhaps a crowd would gather in the street. And, impelled by a sort of despairing hope, she kept her finger on the button.

A key turned in the lock . . . The door was flung wide open. The count appeared on the threshold of the boudoir. And the expression of his face was so terrible that Yvonne began to tremble.

He entered the room. Five or six steps separated him from her. With a supreme effort, she tried to stir, but all movement was impossible; and, when she attempted to speak, she could only flutter her lips and emit incoherent sounds. She felt herself lost. The thought of death unhinged her. Her knees gave way beneath her and she sank into a huddled heap, with a moan.

The count rushed at her and seized her by the throat.

'Hold your tongue . . . don't call out!' he said, in a low voice. 'That will be best for you! . . . '

Seeing that she was not attempting to defend herself, he loosened his hold of her and took from his pocket some strips of canvas ready rolled and of different lengths. In a few minutes, Yvonne was lying on a sofa, with her wrists and ankles bound and her arms fastened close to her body.

It was now dark in the boudoir. The count switched on the electric light and went to a little writing-desk where Yvonne was accustomed to keep her letters. Not succeeding in opening it, he picked the lock with a bent wire, emptied the drawers and collected all the contents into a bundle, which he carried off in a cardboard file.

'Waste of time, eh?' he grinned. 'Nothing but bills and letters of no importance . . . No proof against you . . . Tah! I'll keep my son for all that; and I swear before Heaven that I will not let him go!'

As he was leaving the room, he was joined, near the door, by his man Bernard. The two stopped and talked, in a low voice; but Yvonne heard these words spoken by the servant.

'I have had an answer from the working jeweller. He says he holds himself at my disposal.'

And the count replied: 'The thing is put off until twelve o'clock midday, tomorrow. My mother has just telephoned to say that she could not come before.'

Then Yvonne heard the key turn in the lock and the sound of steps going down to the ground-floor, where her husband's study was.

She long lay inert, her brain reeling with vague, swift ideas that burnt her in passing, like flames. She remembered her husband's infamous behaviour, his humiliating conduct to her, his threats, his plans for a divorce; and she gradually came to understand that she was the victim of a regular conspiracy, that the servants had been sent away until the following evening by their master's orders, that the governess had carried off her son by the count's instructions and with Bernard's assistance, that her son would not come back and that she would never see him again.

'My son!' she cried. 'My son! . . . '

Exasperated by her grief, she stiffened herself, with every nerve, with every muscle tense, to make a violent effort. And she was astonished to find that her right hand, which the count had fastened too hurriedly, still retained a certain freedom.

Then a mad hope invaded her; and, slowly, patiently, she began the work of self-deliverance.

It was long in the doing. She needed a deal of time to widen the knot sufficiently and a deal of time afterward, when the hand was released, to undo those other bonds which tied her arms to her body and those which fastened her ankles.

Still, the thought of her son sustained her; and the last shackle fell as the clock struck eight. She was free!

She was no sooner on her feet than she flew to the window and flung back the latch, with the intention of calling the first passer-by. At that moment a policeman came walking along the pavement. She leant out. But the brisk evening air, striking her face, calmed her. She thought of the scandal, of the judicial investigation, of the cross-examination, of her son. O Heaven! What could she do to get him back? How could she escape? The count might appear at the least sound. And who knew but that, in a moment of fury . . . ?

She shivered from head to foot, seized with a sudden terror. The horror of death mingled, in her poor brain, with the thought of her son; and she stammered, with a choking throat: 'Help! . . . Help! . . . '

She stopped and said to herself, several times over, in a low voice, 'Help! . . . Help! . . . ' as though the word awakened an idea, a memory within her, and as though the hope of assistance no longer seemed to her impossible. For some minutes she remained absorbed in deep meditation, broken by fears and starts. Then, with an almost mechanical series of movements, she put out her arm to a little set of shelves hanging over the writing-desk, took down four books, one after the other, turned the pages with a distraught air, replaced them and ended by finding, between the pages of the fifth, a visiting-card on which her eyes spelt the name.

Horace Velmont

followed by an address written in pencil:

Cercle de la Rue Royale

and her memory conjured up the strange thing which that man had said to her, a few years before, in that same house, on a day when she was at home to her friends.

'If ever a danger threatens you, if you need help, do not hesitate; post this card, which you see me put into this book; and, whatever the hour, whatever the obstacles, I will come.'

With what a curious air he had spoken these words and how well he had conveyed the impression of certainty, of strength, of unlimited power, of indomitable daring!

Abruptly, unconsciously, acting under the impulse of an irresistible determination, the consequences of which she refused to anticipate, Yvonne, with the same automatic gestures, took a pneumatic-delivery envelope, slipped in the card, sealed it, directed it to 'Horace Velmont, Cercle de la Rue Royale' and went to the open window. The policeman was walking up and down outside. She flung out the envelope, trusting to fate. Perhaps it would be picked up, treated as a lost letter and posted.

She had hardly completed this act when she realized its absurdity. It was mad to suppose that the message would reach the address and madder still to hope that the man to whom she was sending could come to her assistance, 'whatever the hour, whatever the obstacles'.

A reaction followed which was all the greater inasmuch as the effort had been swift and violent. Yvonne staggered, leant against a chair and, losing all energy, let herself fall.

The hours passed by, the dreary hours of winter evenings when nothing but the sound of carriages interrupts the silence of the street. The clock struck, pitilessly. In the half-sleep that numbed her limbs, Yvonne counted the strokes. She also heard certain noises, on different floors of the house, which told her that her husband had dined, that he was going up to his room, that he was going down again to his study. But all this seemed very shadowy to her; and her torpor was such that she did not even think of lying down on the sofa, in case he should come in . . .

The twelve strokes of midnight . . . Then half-past twelve . . . then one . . . Yvonne thought of nothing, awaiting the events which were

preparing and against which rebellion was useless. She pictured her
son and herself as one pictures those beings who have suffered much
and who suffer no more and who take each other in their loving
arms. But a nightmare shattered this dream. For now those two
beings were to be torn asunder; and she had the awful feeling, in her
delirium, that she was crying and choking . . .

She leapt from her seat. The key had turned in the lock. The count
was coming, attracted by her cries. Yvonne glanced round for a
weapon with which to defend herself. But the door was pushed back
quickly and, astounded, as though the sight that presented itself
before her eyes seemed to her the most inexplicable prodigy, she
stammered: 'You! . . . You! . . . '

A man was walking up to her, in dress-clothes, with his opera-hat
and cape under his arm, and this man, young, slender and elegant,
she had recognized as Horace Velmont.

'You!' she repeated.

He said, with a bow: 'I beg your pardon, madame, but I did not
receive your letter until very late.'

'Is it possible? Is it possible that this is you . . . that you were able
to . . . ?'

He seemed greatly surprised.

'Did I not promise to come in answer to your call?'

'Yes . . . but . . . '

'Well, here I am,' he said, with a smile.

He examined the strips of canvas from which Yvonne had succeeded in freeing herself and nodded his head, while continuing his
inspection.

'So those are the means employed? The Comte d'Origny, I presume? . . . I also saw that he locked you in . . . But then the pneumatic
letter? . . . Ah, through the window! . . . How careless of you not to
close it!'

He pushed both sides to. Yvonne took fright.

'Suppose they hear!'

'There is no one in the house. I have been over it.'

'Still . . . '

'Your husband went out ten minutes ago.'

'Where is he?'

'With his mother, the Comtesse d'Origny.'

'How do you know?'

'Oh, it's very simple! He was rung up by telephone and I awaited the
result at the corner of this street and the boulevard. As I expected, the

count came out hurriedly, followed by his man. I at once entered, with the aid of special keys.'

He told this in the most natural way, just as one tells a meaningless anecdote in a drawing-room. But Yvonne, suddenly seized with fresh alarm, asked: 'Then it's not true? . . . His mother is not ill? . . . In that case, my husband will be coming back . . . '

'Certainly, the count will see that a trick has been played on him and in three quarters of an hour at the latest . . . '

'Let us go . . . I don't want him to find me here . . . I must go to my son . . . '

'One moment . . . '

'One moment! . . . But don't you know that they have taken him from me? . . . That they are hurting him, perhaps? . . . '

With set face and feverish gestures, she tried to push Velmont back. He, with great gentleness, compelled her to sit down and, leaning over her in a respectful attitude, said, in a serious voice: 'Listen, madame, and let us not waste time, when every minute is valuable. First of all, remember this: we met four times, six years ago . . . And, on the fourth occasion, when I was speaking to you, in the drawing-room of this house, with too much – what shall I say? – with too much feeling, you gave me to understand that my visits were no longer welcome. Since that day I have not seen you. And, nevertheless, in spite of all, your faith in me was such that you kept the card which I put between the pages of that book and, six years later, you send for me and none other. That faith in me I ask you to continue. You must obey me blindly. Just as I surmounted every obstacle to come to you, so I will save you, whatever the position may be.'

Horace Velmont's calmness, his masterful voice, with the friendly intonation, gradually quieted the countess. Though still very weak, she gained a fresh sense of ease and security in that man's presence.

'Have no fear,' he went on. 'The Comtesse d'Origny lives at the other end of the Bois de Vincennes. Allowing that your husband finds a motor-cab, it is impossible for him to be back before a quarter-past three. Well, it is twenty-five to three now. I swear to take you away at three o'clock exactly and to take you to your son. But I will not go before I know everything.'

'What am I to do?' she asked.

'Answer me and very plainly. We have twenty minutes. It is enough. But it is not too much.'

'Ask me what you want to know.'

'Do you think that the count had any . . . any murderous intentions?'

'No.'

'Then it concerns your son?'

'Yes.'

'He is taking him away, I suppose, because he wants to divorce you and marry another woman, a former friend of yours, whom you have turned out of your house. Is that it? Oh, I 'entreat you, answer me frankly! These are facts of public notoriety; and your hesitation, your scruples, must all cease, now that the matter concerns your son. So your husband wished to marry another woman?'

'Yes.'

'The woman has no money. Your husband, on his side, has gambled away all his property and has no means beyond the allowance which he receives from his mother, the Comtesse d'Origny, and the income of a large fortune which your son inherited from two of your uncles. It is this fortune which your husband covets and which he would appropriate more easily if the child were placed in his hands. There is only one way: divorce. Am I right?'

'Yes.'

'And what has prevented him until now is your refusal?'

'Yes, mine and that of my mother-in-law, whose religious feelings are opposed to divorce. The Comtesse d'Origny would only yield in case . . . '

'In case . . . ?'

'In case they could prove me guilty of shameful conduct.'

Velmont shrugged his shoulders.

'Therefore he is powerless to do anything against you or against your son. Both from the legal point of view and from that of his own interests, he stumbles against an obstacle which is the most insurmountable of all: the virtue of an honest woman. And yet, in spite of everything, he suddenly shows fight.'

'What do you mean?'

'I mean that, if a man like the count, after so many hesitations and in the face of so many difficulties, risks so doubtful an adventure, it must be because he thinks he has command of weapons . . . '

'What weapons?'

'I don't know. But they exist . . . or else he would not have begun by taking away your son.'

Yvonne gave way to her despair.

'Oh, this is horrible! . . . How do I know what he may have done, what he may have invented?'

'Try and think . . . Recall your memories . . . Tell me, in this desk which he has broken open, was there any sort of letter which he could possibly turn against you?'

'No . . . only bills and addresses . . . '

'And, in the words he used to you, in his threats, is there nothing that allows you to guess?'

'Nothing.'

'Still . . . still,' Velmont insisted, 'there must be something.' And he continued, 'Has the count a particularly intimate friend . . . in whom he confides?'

'No.'

'Did anybody come to see him yesterday?'

'No, nobody.'

'Was he alone when he bound you and locked you in?'

'At that moment, yes.'

'But afterward?'

'His man, Bernard, joined him near the door and I heard them talking about a working jeweller . . . '

'Is that all?'

'And about something that was to happen the next day, that is, today, at twelve o'clock, because the Comtesse d'Origny could not come earlier.'

Velmont reflected.

'Has that conversation any meaning that throws a light upon your husband's plans?'

'I don't see any.'

'Where are your jewels?'

'My husband has sold them all.'

'You have nothing at all left?'

'No.'

'Not even a ring?'

'No,' she said, showing her hands, 'none except this.'

'Which is your wedding-ring?'

'Which is my . . . wedding- . . . '

She stopped, nonplussed. Velmont saw her flush as she stammered: 'Could it be possible? . . . But no . . . no . . . he doesn't know . . . '

Velmont at once pressed her with questions and Yvonne stood silent, motionless, anxious-faced. At last, she replied, in a low voice: 'This is not my wedding-ring. One day, long ago, it dropped from the mantelpiece in my bedroom, where I had put it a minute before and, hunt for it as I might, I could not find it again. So I ordered another, without saying anything about it . . . and this is the one, on my hand . . . '

'Did the real ring bear the date of your wedding?'

'Yes . . . the 23rd of October.'

'And the second?'

'This one has no date.'

He perceived a slight hesitation in her and a confusion which, in point of fact, she did not try to conceal.

'I implore you,' he exclaimed, 'don't hide anything from me . . . You see how far we have gone in a few minutes, with a little logic and calmness . . . Let us go on, I ask you as a favour.'

'Are you sure,' she said, 'that it is necessary?'

'I am sure that the least detail is of importance and that we are nearly attaining our object. But we must hurry. This is a crucial moment.'

'I have nothing to conceal,' she said, proudly raising her head. 'It was the most wretched and the most dangerous period of my life. While suffering humiliation at home, outside I was surrounded with attentions, with temptations, with pitfalls, like any woman who is seen to be neglected by her husband. Then I remembered: before my marriage, a man had been in love with me. I had guessed his unspoken love; and he has died since. I had the name of that man engraved inside the ring; and I wore it as a talisman. There was no love in me, because I was the wife of another. But, in my secret heart, there was a memory, a sad dream, something sweet and gentle that protected me . . . '

She had spoken slowly, without embarrassment, and Velmont did not doubt for a second that she was telling the absolute truth. He kept silent; and she, becoming anxious again, asked: 'Do you suppose . . . that my husband . . . ?'

He took her hand and, while examining the plain gold ring, said: 'The puzzle lies here. Your husband, I don't know how, knows of the substitution of one ring for the other. His mother will be here at twelve o'clock. In the presence of witnesses, he will compel you to take off your ring; and, in this way, he will obtain the approval of his mother and, at the same time, will be able to obtain his divorce, because he will have the proof for which he was seeking.'

'I am lost!' she moaned. 'I am lost!'

'On the contrary, you are saved! Give me that ring . . . and presently he will find another there, another which I will send you, to reach you before twelve, and which will bear the date of the 23rd of October. So . . . '

He suddenly broke off. While he was speaking, Yvonne's hand had turned ice-cold in his; and, raising his eyes, he saw that the young woman was pale, terribly pale.

'What's the matter? I beseech you . . .'

She yielded to a fit of mad despair.

'This is the matter, that I am lost! . . . This is the matter, that I can't get the ring off! It has grown too small for me! . . . Do you understand? . . . It made no difference and I did not give it a thought . . . But today . . . this proof . . . this accusation . . . Oh, what torture! . . . Look . . . it forms part of my finger . . . it has grown into my flesh . . . and I can't . . . I can't . . .'

She pulled at the ring, vainly, with all her might, at the risk of injuring herself. But the flesh swelled up around the ring; and the ring did not budge.

'Oh!' she cried, seized with an idea that terrified her. 'I remember . . . the other night . . . a nightmare I had . . . It seemed to me that someone entered my room and caught hold of my hand . . . And I could not wake up . . . It was he! It was he! He had put me to sleep, I was sure of it . . . and he was looking at the ring . . . And presently he will pull it off before his mother's eyes . . . Ah, I understand everything: that working jeweller! . . . He will cut it from my hand tomorrow . . . You see, you see . . . I am lost! . . .'

She hid her face in her hands and began to weep. But, amid the silence, the clock struck once . . . and twice . . . and yet once more. And Yvonne drew herself up with a jerk.

'There he is!' she cried. 'He is coming! . . . It is three o'clock! . . . Let us go! . . .'

She grabbed at her cloak and ran to the door . . . Velmont barred the way and, in a masterful tone: 'You shall not go!'

'My son . . . I want to see him, to take him back . . .'

'You don't even know where he is!'

'I want to go.'

'You shall not go! . . . It would be madness . . .'

He took her by the wrists. She tried to release herself; and Velmont had to employ a little force to overcome her resistance. In the end, he succeeded in getting her back to the sofa, then in laying her at full length and, at once, without heeding her lamentations, he took the canvas strips and fastened her wrists and ankles.

'Yes,' he said, 'It would be madness! Who would have set you free? Who would have opened that door for you? An accomplice? What an argument against you and what a pretty use your husband would make of it with his mother! . . . And, besides, what's the good? To run away means accepting divorce . . . and what might that not lead to? . . . You must stay here . . . '

She sobbed: 'I'm frightened . . . I'm frightened . . . this ring burns me . . . Break it . . . Take it away . . . Don't let him find it!'

'And if it is not found on your finger, who will have broken it? Again an accomplice . . . No, you must face the music . . . and face it boldly, for I answer for everything . . . Believe me . . . I answer for everything . . . If I have to tackle the Comtesse d'Origny bodily and thus delay the interview . . . If I had to come myself before noon . . . it is the real wedding-ring that shall be taken from your finger – that I swear! – and your son shall be restored to you.'

Swayed and subdued, Yvonne instinctively held out her hands to the bonds. When he stood up, she was bound as she had been before.

He looked round the room to make sure that no trace of his visit remained. Then he stooped over the countess again and whispered: 'Think of your son and, whatever happens, fear nothing . . . I am watching over you.'

She heard him open and shut the door of the boudoir and, a few minutes later, the hall-door.

At half-past three, a motor-cab drew up. The door downstairs was slammed again; and, almost immediately after, Yvonne saw her husband hurry in, with a furious look in his eyes. He ran up to her, felt to see if she was still fastened and, snatching her hand, examined the ring. Yvonne fainted . . .

*   *   *

She could not tell, when she woke, how long she had slept. But the broad light of day was filling the boudoir; and she perceived, at the first movement which she made, that her bonds were cut. Then she turned her head and saw her husband standing beside her, looking at her.

'My son . . . my son . . . ' she moaned. 'I want my son . . . '

He replied, in a voice of which she felt the jeering insolence: 'Our son is in a safe place. And, for the moment, it's a question not of him, but of you. We are face to face with each other, probably for the last time, and the explanation between us will be a very serious one. I must warn you that it will take place before my mother. Have you any objection?'

Yvonne tried to hide her agitation and answered: 'None at all.'

'Can I send for her?'

'Yes. Leave me, in the meantime. I shall be ready when she comes.'

'My mother is here.'

'Your mother is here?' cried Yvonne, in dismay, remembering Horace Velmont's promise.

'What is there to astonish you in that?'

'And is it now . . . is it at once that you want to . . . ?'

'Yes.'

'Why? . . . Why not this evening? . . . Why not tomorrow?'

'Today and now,' declared the count. 'A rather curious incident happened in the course of last night, an incident which I cannot account for and which decided me to hasten the explanation. Don't you want something to eat first?'

'No . . . no . . . '

'Then I will go and fetch my mother.'

He turned to Yvonne's bedroom. Yvonne glanced at the clock. It marked twenty-five minutes to eleven!

'Ah!' she said, with a shiver of fright.

Twenty-five minutes to eleven! Horace Velmont would not save her and nobody in the world and nothing in the world would save her, for there was no miracle that could place the wedding-ring upon her finger.

The count, returning with the Comtesse d'Origny, asked her to sit down. She was a tall, lank, angular woman, who had always displayed a hostile feeling to Yvonne. She did not even bid her daughter-in-law good-morning, showing that her mind was made up as regards the accusation.

'I don't think,' she said, 'that we need speak at length. In two words, my son maintains . . . '

'I don't maintain, mother,' said the count, 'I declare. I declare on my oath that, three months ago, during the holidays, the upholsterer, when laying the carpet in this room and the boudoir, found the wedding-ring which I gave my wife lying in a crack in the floor. Here is the ring. The date of the 23rd of October is engraved inside.'

'Then,' said the countess, 'the ring which your wife carries . . . '

'That is another ring, which she ordered in exchange for the real one. Acting on my instructions, Bernard, my man, after long searching, ended by discovering in the outskirts of Paris, where he now lives, the little jeweller to whom she went. This man remembers perfectly and is willing to bear witness that his customer did not tell him to engrave a date, but a name. He has forgotten the name, but the man who used to work with him in his shop may be able to remember it. This working jeweller has been informed by letter that I required his services and he replied yesterday, placing himself at my disposal. Bernard went to fetch him at nine o'clock this morning. They are both waiting in my study.'

He turned to his wife.

'Will you give me that ring of your own free will?'

'You know,' she said, 'from the other night, that it won't come off my finger.'

'In that case, can I have the man up? He has the necessary implements with him.'

'Yes,' she said, in a voice faint as a whisper.

She was resigned. She conjured up the future as in a vision: the scandal, the decree of divorce pronounced against herself, the custody of the child awarded to the father; and she accepted this, thinking that she would carry off her son, that she would go with him to the ends of the earth and that the two of them would live alone together and happy . . .

Her mother-in-law said: 'You have been very thoughtless, Yvonne.'

Yvonne was on the point of confessing to her and asking for her protection. But what was the good? How could the Comtesse d'Origny possibly believe her innocent? She made no reply.

Besides, the count at once returned, followed by his servant and by a man carrying a bag of tools under his arm.

And the count said to the man: 'You know what you have to do?'

'Yes,' said the workman. 'It's to cut a ring that's grown too small . . . That's easily done . . . A touch of the nippers . . . '

'And then you will see,' said the count, 'if the inscription inside the ring was the one you engraved.'

Yvonne looked at the clock. It was ten minutes to eleven. She seemed to hear, somewhere in the house, a sound of voices raised in argument; and, in spite of herself, she felt a thrill of hope. Perhaps Velmont has succeeded . . . But the sound was renewed; and she perceived that it was produced by some costermongers passing under her window and moving farther on.

It was all over. Horace Velmont had been unable to assist her. And she understood that, to recover her child, she must rely upon her own strength, for the promises of others are vain.

She made a movement of recoil. She had felt the workman's heavy hand on her hand; and that hateful touch revolted her.

The man apologized, awkwardly. The count said to his wife: 'You must make up your mind, you know.'

Then she put out her slim and trembling hand to the workman, who took it, turned it over and rested it on the table, with the palm upward. Yvonne felt the cold steel. She longed to die, then and there; and, at once attracted by that idea of death, she thought of the poisons which she would buy and which would send her to sleep almost without her knowing it.

The operation did not take long. Inserted on the slant, the little steel pliers pushed back the flesh, made room for themselves and bit the ring. A strong effort . . . and the ring broke. The two ends had only to be separated to remove the ring from the finger. The workman did so.

The count exclaimed, in triumph: 'At last! Now we shall see! . . . The proof is there! And we are all witnesses . . . '

He snatched up the ring and looked at the inscription. A cry of amazement escaped him. The ring bore the date of his marriage to Yvonne: '23rd of October'! . . .

* * *

We were sitting on the terrace at Monte Carlo. Lupin finished his story, lit a cigarette and calmly puffed the smoke into the blue air.

I said: 'Well?'

'Well what?'

'Why, the end of the story . . . '

'The end of the story? But what other end could there be?'

'Come . . . you're joking . . . '

'Not at all. Isn't that enough for you? The countess is saved. The count, not possessing the least proof against her, is compelled by his mother to forego the divorce and to give up the child. That is all. Since then, he has left his wife, who is living happily with her son, a fine lad of sixteen.'

'Yes . . . yes . . . but the way in which the countess was saved?'

Lupin burst out laughing.

'My dear old chap' – Lupin sometimes condescends to address me in this affectionate manner – 'my dear old chap, you may be rather smart at relating my exploits, but, by Jove, you do want to have the i's dotted for you! I assure you, the countess did not ask for explanations!'

'Very likely. But there's no pride about me,' I added, laughing. 'Dot those i's for me, will you?'

He took out a five-franc piece and closed his hand over it.

'What's in my hand?'

'A five-franc piece.'

He opened his hand. The five-franc piece was gone.

'You see how easy it is! A working jeweller, with his nippers, cuts a ring with a date engraved upon it: 23rd of October. It's a simple little trick of sleight-of-hand, one of many which I have in my bag. By Jove, I didn't spend six months with Dickson, the conjurer,* for nothing!'

'But then . . . ?'

'Out with it!'

'The working jeweller?'

'Was Horace Velmont! Was good old Lupin! Leaving the countess at three o'clock in the morning, I employed the few remaining minutes before the husband's return to have a look round his study. On the table I found the letter from the working jeweller. The letter gave me the address. A bribe of a few louis enabled me to take the workman's place; and I arrived with a wedding-ring ready cut and engraved. Hocus-pocus! Pass! . . . The count couldn't make head or tail of it.'

'Splendid!' I cried. And I added, a little chaffingly, in my turn, 'But don't you think that you were humbugged a bit yourself, on this occasion?'

'Oh! And by whom, pray?'

'By the countess?'

'In what way?'

'Hang it all, that name engraved as a talisman! . . . The mysterious Adonis who loved her and suffered for her sake! . . . All that story seems very unlikely; and I wonder whether, Lupin though you be, you did not just drop upon a pretty love-story, absolutely genuine and . . . none too innocent.'

Lupin looked at me out of the corner of his eye.

'No,' he said.

'How do you know?'

'If the countess made a misstatement in telling me that she knew that man before her marriage – and that he was dead – and if she really did love him in her secret heart, I, at least, have a positive proof that it was an ideal love and that he did not suspect it.'

'And where is the proof?'

'It is inscribed inside the ring which I myself broke on the countess's finger . . . and which I carry on me. Here it is. You can read the name she had engraved on it.'

* *The Exploits of Arsène Lupin.* By Maurice Leblanc. Translated by Alexander Teixeira de Mattos (Cassell). IV. The Escape of Arsène Lupin.

He handed me the ring. I read: 'Horace Velmont'.

There was a moment of silence between Lupin and myself; and, noticing it, I also observed on his face a certain emotion, a tinge of melancholy.

I resumed.

'What made you tell me this story . . . to which you have often alluded in my presence?'

'What made me . . . ?'

He drew my attention to a woman, still exceedingly handsome, who was passing on a young man's arm. She saw Lupin and bowed.

'It's she,' he whispered. 'She and her son.'

'Then she recognized you?'

'She always recognizes me, whatever my disguise.'

'But since the burglary at the Château de Thibermesnil,* the police have identified the two names of Arsène Lupin and Horace Velmont.'

'Yes.'

'Therefore she knows who you are.'

'Yes.'

'And she bows to you?' I exclaimed, in spite of myself.

He caught me by the arm and, fiercely: 'Do you think that I am Lupin to her? Do you think that I am a burglar in her eyes, a rogue, a cheat? . . . Why, I might be the lowest of miscreants, I might be a murderer even . . . and still she would bow to me!'

'Why? Because she loved you once?'

'Rot! That would be an additional reason, on the contrary, why she should now despise me.'

'What then?'

'I am the man who gave her back her son!'

* *The Exploits of Arsène Lupin.* IX. Holmlock Shears Arrives Too Late.

The Sign of the Shadow

'I received your telegram and here I am,' said a gentleman with a grey moustache, who entered my study, dressed in a dark-brown frock-coat and a wide-brimmed hat, with a red ribbon in his button-hole. 'What's the matter?'

Had I not been expecting Arsène Lupin, I should certainly never have recognized him in the person of this old half-pay officer.

'What's the matter?' I echoed. 'Oh, nothing much: a rather curious coincidence, that's all. And, as I know that you would just as soon clear up a mystery as plan one . . . '

'Well?'

'You seem in a great hurry!'

'I am . . . unless the mystery in question is worth putting myself out for. So let us get to the point.'

'Very well. Just begin by casting your eye on this little picture, which I picked up, a week or two ago, in a grimy old shop on the other side of the river. I bought it for the sake of its Empire frame, with the palm-leaf ornaments on the mouldings . . . for the painting is execrable.'

'Execrable, as you say,' said Lupin, after he had examined it, 'but the subject itself is rather nice. That corner of an old courtyard, with its rotunda of Greek columns, its sun-dial and its fish-pond and that ruined well with the Renascence roof and those stone steps and stone benches: all very picturesque.'

'And genuine,' I added. 'The picture, good or bad, has never been taken out of its Empire frame. Besides, it is dated . . . There, in the left-hand bottom corner: those red figures, 15. 4. 2, which obviously stand for 15 April, 1802.'

'I dare say . . . I dare say . . . But you were speaking of a coincidence and, so far, I fail to see . . . '

I went to a corner of my study, took a telescope, fixed it on its stand and pointed it, through the open window, at the open window of a little room facing my flat, on the other side of the street. And I asked Lupin to look through it.

He stooped forward. The slanting rays of the morning sun lit up the room opposite, revealing a set of mahogany furniture, all very simple, a large bed and a child's bed hung with cretonne curtains.

'Ah!' cried Lupin, suddenly. 'The same picture!'

'Exactly the same!' I said. 'And the date: do you see the date, in red? 15. 4. 2.'

'Yes, I see . . . And who lives in that room?'

'A lady . . . or, rather, a workwoman, for she has to work for her living . . . needlework, hardly enough to keep herself and her child.'

'What is her name?'

'Louise d'Ernemont . . . From what I hear, she is the great-grand-daughter of a farmer-general who was guillotined during the Terror.'

'Yes, on the same day as André Chénier,' said Lupin. 'According to the memoirs of the time, this d'Ernemont was supposed to be a very rich man.' He raised his head and said, 'It's an interesting story . . . Why did you wait before telling me?'

'Because this is the 15th of April.'

'Well?'

'Well, I discovered yesterday – I heard them talking about it in the porter's box – that the 15th of April plays an important part in the life of Louise d'Ernemont.'

'Nonsense!'

'Contrary to her usual habits, this woman who works every day of her life, who keeps her two rooms tidy, who cooks the lunch which her little girl eats when she comes home from the parish school . . . this woman, on the 15th of April, goes out with the child at ten o'clock in the morning and does not return until nightfall. And this has happened for years and in all weathers. You must admit that there is something queer about this date which I find on an old picture, which is inscribed on another, similar picture and which controls the annual movements of the descendant of d'Ernemont the farmer-general.'

'Yes, it's curious . . . you're quite right,' said Lupin, slowly. 'And don't you know where she goes to?'

'Nobody knows. She does not confide in a soul. As a matter of fact, she talks very little.'

'Are you sure of your information?'

'Absolutely. And the best proof of its accuracy is that here she comes.'

A door had opened at the back of the room opposite, admitting a little girl of seven or eight, who came and looked out of the window. A lady appeared behind her, tall, good-looking still and wearing a sad and gentle air. Both of them were ready and dressed, in clothes which were simple in themselves, but which pointed to a love of neatness and a certain elegance on the part of the mother.

'You see,' I whispered, 'they are going out.'

And presently the mother took the child by the hand and they left the room together.

Lupin caught up his hat.

'Are you coming?'

My curiosity was too great for me to raise the least objection. I went downstairs with Lupin.

As we stepped into the street, we saw my neighbour enter a baker's shop. She bought two rolls and placed them in a little basket which her daughter was carrying and which seemed already to contain some other provisions. Then they went in the direction of the outer boulevards and followed them as far as the Place de l'Étoile, where they turned down the Avenue Kléber to walk toward Passy.

Lupin strolled silently along, evidently obsessed by a train of thought which I was glad to have provoked. From time to time, he uttered a sentence which showed me the thread of his reflections; and I was able to see that the riddle remained as much a mystery to him as to myself.

Louise d'Ernemont, meanwhile, had branched off to the left, along the Rue Raynouard, a quiet old street in which Franklin and Balzac once lived, one of those streets which, lined with old-fashioned houses and walled gardens, give you the impression of being in a country-town. The Seine flows at the foot of the slope which the street crowns; and a number of lanes run down to the river.

My neighbour took one of these narrow, winding, deserted lanes. The first building, on the right, was a house the front of which faced the Rue Raynouard. Next came a moss-grown wall, of a height above the ordinary, supported by buttresses and bristling with broken glass.

Half-way along the wall was a low, arched door. Louise d'Ernemont stopped in front of this door and opened it with a key which seemed to us enormous. Mother and child entered and closed the door.

'In any case,' said Lupin, 'she has nothing to conceal, for she has not looked round once . . .'

He had hardly finished his sentence when we heard the sound of footsteps behind us. It was two old beggars, a man and a woman, tattered, dirty, squalid, covered in rags. They passed us without paying the least attention to our presence. The man took from his wallet a key similar to my neighbour's and put it into the lock. The door closed behind them.

And, suddenly, at the top of the lane, came the noise of a motor-car stopping . . . Lupin dragged me fifty yards lower down, to a corner in which we were able to hide. And we saw coming down the lane, carrying a little dog under her arm, a young and very much over-dressed woman, wearing a quantity of jewellery, a young woman whose eyes were too dark, her lips too red, her hair too fair. In front of the door, the same performance, with the same key . . . The lady and the dog disappeared from view.

'This promises to be most amusing,' said Lupin, chuckling. 'What earthly connection can there be between those different people?'

There hove in sight successively two elderly ladies, lean and rather poverty-stricken in appearance, very much alike, evidently sisters; a footman in livery; an infantry corporal; a fat gentleman in a soiled and patched jacket-suit; and, lastly, a workman's family, father, mother, and four children, all six of them pale and sickly, looking like people who never eat their fill. And each of the newcomers carried a basket or string-bag filled with provisions.

'It's a picnic!' I cried.

'It grows more and more surprising,' said Lupin, 'and I shan't be satisfied till I know what is happening behind that wall.'

To climb it was out of the question. We also saw that it finished, at the lower as well as at the upper end, at a house none of whose windows overlooked the enclosure which the wall contained.

During the next hour, no one else came along. We vainly cast about for a stratagem; and Lupin, whose fertile brain had exhausted every possible expedient, was about to go in search of a ladder, when, suddenly, the little door opened and one of the workman's children came out.

The boy ran up the lane to the Rue Raynouard. A few minutes later he returned, carrying two bottles of water, which he set down on the pavement to take the big key from his pocket.

By that time Lupin had left me and was strolling slowly along the wall. When the child, after entering the enclosure, pushed back the door Lupin sprang forward and stuck the point of his knife into the staple of the lock. The bolt failed to catch; and it became an easy matter to push the door ajar.

'That's done the trick!' said Lupin.

He cautiously put his hand through the doorway and then, to my great surprise, entered boldly. But, on following his example, I saw that, ten yards behind the wall, a clump of laurels formed a sort of curtain which allowed us to come up unobserved.

Lupin took his stand right in the middle of the clump. I joined him and, like him, pushed aside the branches of one of the shrubs. And the sight which presented itself to my eyes was so unexpected that I was unable to suppress an exclamation, while Lupin, on his side, muttered, between his teeth: 'By Jupiter! This is a funny job!'

We saw before us, within the confined space that lay between the two windowless houses, the identical scene represented in the old picture which I had bought at a second-hand dealer's!

The identical scene! At the back, against the opposite wall, the same Greek rotunda displayed its slender columns. In the middle, the same stone benches topped a circle of four steps that ran down to a fish-pond with moss-grown flags. On the left, the same well raised its wrought-iron roof; and, close at hand, the same sun-dial showed its slanting gnomon and its marble face.

The identical scene! And what added to the strangeness of the sight was the memory, obsessing Lupin and myself, of that date of the 15th of April, inscribed in a corner of the picture, and the thought that this very day was the 15th of April and that sixteen or seventeen people, so different in age, condition and manners, had chosen the 15th of April to come together in this forgotten corner of Paris!

All of them, at the moment when we caught sight of them, were sitting in separate groups on the benches and steps; and all were eating. Not very far from my neighbour and her daughter, the workman's family and the beggar couple were sharing their provisions; while the footman, the gentleman in the soiled suit, the infantry corporal and the two lean sisters were making a common stock of their sliced ham, their tins of sardines and their gruyère cheese.

The lady with the little dog alone, who had brought no food with her, sat apart from the others, who made a show of turning their backs upon her. But Louise d'Ernemont offered her a sandwich, whereupon her example was followed by the two sisters; and the corporal at once began to make himself as agreeable to the young person as he could.

It was now half-past one. The beggar-man took out his pipe, as did the fat gentleman; and, when they found that one had no tobacco and the other no matches, their needs soon brought them together.

The men went and smoked by the rotunda and the women joined
them. For that matter, all these people seemed to know one another
quite well.

They were at some distance from where we were standing, so that
we could not hear what they said. However, we gradually perceived
that the conversation was becoming animated. The young person
with the dog, in particular, who by this time appeared to be in great
request, indulged in much voluble talk, accompanying her words
with many gestures, which set the little dog barking furiously.

But, suddenly, there was an outcry, promptly followed by shouts of
rage; and one and all, men and women alike, rushed in disorder
toward the well. One of the workman's brats was at that moment
coming out of it, fastened by his belt to the hook at the end of the
rope; and the three other urchins were drawing him up by turning
the handle. More active than the rest, the corporal flung himself
upon him; and forthwith the footman and the fat gentleman seized
hold of him also, while the beggars and the lean sisters came to blows
with the workman and his family.

In a few seconds the little boy had not a stitch left on him beyond
his shirt. The footman, who had taken possession of the rest of the
clothes, ran away, pursued by the corporal, who snatched away the
boy's breeches, which were next torn from the corporal by one of the
lean sisters.

'They are mad!' I muttered, feeling absolutely at sea.

'Not at all, not at all,' said Lupin.

'What! Do you mean to say that you can make head or tail of what
is going on?'

He did not reply. The young lady with the little dog, tucking her
pet under her arm, had started running after the child in the shirt,
who uttered loud yells. The two of them raced round the laurel-
clump in which we stood hidden; and the brat flung himself into his
mother's arms.

At long last, Louise d'Ernemont, who had played a conciliatory
part from the beginning, succeeded in allaying the tumult. Everybody sat down again; but there was a reaction in all those exasperated
people and they remained motionless and silent, as though worn out
with their exertions.

And time went by. Losing patience and beginning to feel the
pangs of hunger, I went to the Rue Raynouard to fetch something
to eat, which we divided while watching the actors in the incomprehensible comedy that was being performed before our eyes.

They hardly stirred. Each minute that passed seemed to load them with increasing melancholy; and they sank into attitudes of discouragement, bent their backs more and more and sat absorbed in their meditations.

The afternoon wore on in this way, under a grey sky that shed a dreary light over the enclosure.

'Are they going to spend the night here?' I asked, in a bored voice.

But, at five o'clock or so, the fat gentleman in the soiled jacket-suit took out his watch. The others did the same and all, watch in hand, seemed to be anxiously awaiting an event of no little importance to themselves. The event did not take place, for, in fifteen or twenty minutes, the fat gentleman gave a gesture of despair, stood up and put on his hat.

Then lamentations broke forth. The two lean sisters and the workman's wife fell upon their knees and made the sign of the cross. The lady with the little dog and the beggar-woman kissed each other and sobbed; and we saw Louise d'Ernemont pressing her daughter sadly to her.

'Let's go,' said Lupin.

'You think it's over?'

'Yes; and we have only just time to make ourselves scarce.'

We went out unmolested. At the top of the lane, Lupin turned to the left and, leaving me outside, entered the first house in the Rue Raynouard, the one that backed on to the enclosure.

After talking for a few seconds to the porter, he joined me and we stopped a passing taxi-cab.

'No. 34 Rue de Turin,' he said to the driver.

The ground-floor of No. 34 was occupied by a notary's office; and we were shown in, almost without waiting, to Maître Valandier, a smiling, pleasant-spoken man of a certain age.

Lupin introduced himself by the name of Captain Jeanniot, retired from the army. He said that he wanted to build a house to his own liking and that someone had suggested to him a plot of ground situated near the Rue Raynouard.

'But that plot is not for sale,' said Maître Valandier.

'Oh, I was told . . . '

'You have been misinformed, I fear.'

The lawyer rose, went to a cupboard and returned with a picture which he showed us. I was petrified. It was the same picture which I had bought, the same picture that hung in Louise d'Ernemont's room.

'This is a painting,' he said, 'of the plot of ground to which you refer. It is known as the Clos d'Ernemont.'

'Precisely.'

'Well, this close,' continued the notary, 'once formed part of a large garden belonging to d'Ernemont, the farmer-general, who was executed during the Terror. All that could be sold has been sold, piecemeal, by the heirs. But this last plot has remained and will remain in their joint possession . . . unless . . . '

The notary began to laugh.

'Unless what?' asked Lupin.

'Well, it's quite a romance, a rather curious romance, in fact. I often amuse myself by looking through the voluminous documents of the case.'

'Would it be indiscreet, if I asked . . . ?'

'Not at all, not at all,' declared Maître Valandier, who seemed delighted, on the contrary, to have found a listener for his story. And, without waiting to be pressed, he began: 'At the outbreak of the Revolution, Louis Agrippa d'Ernemont, on the pretence of joining his wife, who was staying at Geneva with their daughter Pauline, shut up his mansion in the Faubourg Saint-Germain, dismissed his servants and, with his son Charles, came and took up his abode in his pleasure-house at Passy, where he was known to nobody except an old and devoted serving-woman. He remained there in hiding for three years and he had every reason to hope that his retreat would not be discovered, when, one day, after luncheon, as he was having a nap, the old servant burst into his room. She had seen, at the end of the street, a patrol of armed men who seemed to be making for the house. Louis d'Ernemont got ready quickly and, at the moment when the men were knocking at the front door, disappeared through the door that led to the garden, shouting to his son, in a scared voice, to keep them talking, if only for five minutes. He may have intended to escape and found the outlets through the garden watched. In any case, he returned in six or seven minutes, replied very calmly to the questions put to him and raised no difficulty about accompanying the men. His son Charles, although only eighteen years of age, was arrested also.'

'When did this happen?' asked Lupin.

'It happened on the 26th day of Germinal, Year II, that is to say, on the . . . '

Maître Valandier stopped, with his eyes fixed on a calendar that hung on the wall, and exclaimed: 'Why, it was on this very day! This is the 15th of April, the anniversary of the farmer-general's arrest.'

'What an odd coincidence!' said Lupin. 'And considering the period at which it took place, the arrest, no doubt, had serious consequences?'

'Oh, most serious!' said the notary, laughing. 'Three months later, at the beginning of Thermidor, the farmer-general mounted the scaffold. His son Charles was forgotten in prison and their property was confiscated.'

'The property was immense, I suppose?' said Lupin.

'Well, there you are! That's just where the thing becomes complicated. The property, which was, in fact, immense, could never be traced. It was discovered that the Faubourg Saint-Germain mansion had been sold, before the Revolution, to an Englishman, together with all the country-seats and estates and all the jewels, securities and collections belonging to the farmer-general. The Convention instituted minute inquiries, as did the Directory afterward. But the inquiries led to no result.'

'There remained, at any rate, the Passy house,' said Lupin.

'The house at Passy was bought, for a mere song, by a delegate of the Commune, the very man who had arrested d'Ernemont, one Citizen Broquet. Citizen Broquet shut himself up in the house, barricaded the doors, fortified the walls and, when Charles d'Ernemont was at last set free and appeared outside, received him by firing a musket at him. Charles instituted one law-suit after another, lost them all and then proceeded to offer large sums of money. But Citizen Broquet proved intractable. He had bought the house and he stuck to the house; and he would have stuck to it until his death, if Charles had not obtained the support of Bonaparte. Citizen Broquet cleared out on the 12th of February, 1803; but Charles d'Ernemont's joy was so great and his brain, no doubt, had been so violently unhinged by all that he had gone through, that, on reaching the threshold of the house of which he had at last recovered the ownership, even before opening the door he began to dance and sing in the street. He had gone clean off his head.'

'By Jove!' said Lupin. 'And what became of him?'

'His mother and his sister Pauline, who had ended by marrying a cousin of the same name at Geneva, were both dead. The old servant-woman took care of him and they lived together in the Passy house. Years passed without any notable event; but, suddenly, in 1812, an unexpected incident happened. The old servant made a series of strange revelations on her death-bed, in the presence of two witnesses whom she sent for. She declared that the farmer-general had carried to his house at Passy a number of bags filled with gold and silver and that those bags had disappeared a few days before the arrest. According to earlier confidences made by Charles d'Erne-mont, who had them from his father, the treasures were hidden in the garden, between the rotunda, the sun-dial and the well. In proof of her statement, she produced three pictures, or rather, for they were not yet framed, three canvases, which the farmer-general had painted during his captivity and which he had succeeded in con-veying to her, with instructions to hand them to his wife, his son and his daughter. Tempted by the lure of wealth, Charles and the old servant had kept silence. Then came the law-suits, the recovery of the house, Charles's madness, the servant's own useless searches; and the treasures were still there.'

'And they are there now,' chuckled Lupin.

'And they will be there always,' exclaimed Maître Valandier. 'Un-less . . . unless Citizen Broquet, who no doubt smelt a rat, succeeded in ferreting them out. But this is an unlikely supposition, for Citizen Broquet died in extreme poverty.'

'So then . . . ?'

'So then everybody began to hunt. The children of Pauline, the sister, hastened from Geneva. It was discovered that Charles had been secretly married and that he had sons. All these heirs set to work.'

'But Charles himself?'

'Charles lived in the most absolute retirement. He did not leave his room.'

'Never?'

'Well, that is the most extraordinary, the most astounding part of the story. Once a year, Charles d'Ernemont, impelled by a sort of subconscious will-power, came downstairs, took the exact road which his father had taken, walked across the garden and sat down either on the steps of the rotunda, which you see here, in the picture, or on the curb of the well. At twenty-seven minutes past five, he rose and went indoors again; and until his death, which occurred in 1820, he never once failed to perform this incomprehensible pilgrimage. Well, the day on which this happened was invariably the 15th of April, the anniversary of the arrest.'

Maître Valandier was no longer smiling and himself seemed im-pressed by the amazing story which he was telling us.

'And, since Charles's death?' asked Lupin, after a moment's reflec-tion.

'Since that time,' replied the lawyer, with a certain solemnity of manner, 'for nearly a hundred years, the heirs of Charles and

Pauline d'Ernemont have kept up the pilgrimage of the 15th of April. During the first few years they made the most thorough excavations. Every inch of the garden was searched, every clod of ground dug up. All this is now over. They take hardly any pains. All they do is, from time to time, for no particular reason, to turn over a stone or explore the well. For the most part, they are content to sit down on the steps of the rotunda, like the poor madman; and, like him, they wait. And that, you see, is the sad part of their destiny. In those hundred years, all these people who have succeeded one another, from father to son, have lost – what shall I say? – the energy of life. They have no courage left, no initiative. They wait. They wait for the 15th of April; and, when the 15th of April comes, they wait for a miracle to take place. Poverty has ended by overtaking every one of them. My predecessors and I have sold first the house, in order to build another which yields a better rent, followed by bits of the garden and further bits. But, as to that corner over there,' pointing to the picture, 'they would rather die than sell it. On this they are all agreed: Louise d'Ernemont, who is the direct heiress of Pauline, as well as the beggars, the workman, the footman, the circus-rider and so on, who represent the unfortunate Charles.'

There was a fresh pause; and Lupin asked: 'What is your own opinion, Maître Valandier?'

'My private opinion is that there's nothing in it. What credit can we give to the statements of an old servant enfeebled by age? What importance can we attach to the crotchets of a madman? Besides, if the farmer-general had realized his fortune, don't you think that that fortune would have been found? One could manage to hide a paper, a document, in a confined space like that, but not treasures.'

'Still, the pictures? . . . '

'Yes, of course. But, after all, are they a sufficient proof?'

Lupin bent over the copy which the solicitor had taken from the cupboard and, after examining it at length, said: 'You spoke of three pictures.'

'Yes, the one which you see was handed to my predecessor by the heirs of Charles. Louise d'Ernemont possesses another. As for the third, no one knows what became of it.'

Lupin looked at me and continued.

'And do they all bear the same date?'

'Yes, the date inscribed by Charles d'Ernemont when he had them framed, not long before his death . . . The same date, that is to say the

15th of April, Year II, according to the revolutionary calendar, as the arrest took place in April, 1794.'

'Oh, yes, of course,' said Lupin. 'The figure 2 means . . . '

He thought for a few moments and resumed.

'One more question, if I may. Did no one ever come forward to solve the problem?'

Maître Valandier threw up his arms.

'Goodness gracious me!' he cried. 'Why, it was the plague of the office! One of my predecessors, Maître Turbon, was summoned to Passy no fewer than eighteen times, between 1820 and 1843, by the groups of heirs, whom fortune-tellers, clairvoyants, visionaries, impostors of all sorts had promised that they would discover the farmer-general's treasures. At last, we laid down a rule: any outsider applying to institute a search was to begin by depositing a certain sum.'

'What sum?'

'A thousand francs.'

'And did this have the effect of frightening them off?'

'No. Four years ago, an Hungarian hypnotist tried the experiment and made me waste a whole day. After that, we fixed the deposit at five thousand francs. In case of success, a third of the treasure goes to the finder. In case of failure, the deposit is forfeited to the heirs. Since then, I have been left in peace.'

'Here are your five thousand francs.'

The lawyer gave a start.

'Eh? What do you say?'

'I say,' repeated Lupin, taking five bank-notes from his pocket and calmly spreading them on the table, 'I say that here is the deposit of five thousand francs. Please give me a receipt and invite all the d'Ernemont heirs to meet me at Passy on the 15th of April next year.'

The notary could not believe his senses. I myself, although Lupin had accustomed me to these surprises, was utterly taken back.

'Are you serious?' asked Maître Valandier.

'Perfectly serious.'

'But, you know, I told you my opinion. All these improbable stories rest upon no evidence of any kind.'

'I don't agree with you,' said Lupin.

The notary gave him the look which we give to a person who is not quite right in his head. Then, accepting the situation, he took his pen and drew up a contract on stamped paper, acknowledging the payment of the deposit by Captain Jeanniot and promising him a third of such moneys as he should discover.

'If you change your mind,' he added, 'you might let me know a week before the time comes. I shall not inform the d'Ernemont family until the last moment, so as not to give those poor people too long a spell of hope.'

'You can inform them this very day, Maître Valandier. It will make them spend a happier year.'

We said goodbye. Outside, in the street, I cried: 'So you have hit upon something?'

'I?' replied Lupin. 'Not a bit of it! And that's just what amuses me.'

'But they have been searching for a hundred years!'

'It is not so much a matter of searching as of thinking. Now I have three hundred and sixty-five days to think in. It is a great deal more than I want; and I am afraid that I shall forget all about the business, interesting though it may be. Oblige me by reminding me, will you?'

*   *   *

I reminded him of it several times during the following months, though he never seemed to attach much importance to the matter. Then came a long period during which I had no opportunity of seeing him. It was the period, as I afterward learnt, of his visit to Armenia and of the terrible struggle on which he embarked against Abdul the Damned, a struggle which ended in the tyrant's downfall.

I used to write to him, however, at the address which he gave me and I was thus able to send him certain particulars which I had succeeded in gathering, here and there, about my neighbour Louise d'Ernemont, such as the love which she had conceived, a few years earlier, for a very rich young man, who still loved her, but who had been compelled by his family to throw her over; the young widow's despair, and the plucky life which she led with her little daughter.

Lupin replied to none of my letters. I did not know whether they reached him; and, meantime, the date was drawing near and I could not help wondering whether his numerous undertakings would not prevent him from keeping the appointment which he himself had fixed.

As a matter of fact, the morning of the 15th of April arrived and Lupin was not with me by the time I had finished lunch. It was a quarter-past twelve. I left my flat and took a cab to Passy.

I had no sooner entered the lane than I saw the workman's four brats standing outside the door in the wall. Maître Valandier, informed by them of my arrival, hastened in my direction.

'Well?' he cried. 'Where's Captain Jeanniot?'

'Hasn't he come?'

'No; and I can assure you that everybody is very impatient to see him.'

The different groups began to crowd round the lawyer; and I noticed that all those faces which I recognized had thrown off the gloomy and despondent expression which they wore a year ago.

'They are full of hope,' said Maître Valandier, 'and it is my fault. But what could I do? Your friend made such an impression upon me that I spoke to these good people with a confidence . . . which I cannot say I feel. However, he seems a queer sort of fellow, this Captain Jeanniot of yours . . . '

He asked me many questions and I gave him a number of more or less fanciful details about the captain, to which the heirs listened, nodding their heads in appreciation of my remarks.

'Of course, the truth was bound to be discovered sooner or later,' said the fat gentleman, in a tone of conviction.

The infantry corporal, dazzled by the captain's rank, did not entertain a doubt in his mind.

The lady with the little dog wanted to know if Captain Jeanniot was young.

But Louise d'Ernemont said: 'And suppose he does not come?'

'We shall still have the five thousand francs to divide,' said the beggar-man.

For all that, Louise d'Ernemont's words had damped their enthusiasm. Their faces began to look sullen and I felt an atmosphere as of anguish weighing upon us.

At half-past one, the two lean sisters felt faint and sat down. Then the fat gentleman in the soiled suit suddenly rounded on the notary.

'It's you, Maître Valandier, who are to blame . . . You ought to have brought the captain here by main force . . . He's a humbug, that's quite clear.'

He gave me a savage look, and the footman, in his turn, flung muttered curses at me.

I confess that their reproaches seemed to me well-founded and that Lupin's absence annoyed me greatly.

'He won't come now,' I whispered to the lawyer.

And I was thinking of beating a retreat, when the eldest of the brats appeared at the door, yelling: 'There's someone coming! . . . A motor-cycle! . . . '

A motor was throbbing on the other side of the wall. A man on a motor-bicycle came tearing down the lane at the risk of breaking his neck. Suddenly, he put on his brakes, outside the door, and sprang from his machine.

Under the layer of dust which covered him from head to foot, we could see that his navy-blue reefer-suit, his carefully creased trousers, his black felt hat and patent-leather boots were not the clothes in which a man usually goes cycling.

'But that's not Captain Jeanniot!' shouted the notary, who failed to recognize him.

'Yes, it is,' said Lupin, shaking hands with us. 'I'm Captain Jeanniot right enough . . . only I've shaved off my moustache . . . Besides, Maître Valandier, here's your receipt.'

He caught one of the workman's children by the arm and said: 'Run to the cab-rank and fetch a taxi to the corner of the Rue Raynouard. Look sharp! I have an urgent appointment to keep at two o'clock, or a quarter-past at the latest.'

There was a murmur of protest. Captain Jeanniot took out his watch.

'Well! It's only twelve minutes to two! I have a good quarter of an hour before me. But, by Jingo, how tired I feel! And how hungry into the bargain!'

The corporal thrust his ammunition-bread into Lupin's hand; and he munched away at it as he sat down and said: 'You must forgive me. I was in the Marseilles express, which left the rails between Dijon and Laroche. There were twelve people killed and any number injured, whom I had to help. Then I found this motor-cycle in the luggage-van . . . Maître Valandier, you must be good enough to restore it to the owner. You will find the label fastened to the handle-bar. Ah, you're back, my boy! Is the taxi there? At the corner of the Rue Raynouard? Capital!'

He looked at his watch again.

'Hullo! No time to lose!'

I stared at him with eager curiosity. But how great must the excitement of the d'Ernemont heirs have been! True, they had not the same faith in Captain Jeanniot that I had in Lupin. Nevertheless, their faces were pale and drawn. Captain Jeanniot turned slowly to the left and walked up to the sun-dial. The pedestal represented the figure of a man with a powerful torso, who bore on his shoulders a marble slab the surface of which had been so much worn by time that we could hardly distinguish the engraved lines that marked the hours. Above the slab, a Cupid, with outspread wings, held an arrow that served as a gnomon.

The captain stood leaning forward for a minute, with attentive eyes. Then he said: 'Somebody lend me a knife, please.'

A clock in the neighbourhood struck two. At that exact moment, the shadow of the arrow was thrown upon the sunlit dial along the line of a crack in the marble which divided the slab very nearly in half.

The captain took the knife handed to him. And with the point, very gently, he began to scratch the mixture of earth and moss that filled the narrow cleft.

Almost immediately, at a couple of inches from the edge, he stopped, as though his knife had encountered an obstacle, inserted his thumb and forefinger and withdrew a small object which he rubbed between the palms of his hands and gave to the lawyer.

'Here, Maître Valandier. Something to go on with.'

It was an enormous diamond, the size of a hazelnut and beautifully cut.

The captain resumed his work. The next moment, a fresh stop. A second diamond, magnificent and brilliant as the first, appeared in sight.

And then came a third and a fourth.

In a minute's time, following the crack from one edge to the other and certainly without digging deeper than half an inch, the captain had taken out eighteen diamonds of the same size.

During this minute, there was not a cry, not a movement around the sun-dial. The heirs seemed paralyzed with a sort of stupor. Then the fat gentleman muttered: 'Geminy!'

And the corporal moaned: 'Oh, captain! . . . Oh, captain! . . . '

The two sisters fell in a dead faint. The lady with the little dog dropped on her knees and prayed, while the footman, staggering like a drunken man, held his head in his two hands, and Louise d'Ernemont wept.

When calm was restored and all became eager to thank Captain Jeanniot, they saw that he was gone.

* * *

Some years passed before I had an opportunity of talking to Lupin about this business. He was in a confidential vein and answered: 'The business of the eighteen diamonds? By Jove, when I think that three or four generations of my fellow-men had been hunting for the solution! And the eighteen diamonds were there all the time, under a little mud and dust!'

'But how did you guess? . . . '

'I did not guess. I reflected. I doubt if I need even have reflected. I was struck, from the beginning, by the fact that the whole circumstance was governed by one primary question: the question of time. When Charles d'Ernemont was still in possession of his wits, he wrote a date upon the three pictures. Later, in the gloom in which he was struggling, a faint glimmer of intelligence led him every year to the centre of the old garden; and the same faint glimmer led him away from it every year at the same moment, that is to say, at twenty-seven minutes past five. Something must have acted on the disordered machinery of his brain in this way. What was the superior force that controlled the poor madman's movements? Obviously, the instinctive notion of time represented by the sun-dial in the farmer-general's pictures. It was the annual revolution of the earth around the sun that brought Charles d'Ernemont back to the garden at a fixed date. And it was the earth's daily revolution upon its own axis that took him from it at a fixed hour, that is to say, at the hour, most likely, when the sun, concealed by objects different from those of today, ceased to light the Passy garden. Now of all this the sun-dial was the symbol. And that is why I at once knew where to look.'

'But how did you settle the hour at which to begin looking?'

'Simply by the pictures. A man living at that time, such as Charles d'Ernemont, would have written either 26 Germinal, Year II, or else 15 April, 1794, but not 15 April, Year II. I was astounded that no one had thought of that.'

'Then the figure 2 stood for two o'clock?'

'Evidently. And what must have happened was this: the farmer-general began by turning his fortune into solid gold and silver money. Then, by way of additional precaution, with this gold and silver he bought eighteen wonderful diamonds. When he was surprised by the arrival of the patrol, he fled into his garden. Which was the best place to hide the diamonds? Chance caused his eyes to light upon the sun-dial. It was two o'clock. The shadow of the arrow was then falling along the crack in the marble. He obeyed this sign of the shadow, rammed his eighteen diamonds into the dust and calmly went back and surrendered to the soldiers.'

'But the shadow of the arrow coincides with the crack in the marble every day of the year and not only on the 15th of April.'

'You forget, my dear chap, that we are dealing with a lunatic and that he remembered only this date of the 15th of April.'

'Very well; but you, once you had solved the riddle, could easily have made your way into the enclosure and taken the diamonds.'

'Quite true; and I should not have hesitated, if I had had to do with people of another description. But I really felt sorry for those poor wretches. And then you know the sort of idiot that Lupin is. The idea of appearing suddenly as a benevolent genius and amazing his kind would be enough to make him commit any sort of folly.'

'Tah!' I cried. 'The folly was not so great as all that. Six magnificent diamonds! How delighted the d'Ernemont heirs must have been to fulfil their part of the contract!'

Lupin looked at me and burst into uncontrollable laughter.

'So you haven't heard? Oh, what a joke! The delight of the d'Ernemont heirs! . . . Why, my dear fellow, on the next day, that worthy Captain Jeanniot had so many mortal enemies! On the very next day, the two lean sisters and the fat gentleman organized an opposition. A contract? Not worth the paper it was written on, because, as could easily be proved, there was no such person as Captain Jeanniot. Where did that adventurer spring from? Just let him sue them and they'd soon show him what was what!'

'Louise d'Ernemont too?'

'No, Louise d'Ernemont protested against that piece of rascality. But what could she do against so many? Besides, now that she was rich, she got back her young man. I haven't heard of her since.'

'So . . . ?'

'So, my dear fellow, I was caught in a trap, with not a leg to stand on, and I had to compromise and accept one modest diamond as my share, the smallest and the least handsome of the lot. That comes of doing one's best to help people!'

And Lupin grumbled between his teeth: 'Oh, gratitude! . . . All humbug! . . . Where should we honest men be if we had not our conscience and the satisfaction of duty performed to reward us?'

4

The Infernal Trap

When the race was over, a crowd of people, streaming toward the exit from the grand stand, pushed against Nicolas Dugrival. He brought his hand smartly to the inside pocket of his jacket.

'What's the matter?' asked his wife.

'I still feel nervous . . . with that money on me! I'm afraid of some nasty accident.'

She muttered: 'And I can't understand you. How can you think of carrying such a sum about with you? Every farthing we possess! Lord knows, it cost us trouble enough to earn!'

'Pooh!' he said. 'No one would guess that it is here, in my pocket-book.'

'Yes, yes,' she grumbled. 'That young man-servant whom we discharged last week knew all about it, didn't he, Gabriel?'

'Yes, aunt,' said a youth standing beside her.

Nicolas Dugrival, his wife and his nephew Gabriel were well-known figures at the race-meetings, where the regular frequenters saw them almost every day: Dugrival, a big, fat, red-faced man, who looked as if he knew how to enjoy life; his wife, also built on heavy lines, with a coarse, vulgar face, and always dressed in a plum-coloured silk much the worse for wear; the nephew, quite young, slender, with pale features, dark eyes and fair and rather curly hair.

As a rule, the couple remained seated throughout the afternoon. It was Gabriel who betted for his uncle, watching the horses in the paddock, picking up tips to right and left among the jockeys and stable-lads, running backward and forward between the stands and the *pari-mutuel*.

Luck had favoured them that day, for, three times, Dugrival's neighbours saw the young man come back and hand him money.

The fifth race was just finishing. Dugrival lit a cigar. At that moment, a gentleman in a tight-fitting brown suit, with a face ending in a peaked gray beard, came up to him and asked, in a confidential whisper: 'Does this happen to belong to you, sir?'

And he displayed a gold watch and chain.

Dugrival gave a start.

'Why, yes . . . it's mine . . . Look, here are my initials, N. G.: Nicolas Dugrival!'

And he at once, with a movement of terror, clapped his hand to his jacket-pocket. The note-case was still there.

'Ah,' he said, greatly relieved, 'that's a piece of luck! . . . But, all the same, how on earth was it done? . . . Do you know the scoundrel?'

'Yes, we've got him locked up. Pray come with me and we'll soon look into the matter.'

'Whom have I the honour . . . ?'

'M. Delangle, detective-inspector. I have sent to let M. Marquenne, the magistrate, know.'

Nicolas Dugrival went out with the inspector; and the two of them started for the commissary's office, some distance behind the grand stand. They were within fifty yards of it, when the inspector was accosted by a man who said to him, hurriedly: 'The fellow with the watch has blabbed; we are on the tracks of a whole gang. M. Marquenne wants you to wait for him at the *pari-mutuel* and to keep a look-out near the fourth booth.'

There was a crowd outside the betting-booths and Inspector Delangle muttered: 'It's an absurd arrangement . . . Whom am I to look out for? . . . That's just like M. Marquenne! . . . '

He pushed aside a group of people who were crowding too close upon him.

'By Jove, one has to use one's elbows here and keep a tight hold on one's purse. That's the way you got your watch pinched, M. Dugrival!'

'I can't understand . . . '

'Oh, if you knew how those gentry go to work! One never guesses what they're up to next. One of them treads on your foot, another gives you a poke in the eye with his stick and the third picks your pocket before you know where you are . . . I've been had that way myself.' He stopped and then continued, angrily. 'But, bother it, what's the use of hanging about here! What a mob! It's unbearable! . . . Ah, there's M. Marquenne making signs to us! . . . One moment, please . . . and be sure and wait for me here.'

He shouldered his way through the crowd. Nicolas Dugrival followed him for a moment with his eyes. Once the inspector was out of sight, he stood a little to one side, to avoid being hustled.

A few minutes passed. The sixth race was about to start, when Dugrival saw his wife and nephew looking for him. He explained to them that Inspector Delangle was arranging matters with the magistrate.

'Have you your money still?' asked his wife.

'Why, of course I have!' he replied. 'The inspector and I took good care, I assure you, not to let the crowd jostle us.'

He felt his jacket, gave a stifled cry, thrust his hand into his pocket and began to stammer inarticulate syllables, while Mme Dugrival gasped, in dismay: 'What is it? What's the matter?'

'Stolen!' he moaned. 'The pocket-book . . . the fifty notes! . . . '

'It's not true!' she screamed. 'It's not true!'

'Yes, the inspector . . . a common sharper . . . he's the man . . . '

She uttered absolute yells.

'Thief! Thief! Stop thief! . . . My husband's been robbed! . . . Fifty thousand francs! . . . We are ruined! . . . Thief! Thief . . . '

In a moment they were surrounded by policemen and taken to the commissary's office. Dugrival went like a lamb, absolutely bewildered. His wife continued to shriek at the top of her voice, piling up explanations, railing against the inspector.

'Have him looked for! . . . Have him found! . . . A brown suit . . . A pointed beard . . . Oh, the villain, to think what he's robbed us of! . . . Fifty thousand francs! . . . Why . . . why, Dugrival, what are you doing?'

With one bound, she flung herself upon her husband. Too late! He had pressed the barrel of a revolver against his temple. A shot rang out. Dugrival fell. He was dead.

* * *

The reader cannot have forgotten the commotion made by the newspapers in connection with this case, nor how they jumped at the opportunity once more to accuse the police of carelessness and blundering. Was it conceivable that a pick-pocket could play the part of an inspector like that, in broad daylight and in a public place, and rob a respectable man with impunity?

Nicolas Dugrival's widow kept the controversy alive, thanks to her jeremiads and to the interviews which she granted on every hand. A reporter had secured a snapshot of her in front of her husband's body, holding up her hand and swearing to revenge his death. Her nephew Gabriel was standing beside her, with hatred pictured in his face. He, too, it appeared, in a few words uttered in a whisper, but in a tone of fierce determination, had taken an oath to pursue and catch the murderer.

The accounts described the humble apartment which they occupied at the Batignolles; and, as they had been robbed of all their means, a sporting-paper opened a subscription on their behalf.

As for the mysterious Delangle, he remained undiscovered. Two men were arrested, but had to be released forthwith. The police took up a number of clues, which were at once abandoned; more than one name was mentioned; and, lastly, they accused Arsène Lupin, an action which provoked the famous burglar's celebrated cable, dispatched from New York six days after the incident.

PROTEST INDIGNANTLY AGAINST CALUMNY INVENTED BY BAFFLED POLICE. SEND MY CONDOLENCES TO UNHAPPY VICTIMS. INSTRUCTING MY BANKERS TO REMIT THEM FIFTY THOUSAND FRANCS.

LUPIN

True enough, on the day after the publication of the cable, a stranger rang at Mme Dugrival's door and handed her an envelope. The envelope contained fifty thousand-franc notes.

This theatrical stroke was not at all calculated to allay the universal comment. But an event soon occurred which provided any amount of additional excitement. Two days later, the people living in the same house as Mme Dugrival and her nephew were awakened, at four o'clock in the morning, by horrible cries and shrill calls for help. They rushed to the flat. The porter succeeded in opening the door. By the light of a lantern carried by one of the neighbours, he found Gabriel stretched at full-length in his bedroom, with his wrists and ankles bound and a gag forced into his mouth, while, in the next room, Mme Dugrival lay with her life's blood ebbing away through a great gash in her breast.

She whispered: 'The money . . . I've been robbed . . . All the notes gone . . .'

And she fainted away.

What had happened? Gabriel said – and, as soon as she was able to speak, Mme Dugrival completed her nephew's story – that he was startled from his sleep by finding himself attacked by two men, one of whom gagged him, while the other fastened him down. He was unable to see the men in the dark, but he heard the noise of the struggle between them and his aunt. It was a terrible struggle, Mme Dugrival declared. The ruffians, who obviously knew their way about, guided by some intuition, made straight for the little cupboard containing the money and, in spite of her resistance and outcries, laid hands upon the bundle of bank-notes. As they left, one of them, whom she had bitten in the arm, stabbed her with a knife, whereupon the men had both fled.

'Which way?' she was asked.

'Through the door of my bedroom and afterward, I suppose, through the hall-door.'

'Impossible! The porter would have noticed them.'

For the whole mystery lay in this: how had the ruffians entered the house and how did they manage to leave it? There was no outlet open to them. Was it one of the tenants? A careful inquiry proved the absurdity of such a supposition.

What then?

Chief-inspector Ganimard, who was placed in special charge of the case, confessed that he had never known anything more bewildering.

'It's very like Lupin,' he said, 'and yet it's not Lupin . . . No, there's more in it than meets the eye, something very doubtful and suspicious . . . Besides, if it were Lupin, why should he take back the fifty thousand francs which he sent? There's another question that puzzles me: what is the connection between the second robbery and the first, the one on the race-course? The whole thing is incomprehensible and I have a sort of feeling – which is very rare with me – that it is no use hunting. For my part, I give it up.'

The examining-magistrate threw himself into the case with heart and soul. The reporters united their efforts with those of the police. A famous English sleuth-hound crossed the Channel. A wealthy American, whose head had been turned by detective-stories, offered a big reward to whosoever should supply the first information leading to the discovery of the truth. Six weeks later, no one was any the wiser. The public adopted Ganimard's view; and the examining-magistrate himself grew tired of struggling in a darkness which only became denser as time went on.

And life continued as usual with Dugrival's widow. Nursed by her nephew, she soon recovered from her wound. In the mornings, Gabriel settled her in an easy-chair at the dining-room window, did the rooms and then went out marketing. He cooked their lunch without even accepting the proffered assistance of the porter's wife.

Worried by the police investigations and especially by the requests for interviews, the aunt and nephew refused to see anybody. Not even the portress, whose chatter disturbed and wearied Mme Dugrival, was admitted. She fell back upon Gabriel, whom she accosted each time that he passed her room.

'Take care, M. Gabriel, you're both of you being spied upon. There are men watching you. Why, only last night, my husband caught a fellow staring up at your windows.'

'Nonsense!' said Gabriel. 'It's all right. That's the police, protecting us.'

One afternoon, at about four o'clock, there was a violent altercation between two costermongers at the bottom of the street. The porter's wife at once left her room to listen to the invectives which the adversaries were hurling at each other's heads. Her back was no sooner turned than a man, young, of medium height and dressed in a gray suit of irreproachable cut, slipped into the house and ran up the staircase.

When he came to the third floor, he rang the bell. Receiving no answer, he rang again. At the third summons, the door opened.

'Mme Dugrival?' he asked, taking off his hat.

'Mme Dugrival is still an invalid and unable to see anyone,' said Gabriel, who stood in the hall.

'It's most important that I should speak to her.'

'I am her nephew and perhaps I could take her a message . . .'

'Very well,' said the man. 'Please tell Mme Dugrival that an accident has supplied me with valuable information concerning the robbery from which she has suffered and that I should like to go over the flat and ascertain certain particulars for myself. I am accustomed to this sort of inquiry; and my call is sure to be of use to her.'

Gabriel examined the visitor for a moment, reflected and said: 'In that case, I suppose my aunt will consent . . . Pray come in.'

He opened the door of the dining-room and stepped back to allow the other to pass. The stranger walked to the threshold, but, at the moment when he was crossing it, Gabriel raised his arm and, with a swift movement, struck him with a dagger over the right shoulder.

A burst of laughter rang through the room.

'Got him!' cried Mme Dugrival, darting up from her chair. 'Well done, Gabriel! But, I say, you haven't killed the scoundrel, have you?'

'I don't think so, aunt. It's a small blade and I didn't strike him too hard.'

The man was staggering, with his hands stretched in front of him and his face deathly pale.

'You fool!' sneered the widow. 'So you've fallen into the trap . . . and a good job too! We've been looking out for you a long time. Come, my fine fellow, down with you! You don't care about it, do you? But you can't help yourself, you see. That's right: one knee on the ground, before the missus . . . now the other knee . . . How well we've been brought up! . . . Crash, there we go on the floor! Lord, if my poor Dugrival could only see him like that! . . . And now, Gabriel, to work!'

She went to her bedroom and opened one of the doors of a hanging wardrobe filled with dresses. Pulling these aside, she pushed open another door which formed the back of the wardrobe and led to a room in the next house.

'Help me carry him, Gabriel. And you'll nurse him as well as you can, won't you? For the present, he's worth his weight in gold to us, the artist! . . . '

* * *

The hours succeeded one another. Days passed.

One morning, the wounded man regained a moment's consciousness. He raised his eyelids and looked around him.

He was lying in a room larger than that in which he had been stabbed, a room sparsely furnished, with thick curtains hanging before the windows from top to bottom. There was light enough, however, to enable him to see young Gabriel Dugrival seated on a chair beside him and watching him.

'Ah, it's you, youngster!' he murmured. 'I congratulate you, my lad. You have a sure and pretty touch with the dagger.'

And he fell asleep again.

That day and the following days, he woke up several times and, each time, he saw the stripling's pale face, his thin lips and his dark eyes, with the hard look in them.

'You frighten me,' he said. 'If you have sworn to do for me, don't stand on ceremony. But cheer up, for goodness' sake. The thought of death has always struck me as the most humorous thing in the world. Whereas, with you, old chap, it simply becomes lugubrious. I prefer to go to sleep. Good-night!'

Still, Gabriel, in obedience to Mme Dugrival's orders, continued to nurse him with the utmost care and attention. The patient was almost free from fever and was beginning to take beef-tea and milk. He gained a little strength and jested: 'When will the convalescent be allowed his first drive? Is the bath-chair there? Why, cheer up, stupid!

You look like a weeping-willow contemplating a crime. Come, just one little smile for daddy!'

One day, on waking, he had a very unpleasant feeling of constraint. After a few efforts, he perceived that, during his sleep, his legs, chest and arms had been fastened to the bedstead with thin wire strands that cut into his flesh at the least movements.

'Ah,' he said to his keeper, 'this time it's the great performance! The chicken's going to be bled. Are you operating, Angel Gabriel? If so, see that your razor's nice and clean, old chap! The antiseptic treatment, *if* you please!'

But he was interrupted by the sound of a key grating in the lock. The door opposite opened and Mme Dugrival appeared.

She approached slowly, took a chair and, producing a revolver from her pocket, cocked it and laid it on the table by the bedside.

'Brrrrr!' said the prisoner. 'We might be at the Ambigu! . . . Fourth act: the Traitor's Doom. And the fair sex to do the deed . . . The hand of the Graces . . . What an honour! . . . Mme Dugrival, I rely on you not to disfigure me.'

'Hold your tongue, Lupin.'

'Ah, so you know? . . . By Jove, how clever we are!'

'Hold your tongue, Lupin.'

There was a solemn note in her voice that impressed the captive and compelled him to silence. He watched his two gaolers in turns. The bloated features and red complexion of Mme Dugrival formed a striking contrast with her nephew's refined face; but they both wore the same air of implacable resolve.

The widow leant forward and said: 'Are you prepared to answer my questions?'

'Why not?'

'Then listen to me. How did you know that Dugrival carried all his money in his pocket?'

'Servants' gossip . . . '

'A young man-servant whom we had in our employ: was that it?'

'Yes.'

'And did you steal Dugrival's watch in order to give it back to him and inspire him with confidence?'

'Yes.'

She suppressed a movement of fury.

'You fool! You fool! . . . What! You rob my man, you drive him to kill himself and, instead of making tracks to the uttermost ends of the earth and hiding yourself, you go on playing Lupin in the heart of

Paris! . . . Did you forget that I swore, on my dead husband's head, to find his murderer?'

'That's what staggers me,' said Lupin. 'How did you come to suspect me?'

'How? Why, you gave yourself away!'

'I did? . . . '

'Of course . . . The fifty thousand francs . . . '

'Well, what about it? A present . . . '

'Yes, a present which you gave cabled instructions to have sent to me, so as to make believe that you were in America on the day of the races. A present, indeed! What humbug! The fact is, you didn't like to think of the poor fellow whom you had murdered. So you restored the money to the widow, publicly, of course, because you love playing to the gallery and ranting and posing, like the mountebank that you are. That was all very nicely thought out. Only, my fine fellow, you ought not to have sent me the selfsame notes that were stolen from Dugrival! Yes, you silly fool, the selfsame notes and no others! We knew the numbers, Dugrival and I did. And you were stupid enough to send the bundle to me. Now do you understand your folly?'

Lupin began to laugh.

'It was a pretty blunder, I confess. I'm not responsible; I gave different orders. But, all the same I can't blame anyone except myself.'

'Ah, so you admit it! You signed your theft and you signed your ruin at the same time. There was nothing left to be done but to find you. Find you? No, better than that. Sensible people don't find Lupin: they make him come to them! That was a masterly notion. It belongs to my young nephew, who loathes you as much as I do, if possible, and who knows you thoroughly, through reading all the books that have been written about you. He knows your prying nature, your need to be always plotting, your mania for hunting in the dark and unravelling what others have failed to unravel. He also knows that sort of sham kindness of yours, the drivelling sentimentality that makes you shed crocodile tears over the people you victimize; And he planned the whole farce! He invented the story of the two burglars, the second theft of fifty thousand francs! Oh, I swear to you, before Heaven, that the stab which I gave myself with my own hands never hurt me! And I swear to you, before Heaven, that we spent a glorious time waiting for you, the boy and I, peeping out at your confederates who prowled under our windows, taking their bearings! And there was no mistake about it: you were bound to come! Seeing that you had restored the Widow Dugrival's fifty thousand francs, it was out of the question that you should allow the Widow Dugrival to be robbed of her fifty thousand francs! You were bound to come, attracted by the scent of the mystery. You were bound to come, for swagger, out of vanity! And you come!'

The widow gave a strident laugh.

'Well played, wasn't it? The Lupin of Lupins, the master of masters, inaccessible and invisible, caught in a trap by a woman and a boy! . . . Here he is in flesh and bone . . . here he is with hands and feet tied, no more dangerous than a sparrow . . . here is he . . . here he is! . . . '

She shook with joy and began to pace the room, throwing sidelong glances at the bed, like a wild beast that does not for a moment take its eyes from its victim. And never had Lupin beheld greater hatred and savagery in any human being.

'Enough of this prattle,' she said.

Suddenly restraining herself, she stalked back to him and, in a quite different tone, in a hollow voice, laying stress on every syllable: 'Thanks to the papers in your pocket, Lupin, I have made good use of the last twelve days. I know all your affairs, all your schemes, all your assumed names, all the organization of your band, all the lodgings which you possess in Paris and elsewhere. I have even visited one of them, the most secret, the one where you hide your papers, your ledgers and the whole story of your financial operations. The result of my investigations is very satisfactory. Here are four cheques, taken from four cheque-books and corresponding with four accounts which you keep at four different banks under four different names. I have filled in each of them for ten thousand francs. A larger figure would have been too risky. And, now, sign.'

'By Jove!' said Lupin, sarcastically. 'This is blackmail, my worthy Mme Dugrival.'

'That takes your breath away, what?'

'It takes my breath away, as you say.'

'And you find an adversary who is a match for you?'

'The adversary is far beyond me. So the trap – let us call it infernal – the infernal trap into which I have fallen was laid not merely by a widow thirsting for revenge, but also by a first-rate business woman anxious to increase her capital?'

'Just so.'

'My congratulations. And, while I think of it, used M. Dugrival perhaps to . . . ?'

'You have hit it, Lupin. After all, why conceal the fact? It will relieve your conscience. Yes, Lupin, Dugrival used to work on the same lines as yourself. Oh, not on the same scale! . . . We were modest people: a louis here, a louis there . . . a purse or two which we trained Gabriel to pick up at the races . . . And, in this way, we had made our little pile . . . just enough to buy a small place in the country.'

'I prefer it that way,' said Lupin.

'That's all right! I'm only telling you, so that you may know that I am not a beginner and that you have nothing to hope for. A rescue? No. The room in which we now are communicates with my bedroom. It has a private outlet of which nobody knows. It was Dugrival's special apartment. He used to see his friends here. He kept his implements and tools here, his disguises . . . his telephone even, as you perceive. So there's no hope, you see. Your accomplices have given up looking for you here. I have sent them off on another track. Your goose is cooked. Do you begin to realize the position?'

'Yes.'

'Then sign the cheques.'

'And, when I have signed them, shall I be free?'

'I must cash them first.'

'And after that?'

'After that, on my soul, as I hope to be saved, you will be free.'

'I don't trust you.'

'Have you any choice?'

'That's true. Hand me the cheques.'

She unfastened Lupin's right hand, gave him a pen and said: 'Don't forget that the four cheques require four different signatures and that the handwriting has to be altered in each case.'

'Never fear.'

He signed the cheques.

'Gabriel,' said the widow, 'it is ten o'clock. If I am not back by twelve, it will mean that this scoundrel has played me one of his tricks. At twelve o'clock, blow out his brains. I am leaving you the revolver with which your uncle shot himself. There are five bullets left out of the six. That will be ample.'

She left the room, humming a tune as she went.

Lupin mumbled: 'I wouldn't give twopence for my life.'

He shut his eyes for an instant and then, suddenly, said to Gabriel: 'How much?'

And, when the other did not appear to understand, he grew irritated.

'I mean what I say. How much? Answer me, can't you? We drive the same trade, you and I. I steal, thou stealest, we steal. So we ought to come to terms: that's what we are here for. Well? Is it a bargain? Shall we clear out together. I will give you a post in my gang, an easy, well-paid post. How much do you want for yourself? Ten thousand? Twenty thousand? Fix your own price; don't be shy. There's plenty to be had for the asking.'

An angry shiver passed through his frame as he saw the impassive face of his keeper.

'Oh, the beggar won't even answer! Why, you can't have been so fond of old Dugrival as all that! Listen to me: if you consent to release me . . . '

But he interrupted himself. The young man's eyes wore the cruel expression which he knew so well. What was the use of trying to move him?

'Hang it all!' he snarled. 'I'm not going to croak here, like a dog! Oh, if I could only . . . '

Stiffening all his muscles, he tried to burst his bonds, making a violent effort that drew a cry of pain from him; and he fell back upon his bed, exhausted.

'Well, well,' he muttered, after a moment, 'it's as the widow said: my goose is cooked. Nothing to be done. *De profundis*, Lupin.'

A quarter of an hour passed, half an hour . . .

Gabriel, moving closer to Lupin, saw that his eyes were shut and that his breath came evenly, like that of a man sleeping. But Lupin said: 'Don't imagine that I'm asleep, youngster. No, people don't sleep at a moment like this. Only I am consoling myself. Needs must, eh? . . . And then I am thinking of what is to come after . . . Exactly. I have a little theory of my own about that. You wouldn't think it, to look at me, but I believe in metempsychosis, in the transmigration of souls. It would take too long to explain, however . . . I say, boy . . . suppose we shook hands before we part? You won't? Then goodbye. Good health and a long life to you, Gabriel! . . . '

He closed his eyelids and did not stir again before Mme Dugrival's return.

The widow entered with a lively step, at a few minutes before twelve. She seemed greatly excited.

'I have the money,' she said to her nephew. 'Run away. I'll join you in the motor down below.'

'But . . . '

'I don't want your help to finish him off. I can do that alone. Still, if you feel like seeing the sort of a face a rogue can pull . . . Pass me the weapon.'

Gabriel handed her the revolver and the widow continued: 'Have you burnt our papers?'

'Yes.'

'Then to work. And, as soon as he's done for, be off. The shots may bring the neighbours. They must find both the flats empty.'

She went up to the bed.

'Are you ready, Lupin?'

'Ready's not the word: I'm burning with impatience.'

'Have you any request to make of me?'

'None.'

'Then . . . '

'One word, though.'

'What is it?'

'If I meet Dugrival in the next world, what message am I to give him from you?'

She shrugged her shoulders and put the barrel of the revolver to Lupin's temple.

'That's it,' he said, 'and be sure your hand doesn't shake, my dear lady. It won't hurt you, I swear. Are you ready? At the word of command, eh? One . . . two . . . three . . . '

The widow pulled the trigger. A shot rang out.

'Is this death?' said Lupin. 'That's funny! I should have thought it was something much more different from life!'

There was a second shot. Gabriel snatched the weapon from his aunt's hands and examined it.

'Ah,' he exclaimed, 'the bullets have been removed! . . . There are only the percussion-caps left! . . . '

His aunt and he stood motionless, for a moment, and confused.

'Impossible!' she blurted out. 'Who could have done it? . . . An inspector? . . . The examining-magistrate? . . . '

She stopped and, in a low voice: 'Hark . . . I hear a noise . . . '

They listened and the widow went into the hall. She returned, furious, exasperated by her failure and by the scare which she had received.

'There's nobody there . . . It must have been the neighbours going out . . . We have plenty of time . . . Ah, Lupin, you were beginning to make merry! . . . The knife, Gabriel.'

'It's in my room.'

'Go and fetch it.'

Gabriel hurried away. The widow stamped with rage.

'I've sworn to do it! . . . You've got to suffer, my fine fellow! . . . I swore to Dugrival that I would do it and I have repeated my oath every morning and evening since . . . I have taken it on my knees, yes, on my knees, before Heaven that listens to me! It's my duty and my right to revenge my dead husband! . . . By the way, Lupin, you don't look quite as merry as you did! . . . Lord, one would almost think you were afraid! . . . He's afraid! He's afraid! I can see it in his eyes! . . . Come along, Gabriel, my boy! . . . Look at his eyes! . . . Look at his lips! . . . He's trembling! . . . Give me the knife, so that I may dig it into his heart while he's shivering . . . Oh, you coward! . . . Quick, quick, Gabriel, the knife! . . . '

'I can't find it anywhere,' said the young man, running back in dismay. 'It has gone from my room! I can't make it out!'

'Never mind!' cried the Widow Dugrival, half demented. 'All the better! I will do the business myself.'

She seized Lupin by the throat, clutched him with her ten fingers, digging her nails into his flesh, and began to squeeze with all her might. Lupin uttered a hoarse rattle and gave himself up for lost.

Suddenly, there was a crash at the window. One of the panes was smashed to pieces.

'What's that? What is it?' stammered the widow, drawing herself erect, in alarm.

Gabriel, who had turned even paler than usual, murmured: 'I don't know . . . I can't think . . . '

'Who can have done it?' said the widow.

She dared not move, waiting for what would come next. And one thing above all terrified her, the fact that there was no missile on the floor around them, although the pane of glass, as was clearly visible, had given way before the crash of a heavy and fairly large object, a stone, probably.

After a while, she looked under the bed, under the chest of drawers.

'Nothing,' she said.

'No,' said her nephew, who was also looking.

And, resuming her seat, she said: 'I feel frightened . . . my arms fail me . . . you finish him off . . . '

Gabriel confessed: 'I'm frightened also.'

'Still . . . still,' she stammered, 'it's got to be done . . . I swore it . . . '

Making one last effort, she returned to Lupin and gasped his neck with her stiff fingers. But Lupin, who was watching her pallid face, received a very clear sensation that she would not have the courage to kill him. To her he was becoming something sacred, invulnerable. A mysterious power was protecting him against every attack, a power which had already saved him three times by inexplicable means and which would find other means to protect him against the wiles of death.

She said to him, in a hoarse voice: 'How you must be laughing at me!'

'Not at all, upon my word. I should feel frightened myself, in your place.'

'Nonsense, you scum of the earth! You imagine that you will be rescued . . . that your friends are waiting outside? It's out of the question, my fine fellow.'

'I know. It's not they defending me . . . nobody's defending me . . . '

'Well, then? . . . '

'Well, all the same, there's something strange at the bottom of it, something fantastic and miraculous that makes your flesh creep, my fine lady.'

'You villain! . . . You'll be laughing on the other side of your mouth before long.'

'I doubt it.'

'You wait and see.'

She reflected once more and said to her nephew: 'What would you do?'

'Fasten his arm again and let's be off,' he replied.

A hideous suggestion! It meant condemning Lupin to the most horrible of all deaths, death by starvation.

'No,' said the widow. 'He might still find a means of escape. I know something better than that.'

She took down the receiver of the telephone, waited and asked: 'Number 822.48, please.'

And, after a second or two: 'Hullo! . . . Is that the Criminal Investigation Department? . . . Is Chief-inspector Ganimard there? . . . In twenty minutes, you say? . . . I'm sorry! . . . However! . . . When he comes, give him this message from Mme Dugrival . . . Yes, Mme Nicolas Dugrival . . . Ask him to come to my flat. Tell him to open the looking-glass door of my wardrobe; and, when he has done so, he will see that the wardrobe hides an outlet which makes my bedroom communicate with two other rooms. In one of these, he will find a man bound hand and foot. It is the thief, Dugrival's murderer . . . You don't believe me? . . . Tell M. Ganimard; he'll believe me right enough . . . Oh, I was almost forgetting to give you the man's name: Arsène Lupin!'

And, without another word, she replaced the receiver.

'There, Lupin, that's done. After all, I would just as soon have my revenge this way. How I shall hold my sides when I read the reports of the Lupin trial! . . . Are you coming, Gabriel?'

'Yes, aunt.'

'Goodbye, Lupin. You and I shan't see each other again, I expect, for we are going abroad. But I promise to send you some sweets while you're in prison.'

'Chocolates, mother! We'll eat them together!'

'Goodbye.'

'*Au revoir.*'

The widow went out with her nephew, leaving Lupin fastened down to the bed.

He at once moved his free arm and tried to release himself; but he realized, at the first attempt, that he would never have the strength to break the wire strands that bound him. Exhausted with fever and pain, what could he do in the twenty minutes or so that were left to him before Ganimard's arrival?

Nor did he count upon his friends. True, he had been thrice saved from death; but this was evidently due to an astounding series of accidents and not to any interference on the part of his allies. Otherwise they would not have contented themselves with these extraordinary manifestations, but would have rescued him for good and all.

No, he must abandon all hope. Ganimard was coming. Ganimard would find him there. It was inevitable. There was no getting away from the fact.

And the prospect of what was coming irritated him singularly. He already heard his old enemy's gibes ringing in his ears. He foresaw the roars of laughter with which the incredible news would be greeted on the morrow. To be arrested in action, so to speak, on the battlefield, by an imposing detachment of adversaries, was one thing: but to be arrested, or rather picked up, scraped up, gathered up, in such condition, was really too silly. And Lupin, who had so often scoffed at others, felt all the ridicule that was falling to his share in this ending of the Dugrival business, all the bathos of allowing himself to be caught in the widow's infernal trap and finally of being 'served up' to the police like a dish of game, roasted to a turn and nicely seasoned.

'Blow the widow!' he growled. 'I had rather she had cut my throat and done with it.'

He pricked up his ears. Someone was moving in the next room. Ganimard! No. Great as his eagerness would be, he could not be there yet. Besides, Ganimard would not have acted like that, would not have opened the door as gently as that other person was doing. What other person? Lupin remembered the three miraculous interventions to which he owed his life. Was it possible that there was really somebody who had protected him against the widow, and that that somebody was now attempting to rescue him? But, if so, who?

Unseen by Lupin, the stranger stooped behind the bed. Lupin heard the sound of the pliers attacking the wire strands and releasing him little by little. First his chest was freed, then his arms, then his legs.

And a voice said to him: 'You must get up and dress.'

Feeling very weak, he half-raised himself in bed at the moment when the stranger rose from her stooping posture.

'Who are you?' he whispered. 'Who are you?'

And a great surprise over came him.

By his side stood a woman, a woman dressed in black, with a lace shawl over her head, covering part of her face. And the woman, as far as he could judge, was young and of a graceful and slender stature.

'Who are you?' he repeated.

'You must come now,' said the woman. 'There's no time to lose.'

'Can I?' asked Lupin, making a desperate effort. 'I doubt if I have the strength.'

'Drink this.'

She poured some milk into a cup; and, as she handed it to him, her lace opened, leaving the face uncovered.

'You!' he stammered. 'It's you! . . . It's you who . . . it was you who were . . .'

He stared in amazement at this woman whose features presented so striking a resemblance to Gabriel's, whose delicate, regular face had the same pallor, whose mouth wore the same hard and forbidding expression. No sister could have borne so great a likeness to her brother. There was not a doubt possible: it was the identical person. And, without believing for a moment that Gabriel had concealed himself in a woman's clothes, Lupin, on the contrary, received the distinct impression that it was a woman standing beside him and that the stripling who had pursued him with his hatred and struck him with the dagger was in very deed a woman. In order to follow their trade with greater ease, the Dugrival pair had accustomed her to disguise herself as a boy.

'You . . . you . . . !' he repeated. 'Who would have suspected . . . ?'

She emptied the contents of a phial into the cup.

'Drink this cordial,' she said.

He hesitated, thinking of poison.

She added: 'It was I who saved you.'

'Of course, of course,' he said. 'It was you who removed the bullets from the revolver?'

'Yes.'

'And you who hid the knife?'

'Here it is, in my pocket.'

'And you who smashed the window-pane while your aunt was throttling me?'

'Yes, it was I, with the paper-weight on the table: I threw it into the street.'

'But why? Why?' he asked, in utter amazement.

'Drink the cordial.'

'Didn't you want me to die? But then why did you stab me to begin with?'

'Drink the cordial.'

He emptied the cup at a draught, without quite knowing the reason of his sudden confidence.

'Dress yourself . . . quickly,' she commanded, retiring to the window.

He obeyed and she came back to him, for he had dropped into a chair, exhausted.

'We must go now, we must, we have only just time . . . Collect your strength.'

She bent forward a little, so that he might lean on her shoulder, and turned toward the door and the staircase.

And Lupin walked as one walks in a dream, one of those queer dreams in which the most inconsequent things occur, a dream that was the happy sequel of the terrible nightmare in which he had lived for the past fortnight.

A thought struck him, however. He began to laugh.

'Poor Ganimard! Upon my word, the fellow has no luck, I would give twopence to see him coming to arrest me.'

After descending the staircase with the aid of his companion, who supported him with incredible vigour, he found himself in the street, opposite a motor-car into which she helped him to mount.

'Right away,' she said to the driver.

Lupin, dazed by the open air and the speed at which they were travelling, hardly took stock of the drive and of the incidents on the road. He recovered all his consciousness when he found himself at home in one of the flats which he occupied, looked after by his servant, to whom the girl gave a few rapid instructions.

'You can go,' he said to the man.

But, when the girl turned to go as well, he held her back by a fold of her dress.

'No . . . no . . . you must first explain . . . Why did you save me? Did you return unknown to your aunt? But why did you save me? Was it from pity?'

She did not answer. With her figure drawn up and her head flung back a little, she retained her hard and impenetrable air. Nevertheless, he thought he noticed that the lines of her mouth showed not so much cruelty as bitterness. Her eyes, her beautiful dark eyes, revealed melancholy. And Lupin, without as yet understanding, received a vague intuition of what was passing within her. He seized her hand. She pushed him away, with a start of revolt in which he felt hatred, almost repulsion. And, when he insisted, she cried: 'Let me be, will you? . . . Let me be! . . . Can't you see that I detest you?'

They looked at each other for a moment, Lupin disconcerted, she quivering and full of uneasiness, her pale face all flushed with unwonted colour.

He said to her, gently: 'If you detested me, you should have let me die . . . It was simple enough . . . Why didn't you?'

'Why? . . . Why? . . . How do I know? . . . '

Her face contracted. With a sudden movement, she hid it in her two hands; and he saw tears trickle between her fingers.

Greatly touched, he thought of addressing her in fond words, such as one would use to a little girl whom one wished to console, and of giving her good advice and saving her, in his turn, and snatching her from the bad life which she was leading, perhaps against her better nature.

But such words would have sounded ridiculous, coming from his lips, and he did not know what to say, now that he understood the whole story and was able to picture the young woman sitting beside his sick-bed, nursing the man whom she had wounded, admiring his pluck and gaiety, becoming attached to him, falling in love with him and thrice over, probably in spite of herself, under a sort of instinctive impulse, amid fits of spite and rage, saving him from death.

And all this was so strange, so unforeseen; Lupin was so much unmanned by his astonishment, that, this time, he did not try to retain her when she made for the door, backward, without taking her eyes from him.

She lowered her head, smiled for an instant and disappeared.

He rang the bell, quickly.

'Follow that woman,' he said to his man. 'Or no, stay where you are . . . After all, it is better so . . . '

He sat brooding for a while, possessed by the girl's image. Then he revolved in his mind all that curious, stirring and tragic adventure, in which he had been so very near succumbing; and, taking a hand-glass from the table, he gazed for a long time and with a certain self-complacency at his features, which illness and pain had not succeeded in impairing to any great extent.

'Good looks count for something, after all!' he muttered.

The Red Silk Scarf

On leaving his house one morning, at his usual early hour for going to the Law Courts, Chief-inspector Ganimard noticed the curious behaviour of an individual who was walking along the Rue Per-golèse in front of him. Shabbily dressed and wearing a straw hat, though the day was the first of December, the man stooped at every thirty or forty yards to fasten his boot-lace, or pick up his stick, or for some other reason. And, each time, he took a little piece of orange-peel from his pocket and laid it stealthily on the curb of the pavement. It was probably a mere display of eccentricity, a childish amusement to which no one else would have paid atten-tion; but Ganimard was one of those shrewd observers who are indifferent to nothing that strikes their eyes and who are never satisfied until they know the secret cause of things. He therefore began to follow the man.

Now, at the moment when the fellow was turning to the right, into the Avenue de la Grande-Armée, the inspector caught him exchang-ing signals with a boy of twelve or thirteen, who was walking along the houses on the left-hand side. Twenty yards farther, the man stooped and turned up the bottom of his trousers legs. A bit of orange-peel marked the place. At the same moment, the boy stopped and, with a piece of chalk, drew a white cross, surrounded by a circle, on the wall of the house next to him.

The two continued on their way. A minute later, a fresh halt. The strange individual picked up a pin and dropped a piece of orange-peel; and the boy at once made a second cross on the wall and again drew a white circle round it.

'By Jove!' thought the chief-inspector, with a grunt of satisfaction. 'This is rather promising . . . What on earth can those two merchants be plotting?'

The two 'merchants' went down the Avenue Friedland and the Rue du Faubourg-Saint-Honoré, but nothing occurred that was worthy of special mention. The double performance was repeated at almost regular intervals and, so to speak, mechanically. Nevertheless, it was obvious, on the one hand, that the man with the orange-peel did not do his part of the business until after he had picked out with a glance the house that was to be marked and, on the other hand, that the boy did not mark that particular house until after he had observed his companion's signal. It was certain, therefore, that there was an agreement between the two; and the proceedings presented no small interest in the chief-inspector's eyes.

At the Place Beauveau the man hesitated. Then, apparently making up his mind, he twice turned up and twice turned down the bottom of his trousers legs. Hereupon, the boy sat down on the curb, opposite the sentry who was mounting guard outside the Ministry of the Interior, and marked the flagstone with two little crosses contained within two circles. The same ceremony was gone through a little further on, when they reached the Elysée. Only, on the pavement where the President's sentry was marching up and down, there were three signs instead of two.

'Hang it all!' muttered Ganimard, pale with excitement and thinking, in spite of himself, of his inveterate enemy, Lupin, whose name came to his mind whenever a mysterious circumstance presented itself. 'Hang it all, what does it mean?'

He was nearly collaring and questioning the two 'merchants'. But he was too clever to commit so gross a blunder. The man with the orange-peel had now lit a cigarette; and the boy, also placing a cigarette-end between his lips, had gone up to him, apparently with the object of asking for a light.

They exchanged a few words. Quick as thought, the boy handed his companion an object which looked – at least, so the inspector believed – like a revolver. They both bent over this object; and the man, standing with his face to the wall, put his hand six times in his pocket and made a movement as though he were loading a weapon.

As soon as this was done, they walked briskly to the Rue de Surène; and the inspector, who followed them as closely as he was able to do without attracting their attention, saw them enter the gateway of an old house of which all the shutters were closed, with the exception of those on the third or top floor.

He hurried in after them. At the end of the carriage-entrance he saw a large courtyard, with a house-painter's sign at the back and a staircase on the left.

He went up the stairs and, as soon as he reached the first floor, ran still faster, because he heard, right up at the top, a din as of a free-fight.

When he came to the last landing he found the door open. He entered, listened for a second, caught the sound of a struggle, rushed to the room from which the sound appeared to proceed and remained standing on the threshold, very much out of breath and greatly surprised to see the man of the orange-peel and the boy banging the floor with chairs.

At that moment a third person walked out of an adjoining room. It was a young man of twenty-eight or thirty, wearing a pair of short whiskers in addition to his moustache, spectacles, and a smoking-jacket with an astrakhan collar and looking like a foreigner, a Russian.

'Good morning, Ganimard,' he said. And turning to the two companions, 'Thank you, my friends, and all my congratulations on the successful result. Here's the reward I promised you.'

He gave them a hundred-franc note, pushed them outside and shut both doors.

'I am sorry, old chap,' he said to Ganimard. 'I wanted to talk to you . . . wanted to talk to you badly.'

He offered him his hand and, seeing that the inspector remained flabbergasted and that his face was still distorted with anger, he exclaimed: 'Why, you don't seem to understand! . . . And yet it's clear enough . . . I wanted to see you particularly . . . So what could I do?' And, pretending to reply to an objection, 'No, no, old chap,' he continued. 'You're quite wrong. If I had written or telephoned, you would not have come . . . or else you would have come with a regiment. Now I wanted to see you all alone; and I thought the best thing was to send those two decent fellows to meet you, with orders to scatter bits of orange-peel and draw crosses and circles, in short, to mark out your road to this place . . . Why, you look quite bewildered! What is it? Perhaps you don't recognize me? Lupin . . . Arsène Lupin . . . Ransack your memory . . . Doesn't the name remind you of anything?'

'You dirty scoundrel!' Ganimard snarled between his teeth.

Lupin seemed greatly distressed and, in an affectionate voice: 'Are you vexed? Yes, I can see it in your eyes . . . The Dugrival business, I suppose? I ought to have waited for you to come and take me in charge? . . . There now, the thought never occurred to me! I promise you, next time . . . '

'You scum of the earth!' growled Ganimard.

'And I thinking I was giving you a treat! Upon my word, I did. I said to myself, "That dear old Ganimard! We haven't met for an age. He'll simply rush at me when he sees me!"'

Ganimard, who had not yet stirred a limb, seemed to be waking from his stupor. He looked around him, looked at Lupin, visibly asked himself whether he would not do well to rush at him in reality and then, controlling himself, took hold of a chair and settled himself in it, as though he had suddenly made up his mind to listen to his enemy.

'Speak,' he said. 'And don't waste my time with any nonsense. I'm in a hurry.'

'That's it,' said Lupin, 'let's talk. You can't imagine a quieter place than this. It's an old manor-house, which once stood in the open country, and it belongs to the Duc de Rochelaure. The duke, who has never lived in it, lets this floor to me and the outhouses to a painter and decorator. I always keep up a few establishments of this kind: it's a sound, practical plan. Here, in spite of my looking like a Russian nobleman, I am M. Daubreuil, an ex-cabinet-minister . . . You understand, I had to select a rather overstocked profession, so as not to attract attention . . .'

'Do you think I care a hang about all this?' said Ganimard, interrupting him.

'Quite right, I'm wasting words and you're in a hurry. Forgive me. I shan't be long now . . . Five minutes, that's all . . . I'll start at once . . . Have a cigar? No? Very well, no more will I.'

He sat down also, drummed his fingers on the table, while thinking, and began in this fashion.

'On the 17th of October, 1599, on a warm and sunny autumn day . . . Do you follow me? . . . But, now that I come to think of it, is it really necessary to go back to the reign of Henry IV, and tell you all about the building of the Pont-Neuf? No, I don't suppose you are very well up in French history; and I should only end by muddling you. Suffice it, then, for you to know that, last night, at one o'clock in the morning, a boatman passing under the last arch of the Pont-Neuf aforesaid, along the left bank of the river, heard something drop into the front part of his barge. The thing had been flung from the bridge and its evident destination was the bottom of the Seine. The bargee's dog rushed forward, barking, and, when the man reached the end of his craft, he saw the animal worrying a piece of newspaper that had served to wrap up a number of objects. He took from the dog such of the contents as had not fallen into the water, went to his cabin and examined them carefully. The result struck him as interesting; and, as the man is connected with one of my friends, he sent to let me know. This morning I was waked up and placed in possession of the facts and of the objects which the man had collected. Here they are.'

He pointed to them, spread out on a table. There were, first of all, the torn pieces of a newspaper. Next came a large cut-glass inkstand, with a long piece of string fastened to the lid. There was a bit of broken glass and a sort of flexible cardboard, reduced to shreds. Lastly, there was a piece of bright scarlet silk, ending in a tassel of the same material and colour.

'You see our exhibits, friend of my youth,' said Lupin. 'No doubt, the problem would be more easily solved if we had the other objects which went overboard owing to the stupidity of the dog. But it seems to me, all the same, that we ought to be able to manage, with a little reflection and intelligence. And those are just your great qualities. How does the business strike you?'

Ganimard did not move a muscle. He was willing to stand Lupin's chaff, but his dignity commanded him not to speak a single word in answer nor even to give a nod or shake of the head that might have been taken to express approval or or criticism.

'I see that we are entirely of one mind,' continued Lupin, without appearing to remark the chief-inspector's silence. 'And I can sum up the matter briefly, as told us by these exhibits. Yesterday evening, between nine and twelve o'clock, a showily dressed young woman was wounded with a knife and then caught round the throat and choked to death by a well-dressed gentleman, wearing a single eyeglass and interested in racing, with whom the aforesaid showily dressed young lady had been eating three meringues and a coffee éclair.'

Lupin lit a cigarette and, taking Ganimard by the sleeve: 'Aha, that's up against you, chief-inspector! You thought that, in the domain of police deductions, such feats as those were prohibited to outsiders! Wrong, sir! Lupin juggles with inferences and deductions for all the world like a detective in a novel. My proofs are dazzling and absolutely simple.'

And, pointing to the objects one by one, as he demonstrated his statement, he resumed.

'I said, after nine o'clock yesterday evening. This scrap of news-paper bears yesterday's date, with the words, "Evening edition". Also, you will see here, pasted to the paper, a bit of one of those yellow wrappers in which the subscribers' copies are sent out. These copies are always delivered by the nine o'clock post. Therefore, it was after nine o'clock. I said, a well-dressed man. Please observe that this tiny piece of glass has the round hole of a single eyeglass at one of the edges and that the single eyeglass is an essentially aristocratic article of wear. This well-dressed man walked into a pastry-cook's shop. Here is the very thin cardboard, shaped like a box, and still showing a little of the cream of the meringues and éclairs which were packed in it in the usual way. Having got his parcel, the gentleman with the eyeglass joined a young person whose eccentricity in the matter of dress is pretty clearly indicated by this bright-red silk scarf. Having joined her, for some reason as yet unknown he first stabbed her with a knife and then strangled her with the help of this same scarf. Take your magnifying glass, chief-inspector, and you will see, on the silk, stains of a darker red which are, here, the marks of a knife wiped on the scarf and, there, the marks of a hand, covered with blood, clutching the material. Having committed the murder, his next business is to leave no trace behind him. So he takes from his pocket, first, the newspaper to which he subscribes – a racing-paper, as you will see by glancing at the contents of this scrap; and you will have no difficulty in discovering the title – and, secondly, a cord, which, on inspection, turns out to be a length of whip-cord. These two details prove – do they not? – that our man is interested in racing and that he himself rides. Next, he picks up the fragments of his eyeglass, the cord of which has been broken in the struggle. He takes a pair of scissors – observe the hacking of the scissors – and cuts off the stained part of the scarf, leaving the other end, no doubt, in his victim's clenched hands. He makes a ball of the confectioner's cardboard box. He also puts in certain things that would have betrayed him, such as the knife, which must have slipped into the Seine. He wraps everything in the newspaper, ties it with the cord and fastens this cut-glass inkstand to it, as a make-weight. Then he makes himself scarce. A little later, the parcel falls into the waterman's barge. And there you are. Oof, it's hot work! . . . What do you say to the story?'

He looked at Ganimard to see what impression his speech had produced on the inspector. Ganimard did not depart from his attitude of silence.

Lupin began to laugh.

'As a matter of fact, you're annoyed and surprised. But you're suspicious as well: "Why should that confounded Lupin hand the business over to me," say you, "instead of keeping it for himself, hunting down the murderer and rifling his pockets, if there was a robbery?" The question is quite logical, of course. But – there is a "but" – I have no time, you see. I am full up with work at the present moment: a burglary in London, another at Lausanne, an exchange of children at Marseilles, to say nothing of having to save a young girl who is at this moment shadowed by death. That's always the way: it never rains but it pours. So I said to myself, "Suppose I handed the business over to my dear old Ganimard? Now that it is half-solved for him, he is quite capable of succeeding. And what a service I shall be doing him! How magnificently he will be able to distinguish himself!" No sooner said than done. At eight o'clock in the morning, I sent the joker with the orange-peel to meet you. You swallowed the bait; and you were here by nine, all on edge and eager for the fray.'

Lupin rose from his chair. He went over to the inspector and, with his eyes in Ganimard's, said: 'That's all. You now know the whole story. Presently, you will know the victim: some ballet-dancer, probably, some singer at a music-hall. On the other hand, the chances are that the criminal lives near the Pont-Neuf, most likely on the left bank. Lastly, here are all the exhibits. I make you a present of them. Set to work. I shall only keep this end of the scarf. If ever you want to piece the scarf together, bring me the other end, the one which the police will find round the victim's neck. Bring it me in four weeks from now to the day, that is to say, on the 29th of December, at ten o'clock in the morning. You can be sure of finding me here. And don't be afraid: this is all perfectly serious, friend of my youth; I swear it is. No humbug, honour bright. You can go straight ahead. Oh, by the way, when you arrest the fellow with the eyeglass, be a bit careful: he is left-handed! Goodbye, old dear, and good luck to you!'

Lupin spun round on his heel, went to the door, opened it and disappeared before Ganimard had even thought of taking a decision. The inspector rushed after him, but at once found that the handle of the door, by some trick of mechanism which he did not know, refused to turn. It took him ten minutes to unscrew the lock and ten minutes more to unscrew the lock of the hall-door. By the time that he had scrambled down the three flights of stairs, Ganimard had given up all hope of catching Arsène Lupin.

Besides, he was not thinking of it. Lupin inspired him with a queer, complex feeling, made up of fear, hatred, involuntary admiration and also the vague instinct that he, Ganimard, in spite of all his efforts, in spite of the persistency of his endeavours, would never get the better of this particular adversary. He pursued him from a sense of duty and pride, but with the continual dread of being taken in by that formidable hoaxer and scouted and fooled in the face of a public that was always only too willing to laugh at the chief-inspector's mishaps.

This business of the red scarf, in particular, struck him as most suspicious. It was interesting, certainly, in more ways than one, but so very improbable! And Lupin's explanation, apparently so logical, would never stand the test of a severe examination!

'No,' said Ganimard, 'this is all swank: a parcel of suppositions and guesswork based upon nothing at all. I'm not to be caught with chaff.'

* * *

When he reached the headquarters of police, at 36 Quai des Orfèvres, he had quite made up his mind to treat the incident as though it had never happened.

He went up to the Criminal Investigation Department. Here, one of his fellow-inspectors said: 'Seen the chief?'

'No.'

'He was asking for you just now.'

'Oh, was he?'

'Yes, you had better go after him.'

'Where?'

'To the Rue de Berne . . . there was a murder there last night.'

'Oh! Who's the victim?'

'I don't know exactly . . . a music-hall singer, I believe.'

Ganimard simply muttered: 'By Jove!'

Twenty minutes later he stepped out of the underground railway-station and made for the Rue de Berne.

The victim, who was known in the theatrical world by her stage-name of Jenny Saphir, occupied a small flat on the second floor of one of the houses. A policeman took the chief-inspector upstairs and showed him the way, through two sitting-rooms, to a bedroom, where he found the magistrates in charge of the inquiry, together with the divisional surgeon and M. Dudouis, the head of the detective-service.

Ganimard started at the first glance which he gave into the room. He saw, lying on a sofa, the corpse of a young woman whose hands clutched a strip of red silk! One of the shoulders, which appeared above the low-cut bodice, bore the marks of two wounds surrounded with clotted blood. The distorted and almost blackened features still bore an expression of frenzied terror.

The divisional surgeon, who had just finished his examination, said: 'My first conclusions are very clear. The victim was twice stabbed with a dagger and afterward strangled. The immediate cause of death was asphyxia.'

'By Jove!' thought Ganimard again, remembering Lupin's words and the picture which he had drawn of the crime.

The examining-magistrate objected: 'But the neck shows no discoloration.'

'She may have been strangled with a napkin or a handkerchief,' said the doctor.

'Most probably,' said the chief detective, 'with this silk scarf, which the victim was wearing and a piece of which remains, as though she had clung to it with her two hands to protect herself.'

'But why does only that piece remain?' asked the magistrate. 'What has become of the other?'

'The other may have been stained with blood and carried off by the murderer. You can plainly distinguish the hurried slashing of the scissors.'

'By Jove!' said Ganimard, between his teeth, for the third time. 'That brute of a Lupin saw everything without seeing a thing!'

'And what about the motive of the murder?' asked the magistrate. 'The locks have been forced, the cupboards turned upside down. Have you anything to tell me, M. Dudouis?'

The chief of the detective-service replied: 'I can at least suggest a supposition, derived from the statements made by the servant. The victim, who enjoyed a greater reputation on account of her looks than through her talent as a singer, went to Russia, two years ago, and brought back with her a magnificent sapphire, which she appears to have received from some person of importance at the court. Since then, she went by the name of Jenny Saphir and seems generally to have been very proud of that present, although, for prudence sake, she never wore it. I dare say that we shall not be far out if we presume the theft of the sapphire to have been the cause of the crime.'

'But did the maid know where the stone was?'

'No, nobody did. And the disorder of the room would tend to prove that the murderer did not know either.'

'We will question the maid,' said the examining-magistrate.

M. Dudouis took the chief-inspector aside and said: 'You're looking very old-fashioned, Ganimard. What's the matter? Do you suspect anything?'

'Nothing at all, chief.'

'That's a pity. We could do with a bit of showy work in the department. This is one of a number of crimes, all of the same class, of which we have failed to discover the perpetrator. This time we want the criminal . . . and quickly!'

'A difficult job, chief.'

'It's got to be done. Listen to me, Ganimard. According to what the maid says, Jenny Saphir led a very regular life. For a month past she was in the habit of frequently receiving visits, on her return from the music-hall, that is to say, at about half-past ten, from a man who would stay until midnight or so. "He's a society man," Jenny Saphir used to say, "and he wants to marry me." This society man took every precaution to avoid being seen, such as turning up his coat-collar and lowering the brim of his hat when he passed the porter's box. And Jenny Saphir always made a point of sending away her maid, even before he came. This is the man whom we have to find.'

'Has he left no traces?'

'None at all. It is obvious that we have to deal with a very clever scoundrel, who prepared his crime beforehand and committed it with every possible chance of escaping unpunished. His arrest would be a great feather in our cap. I rely on you, Ganimard.'

'Ah, you rely on me, chief?' replied the inspector. 'Well, we shall see . . . we shall see . . . I don't say no . . . Only . . . '

He seemed in a very nervous condition, and his agitation struck M. Dudouis.

'Only,' continued Ganimard, 'only I swear . . . do you hear, chief? I swear . . . '

'What do you swear?'

'Nothing . . . We shall see, chief . . . we shall see . . . '

Ganimard did not finish his sentence until he was outside, alone. And he finished it aloud, stamping his foot, in a tone of the most violent anger: 'Only, I swear to Heaven that the arrest shall be effected by my own means, without my employing a single one of the clues with which that villain has supplied me. Ah, no! Ah, no! . . . '

Railing against Lupin, furious at being mixed up in this business and resolved, nevertheless, to get to the bottom of it, he wandered aimlessly about the streets. His brain was seething with irritation; and he tried to adjust his ideas a little and to discover, among the chaotic facts, some trifling detail, unperceived by all, unsuspected by Lupin himself, that might lead him to success.

He lunched hurriedly at a bar, resumed his stroll and suddenly stopped, petrified, astounded and confused. He was walking under the gateway of the very house in the Rue de Surène to which Lupin had enticed him a few hours earlier! A force stronger than his own will was drawing him there once more. The solution of the problem lay there. There and there alone were all the elements of the truth. Do and say what he would, Lupin's assertions were so precise, his calculations so accurate, that, worried to the innermost recesses of his being by so prodigious a display of perspicacity, he could not do other than take up the work at the point where his enemy had left it.

Abandoning all further resistance, he climbed the three flights of stairs. The door of the flat was open. No one had touched the exhibits. He put them in his pocket and walked away.

From that moment, he reasoned and acted, so to speak, mechanically, under the influence of the master whom he could not choose but obey.

Admitting that the unknown person whom he was seeking lived in the neighbourhood of the Pont-Neuf, it became necessary to discover, somewhere between that bridge and the Rue de Berne, the first-class confectioner's shop, open in the evenings, at which the cakes were bought. This did not take long to find. A pastry-cook near the Gare Saint-Lazare showed him some little cardboard boxes, identical in material and shape with the one in Ganimard's possession. Moreover, one of the shop-girls remembered having served, on the previous evening, a gentleman whose face was almost concealed in the collar of his fur coat, but whose eyeglass she had happened to notice.

'That's one clue checked,' thought the inspector. 'Our man wears an eyeglass.'

He next collected the pieces of the racing-paper and showed them to a newsvendor, who easily recognized the *Turf Illustré*. Ganimard at once went to the offices of the *Turf* and asked to see the list of subscribers. Going through the list, he jotted down the names and addresses of all those who lived anywhere near the Pont-Neuf and principally – because Lupin had said so – those on the left bank of the river.

He then went back to the Criminal Investigation Department, took half a dozen men and packed them off with the necessary instructions.

At seven o'clock in the evening, the last of these men returned and brought good news with him. A certain M. Prévailles, a subscriber to the *Turf*, occupied an entresol flat on the Quai des Augustins. On the previous evening, he left his place, wearing a fur coat, took his letters and his paper, the *Turf Illustré*, from the porter's wife, walked away and returned home at midnight. This M. Prévailles wore a single eyeglass. He was a regular race-goer and himself owned several hacks which he either rode himself or jobbed out.

The inquiry had taken so short a time and the results obtained were so exactly in accordance with Lupin's predictions that Ganimard felt quite overcome on hearing the detective's report. Once more he was measuring the prodigious extent of the resources at Lupin's disposal. Never in the course of his life – and Ganimard was already well-advanced in years – had he come across such perspicacity, such a quick and far-seeing mind.

He went in search of M. Dudouis.

'Everything's ready, chief. Have you a warrant?'

'Eh?'

'I said, everything is ready for the arrest, chief.'

'You know the name of Jenny Saphir's murderer?'

'Yes.'

'But how? Explain yourself.'

Ganimard had a sort of scruple of conscience, blushed a little and nevertheless replied: 'An accident, chief. The murderer threw everything that was likely to compromise him into the Seine. Part of the parcel was picked up and handed to me.'

'By whom?'

'A boatman who refused to give his name, for fear of getting into trouble. But I had all the clues I wanted. It was not so difficult as I expected.'

And the inspector described how he had gone to work.

'And you call that an accident!' cried M. Dudouis. 'And you say that it was not difficult! Why, it's one of your finest performances! Finish it yourself, Ganimard, and be prudent.'

Ganimard was eager to get the business done. He went to the Quai des Augustins with his men and distributed them around the house. He questioned the portress, who said that her tenant took his meals out of doors, but made a point of looking in after dinner.

A little before nine o'clock, in fact, leaning out of her window, she warned Ganimard, who at once gave a low whistle. A gentleman in a tall hat and a fur coat was coming along the pavement beside the Seine. He crossed the road and walked up to the house.

Ganimard stepped forward.

'M. Prévailles, I believe?'

'Yes, but who are you?'

'I have a commission to . . . '

He had not time to finish his sentence. At the sight of the men appearing out of the shadow, Prévailles quickly retreated to the wall and faced his adversaries, with his back to the door of a shop on the ground-floor, the shutters of which were closed.

'Stand back!' he cried. 'I don't know you!'

His right hand brandished a heavy stick, while his left was slipped behind him and seemed to be trying to open the door.

Ganimard had an impression that the man might escape through this way and through some secret outlet.

'None of this nonsense,' he said, moving closer to him. 'You're caught . . . You had better come quietly.'

But, just as he was laying hold of Prévailles' stick, Ganimard remembered the warning which Lupin gave him: Prévailles was left-handed; and it was his revolver for which he was feeling behind his back.

The inspector ducked his head. He had noticed the man's sudden movement. Two reports rang out. No one was hit.

A second later, Prévailles received a blow under the chin from the butt-end of a revolver, which brought him down where he stood. He was entered at the Dépôt soon after nine o'clock.

*　　*　　*

Ganimard enjoyed a great reputation even at that time. But this capture, so quickly effected, by such very simple means, and at once made public by the police, won him a sudden celebrity. Prévailles was forthwith saddled with all the murders that had remained unpunished; and the newspapers vied with one another in extolling Ganimard's prowess.

The case was conducted briskly at the start. It was first of all ascertained that Prévailles, whose real name was Thomas Derocq, had already been in trouble. Moreover, the search instituted in his rooms, while not supplying any fresh proofs, at least led to the discovery of a ball of whip-cord similar to the cord used for doing up the parcel and also to the discovery of daggers which would have produced a wound similar to the wounds on the victim.

But, on the eighth day, everything was changed. Until then Prévailles had refused to reply to the questions put to him; but now, assisted by his counsel, he pleaded a circumstantial alibi and maintained that he was at the Folies-Bergère on the night of the murder.

As a matter of fact, the pockets of his dinner-jacket contained the counterfoil of a stall-ticket and a programme of the performance, both bearing the date of that evening.

'An alibi prepared in advance,' objected the examining-magistrate.

'Prove it,' said Prévailles.

The prisoner was confronted with the witnesses for the prosecution. The young lady from the confectioner's 'thought she knew' the gentleman with the eyeglass. The hall-porter in the Rue de Berne 'thought he knew' the gentleman who used to come to see Jenny Saphir. But nobody dared to make a more definite statement.

The examination, therefore, led to nothing of a precise character, provided no solid basis whereon to found a serious accusation.

The judge sent for Ganimard and told him of his difficulty.

'I can't possibly persist, at this rate. There is no evidence to support the charge.'

'But surely you are convinced in your own mind, monsieur le juge d'instruction! Prévailles would never have resisted his arrest unless he was guilty.'

'He says that he thought he was being assaulted. He also says that he never set eyes on Jenny Saphir; and, as a matter of fact, we can find no one to contradict his assertion. Then again, admitting that the sapphire has been stolen, we have not been able to find it at his flat.'

'Nor anywhere else,' suggested Ganimard.

'Quite true, but that is no evidence against him. I'll tell you what we shall want, M. Ganimard, and that very soon: the other end of this red scarf.'

'The other end?'

'Yes, for it is obvious that, if the murderer took it away with him, the reason was that the stuff is stained with the marks of the blood on his fingers.'

Ganimard made no reply. For several days he had felt that the whole business was tending to this conclusion. There was no other proof possible. Given the silk scarf – and in no other circumstances – Prévailles' guilt was certain. Now Ganimard's position required that Prévailles' guilt should be established. He was responsible for the arrest, it had cast a glamour around him, he had been praised to the skies as the most formidable adversary of criminals; and he would look absolutely ridiculous if Prévailles were released.

Unfortunately, the one and only indispensable proof was in Lupin's pocket. How was he to get hold of it?

Ganimard cast about, exhausted himself with fresh investigations, went over the inquiry from start to finish, spent sleepless nights in turning over the mystery of the Rue de Berne, studied the records of Prévailles' life, sent ten men hunting after the invisible sapphire. Everything was useless.

On the 28th of December, the examining-magistrate stopped him in one of the passages of the Law Courts.

'Well, M. Ganimard, any news?'

'No, monsieur le juge d'instruction.'

'Then I shall dismiss the case.'

'Wait one day longer.'

'What's the use? We want the other end of the scarf; have you got it?'

'I shall have it tomorrow.'

'Tomorrow!'

'Yes, but please lend me the piece in your possession.'

'What if I do?'

'If you do, I promise to let you have the whole scarf complete.'

'Very well, that's understood.'

Ganimard followed the examining-magistrate to his room and came out with the piece of silk.

'Hang it all!' he growled. 'Yes, I will go and fetch the proof and I shall have it too . . . always presuming that Master Lupin has the courage to keep the appointment.'

In point of fact, he did not doubt for a moment that Master Lupin would have this courage, and that was just what exasperated him. Why had Lupin insisted on this meeting? What was his object, in the circumstances?

Anxious, furious and full of hatred, he resolved to take every precaution necessary not only to prevent his falling into a trap himself, but to make his enemy fall into one, now that the opportunity offered. And, on the next day, which was the 29th of December, the date fixed by Lupin, after spending the night in studying the old manor-house in the Rue de Surène and convincing himself that there was no other outlet than the front door, he warned his men that he was going on a dangerous expedition and arrived with them on the field of battle.

He posted them in a café and gave them formal instructions: if he showed himself at one of the third-floor windows, or if he failed to return within an hour, the detectives were to enter the house and arrest anyone who tried to leave it.

The chief-inspector made sure that his revolver was in working order and that he could take it from his pocket easily. Then he went upstairs.

He was surprised to find things as he had left them, the doors open and the locks broken. After ascertaining that the windows of the principal room looked out on the street, he visited the three other rooms that made up the flat. There was no one there.

'Master Lupin was afraid,' he muttered, not without a certain satisfaction.

'Don't be silly,' said a voice behind him.

Turning round, he saw an old workman, wearing a house-painter's long smock, standing in the doorway.

'You needn't bother your head,' said the man. 'It's I, Lupin. I have been working in the painter's shop since early morning. This is when we knock off for breakfast. So I came upstairs.'

He looked at Ganimard with a quizzing smile and cried.

' 'Pon my word, this is a gorgeous moment I owe you, old chap! I wouldn't sell it for ten years of your life; and yet you know how I love you! What do you think of it, artist? Wasn't it well thought out and well foreseen? Foreseen from alpha to omega? Did I understand the business? Did I penetrate the mystery of the scarf? I'm not saying that there were no holes in my argument, no links missing in the chain . . . But what a masterpiece of intelligence! Ganimard, what a reconstruction of events! What an intuition of everything that had taken place and of everything that was going to take place, from the discovery of the crime to your arrival here in search of a proof! What really marvellous divination! Have you the scarf?'

'Yes, half of it. Have you the other?'

'Here it is. Let's compare.'

They spread the two pieces of silk on the table. The cuts made by the scissors corresponded exactly. Moreover, the colours were identical.

'But I presume,' said Lupin, 'that this was not the only thing you came for. What you are interested in seeing is the marks of the blood. Come with me, Ganimard: it's rather dark in here.'

They moved into the next room, which, though it overlooked the courtyard, was lighter; and Lupin held his piece of silk against the window-pane.

'Look,' he said, making room for Ganimard.

The inspector gave a start of delight. The marks of the five fingers and the print of the palm were distinctly visible. The evidence was undeniable. The murderer had seized the stuff in his bloodstained hand, in the same hand that had stabbed Jenny Saphir, and tied the scarf round her neck.

'And it is the print of a left hand,' observed Lupin. 'Hence my warning, which had nothing miraculous about it, you see. For, though I admit, friend of my youth, that you may look upon me as a superior intelligence, I won't have you treat me as a wizard.'

Ganimard had quickly pocketed the piece of silk. Lupin nodded his head in approval.

'Quite right, old boy, it's for you. I'm so glad you're glad! And, you see, there was no trap about all this . . . only the wish to oblige . . . a service between friends, between pals . . . And also, I confess, a little curiosity . . . Yes, I wanted to examine this other piece of silk, the one the police had . . . Don't be afraid: I'll give it back to you . . . Just a second . . . '

Lupin, with a careless movement, played with the tassel at the end of this half of the scarf, while Ganimard listened to him in spite of himself.

'How ingenious these little bits of women's work are! Did you notice one detail in the maid's evidence? Jenny Saphir was very handy with her needle and used to make all her own hats and frocks. It is obvious that she made this scarf herself . . . Besides, I noticed that from the first. I am naturally curious, as I have already told you, and I made a thorough examination of the piece of silk which you have just put in your pocket. Inside the tassel, I found a little sacred medal, which the poor girl had stitched into it to bring her luck. Touching, isn't it, Ganimard? A little medal of Our Lady of Good Succour.'

The inspector felt greatly puzzled and did not take his eyes off the other. And Lupin continued: 'Then I said to myself, "How interesting it would be to explore the other half of the scarf, the one which the police will find round the victim's neck!" For this other half, which I hold in my hands at last, is finished off in the same way . . . so I shall be able to see if it has a hiding-place too and what's inside it . . . But look, my friend, isn't it cleverly made? And so simple! All you have to do is to take a skein of red cord and braid it round a wooden cup, leaving a little recess, a little empty space in the middle, very small, of course, but large enough to hold a medal of a saint . . . or anything . . . A precious stone, for instance . . . Such as a sapphire . . . '

At that moment he finished pushing back the silk cord and, from the hollow of a cup he took between his thumb and forefinger a wonderful blue stone, perfect in respect of size and purity.

'Ha! What did I tell you, friend of my youth?'

He raised his head. The inspector had turned livid and was staring wild-eyed, as though fascinated by the stone that sparkled before him. He at last realized the whole plot.

'You dirty scoundrel!' he muttered, repeating the insults which he had used at the first interview. 'You scum of the earth!'

The two men were standing one against the other.

'Give me back that,' said the inspector.

Lupin held out the piece of silk.

'And the sapphire,' said Ganimard, in a peremptory tone.

'Don't be silly.'

'Give it back, or . . . '

'Or what, you idiot!' cried Lupin. 'Look here, do you think I put you on to this soft thing for nothing?'

'Give it back!'

'You haven't noticed what I've been about, that's plain! What! For four weeks I've kept you on the move like a deer; and you want to . . . ! Come, Ganimard, old chap, pull yourself together! . . . Don't you see that you've been playing the good dog for four weeks on end? . . . Fetch it, Rover! . . . There's a nice blue pebble over there, which master can't get at. Hunt it, Ganimard, fetch it . . . bring it to master . . . Ah, he's his master's own good little dog! . . . Sit up! Beg! . . . Does 'ms want a bit of sugar, then? . . . '

Ganimard, containing the anger that seethed within him, thought only of one thing, summoning his detectives. And, as the room in which he now was looked out on the courtyard, he tried gradually to work his way round to the communicating door. He would then run to the window and break one of the panes.

'All the same,' continued Lupin, 'what a pack of dunderheads you and the rest must be! You've had the silk all this time and not one of you ever thought of feeling it, not one of you ever asked himself the reason why the poor girl hung on to her scarf. Not one of you! You just acted at haphazard, without reflecting, without foreseeing anything . . . '

The inspector had attained his object. Taking advantage of a second when Lupin had turned away from him, he suddenly wheeled round and grasped the door-handle. But an oath escaped him: the handle did not budge.

Lupin burst into a fit of laughing.

'Not even that! You did not even foresee that! You lay a trap for me and you won't admit that I may perhaps smell the thing out beforehand . . . And you allow yourself to be brought into this room without asking whether I am not bringing you here for a particular reason and without remembering that the locks are fitted with a special mechanism. Come now, speaking frankly, what do you think of it yourself?'

'What do I think of it?' roared Ganimard, beside himself with rage.

He had drawn his revolver and was pointing it straight at Lupin's face.

'Hands up!' he cried. 'That's what I think of it!'

Lupin placed himself in front of him and shrugged his shoulders.

'Sold again!' he said.

'Hands up, I say, once more!'

'And sold again, say I. Your deadly weapon won't go off.'

'What?'

'Old Catherine, your housekeeper, is in my service. She damped the charges this morning while you were having your breakfast coffee.'

Ganimard made a furious gesture, pocketed the revolver and rushed at Lupin.

'Well?' said Lupin, stopping him short with a well-aimed kick on the shin.

Their clothes were almost touching. They exchanged defiant glances, the glances of two adversaries who mean to come to blows. Nevertheless, there was no fight. The recollection of the earlier struggles made any present struggle useless. And Ganimard, who remembered all his past failures, his vain attacks, Lupin's crushing reprisals, did not lift a limb. There was nothing to be done. He felt it. Lupin had forces at his command against which any individual force simply broke to pieces. So what was the good?

'I agree,' said Lupin, in a friendly voice, as though answering Ganimard's unspoken thought, 'you would do better to let things be as they are. Besides, friend of my youth, think of all that this incident has brought you: fame, the certainty of quick promotion and, thanks to that, the prospect of a happy and comfortable old age! Surely, you don't want the discovery of the sapphire and the head of poor Arsène Lupin in addition! It wouldn't be fair. To say nothing of the fact that poor Arsène Lupin saved your life . . . Yes, sir! Who warned you, at this very spot, that Prévailles was left-handed? . . . And is this the way you thank me? It's not pretty of you, Ganimard. Upon my word, you make me blush for you!'

While chattering, Lupin had gone through the same performance as Ganimard and was now near the door. Ganimard saw that his foe was about to escape him. Forgetting all prudence, he tried to block his way and received a tremendous butt in the stomach, which sent him rolling to the opposite wall.

Lupin dexterously touched a spring, turned the handle, opened the door and slipped away, roaring with laughter as he went.

*   *   *

Twenty minutes later, when Ganimard at last succeeded in joining his men, one of them said to him: 'A house-painter left the house, as his mates were coming back from breakfast, and put a letter in my hand. "Give that to your governor," he said. "Which governor?" I asked; but he was gone. I suppose it's meant for you.'

'Let's have it.'

Ganimard opened the letter. It was hurriedly scribbled in pencil and contained these words.

This is to warn you, friend of my youth, against excessive credulity. When a fellow tells you that the cartridges in your revolver are damp, however great your confidence in that fellow may be, even though his name be Arsène Lupin, never allow yourself to be taken in. Fire first; and, if the fellow hops the twig, you will have acquired the proof (1) that the cartridges are not damp; and (2) that old Catherine is the most honest and respectable of housekeepers.

One of these days, I hope to have the pleasure of making her acquaintance.

Meanwhile, friend of my youth, believe me always affectionately and sincerely yours,

Arsène Lupin

6

Shadowed by Death

After he had been round the walls of the property, Arsène Lupin returned to the spot from which he started. It was perfectly clear to him that there was no breach in the walls; and the only way of entering the extensive grounds of the Château de Maupertuis was through a little low door, firmly bolted on the inside, or through the principal gate, which was overlooked by the lodge.

'Very well,' he said. 'We must employ heroic methods.'

Pushing his way into the copsewood where he had hidden his motor-bicycle, he unwound a length of twine from under the saddle and went to a place which he had noticed in the course of his exploration. At this place, which was situated far from the road, on the edge of a wood, a number of large trees, standing inside the park, overlapped the wall.

Lupin fastened a stone to the end of the string, threw it up and caught a thick branch, which he drew down to him and bestraddled. The branch, in recovering its position, raised him from the ground. He climbed over the wall, slipped down the tree, and sprang lightly on the grass.

It was winter; and, through the leafless boughs, across the undulating lawns, he could see the little Château de Maupertuis in the distance. Fearing lest he should be perceived, he concealed himself behind a clump of fir-trees. From there, with the aid of a field-glass, he studied the dark and melancholy front of the manor-house. All the windows were closed and, as it were, barricaded with solid shutters. The house might easily have been uninhabited.

'By Jove!' muttered Lupin. 'It's not the liveliest of residences. I shall certainly not come here to end my days!'

But the clock struck three; one of the doors on the ground-floor opened; and the figure of a woman appeared, a very slender figure wrapped in a brown cloak.

The woman walked up and down for a few minutes and was at once surrounded by birds, to which she scattered crumbs of bread. Then she went down the stone steps that led to the middle lawn and skirted it, taking the path on the right.

With his field-glass, Lupin could distinctly see her coming in his direction. She was tall, fair-haired, graceful in appearance, and seemed to be quite a young girl. She walked with a sprightly step, looking at the pale December sun and amusing herself by breaking the little dead twigs on the shrubs along the road.

She had gone nearly two thirds of the distance that separated her from Lupin when there came a furious sound of barking and a huge dog, a colossal Danish boarhound, sprang from a neighbouring kennel and stood erect at the end of the chain by which it was fastened.

The girl moved a little to one side, without paying further attention to what was doubtless a daily incident. The dog grew angrier than ever, standing on its legs and dragging at its collar, at the risk of strangling itself.

Thirty or forty steps farther, yielding probably to an impulse of impatience, the girl turned round and made a gesture with her hand. The great Dane gave a start of rage, retreated to the back of its kennel and rushed out again, this time unfettered. The girl uttered a cry of mad terror. The dog was covering the space between them, trailing its broken chain behind it.

She began to run, to run with all her might, and screamed out desperately for help. But the dog came up with her in a few bounds.

She fell, at once exhausted, giving herself up for lost. The animal was already upon her, almost touching her.

At that exact moment a shot rang out. The dog turned a complete somersault, recovered its feet, tore the ground and then lay down, giving a number of hoarse, breathless howls, which ended in a dull moan and an indistinct gurgling. And that was all.

'Dead,' said Lupin, who had hastened up at once, prepared, if necessary, to fire his revolver a second time.

The girl had risen and stood pale, still staggering. She looked in great surprise at this man whom she did not know and who had saved her life; and she whispered: 'Thank you . . . I have had a great fright . . . You were in the nick of time . . . I thank you, monsieur.'

Lupin took off his hat.

'Allow me to introduce myself, mademoiselle . . . My name is Paul Daubreuil . . . But before entering into any explanations, I must ask for one moment . . . '

He stooped over the dog's dead body and examined the chain at the part where the brute's effort had snapped it.

'That's it,' he said, between his teeth. 'It's just as I suspected. By Jupiter, things are moving rapidly! . . . I ought to have come earlier.'

Returning to the girl's side, he said to her, speaking very quickly: 'Mademoiselle, we have not a minute to lose. My presence in these grounds is quite irregular. I do not wish to be surprised here; and this for reasons that concern yourself alone. Do you think that the report can have been heard at the house?'

The girl seemed already to have recovered from her emotion; and she replied, with a calmness that revealed all her pluck: 'I don't think so.'

'Is your father in the house today?'

'My father is ill and has been in bed for months. Besides, his room looks out on the other front.'

'And the servants?'

'Their quarters and the kitchen are also on the other side. No one ever comes to this part. I walk here myself, but nobody else does.'

'It is probable, therefore, that I have not been seen either, especially as the trees hide us?'

'It is most probable.'

'Then I can speak to you freely?'

'Certainly, but I don't understand . . . '

'You will, presently. Permit me to be brief. The point is this: four days ago, Mlle Jeanne Darcieux . . . '

'That is my name,' she said, smiling.

'Mlle Jeanne Darcieux,' continued Lupin, 'wrote a letter to one of her friends, called Marceline, who lives at Versailles . . . '

'How do you know all that?' asked the girl, in astonishment. 'I tore up the letter before I had finished it.'

'And you flung the pieces on the edge of the road that runs from the house to Vendôme.'

'That's true . . . I had gone out walking . . . '

'The pieces were picked up and they came into my hands next day.'

'Then . . . you must have read them,' said Jeanne Darcieux, betraying a certain annoyance by her manner.

'Yes, I committed that indiscretion; and I do not regret it, because I can save you.'

'Save me? From what?'

'From death.'

Lupin spoke this little sentence in a very distinct voice. The girl gave a shudder. Then she said: 'I am not threatened with death.'

'Yes, you are, mademoiselle. At the end of October, you were reading on a bench on the terrace where you were accustomed to sit at the same hour every day, when a block of stone fell from the cornice above your head and you were within a few inches of being crushed.'

'An accident . . . '

'One fine evening in November, you were walking in the kitchen-garden, by moonlight. A shot was fired. The bullet whizzed past your ear.'

'At least, I thought so.'

'Lastly, less than a week ago, the little wooden bridge that crosses the river in the park, two yards from the waterfall, gave way while you were on it. You were just able, by a miracle, to catch hold of the root of a tree.'

Jeanne Darcieux tried to smile.

'Very well. But, as I wrote to Marceline, these are only a series of coincidences, of accidents . . . '

'No, mademoiselle, no. One accident of this sort is allowable . . . So are two . . . and even then! . . . But we have no right to suppose that the chapter of accidents, repeating the same act three times in such different and extraordinary circumstances, is a mere amusing coincidence. That is why I thought that I might presume to come to your assistance. And, as my intervention can be of no use unless it remains secret, I did not hesitate to make my way in here . . . without walking through the gate. I came in the nick of time, as you said. Your enemy was attacking you once more.'

'What! . . . Do you think? . . . No, it is impossible . . . I refuse to believe . . . '

Lupin picked up the chain and, showing it to her: 'Look at the last link. There is no question but that it has been filed. Otherwise, so powerful a chain as this would never have yielded. Besides, you can see the mark of the file here.'

Jeanne turned pale and her pretty features were distorted with terror.

'But who can bear me such a grudge?' she gasped. 'It is terrible . . . I have never done anyone harm . . . And yet you are certainly right . . . Worse still . . . '

She finished her sentence in a lower voice: 'Worse still, I am wondering whether the same danger does not threaten my father.'

'Has he been attacked also?'

'No, for he never stirs from his room. But his is such a mysterious illness! ... He has no strength ... he cannot walk at all ... In addition to that, he is subject to fits of suffocation, as though his heart stopped beating ... Oh, what an awful thing!'

Lupin realized all the authority which he was able to assert at such a moment, and he said: 'Have no fear, mademoiselle. If you obey me blindly, I shall be sure to succeed.'

'Yes ... yes ... I am quite willing ... but all this is so terrible ... '

'Trust me, I beg of you. And please listen to me, I shall want a few particulars.'

He rapped out a number of questions, which Jeanne Darcieux answered hurriedly: 'That animal was never let loose, was he?'

'Never.'

'Who used to feed him?'

'The lodge-keeper. He brought him his food every evening.'

'Consequently, he could go near him without being bitten?'

'Yes; and he only, for the dog was very savage.'

'You don't suspect the man?'

'Oh, no! ... Baptiste? ... Never!'

'And you can't think of anybody?'

'No. Our servants are quite devoted to us. They are very fond of me.'

'You have no friends staying in the house?'

'No.'

'No brother?'

'No.'

'Then your father is your only protector?'

'Yes; and I have told you the condition he is in.'

'Have you told him of the different attempts?'

'Yes; and it was wrong of me to do so. Our doctor, old Dr Guéroult, forbade me to cause him the least excitement.'

'Your mother? ... '

'I don't remember her. She died sixteen years ago ... just sixteen years ago.'

'How old were you then?'

'I was not quite five years old.'

'And were you living here?'

'We were living in Paris. My father only bought this place the year after.'

Lupin was silent for a few moments. Then he concluded: 'Very well, mademoiselle, I am obliged to you. Those particulars are all I need for the present. Besides, it would not be wise for us to remain together longer.'

'But,' she said, 'the lodge-keeper will find the dog soon . . . Who will have killed him?'

'You, mademoiselle, to defend yourself against an attack.'

'I never carry firearms.'

'I am afraid you do,' said Lupin, smiling, 'because you killed the dog and there is no one but you who could have killed him. For that matter, let them think what they please. The great thing is that I shall not be suspected when I come to the house.'

'To the house? Do you intend to?'

'Yes. I don't yet know how . . . But I shall come . . . This very evening . . . So, once more, be easy in your mind. I will answer for everything.'

Jeanne looked at him and, dominated by him, conquered by his air of assurance and good faith, she said, simply: 'I am quite easy.'

'Then all will go well. Till this evening, mademoiselle.'

'Till this evening.'

She walked away; and Lupin, following her with his eyes until the moment when she disappeared round the corner of the house, murmured: 'What a pretty creature! It would be a pity if any harm were to come to her. Luckily, Arsène Lupin is keeping his weather-eye open.'

Taking care not to be seen, with eyes and ears attentive to the least sight or sound, he inspected every nook and corner of the grounds, looked for the little low door which he had noticed outside and which was the door of the kitchen garden, drew the bolt, took the key and then skirted the walls and found himself once more near the tree which he had climbed. Two minutes later, he was mounting his motor-cycle.

*   *   *

The village of Maupertuis lay quite close to the estate. Lupin inquired and learnt that Dr Guéroult lived next door to the church.

He rang, was shown into the consulting-room and introduced himself by his name of Paul Daubreuil, of the Rue de Surène, Paris, adding that he had official relations with the detective-service, a fact which he requested might be kept secret. He had become acquainted, by means of a torn letter, with the incidents that had endangered Mlle Darcieux's life; and he had come to that young lady's assistance.

Dr Guéroult, an old country practitioner, who idolized Jeanne, on hearing Lupin's explanations at once admitted that those incidents constituted undeniable proofs of a plot. He showed great concern, offered his visitor hospitality and kept him to dinner.

The two men talked at length. In the evening, they walked round to the manor-house together.

The doctor went to the sick man's room, which was on the first floor, and asked leave to bring up a young colleague, to whom he intended soon to make over his practice, when he retired.

Lupin, on entering, saw Jeanne Darcieux seated by her father's bedside. She suppressed a movement of surprise and, at a sign from the doctor, left the room.

The consultation thereupon took place in Lupin's presence. M. Darcieux's face was worn with much suffering, and his eyes were bright with fever. He complained particularly, that day, of his heart. After the auscultation, he questioned the doctor with obvious anxiety; and each reply seemed to give him relief. He also spoke of Jeanne and expressed his conviction that they were deceiving him and that his daughter had escaped yet more accidents. He continued perturbed, in spite of the doctor's denials. He wanted to have the police informed and inquiries set on foot.

But his excitement tired him and he gradually dropped off to sleep.

Lupin stopped the doctor in the passage.

'Come, doctor, give me your exact opinion. Do you think that M. Darcieux's illness can be attributed to an outside cause?'

'How do you mean?'

'Well, suppose that the same enemy should be interested in removing both father and daughter.'

The doctor seemed struck by the suggestion.

'Upon my word, there is something in what you say . . . The father's illness at times adopts such a very unusual character! . . . For instance, the paralysis of the legs, which is almost complete, ought to be accompanied by . . . '

The doctor reflected for a moment and then said in a low voice: 'You think it's poison, of course . . . but what poison? . . . Besides, I see no toxic symptoms . . . It would have to be . . . But what are you doing? What's the matter? . . . '

The two men were talking outside a little sitting-room on the first floor, where Jeanne, seizing the opportunity while the doctor was with her father, had begun her evening meal. Lupin, who was watching her through the open door, saw her lift a cup to her lips and take a few sups.

Suddenly, he rushed at her and caught her by the arm.

'What are you drinking there?'

'Why,' she said, taken aback, 'only tea!'

'You pulled a face of disgust . . . what made you do that?'

'I don't know . . . I thought . . . '

'You thought what?'

'That . . . that it tasted rather bitter . . . But I expect that comes from the medicine I mixed with it.'

'What medicine?'

'Some drops which I take at dinner . . . the drops which you prescribed for me, you know, doctor.'

'Yes,' said Dr Guéroult, 'but that medicine has no taste of any kind . . . You know it hasn't, Jeanne, for you have been taking it for a fortnight and this is the first time . . . '

'Quite right,' said the girl, 'and this does have a taste . . . There – oh! – my mouth is still burning.'

Dr Guéroult now took a sip from the cup.

'Faugh!' he exclaimed, spitting it out again. 'There's no mistake about it . . . '

Lupin, on his side, was examining the bottle containing the medicine; and he asked: 'Where is this bottle kept in the daytime?'

But Jeanne was unable to answer. She had put her hand to her heart and, wan-faced, with staring eyes, seemed to be suffering great pain.

'It hurts . . . it hurts,' she stammered.

The two men quickly carried her to her room and laid her on the bed.

'She ought to have an emetic,' said Lupin.

'Open the cupboard,' said the doctor. 'You'll see a medicine-case . . . Have you got it? . . . Take out one of those little tubes . . . Yes, that one . . . And now some hot water . . . You'll find some on the tea-tray in the other room.'

Jeanne's own maid came running up in answer to the bell. Lupin told her that Mlle Darcieux had been taken unwell, for some unknown reason.

He next returned to the little dining-room, inspected the sideboard and the cupboards, went down to the kitchen and pretended that the doctor had sent him to ask about M. Darcieux's diet. Without appearing to do so, he catechized the cook, the butler, and Baptiste, the lodge-keeper, who had his meals at the manor-house with the servants. Then he went back to the doctor.

'Well?'

'She's asleep.'

'Any danger?'

'No. Fortunately, she had only taken two or three sips. But this is the second time today that you have saved her life, as the analysis of this bottle will show.'

'Quite superfluous to make an analysis, doctor. There is no doubt about the fact that there has been an attempt at poisoning.'

'By whom?'

'I can't say. But the demon who is engineering all this business clearly knows the ways of the house. He comes and goes as he pleases, walks about in the park, files the dog's chain, mixes poison with the food and, in short, moves and acts precisely as though he were living the very life of her – or rather of those – whom he wants to put away.'

'Ah! You really believe that M. Darcieux is threatened with the same danger?'

'I have not a doubt of it.'

'Then it must be one of the servants? But that is most unlikely! Do you think . . . ?'

'I think nothing, doctor. I know nothing. All I can say is that the situation is most tragic and that we must be prepared for the worst. Death is here, doctor, shadowing the people in this house; and it will soon strike at those whom it is pursuing.'

'What's to be done?'

'Watch, doctor. Let us pretend that we are alarmed about M. Darcieux's health and spend the night in here. The bedrooms of both the father and daughter are close by. If anything happens, we are sure to hear.'

There was an easy-chair in the room. They arranged to sleep in it turn and turn about.

In reality, Lupin slept for only two or three hours. In the middle of the night he left the room, without disturbing his companion, carefully looked round the whole of the house and walked out through the principal gate.

* * *

He reached Paris on his motor-cycle at nine o'clock in the morning. Two of his friends, to whom he telephoned on the road, met him there. They all three spent the day in making searches which Lupin had planned out beforehand.

He set out again hurriedly at six o'clock; and never, perhaps, as he told me subsequently, did he risk his life with greater temerity than in his breakneck ride, at a mad rate of speed, on a foggy December evening, with the light of his lamp hardly able to pierce through the darkness.

He sprang from his bicycle outside the gate, which was still open, ran to the house and reached the first floor in a few bounds.

There was no one in the little dining-room.

Without hesitating, without knocking, he walked into Jeanne's bedroom.

'Ah, here you are!' he said, with a sigh of relief, seeing Jeanne and the doctor sitting side by side, talking.

'What? Any news?' asked the doctor, alarmed at seeing such a state of agitation in a man whose coolness he had had occasion to observe.

'No,' said Lupin. 'No news. And here?'

'None here, either. We have just left M. Darcieux. He has had an excellent day and he ate his dinner with a good appetite. As for Jeanne, you can see for yourself, she has all her pretty colour back again.'

'Then she must go.'

'Go? But it's out of the question!' protested the girl.

'You must go, you must!' cried Lupin, with real violence, stamping his foot on the floor.

He at once mastered himself, spoke a few words of apology and then, for three or four minutes, preserved a complete silence, which the doctor and Jeanne were careful not to disturb.

At last, he said to the young girl: 'You shall go tomorrow morning, mademoiselle. It will be only for one or two weeks. I will take you to your friend at Versailles, the one to whom you were writing. I entreat you to get everything ready tonight . . . without concealment of any kind. Let the servants know that you are going . . . On the other hand, the doctor will be good enough to tell M. Darcieux and give him to understand, with every possible precaution, that this journey is essential to your safety. Besides, he can join you as soon as his strength permits . . . That's settled, is it not?'

'Yes,' she said, absolutely dominated by Lupin's gentle and imperious voice.

'In that case,' he said, 'be as quick as you can . . . and do not stir from your room . . . '

'But,' said the girl, with a shudder, 'am I to stay alone tonight?'

'Fear nothing. Should there be the least danger, the doctor and I will come back. Do not open your door unless you hear three very light taps.'

Jeanne at once rang for her maid. The doctor went to M. Darcieux, while Lupin had some supper brought to him in the little dining-room.

'That's done,' said the doctor, returning to him in twenty minutes' time. 'M. Darcieux did not raise any great difficulty. As a matter of fact, he himself thinks it just as well that we should send Jeanne away.'

They then went downstairs together and left the house.

On reaching the lodge, Lupin called the keeper.

'You can shut the gate, my man. If M. Darcieux should want us, send for us at once.'

The clock of Maupertuis church struck ten. The sky was overcast with black clouds, through which the moon broke at moments.

The two men walked on for sixty or seventy yards.

They were nearing the village, when Lupin gripped his companion by the arm.

'Stop!'

'What on earth's the matter?' exclaimed the doctor.

'The matter is this,' Lupin jerked out, 'that, if my calculations turn out right, if I have not misjudged the business from start to finish, Mlle Darcieux will be murdered before the night is out.'

'Eh? What's that?' gasped the doctor, in dismay. 'But then why did we go?'

'With the precise object that the miscreant, who is watching all our movements in the dark, may not postpone his crime and may per-petrate it, not at the hour chosen by himself, but at the hour which I have decided upon.'

'Then we are returning to the manor-house?'

'Yes, of course we are, but separately.'

'In that case, let us go at once.'

'Listen to me, doctor,' said Lupin, in a steady voice, 'and let us waste no time in useless words. Above all, we must defeat any attempt to watch us. You will therefore go straight home and not come out again until you are quite certain that you have not been followed. You will then make for the walls of the property, keeping to the left, till you come to the little door of the kitchen-garden. Here is the key. When the church clock strikes eleven, open the door very gently and walk right up to the terrace at the back of the house. The fifth window is badly fastened. You have only to climb over the balcony. As soon as you are inside Mlle Darcieux's room, bolt the door and don't budge. You quite understand, don't budge, either of you, whatever happens. I have noticed that Mlle Darcieux leaves her dressing-room window ajar, isn't that so?'

'Yes, it's a habit which I taught her.'

'That's the way they'll come.'

'And you?'

'That's the way I shall come also.'

'And do you know who the villain is?'

Lupin hesitated and then replied: 'No, I don't know . . . And that is just how we shall find out. But, I implore you, keep cool. Not a word, not a movement, *whatever happens*!'

'I promise you.'

'I want more than that, doctor. You must give me your word of honour.'

'I give you my word of honour.'

The doctor went away. Lupin at once climbed a neighbouring mound from which he could see the windows of the first and second floor. Several of them were lighted.

He waited for some little time. The lights went out one by one. Then, taking a direction opposite to that in which the doctor had gone, he branched off to the right and skirted the wall until he came to the clump of trees near which he had hidden his motor-cycle on the day before.

Eleven o'clock struck. He calculated the time which it would take the doctor to cross the kitchen-garden and make his way into the house.

'That's one point scored!' he muttered. 'Everything's all right on that side. And now, Lupin to the rescue? The enemy won't be long before he plays his last trump . . . and, by all the gods, I must be there! . . . '

He went through the same performance as on the first occasion, pulled down the branch and hoisted himself to the top of the wall, from which he was able to reach the bigger boughs of the tree.

Just then he pricked up his ears. He seemed to hear a rustling of dead leaves. And he actually perceived a dark form moving on the level thirty yards away.

'Hang it all!' he said to himself. 'I'm done: the scoundrel has smelt a rat.'

A moonbeam pierced through the clouds. Lupin distinctly saw the man take aim. He tried to jump to the ground and turned his head.

But he felt something hit him in the chest, heard the sound of a report, uttered an angry oath and came crashing down from branch to branch, like a corpse.

* * *

Meanwhile, Doctor Guéroult, following Arsène Lupin's instructions, had climbed the ledge of the fifth window and groped his way to the first floor. On reaching Jeanne's room, he tapped lightly, three times, at the door and, immediately on entering, pushed the bolt.

'Lie down at once,' he whispered to the girl, who had not taken off her things. 'You must appear to have gone to bed. Brrrr, it's cold in here! Is the window open in your dressing-room?'

'Yes . . . would you like me to . . . ?'

'No, leave it as it is. They are coming.'

'They are coming!' spluttered Jeanne, in affright.

'Yes, beyond a doubt.'

'But who? Do you suspect anyone?'

'I don't know who . . . I expect that there is someone hidden in the house . . . or in the park.'

'Oh, I feel so frightened!'

'Don't be frightened. The sportsman who's looking after you seems jolly clever and makes a point of playing a safe game. I expect he's on the look-out in the court.'

The doctor put out the night-light, went to the window and raised the blind. A narrow cornice, running along the first storey, prevented him from seeing more than a distant part of the courtyard; and he came back and sat down by the bed.

Some very painful minutes passed, minutes that appeared to them interminably long. The clock in the village struck; but, taken up as they were with all the little noises of the night, they hardly noticed the sound. They listened, listened, with all their nerves on edge.

'Did you hear?' whispered the doctor.

'Yes . . . yes,' said Jeanne, sitting up in bed.

'Lie down . . . lie down,' he said, presently. 'There's someone coming.'

There was a little tapping sound outside, against the cornice. Next came a series of indistinct noises, the nature of which they could not make out for certain. But they had a feeling that the window in the dressing-room was being opened wider, for they were buffeted by gusts of cold air.

Suddenly, it became quite clear: there was someone next door.

The doctor, whose hand was trembling a little, seized his revolver. Nevertheless, he did not move, remembering the formal orders which he had received and fearing to act against them.

The room was in absolute darkness; and they were unable to see where the adversary was. But they felt his presence.

They followed his invisible movements, the sound of his footsteps deadened by the carpet; and they did not doubt but that he had already crossed the threshold of the room.

And the adversary stopped. Of that they were certain. He was standing six steps away from the bed, motionless, undecided perhaps, seeking to pierce the darkness with his keen eyes.

Jeanne's hand, icy-cold and clammy, trembled in the doctor's grasp.

With his other hand, the doctor clutched his revolver, with his finger on the trigger. In spite of his pledged word, he did not hesitate. If the adversary touched the end of the bed, the shot would be fired at a venture.

The adversary took another step and then stopped again. And there was something awful about that silence, that impassive silence, that darkness in which those human beings were peering at one another, wildly.

Who was it looming in the murky darkness? Who was the man? What horrible enmity was it that turned his hand against the girl and what abominable aim was he pursuing?

Terrified though they were, Jeanne and the doctor thought only of that one thing: to see, to learn the truth, to gaze upon the adversary's face.

He took one more step and did not move again. It seemed to them that his figure stood out, darker, against the dark space and that his arm rose slowly, slowly . . .

A minute passed and then another minute . . .

And, suddenly, beyond the man, on the right a sharp click . . . A bright light flashed, was flung upon the man, lit him full in the face, remorselessly.

Jeanne gave a cry of affright. She had seen – standing over her, with a dagger in his hand – she had seen . . . her father!

Almost at the same time, though the light was already turned off, there came a report: the doctor had fired.

'Dash it all, don't shoot!' roared Lupin.

He threw his arms round the doctor, who choked out: 'Didn't you see? . . . Didn't you see? . . . Listen! . . . He's escaping! . . . '

'Let him escape: it's the best thing that could happen.'

He pressed the spring of his electric lantern again, ran to the dressing-room, made certain that the man had disappeared and, returning quietly to the table, lit the lamp.

Jeanne lay on her bed, pallid, in a dead faint.

The doctor, huddled in his chair, emitted inarticulate sounds.

'Come,' said Lupin, laughing, 'pull yourself together. There is nothing to excite ourselves about: it's all over.'

'Her father! . . . Her father!' moaned the old doctor.

'If you please, doctor, Mlle Darcieux is ill. Look after her.'

Without more words, Lupin went back to the dressing-room and stepped out on the window-ledge. A ladder stood against the ledge. He ran down it. Skirting the wall of the house, twenty steps farther, he tripped over the rungs of a rope-ladder, which he climbed and found himself in M. Darcieux's bedroom. The room was empty.

'Just so,' he said. 'My gentleman did not like the position and has cleared out. Here's wishing him a good journey . . . And, of course, the door is bolted? . . . Exactly! . . . That is how our sick man, tricking his worthy medical attendant, used to get up at night in full security, fasten his rope-ladder to the balcony and prepare his little games. He's no fool, is friend Darcieux!'

He drew the bolts and returned to Jeanne's room. The doctor, who was just coming out of the doorway, drew him to the little dining-room.

'She's asleep, don't let us disturb her. She has had a bad shock and will take some time to recover.'

Lupin poured himself out a glass of water and drank it down. Then he took a chair and, calmly: 'Pooh! She'll be all right by tomorrow.'

'What do you say?'

'I say that she'll be all right by tomorrow.'

'Why?'

'In the first place, because it did not strike me that Mlle Darcieux felt any very great affection for her father.'

'Never mind! Think of it: a father who tries to kill his daughter! A father who, for months on end, repeats his monstrous attempt four, five, six times over again! . . . Well, isn't that enough to blight a less sensitive soul than Jeanne's for good and all? What a hateful memory!'

'She will forget.'

'One does not forget such a thing as that.'

'She will forget, doctor, and for a very simple reason . . .'

'Explain yourself!'

'She is not M. Darcieux's daughter!'

'Eh?'

'I repeat, she is not that villain's daughter.'

'What do you mean? M. Darcieux . . . '

'M. Darcieux is only her step-father. She had just been born when her father, her real father, died. Jeanne's mother then married a cousin of her husband's, a man bearing the same name, and she died within a year of her second wedding. She left Jeanne in M. Darcieux's charge. He first took her abroad and then bought this country-house; and, as nobody knew him in the neighbourhood, he represented the child as being his daughter. She herself did not know the truth about her birth.'

The doctor sat confounded. He asked: 'Are you sure of your facts?'

'I spent my day in the town-halls of the Paris municipalities. I searched the registers, I interviewed two solicitors, I have seen all the documents. There is no doubt possible.'

'But that does not explain the crime, or rather the series of crimes.'

'Yes, it does,' declared Lupin. 'And, from the start, from the first hour when I meddled in this business, some words which Mlle Darcieux used made me suspect that direction which my investigations must take. "I was not quite five years old when my mother died," she said. "That was sixteen years ago." Mlle Darcieux, therefore, was nearly twenty-one, that is to say, she was on the verge of attaining her majority. I at once saw that this was an important detail. The day on which you reach your majority is the day on which your accounts are rendered. What was the financial position of Mlle Darcieux, who was her mother's natural heiress? Of course, I did not think of the father for a second. To begin with, one can't imagine a thing like that; and then the farce which M. Darcieux was playing . . . helpless, bedridden, ill . . . '

'Really ill,' interrupted the doctor.

'All this diverted suspicion from him . . . the more so as I believe that he himself was exposed to criminal attacks. But was there not in the family some person who would be interested in their removal? My journey to Paris revealed the truth to me: Mlle Darcieux inherits a large fortune from her mother, of which her step-father draws the income. The solicitor was to have called a meeting of the family in Paris next month. The truth would have been out. It meant ruin to M. Darcieux.'

'Then he had put no money by?'

'Yes, but he had lost a great deal as the result of unfortunate speculations.'

'But, after all, Jeanne would not have taken the management of her fortune out of his hands!'

'There is one detail which you do not know, doctor, and which I learnt from reading the torn letter. Mlle Darcieux is in love with the brother of Marceline, her Versailles friend; M. Darcieux was opposed to the marriage; and – you now see the reason – she was waiting until she came of age to be married.'

'You're right,' said the doctor, 'you're right . . . It meant his ruin.'

'His absolute ruin. One chance of saving himself remained, the death of his step-daughter, of whom he is the next heir.'

'Certainly, but on condition that no one suspected him.'

'Of course; and that is why he contrived the series of accidents, so that the death might appear to be due to misadventure. And that is why I, on my side, wishing to bring things to a head, asked you to tell him of Mlle Darcieux's impending departure. From that moment, it was no longer enough for the would-be sick man to wander about the grounds and the passages, in the dark, and execute some leisurely thought-out plan. No, he had to act, to act at once, without preparation, violently, dagger in hand. I had no doubt that he would decide to do it. And he did.'

'Then he had no suspicions?'

'Of me, yes. He felt that I would return tonight, and he kept a watch at the place where I had already climbed the wall.'

'Well?'

'Well,' said Lupin, laughing, 'I received a bullet full in the chest . . . or rather my pocket-book received a bullet . . . Here, you can see the hole . . . So I tumbled from the tree, like a dead man. Thinking that he was rid of his only adversary, he went back to the house. I saw him prowl about for two hours. Then, making up his mind, he went to the coach-house, took a ladder and set it against the window. I had only to follow him.'

The doctor reflected and said: 'You could have collared him earlier. Why did you let him come up? It was a sore trial for Jeanne . . . and unnecessary.'

'On the contrary, it was indispensable! Mlle Darcieux would never have accepted the truth. It was essential that she should see the murderer's very face. You must tell her all the circumstances when she wakes. She will soon be well again.'

'But . . . M. Darcieux?'

'You can explain his disappearance as you think best . . . a sudden journey . . . a fit of madness . . . There will be a few inquiries . . . And you may be sure that he will never be heard of again.'

The doctor nodded his head.

'Yes . . . that is so . . . that is so . . . you are right. You have managed all this business with extraordinary skill; and Jeanne owes you her life. She will thank you in person . . . But now, can I be of use to you in any way? You told me that you were connected with the detective-service . . . Will you allow me to write and praise your conduct, your courage?'

Lupin began to laugh.

'Certainly! A letter of that kind will do me a world of good. You might write to my immediate superior, Chief-inspector Ganimard. He will be glad to hear that his favourite officer, Paul Daubreuil, of the Rue de Surène, has once again distinguished himself by a brilliant action. As it happens, I have an appointment to meet him about a case of which you may have heard: the case of the red scarf . . . How pleased my dear M. Ganimard will be!'

A Tragedy in the Forest of Morgues

The village was terror-stricken.

It was on a Sunday morning. The peasants of Saint-Nicolas and the neighbourhood were coming out of church and spreading across the square, when, suddenly, the women who were walking ahead and who had already turned into the high-road fell back with loud cries of dismay.

At the same moment, an enormous motor-car, looking like some appalling monster, came tearing into sight at a headlong rate of speed. Amid the shouts of the madly scattering people, it made straight for the church, swerved, just as it seemed about to dash itself to pieces against the steps, grazed the wall of the presbytery, regained the continuation of the national road, dashed along, turned the corner and disappeared without, by some incomprehensible miracle, having so much as brushed against any of the persons crowding the square.

But they had seen! They had seen a man in the driver's seat, wrapped in a goat-skin coat, with a fur cap on his head and his face disguised in a pair of large goggles, and, with him, on the front of that seat, flung back, bent in two, a woman whose head, all covered with blood, hung down over the bonnet . . .

And they had heard! They had heard the woman's screams, screams of horror, screams of agony . . .

And it was all such a vision of hell and carnage that the people stood, for some seconds, motionless, stupefied.

'Blood!' roared somebody.

There was blood everywhere, on the cobblestones of the square, on the ground hardened by the first frosts of autumn; and, when a number of men and boys rushed off in pursuit of the motor, they had but to take those sinister marks for their guide.

The marks, on their part, followed the high-road, but in a very strange manner, going from one side to the other and leaving a zigzag track, in the wake of the tires, that made those who saw it shudder. How was it that the car had not bumped against that tree? How had it been righted, instead of smashing into that bank? What novice, what madman, what drunkard, what frightened criminal was driving that motor-car with such astounding bounds and swerves?

One of the peasants declared: 'They will never do the turn in the forest.'

And another said: 'Of course they won't! She's bound to upset!'

The Forest of Morgues began at half a mile beyond Saint-Nicolas; and the road, which was straight up to that point, except for a slight bend where it left the village, started climbing, immediately after entering the forest, and made an abrupt turn among the rocks and trees. No motor-car was able to take this turn without first slackening speed. There were posts to give notice of the danger.

The breathless peasants reached the quincunx of beeches that formed the edge of the forest. And one of them at once cried: 'There you are!'

'What?'

'Upset!'

The car, a limousine, had turned turtle and lay smashed, twisted and shapeless. Beside it, the woman's dead body. But the most horrible, sordid, stupefying thing was the woman's head, crushed, flattened, invisible under a block of stone, a huge block of stone lodged there by some unknown and prodigious agency. As for the man in the goat-skin coat, he was nowhere to be found.

*　*　*

He was not found on the scene of the accident. He was not found either in the neighbourhood. Moreover, some workmen coming down the Côte de Morgues declared that they had not seen anybody.

The man, therefore, had taken refuge in the woods.

The gendarmes, who were at once sent for, made a minute search, assisted by the peasants, but discovered nothing. In the same way, the examining-magistrates, after a close inquiry lasting for several days, found no clue capable of throwing the least light upon this inscrutable tragedy. On the contrary, the investigations only led to further mysteries and further improbabilities.

Thus it was ascertained that the block of stone came from where there had been a landslip, at least forty yards away. And the murderer, in a few minutes, had carried it all that distance and flung it on his victim's head.

On the other hand, the murderer, who was most certainly not hiding in the forest – for, if so, he must inevitably have been discovered, the forest being of limited extent – had the audacity, eight days after the crime, to come back to the turn on the hill and leave his goat-skin coat there. Why? With what object? There was nothing in the pockets of the coat, except a corkscrew and a napkin. What did it all mean?

Inquiries were made of the builder of the motor-car, who recognized the limousine as one which he had sold, three years ago, to a Russian. The said Russian, declared the manufacturer, had sold it again at once. To whom? No one knew. The car bore no number.

Then again, it was impossible to identify the dead woman's body. Her clothes and underclothing were not marked in any way. And the face was quite unknown.

Meanwhile, detectives were going along the national road in the direction opposite to that taken by the actors in this mysterious tragedy. But who was to prove that the car had followed that particular road on the previous night?

They examined every yard of the ground, they questioned everybody. At last, they succeeded in learning that, on the Saturday evening, a limousine had stopped outside a grocer's shop in a small town situated about two hundred miles from Saint-Nicolas, on a highway branching out of the national road. The driver had first filled his tank, bought some spare cans of petrol and lastly taken away a small stock of provisions: a ham, fruit, biscuits, wine and a half-bottle of Three Star brandy.

There was a lady on the driver's seat. She did not get down. The blinds of the limousine were drawn. One of these blinds was seen to move several times. The shopman was positive that there was somebody inside.

Presuming the shopman's evidence to be correct, then the problem became even more complicated, for, so far, no clue had revealed the presence of a third person.

Meanwhile, as the travellers had supplied themselves with provisions, it remained to be discovered what they had done with them and what had become of the remains.

The detectives retraced their steps. It was not until they came to the fork of the two roads, at a spot eleven or twelve miles from Saint-Nicolas, that they met a shepherd who, in answer to their questions,

directed them to a neighbouring field, hidden from view behind the
screen of bushes, where he had seen an empty bottle and other things.

The detectives were convinced at the first examination. The motor-
car had stopped there; and the unknown travellers, probably after a
night's rest in their car, had breakfasted and resumed their journey in
the course of the morning.

One unmistakable proof was the half-bottle of Three Star brandy
sold by the grocer. This bottle had its neck broken clean off with a
stone. The stone employed for the purpose was picked up, as was the
neck of the bottle, with its cork, covered with a tin-foil seal. The seal
showed marks of attempts that had been made to uncork the bottle in
the ordinary manner.

The detectives continued their search and followed a ditch that ran
along the field at right angles to the road. It ended in a little spring,
hidden under brambles, which seemed to emit an offensive smell. On
lifting the brambles, they perceived a corpse, the corpse of a man
whose head had been smashed in, so that it formed little more than a
sort of pulp, swarming with vermin. The body was dressed in jacket
and trousers of dark-brown leather. The pockets were empty: no
papers, no pocket-book, no watch.

The grocer and his shopman were summoned and, two days later,
formally identified, by his dress and figure, the traveller who had
bought the petrol and provisions on the Saturday evening.

The whole case, therefore, had to be reopened on a fresh basis.
The authorities were confronted with a tragedy no longer enacted by
two persons, a man and a woman, of whom one had killed the other,
but by three persons, including two victims, of whom one was the
very man who was accused of killing his companion.

As to the murderer, there was no doubt: he was the person who
travelled inside the motor-car and who took the precaution to remain
concealed behind the curtains. He had first got rid of the driver and
rifled his pockets and then, after wounding the woman, carried her off
in a mad dash for death.

*   *   *

Given a fresh case, unexpected discoveries, unforeseen evidence,
one might have hoped that the mystery would be cleared up, or
at least, that the inquiry would point a few steps along the road
to the truth. But not at all. The corpse was simply placed beside
the first corpse. New problems were added to the old. The accusation of murder was shifted from the one to the other. And there

it ended. Outside those tangible, obvious facts there was nothing but darkness. The name of the woman, the name of the man, the name of the murderer were so many riddles. And then what had become of the murderer? If he had disappeared from one moment to the other, that in itself would have been a tolerably curious phenomenon. But the phenomenon was actually something very like a miracle, inasmuch as the murderer had not absolutely disappeared. He was there! He made a practice of returning to the scene of the catastrophe! In addition to the goat-skin coat, a fur cap was picked up one day; and, by way of an unparalleled prodigy, one morning, after a whole night spent on guard in the rock, beside the famous turning, the detectives found, on the grass of the turning itself, a pair of motor-goggles, broken, rusty, dirty, done for. How had the murderer managed to bring back those goggles unseen by the detectives? And, above all, why had he brought them back?

Men's brains reeled in the presence of such abnormalities. They were almost afraid to pursue the ambiguous adventure. They received the impression of a heavy, stifling, breathless atmosphere, which dimmed the eyes and baffled the most clear-sighted.

The magistrate in charge of the case fell ill. Four days later, his successor confessed that the matter was beyond him.

Two tramps were arrested and at once released. Another was pursued, but not caught; moreover, there was no evidence of any sort or kind against him. In short, it was nothing but one helpless muddle of mist and contradiction.

An accident, the merest accident led to the solution, or rather produced a series of circumstances that ended by leading to the solution. A reporter on the staff of an important Paris paper, who had been sent to make investigations on the spot, concluded his article with the following words.

I repeat, therefore, that we must wait for fresh events, fresh facts; we must wait for some lucky accident. As things stand, we are simply wasting our time. The elements of truth are not even sufficient to suggest a plausible theory. We are in the midst of the most absolute, painful, impenetrable darkness. There is nothing to be done. All the Sherlock Holmeses in the world would not know what to make of the mystery, and Arsène Lupin himself, if he will allow me to say so, would have to pay forfeit here.

* * *

On the day after the appearance of that article, the newspaper in question printed this telegram.

HAVE SOMETIMES PAID FORFEIT, BUT NEVER OVER SUCH A SILLY THING AS THIS. THE SAINT-NICOLAS TRAGEDY IS A MYSTERY FOR BABIES.

ARSÈNE LUPIN

And the editor added.

We insert this telegram as a matter of curiosity, for it is obviously the work of a wag. Arsène Lupin, past-master though he be in the art of practical joking, would be the last man to display such childish flippancy.'

Two days elapsed; and then the paper published the famous letter, so precise and categorical in its conclusions, in which Arsène Lupin furnished the solution of the problem. I quote it in full.

Sir.

You have taken me on my weak side by defying me. You challenge me, and I accept the challenge. And I will begin by declaring once more that the Saint-Nicolas tragedy is a mystery for babies. I know nothing so simple, so natural; and the proof of the simplicity shall lie in the succinctness of my demonstration. It is contained in these few words: when a crime seems to go beyond the ordinary scope of things, when it seems unusual and stupid, then there are many chances that its explanation is to be found in superordinary, supernatural, superhuman motives.

I say that there are many chances, for we must always allow for the part played by absurdity in the most logical and commonplace events. But, of course, it is impossible to see things as they are and not to take account of the absurd and the disproportionate.

I was struck from the very beginning by that very evident character of unusualness. We have, first of all, the awkward, zigzag course of the motor-car, which would give one the impression that the car was driven by a novice. People have spoken of a drunkard or a madman, a justifiable supposition in itself. But neither madness nor drunkenness would account for the incredible strength required to transport, especially in so short a space of time, the stone with which the unfortunate woman's head was crushed. That proceeding called for a muscular power so great that I do not hesitate to look upon it as a second sign of the unusualness that marks the whole tragedy. And why move that enormous stone, to finish off the victim, when a mere pebble would have done the work? Why again was the murderer not killed, or at least reduced to a temporary state of helplessness, in the terrible somersault turned by the car? How did he disappear? And why, having disappeared, did he return to the scene of the accident? Why did he throw his fur coat there; then, on another day, his cap; then, on another day, his goggles?

Unusual, useless, stupid acts.

Why, besides, convey that wounded, dying woman on the driver's seat of the car, where everybody could see her? Why do that, instead of putting her inside, or flinging her into some corner, dead, just as the man was flung under the brambles in the ditch?

Unusualness, stupidity.

Everything in the whole story is absurd. Everything points to hesitation, incoherency, awkwardness, the silliness of a child or rather of a mad, blundering savage, of a brute.

Look at the bottle of brandy. There was a corkscrew: it was found in the pocket of the great coat. Did the murderer use it? Yes, the marks of the corkscrew can be seen on the seal. But the operation was too complicated for him. He broke the neck with a stone. Always stones: observe that detail. They are the only weapon, the only implement which the creature employs. It is his customary weapon, his familiar implement. He kills the man with a stone, he kills the woman with a stone and he opens bottles with a stone!

A brute, I repeat, a savage; disordered, unhinged, suddenly driven mad. By what? Why, of course, by that same brandy, which he swallowed at a draught while the driver and his companion were having breakfast in the field. He got out of the limousine, in which he was travelling, in his goat-skin coat and his fur cap, took the bottle, broke off the neck and drank. There is the whole story. Having drunk, he went raving mad and hit out at random, without reason. Then, seized with instinctive fear, dreading the inevitable punishment, he hid the body of the man. Then, like an idiot, he took up the wounded woman and ran away. He ran away in that motor-car which he did not know how to work, but which to him represented safety, escape from capture.

But the money, you will ask, the stolen pocket-book? Why, who says that he was the thief? Who says that it was not some passing tramp, some labourer, guided by the stench of the corpse?

Very well, you object, but the brute would have been found, as he is hiding somewhere near the turn, and as, after all, he must eat and drink.

Well, well, I see that you have not yet understood. The simplest way, I suppose, to have done and to answer your objections is to make straight for the mark. Then let the gentlemen of the police and the gendarmerie themselves make straight for the mark. Let them take firearms. Let them explore the forest within a radius of two or three hundred yards from the turn, no more. But, instead of exploring with their heads down and their eyes fixed on the ground, let them look up into the air, yes, into the air, among the leaves and branches of the tallest oaks and the most unlikely beeches. And, believe me, they will see him. For he is there. He is there, bewildered, piteously at a loss, seeking for the man and woman whom he has killed, looking for them and waiting for them and not daring to go away and quite unable to understand.

I myself am exceedingly sorry that I am kept in town by urgent private affairs and by some complicated matters of business which I have to set going, for I should much have liked to see the end of this rather curious adventure.

Pray, therefore excuse me to my kind friends in the police and permit me to be, sir,

Your obedient servant,

Arsène Lupin

* * *

The upshot will be remembered. The 'gentlemen of the police and the gendarmerie' shrugged their shoulders and paid no attention to this lucubration. But four of the local country gentry took their rifles and went shooting, with their eyes fixed skyward, as though they meant to pot a few rooks. In half an hour they had caught sight of the murderer. Two shots, and he came tumbling from bough to bough. He was only wounded, and they took him alive.

That evening, a Paris paper, which did not yet know of the capture, printed the following paragraphs.

Enquiries are being made after a M. and Mme Bragoff, who landed at Marseilles six weeks ago and there hired a motor-car. They had been living in Australia for many years, during which time they had not visited Europe; and they wrote to the director of the Jardin d'Acclimatation, with whom they were in the habit of corresponding, that they were bringing with them a curious creature, of an entirely unknown species, of which it was difficult to say whether it was a man or a monkey.

According to M. Bragoff, who is an eminent archæologist, the specimen in question is the anthropoid ape, or rather the ape-man, the existence of which had not hitherto been definitely proved. The structure is said to be exactly similar to that of *Pithecanthropus erectus*, discovered by Dr Dubois in Java in 1891.

This curious, intelligent and observant animal acted as its owner's servant on their property in Australia and used to clean their motor-car and even attempt to drive it.

The question that is being asked is where are M. and Mme Bragoff? Where is the strange primate that landed with them at Marseilles?'

The answer to this question was now made easy. Thanks to the hints supplied by Arsène Lupin, all the elements of the tragedy were known. Thanks to him, the culprit was in the hands of the law.

You can see him at the Jardin d'Acclimatation, where he is locked up under the name of 'Three Stars'. He is, in point of fact, a monkey; but he is also a man. He has the gentleness and the wisdom of the domestic animals and the sadness which they feel when their master dies. But he has many other qualities that bring him much closer to humanity: he is treacherous, cruel, idle, greedy and quarrelsome; and, above all, he is immoderately fond of brandy.

Apart from that, he is a monkey. Unless indeed . . . !

* * *

A few days after Three Stars' arrest, I saw Arsène Lupin standing in front of his cage. Lupin was manifestly trying to solve this interesting problem for himself. I at once said, for I had set my heart upon having the matter out with him.

'You know, Lupin, that intervention of yours, your argument, your letter, in short, did not surprise me so much as you might think!'

'Oh, really?' he said, calmly. 'And why?'

'Why? Because the incident has occurred before, seventy or eighty years ago. Edgar Allan Poe made it the subject of one of his finest tales. In those circumstances, the key to the riddle was easy enough to find.'

Arsène Lupin took my arm, and walking away with me, said: 'When did you guess it, yourself?'

'On reading your letter,' I confessed.

'And at what part of my letter?'

'At the end.'

'At the end, eh? After I had dotted all the i's. So here is a crime which accident causes to be repeated, under quite different conditions, it is true, but still with the same sort of hero; and your eyes had to be opened, as well as other people's. It needed the assistance of my letter, the letter in which I amused myself – apart from the exigencies of the facts – by employing the argument and sometimes the identical words used by the American poet in a story which everybody has read. So you see that my letter was not absolutely useless and that one may safely venture to repeat to people things which they have learnt only to forget them.'

Wherewith Lupin turned on his heel and burst out laughing in the face of an old monkey, who sat with the air of a philosopher, gravely meditating.

Lupin's Marriage

Monsieur Arsène Lupin has the honour to inform you of his approaching marriage with Mademoiselle Angélique de Sarzeau-Vendôme, Princesse de Bourbon-Condé, and to request the pleasure of your company at the wedding, which will take place at the church of Sainte-Clotilde . . .

The Duc de Sarzeau-Vendôme has the honour to inform you of the approaching marriage of his daughter Angélique, Princesse de Bourbon-Condé, with Monsieur Arsène Lupin, and to request . . .

Jean Duc de Sarzeau-Vendôme could not finish reading the invitations which he held in his trembling hand. Pale with anger, his long, lean body shaking with tremors: 'There!' he gasped, handing the two communications to his daughter. 'This is what our friends have received! This has been the talk of Paris since yesterday! What do you say to that dastardly insult, Angélique? What would your poor mother say to it, if she were alive?'

Angélique was tall and thin like her father, skinny and angular like him. She was thirty-three years of age, always dressed in black stuff, shy and retiring in manner, with a head too small in proportion to her height and narrowed on either side until the nose seemed to jut forth in protest against such parsimony. And yet it would be impossible to say that she was ugly, for her eyes were extremely beautiful, soft and grave, proud and a little sad: pathetic eyes which to see once was to remember.

She flushed with shame at hearing her father's words, which told her the scandal of which she was the victim. But, as she loved him, notwithstanding his harshness to her, his injustice and despotism, she said: 'Oh, I think it must be meant for a joke, father, to which we need pay no attention!'

'A joke? Why, everyone is gossiping about it! A dozen papers have printed the confounded notice this morning, with satirical comments.

They quote our pedigree, our ancestors, our illustrious dead. They pretend to take the thing seriously . . . '

'Still, no one could believe . . . '

'Of course not. But that doesn't prevent us from being the by-word of Paris.'

'It will all be forgotten by tomorrow.'

'Tomorrow, my girl, people will remember that the name of Angélique de Sarzeau-Vendôme has been bandied about as it should not be. Oh, if I could find out the name of the scoundrel who has dared . . . '

At that moment, Hyacinthe, the duke's valet, came in and said that monsieur le duc was wanted on the telephone. Still fuming, he took down the receiver and growled: 'Well? Who is it? Yes, it's the Duc de Sarzeau-Vendôme speaking.'

A voice replied: 'I want to apologize to you, monsieur le duc, and to Mlle Angélique. It's my secretary's fault.'

'Your secretary?'

'Yes, the invitations were only a rough draft which I meant to submit to you. Unfortunately my secretary thought . . . '

'But, tell me, monsieur, who are you?'

'What, monsieur le duc, don't you know my voice? The voice of your future son-in-law?'

'What!'

'Arsène Lupin.'

The duke dropped into a chair. His face was livid.

'Arsène Lupin . . . it's he . . . Arsène Lupin . . . '

Angélique gave a smile.

'You see, father, it's only a joke, a hoax.'

But the duke's rage broke out afresh and he began to walk up and down, moving his arms.

'I shall go to the police! . . . The fellow can't be allowed to make a fool of me in this way! . . . If there's any law left in the land, it must be stopped!'

Hyacinthe entered the room again. He brought two visiting-cards.

'Chotois? Lepetit? Don't know them.'

'They are both journalists, monsieur le duc.'

'What do they want?'

'They would like to speak to monsieur le duc with regard to . . . the marriage . . . '

'Turn them out!' exclaimed the duke. 'Kick them out! And tell the porter not to admit scum of that sort to my house in future.'

'Please, father . . . ' Angélique ventured to say.

'As for you, shut up! If you had consented to marry one of your cousins when I wanted you to this wouldn't have happened.'

The same evening, one of the two reporters printed, on the front page of his paper, a somewhat fanciful story of his expedition to the family mansion of the Sarzeau-Vendômes, in the Rue de Varennes, and expatiated pleasantly upon the old nobleman's wrathful protests.

The next morning, another newspaper published an interview with Arsène Lupin which was supposed to have taken place in a lobby at the Opera. Arsène Lupin retorted in a letter to the editor.

I share my prospective father-in-law's indignation to the full. The sending out of the invitations was a gross breach of etiquette for which I am not responsible, but for which I wish to make a public apology. Why, sir, the date of the marriage is not yet fixed. My bride's father suggests early in May. She and I think that six weeks is really too long to wait! . . .

That which gave a special piquancy to the affair and added immensely to the enjoyment of the friends of the family was the duke's well-known character: his pride and the uncompromising nature of his ideas and principles. Duc Jean was the last descendant of the Barons de Sarzeau, the most ancient family in Brittany; he was the lineal descendant of that Sarzeau who, upon marrying a Vendôme, refused to bear the new title which Louis XV forced upon him until after he had been imprisoned for ten years in the Bastille; and he had abandoned none of the prejudices of the old régime. In his youth, he followed the Comte de Chambord into exile. In his old age, he refused a seat in the Chamber on the pretext that a Sarzeau could only sit with his peers.

The incident stung him to the quick. Nothing could pacify him. He cursed Lupin in good round terms, threatened him with every sort of punishment, and rounded on his daughter.

'There, if you had only married! . . . After all you had plenty of chances. Your three cousins, Mussy, d'Emboise and Caorches, are noblemen of good descent, allied to the best families, fairly well-off; and they are still anxious to marry you. Why do you refuse them? Ah, because miss is a dreamer, a sentimentalist; and because her cousins are too fat, or too thin, or too coarse for her . . . '

She was, in fact, a dreamer. Left to her own devices from childhood, she had read all the books of chivalry, all the colourless romances of olden-time that littered the ancestral presses; and she looked upon life as a fairy-tale in which the beauteous maidens are always happy, while the others wait till death for the bridegroom who does not come. Why should she marry one of her cousins when they were only after her money, the millions which she had inherited from her mother? She might as well remain an old maid and go on dreaming . . .

She answered, gently: 'You will end by making yourself ill, father. Forget this silly business.'

But how could he forget it? Every morning, some pin-prick renewed his wound. Three days running, Angélique received a wonderful sheaf of flowers, with Arsène Lupin's card peeping from it. The duke could not go to his club but a friend accosted him.

'That was a good one today!'

'What was?'

'Why, your son-in-law's latest! Haven't you seen it? Here, read it for yourself: "M. Arsène Lupin is petitioning the Council of State for permission to add his wife's name to his own and to be known henceforth as Lupin de Sarzeau-Vendôme." '

And, the next day, he read.

As the young bride, by virtue of an unrepealed decree of Charles X, bears the title and arms of the Bourbon-Condés, of whom she is the heiress-of-line, the eldest son of the Lupins de Sarzeau-Vendôme will be styled Prince de Bourbon-Condé.

And, the day after, an advertisement.

Exhibition of Mlle de Sarzeau-Vendôme's trousseau at Messrs — — 's Great Linen Warehouse. Each article marked with initials L. S. V.

Then an illustrated paper published a photographic scene: the duke, his daughter and his son- in-law sitting at a table playing three-handed auction-bridge.

And the date also was announced with a great flourish of trumpets: the 4th of May.

And particulars were given of the marriage-settlement. Lupin showed himself wonderfully disinterested. He was prepared to sign, the newspapers said, with his eyes closed, without knowing the figure of the dowry.

All these things drove the old duke crazy. His hatred of Lupin assumed morbid proportions. Much as it went against the grain, he called on the prefect of police, who advised him to be on his guard.

'We know the gentleman's ways; he is employing one of his favourite dodges. Forgive the expression, monsieur le duc, but he is "nursing" you. Don't fall into the trap.'

'What dodge? What trap?' asked the duke, anxiously.

'He is trying to make you lose your head and to lead you, by intimidation, to do something which you would refuse to do in cold blood.'

'Still, M. Arsène Lupin can hardly hope that I will offer him my daughter's hand!'

'No, but he hopes that you will commit, to put it mildly, a blunder.'

'What blunder?'

'Exactly that blunder which he wants you to commit.'

'Then you think, monsieur le préfet . . . ?'

'I think the best thing you can do, monsieur le duc, is to go home, or, if all this excitement worries you, to run down to the country and stay there quietly, without upsetting yourself.'

This conversation only increased the old duke's fears. Lupin appeared to him in the light of a terrible person, who employed diabolical methods and kept accomplices in every sphere of society. Prudence was the watchword.

And life, from that moment, became intolerable. The duke grew more crabbed and silent than ever and denied his door to all his old friends and even to Angélique's three suitors, her Cousins de Mussy, d'Emboise and de Caorches, who were none of them on speaking terms with the others, in consequence of their rivalry, and who were in the habit of calling, turn and turn about, every week.

For no earthly reason, he dismissed his butler and his coachman. But he dared not fill their places, for fear of engaging creatures of Arsène Lupin's; and his own man, Hyacinthe, in whom he had every confidence, having had him in his service for over forty years, had to take upon himself the laborious duties of the stables and the pantry.

'Come, father,' said Angélique, trying to make him listen to common-sense. 'I really can't see what you are afraid of. No one can force me into this ridiculous marriage.'

'Well, of course, that's not what I'm afraid of.'

'What then, father?'

'How can I tell? An abduction! A burglary! An act of violence! There is no doubt that the villain is scheming something; and there is also no doubt that we are surrounded by spies.'

One afternoon, he received a newspaper in which the following paragraph was marked in red pencil.

The signing of the marriage-contract is fixed for this evening, at the Sarzeau-Vendôme town-house. It will be quite a private ceremony and only a few privileged friends will be present to congratulate the happy pair. The witnesses to the contract on behalf of Mlle de Sarzeau-Vendôme, the Prince de la Roche-foucauld-Limours and the Comte de Chartres, will be introduced by M. Arsène Lupin to the two gentlemen who have claimed the honour of acting as his groomsmen, namely, the prefect of police and the governor of the Santé Prison.'

Ten minutes later, the duke sent his servant Hyacinthe to the post with three express messages. At four o'clock, in Angélique's presence, he saw the three cousins: Mussy, fat, heavy, pasty-faced; d'Emboise, slender, fresh-coloured and shy: Caorches, short, thin and unhealthy-looking: all three, old bachelors by this time, lacking distinction in dress or appearance.

The meeting was a short one. The duke had worked out his whole plan of campaign, a defensive campaign, of which he set forth the first stage in explicit terms.

'Angélique and I will leave Paris tonight for our place in Brittany. I rely on you, my three nephews, to help us get away. You, d'Emboise, will come and fetch us in your car, with the hood up. You, Mussy, will bring your big motor and kindly see to the luggage with Hyacinthe, my man. You, Caorches, will go to the Gare d'Orléans and book our berths in the sleeping-car for Vannes by the 10.40 train. Is that settled?'

The rest of the day passed without incident. The duke, to avoid any accidental indiscretion, waited until after dinner to tell Hyacinthe to pack a trunk and a portmanteau. Hyacinthe was to accompany them, as well as Angélique's maid.

At nine o'clock, all the other servants went to bed, by their master's order. At ten minutes to ten, the duke, who was completing his preparations, heard the sound of a motor-horn. The porter opened the gates of the courtyard. The duke, standing at the window, recognized d'Emboise's landaulette.

'Tell him I shall be down presently,' he said to Hyacinthe, 'and let mademoiselle know.'

In a few minutes, as Hyacinthe did not return, he left his room. But he was attacked on the landing by two masked men, who gagged and bound him before he could utter a cry. And one of the men said to him, in a low voice: 'Take this as a first warning, monsieur le duc. If you persist in leaving Paris and refusing your consent, it will be a more serious matter.'

And the same man said to his companion: 'Keep an eye on him. I will see to the young lady.'

By that time, two other confederates had secured the lady's maid; and Angélique, herself gagged, lay fainting on a couch in her boudoir.

She came to almost immediately, under the stimulus of a bottle of salts held to her nostrils; and, when she opened her eyes, she saw bending over her a young man, in evening-clothes, with a smiling and friendly face, who said: 'I implore your forgiveness, mademoiselle. All these happenings are a trifle sudden and this behaviour rather out of the way. But circumstances often compel us to deeds of which our conscience does not approve. Pray pardon me.'

He took her hand very gently and slipped a broad gold ring on the girl's finger, saying: 'There, now we are engaged. Never forget the man who gave you this ring. He entreats you not to run away from him . . . and to stay in Paris and await the proofs of his devotion. Have faith in him.'

He said all this in so serious and respectful a voice, with so much authority and deference, that she had not the strength to resist. Their eyes met. He whispered: 'The exquisite purity of your eyes! It would be heavenly to live with those eyes upon one. Now close them . . . '

He withdrew. His accomplices followed suit. The car drove off, and the house in the Rue de Varennes remained still and silent until the moment when Angélique, regaining complete consciousness, called out for the servants.

They found the duke, Hyacinthe, the lady's maid and the porter and his wife all tightly bound. A few priceless ornaments had disappeared, as well as the duke's pocket-book and all his jewellery; tie pins, pearl studs, watch and so on.

The police were advised without delay. In the morning it appeared that, on the evening before, d'Emboise, when leaving his house in the motor-car, was stabbed by his own chauffeur and thrown, half-dead, into a deserted street. Mussy and Caorches had each received a telephone-message, purporting to come from the duke, countermanding their attendance.

Next week, without troubling further about the police investigation, without obeying the summons of the examining-magistrate, without even reading Arsène Lupin's letters to the papers on 'the

Varennes Flight', the duke, his daughter and his valet stealthily took a slow train for Vannes and arrived one evening at the old feudal castle that towers over the headland of Sarzeau. The duke at once organized a defence with the aid of the Breton peasants, true medieval vassals to a man. On the fourth day, Mussy arrived; on the fifth, Caorches; and on the seventh, d'Emboise, whose wound was not as severe as had been feared.

The duke waited two days longer before communicating to those about him what, now that his escape had succeeded in spite of Lupin, he called the second part of his plan. He did so, in the presence of the three cousins, by a dictatorial order to Angélique, expressed in these peremptory terms: 'All this bother is upsetting me terribly. I have entered on a struggle with this man whose daring you have seen for yourself; and the struggle is killing me. I want to end it at all costs. There is only one way of doing so, Angélique, and that is for you to release me from all responsibility by accepting the hand of one of your cousins. Before a month is out, you must be the wife of Mussy, Caorches or d'Emboise. You have a free choice. Make your decision.'

For four whole days Angélique wept and entreated her father, but in vain. She felt that he would be inflexible and that she must end by submitting to his wishes. She accepted.

'Whichever you please, father. I love none of them. So I may as well be unhappy with one as with the other.'

Thereupon a fresh discussion ensued, as the duke wanted to compel her to make her own choice. She stood firm. Reluctantly and for financial considerations, he named d'Emboise.

The banns were published without delay.

From that moment, the watch in and around the castle was increased twofold, all the more inasmuch as Lupin's silence and the sudden cessation of the campaign which he had been conducting in the press could not but alarm the Duc de Sarzeau-Vendôme. It was obvious that the enemy was getting ready to strike and would endeavour to oppose the marriage by one of his characteristic moves.

Nevertheless, nothing happened: nothing two days before the ceremony, nothing on the day before, nothing on the morning itself. The marriage took place in the mayor's office, followed by the religious celebration in church; and the thing was done.

Then and not till then, the duke breathed freely. Notwithstanding his daughter's sadness, notwithstanding the embarrassed silence of his son-in-law, who found the situation a little trying, he rubbed his hands with an air of pleasure, as though he had achieved a brilliant victory.

'Tell them to lower the drawbridge,' he said to Hyacinthe, 'and to admit everybody. We have nothing more to fear from that scoundrel.'

After the wedding-breakfast, he had wine served out to the peasants and clinked glasses with them. They danced and sang.

At three o'clock, he returned to the ground-floor rooms. It was the hour for his afternoon nap. He walked to the guard-room at the end of the suite. But he had no sooner placed his foot on the threshold than he stopped suddenly and exclaimed: 'What are you doing here, d'Emboise? Is this a joke?'

D'Emboise was standing before him, dressed as a Breton fisherman, in a dirty jacket and breeches, torn, patched and many sizes too large for him.

The duke seemed dumbfounded. He stared with eyes of amazement at that face which he knew and which, at the same time, roused memories of a very distant past within his brain. Then he strode abruptly to one of the windows overlooking the castle-terrace and called: 'Angélique!'

'What is it, father?' she asked, coming forward.

'Where's your husband?'

'Over there, father,' said Angélique, pointing to d'Emboise, who was smoking a cigarette and reading, some way off.

The duke stumbled and fell into a chair, with a great shudder of fright.

'Oh, I shall go mad!'

But the man in the fisherman's garb knelt down before him and said: 'Look at me, uncle. You know me, don't you? I'm your nephew, the one who used to play here in the old days, the one whom you called Jacquot . . . Just think a minute . . . Here, look at this scar . . . '

'Yes, yes,' stammered the duke, 'I recognize you. It's Jacques. But the other one . . . '

He put his hands to his head.

'And yet, no, it can't be . . . Explain yourself . . . I don't under-stand . . . I don't want to understand . . . '

There was a pause, during which the newcomer shut the window and closed the door leading to the next room. Then he came up to the old duke, touched him gently on the shoulder, to wake him from his torpor, and without further preface, as though to cut short any explanation that was not absolutely necessary, spoke as follows.

'Four years ago, that is to say, in the eleventh year of my voluntary exile, when I settled in the extreme south of Algeria, I made the acquaintance, in the course of a hunting-expedition arranged by a big Arab chief, of a man whose geniality, whose charm of manner, whose consummate prowess, whose indomitable pluck, whose combined humour and depth of mind fascinated me in the highest degree. The Comte d'Andrésy spent six weeks as my guest. After he left, we kept up a correspondence at regular intervals. I also often saw his name in the papers, in the society and sporting columns. He was to come back and I was preparing to receive him, three months ago, when, one evening as I was out riding, my two Arab attendants flung themselves upon me, bound me, blindfolded me and took me, travelling day and night, for a week, along deserted roads, to a bay on the coast, where five men awaited them. I was at once carried on board a small steam-yacht, which weighed anchor without delay. There was nothing to tell me who the men were nor what their object was in kidnapping me. They had locked me into a narrow cabin, secured by a massive door and lighted by a port-hole protected by two iron cross-bars. Every morning, a hand was inserted through a hatch between the next cabin and my own and placed on my bunk two or three pounds of bread, a good helping of food and a flagon of wine and removed the remains of yesterday's meals, which I put there for the purpose. From time to time, at night, the yacht stopped and I heard the sound of the boat rowing to some harbour and then returning, doubtless with provisions. Then we set out once more, without hurrying, as though on a cruise of people of our class, who travel for pleasure and are not pressed for time. Sometimes, standing on a chair, I would see the coastline, through my port-hole, too indistinctly, however, to locate it. And this lasted for weeks. One morning, in the ninth week, I perceived that the hatch had been left unfastened and I pushed it open. The cabin was empty at the time. With an effort, I was able to take a nail-file from a dressing-table. Two weeks after that, by dint of patient perseverance, I had succeeded in filing through the bars of my port-hole and I could have escaped that way, only, though I am a good swimmer, I soon grow tired. I had therefore to choose a moment when the yacht was not too far from the land. It was not until yesterday that, perched on my chair, I caught sight of the coast; and, in the evening, at sunset, I recognized, to my astonishment, the outlines of the Château de Sarzeau, with its pointed turrets and its square keep. I wondered if this was the goal of my mysterious voyage. All night long, we cruised in the offing. The same all day yesterday. At last, this morning, we put in at a distance which I considered favourable, all the more so as we were steaming through rocks under cover of which I could swim unobserved. But, just as I was about to make my escape, I noticed that the shutter of the hatch, which they thought they had closed, had once more opened of itself and was flapping against the partition. I again pushed it ajar from curiosity. Within arm's length was a little cupboard which I managed to open and in which my hand, groping at random, laid hold of a bundle of papers. This consisted of letters, letters containing instructions addressed to the pirates who held me prisoner. An hour later, when I wriggled through the port-hole and slipped into the sea, I knew all: the reasons for my abduction, the means employed, the object in view and the infamous scheme plotted during the last three months against the Duc de Sarzeau-Vendôme and his daughter. Unfortunately, it was too late. I was obliged, in order not to be seen from the yacht, to crouch in the cleft of a rock and did not reach land until mid-day. By the time that I had been to a fisherman's cabin, exchanged my clothes for his and come on here, it was three o'clock. On my arrival. I learnt that Angélique's marriage was celebrated this morning.'

The old duke had not spoken a word. With his eyes riveted on the stranger's, he was listening in ever-increasing dismay. At times, the thought of the warnings given him by the prefect of police returned to his mind.

'They're nursing you, monsieur le duc, they are nursing you.'

He said, in a hollow voice: 'Speak on . . . finish your story . . . All this is ghastly . . . I don't understand it yet . . . and I feel nervous . . .'

The stranger resumed.

'I am sorry to say, the story is easily pieced together and is summed up in a few sentences. It is like this: the Comte d'Andrésy remembered several things from his stay with me and from the confidences which I was foolish enough to make to him. First of all, I was your nephew and yet you had seen comparatively little of me, because I left Sarzeau when I was quite a child, and since then our intercourse was limited to the few weeks which I spent here, fifteen years ago, when I proposed for the hand of my Cousin Angélique; secondly, having broken with the past, I received no letters; lastly, there was a certain physical resemblance between d'Andrésy and myself which could be accentuated to such an extent as to become striking. His scheme was built up on those three points. He bribed my Arab servants to give him warning in case I left Algeria. Then he went back to Paris, bearing my name and made up to look exactly like me, came to see you, was invited to your house once a fortnight and lived under my name, which thus became one of the many aliases beneath which he conceals his real identity. Three months ago, when "the apple was ripe", as he says in his letters, he began the attack by a series of communications to the press; and, at the same time, fearing no doubt that some newspaper would tell me in Algeria the part that was being played under my name in Paris, he had me assaulted by my servants and kidnapped by his confederates. I need not explain any more in so far as you are concerned, uncle.'

The Duc de Sarzeau-Vendôme was shaken with a fit of nervous trembling. The awful truth to which he refused to open his eyes appeared to him in its nakedness and assumed the hateful countenance of the enemy. He clutched his nephew's hands and said to him, fiercely, despairingly.

'It's Lupin, is it not?'

'Yes, uncle.'

'And it's to him . . . it's to him that I have given my daughter!'

'Yes, uncle, to him, who has stolen my name of Jacques d'Emboise from me and stolen your daughter from you. Angélique is the wedded wife of Arsène Lupin; and that in accordance with your orders. This letter in his handwriting bears witness to it. He has upset your whole life, thrown you off your balance, besieging your hours of waking and your nights of dreaming, rifling your town-house, until the moment when, seized with terror, you took refuge here, where, thinking that you would escape his artifices and his rapacity, you told your daughter to choose one of her three cousins, Mussy, d'Emboise or Caorches, as her husband.

'But why did she select that one rather than the others?'

'It was you who selected him, uncle.'

'At random . . . because he had the biggest income . . . '

'No, not at random, but on the insidious, persistent and very clever advice of your servant Hyacinthe.'

The duke gave a start.

'What! Is Hyacinthe an accomplice?'

'No, not of Arsène Lupin, but of the man whom he believes to be d'Emboise and who promised to give him a hundred thousand francs within a week after the marriage.'

'Oh, the villain! . . . He planned everything, foresaw everything . . . '

'Foresaw everything, uncle, down to shamming an attempt upon his life so as to avert suspicion, down to shamming a wound received in your service.'

'But with what object? Why all these dastardly tricks?'

'Angélique has a fortune of eleven million francs. Your solicitor in Paris was to hand the securities next week to the counterfeit d'Emboise, who had only to realize them forthwith and disappear. But, this very morning, you yourself were to hand your son-in-law, as a personal wedding-present, five hundred thousand francs' worth of bearer-stock, which he has arranged to deliver to one of his accomplices at nine o'clock this evening, outside the castle, near the Great Oak, so that they may be negotiated tomorrow morning in Brussels.'

The Duc de Sarzeau-Vendôme had risen from his seat and was stamping furiously up and down the room.

'At nine o'clock this evening?' he said. 'We'll see about that . . . We'll see about that . . . I'll have the gendarmes here before then . . . '

'Arsène Lupin laughs at gendarmes.'

'Let's telegraph to Paris.'

'Yes, but how about the five hundred thousand francs? . . . And, still worse, uncle, the scandal? . . . Think of this: your daughter, Angélique de Sarzeau-Vendôme, married to that swindler, that thief . . . No, no, it would never do . . . '

'What then?'

'What? . . . '

The nephew now rose and, stepping to a gun-rack, took down a rifle and laid it on the table, in front of the duke.

'Away in Algeria, uncle, on the verge of the desert, when we find ourselves face to face with a wild beast, we do not send for the gendarmes. We take our rifle and we shoot the wild beast. Otherwise, the beast would tear us to pieces with its claws.'

'What do you mean?'

'I mean that, over there, I acquired the habit of dispensing with the gendarmes. It is a rather summary way of doing justice, but it is the best way, believe me, and today, in the present case, it is the only way. Once the beast is killed, you and I will bury it in some corner, unseen and unknown.'

'And Angélique?'

'We will tell her later.'

'What will become of her?'

'She will be my wife, the wife of the real d'Emboise. I desert her tomorrow and return to Algeria. The divorce will be granted in two months' time.'

The duke listened, pale and staring, with set jaws. He whispered: 'Are you sure that his accomplices on the yacht will not inform him of your escape?'

'Not before tomorrow.'

'So that . . . ?'

'So that inevitably, at nine o'clock this evening, Arsène Lupin, on his way to the Great Oak, will take the patrol-path that follows the old ramparts and skirts the ruins of the chapel. I shall be there, in the ruins.'

'I shall be there too,' said the Duc de Sarzeau-Vendôme, quietly, taking down a gun.

It was now five o'clock. The duke talked some time longer to his nephew, examined the weapons, loaded them with fresh cartridges. Then, when night came, he took d'Emboise through the dark passages to his bedroom and hid him in an adjoining closet.

Nothing further happened until dinner. The duke forced himself to keep calm during the meal. From time to time, he stole a glance at his son-in-law and was surprised at the likeness between him and the real d'Emboise. It was the same complexion, the same cast of features, the same cut of hair. Nevertheless, the look of the eye was different, keener in this case and brighter; and gradually the duke discovered minor details which had passed unperceived till then and which proved the fellow's imposture.

The party broke up after dinner. It was eight o'clock. The duke went to his room and released his nephew. Ten minutes later, under cover of the darkness, they slipped into the ruins, gun in hand.

Meanwhile, Angélique, accompanied by her husband, had gone to the suite of rooms which she occupied on the ground-floor of a tower that flanked the left wing. Her husband stopped at the entrance to the rooms and said: 'I am going for a short stroll, Angélique. May I come to you here, when I return?'

'Yes,' she replied.

He left her and went up to the first floor, which had been assigned to him as his quarters. The moment he was alone, he locked the door, noiselessly opened a window that looked over the landscape and leant out. He saw a shadow at the foot of the tower, some hundred feet or more below him. He whistled and received a faint whistle in reply.

He then took from a cupboard a thick leather satchel, crammed with papers, wrapped it in a piece of black cloth and tied it up. Then he sat down at the table and wrote.

Glad you got my message, for I think it unsafe to walk out of the castle with that large bundle of securities. Here they are. You will be in Paris, on your motor-cycle, in time to catch the morning train to Brussels, where you will hand over the bonds to Z.; and he will negotiate them at once.

A. L.

P. S. – As you pass by the Great Oak, tell our chaps that I'm coming. I have some instructions to give them. But everything is going well. No one here has the least suspicion.

He fastened the letter to the parcel and lowered both through the window with a length of string.

'Good,' he said. 'That's all right. It's a weight off my mind.'

He waited a few minutes longer, stalking up and down the room and smiling at the portraits of two gallant gentlemen hanging on the wall.

'Horace de Sarzeau-Vendôme, marshal of France . . . And you, the Great Condé . . . I salute you, my ancestors both. Lupin de Sarzeau-Vendôme will show himself worthy of you.'

At last, when the time came, he took his hat and went down. But, when he reached the ground-floor, Angélique burst from her rooms and exclaimed, with a distraught air: 'I say . . . if you don't mind . . . I think you had better . . . '

And then, without saying more, she went in again, leaving a vision of irresponsible terror in her husband's mind.

'She's out of sorts,' he said to himself. 'Marriage doesn't suit her.'

He lit a cigarette and went out, without attaching importance to an incident that ought to have impressed him.

'Poor Angélique! This will all end in a divorce . . . '

The night outside was dark, with a cloudy sky.

The servants were closing the shutters of the castle. There was no light in the windows, it being the duke's habit to go to bed soon after dinner.

Lupin passed the gate-keeper's lodge and, as he put his foot on the drawbridge, said: 'Leave the gate open. I am going for a breath of air; I shall be back soon.'

The patrol-path was on the right and ran along one of the old ramparts, which used to surround the castle with a second

and much larger enclosure, until it ended at an almost demolished
postern-gate. The park, which skirted a hillock and afterward followed the side of a deep valley, was bordered on the left by thick
coppices.

'What a wonderful place for an ambush!' he said. 'A regular cut-
throat spot!'

He stopped, thinking that he heard a noise. But no, it was a
rustling of the leaves. And yet a stone went rattling down the slopes,
bounding against the rugged projections of the rock. But, strange to
say, nothing seemed to disquiet him. The crisp sea-breeze came
blowing over the plains of the headland; and he eagerly filled his
lungs with it.

'What a thing it is to be alive!' he thought. 'Still young, a member
of the old nobility, a multi-millionaire: what could a man want
more?'

At a short distance, he saw against the darkness the yet darker
outline of the chapel, the ruins of which towered above the path. A
few drops of rain began to fall; and he heard a clock strike nine. He
quickened his pace. There was a short descent; then the path rose
again. And suddenly, he stopped once more.

A hand had seized his.

He drew back, tried to release himself.

But someone stepped from the clump of trees against which he was
brushing; and a voice said; 'Ssh! . . . Not a word! . . . '

He recognized his wife, Angélique.

'What's the matter?' he asked.

She whispered, so low that he could hardly catch the words: 'They
are lying in wait for you . . . they are in there, in the ruins, with their
guns . . . '

'Who?'

'Keep quiet . . . Listen . . . '

They stood for a moment without stirring; then she said: 'They are
not moving . . . Perhaps they never heard me . . . Let's go back . . . '

'But . . . '

'Come with me.'

Her accent was so imperious that he obeyed without further question. But suddenly she took fright.

'Run! . . . They are coming! . . . I am sure of it! . . . '

True enough, they heard a sound of footsteps.

Then, swiftly, still holding him by the hand, she dragged him,
with irresistible energy, along a shortcut, following its turns without

hesitation in spite of the darkness and the brambles. And they very soon arrived at the drawbridge.

She put her arm in his. The gate-keeper touched his cap. They crossed the courtyard and entered the castle; and she led him to the corner tower in which both of them had their apartments.

'Come in here,' she said.

'To your rooms?'

'Yes.'

Two maids were sitting up for her. Their mistress ordered them to retire to their bedrooms, on the third floor.

Almost immediately after, there was a knock at the door of the outer room; and a voice called: 'Angélique!'

'Is that you, father?' she asked, suppressing her agitation.

'Yes. Is your husband here?'

'We have just come in.'

'Tell him I want to speak to him. Ask him to come to my room. It's important.'

'Very well, father, I'll send him to you.'

She listened for a few seconds, then returned to the boudoir where her husband was and said: 'I am sure my father is still there.'

He moved as though to go out.

'In that case, if he wants to speak to me . . . '

'My father is not alone,' she said, quickly, blocking his way.

'Who is with him?'

'His nephew, Jacques d'Emboise.'

There was a moment's silence. He looked at her with a certain astonishment, failing quite to understand his wife's attitude. But, without pausing to go into the matter: 'Ah, so that dear old d'Emboise is there?' he chuckled. 'Then the fat's in the fire? Unless, indeed . . . '

'My father knows everything,' she said. 'I overheard a conversation between them just now. His nephew has read certain letters . . . I hesitated at first about telling you . . . Then I thought that my duty . . . '

He studied her afresh. But, at once conquered by the queerness of the situation, he burst out laughing.

'What? Don't my friends on board ship burn my letters? And they have let their prisoner escape? The idiots! Oh, when you don't see to everything yourself! . . . No matter, it's distinctly humorous . . . D'Emboise versus d'Emboise . . . Oh, but suppose I were no longer recognized? Suppose d'Emboise himself were to confuse me with himself?'

He turned to a wash-hand-stand, took a towel, dipped it in the basin and soaped it and, in the twinkling of an eye, wiped the make-up from his face and altered the set of his hair.

'That's it,' he said, showing himself to Angélique under the aspect in which she had seen him on the night of the burglary in Paris. 'I feel more comfortable like this for a discussion with my father-in-law.'

'Where are you going?' she cried, flinging herself in front of the door.

'Why, to join the gentlemen.'

'You shall not pass!'

'Why not?'

'Suppose they kill you?'

'Kill me?'

'That's what they mean to do, to kill you . . . to hide your body somewhere . . . Who would know of it?'

'Very well,' he said, 'from their point of view, they are quite right. But, if I don't go to them, they will come here. That door won't stop them . . . Nor you, I'm thinking. Therefore, it's better to have done with it.'

'Follow me,' commanded Angélique.

She took up the lamp that lit the room, went into her bedroom, pushed aside the wardrobe, which slid easily on hidden castors, pulled back an old tapestry-hanging, and said: 'Here is a door that has not been used for years. My father believes the key to be lost. I have it here. Unlock the door with it. A staircase in the wall will take you to the bottom of the tower. You need only draw the bolts of another door and you will be free.'

He could hardly believe his ears. Suddenly, he grasped the meaning of Angélique's whole behaviour. In front of that sad, plain, but wonderfully gentle face, he stood for a moment discountenanced, almost abashed. He no longer thought of laughing. A feeling of respect, mingled with remorse and kindness, overcame him.

'Why are you saving me?' he whispered.

'You are my husband.'

He protested: 'No, no . . . I have stolen that title. The law will never recognize my marriage.'

'My father does not want a scandal,' she said.

'Just so,' he replied, sharply, 'just so. I foresaw that; and that was why I had your cousin d'Emboise near at hand. Once I disappear, he becomes your husband. He is the man you have married in the eyes of men.'

'You are the man I have married in the eyes of the Church.'

'The Church! The Church! There are means of arranging matters with the Church . . . Your marriage can be annulled.'

'On what pretext that we can admit?'

He remained silent, thinking over all those points which he had not considered, all those points which were trivial and absurd for him, but which were serious for her, and he repeated several times: 'This is terrible . . . this is terrible . . . I should have anticipated . . . '

And, suddenly, seized with an idea, he clapped his hands and cried: 'There, I have it! I'm hand in glove with one of the chief figures at the Vatican. The Pope never refuses me anything. I shall obtain an audience and I have no doubt that the Holy Father, moved by my entreaties . . . '

His plan was so humorous and his delight so artless that Angélique could not help smiling; and she said: 'I am your wife in the eyes of God.'

She gave him a look that showed neither scorn nor animosity, nor even anger; and he realized that she omitted to see in him the outlaw and the evil-doer and remembered only the man who was her husband and to whom the priest had bound her until the hour of death.

He took a step toward her and observed her more attentively. She did not lower her eyes at first. But she blushed. And never had he seen so pathetic a face, marked with such modesty and such dignity. He said to her, as on that first evening in Paris: 'Oh, your eyes . . . the calm and sadness of your eyes . . . the beauty of your eyes!'

She dropped her head and stammered: 'Go away . . . go . . . '

In the presence of her confusion, he received a quick intuition of the deeper feelings that stirred her, unknown to herself. To that spinster soul, of which he recognized the romantic power of imagination, the unsatisfied yearnings, the poring over old-world books, he suddenly represented, in that exceptional moment and in consequence of the unconventional circumstances of their meetings, somebody special, a Byronic hero, a chivalrous brigand of romance. One evening, in spite of all obstacles, he, the world-famed adventurer, already ennobled in song and story and exalted by his own audacity, had come to her and slipped the magic ring upon her finger: a mystic and passionate betrothal, as in the days of *The Corsair* and *Hernani* . . . Greatly moved and touched, he was on the verge of giving way to an enthusiastic impulse and exclaiming: 'Let us go away together! . . . Let us fly! . . . You are my bride . . . my wife . . .

Share my dangers, my sorrows and my joys . . . It will be a strange and vigorous, a proud and magnificent life . . . '

But Angélique's eyes were raised to his again; and they were so pure and so noble that he blushed in his turn. This was not the woman to whom such words could be addressed.

He whispered: 'Forgive me . . . I am a contemptible wretch . . . I have wrecked your life . . . '

'No,' she replied, softly. 'On the contrary, you have shown me where my real life lies.'

He was about to ask her to explain. But she had opened the door and was pointing the way to him. Nothing more could be spoken between them. He went out without a word, bowing very low as he passed.

* * *

A month later, Angélique de Sarzeau-Vendôme, Princesse de Bourbon-Condé, lawful wife of Arsène Lupin, took the veil and, under the name of Sister Marie-Auguste, buried herself within the walls of the Visitation Convent.

On the day of the ceremony, the mother superior of the convent received a heavy sealed envelope containing a letter with the following words.

'For Sister Marie-Auguste's poor.'

Enclosed with the letter were five hundred bank-notes of a thousand francs each.

The Invisible Prisoner

One day, at about four o'clock, as evening was drawing in, Farmer Goussot, with his four sons, returned from a day's shooting. They were stalwart men, all five of them, long of limb, broad-chested, with faces tanned by sun and wind. And all five displayed, planted on an enormous neck and shoulders, the same small head with the low fore-head, thin lips, beaked nose and hard and repellent cast of counten-ance. They were feared and disliked by all around them. They were a money-grubbing, crafty family; and their word was not to be trusted.

On reaching the old barbican-wall that surrounds the Héberville property, the farmer opened a narrow, massive door, putting the big key back in his pocket after his sons had passed in. And he walked behind them, along the path that led through the orchards. Here and there stood great trees, stripped by the autumn winds, and clumps of pines, the last survivors of the ancient park now covered by old Goussot's farm.

One of the sons said: 'I hope mother has lit a log or two.'

'There's smoke coming from the chimney,' said the father.

The outhouses and the homestead showed at the end of a lawn; and, above them, the village church, whose steeple seemed to prick the clouds that trailed along the sky.

'All the guns unloaded?' asked old Goussot.

'Mine isn't,' said the eldest. 'I slipped in a bullet to blow a kestrel's head off . . . '

He was the one who was proudest of his skill. And he said to his brothers: 'Look at that bough, at the top of the cherry tree. See me snap it off.'

On the bough sat a scarecrow, which had been there since spring and which protected the leafless branches with its idiot arms.

He raised his gun and fired.

The figure came tumbling down with large, comic gestures, and was caught on a big, lower branch, where it remained lying stiff on its stomach, with a great top hat on its head of rags and its hay-stuffed legs swaying from right to left above some water that flowed past the cherry tree through a wooden trough.

They all laughed. The father approved.

'A fine shot, my lad. Besides, the old boy was beginning to annoy me. I couldn't take my eyes from my plate at meals without catching sight of that oaf . . .'

They went a few steps farther. They were not more than thirty yards from the house, when the father stopped suddenly and said: 'Hullo! What's up?'

The sons also had stopped and stood listening. One of them said, under his breath: 'It comes from the house . . . from the linen-room . . .'

And another spluttered: 'Sounds like moans . . . And mother's alone!'

Suddenly, a frightful scream rang out. All five rushed forward. Another scream, followed by cries of despair.

'We're here! We're coming!' shouted the eldest, who was leading.

And, as it was a roundabout way to the door, he smashed in a window with his fist and sprang into the old people's bedroom. The room next to it was the linen-room, in which Mother Goussot spent most of her time.

'Damnation!' he said, seeing her lying on the floor, with blood all over her face. 'Dad! Dad!'

'What? Where is she?' roared old Goussot, appearing on the scene. 'Good lord, what's this? . . . What have they done to your mother?'

She pulled herself together and, with outstretched arm, stammered: 'Run after him! . . . This way! . . . This way! . . . I'm all right . . . only a scratch or two . . . But run, you! He's taken the money.'

The father and sons gave a bound.

'He's taken the money!' bellowed old Goussot, rushing to the door to which his wife was pointing. 'He's taken the money! Stop thief!'

But a sound of several voices rose at the end of the passage through which the other three sons were coming.

'I saw him! I saw him!'

'So did I! He ran up the stairs.'

'No, there he is, he's coming down again!'

A mad steeplechase shook every floor in the house. Farmer Goussot, on reaching the end of the passage, caught sight of a man standing by the front door trying to open it. If he succeeded, it meant safety, escape through the market square and the back lanes of the village.

Interrupted as he was fumbling at the bolts, the man turning stupid, lost his head, charged at old Goussot and sent him spinning, dodged the eldest brother and, pursued by the four sons, doubled back down the long passage, ran into the old couple's bedroom, flung his legs through the broken window and disappeared.

The sons rushed after him across the lawns and orchards, now darkened by the falling night.

'The villain's done for,' chuckled old Goussot. 'There's no way out for him. The walls are too high. He's done for, the scoundrel!'

The two farm-hands returned, at that moment, from the village; and he told them what had happened and gave each of them a gun.

'If the swine shows his nose anywhere near the house,' he said, 'let fly at him. Give him no mercy!'

He told them where to stand, went to make sure that the farm-gates, which were only used for the carts, were locked, and, not till then, remembered that his wife might perhaps be in need of aid.

'Well, mother, how goes it?'

'Where is he? Have you got him?' she asked, in a breath.

'Yes, we're after him. The lads must have collared him by now.'

The news quite restored her; and a nip of rum gave her the strength to drag herself to the bed, with old Goussot's assistance, and to tell her story. For that matter, there was not much to tell. She had just lit the fire in the living-hall; and she was knitting quietly at her bedroom window, waiting for the men to return, when she thought that she heard a slight grating sound in the linen-room next door.

'I must have left the cat in there,' she thought to herself.

She went in, suspecting nothing, and was astonished to see the two doors of one of the linen-cupboards, the one in which they hid their money, wide open. She walked up to it, still without suspicion. There was a man there, hiding, with his back to the shelves.

'But how did he get in?' asked old Goussot.

'Through the passage, I suppose. We never keep the back door shut.'

'And then did he go for you?'

'No, I went for him. He tried to get away.'

'You should have let him.'

'And what about the money?'

'Had he taken it by then?'

'Had he taken it! I saw the bundle of bank-notes in his hands, the sweep! I would have let him kill me sooner . . . Oh, we had a sharp tussle, I give you my word!'

'Then he had no weapon?'

'No more than I did. We had our fingers, our nails and our teeth. Look here, where he bit me. And I yelled and screamed! Only, I'm an old woman you see . . . I had to let go of him . . . '

'Do you know the man?'

'I'm pretty sure it was old Trainard.'

'The tramp? Why, of course it's old Trainard!' cried the farmer. 'I thought I knew him too . . . Besides, he's been hanging round the house these last three days. The old vagabond must have smelt the money. Aha, Trainard, my man, we shall see some fun! A number-one hiding in the first place; and then the police . . . I say, mother, you can get up now, can't you? Then go and fetch the neighbours . . . Ask them to run for the gendarmes . . . By the by, the attorney's youngster has a bicycle . . . How that damned old Trainard scooted! He's got good legs for his age, he has. He can run like a hare!'

Goussot was holding his sides, revelling in the occurrence. He risked nothing by waiting. No power on earth could help the tramp escape or keep him from the sound thrashing which he had earned and from being conveyed, under safe escort, to the town gaol.

The farmer took a gun and went out to his two labourers.

'Anything fresh?'

'No, Farmer Goussot, not yet.'

'We shan't have long to wait. Unless old Nick carries him over the walls . . . '

From time to time, they heard the four brothers hailing one another in the distance. The old bird was evidently making a fight for it, was more active than they would have thought. Still, with sturdy fellows like the Goussot brothers . . .

However, one of them returned, looking rather crestfallen, and made no secret of his opinion.

'It's no use keeping on at it for the present. It's pitch dark. The old chap must have crept into some hole. We'll hunt him out tomorrow.'

'Tomorrow! Why, lad, you're off your chump!' protested the farmer.

The eldest son now appeared, quite out of breath, and was of the same opinion as his brother. Why not wait till next day, seeing that the ruffian was as safe within the demesne as between the walls of a prison?

'Well, I'll go myself,' cried old Goussot. 'Light me a lantern, somebody!'

But, at that moment, three gendarmes arrived; and a number of village lads also came up to hear the latest.

The sergeant of gendarmes was a man of method. He first insisted on hearing the whole story, in full detail; then he stopped to think; then he questioned the four brothers, separately, and took his time for reflection after each deposition. When he had learnt from them that the tramp had fled toward the back of the estate, that he had been lost sight of repeatedly and that he had finally disappeared near a place known as the Crows' Knoll, he meditated once more and announced his conclusion.

'Better wait. Old Trainard might slip through our hands, amidst all the confusion of a pursuit in the dark, and then good-night, everybody!'

The farmer shrugged his shoulders and, cursing under his breath, yielded to the sergeant's arguments. That worthy organized a strict watch, distributed the brothers Goussot and the lads from the village under his men's eyes, made sure that the ladders were locked away and established his headquarters in the dining-room, where he and Farmer Goussot sat and nodded over a decanter of old brandy.

The night passed quietly. Every two hours, the sergeant went his rounds and inspected the posts. There were no alarms. Old Trainard did not budge from his hole.

The battle began at break of day.

It lasted four hours.

In those four hours, the thirteen acres of land within the walls were searched, explored, gone over in every direction by a score of men who beat the bushes with sticks, trampled over the tall grass, rummaged in the hollows of the trees and scattered the heaps of dry leaves. And old Trainard remained invisible.

'Well, this is a bit thick!' growled Goussot.

'Beats me altogether,' retorted the sergeant.

And indeed there was no explaining the phenomenon. For, after all, apart from a few old clumps of laurels and spindle-trees, which were thoroughly beaten, all the trees were bare. There was no building, no shed, no stack, nothing, in short, that could serve as a hiding-place.

As for the wall, a careful inspection convinced even the sergeant that it was physically impossible to scale it.

In the afternoon, the investigations were begun all over again in the presence of the examining-magistrate and the public-prosecutor's deputy. The results were no more successful. Nay, worse, the officials looked upon the matter as so suspicious that they could not restrain their ill-humour and asked: 'Are you quite sure, Farmer Goussot, that you and your sons haven't been seeing double?'

'And what about my wife?' retorted the farmer, red with anger. 'Did she see double when the scamp had her by the throat? Go and look at the marks, if you doubt me!'

'Very well. But then where is the scamp?'

'Here, between those four walls.'

'Very well. Then ferret him out. We give it up. It's quite clear, that if a man were hidden within the precincts of this farm, we should have found him by now.'

'I swear I'll lay hands on him, true as I stand here!' shouted Farmer Goussot. 'It shall not be said that I've been robbed of six thousand francs. Yes, six thousand! There were three cows I sold; and then the wheat-crop; and then the apples. Six thousand-franc notes, which I was just going to take to the bank. Well, I swear to Heaven that the money's as good as in my pocket!'

'That's all right and I wish you luck,' said the examining magistrate, as he went away, followed by the deputy and the gendarmes.

The neighbours also walked off in a more or less facetious mood. And, by the end of the afternoon, none remained but the Goussots and the two farm-labourers.

Old Goussot at once explained his plan. By day, they were to search. At night, they were to keep an incessant watch. It would last as long as it had to. Hang it, old Trainard was a man like other men; and men have to eat and drink! Old Trainard must needs, therefore, come out of his earth to eat and drink.

'At most,' said Goussot, 'he can have a few crusts of bread in his pocket, or even pull up a root or two at night. But, as far as drink's concerned, no go. There's only the spring. And he'll be a clever dog if he gets near that.'

He himself, that evening, took up his stand near the spring. Three hours later, his eldest son relieved him. The other brothers and the farm-hands slept in the house, each taking his turn of the watch and keeping all the lamps and candles lit, so that there might be no surprise.

So it went on for fourteen consecutive nights. And for fourteen days, while two of the men and Mother Goussot remained on guard, the five others explored the Héberville ground.

At the end of that fortnight, not a sign.

The farmer never ceased storming. He sent for a retired detective-inspector who lived in the neighbouring town. The inspector stayed with him for a whole week. He found neither old Trainard nor the least clue that could give them any hope of finding old Trainard.

'It's a bit thick!' repeated Farmer Goussot. 'For he's there, the rascal! As far as being anywhere goes, he's there. So . . . '

Planting himself on the threshold, he railed at the enemy at the top of his voice.

'You blithering idiot, would you rather croak in your hole than fork out the money? Then croak, you pig!'

And Mother Goussot, in her turn, yelped, in her shrill voice: 'Is it prison you're afraid of? Hand over the notes and you can hook it!'

But old Trainard did not breathe a word; and the husband and wife tired their lungs in vain.

Shocking days passed. Farmer Goussot could no longer sleep, lay shivering with fever. The sons became morose and quarrelsome and never let their guns out of their hands, having no other idea but to shoot the tramp.

It was the one topic of conversation in the village; and the Goussot story, from being local at first, soon went the round of the press. Newspaper-reporters came from the assize-town, from Paris itself, and were rudely shown the door by Farmer Goussot.

'Each man his own house,' he said. 'You mind your business. I mind mine. It's nothing to do with anyone.'

'Still, Farmer Goussot . . . '

'Go to blazes!'

And he slammed the door in their face.

Old Trainard had now been hidden within the walls of Héberville for something like four weeks. The Goussots continued their search as doggedly and confidently as ever, but with daily decreasing hope, as though they were confronted with one of those mysterious obstacles which discourage human effort. And the idea that they would never see their money again began to take root in them.

*   *   *

One fine morning, at about ten o'clock, a motor-car, crossing the village square at full speed, broke down and came to a dead stop.

The driver, after a careful inspection, declared that the repairs would take some little time, whereupon the owner of the car resolved to wait at the inn and lunch. He was a gentleman on the right side of forty, with close-cropped side-whiskers and a pleasant expression of face; and he soon made himself at home with the people at the inn.

Of course, they told him the story of the Goussots. He had not heard it before, as he had been abroad; but it seemed to interest him greatly. He made them give him all the details, raised objections, discussed various theories with a number of people who were eating at the same table and ended by exclaiming: 'Nonsense! It can't be so intricate as all that. I have had some experience of this sort of thing. And, if I were on the premises . . . '

'That's easily arranged,' said the inn-keeper. 'I know Farmer Goussot . . . He won't object . . . '

The request was soon made and granted. Old Goussot was in one of those frames of mind when we are less disposed to protest against outside interference. His wife, at any rate, was very firm.

'Let the gentleman come, if he wants to.'

The gentleman paid his bill and instructed his driver to try the car on the high-road as soon as the repairs were finished.

'I shall want an hour,' he said, 'no more. Be ready in an hour's time.'

Then he went to Farmer Goussot's.

He did not say much at the farm. Old Goussot, hoping against hope, was lavish with information, took his visitor along the walls down to the little door opening on the fields, produced the key and gave minute details of all the searches that had been made so far.

Oddly enough, the stranger, who hardly spoke, seemed not to listen either. He merely looked, with a rather vacant gaze. When they had been round the estate, old Goussot asked, anxiously: 'Well?'

'Well what?'

'Do you think you know?'

The visitor stood for a moment without answering. Then he said: 'No, nothing.'

'Why, of course not!' cried the farmer, throwing up his arms. 'How should you know! It's all hanky-panky. Shall I tell you what I think? Well, that old Trainard has been so jolly clever that he's lying dead in his hole . . . and the bank-notes are rotting with him. Do you hear? You can take my word for it.'

The gentleman said, very calmly: 'There's only one thing that interests me. The tramp, all said and done, was free at night and able to feed on what he could pick up. But how about drinking?'

'Out of the question!' shouted the farmer. 'Quite out of the question! There's no water except this; and we have kept watch beside it every night.'

'It's a spring. Where does it rise?'

'Here, where we stand.'

'Is there enough pressure to bring it into the pool of itself?'

'Yes.'

'And where does the water go when it runs out of the pool?'

'Into this pipe here, which goes under ground and carries it to the house, for use in the kitchen. So there's no way of drinking, seeing that we were there and that the spring is twenty yards from the house.'

'Hasn't it rained during the last four weeks?'

'Not once: I've told you that already.'

The stranger went to the spring and examined it. The trough was formed of a few boards of wood joined together just above the ground; and the water ran through it, slow and clear.

'The water's not more than a foot deep, is it?' he asked.

In order to measure it, he picked up from the grass a straw which he dipped into the pool. But, as he was stooping, he suddenly broke off and looked around him.

'Oh, how funny!' he said, bursting into a peal of laughter.

'Why, what's the matter?' spluttered old Goussot, rushing toward the pool, as though a man could have lain hidden between those narrow boards.

And Mother Goussot clasped her hands.

'What is it? Have you seen him? Where is he?'

'Neither in it nor under it,' replied the stranger, who was still laughing.

He made for the house, eagerly followed by the farmer, the old woman and the four sons. The inn-keeper was there also, as were the people from the inn who had been watching the stranger's movements. And there was a dead silence, while they waited for the extraordinary disclosure.

'It's as I thought,' he said, with an amused expression. 'The old chap had to quench his thirst somewhere; and, as there was only the spring . . .'

'Oh, but look here,' growled Farmer Goussot, 'we should have seen him!'

'It was at night.'

'We should have heard him . . . and seen him too, as we were close by.'

'So was he.'

'And he drank the water from the pool?'

'Yes.'

'How?'

'From a little way off.'

'With what?'

'With this.'

And the stranger showed the straw which he had picked up.

'There, here's the straw for the customer's long drink. You will see, there's more of it than usual: in fact, it is made of three straws stuck into one another. That was the first thing I noticed: those three straws fastened together. The proof is conclusive.'

'But, hang it all, the proof of what?' cried Farmer Goussot, irritably.

The stranger took a shotgun from the rack.

'Is it loaded?' he asked.

'Yes,' said the youngest of the brothers. 'I use it to kill the sparrows with, for fun. It's small shot.'

'Capital! A peppering where it won't hurt him will do the trick.'

His face suddenly assumed a masterful look. He gripped the farmer by the arm and rapped out, in an imperious tone: 'Listen to me, Farmer Goussot. I'm not here to do policeman's work; and I won't have the poor beggar locked up at any price. Four weeks of starvation and fright is good enough for anybody. So you've got to swear to me, you and your sons, that you'll let him off without hurting him.'

'He must hand over the money!'

'Well, of course. Do you swear?'

'I swear.'

The gentleman walked back to the door-sill, at the entrance to the orchard. He took a quick aim, pointing his gun a little in the air, in the direction of the cherry tree which overhung the spring. He fired. A hoarse cry rang from the tree; and the scarecrow which had been straddling the main branch for a month past came tumbling to the ground, only to jump up at once and make off as fast as its legs could carry it.

There was a moment's amazement, followed by outcries. The sons darted in pursuit and were not long in coming up with the runaway, hampered as he was by his rags and weakened by privation. But the stranger was already protecting him against their wrath.

'Hands off there! This man belongs to me. I won't have him touched . . . I hope I haven't stung you up too much, Trainard?'

Standing on his straw legs wrapped round with strips of tattered cloth, with his arms and his whole body clad in the same materials, his head swathed in linen, tightly packed like a sausage, the old chap still had the stiff appearance of a lay-figure. And the whole effect was so ludicrous and so unexpected that the onlookers screamed with laughter.

The stranger unbound his head; and they saw a veiled mask of tangled gray beard encroaching on every side upon a skeleton face lit up by two eyes burning with fever.

The laughter was louder than ever.

'The money! The six notes!' roared the farmer.

The stranger kept him at a distance.

'One moment . . . we'll give you that back, shan't we, Trainard?'

And, taking his knife and cutting away the straw and cloth, he jested, cheerily: 'You poor old beggar, what a guy you look! But how on earth did you manage to pull off that trick? You must be confoundedly clever, or else you had the devil's own luck . . . So, on the first night, you used the breathing-time they left you to rig yourself in these togs! Not a bad idea. Who could ever suspect a scarecrow? . . . They were so accustomed to seeing it stuck up in its tree! But, poor old daddy, how uncomfortable you must have felt, lying flat up there on your stomach, with your arms and legs dangling down! All day long, like that! The deuce of an attitude! And how you must have been put to it, when you ventured to move a limb, eh? And how you must have funked going to sleep! . . . And then you had to eat! And drink! And you heard the sentry and felt the barrel of his gun within a yard of your nose! Brrrr! . . . But the trickiest of all, you know, was your bit of straw! . . . Upon my word, when I think that, without a sound, without a movement so to speak, you had to fish out lengths of straw from your toggery, fix them end to end, let your apparatus down to the water and suck up the heavenly moisture drop by drop . . . Upon my word, one could scream with admiration . . . Well done, Trainard . . .'

And he added, between his teeth, 'Only you're in a very unappetizing state, my man. Haven't you washed yourself all this month, you old pig? After all, you had as much water as you wanted! . . . Here, you people, I hand him over to you. I'm going to wash my hands, that's what I'm going to do.'

Farmer Goussot and his four sons grabbed at the prey which he was abandoning to them.

'Now then, come along, fork out the money.'

Dazed as he was, the tramp still managed to simulate astonishment.

'Don't put on that idiot look,' growled the farmer. 'Come on. Out with the six notes . . . '

'What? . . . What do you want of me?' stammered old Trainard.

'The money . . . on the nail . . . '

'What money?'

'The bank-notes.'

'The bank-notes?'

'Oh, I'm getting sick of you! Here, lads . . . '

They laid the old fellow flat, tore off the rags that composed his clothes, felt and searched him all over.

There was nothing on him.

'You thief and you robber!' yelled old Goussot. 'What have you done with it?'

The old beggar seemed more dazed than ever. Too cunning to confess, he kept on whining: 'What do you want of me? . . . Money? I haven't three sous to call my own . . . '

But his eyes, wide with wonder, remained fixed upon his clothes; and he himself seemed not to understand.

The Goussots' rage could no longer be restrained. They rained blows upon him, which did not improve matters. But the farmer was convinced that Trainard had hidden the money before turning himself into the scarecrow.

'Where have you put it, you scum? Out with it! In what part of the orchard have you hidden it?'

'The money?' repeated the tramp with a stupid look.

'Yes, the money! The money which you've buried somewhere . . . Oh, if we don't find it, your goose is cooked! . . . We have witnesses, haven't we? . . . All of you, friends, eh? And then the gentleman . . . '

He turned, with the intention of addressing the stranger, in the direction of the spring, which was thirty or forty steps to the left. And he was quite surprised not to see him washing his hands there.

'Has he gone?' he asked.

Someone answered.

'No, he lit a cigarette and went for a stroll in the orchard.'

'Oh, that's all right!' said the farmer. 'He's the sort to find the notes for us, just as he found the man.'

'Unless . . . ' said a voice.

'Unless what?' echoed the farmer. 'What do you mean? Have you something in your head? Out with it, then! What is it?'

But he interrupted himself suddenly, seized with a doubt; and there was a moment's silence. The same idea dawned on all the country-folk. The stranger's arrival at Héberville, the breakdown of his motor, his manner of questioning the people at the inn and of gaining admission to the farm: were not all these part and parcel of a put-up job, the trick of a cracksman who had learnt the story from the papers and who had come to try his luck on the spot? . . .

'Jolly smart of him!' said the inn-keeper. 'He must have taken the money from old Trainard's pocket, before our eyes, while he was searching him.'

'Impossible!' spluttered Farmer Goussot. 'He would have been seen going out that way . . . by the house . . . whereas he's strolling in the orchard.'

Mother Goussot, all of a heap, suggested: 'The little door at the end, down there? . . . '

'The key never leaves me.'

'But you showed it to him.'

'Yes; and I took it back again . . . Look, here it is.'

He clapped his hand to his pocket and uttered a cry.

'Oh, dash it all, it's gone! . . . He's sneaked it! . . . '

He at once rushed away, followed and escorted by his sons and a number of the villagers.

When they were halfway down the orchard, they heard the throb of a motor-car, obviously the one belonging to the stranger, who had given orders to his chauffeur to wait for him at that lower entrance.

When the Goussots reached the door, they saw scrawled with a brick, on the worm-eaten panel, the two words:

ARSÈNE LUPIN

*   *   *

Stick to it as the angry Goussots might, they found it impossible to prove that old Trainard had stolen any money. Twenty persons had to bear witness that, when all was said, nothing was discovered on his person. He escaped with a few months' imprisonment for the assault.

He did not regret them. As soon as he was released, he was secretly informed that, every quarter, on a given date, at a given hour, under a given milestone on a given road, he would find three gold louis.

To a man like old Trainard that means wealth.

Edith Swan-neck

'Arsène Lupin, what's your real opinion of Inspector Ganimard?'

'A very high one, my dear fellow.'

'A very high one? Then why do you never miss a chance of turning him into ridicule?'

'It's a bad habit; and I'm sorry for it. But what can I say? It's the way of the world. Here's a decent detective-chap, here's a whole pack of decent men, who stand for law and order, who protect us against the apaches, who risk their lives for honest people like you and me; and we have nothing to give them in return but flouts and gibes. It's preposterous!'

'Bravo, Lupin! you're talking like a respectable ratepayer!'

'What else am I? I may have peculiar views about other people's property; but I assure you that it's very different when my own's at stake. By Jove, it doesn't do to lay hands on what belongs to me! Then I'm out for blood! Aha! It's *my* pocket, *my* money, *my* watch . . . hands off! I have the soul of a conservative, my dear fellow, the instincts of a retired tradesman and a due respect for every sort of tradition and authority. And that is why Ganimard inspires me with no little gratitude and esteem.'

'But not much admiration?'

'Plenty of admiration too. Over and above the dauntless courage which comes natural to all those gentry at the Criminal Investigation Department, Ganimard possesses very sterling qualities: decision, insight and judgment. I have watched him at work. He's somebody, when all's said. Do you know the Edith Swan-neck story, as it was called?'

'I know as much as everybody knows.'

'That means that you don't know it at all. Well, that job was, I dare say, the one which I thought out most cleverly, with the utmost care and the utmost precaution, the one which I shrouded in the greatest darkness and mystery, the one which it took the biggest generalship to carry through. It was a regular game of chess, played according to strict scientific and mathematical rules. And yet Ganimard ended by unravelling the knot. Thanks to him, they know the truth today on the Quai des Orfèvres. And it is a truth quite out of the common, I assure you.'

'May I hope to hear it?'

'Certainly . . . one of these days . . . when I have time . . . But the Brunelli is dancing at the Opera tonight; and, if she were not to see me in my stall . . . !'

I do not meet Lupin often. He confesses with difficulty, when it suits him. It was only gradually, by snatches, by odds and ends of confidences, that I was able to obtain the different incidents and to piece the story together in all its details.

*   *   *

The main features are well known and I will merely mention the facts.

Three years ago, when the train from Brest arrived at Rennes, the door of one of the luggage vans was found smashed in. This van had been booked by Colonel Sparmiento, a rich Brazilian, who was travelling with his wife in the same train. It contained a complete set of tapestry-hangings. The case in which one of these was packed had been broken open and the tapestry had disappeared.

Colonel Sparmiento started proceedings against the railway company, claiming heavy damages, not only for the stolen tapestry, but also for the loss in value which the whole collection suffered in consequence of the theft.

The police instituted inquiries. The company offered a large reward. A fortnight later, a letter which had come undone in the post was opened by the authorities and revealed the fact that the theft had been carried out under the direction of Arsène Lupin and that a package was to leave next day for the United States. That same evening, the tapestry was discovered in a trunk deposited in the cloak-room at the Gare Saint-Lazare.

The scheme, therefore, had miscarried. Lupin felt the disappointment so much that he vented his ill-humour in a communication to Colonel Sparmiento, ending with the following words, which were clear enough for anybody.

It was very considerate of me to take only one. Next time, I shall take the twelve. *Verbum sap.*

A. L.

Colonel Sparmiento had been living for some months in a house standing at the end of a small garden at the corner of the Rue de la Faisanderie and the Rue Dufresnoy. He was a rather thick-set, broad-shouldered man, with black hair and a swarthy skin, always well and quietly dressed. He was married to an extremely pretty but delicate Englishwoman, who was much upset by the business of the tapestries. From the first she implored her husband to sell them for what they would fetch. The Colonel had much too forcible and dogged a nature to yield to what he had every right to describe as a woman's fancies. He sold nothing, but he redoubled his precautions and adopted every measure that was likely to make an attempt at burglary impossible.

To begin with, so that he might confine his watch to the garden-front, he walled up all the windows on the ground-floor and the first floor overlooking the Rue Dufresnoy. Next, he enlisted the services of a firm which made a speciality of protecting private houses against robberies. Every window of the gallery in which the tapestries were hung was fitted with invisible burglar alarms, the position of which was known to none but himself. These, at the least touch, switched on all the electric lights and set a whole system of bells and gongs ringing.

In addition to this, the insurance companies to which he applied refused to grant policies to any considerable amount unless he consented to let three men, supplied by the companies and paid by himself, occupy the ground-floor of his house every night. They selected for the purpose three ex-detectives, tried and trustworthy men, all of whom hated Lupin like poison. As for the servants, the colonel had known them for years and was ready to vouch for them.

After taking these steps and organizing the defence of the house as though it were a fortress, the colonel gave a great house-warming, a sort of private view, to which he invited the members of both his clubs, as well as a certain number of ladies, journalists, art-patrons and critics.

They felt, as they passed through the garden-gate, much as if they were walking into a prison. The three private detectives, posted at the foot of the stairs, asked for each visitor's invitation card and eyed him up and down suspiciously, making him feel as though they were going to search his pockets or take his finger-prints.

The colonel, who received his guests on the first floor, made laughing apologies and seemed delighted at the opportunity of explaining the arrangements which he had invented to secure the safety of his hangings. His wife stood by him, looking charmingly young and pretty, fair-haired, pale and sinuous, with a sad

and gentle expression, the expression of resignation often worn by
those who are threatened by fate.

When all the guests had come, the garden-gates and the hall-doors
were closed. Then everybody filed into the middle gallery, which
was reached through two steel doors, while its windows, with their
huge shutters, were protected by iron bars. This was where the
twelve tapestries were kept.

They were matchless works of art and, taking their inspiration
from the famous Bayeux Tapestry, attributed to Queen Matilda,
they represented the story of the Norman Conquest. They had been
ordered in the fourteenth century by the descendant of a man-at-
arms in William the Conqueror's train; were executed by Jehan
Gosset, a famous Arras weaver; and were discovered, five hundred
years later, in an old Breton manor-house. On hearing of this, the
colonel had struck a bargain for fifty thousand francs. They were
worth ten times the money.

But the finest of the twelve hangings composing the set, the most
uncommon because the subject had not been treated by Queen
Matilda, was the one which Arsène Lupin had stolen and which had
been so fortunately recovered. It portrayed Edith Swan-neck on the
battlefield of Hastings, seeking among the dead for the body of her
sweetheart Harold, last of the Saxon kings.

The guests were lost in enthusiasm over this tapestry, over the
unsophisticated beauty of the design, over the faded colours, over
the life-like grouping of the figures and the pitiful sadness of the
scene. Poor Edith Swan-neck stood drooping like an overweighted
lily. Her white gown revealed the lines of her languid figure. Her
long, tapering hands were outstretched in a gesture of terror and
entreaty. And nothing could be more mournful than her profile, over
which flickered the most dejected and despairing of smiles.

'A harrowing smile,' remarked one of the critics, to whom the
others listened with deference. 'A very charming smile, besides; and
it reminds me, Colonel, of the smile of Mme Sparmiento.'

And seeing that the observation seemed to meet with approval, he
enlarged upon his idea.

'There are other points of resemblance that struck me at once,
such as the very graceful curve of the neck and the delicacy of the
hands . . . and also something about the figure, about the general
attitude . . .'

'What you say is so true,' said the colonel, 'that I confess that it
was this likeness that decided me to buy the hangings. And there

was another reason, which was that, by a really curious chance, my wife's name happens to be Edith. I have called her Edith Swan-neck ever since.' And the colonel added, with a laugh, 'I hope that the coincidence will stop at this and that my dear Edith will never have to go in search of her true-love's body, like her prototype.'

He laughed as he uttered these words, but his laugh met with no echo; and we find the same impression of awkward silence in all the accounts of the evening that appeared during the next few days. The people standing near him did not know what to say. One of them tried to jest.

'Your name isn't Harold, Colonel?'

'No, thank you,' he declared, with continued merriment. 'No, that's not my name; nor am I in the least like the Saxon king.'

All have since agreed in stating that at that moment, as the colonel finished speaking, the first alarm rang from the windows – the right or the middle window: opinions differ on this point – rang short and shrill on a single note. The peal of the alarm-bell was followed by an exclamation of terror uttered by Mme Sparmiento, who caught hold of her husband's arm. He cried: 'What's the matter? What does this mean?'

The guests stood motionless, with their eyes staring at the windows. The colonel repeated: 'What does it mean? I don't understand. No one but myself knows where that bell is fixed . . . '

And, at that moment – here again the evidence is unanimous – at that moment came sudden, absolute darkness, followed immediately by the maddening din of all the bells and all the gongs, from top to bottom of the house, in every room and at every window.

For a few seconds, a stupid disorder, an insane terror, reigned. The women screamed. The men banged with their fists on the closed doors. They hustled and fought. People fell to the floor and were trampled under foot. It was like a panic-stricken crowd, scared by threatening flames or by a bursting shell. And, above the uproar, rose the colonel's voice, shouting: 'Silence! . . . Don't move! . . . It's all right! . . . The switch is over there, in the corner . . . Wait a bit . . . Here!'

He had pushed his way through his guests and reached a corner of the gallery; and, all at once, the electric light blazed up again, while the pandemonium of bells stopped.

Then, in the sudden light, a strange sight met the eyes. Two ladies had fainted. Mme Sparmiento, hanging to her husband's arm, with her knees dragging on the floor, and livid in the face, appeared half dead. The men, pale, with their neckties awry, looked as if they had all been in the wars.

'The tapestries are there!' cried someone.

There was a great surprise, as though the disappearance of those hangings ought to have been the natural result and the only plausible explanation of the incident. But nothing had been moved. A few valuable pictures, hanging on the walls, were there still. And, though the same din had reverberated all over the house, though all the rooms had been thrown into darkness, the detectives had seen no one entering or trying to enter.

'Besides,' said the colonel, 'it's only the windows of the gallery that have alarms. Nobody but myself understands how they work; and I had not set them yet.'

People laughed loudly at the way in which they had been frightened, but they laughed without conviction and in a more or less shamefaced fashion, for each of them was keenly alive to the absurdity of his conduct. And they had but one thought – to get out of that house where, say what you would, the atmosphere was one of agonizing anxiety.

Two journalists stayed behind, however; and the colonel joined them, after attending to Edith and handing her over to her maids. The three of them, together with the detectives, made a search that did not lead to the discovery of anything of the least interest. Then the colonel sent for some champagne; and the result was that it was not until a late hour – to be exact, a quarter to three in the morning – that the journalists took their leave, the colonel retired to his quarters, and the detectives withdrew to the room which had been set aside for them on the ground-floor.

They took the watch by turns, a watch consisting, in the first place, in keeping awake and, next, in looking round the garden and visiting the gallery at intervals.

These orders were scrupulously carried out, except between five and seven in the morning, when sleep gained the mastery and the men ceased to go their rounds. But it was broad daylight out of doors. Besides, if there had been the least sound of bells, would they not have woke up?

Nevertheless, when one of them, at twenty minutes past seven, opened the door of the gallery and flung back the shutters, he saw that the twelve tapestries were gone.

This man and the others were blamed afterward for not giving the alarm at once and for starting their own investigations before informing the colonel and telephoning to the local commissary. Yet this very excusable delay can hardly be said to have hampered the action of the police. In any case, the colonel was not told until half-past eight. He was dressed and ready to go out. The news did not seem to upset him beyond measure, or, at least, he managed to control his emotion. But the effort must have been too much for him, for he suddenly dropped into a chair and, for some moments, gave way to a regular fit of despair and anguish, most painful to behold in a man of his resolute appearance.

Recovering and mastering himself, he went to the gallery, stared at the bare walls and then sat down at a table and hastily scribbled a letter, which he put into an envelope and sealed.

'There,' he said. 'I'm in a hurry . . . I have an important engage-ment . . . Here is a letter for the commissary of police.' And, seeing the detectives' eyes upon him, he added, 'I am giving the commissary my views . . . telling him of a suspicion that occurs to me . . . He must follow it up . . . I will do what I can . . . '

He left the house at a run, with excited gestures which the detec-tives were subsequently to remember.

A few minutes later, the commissary of police arrived. He was handed the letter, which contained the following words.

I am at the end of my tether. The theft of those tapestries com-pletes the crash which I have been trying to conceal for the past year. I bought them as a speculation and was hoping to get a million francs for them, thanks to the fuss that was made about them. As it was, an American offered me six hundred thousand. It meant my salvation. This means utter destruction.

I hope that my dear wife will forgive the sorrow which I am bring-ing upon her. Her name will be on my lips at the last moment.

Mme Sparmiento was informed. She remained aghast with horror, while inquiries were instituted and attempts made to trace the col-onel's movements.

Late in the afternoon, a telephone-message came from Ville d'Avray. A gang of railway-men had found a man's body lying at the entrance to a tunnel after a train had passed. The body was hideously mutilated; the face had lost all resemblance to anything human. There were no papers in the pockets. But the description answered to that of the colonel.

Mme Sparmiento arrived at Ville d'Avray, by motor-car, at seven o'clock in the evening. She was taken to a room at the railway station. When the sheet that covered it was removed, Edith, Edith Swan-neck, recognized her husband's body.

*   *   *

In these circumstances, Lupin did not receive his usual good notices in the press.

> Let him look to himself, jeered one leader-writer, summing up the general opinion. It would not take many exploits of this kind for him to forfeit the popularity which has not been grudged him hitherto. We have no use for Lupin, except when his roguer-ies are perpetrated at the expense of shady company-promoters, foreign adventurers, German barons, banks and financial compa-nies. And, above all, no murders! A burglar we can put up with; but a murderer, no! If he is not directly guilty, he is at least responsible for this death. There is blood upon his hands; the arms on his escutcheon are stained gules . . .

The public anger and disgust were increased by the pity which Edith's pale face aroused. The guests of the night before gave their version of what had happened, omitting none of the impressive details; and a legend formed straightway around the fair-haired Englishwoman, a legend that assumed a really tragic character, owing to the popular story of the swan-necked heroine.

And yet the public could not withhold its admiration of the extra-ordinary skill with which the theft had been effected. The police explained it, after a fashion. The detectives had noticed from the first and subsequently stated that one of the three windows of the gallery was wide open. There could be no doubt that Lupin and his confed-erates had entered through this window. It seemed a very plausible suggestion. Still, in that case, how were they able, first, to climb the garden railings, in coming and going, without being seen; secondly, to cross the garden and put up a ladder on the flower-border, without leaving the least trace behind; thirdly, to open the shutters and the win-dow, without starting the bells and switching on the lights in the house?

The police accused the three detectives of complicity. The magis-trate in charge of the case examined them at length, made minute inquiries into their private lives and stated formally that they were above all suspicion. As for the tapestries, there seemed to be no hope that they would be recovered.

It was at this moment that Chief-inspector Ganimard returned from India, where he had been hunting for Lupin on the strength of a number of most convincing proofs supplied by former confederates of Lupin himself. Feeling that he had once more been tricked by his everlasting adversary, fully believing that Lupin had dispatched him on this wild-goose chase so as to be rid of him during the business of the tapestries, he asked for a fortnight's leave of absence, called on Mme Sparmiento and promised to avenge her husband.

Edith had reached the point at which not even the thought of vengeance relieves the sufferer's pain. She had dismissed the three detectives on the day of the funeral and engaged just one man and an old cook-housekeeper to take the place of the large staff of servants the sight of whom reminded her too cruelly of the past. Not caring what happened, she kept her room and left Ganimard free to act as he pleased.

He took up his quarters on the ground-floor and at once instituted a series of the most minute investigations. He started the inquiry afresh, questioned the people in the neighbourhood, studied the distribution of the rooms and set each of the burglar-alarms going thirty and forty times over.

At the end of the fortnight, he asked for an extension of leave. The chief of the detective-service, who was at that time M. Dudouis, came to see him and found him perched on the top of a ladder, in the gallery. That day, the chief-inspector admitted that all his searches had proved useless.

Two days later, however, M. Dudouis called again and discovered Ganimard in a very thoughtful frame of mind. A bundle of news-papers lay spread in front of him. At last, in reply to his superior's urgent questions, the chief-inspector muttered: 'I know nothing, chief, absolutely nothing; but there's a confounded notion worry-ing me . . . Only it seems so absurd . . . And then it doesn't explain things . . . On the contrary, it confuses them rather . . . '

'Then . . . ?'

'Then I implore you, chief, to have a little patience . . . to let me go my own way. But if I telephone to you, some day or other, suddenly, you must jump into a taxi, without losing a minute. It will mean that I have discovered the secret.'

Forty-eight hours passed. Then, one morning, M. Dudouis re-ceived a telegram.

GOING TO LILLE — GANIMARD

'What the dickens can he want to go to Lille for?' wondered the chief-detective.

The day passed without news, followed by another day. But M. Dudouis had every confidence in Ganimard. He knew his man, knew that the old detective was not one of those people who excite themselves for nothing. When Ganimard 'got a move on him', it meant that he had sound reasons for doing so.

As a matter of fact, on the evening of that second day, M. Dudouis was called to the telephone.

'Is that you, chief?'

'Is it Ganimard speaking?'

Cautious men both, they began by making sure of each other's identity. As soon as his mind was eased on this point, Ganimard continued, hurriedly.

'Ten men, chief, at once. And please come yourself.'

'Where are you?'

'In the house, on the ground-floor. But I will wait for you just inside the garden-gate.'

'I'll come at once. In a taxi, of course?'

'Yes, chief. Stop the taxi fifty yards from the house. I'll let you in when you whistle.'

Things took place as Ganimard had arranged. Shortly after midnight, when all the lights were out on the upper floors, he slipped into the street and went to meet M. Dudouis. There was a hurried consultation. The officers distributed themselves as Ganimard ordered. Then the chief and the chief-inspector walked back together, noiselessly crossed the garden and closeted themselves with every precaution.

'Well, what's it all about?' asked M. Dudouis. 'What does all this mean? Upon my word, we look like a pair of conspirators!'

But Ganimard was not laughing. His chief had never seen him in such a state of perturbation, nor heard him speak in a voice denoting such excitement.

'Any news, Ganimard?'

'Yes, chief, and . . . this time . . . ! But I can hardly believe it myself . . . And yet I'm not mistaken: I know the real truth . . . It may be as unlikely as you please, but it is the truth, the whole truth and nothing but the truth.'

He wiped away the drops of perspiration that trickled down his forehead and, after a further question from M. Dudouis, pulled himself together, swallowed a glass of water and began.

'Lupin has often got the better of me . . . '

'Look here, Ganimard,' said M. Dudouis, interrupting him.'Why can'tyou come straight to the point?Tell me, in two words,what's happened.'

'No, chief,' retorted the chief-inspector, 'it is essential that you should know the different stages which I have passed through. Excuse me, but I consider it indispensable.' And he repeated: 'I was saying, chief, that Lupin has often got the better of me and led me many a dance. But, in this contest in which I have always come out worst . . . so far . . . I have at least gained experience of his manner of play and learnt to know his tactics. Now, in the matter of the tapestries, it occurred to me almost from the start to set myself two problems. In the first place, Lupin, who never makes a move without knowing what he is after, was obviously aware that Colonel Sparmiento had come to the end of his money and that the loss of the tapestries might drive him to suicide. Nevertheless, Lupin, who hates the very thought of bloodshed, stole the tapestries.'

'There was the inducement,' said M. Dudouis, 'of the five or six hundred thousand francs which they are worth.'

'No, chief, I tell you once more, whatever the occasion might be, Lupin would not take life, nor be the cause of another person's death, for anything in this world, for millions and millions. That's the first point. In the second place, what was the object of all that disturbance, in the evening, during the house-warming party? Obviously, don't you think, to surround the business with an atmosphere of anxiety and terror, in the shortest possible time, and also to divert suspicion from the truth, which, otherwise, might easily have been suspected? . . . You seem not to understand, chief?'

'Upon my word, I do not!'

'As a matter of fact,' said Ganimard, 'as a matter of fact, it is not particularly plain. And I myself, when I put the problem before my mind in those same words, did not understand it very clearly . . . And yet I felt that I was on the right track . . . Yes, there was no doubt about it that Lupin wanted to divert suspicions . . . to divert them to himself, Lupin, mark you . . . so that the real person who was working the business might remain unknown . . . '

'A confederate,' suggested M. Dudouis. 'A confederate, moving among the visitors, who set the alarms going . . . and who managed to hide in the house after the party had broken up.'

'You're getting warm, chief, you're getting warm! It is certain that the tapestries, as they cannot have been stolen by anyone making his way surreptitiously into the house, were stolen by somebody who remained in the house; and it is equally certain that, by taking the list of the people invited and inquiring into the antecedents of each of them, one might . . . '

'Well?'

'Well, chief, there's a "but", namely, that the three detectives had this list in their hands when the guests arrived and that they still had it when the guests left. Now sixty-three came in and sixty-three went away. So you see . . . '

'Then do you suppose a servant? . . . '

'No.'

'The detectives?'

'No.'

'But, still . . . but, still,' said the chief, impatiently, 'if the robbery was committed from the inside . . . '

'That is beyond dispute,' declared the inspector, whose excitement seemed to be nearing fever-point. 'There is no question about it. All my investigations led to the same certainty. And my conviction gradually became so positive that I ended, one day, by drawing up this startling axiom: in theory and in fact, the robbery can only have been committed with the assistance of an accomplice staying in the house. Whereas there was no accomplice!'

'That's absurd,' said Dudouis.

'Quite absurd,' said Ganimard. 'But, at the very moment when I uttered that absurd sentence, the truth flashed upon me.'

'Eh?'

'Oh, a very dim, very incomplete, but still sufficient truth! With that clue to guide me, I was bound to find the way. Do you follow me, chief?'

M. Dudouis sat silent. The same phenomenon that had taken place in Ganimard was evidently taking place in him. He muttered: 'If it's not one of the guests, nor the servants, nor the private detectives, then there's no one left . . . '

'Yes, chief, there's one left . . . '

M. Dudouis started as though he had received a shock; and, in a voice that betrayed his excitement: 'But, look here, that's preposterous.'

'Why?'

'Come, think for yourself!'

'Go on, chief: say what's in your mind.'

'Nonsense! What do you mean?'

'Go on, chief.'

'It's impossible! How can Sparmiento have been Lupin's accomplice?'

Ganimard gave a little chuckle.

'Exactly, Arsène Lupin's accomplice! . . . That explains everything. During the night, while the three detectives were downstairs watching, or sleeping rather, for Colonel Sparmiento had given them champagne to drink and perhaps doctored it beforehand, the said colonel took down the hangings and passed them out through the window of his bedroom. The room is on the second floor and looks out on another street, which was not watched, because the lower windows are walled up.'

M. Dudouis reflected and then shrugged his shoulders.

'It's preposterous!' he repeated.

'Why?'

'Why? Because, if the colonel had been Arsène Lupin's accomplice, he would not have committed suicide after achieving his success.'

'Who says that he committed suicide?'

'Why, he was found dead on the line!'

'I told you, there is no such thing as death with Lupin.'

'Still, this was genuine enough. Besides, Mme Sparmiento identified the body.'

'I thought you would say that, chief. The argument worried me too. There was I, all of a sudden, with three people in front of me instead of one: first, Arsène Lupin, cracksman; secondly, Colonel Sparmiento, his accomplice; thirdly, a dead man. Spare us! It was too much of a good thing!'

Ganimard took a bundle of newspapers, untied it and handed one of them to Mr Dudouis.

'You remember, chief, last time you were here, I was looking through the papers . . . I wanted to see if something had not happened, at that period, that might bear upon the case and confirm my supposition. Please read this paragraph.'

M. Dudouis took the paper and read aloud.

Our Lille correspondent informs us that a curious incident has occurred in that town. A corpse has disappeared from the local morgue, the corpse of a man unknown who threw himself under the wheels of a steam tram-car on the day before. No one is able to suggest a reason for this disappearance.

M. Dudouis sat thinking and then asked: 'So . . . you believe . . . ?'

'I have just come from Lille,' replied Ganimard, 'and my inquiries leave not a doubt in my mind. The corpse was removed on the same night on which Colonel Sparmiento gave his house-warming. It was taken straight to Ville d'Avray by motor-car; and the car remained near the railway-line until the evening.'

'Near the tunnel, therefore,' said M. Dudouis.

'Next to it, chief.'

'So that the body which was found is merely that body, dressed in Colonel Sparmiento's clothes.'

'Precisely, chief.'

'Then Colonel Sparmiento is not dead?'

'No more dead than you or I, chief.'

'But then why all these complications? Why the theft of one tapestry, followed by its recovery, followed by the theft of the twelve? Why that house-warming? Why that disturbance? Why everything? Your story won't hold water, Ganimard.'

'Only because you, chief, like myself, have stopped halfway; because, strange as this story already sounds, we must go still farther, very much farther, in the direction of the improbable and the astounding. And why not, after all? Remember that we are dealing with Arsène Lupin. With him, is it not always just the improbable and the astounding that we must look for? Must we not always go straight for the maddest suppositions? And, when I say the maddest, I am using the wrong word. On the contrary, the whole thing is wonderfully logical and so simple that a child could understand it. Confederates only betray you. Why employ confederates, when it is so easy and so natural to act for yourself, by yourself, with your own hands and by the means within your own reach?'

'What are you saying? . . . What are you saying? . . . What are you saying?' cried M. Dudouis, in a sort of sing-song voice and a tone of bewilderment that increased with each separate exclamation.

Ganimard gave a fresh chuckle.

'Takes your breath away, chief, doesn't it? So it did mine, on the day when you came to see me here and when the notion was beginning to grow upon me. I was flabbergasted with astonishment. And yet I've had experience of my customer. I know what he's capable of . . . But this, no, this was really a bit too stiff!'

'It's impossible! It's impossible!' said M. Dudouis, in a low voice.

'On the contrary, chief, it's quite possible and quite logical and quite normal. It's the threefold incarnation of one and the same individual. A schoolboy would solve the problem in a minute, by a simple process of elimination. Take away the dead man: there remains Sparmiento and Lupin. Take away Sparmiento . . . '

'There remains Lupin,' muttered the chief-detective.

'Yes, chief, Lupin simply, Lupin in five letters and two syllables, Lupin taken out of his Brazilian skin, Lupin revived from the dead, Lupin translated, for the past six months, into Colonel Sparmiento, travelling in Brittany, hearing of the discovery of the twelve tapestries, buying them, planning the theft of the best of them, so as to draw attention to himself, Lupin, and divert it from himself, Sparmiento. Next, he brings about, in full view of the gaping public, a noisy contest between Lupin and Sparmiento or Sparmiento and Lupin, plots and gives the house-warming party, terrifies his guests and, when everything is ready, arranges for Lupin to steal Sparmiento's tapestries and for Sparmiento, Lupin's victim, to disappear from sight and die unsuspected, unsuspectable, regretted by his friends, pitied by the public and leaving behind him, to pocket the profits of the swindle . . . '

Ganimard stopped, looked the chief in the eyes and, in a voice that emphasized the importance of his words, concluded: 'Leaving behind him a disconsolate widow.'

'Mme Sparmiento! You really believe . . . ?

'Hang it all!' said the chief-inspector. 'People don't work up a whole business of this sort, without seeing something ahead of them . . . solid profits.'

'But the profits, it seems to me, lie in the sale of the tapestries which Lupin will effect in America or elsewhere.'

'First of all, yes. But Colonel Sparmiento could effect that sale just as well. And even better. So there's something more.'

'Something more?'

'Come, chief, you're forgetting that Colonel Sparmiento has been the victim of an important robbery and that, though he may be dead, at least his widow remains. So it's his widow who will get the money.'

'What money?'

'What money? Why, the money due to her! The insurance-money, of course!'

M. Dudouis was staggered. The whole business suddenly became clear to him, with its real meaning. He muttered: 'That's true! . . . That's true! . . . The colonel had insured his tapestries . . . '

'Rather! And for no trifle either.'

'For how much?'

'Eight hundred thousand francs.'

'Eight hundred thousand?'

'Just so. In five different companies.'

'And has Mme Sparmiento had the money?'

'She got a hundred and fifty thousand francs yesterday and two hundred thousand today, while I was away. The remaining payments are to be made in the course of this week.'

'But this is terrible! You ought to have . . . '

'What, chief? To begin with, they took ad vantage of my absence to settle up accounts with the companies. I only heard about it on my return when I ran up against an insurance-manager whom I happen to know and took the opportunity of drawing him out.'

The chief-detective was silent for some time, not knowing what to say. Then he mumbled: 'What a fellow, though!'

Ganimard nodded his head.

'Yes, chief, a blackguard, but, I can't help saying, a devil of a clever fellow. For his plan to succeed, he must have managed in such a way that, for four or five weeks, no one could express or even conceive the least suspicion of the part played by Colonel Sparmiento. All the indignation and all the inquiries had to be concentrated upon Lupin alone. In the last resort, people had to find themselves faced simply with a mournful, pitiful, penniless widow, poor Edith Swan-neck, a beautiful and legendary vision, a creature so pathetic that the gentlemen of the insurance-companies were almost glad to place something in her hands to relieve her poverty and her grief. That's what was wanted and that's what happened.'

The two men were close together and did not take their eyes from each other's faces.

The chief asked: 'Who is that woman?'

'Sonia Kritchnoff.'

'Sonia Kritchnoff?'

'Yes, the Russian girl whom I arrested last year at the time of the theft of the coronet, and whom Lupin helped to escape.' *

'Are you sure?'

'Absolutely. I was put off the scent, like everybody else, by Lupin's machinations, and had paid no particular attention to her. But, when I knew the part which she was playing, I remembered. She is certainly Sonia, metamorphosed into an Englishwoman; Sonia, the most innocent-looking and the trickiest of actresses; Sonia, who would not hesitate to face death for love of Lupin.'

'A good capture, Ganimard,' said M. Dudouis, approvingly.

'I've something better still for you, chief!'

'Really? What?'

'Lupin's old foster-mother.'

* *Arsène Lupin.* The Novel of the Play. By Edgar Jepson and Maurice Leblanc (Mills & Boon).

'Victoire?' *

'She has been here since Mme Sparmiento began playing the widow; she's the cook.'

'Oho!' said M. Dudouis. 'My congratulations, Ganimard!'

'I've something for you, chief, that's even better than that!'

M. Dudouis gave a start. The inspector's hand clutched his and was shaking with excitement.

'What do you mean, Ganimard?'

'Do you think, chief, that I would have brought you here, at this late hour, if I had had nothing more attractive to offer you than Sonia and Victoire? Pah! They'd have kept!'

'You mean to say . . . ?' whispered M. Dudouis, at last understanding the chief-inspector's agitation.

'You've guessed it, chief!'

'Is he here?'

'He's here.'

'In hiding?'

'Not a bit of it. Simply in disguise. He's the man-servant.'

This time, M. Dudouis did not utter a word nor make a gesture. Lupin's audacity confounded him.

Ganimard chuckled.

'It's no longer a threefold, but a fourfold incarnation. Edith Swanneck might have blundered. The master's presence was necessary; and he had the cheek to return. For three weeks, he has been beside me during my inquiry, calmly following the progress made.'

'Did you recognize him?'

'One doesn't recognize him. He has a knack of making-up his face and altering the proportions of his body so as to prevent anyone from knowing him. Besides, I was miles from suspecting . . . But, this evening, as I was watching Sonia in the shadow of the stairs, I heard Victoire speak to the man-servant and call him "Dearie". A light flashed in upon me. "Dearie!" That was what she always used to call him. And I knew where I was.'

M. Dudouis seemed flustered, in his turn, by the presence of the enemy, so often pursued and always so intangible.

'We've got him, this time,' he said, between his teeth. 'We've got him; and he can't escape us.'

'No, chief, he can't: neither he nor the two women.'

* *The Hollow Needle.* By Maurice Leblanc. Translated by Alexander Teixeira de Mattos (Nash). *813* By Maurice Leblanc. Translated by Alexander Teixeira de Mattos (Mills & Boon).

'Where are they?'

'Sonia and Victoire are on the second floor; Lupin is on the third.'

M. Dudouis suddenly became anxious.

'Why, it was through the windows of one of those floors that the tapestries were passed when they disappeared!'

'That's so, chief.'

'In that case, Lupin can get away too. The windows look out on the Rue Dufresnoy.'

'Of course they do, chief; but I have taken my precautions. The moment you arrived, I sent four of our men to keep watch under the windows in the Rue Dufresnoy. They have strict instructions to shoot, if anyone appears at the windows and looks like coming down. Blank cartridges for the first shot, ball-cartridges for the next.'

'Good, Ganimard! You have thought of everything. We'll wait here; and, immediately after sunrise . . . '

'Wait, chief? Stand on ceremony with that rascal? Bother about rules and regulations, legal hours and all that rot? And suppose he's not quite so polite to us and gives us the slip meanwhile? Suppose he plays us one of his Lupin tricks? No, no, we must have no nonsense! We've got him: let's collar him; and that without delay!'

And Ganimard, all a-quiver with indignant impatience, went out, walked across the garden and presently returned with half-a-dozen men.

'It's all right, chief. I've told them, in the Rue Dufresnoy, to get their revolvers out and aim at the windows. Come along.'

These alarums and excursions had not been effected without a certain amount of noise, which was bound to be heard by the inhabitants of the house. M. Dudouis felt that his hand was forced. He made up his mind to act.

'Come on, then,' he said.

The thing did not take long. The eight of them, Browning pistols in hand, went up the stairs without overmuch precaution, eager to surprise Lupin before he had time to organize his defences.

'Open the door!' roared Ganimard, rushing at the door of Mme Sparmiento's bedroom.

A policeman smashed it in with his shoulder.

There was no one in the room; and no one in Victoire's bedroom either.

'They're all upstairs!' shouted Ganimard. 'They've gone up to Lupin in his attic. Be careful now!'

All the eight ran up the third flight of stairs. To his great astonishment, Ganimard found the door of the attic open and the attic empty. And the other rooms were empty too.

'Blast them!' he cursed. 'What's become of them?'

But the chief called him. M. Dudouis, who had gone down again to the second floor, noticed that one of the windows was not latched, but just pushed to.

'There,' he said, to Ganimard, 'that's the road they took, the road of the tapestries. I told you as much: the Rue Dufresnoy . . .'

'But our men would have fired on them,' protested Ganimard, grinding his teeth with rage. 'The street's guarded.'

'They must have gone before the street was guarded.'

'They were all three of them in their rooms when I rang you up, chief!'

'They must have gone while you were waiting for me in the garden.'

'But why? Why? There was no reason why they should go today rather than tomorrow, or the next day, or next week, for that matter, when they had pocketed all the insurance-money!'

Yes, there was a reason; and Ganimard knew it when he saw, on the table, a letter addressed to himself and opened it and read it. The letter was worded in the style of the testimonials which we hand to people in our service who have given satisfaction.

I, the undersigned, Arsène Lupin, gentleman-burglar, ex-colonel, ex-man-of-all-work, ex-corpse, hereby certify that the person of the name of Ganimard gave proof of the most remarkable qualities during his stay in this house. He was exemplary in his behaviour, thoroughly devoted and attentive; and, unaided by the least clue, he foiled a part of my plans and saved the insurance-companies four hundred and fifty thousand francs. I congratulate him; and I am quite willing to overlook his blunder in not anticipating that the downstairs telephone communicates with the telephone in Sonia Kritchnoff's bedroom and that, when telephoning to Mr Chief-detective, he was at the same time telephoning to me to clear out as fast as I could. It was a pardonable slip, which must not be allowed to dim the glamour of his services nor to detract from the merits of his victory.

Having said this, I beg him to accept the homage of my admiration and of my sincere friendship.

Arsène Lupin

THE END

THE GOLDEN TRIANGLE

Chapter 1
Coralie

It was close upon half-past six and the evening shadows were growing denser when two soldiers reached the little space, planted with trees, opposite the Musée Galliéra, where the Rue de Chaillot and the Rue Pierre-Charron meet. One wore an infantryman's sky-blue great-coat; the other, a Senegalese, those clothes of undyed wool, with baggy breeches and a belted jacket, in which the Zouaves and the native African troops have been dressed since the war. One of them had lost his right leg, the other his left arm.

They walked round the open space, in the center of which stands a fine group of Silenus figures, and stopped. The infantryman threw away his cigarette. The Senegalese picked it up, took a few quick puffs at it, put it out by squeezing it between his fore-finger and thumb and stuffed it into his pocket. All this without a word.

Almost at the same time two more soldiers came out of the Rue Galliéra. It would have been impossible to say to what branch they belonged, for their military attire was composed of the most incongruous civilian garments. However, one of them sported a Zouave's *chechia*, the other an artilleryman's *képi*. The first walked on crutches, the other on two sticks. These two kept near the newspaper-kiosk which stands at the edge of the pavement.

Three others came singly by the Rue Pierre-Charron, the Rue Brignoles and the Rue de Chaillot: a one-armed rifleman, a limping sapper and a marine with a hip that looked as if it was twisted. Each of them made straight for a tree and leant against it.

Not a word was uttered among them. None of the seven crippled soldiers seemed to know his companions or to trouble about or even perceive their presence. They stood behind their trees or behind the kiosk or behind the group of Silenus figures without stirring. And the few wayfarers who, on that evening of the 3rd of April, 1915, crossed this unfrequented square, which received hardly any light from the shrouded street-lamps, did not slacken pace to observe the men's motionless outlines.

A clock struck half-past six. At that moment the door of one of the houses overlooking the square opened. A man came out, closed the door behind him, crossed the Rue de Chaillot and walked round the open space in front of the museum. It was an officer in khaki. Under his red forage-cap, with its three lines of gold braid, his head was wrapped in a wide linen bandage, which hid his forehead and neck. He was tall and very slenderly built. His right leg ended in a wooden stump with a rubber foot to it. He leant on a stick.

Leaving the square, he stepped into the roadway of the Rue Pierre-Charron. Here he turned and gave a leisurely look to his surroundings on every side. This minute inspection brought him to one of the trees facing the museum. With the tip of his cane he gently tapped a protruding stomach. The stomach pulled itself in.

The officer moved off again. This time he went definitely down the Rue Pierre-Charron towards the center of Paris. He thus came to the Avenue des Champs-Élysées, which he went up, taking the left pavement.

Two hundred yards further on was a large house, which had been transformed, as a flag proclaimed, into a hospital. The officer took up his position at some distance, so as not to be seen by those leaving, and waited.

It struck a quarter to seven and seven o'clock. A few more minutes passed. Five persons came out of the house, followed by two more. At last a lady appeared in the hall, a nurse wearing a wide blue cloak marked with the Red Cross.

'Here she comes,' said the officer.

She took the road by which he had arrived and turned down the Rue Pierre-Charron, keeping to the right-hand pavement and thus making for the space where the street meets the Rue de Chaillot. Her walk was light, her step easy and well-balanced. The wind, buffeting against her as she moved quickly on her way, swelled out the long blue veil floating around her shoulders. Notwithstanding the width of the cloak, the rhythmical swing of her body and the youthfulness of her figure were revealed. The officer kept behind her and walked along with an absent-minded air, twirling his stick, like a man taking an aimless stroll.

At this moment there was nobody in sight, in that part of the street, except him and her. But, just after she had crossed the Avenue Marceau and some time before he reached it, a motor standing in the avenue started driving in the same direction as the nurse, at a fixed distance from her.

It was a taxi-cab. And the officer noticed two things: first, that there were two men inside it and, next, that one of them leant out of the window almost the whole time, talking to the driver. He was able to catch a momentary glimpse of this man's face, cut in half by a heavy mustache and surmounted by a gray felt hat.

Meanwhile, the nurse walked on without turning round. The officer had crossed the street and now hurried his pace, the more so as it struck him that the cab was also increasing its speed as the girl drew near the space in front of the museum.

From where he was the officer could take in almost the whole of the little square at a glance; and, however sharply he looked, he discerned nothing in the darkness that revealed the presence of the seven crippled men. No one, moreover, was passing on foot or driving. In the distance only, in the dusk of the wide crossing avenues, two tram-cars, with lowered blinds, disturbed the silence.

Nor did the girl, presuming that she was paying attention to the sights of the street, appear to see anything to alarm her. She gave not the least sign of hesitation. And the behavior of the motor-cab following her did not seem to strike her either, for she did not look round once.

The cab, however, was gaining ground. When it neared the square, it was ten or fifteen yards, at most, from the nurse; and, by the time that she, still noticing nothing, had reached the first trees, it came closer yet and, leaving the middle of the road, began to hug the pavement, while, on the side opposite the pavement, the left-hand side, the man who kept leaning out had opened the door and was now standing on the step.

The officer crossed the street once more, briskly, without fear of being seen, so heedless did the two men now appear of anything but their immediate business. He raised a whistle to his lips. There was no doubt that the expected event was about to take place.

The cab, in fact, pulled up suddenly. The two men leapt from the doors on either side and rushed to the pavement of the square, a few yards from the kiosk. At the same moment there was a cry of terror from the girl and a shrill whistle from the officer. And, also at the same time, the two men caught up and seized their victim and dragged her towards the cab, while the seven wounded soldiers, seeming to spring from the very trunks of the trees that hid them, fell upon the two aggressors.

The battle did not last long. Or rather there was no battle. At the outset the driver of the taxi, perceiving that the attack was being countered, made off and drove away as fast as he could. As for the two men, realizing that their enterprise had failed and finding themselves faced with a threatening array of uplifted sticks and crutches, not to mention the barrel of a revolver which the officer pointed at them, they let go the girl, tacked from side to side, to prevent the officer from taking aim, and disappeared in the darkness of the Rue Brignoles.

'Run for all you're worth, Ya-Bon,' said the officer to the one-armed Senegalese, 'and bring me back one of them by the scruff of the neck!'

He supported the girl with his arm. She was trembling all over and seemed ready to faint.

'Don't be frightened, Little Mother Coralie,' he said, very anxiously. 'It's I, Captain Belval, Patrice Belval.'

'Ah, it's you, captain!' she stammered.

'Yes; all your friends have gathered round to defend you, all your old patients from the hospital, whom I found in the convalescent home.'

'Thank you. Thank you.' And she added, in a quivering voice, 'The others? Those two men?'

'Run away. Ya-Bon's gone after them.'

'But what did they want with me? And what miracle brought you all here?'

'We'll talk about that later, Little Mother Coralie. Let's speak of you first. Where am I to take you? Don't you think you'd better come in here with me, until you've recovered and taken a little rest?'

Assisted by one of the soldiers, he helped her gently to the house which he himself had left three-quarters of an hour before. The girl let him do as he pleased. They all entered an apartment on the ground-floor and went into the drawing-room, where a bright fire of logs was burning. He switched on the electric light.

'Sit down,' he said.

She dropped into a chair; and the captain at once gave his orders.

'You, Poulard, go and fetch a glass in the dining-room. And you, Ribrac, draw a jug of cold water in the kitchen . . . Chatelain, you'll find a decanter of rum in the pantry . . . Or, stay, she doesn't like rum . . . Then . . .'

'Then,' she said, smiling, 'just a glass of water, please.'

Her cheeks, which were naturally pale, recovered a little of their warmth. The blood flowed back to her lips; and the smile on her face was full of confidence. Her face, all charm and gentleness, had a pure outline, features almost too delicate, a fair complexion and the ingenuous expression of a wondering child that looks on life with eyes always wide open. And all this, which was dainty and exquisite, nevertheless at certain moments gave an impression of energy, due no doubt to her shining, dark eyes and to the line of smooth, black hair that came down on either side from under the white cap in which her forehead was imprisoned.

'Aha!' cried the captain, gaily, when she had drunk the water. 'You're feeling better, I think, eh, Little Mother Coralie?'

'Much better.'

'Capital. But that was a bad minute we went through just now! What an adventure! We shall have to talk it all over and get some light on it, shan't we? Meanwhile, my lads, pay your respects to Little Mother Coralie. Eh, my fine fellows, who would have thought, when she was coddling you and patting your pillows for your fat pates to sink into, that one day we should be taking care of her and that the children would be coddling their little mother?'

They all pressed round her, the one-armed and the one-legged, the crippled and the sick, all glad to see her. And she shook hands with them affectionately.

'Well, Ribrac, how's that leg of yours?'

'I don't feel it any longer, Little Mother Coralie.'

'And you, Vatinel? That wound in your shoulder?'

'Not a sign of it, Little Mother Coralie.'

'And you, Poulard? And you, Jorisse?'

Her emotion increased at seeing them again, the men whom she called her children. And Patrice Belval exclaimed.

'Ah, Little Mother Coralie, now you're crying! Little mother, little mother, that's how you captured all our hearts. When we were trying our hardest not to call out, on our bed of pain, we used to see your eyes filling with great tears. Little Mother Coralie was weeping over her children. Then we clenched our teeth still firmer.'

'And I used to cry still more,' she said, 'just because you were afraid of hurting me.'

'And today you're at it again. No, you are too soft-hearted! You love us. We love you. There's nothing to cry about in that. Come, Little Mother Coralie, a smile . . . And, I say, here's Ya-Bon coming; and Ya-Bon always laughs.'

She rose suddenly.

'Do you think he can have overtaken one of the two men?'

'Do I think so? I told Ya-Bon to bring one back by the neck. He won't fail. I'm only afraid of one thing . . .'

They had gone towards the hall. The Senegalese was already on the steps. With his right hand he was clutching the neck of a man, of a limp rag, rather, which he seemed to be carrying at arm's length, like a dancing-doll.

'Drop him,' said the captain.

Ya-Bon loosened his fingers. The man fell on the flags in the hall.

'That's what I feared,' muttered the officer. 'Ya-Bon has only his right hand; but, when that hand holds anyone by the throat, it's a miracle if it doesn't strangle him. The Boches know something about it.'

Ya-Bon was a sort of colossus, the color of gleaming coal, with a woolly head and a few curly hairs on his chin, with an empty sleeve fastened to his left shoulder and two medals pinned to his jacket. Ya-Bon had had one cheek, one side of his jaw, half his mouth and the whole of his palate smashed by a splinter of shell. The other half of that mouth was split to the ear in a laugh which never seemed to cease and which was all the more surprising because the wounded portion of the face, patched up as best it could be and covered with a grafted skin, remained impassive.

Moreover, Ya-Bon had lost his power of speech. The most that he could do was to emit a sequence of indistinct grunts in which his nickname of Ya-Bon was everlastingly repeated.

He uttered it once more with a satisfied air, glancing by turns at his master and his victim, like a good sporting-dog standing over the bird which he has retrieved.

'Good,' said the officer. 'But, next time, go to work more gently.'

He bent over the man, felt his heart and, on seeing that he had only fainted, asked the nurse.

'Do you know him?'

'No,' she said.

'Are you sure? Have you never seen that head anywhere?'

It was a very big head, with black hair, plastered down with grease, and a thick beard. The man's clothes, which were of dark-blue serge and well-cut, showed him to be in easy circumstances.

'Never . . . never,' the girl declared.

Captain Belval searched the man's pockets. They contained no papers.

'Very well,' he said, rising to his feet, 'we will wait till he wakes up and question him then. Ya-Bon, tie up his arms and legs and stay here, in the hall. The rest of you fellows, go back to the home: it's time you were indoors. I have my key. Say goodbye to Little Mother Coralie and trot off.'

And, when goodbye had been said, he pushed them outside, came back to the nurse, led her into the drawing-room and said.

'Now let's talk, Little Mother Coralie. First of all, before we try to explain things, listen to me. It won't take long.'

They were sitting before the merrily blazing fire. Patrice Belval slipped a hassock under Little Mother Coralie's feet, put out a light that seemed to worry her and, when he felt certain that she was comfortable, began.

'As you know, Little Mother Coralie, I left the hospital a week ago and am staying on the Boulevard Maillot, at Neuilly, in the home reserved for the convalescent patients of the hospital. I sleep there at night and have my wounds dressed in the morning. The rest of the time I spend in loafing: I stroll about, lunch and dine where the mood takes me and go and call on my friends. Well, this morning I was waiting for one of them in a big café-restaurant on the boule-vard, when I overheard the end of a conversation . . . But I must tell you that the place is divided into two by a partition standing about six feet high, with the customers of the café on one side and those of the restaurant on the other. I was all by myself in the restaurant; and the two men, who had their backs turned to me and who in any case were out of sight, probably thought that there was no one there at all, for they were speaking rather louder than they need have done, considering the sentences which I overheard . . . and which I after-wards wrote down in my little note-book.'

He took the note-book from his pocket and went on.

'These sentences, which caught my attention for reasons which you will understand presently, were preceded by some others in which there was a reference to sparks, to a shower of sparks that had already occurred twice before the war, a sort of night signal for the possible repetition of which they proposed to watch, so that they might act quickly as soon as it appeared. Does none of this tell you anything?'

'No. Why?'

'You shall see. By the way, I forgot to tell you that the two were talking English, quite correctly, but with an accent which assured me that neither of them was an Englishman. Here is what they said, faithfully translated: "To finish up, therefore," said one, "every-thing is decided. You and he will be at the appointed place at a little before seven this evening." "We shall be there, colonel. We have engaged our taxi." "Good. Remember that the little woman leaves her hospital at seven o'clock." "Have no fear. There can't be any mistake, because she always goes the same way, down the Rue Pierre-Charron." "And your whole plan is settled?" "In every particular. The thing will happen in the square at the end of the Rue de Chaillot. Even granting that there may be people about, they will have no time to rescue her, for we shall act too quickly." "Are you certain of your driver?" "I am certain that we shall pay him enough to secure his obedience. That's all we want." "Capital. I'll wait for you at the place you know of, in a motor-car. You'll hand the little woman over to me. From that moment, we shall be masters of the situation." "And you of the little woman, colonel, which isn't bad for you, for she's deucedly pretty." "Deucedly, as you say. I've known her a long time by sight; and, upon my word . . . ." The two began to laugh coarsely and called for their bill. I at once got up and went to the door on the boulevard, but only one of them came out by that door, a man with a big drooping mustache and a gray felt hat. The other had left by the door in the street round the corner. There was only one taxi in the road. The man took it and I had to give up all hope of following him. Only . . . only, as I knew that you left the hospital at seven o'clock every evening and that you went along the Rue Pierre-Charron, I was justified, wasn't I, in believing . . . ?'

The captain stopped. The girl reflected, with a thoughtful air. Presently she asked.

'Why didn't you warn me?'

'Warn you!' he exclaimed. 'And, if, after all, it wasn't you? Why alarm you? And, if, on the other hand, it was you, why put you on your guard? After the attempt had failed, your enemies would have laid another trap for you; and we, not knowing of it, would have been unable to prevent it. No, the best thing was to accept the fight. I enrolled a little band of your former patients who were being treated at the home; and, as the friend whom I was expecting to meet happened to live in the square, here, in this house, I asked him to place his rooms at my disposal from six to nine o'clock. That's what I did, Little Mother Coralie. And now that you know as much as I do, what do you think of it?'

She gave him her hand.

'I think you have saved me from an unknown danger that looks like a very great one; and I thank you.'

'No, no,' he said, 'I can accept no thanks. I was so glad to have succeeded! What I want to know is your opinion of the business itself?'

Without a second's hesitation, she replied: 'I have none. Not a word, not an incident, in all that you have told me, suggests the least idea to me.'

'You have no enemies, to your knowledge?'

'Personally, no.'

'What about that man to whom your two assailants were to hand you over and who says that he knows you?'

'Doesn't every woman,' she said, with a slight blush, 'come across men who pursue her more or less openly? I can't tell who it is.'

The captain was silent for a while and then went on.

'When all is said, our only hope of clearing up the matter lies in questioning our prisoner. If he refuses to answer, I shall hand him over to the police, who will know how to get to the bottom of the business.'

The girl gave a start.

'The police?'

'Well, of course. What would you have me do with the fellow? He doesn't belong to me. He belongs to the police.'

'No, no, no!' she exclaimed, excitedly. 'Not on any account! What, have my life gone into? . . . Have to appear before the magistrate? . . . Have my name mixed up in all this? . . . '

'And yet, Little Mother Coralie, I can't . . . '

'Oh, I beg, I beseech you, as my friend, find some way out of it, but don't have me talked about! I don't want to be talked about!'

The captain looked at her, somewhat surprised to see her in such a state of agitation, and said.

'You shan't be talked about, Little Mother Coralie, I promise you.'

'Then what will you do with that man?'

'Well,' he said, with a laugh, 'I shall begin by asking him politely if he will condescend to answer my questions; then thank him for his civil behavior to you; and lastly beg him to be good enough to go away.'

He rose.

'Do you wish to see him, Little Mother Coralie?'

'No,' she said, 'I am so tired! If you don't want me, question him by yourself. You can tell me about it afterwards . . . '

She seemed quite exhausted by all this fresh excitement and strain, added to all those which already rendered her life as a nurse so hard.

The captain did not insist and went out, closing the door of the drawing-room after him.

She heard him saying.

'Well, Ya-Bon, have you kept a good watch! No news? And how's your prisoner? ... Ah, there you are, my fine fellow! Have you got your breath back? Oh, I know Ya-Bon's hand is a bit heavy! ... What's this? Won't you answer? ... Hallo, what's happened? Hanged if I don't think ... '

A cry escaped him. The girl ran to the hall. She met the captain, who tried to bar her way.

'Don't come,' he said, in great agitation. 'What's the use!'

'But you're hurt!' she exclaimed.

'I?'

'There's blood on your shirt-cuff.'

'So there is, but it's nothing: it's the man's blood that must have stained me.'

'Then he was wounded?'

'Yes, or at least his mouth was bleeding. Some blood-vessel ... '

'Why, surely Ya-Bon didn't grip as hard as that?'

'It wasn't Ya-Bon.'

'Then who was it?'

'His accomplices.'

'Did they come back?'

'Yes; and they've strangled him.'

'But it's not possible!'

She pushed by and went towards the prisoner. He did not move. His face had the pallor of death. Round his neck was a red-silk string, twisted very thin and with a buckle at either end.

Chapter 2
Right Hand and Left Leg

'One rogue less in the world, Little Mother Coralie!' cried Patrice Belval, after he had led the girl back to the drawing-room and made a rapid investigation with Ya-Bon. 'Remember his name – I found it engraved on his watch – Mustapha Rovalaïof, the name of a rogue!'

He spoke gaily, with no emotion in his voice, and continued, as he walked up and down the room.

'You and I, Little Mother Coralie, who have witnessed so many tragedies and seen so many good fellows die, need not waste tears over the death of Mustapha Rovalaïof or his murder by his accomplices. Not even a funeral oration, eh? Ya-Bon has taken him under his arm, waited until the square was clear and carried him to the Rue Brignoles, with orders to fling the gentleman over the railings into the garden of the Musée Galliéra. The railings are high. But Ya-Bon's right hand knows no obstacles. And so, Little Mother Coralie, the matter is buried. You won't be talked about; and, this time, I claim a word of thanks.'

He stopped to laugh.

'A word of thanks, but no compliments. By Jove, I don't make much of a warder! It was clever the way those beggars snatched my prisoner. Why didn't I foresee that your other assailant, the man in the gray-felt hat, would go and tell the third, who was waiting in his motor, and that they would both come back together to rescue their companion? And they came back. And, while you and I were chatting, they must have forced the servants' entrance, passed through the kitchen, come to the little door between the pantry and the hall and pushed it open. There, close by them, lay their man, still unconscious and firmly bound, on his sofa. What were they to do? It was impossible to get him out of the hall without alarming Ya-Bon. And yet, if they didn't release him, he would speak, give away his accomplices and ruin a carefully prepared plan. So one of the two must have leant forward stealthily, put out his arm, thrown his string round that throat which Ya-Bon had already handled pretty roughly, gathered the buckles at the two ends and pulled, pulled, quietly, until death came. Not a sound. Not a sigh. The whole operation performed in silence. We come, we kill and we go away. Good-night. The trick is done and our friend won't talk.'

Captain Belval's merriment increased.

'Our friend won't talk,' he repeated, 'and the police, when they find his body tomorrow morning inside a railed garden, won't understand a word of the business. Nor we either, Little Mother Coralie; and we shall never know why those men tried to kidnap you. It's only too true! I may not be up to much as a warder, but I'm beneath contempt as a detective!'

He continued to walk up and down the room. The fact that his leg or rather his calf had been amputated seemed hardly to inconvenience him; and, as the joints of the knee and thighbone had retained their mobility, there was at most a certain want of rhythm in the action of his hips and shoulders. Moreover, his tall figure tended to correct this lameness, which was reduced to insignificant proportions by the ease of his movements and the indifference with which he appeared to accept it.

He had an open countenance, rather dark in color, burnt by the sun and tanned by the weather, with an expression that was frank, cheerful and often bantering. He must have been between twenty-eight and thirty. His manner suggested that of the officers of the First Empire, to whom their life in camp imparted a special air which they subsequently brought into the ladies' drawing-rooms.

He stopped to look at Coralie, whose shapely profile stood out against the gleams from the fireplace. Then he came and sat beside her.

'I know nothing about you,' he said softly. 'At the hospital the doctors and nurses call you Madame Coralie. Your patients prefer to say Little Mother. What is your married or your maiden name? Have you a husband or are you a widow? Where do you live? Nobody knows. You arrive every day at the same time and you go away by the same street. Sometimes an old serving-man, with long gray hair and a bristly beard, with a comforter round his neck and a pair of yellow spectacles on his nose, brings you or fetches you. Sometimes also he waits for you, always sitting on the same chair in the covered yard. He has been asked questions, but he never gives an answer. I know only one thing, therefore, about you, which is that you are adorably good and kind and that you are also – I may say it, may I not? – adorably beautiful. And it is perhaps, Little Mother Coralie, because I know nothing about your life that I imagine it so mysterious, and, in some way, so sad. You give the impression of living amid sorrow and anxiety; the feeling that you are all alone. There is no one who devotes himself to making you happy and taking care of you. So I thought – I have long thought and waited for an opportunity of telling you – I thought that you must need a friend, a brother, who would advise and protect you. Am I not right, Little Mother Coralie?'

As he went on, Coralie seemed to shrink into herself and to place a greater distance between them, as though she did not wish him to penetrate those secret regions of which he spoke.

'No,' she murmured, 'you are mistaken. My life is quite simple. I do not need to be defended.'

'You do not need to be defended!' he cried, with increasing animation. 'What about those men who tried to kidnap you? That plot hatched against you? That plot which your assailants are so afraid to see discovered that they go to the length of killing the one who allowed himself to be caught? Is that nothing? Is it mere delusion on my part when I say that you are surrounded by dangers, that you have enemies who stick at nothing, that you have to be defended against their attempts and that, if you decline the offer of my assistance, I . . . Well, I . . . ?'

She persisted in her silence, showed herself more and more distant, almost hostile. The officer struck the marble mantelpiece with his fist, and, bending over her, finished his sentence in a determined tone.

'Well, if you decline the offer of my assistance, I shall force it on you.'

She shook her head.

'I shall force it on you,' he repeated, firmly. 'It is my duty and my right.'

'No,' she said, in an undertone.

'My absolute right,' said Captain Belval, 'for a reason which outweighs all the others and makes it unnecessary for me even to consult you.'

'What do you mean?'

'I love you.'

He brought out the words plainly, not like a lover venturing on a timid declaration, but like a man proud of the sentiment that he feels and happy to proclaim it.

She lowered her eyes and blushed; and he cried, exultantly: 'You can take it, Little Mother, from me. No impassioned outbursts, no sighs, no waving of the arms, no clapping of the hands. Just three little words, which I tell you without going on my knees. And it's the easier for me because you know it. Yes, Madame Coralie, it's all very well to look so shy, but you know my love for you and you've known it as long as I have. We saw it together take birth when your dear little hands touched my battered head. The others used to torture me. With you, it was nothing but caresses. So was the pity in your eyes and the tears that fell because I was in pain. But can anyone see you without loving you? Your seven patients who were here just now are all in love with you, Little Mother Coralie. Ya-Bon worships the ground you walk on. Only they are privates. They cannot speak. I am an officer; and I speak without hesitation or embarrassment, believe me.'

Coralie had put her hands to her burning cheeks and sat silent, bending forward.

'You understand what I mean, don't you,' he went on, in a voice that rang, 'when I say that I speak without hesitation or embarrassment? If I had been before the war what I am now, a maimed man, I should not have had the same assurance and I should have declared my love for you humbly and begged your pardon for my boldness. But now! . . . Believe me, Little Mother Coralie, when I sit here face to face with the woman I adore, I do not think of my infirmity. Not for a moment do I feel the impression that I can appear ridiculous or presumptuous in your eyes.'

He stopped, as though to take breath, and then, rising, went on: 'And it must needs be so. People will have to understand that those who have been maimed in this war do not look upon themselves as outcasts, lame ducks, or lepers, but as absolutely normal men. Yes, normal! One leg short? What about it? Does that rob a man of his brain or heart? Then, because the war has deprived me of a leg, or an arm, or even both legs or both arms, I have no longer the right to love a woman save at the risk of meeting with a rebuff or imagining that she pities me? Pity! But we don't want the woman to pity us, nor to make an effort to love us, nor even to think that she is doing a charity because she treats us kindly. What we demand, from women and from the world at large, from those whom we meet in the street and from those who belong to the same set as ourselves, is absolute equality with the rest, who have been saved from our fate by their lucky stars or their cowardice.'

The captain once more struck the mantelpiece.

'Yes, absolute equality! We all of us, whether we have lost a leg or an arm, whether blind in one eye or two, whether crippled or deformed, claim to be just as good, physically and morally, as anyone you please; and perhaps better. What! Shall men who have used their legs to rush upon the enemy be outdistanced in life, because they no longer have those legs, by men who have sat and warmed their toes at an office-fire? What nonsense! We want our place in the sun as well as the others. It is our due; and we shall know how to get it and keep it. There is no happiness to which we are not entitled and no work for which we are not capable with a little exercise and training. Ya-Bon's right hand is already worth any pair of hands in the wide world; and Captain Belval's left leg allows him to do his five miles an hour if he pleases.'

He began to laugh.

'Right hand and left leg; left hand and right leg: what does it matter which we have saved, if we know how to use it? In what respect have we fallen off? Whether it's a question of obtaining a position or perpetuating our race, are we not as good as we were? And perhaps even better. I venture to say that the children which we shall give to the country will be just as well-built as ever, with arms and legs and the rest . . . not to mention a mighty legacy of pluck and spirit. That's what we claim, Little Mother Coralie. We refuse to admit that our wooden legs keep us back or that we cannot stand as upright on our crutches as on legs of flesh and bone. We do not consider that devotion to us is any sacrifice or that it's necessary to talk of heroism when a girl has the honor to marry a blind soldier! Once more, we are not creatures outside the pale. We have not fallen off in any way whatever; and this is a truth before which everybody will bow for the next two or three generations. You can understand that, in a country like France, when maimed men are to be met by the hundred thousand, the conception of what makes a perfect man will no longer be as hard and fast as it was. In the new form of humanity which is preparing, there will be men with two arms and men with only one, just as there are fair men and dark, bearded men and clean-shaven. And it will all seem quite natural. And everyone will lead the life he pleases, without needing to be complete in every limb. And, as my life is wrapped up in you, Little Mother Coralie, and as my happiness depends on you, I thought I would wait no longer before making you my little speech . . . Well! That's finished! I have plenty more to say on the subject, but it can't all be said in a day, can it? . . .'

He broke off, thrown out of his stride after all by Coralie's silence. She had not stirred since the first words of love that he uttered. Her hands had sought her forehead; and her shoulders were shaking slightly.

He stooped and, with infinite gentleness, drawing aside the slender fingers, uncovered her beautiful face.

'Why are you crying, Little Mother Coralie?'

He was calling her *tu* now, but she did not mind. Between a man and the woman who has bent over his wounds relations of a special kind arise; and Captain Belval in particular had those rather familiar, but still respectful, ways at which it seems impossible to take offence.

'Have *I* made you cry?' he asked.

'No,' she said, in a low voice, 'it's all of you who upset me. It's your cheerfulness, your pride, your way not of submitting to fate, but mastering it. The humblest of you raises himself above his nature without an effort; and I know nothing finer or more touching than that indifference.'

He sat down beside her.

'Then you're not angry with me for saying . . . what I said?'

'Angry with you?' she replied, pretending to mistake his meaning. 'Why, every woman thinks as you do. If women, in bestowing their affection, had to choose among the men returning from the war, the choice I am sure would be in favor of those who have suffered most cruelly.'

He shook his head.

'You see, I am asking for something more than affection and a more definite answer to what I said. Shall I remind you of my words?'

'No.'

'Then your answer . . . ?'

'My answer, dear friend, is that you must not speak those words again.'

He put on a solemn air.

'You forbid me?'

'I do.'

'In that case, I swear to say nothing more until I see you again.'

'You will not see me again,' she murmured.

Captain Belval was greatly amused at this.

'I say, I say! And why shan't I see you again, Little Mother Coralie?'

'Because I don't wish it.'

'And your reason, please?'

'My reason?'

She turned her eyes to him and said, slowly: 'I am married.'

Belval seemed in no way disconcerted by this news. On the contrary, he said, in the calmest of tones: 'Well, you must marry again! No doubt your husband is an old man and you do not love him. He will therefore understand that, as you have someone in love with you . . .'

'Don't jest, please.'

He caught hold of her hand, just as she was rising to go.

'You are right, Little Mother Coralie, and I apologize for not adopting a more serious manner to speak to you of very serious things. It's a question of our two lives. I am profoundly convinced that they are moving towards each other and that you are powerless to restrain them. That is why your answer is beside the point. I ask nothing of you. I expect everything from fate. It is fate that will bring us together.'

'No,' she said.

'Yes,' he declared, 'that is how things will happen.'

'It is not. They will not and shall not happen like that. You must give me your word of honor not to try to see me again nor even to learn my name. I might have granted more if you had been content to remain friends. The confession which you have made sets a barrier between us. I want nobody in my life . . . nobody!'

She made this declaration with a certain vehemence and at the same time tried to release her arm from his grasp. Patrice Belval resisted her efforts and said: 'You are wrong . . . You have no right to expose yourself to danger like this . . . Please reflect . . .'

She pushed him away. As she did so, she knocked off the mantelpiece a little bag which she had placed there. It fell on the carpet and opened. Two or three things escaped, and she picked them up, while Patrice Belval knelt down on the floor to help her.

'Here,' he said, 'you've missed this.'

It was a little case in plaited straw, which had also come open; the beads of a rosary protruded from it.

They both stood up in silence. Captain Belval examined the rosary.

'What a curious coincidence!' he muttered. 'These amethyst beads! This old-fashioned gold filigree setting! . . . It's strange to find the same materials and the same workmanship . . .'

He gave a start, and it was so marked that Coralie asked: 'Why, what's the matter?'

He was holding in his fingers a bead larger than most of the others, forming a link between the string of tens and the shorter prayer-chain. And this bead was broken half-way across, almost level with the gold setting which held it.

'The coincidence,' he said, 'is so inconceivable that I hardly dare . . . And yet the face can be verified at once. But first, one question: who gave you this rosary?'

'Nobody gave it to me. I've always had it.'

'But it must have belonged to somebody before?'

'To my mother, I suppose.'

'Your mother?'

'I expect so, in the same way as the different jewels which she left me.'

'Is your mother dead?'

'Yes, she died when I was four years old. I have only the vaguest recollection of her. But what has all this to do with a rosary?'

'It's because of this,' he said. 'Because of this amethyst bead broken in two.'

He undid his jacket and took his watch from his waistcoat-pocket. It had a number of trinkets fastened to it by a little leather and silver strap. One of these trinkets consisted of the half of an amethyst bead, also broken across, also held in a filigree setting. The original size of the two beads seemed to be identical. The two amethysts were of the same color and contained in the same filigree.

Coralie and Belval looked at each other anxiously. She stammered: 'It's only an accident, nothing else . . . '

'I agree,' he said. 'But, supposing these two halves fit each other exactly . . . '

'It's impossible,' she said, herself frightened at the thought of the simple little act needed for the indisputable proof.

The officer, however, decided upon that act. He brought his right hand, which held the rosary-bead, and his left, which held the trinket, together. The hands hesitated, felt about and stopped. The contact was made.

The projections and indentations of the broken stones corresponded precisely. Each protruding part found a space to fit it. The two half amethysts were the two halves of the same amethyst. When joined, they formed one and the same bead.

There was a long pause, laden with excitement and mystery. Then, speaking in a low voice: 'I do not know either exactly where this trinket comes from,' Captain Belval said. 'Ever since I was a child, I used to see it among other things of trifling value which I kept in a cardboard box: watch-keys, old rings, old-fashioned seals. I picked out these trinkets from among them two or three years ago. Where does this one come from? I don't know. But what I do know . . . '

He had separated the two pieces and, examining them carefully, concluded: 'What I do know, beyond a doubt, is that the largest bead in this rosary came off one day and broke; and that the other, with its setting, went to form the trinket which I now have. You and I therefore possess the two halves of a thing which somebody else possessed twenty years ago.'

He went up to her and, in the same low and rather serious voice, said: 'You protested just now when I declared my faith in destiny and my certainty that events were leading us towards each other. Do you still deny it? For, after all, this is either an accident so extraordinary that we have no right to admit it or an actual fact which proves that our two lives have already touched in the past at some mysterious point and that they will meet again in the future, never to part. And that is why, without waiting for the perhaps distant future, I offer you today, when danger hangs over you, the support of my friendship. Observe that I am no longer speaking of love but only of friendship. Do you accept?'

She was nonplussed and so much perturbed by that miracle of the two broken amethysts, fitting each other exactly, that she appeared not to hear Belval's voice.

'Do you accept?' he repeated.

After a moment she replied: 'No.'

'Then the proof which destiny has given you of its wishes does not satisfy you?' he said, good-humoredly.

'We must not see each other again,' she declared.

'Very well. I will leave it to chance. It will not be for long. Meanwhile, I promise to make no effort to see you.'

'Nor to find out my name?'

'Yes, I promise you.'

'Goodbye,' she said, giving him her hand.

'*Au revoir*,' he answered.

She moved away. When she reached the door, she seemed to hesitate. He was standing motionless by the chimney. Once more she said: 'Goodbye.'

'*Au revoir*, Little Mother Coralie.'

Then she went out.

Only when the street-door had closed behind her did Captain Belval go to one of the windows. He saw Coralie passing through the trees, looking quite small in the surrounding darkness. He felt a pang at his heart. Would he ever see her again?

'Shall I? Rather!' he exclaimed. 'Why, tomorrow perhaps. Am I not the favorite of the gods?'

And, taking his stick, he set off, as he said, with his wooden leg foremost.

That evening, after dining at the nearest restaurant, Captain Belval went to Neuilly. The home run in connection with the hospital was a pleasant villa on the Boulevard Maillot, looking out on the Bois de Boulogne. Discipline was not too strictly enforced. The captain could come in at any hour of the night; and the man easily obtained leave from the matron.

'Is Ya-Bon there?' he asked this lady.

'Yes, he's playing cards with his sweetheart.'

'He has the right to love and be loved,' he said. 'Any letters for me?'

'No, only a parcel.'

'From whom?'

'A commissionaire brought it and just said that it was "for Captain Belval". I put it in your room.'

The officer went up to his bedroom on the top floor and saw the parcel, done up in paper and string, on the table. He opened it and discovered a box. The box contained a key, a large, rusty key, of a shape and manufacture that were obviously old.

What could it all mean? There was no address on the box and no mark. He presumed that there was some mistake which would come to light of itself; and he slipped the key into his pocket.

'Enough riddles for one day,' he thought. 'Let's go to bed.'

But when he went to the window to draw the curtains he saw, across the trees of the Bois, a cascade of sparks which spread to some distance in the dense blackness of the night. And he remembered the conversation which he had overheard in the restaurant and the rain of sparks mentioned by the men who were plotting to kidnap Little Mother Coralie . . .

Chapter 3
The Rusty Key

When Patrice Belval was eight years old he was sent from Paris, where he had lived till then, to a French boarding-school in London. Here he remained for ten years. At first he used to hear from his father weekly. Then, one day, the head-master told him that he was an orphan, that provision had been made for the cost of his education and that, on his majority, he would receive through an English solicitor his paternal inheritance, amounting to some eight thousand pounds.

Two hundred thousand francs could never be enough for a young man who soon proved himself to possess expensive tastes and who, when sent to Algeria to perform his military service, found means to run up twenty thousand francs of debts before coming into his money. He therefore started by squandering his patrimony and, having done so, settled down to work. Endowed with an active temperament and an ingenious brain, possessing no special vocation, but capable of anything that calls for initiative and resolution, full of ideas, with both the will and the knowledge to carry out an enterprise, he inspired confidence in others, found capital as he needed it and started one venture after another, including electrical schemes, the purchase of rivers and waterfalls, the organization of motor services in the colonies, of steamship lines and of mining companies. In a few years he had floated a dozen of such enterprises, all of which succeeded.

The war came to him as a wonderful adventure. He flung himself into it with heart and soul. As a sergeant in a colonial regiment, he won his lieutenant's stripes on the Marne. He was wounded in the calf on the 15th of September and had it amputated the same day. Two months after, by some mysterious wirepulling, cripple though he was, he began to go up as observer in the aeroplane of one of our best pilots. A shrapnel-shell put an end to the exploits of both heroes on the 10th of January. This time, Captain Belval, suffering from a serious wound in the head, was discharged and sent to the hospital in the Avenue des Champs-Élysées. About the same period, the lady whom he was to call Little Mother Coralie also entered the hospital as a nurse.

There he was trepanned. The operation was successful, but complications remained. He suffered a good deal of pain, though he never uttered a complaint and, in fact, with his own good-humor kept up the spirits of his companions in misfortune, all of whom were devoted to him. He made them laugh, consoled them and stimulated them with his cheeriness and his constant happy manner of facing the worst positions.

Not one of them is ever likely to forget the way in which he received a manufacturer who called to sell him a mechanical leg.

'Aha, a mechanical leg! And what for, sir? To take in people, I suppose, so that they may not notice that I've lost a bit of mine? Then you consider, sir, that it's a blemish to have your leg amputated, and that I, a French officer, ought to hide it as a disgrace?'

'Not at all, captain. Still . . . '

'And what's the price of that apparatus of yours?'

'Five hundred francs.'

'Five hundred francs! And you think me capable of spending five hundred francs on a mechanical leg, when there are a hundred thousand poor devils who have been wounded as I have and who will have to go on showing their wooden stumps?'

The men sitting within hearing reveled with delight. Little Mother Coralie herself listened with a smile. And what would Patrice Belval not have given for a smile from Little Mother Coralie?

As he told her, he had fallen in love with her from the first, touched by her appealing beauty, her artless grace, her soft eyes, her gentle soul, which seemed to bend over the patients and to fondle them like a soothing caress. From the very first, the charm of her stole into his being and at the same time compassed it about. Her voice gave him new life. She bewitched him with the glance of her eyes and with her fragrant presence. And yet, while yielding to the empire of this love, he had an immense craving to devote himself to and to place his strength at the service of this delicate little creature, whom he felt to be surrounded with danger.

And now events were proving that he was right, the danger was taking definite shape and he had had the happiness to snatch Coralie from the grasp of her enemies. He rejoiced at the result of the first battle, but could not look upon it as over. The attacks were bound to be repeated. And even now was he not entitled to ask himself if there was not some close connection between the plot prepared against Coralie that morning and the sort of signal given by the shower of sparks? Did the two facts announced by the speakers at the restaurant not form part of the same suspicious machination?

The sparks continued to glitter in the distance. So far as Patrice Belval could judge, they came from the riverside, at some spot between two extreme points which might be the Trocadéro on the left and the Gare de Passy on the right.

'A mile or two at most, as the crow flies,' he said to himself. 'Why not go there? We'll soon see.'

A faint light filtered through the key-hole of a door on the second floor. It was Ya-Bon's room; and the matron had told him that Ya-Bon was playing cards with his sweetheart. He walked in.

Ya-Bon was no longer playing. He had fallen asleep in an arm-chair, in front of the outspread cards, and on the pinned-back sleeve hanging from his left shoulder lay the head of a woman, an appallingly common head, with lips as thick as Ya-Bon's, revealing a set of black teeth, and with a yellow, greasy skin that seemed soaked in oil. It was Angèle, the kitchen-maid, Ya-Bon's sweetheart. She snored aloud.

Patrice looked at them contentedly. The sight confirmed the truth of his theories. If Ya-Bon could find someone to care for him, might not the most sadly mutilated heroes aspire likewise to all the joys of love?

He touched the Senegalese on the shoulder. Ya-Bon woke up and smiled, or rather, divining the presence of his captain, smiled even before he woke.

'I want you, Ya-Bon.'

Ya-Bon uttered a grunt of pleasure and gave a push to Angèle, who fell over on the table and went on snoring.

Coming out of the house, Patrice saw no more sparks. They were hidden behind the trees. He walked along the boulevard and, to save time, went by the Ceinture railway to the Avenue Henri-Martin. Here he turned down the Rue de la Tour, which runs to Passy.

On the way he kept talking to Ya-Bon about what he had in his mind, though he well knew that the negro did not understand much of what he said. But this was a habit with him. Ya-Bon, first his comrade-in-arms and then his orderly, was as devoted to him as a dog. He had lost a limb on the same day as his officer and was wounded in the head on the same day; he believed himself destined to undergo the same experiences throughout; and he rejoiced at having been twice wounded just as he would have rejoiced at dying at the same time as Captain Belval. On his side, the captain rewarded this humble, dumb devotion by unbending genially to his companion; he treated him with an ironical and sometimes impatient humor which heightened the negro's love for him. Ya-Bon played the part of the passive confidant who is consulted without being regarded and who is made to bear the brunt of his interlocutor's hasty temper.

'What do you think of all this, Master Ya-Bon?' asked the captain, walking arm-in-arm with him. 'I have an idea that it's all part of the same business. Do you think so too?'

Ya-Bon had two grunts, one of which meant yes, the other no. He grunted out: 'Yes.'

'So there's no doubt about it,' the officer declared, 'and we must admit that Little Mother Coralie is threatened with a fresh danger. Is that so?'

'Yes,' grunted Ya-Bon, who always approved, on principle.

'Very well. It now remains to be seen what that shower of sparks means. I thought for a moment that, as we had our first visit from the Zeppelins a week ago . . . are you listening to me?'

'Yes.'

'I thought that it was a treacherous signal with a view to a second Zeppelin visit . . . '

'Yes.'

'No, you idiot, it's not yes. How could it be a Zeppelin signal when, according to the conversation which I overheard, the signal had already been given twice before the war. Besides, is it really a signal?'

'No.'

'How do you mean, no? What else could it be, you silly ass? You'd do better to hold your tongue and listen to me, all the more as you don't even know what it's all about . . . No more do I, for that matter, and I confess that I'm at an utter loss. Lord, it's a complicated business, and I'm not much of a hand at solving these problems.'

Patrice Belval was even more perplexed when he came to the bottom of the Rue de la Tour. There were several roads in front of him, and he did not know which to take. Moreover, though he was in the middle of Passy, not a spark shone in the dark sky.

'It's finished, I expect,' he said, 'and we've had our trouble for nothing. It's your fault, Ya-Bon. If you hadn't made me lose precious moments in snatching you from the arms of your beloved we should have arrived in time. I admit Angèle's charms, but, after all . . . '

He took his bearings, feeling more and more undecided. The expedition undertaken on chance and with insufficient information was certainly yielding no results; and he was thinking of abandoning it when a closed private car came out of the Rue Franklin, from the direction of the Trocadéro, and someone inside shouted through the speaking-tube: 'Bear to the left . . . and then straight on, till I stop you.'

Now it appeared to Captain Belval that this voice had the same foreign inflection as one of those which he had heard that morning at the restaurant.

'Can it be the beggar in the gray hat,' he muttered, 'one of those who tried to carry off Little Mother Coralie?'

'Yes,' grunted Ya-Bon.

'Yes. The signal of the sparks explains his presence in these parts. We mustn't lose sight of this track. Off with you, Ya-Bon.'

But there was no need for Ya-Bon to hurry. The car had gone down the Rue Raynouard, and Belval himself arrived just as it was stopping three or four hundred yards from the turning, in front of a large carriage-entrance on the left-hand side.

Five men alighted. One of them rang. Thirty or forty seconds passed. Then Patrice heard the bell tinkle a second time. The five men waited, standing packed close together on the pavement. At last, after a third ring, a small wicket contrived in one of the folding-doors was opened.

There was a pause and some argument. Whoever had opened the wicket appeared to be asking for explanations. But suddenly two of the men bore heavily on the folding-door, which gave way before their thrust and let the whole gang through.

There was a loud noise as the door slammed to. Captain Belval at once studied his surroundings.

The Rue Raynouard is an old country-road which at one time used to wind among the houses and gardens of the village of Passy, on the side of the hills bathed by the Seine. In certain places, which unfortunately are becoming more and more rare, it has retained a provincial aspect. It is skirted by old properties. Old houses stand hidden amidst the trees: that in which Balzac lived has been piously preserved. It was in this street that the mysterious garden lay where Arsène Lupin discovered a farmer-general's diamonds hidden in a crack of an old sundial.*

* *The Confessions of Arsène Lupin.* By Maurice Leblanc. Translated by Alexander Teixeira de Mattos. III. The Sign of the Shadow.

The car was still standing outside the house into which the five men had forced their way; and this prevented Patrice Belval from coming nearer. It was built in continuation of a wall and seemed to be one of the private mansions dating back to the First Empire. It had a very long front with two rows of round windows, protected by gratings on the ground-floor and solid shutters on the storey above. There was another building farther down, forming a separate wing.

'There's nothing to be done on this side,' said the captain. 'It's as impregnable as a feudal stronghold. Let's look elsewhere.'

From the Rue Raynouard, narrow lanes, which used to divide the old properties, make their way down to the river. One of them skirted the wall that preceded the house. Belval turned down it with Ya-Bon. It was constructed of ugly pointed pebbles, was broken into steps and faintly lighted by the gleam of a street-lamp.

'Lend me a hand, Ya-Bon. The wall is too high. But perhaps with the aid of the lamp-post . . .'

Assisted by the negro, he hoisted himself to the lamp and was stretching out one of his hands when he noticed that all this part of the wall bristled with broken glass, which made it absolutely impossible to grasp. He slid down again.

'Upon my word, Ya-Bon,' he said, angrily, 'you might have warned me! Another second and you would have made me cut my hands to pieces. What are you thinking of? In fact, I can't imagine what made you so anxious to come with me at all costs.'

There was a turn in the lane, hiding the light, so that they were now in utter darkness, and Captain Belval had to grope his way along. He felt the negro's hand come down upon his shoulder.

'What do you want, Ya-Bon?'

The hand pushed him against the wall. At this spot there was a door in an embrasure.

'Well, yes,' he said, 'that's a door. Do you think I didn't see it? Oh, no one has eyes but Master Ya-Bon, I suppose.'

Ya-Bon handed him a box of matches. He struck several, one after the other, and examined the door.

'What did I tell you?' he said between his teeth. 'There's nothing to be done. Massive wood, barred and studded with iron . . . Look, there's no handle on this side, merely a key-hole . . . Ah, what we want is a key, made to measure and cut for the purpose! . . . For instance, a key like the one which the commissionaire left for me at the home just now . . .'

He stopped. An absurd idea flitted through his brain; and yet, absurd as it was, he felt that he was bound to perform the trifling action which it suggested to him. He therefore retraced his steps. He had the key on him. He took it from his pocket.

He struck a fresh light. The key-hole appeared. Belval inserted the key at the first attempt. He bore on it to the left: the key turned in the lock. He pushed the door: it opened.

'Come along in,' he said.

The negro did not stir a foot. Patrice could understand his amazement. All said, he himself was equally amazed. By what unprecedented miracle was the key just the key of this very door? By what miracle was the unknown person who had sent it him able to guess that he would be in a position to use it without further instructions? A miracle indeed!

But Patrice had resolved to act without trying to solve the riddle which a mischievous chance seemed bent upon setting him.

'Come along in,' he repeated, triumphantly.

Branches struck him in the face and he perceived that he was walking on grass and that there must be a garden lying in front of him. It was so dark that he could not see the paths against the blackness of the turf; and, after walking for a minute or two, he hit his foot against some rocks with a sheet of water on them.

'Oh, confound it!' he cursed. 'I'm all wet. Damn you, Ya-Bon!'

He had not finished speaking when a furious barking was heard at the far end of the garden; and the sound at once came nearer, with extreme rapidity. Patrice realized that a watchdog, perceiving their presence, was rushing upon them, and, brave as he was, he shuddered, because of the impressiveness of this attack in complete darkness. How was he to defend himself? A shot would betray them; and yet he carried no weapon but his revolver.

The dog came dashing on, a powerful animal, to judge by the noise it made, suggesting the rush of a wild boar through the copsewood. It must have broken its chain, for it was accompanied by the clatter of iron. Patrice braced himself to meet it. But through the darkness he saw Ya-Bon pass before him to protect him, and the impact took place almost at once.

'Here, I say, Ya-Bon! Why did you get in front of me? It's all right, my lad, I'm coming!'

The two adversaries had rolled over on the grass. Patrice stooped down, seeking to rescue the negro. He touched the hair of an animal and then Ya-Bon's clothes. But the two were wriggling on the ground in so compact a mass and fighting so frantically that his interference was useless.

Moreover, the contest did not last long. In a few minutes the adversaries had ceased to move. A strangled death-rattle issued from the group.

'Is it all right, Ya-Bon?' whispered the captain, anxiously.

The negro stood up with a grunt. By the light of a match Patrice saw that he was holding at the end of his outstretched arm, of the one arm with which he had had to defend himself, a huge dog, which was gurgling, clutched round the throat by Ya-Bon's implacable fingers. A broken chain hung from its neck.

'Thank you, Ya-Bon. I've had a narrow escape. You can let him go now. He can't do us any harm, I think.'

Ya-Bon obeyed. But he had no doubt squeezed too tight. The dog writhed for a moment on the grass, gave a few moans and then lay without moving.

'Poor brute!' said Patrice. 'After all, he only did his duty in going for the burglars that we are. Let us do ours, Ya-Bon, which is nothing like as plain.'

Something that shone like a window-pane guided his steps and led him, by a series of stairs cut in the rocks and of successive terraces, to the level ground on which the house was built. On this side also, all the windows were round and high up, like those in the streets, and barricaded with shutters. But one of them allowed the light which he had seen from below to filter through.

Telling Ya-Bon to hide in the shrubberies, he went up to the house, listened, caught an indistinct sound of voices, discovered that the shutters were too firmly closed to enable him either to see or to hear and, in this way, after the fourth window, reached a flight of steps. At the top of the steps was a door.

'Since they sent me the key of the garden,' he said to himself, 'there's no reason why this door, which leads from the house into the garden, should not be open.'

It was open.

The voices indoors were now more clearly perceptible, and Belval observed that they reached him by the well of the staircase and that this staircase, which seemed to lead to an unoccupied part of the house, showed with an uncertain light above him.

He went up. A door stood ajar on the first floor. He slipped his head through the opening and went in. He found that he was on a narrow balcony which ran at mid-height around three sides of a large room, along book-shelves rising to the ceiling. Against the wall at either end of the room was an iron spiral staircase. Stacks of books were also piled against the bars of the railing which protected the gallery, thus hiding Patrice from the view of the people on the ground-floor, ten or twelve feet below.

He gently separated two of these stacks. At that moment the sound of voices suddenly increased to a great uproar and he saw five men, shouting like lunatics, hurl themselves upon a sixth and fling him to the ground before he had time to lift a finger in self-defense.

Belval's first impulse was to rush to the victim's rescue. With the aid of Ya-Bon, who would have hastened to his call, he would certainly have intimidated the five men. The reason why he did not act was that, at any rate, they were using no weapons and appeared to have no murderous intentions. After depriving their victim of all power of movement, they were content to hold him by the throat, shoulders and ankles. Belval wondered what would happen next.

One of the five drew himself up briskly and, in a tone of command, said: 'Bind him . . . Put a gag in his mouth . . . Or let him call out, if he wants to: there's no one to hear him.'

Patrice at once recognized one of the voices which he had heard that morning in the restaurant. Its owner was a short, slim-built, well-dressed man, with an olive complexion and a cruel face.

'At last we've got him,' he said, 'the rascal! And I think we shall get him to speak this time. Are you prepared to go all lengths, friends?'

One of the other four growled, spitefully: 'Yes. And at once, whatever happens!'

The last speaker had a big black mustache; and Patrice recognized the other man whose conversation at the restaurant he had overheard, that is to say, one of Coralie's assailants, the one who had taken to flight. His gray-felt hat lay on a chair.

'All lengths, Bournef, whatever happens, eh?' grinned the leader. 'Well, let's get on with the work. So you refuse to give up your secret, Essarès, old man? We shall have some fun.'

All their movements must have been prepared beforehand and the parts carefully arranged, for the actions which they carried out were performed in an incredibly prompt and methodical fashion.

After the man was tied up, they lifted him into an easy-chair with a very low back, to which they fastened him round the chest and waist with a rope. His legs, which were bound together, were placed on the seat of a heavy chair of the same height as the arm-chair, with the two feet projecting. Then the victim's shoes and socks were removed.

'Roll him along!' said the leader.

Between two of the four windows that overlooked the chimney was a large fire-place, in which burnt a red coal-fire, white in places with the intense heat of the hearth. The men pushed the two chairs bearing the victim until his bare feet were within twenty inches of the blazing coals.

In spite of his gag, the man uttered a hideous yell of pain, while his legs, in spite of their bonds, succeeded in contracting and curling upon themselves.

'Go on!' shouted the leader, passionately. 'Go on! Nearer!'

Patrice Belval grasped his revolver.

'Oh, I'm going on too!' he said to himself. 'I won't let that wretch be . . .'

But, at this very moment, when he was on the point of drawing himself up and acting, a chance movement made him behold the most extraordinary and unexpected sight. Opposite him, on the other side of the room, in a part of the balcony corresponding with that where he was, he saw a woman's head, a head glued to the rails, livid and terror-stricken, with eyes wide-open in horror gazing frenziedly at the awful scene that was being enacted below by the glowing fire.

Patrice had recognized Little Mother Coralie.

Chapter 4
Before the Flames

Little Mother Coralie! Coralie concealed in this house into which her assailants had forced their way and in which she herself was hiding, through force of circumstances which were incapable of explanation.

His first idea, which would at least have solved one of the riddles, was that she also had entered from the lane, gone into the house by the steps and in this way opened a passage for him. But, in that case, how had she procured the means of carrying out this enterprise? And, above all, what brought her here?

All these questions occurred to Captain Belval's mind without his trying to reply to them. He was far too much impressed by the absorbed expression on Coralie's face. Moreover, a second cry, even wilder than the first, came from below; and he saw the victim's face writhing before the red curtain of fire from the hearth.

But this time Patrice, held back by Coralie's presence, had no inclination to go to the sufferer's assistance. He decided to model himself entirely upon her and not to move or do anything to attract her attention.

'Easy!' the leader commanded. 'Pull him back. I expect he's had enough.'

He went up to the victim.

'Well, my dear Essarès,' he asked, 'what do you think of it? Are you happy? And, you know, we're only beginning. If you don't speak, we shall go on to the end, as the real *chauffeurs* used to do in the days of the Revolution. So it's settled, I presume: you're going to speak?'

There was no answer. The leader rapped out an oath and went on: 'What do you mean? Do you refuse? But, you obstinate brute, don't you understand the situation? Or have you a glimmer of hope? Hope, indeed! You're mad. Who would rescue you? Your servants? The porter, the footman and the butler are in my pay. I gave them a week's notice. They're gone by now. The housemaid? The cook? They sleep at the other end of the house; and you yourself have told me, time after time, that one can't hear anything over there. Who else? Your wife? Her room also is far away; and she hasn't heard anything either? Siméon, your old secretary? We made him fast when he opened the front door to us just now. Besides, we may as well finish the job here. Bournef!'

The man with the big mustache, who was still holding the chair, drew himself up.

'Bournef, where did you lock up the secretary?'

'In the porter's lodge.'

'You know where to find Mme Essarès' bedroom?'

'Yes, you told me the way.'

'Go, all four of you, and bring the lady and the secretary here!'

The four men went out by a door below the spot where Coralie was standing. They were hardly out of sight when the leader stooped eagerly over his victim and said: 'We're alone, Essarès. It's what I intended. Let's make the most of it.'

He bent still lower and whispered so that Patrice found it difficult to hear what he said.

'Those men are fools. I twist them round my finger and tell them no more of my plans than I can help. You and I, on the other hand, Essarès, are the men to come to terms. That is what you refused to admit; and you see where it has landed you. Come, Essarès, don't be obstinate and don't shuffle. You are caught in a trap, you are helpless, you are absolutely in my power. Well, rather than allow yourself to be broken down by tortures which would certainly end by overcoming your resistance, strike a bargain with me. We'll go halves, shall we? Let's make peace and treat upon that basis. I'll give you a hand in my game and you'll give me one in yours. As allies, we are bound to win. As enemies, who knows whether the victor will surmount all the obstacles that will still stand in his path? That's why I say again, halves! Answer me. Yes or no.'

He loosened the gag and listened. This time, Patrice did not hear the few words which the victim uttered. But the other, the leader, almost immediately burst into a rage.

'Eh? What's that you're proposing? Upon my word, but you're a cool hand! An offer of this kind to me! That's all very well for Bournef or his fellows. They'll understand, they will. But it won't do for me, it won't do for Colonel Fakhi. No, no, my friend, I open my mouth wider! I'll consent to go halves, but accept an alms, never!'

Patrice listened eagerly and, at the same time, kept his eyes on Coralie, whose face still contorted with anguish, wore an expression of the same rapt attention. And he looked back at the victim, part of whose body was reflected in the glass above the mantelpiece. The man was dressed in a braided brown-velvet smoking-suit and appeared to be about fifty years of age, quite bald, with a fleshy face, a large hooked nose, eyes deep set under a pair of thick eyebrows, and puffy cheeks covered with a thick grizzled beard. Patrice was also able to examine his features more closely in a portrait of him which hung to the left of the fireplace, between the first and second windows, and which represented a strong, powerful countenance with an almost fierce expression.

'It's an Eastern face,' said Patrice to himself. 'I've seen heads like that in Egypt and Turkey.'

The names of all these men too – Colonel Fakhi, Mustapha, Bournef, Essarès – their accent in talking, their way of holding themselves, their features, their figures, all recalled impressions which he had gathered in the Near East, in the hotels at Alexandria or on the banks of the Bosphorus, in the bazaars of Adrianople or in the Greek boats that plow the Ægean Sea. They were Levantine types, but of Levantines who had taken root in Paris. Essarès Bey was a name which Patrice recognized as well-known in the financial world, even as he knew that of Colonel Fakhi, whose speech and intonation marked him for a seasoned Parisian.

But a sound of voices came from outside the door. It was flung open violently and the four men appeared, dragging in a bound man, whom they dropped to the floor as they entered.

'Here's old Siméon,' cried the one whom Fakhi had addressed as Bournef.

'And the wife?' asked the leader. 'I hope you've got her too!'

'Well, no.'

'What is that? Has she escaped?'

'Yes, through her window.'

'But you must run after her. She can only be in the garden. Remember, the watch-dog was barking just now.'

'And suppose she's got away?'

'How?'

'By the door on the lane?'

'Impossible!'

'Why?'

'The door hasn't been used for years. There's not even a key to it.'

'That's as may be,' Bournef rejoined. 'All the same, we're surely not going to organize a battue with lanterns and rouse the whole district for the sake of finding a woman . . . '

'Yes, but that woman . . . '

Colonel Fakhi seemed exasperated. He turned to the prisoner.

'You're in luck, you old rascal! This is the second time today that minx of yours has slipped through my fingers! Did she tell you what happened this afternoon? Oh, if it hadn't been for an infernal officer who happened to be passing! . . . But I'll get hold of him yet and he shall pay dearly for his interference . . . '

Patrice clenched his fists with fury. He understood: Coralie was hiding in her own house. Surprised by the sudden arrival of the five men, she had managed to climb out of her window and, making her way along the terrace to the steps, had gone to the part of the house opposite the rooms that were in use and taken refuge in the gallery of the library, where she was able to witness the terrible assault levied at her husband.

'Her husband!' thought Patrice, with a shudder. 'Her husband!'

And, if he still entertained any doubts on the subject, the hurried course of events soon removed them, for the leader began to chuckle.

'Yes, Essarès, old man, I confess that she attracts me more than I can tell you; and, as I failed to catch her earlier in the day, I did hope this evening, as soon as I had settled my business with you, to settle something infinitely more agreeable with your wife. Not to mention that, once in my power, the little woman would be serving me as a hostage and that I would only have restored her to you – oh, safe and sound, believe me! – after specific performance of our agreement. And you would have run straight, Essarès! For you love your Coralie passionately! And quite right too!'

He went to the right-hand side of the fireplace and, touching a switch, lit an electric lamp under a reflector between the third and fourth windows. There was a companion picture here to Essarès' portrait, but it was covered over. The leader drew the curtain, and Coralie appeared in the full light.

'The monarch of all she surveys! The idol! The witch! The pearl of pearls! The imperial diamond of Essarès Bey, banker! Isn't she beautiful? I ask you. Admire the delicate outline of her face, the purity of that oval; and the pretty neck; and those graceful shoulders. Essarès, there's not a favorite in the country we come from who can hold a candle to your Coralie! My Coralie, soon! For I shall know how to find her. Ah, Coralie, Coralie! . . . '

Patrice looked across at her, and it seemed to him that her face was reddened with a blush of shame. He himself was shaken by indignation and anger at each insulting word. It was a violent enough sorrow to him to know that Coralie was the wife of another; and added to this sorrow was his rage at seeing her thus exposed to these men's gaze and promised as a helpless prey to whosoever should prove himself the strongest.

At the same time, he wondered why Coralie remained in the room. Supposing that she could not leave the garden, nevertheless she was free to move about in that part of the house and might well have opened a window and called for help. What prevented her from doing so? Of course she did not love her husband. If she had loved him, she would have faced every danger to defend him. But how was it possible for her to allow that man to be tortured, worse still, to be present at his sufferings, to contemplate that most hideous of sights and to listen to his yells of pain?

'Enough of this nonsense!' cried the leader, pulling the curtain back into its place. 'Coralie, you shall be my final reward; but I must first win you. Comrades, to work; let's finish our friend's job. First of all, twenty inches nearer, no more. Good! Does it burn, Essarès? All the same, it's not more than you can stand. Bear up, old fellow.'

He unfastened the prisoner's right arm, put a little table by his side, laid a pencil and paper on it and continued: 'There's writing-materials for you. As your gag prevents you from speaking, write. You know what's wanted of you, don't you? Scribble a few letters, and you're free. Do you consent? No? Comrades, three inches nearer.'

He moved away and stooped over the secretary, whom Patrice, by the brighter light, had recognized as the old fellow who sometimes escorted Coralie to the hospital.

'As for you, Siméon,' he said, 'you shall come to no harm. I know that you are devoted to your master, but I also know that he tells you none of his private affairs. On the other hand, I am certain that you will keep silent as to all this, because a single word of betrayal would involve your master's ruin even more than ours. That's understood between us, isn't it? Well, why don't you answer? Have they squeezed your throat a bit too tight with their cords? Wait, I'll give you some air . . .'

Meanwhile the ugly work at the fireplace pursued its course. The two feet were reddened by the heat until it seemed almost as though the bright flames of the fire were glowing through them. The sufferer exerted all his strength in trying to bend his legs and to draw back; and a dull, continuous moan came through his gag.

'Oh, hang it all!' thought Patrice. 'Are we going to let him roast like this, like a chicken on a spit?'

He looked at Coralie. She did not stir. Her face was distorted beyond recognition, and her eyes seemed fascinated by the terrifying sight.

'Couple of inches nearer!' cried the leader, from the other end of the room, as he unfastened Siméon's bonds.

The order was executed. The victim gave such a yell that Patrice's blood froze in his veins. But, at the same moment, he became aware of something that had not struck him so far, or at least he had attached no significance to it. The prisoner's hand, as the result of a sequence of little movements apparently due to nervous twitches, had seized the opposite edge of the table, while his arm rested on the marble top. And gradually, unseen by the torturers, all whose efforts were directed to keeping his legs in position, or by the leader, who was still engaged with Siméon, this hand opened a drawer which swung on a hinge, dipped into the drawer, took out a revolver and, resuming its original position with a jerk, hid the weapon in the chair.

The act, or rather the intention which it indicated, was foolhardy in the extreme, for, when all was said, reduced to his present state of helplessness, the man could not hope for victory against five adversaries, all free and all armed. Nevertheless, as Patrice looked at the glass in which he beheld him, he saw a fierce determination pictured in the man's face.

'Another two inches,' said Colonel Fakhi, as he walked back to the fireplace.

He examined the condition of the flesh and said, with a laugh: 'The skin is blistering in places; the veins are ready to burst. Essarès Bey, you can't be enjoying yourself, and it strikes me that you mean to do the right thing at last. Have you started scribbling yet? No? And don't you mean to? Are you still hoping? Counting on your wife, perhaps? Come, come, you must see that, even if she has succeeded in escaping, she won't say anything! Well, then, are you humbugging me, or what? . . .'

He was seized with a sudden burst of rage and shouted: 'Shove his feet into the fire! And let's have a good smell of burning for once! Ah, you would defy me, would you? Well, wait a bit, old chap, and let me have a go at you! I'll cut off an ear or two: you know, the way we have in our country!'

He drew from his waistcoat a dagger that gleamed in the firelight. His face was hideous with animal cruelty. He gave a fierce cry, raised his arm and stood over the other relentlessly.

But, swift as his movement was, Essarès was before him. The revolver, quickly aimed, was discharged with a loud report. The dagger dropped from the colonel's hand. For two or three seconds he maintained his threatening attitude, with one arm lifted on high and a haggard look in his eyes, as though he did not quite understand what had happened to him. And then, suddenly, he fell upon his victim in a huddled heap, paralyzing his arm with the full weight of his body, at the moment when Essarès was taking aim at one of the other confederates.

He was still breathing.

'Oh, the brute, the brute!' he panted. 'He's killed me! . . . But you'll lose by it, Essarès . . . I was prepared for this. If I don't come home tonight, the prefect of police will receive a letter . . . They'll know about your treason, Essarès . . . all your story . . . your plans . . . Oh, you devil! . . . And what a fool! . . . We could so easily have come to terms . . . '

He muttered a few inaudible words and rolled down to the floor. It was all over.

A moment of stupefaction was produced not so much by this unexpected tragedy as by the revelation which the leader had made before dying and by the thought of that letter, which no doubt implicated the aggressors as well as their victim. Bournef had disarmed Essarès. The latter, now that the chair was no longer held in position, had succeeded in bending his legs. No one moved.

Meanwhile, the sense of terror which the whole scene had produced seemed rather to increase with the silence. On the ground was the corpse, with the blood flowing on the carpet. Not far away lay Siméon's motionless form. Then there was the prisoner, still bound in front of the flames waiting to devour his flesh. And standing near him were the four butchers, hesitating perhaps what to do next, but showing in every feature an implacable resolution to defeat the enemy by all and every means.

His companions glanced at Bournef, who seemed the kind of man to go any length. He was a short, stout, powerfully-built man; his upper lip bristled with the mustache which had attracted Patrice Belval's attention. He was less cruel in appearance than his chief, less elegant in his manner and less masterful, but displayed far greater coolness and self-command. As for the colonel, his accomplices seemed not to trouble about him. The part which they were playing dispensed them from showing any empty compassion.

At last Bournef appeared to have made up his mind how to act. He went to his hat, the gray-felt hat lying near the door, turned back the lining and took from it a tiny coil the sight of which made Patrice start. It was a slender red cord, exactly like that which he had found round the neck of Mustapha Rovalaïof, the first accomplice captured by Ya-Bon.

Bournef unrolled the cord, took it by the two buckles, tested its strength across his knee and then, going back to Essarès, slipped it over his neck after first removing his gag.

'Essarès,' he said, with a calmness which was more impressive than the colonel's violence and sneers, 'Essarès, I shall not put you to any pain. Torture is a revolting process; and I shall not have recourse to it. You know what to do; I know what to do. A word on your side, an action on my side; and the thing is done. The word is the yes or no which you will now speak. The action which I shall accomplish in reply to your yes or no will mean either your release or else . . .'

He stopped for a second or two. Then he declared: 'Or else your death.'

The brief phrase was uttered very simply but with a firmness that gave it the full significance of an irrevocable sentence. It was clear that Essarès was faced with a catastrophe which he could no longer avoid save by submitting absolutely. In less than a minute, he would have spoken or he would be dead.

Once again Patrice fixed his eyes on Coralie, ready to interfere should he perceive in her any other feeling than one of passive terror. But her attitude did not change. She was therefore accepting the worst, it appeared, even though this meant her husband's death; and Patrice held his hand accordingly.

'Are we all agreed?' Bournef asked, turning to his accomplices.

'Quite,' said one of them.

'Do you take your share of the responsibility?'

'We do.'

Bournef brought his hands together and crossed them, which had the result of knotting the cord round Essarès' neck. Then he pulled slightly, so as to make the pressure felt, and asked, unemotionally: 'Yes or no?'

'Yes.'

There was a murmur of satisfaction. The accomplices heaved a breath; and Bournef nodded his head with an air of approval.

'Ah, so you accept! It was high time: I doubt if anyone was ever nearer death than you were, Essarès.' Retaining his hold of the cord, he continued, 'Very well. You will speak. But I know you; and your answer surprises me, for I told the colonel that not even the certainty of death would make you confess your secret. Am I wrong?'

'No,' replied Essarès. 'Neither death nor torture.'

'Then you have something different to propose?'

'Yes.'

'Something worth our while?'

'Yes. I suggested it to the colonel just now, when you were out of the room. But, though he was willing to betray you and go halves with me in the secret, he refused the other thing.'

'Why should I accept it?'

'Because you must take it or leave it and because you will understand what he did not.'

'It's a compromise, I suppose?'

'Yes.'

'Money?'

'Yes.'

Bournef shrugged his shoulders.

'A few thousand-franc notes, I expect. And you imagine that Bournef and his friends will be such fools? . . . Come, Essarès, why do you want us to compromise? We know your secret almost entirely . . .'

'You know what it is, but not how to use it. You don't know how to get at it; and that's just the point.'

'We shall discover it.'

'Never.'

'Yes, your death will make it easier for us.'

'My death? Thanks to the information lodged by the colonel, in a few hours you will be tracked down and most likely caught: in any case, you will be unable to pursue your search. Therefore you have hardly any choice. It's the money which I'm offering you, or else . . . prison.'

'And, if we accept,' asked Bournef, to whom the argument seemed to appeal, 'when shall we be paid?'

'At once.'

'Then the money is here?'

'Yes.'

'A contemptible sum, as I said before?'

'No, a much larger sum than you hope for; infinitely larger.'

'How much?'

'Four millions.'

Chapter 5
Husband and Wife

The accomplices started, as though they had received an electric shock. Bournef darted forward.

'What did you say?'

'I said four millions, which means a million for each of you.'

'Look here! . . . Do you mean it? . . . Four millions? . . . '

'Four millions is what I said.'

The figure was so gigantic and the proposal so utterly unexpected that the accomplices had the same feeling which Patrice Belval on his side underwent. They suspected a trap; and Bournef could not help saying: 'The offer is more than we expected . . . And I am wondering what induced you to make it.'

'Would you have been satisfied with less?'

'Yes,' said Bournef, candidly.

'Unfortunately, I can't make it less. I have only one means of escaping death; and that is to open my safe for you. And my safe contains four bundles of a thousand bank-notes each.'

Bournef could not get over his astonishment and became more and more suspicious.

'How do you know that, after taking the four millions, we shall not insist on more?'

'Insist on what? The secret of the site?'

'Yes.'

'Because you know that I would as soon die as tell it you. The four millions are the maximum. Do you want them or don't you? I ask for no promise in return, no oath of any kind, for I am convinced that, when you have filled your pockets, you will have but one thought, to clear off, without handicapping yourselves with a murder which might prove your undoing.'

The argument was so unanswerable that Bournef ceased discussing and asked: 'Is the safe in this room?'

'Yes, between the first and second windows, behind my portrait.'

Bournef took down the picture and said: 'I see nothing.'

'It's all right. The lines of the safe are marked by the moldings of the central panel. In the middle you will see what looks like a rose, not of wood but of iron; and there are four others at the four corners of the panel. These four turn to the right, by successive notches, forming a word which is the key to the lock, the word Cora.'

'The first four letters of Coralie?' asked Bournef, following Essarès' instructions as he spoke.

'No,' said Essarès Bey, 'the first four letters of the Coran. Have you done that?'

After a moment, Bournef answered: 'Yes, I've finished. And the key?'

'There's no key. The fifth letter of the word, the letter N, is the letter of the central rose.'

Bournef turned this fifth rose; and presently a click was heard.

'Now pull,' said Essarès. 'That's it. The safe is not deep: it's dug in one of the stones of the front wall. Put in your hand. You'll find four pocket-books.'

It must be admitted that Patrice Belval expected to see something startling interrupt Bournef's quest and hurl him into some pit suddenly opened by Essarès' trickery. And the three confederates seemed to share this unpleasant apprehension, for they were gray in the face, while Bournef himself appeared to be working very cautiously and suspiciously.

At last he turned round and came and sat beside Essarès. In his hands he held a bundle of four pocket-books, short but extremely bulky and bound together with a canvas strap. He unfastened the buckle of the strap and opened one of the pocket-books.

His knees shook under their precious burden, and, when he had taken a huge sheaf of notes from one of the compartments, his hands were like the hands of a very old man trembling with fever.

'Thousand-franc notes,' he murmured. 'Ten packets of thousand-franc notes.'

Brutally, like men prepared to fight one another, each of the other three laid hold of a pocket-book, felt inside and mumbled: 'Ten packets . . . they're all there . . . Thousand-franc notes . . . '

And one of them forthwith cried, in a choking voice: 'Let's clear out! . . . Let's go!'

A sudden fear was sending them off their heads. They could not imagine that Essarès would hand over such a fortune to them unless he had some plan which would enable him to recover it before they had left the room. That was a certainty. The ceiling would come down on their heads. The walls would close up and crush them to death, while sparing their unfathomable adversary.

Nor had Patrice Belval any doubt of it. The disaster was preparing. Essarès' revenge was inevitably at hand. A man like him, a fighter as able as he appeared to be, does not so easily surrender four million francs if he has not some scheme at the back of his head. Patrice felt himself breathing heavily. His present excitement was more violent than any with which he had thrilled since the very beginning of the tragic scenes which he had been witnessing; and he saw that Coralie's face was as anxious as his own.

Meanwhile Bournef partially recovered his composure and, holding back his companions, said: 'Don't be such fools! He would be capable, with old Siméon, of releasing himself and running after us.'

Using only one hand, for the other was clutching a pocket-book, all four fastened Essarès' arm to the chair, while he protested angrily: 'You idiots! You came here to rob me of a secret of immense importance, as you well knew, and you lose your heads over a trifle of four millions. Say what you like, the colonel had more backbone than that!'

They gagged him once more and Bournef gave him a smashing blow with his fist which laid him unconscious.

'That makes our retreat safe,' said Bournef.

'What about the colonel?' asked one of the others. 'Are we to leave him here?'

'Why not?'

But apparently he thought this unwise; for he added: 'On second thoughts, no. It's not to our interest to compromise Essarès any further. What we must do, Essarès as well as ourselves, is to make ourselves scarce as fast as we can, before that damned letter of the colonel's is delivered at headquarters, say before twelve o'clock in the day.'

'Then what do you suggest?'

'We'll take the colonel with us in the motor and drop him any-where. The police must make what they can of it.'

'And his papers?'

'We'll look through his pockets as we go. Lend me a hand.'

They bandaged the wound to stop the flow of blood, took up the body, each holding it by an arm or leg, and walked out without any one of them letting go his pocket-book for a second.

Patrice Belval heard them pass through another room and then tramp heavily over the echoing flags of a hall.

'This is the moment,' he said. 'Essarès or Siméon will press a button and the rogues will be nabbed.'

Essarès did not budge.

Siméon did not budge.

Patrice heard all the sounds accompanying their departure: the slamming of the carriage-gate, the starting-up of the engine and the drone of the car as it moved away. And that was all. Nothing had happened. The confederates were getting off with their four millions.

A long silence followed, during which Patrice remained on tenter-hooks. He did not believe that the drama had reached its last phase; and he was so much afraid of the unexpected which might still occur that he determined to make Coralie aware of his presence.

A fresh incident prevented him. Coralie had risen to her feet.

Her face no longer wore its expression of horror and affright, but Patrice was perhaps more scared at seeing her suddenly animated with a sinister energy that gave an unwonted sparkle to her eyes and set her eyebrows and her lips twitching. He realized that Coralie was preparing to act.

In what way? Was this the end of the tragedy?

She walked to the corner on her side of the gallery where one of the two spiral staircases stood and went down slowly, without, how-ever, trying to deaden the sound of her feet. Her husband could not help hearing her. Patrice, moreover, saw in the mirror that he had lifted his head and was following her with his eyes.

She stopped at the foot of the stairs. But there was no indecision in her attitude. Her plan was obviously quite clear; and she was only thinking out the best method of putting it into execution.

'Ah!' whispered Patrice to himself, quivering all over. 'What are you doing, Little Mother Coralie?'

He gave a start. The direction in which Coralie's eyes were turned, together with the strange manner in which they stared, revealed her secret resolve to him. She had caught sight of the dagger, lying on the floor where it had slipped from the colonel's grasp.

Not for a second did Patrice believe that she meant to pick up that dagger with any other thought than to stab her husband. The intention of murder was so plainly written on her livid features that, even before she stirred a limb, Essarès was seized with a fit of terror and strained every muscle to break the bonds that hampered his movements.

She came forward, stopped once more and, suddenly bending, seized the dagger. Without waiting, she took two more steps. These

brought her to the right of the chair in which Essarès lay. He had only
to turn his head a little way to see her. And an awful minute passed,
during which the husband and wife looked into each other's eyes.

The whirl of thoughts, of fear, of hatred, of vagrant and conflicting
passions that passed through the brains of her who was about to kill
and him who was about to die, was reproduced in Patrice Belval's
mind and deep down in his inner consciousness. What was he to do?
What part ought he to play in the tragedy that was being enacted
before his eyes? Should he intervene? Was it his duty to prevent
Coralie from committing the irreparable deed? Or should he commit
it himself by breaking the man's head with a bullet from his revolver?

Yet, from the beginning, Patrice had really been swayed by a feeling
which, mingling with all the others, gradually paralyzed him and
rendered any inward struggle illusory: a feeling of curiosity driven to
its utmost pitch. It was not the everyday curiosity of unearthing a
squalid secret, but the higher curiosity of penetrating the mysterious
soul of a woman whom he loved, who was carried away by the rush of
events and who suddenly, becoming once more mistress of herself,
was of her own accord and with impressive calmness taking the most
fearful resolution. Thereupon other questions forced themselves upon
him. What prompted her to take this resolution? Was it revenge? Was
it punishment? Was it the gratification of hatred?

Patrice Belval remained where he was.

Coralie raised her arm. Her husband, in front of her, no longer
even attempted to make those movements of despair which indicate
a last effort. There was neither entreaty nor menace in his eyes. He
waited in resignation.

Not far from them, old Siméon, still bound, half-lifted himself on
his elbows and stared at them in dismay.

Coralie raised her arm again. Her whole frame seemed to grow
larger and taller. An invisible force appeared to strengthen and stiffen
her whole being, summoning all her energies to the service of her will.
She was on the point of striking. Her eyes sought the place at which
she should strike.

Yet her eyes became less hard and less dark. It even seemed to
Patrice that there was a certain hesitation in her gaze and that she
was recovering not her usual gentleness, but a little of her womanly
grace.

'Ah, Little Mother Coralie,' murmured Patrice, 'you are yourself
again! You are the woman I know. Whatever right you may think
you have to kill that man, you will not kill him . . . and I prefer it so.'

Slowly Coralie's arm dropped to her side. Her features relaxed. Patrice could guess the immense relief which she felt at escaping from the obsessing purpose that was driving her to murder. She looked at her dagger with astonishment, as though she were waking from a hideous nightmare. And, bending over her husband she began to cut his bonds.

She did so with visible repugnance, avoiding his touch, as it were, and shunning his eyes. The cords were severed one by one. Essarès was free.

What happened next was in the highest measure unexpected. With not a word of thanks to his wife, with not a word of anger either, this man who had just undergone the most cruel torture and whose body still throbbed with pain hurriedly tottered barefoot to a telephone standing on a table. He was like a hungry man who suddenly sees a piece of bread and snatches at it greedily as the means of saving himself and returning to life. Panting for breath, Essarès took down the receiver and called out: 'Central 40.39.'

Then he turned abruptly to his wife. 'Go away,' he said.

She seemed not to hear. She had knelt down beside old Siméon and was setting him free also.

Essarès at the telephone began to lose patience.

'Are you there? . . . Are you there? . . . I want that number today, please, not next week! It's urgent . . . 40.39 . . . It's urgent, I tell you!'

And, turning to Coralie, he repeated, in an imperious tone: 'Go away!'

She made a sign that she would not go away and that, on the contrary, she meant to listen. He shook his fist at her and again said: 'Go away, go away! . . . I won't have you stay in the room. You go away too, Siméon.'

Old Siméon got up and moved towards Essarès. It looked as though he wished to speak, no doubt to protest. But his action was undecided; and, after a moment's reflection, he turned to the door and went without uttering a word.

'Go away, will you, go away!' Essarès repeated, his whole body expressing menace.

But Coralie came nearer to him and crossed her arms obstinately and defiantly. At that moment, Essarès appeared to get his call, for he asked: 'Is that 40.39? Ah, yes . . . '

He hesitated. Coralie's presence obviously displeased him greatly, and he was about to say things which he did not wish her to know. But time, no doubt, was pressing. He suddenly made up his mind and, with both receivers glued to his ears, said, in English: 'Is that you, Grégoire? . . . Essarès speaking . . . Hullo! . . . Yes, I'm speaking from the Rue Raynouard . . . There's no time to lose . . . Listen . . .'

He sat down and went on: 'Look here. Mustapha's dead. So is the colonel . . . Damn it, don't interrupt, or we're done for! . . . Yes, done for; and you too . . . Listen, they all came, the colonel, Bournef, the whole gang, and robbed me by means of violence and threats . . . I finished the colonel, only he had written to the police, giving us all away. The letter will be delivered soon. So you understand, Bournef and his three ruffians are going to disappear. They'll just run home and pack up their papers; and I reckon they'll be with you in an hour, or two hours at most. It's the refuge they're sure to make for. They prepared it themselves, without suspecting that you and I know each other. So there's no doubt about it. They're sure to come . . .'

Essarès stopped. He thought for a moment and resumed: 'You still have a second key to each of the rooms which they use as bedrooms? Is that so? . . . Good. And you have duplicates of the keys that open the cupboards in the walls of those rooms, haven't you? . . . Capital. Well, as soon as they get to sleep, or rather as soon as you are certain that they are sound asleep, go in and search the cupboards. Each of them is bound to hide his share of the booty there. You'll find it quite easily. It's the four pocket-books which you know of. Put them in your bag, clear out as fast as you can and join me.'

There was another pause. This time it was Essarès listening. He replied: 'What's that you say? Rue Raynouard? Here? Join me here? Why, you must be mad! Do you imagine that I can stay now, after the colonel's given me away? No, go and wait for me at the hotel, near the station. I shall be there by twelve o'clock or one in the afternoon, perhaps a little later. Don't be uneasy. Have your lunch quietly and we'll talk things over . . . Hullo! Did you hear? . . . Very well, I'll see that everything's all right. Goodbye for the present.'

The conversation was finished; and it looked as if Essarès, having taken all his measures to recover possession of the four million francs, had no further cause for anxiety. He hung up the receiver, went back to the lounge-chair in which he had been tortured, wheeled it round with its back to the fire, sat down, turned down the bottoms of his trousers and pulled on his socks and shoes, all a little painfully and accompanied by a few grimaces, but calmly, in the manner of a man who has no need to hurry.

Coralie kept her eyes fixed on his face.

'I really ought to go,' thought Captain Belval, who felt a trifle embarrassed at the thought of overhearing what the husband and wife were about to say.

Nevertheless he stayed. He was not comfortable in his mind on Coralie's account.

Essarès fired the first shot.

'Well,' he asked, 'what are you looking at me like that for?'

'So it's true?' she murmured, maintaining her attitude of defiance. 'You leave me no possibility of doubt?'

'Why should I lie?' he snarled. 'I should not have telephoned in your hearing if I hadn't been sure that you were here all the time.'

'I was up there.'

'Then you heard everything?'

'Yes.'

'And saw everything?'

'Yes.'

'And, seeing the torture which they inflicted on me and hearing my cries, you did nothing to defend me, to defend me against torture, against death!'

'No, for I knew the truth.'

'What truth?'

'The truth which I suspected without daring to admit it.'

'What truth?' he repeated, in a louder voice.

'The truth about your treason.'

'You're mad. I've committed no treason.'

'Oh, don't juggle with words! I confess that I don't know the whole truth: I did not understand all that those men said or what they were demanding of you. But the secret which they tried to force from you was a treasonable secret.'

'A man can only commit treason against his country,' he said, shrugging his shoulders. 'I'm not a Frenchman.'

'You were a Frenchman!' she cried. 'You asked to be one and you became one. You married me, a Frenchwoman, and you live in France and you've made your fortune in France. It's France that you're betraying.'

'Don't talk nonsense! And for whose benefit?'

'I don't know that, either. For months, for years indeed, the colonel, Bournef, all your former accomplices and yourself have been engaged on an enormous work – yes, enormous, it's their own word – and now it appears that you are fighting over the profits of the common enterprise and the others accuse you of pocketing those profits for yourself alone and of keeping a secret that doesn't belong to you. So that I seem to see something dirtier and more hateful even than treachery, something worthy of a common pickpocket . . .'

The man struck the arm of his chair with his fist.

'Enough!' he cried.

Coralie seemed in no way alarmed.

'Enough,' she echoed, 'you are right. Enough words between us. Besides, there is one fact that stands out above everything: your flight. That amounts to a confession. You're afraid of the police.'

He shrugged his shoulders a second time.

'I'm afraid of nobody.'

'Very well, but you're going.'

'Yes.'

'Then let's have it out. When are you going?'

'Presently, at twelve o'clock.'

'And if you're arrested?'

'I shan't be arrested.'

'If you are arrested, however?'

'I shall be let go.'

'At least there will be an inquiry, a trial?'

'No, the matter will be hushed up.'

'You hope so.'

'I'm sure of it.'

'God grant it! And you will leave France, of course?'

'As soon as I can.'

'When will that be?'

'In a fortnight or three weeks.'

'Send me word of the day, so that I may know when I can breathe again.'

'I shall send you word, Coralie, but for another reason.'

'What reason?'

'So that you may join me.'

'Join you!'

He gave a cruel smile.

'You are my wife,' he said. 'Where the husband goes the wife goes; and you know that, in my religion, the husband has every right over his wife, including that of life and death. Well, you're my wife.'

Coralie shook her head, and, in a tone of indescribable contempt, answered: 'I am not your wife. I feel nothing for you but loathing and horror. I don't wish to see you again, and, whatever happens, whatever you may threaten, I shall not see you again.'

He rose, and, walking to her, bent in two, all trembling on his legs, he shouted, while again he shook his clenched fists at her, 'What's that you say? What's that you dare to say? I, I, your lord and master, order you to join me the moment that I send for you.'

'I shall not join you. I swear it before God! I swear it as I hope to be saved.'

He stamped his feet with rage. His face underwent a hideous contortion; and he roared: 'That means that you want to stay! Yes, you have reasons which I don't know, but which are easy to guess! An affair of the heart, I suppose. There's someone in your life, no doubt . . . Hold your tongue, will you? . . . Haven't you always detested me? . . . Your hatred does not date from today. It dates back to the first time you saw me, to a time even before our marriage . . . We have always lived like mortal enemies. I loved you. I worshipped you. A word from you would have brought me to your feet. The mere sound of your steps thrilled me to the marrow . . . But your feeling for me is one of horror. And you imagine that you are going to start a new life, without me? Why, I'd sooner kill you, my beauty!'

He had unclenched his fists; and his open hands were clutching on either side of Coralie, close to her head, as though around a prey which they seemed on the point of throttling. A nervous shiver made his jaws clash together. Beads of perspiration gleamed on his bald head.

In front of him, Coralie stood impassive, looking very small and frail. Patrice Belval, in an agony of suspense and ready at any moment to act, could read nothing on her calm features but aversion and contempt.

Mastering himself at last, Essarès said: 'You shall join me, Coralie. Whether you like it or not, I am your husband. You felt it just now, when the lust to murder me made you take up a weapon and left you without the courage to carry out your intention. It will always be like that. Your independent fit will pass away and you will join the man who is your master.'

'I shall remain behind to fight against you,' she replied, 'here, in this house. The work of treason which you have accomplished I shall destroy. I shall do it without hatred, for I am no longer capable of hatred, but I shall do it without intermission, to repair the evil which you have wrought.'

He answered, in a low voice: 'I *am* capable of hatred. Beware, Coralie. The very moment when you believe that you have nothing more to fear will perhaps be the moment when I shall call you to account. Take care.'

He pushed an electric bell. Old Siméon appeared.

'So the two men-servants have decamped?' asked Essarès. And, without waiting for the answer, he went on, 'A good riddance. The housemaid and the cook can do all I want. They heard nothing, did they? No, their bedroom is too far away. No matter, Siméon: you must keep a watch on them after I am gone.'

He looked at his wife, surprised to see her still there, and said to his secretary: 'I must be up at six to get everything ready; and I am dead tired. Take me to my room. You can come back and put out the lights afterwards.'

He went out, supported by Siméon. Patrice Belval at once perceived that Coralie had done her best to show no weakness in her husband's presence, but that she had come to the end of her strength and was unable to walk. Seized with faintness, she fell on her knees, making the sign of the cross.

When she was able to rise, a few minutes later, she saw on the carpet, between her and the door, a sheet of note-paper with her name on it. She picked it up and read.

'Little Mother Coralie, the struggle is too much for you. Why not appeal to me, your friend? Give a signal and I am with you.'

She staggered, dazed by the discovery of the letter and dismayed by Belval's daring. But, making a last effort to summon up her power of will, she left the room, without giving the signal for which Patrice was longing.

Chapter 6

Nineteen Minutes Past Seven

Patrice, in his bedroom at the home, was unable to sleep that night. He had a continual waking sensation of being oppressed and hunted down, as though he were suffering the terrors of some monstrous nightmare. He had an impression that the frantic series of events in which he was playing the combined parts of a bewildered spectator and a helpless actor would never cease so long as he tried to rest; that, on the contrary, they would rage with greater violence and intensity. The leave-taking of the husband and wife did not put an end, even momentarily, to the dangers incurred by Coralie. Fresh perils arose on every side; and Patrice Belval confessed himself incapable of foreseeing and still more of allaying them.

After lying awake for two hours, he switched on his electric light and began hurriedly to write down the story of the past twelve hours. He hoped in this way to some small extent to unravel the tangled knot.

At six o'clock he went and roused Ya-Bon and brought him back with him. Then, standing in front of the astonished negro, he crossed his arms and exclaimed: 'So you consider that your job is over! While I lie tossing about in the dark, my lord sleeps and all's well! My dear man, you have a jolly elastic conscience.'

The word elastic amused the Senegalese mightily. His mouth opened wider than ever; and he gave a grunt of enjoyment.

'That'll do, that'll do,' said the captain. 'There's no getting a word in, once you start talking. Here, take a chair, read this report and give me your reasoned opinion. What? You don't know how to read? Well, upon my word! What was the good, then, of wearing out the seat of your trousers on the benches of the Senegal schools and colleges? A queer education, I must say!'

He heaved a sigh, and, snatching the manuscript, said: 'Listen, reflect, argue, deduct and conclude. This is how the matter briefly stands. First, we have one Essarès Bey, a banker, rich as Crœsus, and the lowest of rapscallions, who betrays at one and the same time

France, Egypt, England, Turkey, Bulgaria and Greece . . . as is proved by the fact that his accomplices roast his feet for him. Thereupon he kills one of them and gets rid of four with the aid of as many millions, which millions he orders another accomplice to get back for him before five minutes are passed. And all these bright spirits will duck underground at eleven o'clock this morning, for at twelve o'clock the police propose to enter on the scene. Good.'

Patrice Belval paused to take breath and continued: 'Secondly, Little Mother Coralie – upon my word, I can't say why – is married to Rapscallion Bey. She hates him and wants to kill him. He loves her and wants to kill her. There is also a colonel who loves her and for that reason loses his life and a certain Mustapha, who tries to kidnap her on the colonel's account and also loses his life for that reason, strangled by a Senegalese. Lastly, there is a French captain, a dot-and-carry-one, who likewise loves her, but whom she avoids because she is married to a man whom she abhors. And with this captain, in a previous incarnation, she has halved an amethyst bead. Add to all this, by way of accessories, a rusty key, a red silk bowstring, a dog choked to death and a grate filled with red coals. And, if you dare to understand a single word of my explanation, I'll catch you a whack with my wooden leg, for I don't understand it a little bit and I'm your captain.'

Ya-Bon laughed all over his mouth and all over the gaping scar that cut one of his cheeks in two. As ordered by his captain, he understood nothing of the business and very little of what Patrice had said; but he always quivered with delight when Patrice addressed him in that gruff tone.

'That's enough,' said the captain. 'It's my turn now to argue, deduct and conclude.'

He leant against the mantelpiece, with his two elbows on the marble shelf and his head tight-pressed between his hands. His merriment, which sprang from temperamental lightness of heart, was this time only a surface merriment. Deep down within himself he did nothing but think of Coralie with sorrowful apprehension. What could he do to protect her? A number of plans occurred to him: which was he to choose? Should he hunt through the numbers in the telephone-book till he hit upon the whereabouts of that Grégoire, with whom Bournef and his companions had taken refuge? Should he inform the police? Should he return to the Rue Raynouard? He did not know. Yes, he was capable of acting, if the act to be performed consisted in flinging himself into the conflict with furious ardor. But to prepare the action, to divine the obstacles, to rend the darkness, and, as he said, to see the invisible and grasp the intangible, that was beyond his powers.

He turned suddenly to Ya-Bon, who was standing depressed by his silence. 'What's the matter with you, putting on that lugubrious air? Of course it's you that throw a gloom over me! You always look at the black side of things . . . like a nigger! . . . Be off.'

Ya-Bon was going away discomfited, when someone tapped at the door and a voice said: 'Captain Belval, you're wanted on the telephone.'

Patrice hurried out. Who on earth could be telephoning to him so early in the morning?

'Who is it?' he asked the nurse.

'I don't know, captain . . . It's a man's voice; he seemed to want you urgently. The bell had been ringing some time. I was downstairs, in the kitchen . . . '

Before Patrice's eyes there rose a vision of the telephone in the Rue Raynouard, in the big room at the Essarès' house. He could not help wondering if there was anything to connect the two incidents.

He went down one flight of stairs and along a passage. The telephone was through a small waiting-room, in a room that had been turned into a linen-closet. He closed the door behind him.

'Hullo! Captain Belval speaking. What is it?'

A voice, a man's voice which he did not know, replied in breathless, panting tones: 'Ah! . . . Captain Belval! . . . It's you! . . . Look here . . . but I'm almost afraid that it's too late . . . I don't know if I shall have time to finish . . . Did you get the key and the letter? . . . '

'Who are you?' asked Patrice.

'Did you get the key and the letter?' the voice insisted.

'The key, yes,' Patrice replied, 'but not the letter.'

'Not the letter? But this is terrible! Then you don't know . . . '

A hoarse cry struck Patrice's ear and the next thing he caught was incoherent sounds at the other end of the wire, the noise of an altercation. Then the voice seemed to glue itself to the instrument and he distinctly heard it gasping: 'Too late! . . . Patrice . . . is that you? . . . Listen, the amethyst pendant . . . yes, I have it on me . . . The pendant . . . Ah, it's too late! . . . I should so much have liked to . . . Patrice . . . Coralie . . . '

Then again a loud cry, a heart-rending cry, and confused sounds growing more distant, in which he seemed to distinguish: 'Help! . . . Help! . . . '

These grew fainter and fainter. Silence followed. And suddenly there was a little click. The murderer had hung up the receiver.

All this had not taken twenty seconds. But, when Patrice wanted to replace the telephone, his fingers were gripping it so hard that it needed an effort to relax them.

He stood utterly dumbfounded. His eyes had fastened on a large clock which he saw, through the window, on one of the buildings in the yard, marking nineteen minutes past seven; and he mechanically repeated these figures, attributing a documentary value to them. Then he asked himself – so unreal did the scene appear to him – if all this was true and if the crime had not been penetrated within himself, in the depths of his aching heart. But the shouting still echoed in his ears; and suddenly he took up the receiver again, like one clinging desperately to some undefined hope.

'Hullo!' he cried. 'Exchange! ... Who was it rang me up just now? ... Are you there? Did you hear the cries? ... Are you there? ... Are you there? ... '

There was no reply. He lost his temper, insulted the exchange, left the linen-closet, met Ya-Bon and pushed him about.

'Get out of this! It's your fault. Of course you ought to have stayed and looked after Coralie. Be off there now and hold yourself at my disposal. I'm going to inform the police. If you hadn't prevented me, it would have been done long ago and we shouldn't be in this predicament. Off you go!'

He held him back.

'No, don't stir. Your plan's ridiculous. Stay here. Oh, not here in my pocket! You're too impetuous for me, my lad!'

He drove him out and returned to the linen-closet, striding up and down and betraying his excitement in irritable gestures and angry words. Nevertheless, in the midst of his confusion, one idea gradually came to light, which was that, after all, he had no proof that the crime which he suspected had happened at the house in the Rue Raynouard. He must not allow himself to be obsessed by the facts that lingered in his memory to the point of always seeing the same vision in the same tragic setting. No doubt the drama was being continued, as he had felt that it would be, but perhaps elsewhere and far away from Coralie.

And this first thought led to another: why not investigate matters at once?

'Yes, why not?' he asked himself. 'Before bothering the police, discovering the number of the person who rang me up and thus working back to the start, a process which it will be time enough to employ later, why shouldn't I telephone to the Rue Raynouard at once, on any pretext and in anybody's name? I shall then have a chance of knowing what to think . . . '

Patrice felt that this measure did not amount to much. Suppose that no one answered, would that prove that the murder had been committed in the house, or merely that no one was yet about? Nevertheless, the need to do something decided him. He looked up Essarès Bey's number in the telephone-directory and resolutely rang up the exchange.

The strain of waiting was almost more than he could bear. And then he was conscious of a thrill which vibrated through him from head to foot. He was connected; and someone at the other end was answering the call.

'Hullo!' he said.

'Hullo!' said a voice. 'Who are you?'

It was the voice of Essarès Bey.

Although this was only natural, since at that moment Essarès must be getting his papers ready and preparing his flight, Patrice was so much taken aback that he did not know what to say and spoke the first words that came into his head.

'Is that Essarès Bey?'

'Yes. Who are you?'

'I'm one of the wounded at the hospital, now under treatment at the home . . . '

'Captain Belval, perhaps?'

Patrice was absolutely amazed. So Coralie's husband knew him by name? He stammered: 'Yes . . . Captain Belval.'

'What a lucky thing!' cried Essarès Bey, in a tone of delight. 'I rang you up a moment ago, at the home, Captain Belval, to ask . . . '

'Oh, it was you!' interrupted Patrice, whose astonishment knew no bounds.

'Yes, I wanted to know at what time I could speak to Captain Belval in order to thank him.'

'It was *you*! . . . It was *you*! . . . ' Patrice repeated, more and more thunderstruck.

Essarès' intonation denoted a certain surprise.

'Yes, wasn't it a curious coincidence?' he said. 'Unfortunately, I was cut off, or rather my call was interrupted by somebody else.'

'Then you heard?'

'What, Captain Belval?'

'Cries.'

'Cries?'

'At least, so it seemed to me; but the connection was very indistinct.'

'All that I heard was somebody asking for you, somebody who was in a great hurry; and, as I was not, I hung up the telephone and postponed the pleasure of thanking you.'

'Of thanking me?'

'Yes, I have heard how my wife was assaulted last night and how you came to her rescue. And I am anxious to see you and express my gratitude. Shall we make an appointment? Could we meet at the hospital, for instance, at three o'clock this afternoon?'

Patrice made no reply. The audacity of this man, threatened with arrest and preparing for flight, baffled him. At the same time, he was wondering what Essarès' real object had been in telephoning to him without being in any way obliged to. But Belval's silence in no way troubled the banker, who continued his civilities and ended the inscrutable conversation with a monologue in which he replied with the greatest ease to questions which he kept putting to himself.

In spite of everything, Patrice felt more comfortable. He went back to his room, lay down on his bed and slept for two hours. Then he sent for Ya-Bon.

'This time,' he said, 'try to control your nerves and not to lose your head as you did just now. You were absurd. But don't let's talk about it. Have you had your breakfast? No? No more have I. Have you seen the doctor? No? No more have I. And the surgeon has just promised to take off this beastly bandage. You can imagine how pleased I am. A wooden leg is all very well; but a head wrapped up in lint, for a lover, never! Get on, look sharp. When we're ready, we'll start for the hospital. Little Mother Coralie can't forbid me to see her there!'

Patrice was as happy as a schoolboy. As he said to Ya-Bon an hour later, on their way to the Porte-Maillot, the clouds were beginning to roll by.

'Yes, Ya-Bon, yes, they are. And this is where we stand. To begin with, Coralie is not in danger. As I hoped, the battle is being fought far away from her, among the accomplices no doubt, over their millions. As for the unfortunate man who rang me up and whose dying cries I overheard, he was obviously some unknown friend, for he addressed me familiarly and called me by my Christian name. It was certainly he who sent me the key of the garden. Unfortunately, the letter that came with the key went astray. In the end, he felt constrained to tell me everything. Just at that moment he was attacked. By whom, you ask. Probably by one of the accomplices, who was frightened of his revelations. There you are, Ya-Bon. It's all as clear as noonday. For that matter, the truth may just as easily be the exact opposite of what I suggest. But I don't care. The great thing is to take one's stand upon a theory, true or false. Besides, if mine is false, I reserve the right to shift the responsibility on you. So you know what you're in for . . . '

At the Porte-Maillot they took a cab and it occurred to Patrice to drive round by the Rue Raynouard. At the junction of this street with the Rue de Passy, they saw Coralie leaving the Rue Raynouard, accompanied by old Siméon.

She had hailed a taxi and stepped inside. Siméon sat down by the driver. They went to the hospital in the Champs-Élysées, with Patrice following. It was eleven o'clock when they arrived.

'All's well,' said Patrice. 'While her husband is running away, she refuses to make any change in her daily life.'

He and Ya-Bon lunched in the neighborhood, strolled along the avenue, without losing sight of the hospital, and called there at half-past one.

Patrice at once saw old Siméon, sitting at the end of a covered yard where the soldiers used to meet. His head was half wrapped up in the usual comforter; and, with his big yellow spectacles on his nose, he sat smoking his pipe on the chair which he always occupied.

As for Coralie, she was in one of the rooms allotted to her on the first floor, seated by the bedside of a patient whose hand she held between her own. The man was asleep.

Coralie appeared to Patrice to be very tired. The dark rings round her eyes and the unusual pallor of her cheeks bore witness to her fatigue.

'Poor child!' he thought. 'All those blackguards will be the death of you.'

He now understood, when he remembered the scenes of the night before, why Coralie kept her private life secret and endeavored, at least to the little world of the hospital, to be merely the kind sister whom people call by her Christian name. Suspecting the web of crime with which she was surrounded, she dropped her husband's name and told nobody where she lived. And so well was she protected by the defenses set up by her modesty and determination that Patrice dared not go to her and stood rooted to the threshold.

'Yet surely,' he said to himself, as he looked at Coralie without being seen by her, 'I'm not going to send her in my card!'

He was making up his mind to enter, when a woman who had come up the stairs, talking loudly as she went, called out: 'Where is madame? . . . M. Siméon, she must come at once!'

Old Siméon, who had climbed the stairs with her, pointed to where Coralie sat at the far end of the room; and the woman rushed in. She said a few words to Coralie, who seemed upset and at once ran to the door, passing in front of Patrice, and down the stairs, followed by Siméon and the woman.

'I've got a taxi, ma'am,' stammered the woman, all out of breath. 'I had the luck to find one when I left the house and I kept it. We must be quick, ma'am . . . The commissary of police told me to . . . '

Patrice, who was downstairs by this time, heard nothing more; but the last words decided him. He seized hold of Ya-Bon as he passed; and the two of them leapt into a cab, telling the driver to follow Coralie's taxi.

'There's news, Ya-Bon, there's news!' said Patrice. 'The plot is thickening. The woman is obviously one of the Essarès servants and she has come for her mistress by the commissary's orders. Therefore the colonel's disclosures are having their effect. House searched; magistrate's inquest; every sort of worry for Little Mother Coralie; and you have the cheek to advise me to be careful! You imagine that I would leave her to her own devices at such a moment! What a mean nature you must have, my poor Ya-Bon!'

An idea occurred to him; and he exclaimed: 'Heavens! I hope that ruffian of an Essarès hasn't allowed himself to be caught! That would be a disaster! But he was far too sure of himself. I expect he's been trifling away his time . . . '

All through the drive this fear excited Captain Belval and removed his last scruples. In the end his certainty was absolute. Nothing short of Essarès' arrest could have produced the servant's attitude of panic or Coralie's precipitate departure. Under these conditions, how could he hesitate to interfere in a matter in which his revelations would enlighten the police? All the more so as, by revealing less or more, according to circumstances, he could make his evidence subservient to Coralie's interests.

The two cabs pulled up almost simultaneously outside the Essarès house, where a car was already standing. Coralie alighted and disappeared through the carriage-gate. The maid and Siméon also crossed the pavement.

'Come along,' said Patrice to the Senegalese.

The front-door was ajar and Patrice entered. In the big hall were two policemen on duty. Patrice acknowledged their presence with a hurried movement of his hand and passed them with the air of a man who belonged to the house and whose importance was so great that nothing done without him could be of any use.

The sound of his footsteps echoing on the flags reminded him of the flight of Bournef and his accomplices. He was on the right road. Moreover, there was a drawing-room on the left, the room communicating with the library, to which the accomplices had carried the colonel's body. Voices came from the library. He walked across the drawing-room.

At that moment he heard Coralie exclaim in accents of terror: 'Oh, my God, it can't be! . . . '

Two other policemen barred the doorway.

'I am a relation of Mme Essarès',' he said, 'her only relation . . . '

'We have our orders, captain . . . '

'I know, of course. Be sure and let no one in! Ya-Bon, stay here.'

And he went in.

But, in the immense room, a group of six or seven gentlemen, no doubt commissaries of police and magistrates, stood in his way, bending over something which he was unable to distinguish. From amidst this group Coralie suddenly appeared and came towards him, tottering and wringing her hands. The housemaid took her round the waist and pressed her into a chair.

'What's the matter?' asked Patrice.

'Madame is feeling faint,' replied the woman, still quite distraught. 'Oh, I'm nearly off my head!'

'But why? What's the reason?'

'It's the master . . . just think! . . . Such a sight! . . . It gave me a turn, too . . . '

'What sight?'

One of the gentlemen left the group and approached.

'Is Mme Essarès ill?'

'It's nothing,' said the maid. 'A fainting-fit . . . She is liable to these attacks.'

'Take her away as soon as she can walk. We shall not need her any longer.'

And, addressing Patrice Belval with a questioning air: 'Captain? . . . '

Patrice pretended not to understand.

'Yes, sir,' he said, 'we will take Mme Essarès away. Her presence, as you say, is unnecessary. Only I must first . . . '

He moved aside to avoid his interlocutor, and, perceiving that the group of magistrates had opened out a little, stepped forward. What he now saw explained Coralie's fainting-fit and the servant's agitation. He himself felt his flesh creep at a spectacle which was infinitely more horrible than that of the evening before.

On the floor, near the fireplace, almost at the place where he had undergone his torture, Essarès Bey lay upon his back. He was wearing the same clothes as on the previous day: a brown-velvet smoking-suit with a braided jacket. His head and shoulders had been covered with a napkin. But one of the men standing around, a divisional surgeon no doubt, was holding up the napkin with one hand and pointing to the dead man's face with the other, while he offered an explanation in a low voice.

And that face . . . but it was hardly the word for the unspeakable mass of flesh, part of which seemed to be charred while the other part formed no more than a bloodstained pulp, mixed with bits of bone and skin, hairs and a broken eye-ball.

'Oh,' Patrice blurted out, 'how horrible! He was killed and fell with his head right in the fire. That's how they found him, I suppose?'

The man who had already spoken to him and who appeared to be the most important figure present came up to him once more.

'May I ask who you are?' he demanded.

'Captain Belval, sir, a friend of Mme Essarès, one of the wounded officers whose lives she has helped to save . . . '

'That may be, sir,' replied the important figure, 'but you can't stay here. Nobody must stay here, for that matter. Monsieur le commissaire, please order everyone to leave the room, except the doctor, and have the door guarded. Let no one enter on any pretext whatever . . . '

'Sir,' Patrice insisted, 'I have some very serious information to communicate.'

'I shall be pleased to receive it, captain, but later on. You must excuse me now.'

Chapter 7

Twenty-three Minutes past Twelve

The great hall that ran from Rue Raynouard to the upper terrace of the garden was filled to half its extent by a wide staircase and divided the Essarès house into two parts communicating only by way of the hall.

On the left were the drawing-room and the library, which was followed by an independent block containing a private staircase. On the right were a billiard-room and the dining-room, both with lower ceilings. Above these were Essarès Bey's bedroom, on the street side, and Coralie's, overlooking the garden. Beyond was the servants' wing, where old Siméon also used to sleep.

Patrice was asked to wait in the billiard-room, with the Senegalese. He had been there about a quarter of an hour when Siméon and the maid were shown in.

The old secretary seemed quite paralyzed by the death of his employer and was holding forth under his breath, making queer gestures as he spoke. Patrice asked him how things were going; and the old fellow whispered in his ear: 'It's not over yet . . . There's something to fear . . . to fear! . . . Today . . . presently.'

'Presently?' asked Patrice.

'Yes . . . yes,' said the old man, trembling.

He said nothing more. As for the housemaid, she readily told her story in reply to Patrice's questions.

'The first surprise, sir, this morning was that there was no butler, no footman, no porter. All the three were gone. Then, at half-past six, M. Siméon came and told us from the master that the master had locked himself in his library and that he wasn't to be disturbed even for breakfast. The mistress was not very well. She had her chocolate at nine o'clock . . . At ten o'clock she went out with M. Siméon. Then, after we had done the bedrooms, we never left the kitchen. Eleven o'clock came, twelve . . . and, just as the hour was striking, we heard a loud ring at the front-door. I looked out of the window. There was a motor, with four gentlemen inside. I went to the door.

The commissary of police explained who he was and wanted to see the master. I showed them the way. The library-door was locked. We knocked: no answer. We shook it: no answer. In the end, one of the gentlemen, who knew how, picked the lock ... Then ... then ... you can imagine what we saw ... But you can't, it was much worse, because the poor master at that moment had his head almost under the grate ... Oh, what scoundrels they must have been! ... For they did kill him, didn't they? I know one of the gentlemen said at once that the master had died of a stroke and fallen into the fire. Only my firm belief is ... '

Old Siméon had listened without speaking, with his head still half wrapped up, showing only his bristly gray beard and his eyes hidden behind their yellow spectacles. But at this point of the story he gave a little chuckle, came up to Patrice and said in his ear: 'There's something to fear ... to fear! ... Mme Coralie ... Make her go away at once ... make her go away ... If not, it'll be the worse for her ... '

Patrice shuddered and tried to question him, but could learn nothing more. Besides, the old man did not remain. A policeman came to fetch him and took him to the library.

His evidence lasted a long time. It was followed by the depositions of the cook and the housemaid. Next, Coralie's evidence was taken, in her own room. At four o'clock another car arrived. Patrice saw two gentlemen pass into the hall, with everybody bowing very low before them. He recognized the minister of justice and the minister of the interior. They conferred in the library for half an hour and went away again.

At last, shortly before five o'clock, a policeman came for Patrice and showed him up to the first floor. The man tapped at a door and stood aside. Patrice entered a small boudoir, lit up by a wood fire by which two persons were seated: Coralie, to whom he bowed, and, opposite her, the gentleman who had spoken to him on his arrival and who seemed to be directing the whole enquiry.

He was a man of about fifty, with a thickset body and a heavy face, slow of movement, but with bright, intelligent eyes.

'The examining-magistrate, I presume, sir?' asked Patrice.

'No,' he replied, 'I am M. Masseron, a retired magistrate, specially appointed to clear up this affair ... not to examine it, as you think, for it does not seem to me that there is anything to examine.'

'What?' cried Patrice, in great surprise. 'Nothing to examine?'

He looked at Coralie, who kept her eyes fixed upon him attentively. Then she turned them on M. Masseron, who resumed: 'I have no doubt, Captain Belval, that, when we have said what we have to say, we shall be agreed at all points . . . just as madame and I are already agreed.'

'I don't doubt it either,' said Patrice. 'All the same, I am afraid that many of those points remain unexplained.'

'Certainly, but we shall find an explanation, we shall find it together. Will you please tell me what you know?'

Patrice waited for a moment and then said: 'I will not disguise my astonishment, sir. The story which I have to tell is of some importance; and yet there is no one here to take it down. Is it not to count as evidence given on oath, as a deposition which I shall have to sign?'

'You yourself, captain, shall determine the value of your words and the innuendo which you wish them to bear. For the moment, we will look on this as a preliminary conversation, as an exchange of views relating to facts . . . touching which Mme Essarès has given me, I believe, the same information that you will be able to give me.'

Patrice did not reply at once. He had a vague impression that there was a private understanding between Coralie and the magistrate and that, in face of that understanding, he, both by his presence and by his zeal, was playing the part of an intruder whom they would gladly have dismissed. He resolved therefore to maintain an attitude of reserve until the magistrate had shown his hand.

'Of course,' he said, 'I dare say madame has told you. So you know of the conversation which I overheard yesterday at the restaurant?'

'Yes.'

'And the attempt to kidnap Mme Essarès?'

'Yes.'

'And the murder? . . . '

'Yes.'

'Mme Essarès has described to you the blackmailing scene that took place last night, with M. Essarès for a victim, the details of the torture, the death of the colonel, the handing over of the four millions, the conversation on the telephone between M. Essarès and a certain Grégoire and, lastly, the threats uttered against madame by her husband?'

'Yes, Captain Belval, I know all this, that is to say, all that you know; and I know, in addition, all that I discovered through my own investigations.'

'Of course, of course,' Patrice repeated. 'I see that my story becomes superfluous and that you are in possession of all the necessary factors to enable you to draw your conclusions.' And, continuing to put

rather than answer questions, he added, 'May I ask what inference you
have arrived at?'

'To tell you the truth, captain, my inferences are not definite.
However, until I receive some proof to the contrary, I propose to
remain satisfied with the actual words of a letter which M. Essarès
wrote to his wife at about twelve o'clock this morning and which we
found lying on his desk, unfinished. Mme Essarès asked me to read it
and, if necessary, to communicate the contents to you. Listen.'

M. Masseron proceeded to read the letter aloud.

Coralie,
You were wrong yesterday to attribute my departure to reasons
which I dared not acknowledge; and perhaps I also was wrong
not to defend myself more convincingly against your accusation.
The only motive for my departure is the hatred with which I
am surrounded. You have seen how fierce it is. In the face of
these enemies who are seeking to despoil me by every possible
means, my only hope of salvation lies in flight. That is why I am
going away.
    But let me remind you, Coralie, of my clearly expressed wish.
You are to join me at the first summons. If you do not leave Paris
then, nothing shall protect you against my lawful resentment:
nothing, not even my death. I have made all my arrangements
so that, even in the contingency . . .

'The letter ends there,' said M. Masseron, handing it back to
Coralie, 'and we know by an unimpeachable sign that the last lines
were written immediately before M. Essarès' death, because, in
falling, he upset a little clock which stood on his desk and which
marked twenty-three minutes past twelve. I assume that he felt
unwell and that, on trying to rise, he was seized with a fit of
giddiness and fell to the floor. Unfortunately, the fireplace was
near, with a fierce fire blazing in it; his head struck the grate; and
the wound that resulted was so deep – the surgeon testified to this –
that he fainted. Then the fire close at hand did its work . . . with the
effects which you have seen . . . '

Patrice had listened in amazement to this unexpected explanation.

'Then in your opinion,' he asked, 'M. Essarès died of an accident?
He was not murdered?'

'Murdered? Certainly not! We have no clue to support any such
theory.'

'Still . . .'

'Captain Belval, you are the victim of an association of ideas which, I admit, is perfectly justifiable. Ever since yesterday you have been witnessing a series of tragic incidents; and your imagination naturally leads you to the most tragic solution, that of murder. Only – reflect – why should a murder have been committed? And by whom? By Bournef and his friends? With what object? They were crammed full with bank-notes; and, even admitting that the man called Grégoire recovered those millions from them, they would certainly not have got them back by killing M. Essarès. Then again, how would they have entered the house? And how can they have gone out? . . . No, captain, you must excuse me, but M. Essarès died an accidental death. The facts are undeniable; and this is the opinion of the divisional surgeon, who will draw up his report in that sense.'

Patrice turned to Coralie: 'Is it Mme Essarès' opinion also?'

She reddened slightly and answered: 'Yes.'

'And old Siméon's?'

'Oh,' replied the magistrate, 'old Siméon is wandering in his mind! To listen to him, you would think that everything was about to happen all over again, that Mme Essarès is threatened with danger and that she ought to take to flight at once. That is all that I have been able to get out of him. However, he took me to an old disused door that opens out of the garden on a lane running at right angles with the Rue Raynouard; and here he showed me first the watch-dog's dead body and next some footprints between the door and the flight of steps near the library. But you know those footprints, do you not? They belong to you and your Senegalese. As for the death of the watch-dog, I can put that down to your Senegalese, can't I?'

Patrice was beginning to understand. The magistrate's reticence, his explanation, his agreement with Coralie: all this was gradually becoming plain. He put the question frankly: 'So there was no murder?'

'No.'

'Then there will be no magistrate's examination?'

'No.'

'And no talk about the matter; it will all be kept quiet, in short, and forgotten?'

'Just so.'

Captain Belval began to walk up and down, as was his habit. He now remembered Essarès' prophecy.

'I shan't be arrested . . . If I am, I shall be let go . . . The matter will be hushed up . . .'

Essarès was right. The hand of justice was arrested; and there was no way for Coralie to escape silent complicity.

Patrice was intensely annoyed by the manner in which the case was being handled. It was certain that a compact had been concluded between Coralie and M. Masseron. He suspected the magistrate of circumventing Coralie and inducing her to sacrifice her own interests to other considerations. To effect this, the first thing was to get rid of him, Patrice.

'Ugh!' said Patrice to himself. 'I'm fairly sick of this sportsman, with his cool ironical ways. It looks as if he were doing a considerable piece of thimble-rigging at my expense.'

He restrained himself, however, and, with a pretense of wanting to keep on good terms with the magistrate, came and sat down beside him.

'You must forgive me, sir,' he said, 'for insisting in what may appear to you an indiscreet fashion. But my conduct is explained not only by such sympathy or feeling as I entertain for Mme Essarès at a moment in her life when she is more lonely than ever, a sympathy and feeling which she seems to repulse even more firmly than she did before. It is also explained by certain mysterious links which unite us to each other and which go back to a period too remote for our eyes to focus. Has Mme Essarès told you those details? In my opinion, they are most important; and I cannot help associating them with the events that interest us.'

M. Masseron glanced at Coralie, who nodded. He answered: 'Yes, Mme Essarès has informed me and even . . . '

He hesitated once more and again consulted Coralie, who flushed and seemed put out of countenance. M. Masseron, however, waited for a reply which would enable him to proceed. She ended by saying, in a low voice: 'Captain Belval is entitled to know what we have discovered. The truth belongs as much to him as to me; and I have no right to keep it from him. Pray speak, monsieur.'

'I doubt if it is even necessary to speak,' said the magistrate. 'It will be enough, I think, to show the captain this photograph-album which I have found. Here you are, Captain Belval.'

And he handed Patrice a very slender album, covered in gray canvas and fastened with an india-rubber band.

Patrice took it with a certain anxiety. But what he saw on opening it was so utterly unexpected that he gave an exclamation: 'It's incredible!'

On the first page, held in place by their four corners, were two photographs: one, on the right, representing a small boy in an Eton jacket; the other, on the left, representing a very little girl. There was an inscription under each. On the right: 'Patrice, at ten.' On the left: 'Coralie, at three.'

Moved beyond expression, Patrice turned the leaf. On the second page they appeared again, he at the age of fifteen, she at the age of eight. And he saw himself at nineteen and at twenty-three and at twenty-eight, always accompanied by Coralie, first as a little girl, then as a young girl, next as a woman.

'This is incredible!' he cried. 'How is it possible? Here are portraits of myself which I had never seen, amateur photographs obviously, which trace my whole life. Here's one when I was doing my military training . . . Here I am on horseback . . . Who can have ordered these photographs? And who can have collected them together with yours, madame?'

He fixed his eyes on Coralie, who evaded their questioning gaze and lowered her head as though the close connection between their two lives, to which those pages bore witness, had shaken her to the very depths of her being.

'Who can have brought them together?' he repeated. 'Do you know? And where does the album come from?'

M. Masseron supplied the answer.

'It was the surgeon who found it. M. Essarès wore a vest under his shirt; and the album was in an inner pocket, a pocket sewn inside the vest. The surgeon felt the boards through it when he was undressing M. Essarès' body.'

This time, Patrice's and Coralie's eyes met. The thought that M. Essarès had been collecting both their photographs during the past twenty years and that he wore them next to his breast and that he had lived and died with them upon him, this thought amazed them so much that they did not even try to fathom its strange significance.

'Are you sure of what you are saying, sir?' asked Patrice.

'I was there,' said M. Masseron. 'I was present at the discovery. Besides, I myself made another which confirms this one and completes it in a really surprising fashion. I found a pendant, cut out of a solid block of amethyst and held in a setting of filigree-work.'

'What's that?' cried Captain Belval. 'What's that? A pendant? An amethyst pendant?'

'Look for yourself, sir,' suggested the magistrate, after once more consulting Mme Essarès with a glance.

And he handed Captain Belval an amethyst pendant, larger than the ball formed by joining the two halves which Coralie and Patrice possessed, she on her rosary and he on his bunch of seals; and this new ball was encircled with a specimen of gold filigree-work exactly like that on the rosary and on the seal.

The setting served as a clasp.

'Am I to open it?' he asked.

Coralie nodded. He opened the pendant. The inside was divided by a movable glass disk, which separated two miniature photographs, one of Coralie as a nurse, the other of himself, wounded, in an officer's uniform.

Patrice reflected, with pale cheeks. Presently he asked: 'And where does this pendant come from? Did you find it, sir?'

'Yes, Captain Belval.'

'Where?'

The magistrate seemed to hesitate. Coralie's attitude gave Patrice the impression that she was unaware of this detail. M. Masseron at last said: 'I found it in the dead man's hand.'

'In the dead man's hand? In M. Essarès' hand?'

Patrice had given a start, as though under an unexpected blow, and was now leaning over the magistrate, greedily awaiting a reply which he wanted to hear for the second time before accepting it as certain.

'Yes, in his hand. I had to force back the clasped fingers in order to release it.'

Belval stood up and, striking the table with his fist, exclaimed: 'Well, sir, I will tell you one thing which I was keeping back as a last argument to prove to you that my collaboration is of use; and this thing becomes of great importance after what we have just learnt. Sir, this morning someone asked to speak to me on the telephone; and I had hardly answered the call when this person, who seemed greatly excited, was the victim of a murderous assault, committed in my hearing. And, amid the sound of the scuffle and the cries of agony, I caught the following words, which the unhappy man insisted on trying to get to me as so many last instructions: "Patrice! . . . Coralie! . . . The amethyst pendant . . . Yes, I have it on me . . . The pendant . . . Ah, it's too late! . . . I should so much have liked . . . Patrice . . . Coralie . . ." There's what I heard, sir, and here are the two facts which we cannot escape. This morning, at nineteen minutes past seven, a man was murdered having upon him an amethyst pendant. This is the first undeniable fact. A few hours later, at twenty-three minutes past twelve, this same amethyst pendant is discovered clutched in the hand of another man. This is the second undeniable fact. Place these facts side by side and you are bound to come to the conclusion that the first murder, the one of which I caught the distant echo, was committed here, in this house, in the same library which, since yesterday evening, witnessed the end of every scene in the tragedy which we are contemplating.'

This revelation, which in reality amounted to a fresh accusation against Essarès, seemed to affect the magistrate profoundly. Patrice had flung himself into the discussion with a passionate vehemence and a logical reasoning which it was impossible to disregard without evident insincerity.

Coralie had turned aside slightly and Patrice could not see her face; but he suspected her dismay in the presence of all this infamy and shame.

M. Masseron raised an objection.

'Two undeniable facts, you say, Captain Belval? As to the first point, let me remark that we have not found the body of the man who is supposed to have been murdered at nineteen minutes past seven this morning.'

'It will be found in due course.'

'Very well. Second point: as regards the amethyst pendant discovered in Essarès' hand, how can we tell that Essarès Bey found it in the murdered man's hand and not somewhere else? For, after all, we do not know if he was at home at that time and still less if he was in his library.'

'But I do know.'

'How?'

'I telephoned to him a few minutes later and he answered. More than that, to sweep away any trace of doubt, he told me that he had rung me up but that he had been cut off.'

M. Masseron thought for a moment and then said: 'Did he go out this morning?'

'Ask Mme Essarès.'

Without turning round, manifestly wishing to avoid Belval's eyes, Coralie answered: 'I don't think that he went out. The suit he was wearing at the time of his death was an indoor suit.'

'Did you see him after last night?'

'He came and knocked at my room three times this morning, between seven and nine o'clock. I did not open the door. At about eleven o'clock I started off alone; I heard him call old Siméon and tell him to go with me. Siméon caught me up in the street. That is all I know.'

A prolonged silence ensued. Each of the three was meditating upon this strange series of adventures. In the end, M. Masseron, who had realized that a man of Captain Belval's stamp was not the sort to be easily thrust aside, spoke in the tone of one who, before coming to terms, wishes to know exactly what his adversary's last word is likely to be.

'Let us come to the point, captain. You are building up a theory which strikes me as very vague. What is it precisely? And what are you proposing to do if I decline to accept it? I have asked you two very plain questions. Do you mind answering them?'

'I will answer them, sir, as plainly as you put them.'

He went up to the magistrate and said: 'Here, sir, is the field of battle and of attack – yes, of attack, if need be – which I select. A man who used to know me, who knew Mme Essarès as a child and who was interested in both of us, a man who used to collect our portraits at different ages, who had reasons for loving us unknown to me, who sent me the key of that garden and who was making arrangements to bring us together for a purpose which he would have told us, this man was murdered at the moment when he was about to execute his plan. Now everything tells me that he was murdered by M. Essarès. I am therefore resolved to lodge an information, whatever the results of my action may be. And believe me, sir, my charge will not be hushed up. There are always means of making one's self heard ... even if I am reduced to shouting the truth from the house-tops.'

M. Masseron burst out laughing.

'By Jove, captain, but you're letting yourself go!'

'I'm behaving according to my conscience; and Mme Essarès, I feel sure, will forgive me. She knows that I am acting for her good. She knows that all will be over with her if this case is hushed up and if the authorities do not assist her. She knows that the enemies who threaten her are implacable. They will stop at nothing to attain their object and to do away with her, for she stands in their way. And the terrible thing about it is that the most clear-seeing eyes are unable to make out what that object is. We are playing the most formidable game against these enemies; and we do not even know what the stakes are. Only the police can discover those stakes.'

M. Masseron waited for a second or two and then, laying his hand on Patrice's shoulder, said, calmly: 'And, suppose the authorities knew what the stakes were?'

Patrice looked at him in surprise.

'What? Do you mean to say you know?'

'Perhaps.'

'And can you tell me?'

'Oh, well, if you force me to!'

'What are they?'

'Not much! A trifle!'

'But what sort of trifle?'

'A thousand million francs.'

'A thousand millions?'

'Just that. A thousand millions, of which two-thirds, I regret to say, if not three-quarters, had already left France before the war. But the remaining two hundred and fifty or three hundred millions are worth more than a thousand millions all the same, for a very good reason.'

'What reason?'

'They happen to be in gold.'

Chapter 8

Essarès Bey's Work

This time Captain Belval seemed to relax to some extent. He vaguely perceived the consideration that compelled the authorities to wage the battle prudently.

'Are you sure?' he asked.

'Yes, I was instructed to investigate this matter two years ago; and my enquiries proved that really remarkable exports of gold were being effected from France. But, I confess, it is only since my conversation with Mme Essarès that I have seen where the leakage came from and who it was that set on foot, all over France, down to the least important market-towns, the formidable organization through which the indispensable metal was made to leave the country.'

'Then Mme Essarès knew?'

'No, but she suspected a great deal; and last night, before you arrived, she overheard some words spoken between Essarès and his assailants which she repeated to me, thus giving me the key to the riddle. I should have been glad to work out the complete solution without your assistance – for one thing, those were the orders of the minister of the interior; and Mme Essarès displayed the same wish – but your impetuosity overcomes my hesitation; and, since I can't manage to get rid of you, Captain Belval, I will tell you the whole story frankly . . . especially as your cooperation is not to be despised.'

'I am all ears,' said Patrice, who was burning to know more.

'Well, the motive force of the plot was here, in this house. Essarès Bey, president of the Franco-Oriental Bank, 6, Rue Lafayette, apparently an Egyptian, in reality a Turk, enjoyed the greatest influence in the Paris financial world. He had been naturalized an Englishman, but had kept up secret relations with the former possessors of Egypt; and he had received instructions from a foreign power, which I am not yet able to name with certainty, to bleed – there is no other word for it – to bleed France of all the gold that he could cause to flow into his coffers. According to documents which I have seen, he succeeded in exporting in this way some seven hundred million francs in two years. A last consignment was preparing when war was declared. You can understand that thenceforth such important sums could not be smuggled out of the country so easily as in times of peace. The railway-wagons are inspected on the frontiers; the outgoing vessels are searched in the harbors. In short, the gold was not sent away. Those two hundred and fifty or three hundred millions remained in France. Ten months passed; and the inevitable happened, which was that Essarès Bey, having this fabulous treasure at his disposal, clung to it, came gradually to look upon it as his own and, in the end, resolved to appropriate it. Only there were accomplices . . .'

'The men I saw last night?'

'Yes, half-a-dozen shady Levantines, sham naturalized French citizens, more or less well-disguised Bulgarians, secret agents of the little German courts in the Balkans. This gang ran provincial branches of Essarès' bank. It had in its pay, on Essarès' account, hundreds of minor agents, who scoured the villages, visited the fairs, were hail-fellow-well-met with the peasants, offered them bank-notes and government securities in exchange for French gold and trousered all their savings. When war broke out the gang shut up shop and gathered round Essarès Bey, who also had closed his offices in the Rue Lafayette.'

'What happened then?'

'Things that we don't know. No doubt the accomplices learnt from their governments that the last despatch of gold had never taken place; and no doubt they also guessed that Essarès Bey was trying to keep for himself the three hundred millions collected by the gang. One thing is certain, that a struggle began between the former partners, a fierce, implacable struggle, the accomplices wanting their share of the plunder, while Essarès Bey was resolved to part with none of it and pretended that the millions had left the country. Yesterday the struggle attained its culminating-point. In the afternoon the accomplices tried to get hold of Mme Essarès so that they might have a hostage to use against her husband. In the evening . . . in the evening you yourself witnessed the final episode.'

'But why yesterday evening rather than another?'

'Because the accomplices had every reason to think that the millions were intended to disappear yesterday evening. Though they did not know the methods employed by Essarès Bey when he made his last remittances, they believed that each of the remittances, or rather each removal of the sacks, was preceded by a signal.'

'Yes, a shower of sparks, was it not?'

'Exactly. In a corner of the garden are some old conservatories, above which stands the furnace that used to heat them. This grimy furnace, full of soot and rubbish, sends forth, when you light it, flakes of fire and sparks which are seen at a distance and serve as an intimation. Essarès Bey lit it last night himself. The accomplices at once took alarm and came prepared to go any lengths.'

'And Essarès' plan failed.'

'Yes. But so did theirs. The colonel is dead. The others were only able to get hold of a few bundles of notes which have probably been taken from them by this time. But the struggle was not finished; and its dying agony has been a most shocking tragedy. According to your statement, a man who knew you and who was seeking to get into touch with you, was killed at nineteen minutes past seven, most likely by Essarès Bey, who dreaded his intervention. And, five hours later, at twenty-three past twelve, Essarès Bey himself was murdered, presumably by one of his accomplices. There is the whole story, Captain Belval. And, now that you know as much of it as I do, don't you think that the investigation of this case should remain secret and be pursued not quite in accordance with the ordinary rules?'

After a moment's reflection Patrice said: 'Yes, I agree.'

'There can be no doubt about it!' cried M. Masseron. 'Not only will it serve no purpose to publish this story of gold which has disappeared and which can't be found, which would startle the public and excite their imaginations, but you will readily imagine that an operation which consisted in draining off such a quantity of gold in two years cannot have been effected without compromising a regrettable number of people. I feel certain that my own enquiries will reveal a series of weak concessions and unworthy bargains on the part of certain more or less important banks and credit-houses, transactions on which I do not wish to insist, but which it would be the gravest of blunders to publish. Therefore, silence.'

'But is silence possible?'

'Why not?'

'Bless my soul, there are a good few corpses to be explained away! Colonel Fakhi's, for instance?'

'Suicide.'

'Mustapha's, which you will discover or which you have already discovered in the Galliéra garden?'

'Found dead.'

'Essarès Bey's?'

'An accident.'

'So that all these manifestations of the same power will remain separated?'

'There is nothing to show the link that connects them.'

'Perhaps the public will think otherwise.'

'The public will think what we wish it to think. This is war-time.'

'The press will speak.'

'The press will do nothing of the kind. We have the censorship.'

'But, if some fact or, rather, a fresh crime . . . ?'

'Why should there be a fresh crime? The matter is finished, at least on its active and dramatic side. The chief actors are dead. The curtain falls on the murder of Essarès Bey. As for the supernumeraries, Bournef and the others, we shall have them stowed away in an internment-camp before a week is past. We therefore find ourselves in the presence of a certain number of millions, with no owner, with no one who dares to claim them, on which France is entitled to lay hands. I shall devote my activity to securing the money for the republic.'

Patrice Belval shook his head.

'Mme Essarès remains, sir. We must not forget her husband's threats.'

'He is dead.'

'No matter, the threats are there. Old Siméon tells you so in a striking fashion.'

'He's half mad.'

'Exactly, his brain retains the impression of great and imminent danger. No, the struggle is not ended. Perhaps indeed it is only beginning.'

'Well, captain, are we not here? Make it your business to protect and defend Mme Essarès by all the means in your power and by all those which I place at your disposal. Our collaboration will be uninterrupted, because my task lies here and because, if the battle – which you expect and I do not – takes place, it will be within the walls of this house and garden.'

'What makes you think that?'

'Some words which Mme Essarès overheard last night. The colonel repeated several times, "The gold is here, Essarès." He added, "For years past, your car brought to this house all that there was at your bank in the Rue Lafayette. Siméon, you and the chauffeur used to let the sacks down the last grating on the left. How you used

to send it away I do not know. But of what was here on the day
when the war broke out, of the seventeen or eighteen hundred
bags which they were expecting out yonder, none has left your
place. I suspected the trick; and we kept watch night and day. The
gold is here." '

'And have you no clue?'

'Not one. Or this at most; but I attach comparatively little value
to it.'

He took a crumpled paper from his pocket, unfolded it and continued: 'Besides the pendant, Essarès Bey held in his hand this bit of
blotted paper, on which you can see a few straggling, hurriedly-
written words. The only ones that are more or less legible are these:
"golden triangle". What this golden triangle means, what it has
to do with the case in hand, I can't for the present tell. The most
that I am able to presume is that, like the pendant, the scrap of
paper was snatched by Essarès Bey from the man who died at
nineteen minutes past seven this morning and that, when he himself was killed at twenty-three minutes past twelve, he was occupied
in examining it.'

'And then there is the album,' said Patrice, making his last point.
'You see how all the details are linked together. You may safely
believe that it is all one case.'

'Very well,' said M. Masseron. 'One case in two parts. You, captain,
had better follow up the second. I grant you that nothing could be
stranger than this discovery of photographs of Mme Essarès and
yourself in the same album and in the same pendant. It sets a problem
the solution of which will no doubt bring us very near to the truth. We
shall meet again soon, Captain Belval, I hope. And, once more, make
use of me and of my men.'

He shook Patrice by the hand. Patrice held him back.

'I shall make use of you, sir, as you suggest. But is this not the time
to take the necessary precautions?'

'They are taken, captain. We are in occupation of the house.'

'Yes ... yes ... I know; but, all the same ... I have a sort of
presentiment that the day will not end without ... Remember old
Siméon's strange words ...'

M. Masseron began to laugh.

'Come, Captain Belval, we mustn't exaggerate things. If any enemies
remain for us to fight, they must stand in great need, for the moment,
of taking council with themselves. We'll talk about this tomorrow,
shall we, captain?'

He shook hands with Patrice again, bowed to Mme Essarès and left the room.

Belval had at first made a discreet movement to go out with him. He stopped at the door and walked back again. Mme Essarès, who seemed not to hear him, sat motionless, bent in two, with her head turned away from him.

'Coralie,' he said.

She did not reply; and he uttered her name a second time, hoping that again she might not answer, for her silence suddenly appeared to him to be the one thing in the world for him to desire. That silence no longer implied either constraint or rebellion. Coralie accepted the fact that he was there, by her side, as a helpful friend. And Patrice no longer thought of all the problems that harassed him, nor of the murders that had mounted up, one after another, around them, nor of the dangers that might still encompass them. He thought only of Coralie's yielding gentleness.

'Don't answer, Coralie, don't say a word. It is for me to speak. I must tell you what you do not know, the reasons that made you wish to keep me out of this house . . . out of this house and out of your very life.'

He put his hand on the back of the chair in which she was sitting; and his hand just touched Coralie's hair.

'Coralie, you imagine that it is the shame of your life here that keeps you away from me. You blush at having been that man's wife; and this makes you feel troubled and anxious, as though you yourself had been guilty. But why should you? It was not your fault. Surely you know that I can guess the misery and hatred that must have passed between you and him and the constraint that was brought to bear upon you, by some machination, in order to force your consent to the marriage! No, Coralie, there is something else; and I will tell you what it is. There is something else . . .'

He was bending over her still more. He saw her beautiful profile lit up by the blazing logs and, speaking with increasing fervor and adopting the familiar *tu* and *toi* which, in his mouth, retained a note of affectionate respect, he cried: 'Am I to speak, Little Mother Coralie? I needn't, need I? You have understood; and you read yourself clearly. Ah, I feel you trembling from head to foot! Yes, yes, I tell you, I knew your secret from the very first day. From the very first day you loved your great beggar of a wounded man, all scarred and maimed though he was. Hush! Don't deny it! . . . Yes, I understand: you are rather shocked to hear such words as these spoken today. I ought perhaps to have waited. And yet why should I? I am asking you nothing. I know; and that is enough for me. I shan't speak of it again for a long time to come, until the inevitable hour arrives when you are forced to tell it to me yourself. Till then I shall keep silence. But our love will always be between us; and it will be exquisite, Little Mother Coralie, it will be exquisite for me to know that you love me. Coralie . . . There, now you're crying! And you would still deny the truth? Why, when you cry – I know you, Little Mother – it means that your dear heart is overflowing with tenderness and love! You are crying? Ah, Little Mother, I never thought you loved me to that extent!'

Patrice also had tears in his eyes. Coralie's were coursing down her pale cheeks; and he would have given much to kiss that wet face. But the least outward sign of affection appeared to him an offense at such a moment. He was content to gaze at her passionately.

And, as he did so, he received an impression that her thoughts were becoming detached from his own, that her eyes were being attracted by an unexpected sight and that, amid the great silence of their love, she was listening to something that he himself had not heard.

And suddenly he too heard that thing, though it was almost imperceptible. It was not so much a sound as the sensation of a presence mingling with the distant rumble of the town. What could be happening?

The light had begun to fade, without his noticing it. Also unperceived by Patrice, Mme Essarès had opened the window a little way, for the boudoir was small and the heat of the fire was becoming oppressive. Nevertheless, the two casements were almost touching. It was at this that she was staring; and it was from there that the danger threatened.

Patrice's first impulse was to run to the window, but he restrained himself. The danger was becoming defined. Outside, in the twilight, he distinguished through the slanting panes a human form. Next, he saw between the two casements something which gleamed in the light of the fire and which looked like the barrel of a revolver.

'Coralie is done for,' he thought, 'if I allow it to be suspected for an instant that I am on my guard.'

She was in fact opposite the window, with no obstacle intervening. He therefore said aloud, in a careless tone: 'Coralie, you must be a little tired. We will say goodbye.'

At the same time, he went round her chair to protect her.

But he had not the time to complete his movement. She also no doubt had seen the glint of the revolver, for she drew back abruptly, stammering: 'Oh, Patrice! . . . Patrice! . . . '

Two shots rang out, followed by a moan.

'You're wounded!' cried Patrice, springing to her side.

'No, no,' she said, 'but the fright . . . '

'Oh, if he's touched you, the scoundrel!'

'No, he hasn't.'

'Are you quite sure?'

He lost thirty or forty seconds, switching on the electric light, looking at Coralie for signs of a wound and waiting in an agony of suspense for her to regain full consciousness. Only then did he rush to the window, open it wide and climb over the balcony. The room was on the first floor. There was plenty of lattice-work on the wall. But, because of his leg, Patrice had some difficulty in making his way down.

Below, on the terrace, he caught his foot in the rungs of an over-turned ladder. Next, he knocked against some policemen who were coming from the ground-floor. One of them shouted: 'I saw the figure of a man making off that way.'

'Which way?' asked Patrice.

The man was running in the direction of the lane. Patrice followed him. But, at that moment, from close beside the little door, there came shrill cries and the whimper of a choking voice: 'Help! . . . Help! . . . '

When Patrice came up, the policeman was already flashing his electric lantern over the ground; and they both saw a human form writhing in the shrubbery.

'The door's open!' shouted Patrice. 'The assassin has escaped! Go after him!'

The policeman vanished down the lane; and, Ya-Bon appearing on the scene, Patrice gave him his orders.

'Quick as you can, Ya-Bon! . . . If the policeman is going up the lane, you go down. Run! I'll look after the victim.'

All this time, Patrice was stooping low, flinging the light of the policeman's lantern on the man who lay struggling on the ground. He recognized old Siméon, nearly strangled, with a red-silk cord round his neck.

'How do you feel?' he asked. 'Can you understand what I'm saying?'

He unfastened the cord and repeated his question. Siméon stuttered out a series of incoherent syllables and then suddenly began to sing and laugh, a very low, jerky laugh, alternating with hiccoughs. He had gone mad.

When M. Masseron arrived, Patrice told him what had happened. 'Do you really believe it's all over?' he asked.

'No. You were right and I was wrong,' said M. Masseron. 'We must take every precaution to ensure Mme Essarès' safety. The house shall be guarded all night.'

A few minutes later the policeman and Ya-Bon returned, after a vain search. The key that had served to open the door was found in the lane. It was exactly similar to the one in Patrice Belval's possession, equally old and equally rusty. The would-be murderer had thrown it away in the course of his flight.

*　　*　　*

It was seven o'clock when Patrice, accompanied by Ya-Bon, left the house in the Rue Raynouard and turned towards Neuilly. As usual, Patrice took Ya-Bon's arm and, leaning upon him for support as he walked, he said: 'I can guess what you're thinking, Ya-Bon.'

Ya-Bon grunted.

'That's it,' said Captain Belval, in a tone of approval. 'We are entirely in agreement all along the line. What strikes you first and foremost is the utter incapacity displayed by the police. A pack of addle-pates, you say? When you speak like that, Master Ya-Bon, you are talking impertinent nonsense, which, coming from you, does not astonish me and which might easily make me give you the punishment you deserve. But we will overlook it this time. What-ever you may say, the police do what they can, not to mention that, in war-time, they have other things to do than to occupy themselves with the mysterious relations between Captain Belval and Mme Essarès. It is I therefore who will have to act; and I have hardly anyone to reckon on but myself. Well, I wonder if I am a match for such adversaries. To think that here's one who has the cheek to come back to the house while it is being watched by the police, to put up a ladder, to listen no doubt to my conversation with M. Masseron and afterwards to what I said to Little Mother Coralie and, lastly, to send a couple of bullets whizzing past our ears! What do you say? Am I the man for the job? And could all the French police, overworked as they are, give me the indispensable assist-ance? No, the man I need for clearing up a thing like this is an exceptional sort of chap, one who unites every quality in himself, in short the type of man one never sees.'

Patrice leant more heavily on his companion's arm.

'You, who know so many good people, haven't you the fellow I want concealed about your person? A genius of sorts? A demigod?'

Ya-Bon grunted again, merrily this time, and withdrew his arm. He always carried a little electric lamp. Switching on the light, he put the handle between his teeth. Then he took a bit of chalk out of his jacket-pocket.

A grimy, weather-beaten plaster wall ran along the street. Ya-Bon took his stand in front of the wall and, turning the light upon it, began to write with an unskilful hand, as though each letter cost him a measureless effort and as though the sum total of those letters were the only one that he had ever succeeded in composing and remembering. In this way he wrote two words which Patrice read out.

Arsène Lupin

'Arsène Lupin,' said Patrice, under his breath. And, looking at Ya-Bon in amazement, 'Are you in your right mind? What do you mean by Arsène Lupin? Are you suggesting Arsène Lupin to me?'

Ya-Bon nodded his head.

'Arsène Lupin? Do you know him?'

'Yes,' Ya-Bon signified.

Patrice then remembered that the Senegalese used to spend his days at the hospital getting his good-natured comrades to read all the adventures of Arsène Lupin aloud to him; and he grinned.

'Yes, you know him as one knows somebody whose history one has read.'

'No,' protested Ya-Bon.

'Do you know him personally?'

'Yes.'

'Get out, you silly fool! Arsène Lupin is dead. He threw himself into the sea from a rock;[*] and you pretend that you know him?'

'Yes.'

'Do you mean to say that you have met him since he died?'

'Yes.'

'By Jove! And Master Ya-Bon's influence with Arsène Lupin is enough to make him come to life again and put himself out at a sign from Master Ya-Bon?'

'Yes.'

'I say! I had a high opinion of you as it was, but now there is nothing for me but to make you my bow. A friend of the late Arsène

[*] *813.* By Maurice Leblanc. Translated by Alexander Teixeira de Mattos.

Lupin! We're going it! . . . And how long will it take you to place his ghost at our disposal? Six months? Three months? One month? A fortnight?'

Ya-Bon made a gesture.

'About a fortnight,' Captain Belval translated. 'Very well, evoke your friend's spirit; I shall be delighted to make his acquaintance. Only, upon my word, you must have a very poor idea of me to imagine that I need a collaborator! What next! Do you take me for a helpless dunderhead?'

Chapter 9
Patrice and Coralie

Everything happened as M. Masseron had foretold. The press did not speak. The public did not become excited. The various deaths were casually paragraphed. The funeral of Essarès Bey, the wealthy banker, passed unnoticed.

But, on the day following the funeral, after Captain Belval, with the support of the police, had made an application to the military authorities, a new order of things was established in the house in the Rue Raynouard. It was recognized as Home No. 2 attached to the hospital in the Champs-Élysées; Mme Essarès was appointed matron; and it became the residence of Captain Belval and his seven wounded men exclusively.

Coralie, therefore, was the only woman remaining. The cook and housemaid were sent away. The seven cripples did all the work of the house. One acted as hall-porter, another as cook, a third as butler. Ya-Bon, promoted to parlor-maid, made it his business to wait on Little Mother Coralie. At night he slept in the passage outside her door. By day he mounted guard outside her window.

'Let no one near that door or that window!' Patrice said to him. 'Let no one in! You'll catch it if so much as a mosquito succeeds in entering her room.'

Nevertheless, Patrice was not easy in his mind. The enemy had given him too many proofs of reckless daring to let him imagine that he could take any steps to ensure her perfect protection. Danger always creeps in where it is least expected; and it was all the more difficult to ward off in that no one knew whence it threatened. Now that Essarès Bey was dead, who was continuing his work? Who had inherited the task of revenge upon Coralie announced in his last letter?

M. Masseron had at once begun his work of investigation, but the dramatic side of the case seemed to leave him indifferent. Since he had not found the body of the man whose dying cries reached Patrice Belval's ears, since he had discovered no clue to the mysterious

assailant who had fired at Patrice and Coralie later in the day, since
he was not able to trace where the assailant had obtained his ladder,
he dropped these questions and confined his efforts entirely to the
search of the eighteen hundred bags of gold. These were all that
concerned him.

'We have every reason to believe that they are here,' he said,
'between the four sides of the quadrilateral formed by the garden and
the house. Obviously, a bag of gold weighing a hundredweight does
not take up as much room, by a long way, as a sack of coal of the same
weight. But, for all that, eighteen hundred bags represent a cubic
content; and a content like that is not easily concealed.'

In two days he had assured himself that the treasure was hidden
neither in the house nor under the house. On the evenings when
Essarès Bey's car brought the gold out of the coffers of the Franco-
Oriental Bank to the Rue Raynouard, Essarès, the chauffeur and
the man known as Grégoire used to pass a thick wire through
the grating of which the accomplices spoke. This wire was found.
Along the wire ran hooks, which were also found; and on these the
bags were slung and afterwards stacked in a large cellar situated
exactly under the library. It is needless to say that M. Masseron and
his detectives devoted all their ingenuity and all the painstaking
patience of which they were capable to the task of searching every
corner of this cellar. Their efforts only established beyond doubt
that it contained no secret, save that of a staircase which ran down
from the library and which was closed at the top by a trap-door
concealed by the carpet.

In addition to the grating on the Rue Raynouard, there was another
which overlooked the garden, on the level of the first terrace. These
two openings were barricaded on the inside by very heavy shutters,
so that it was an easy matter to stack thousands and thousands of
rouleaus of gold in the cellar before sending them away.

'But how were they sent away?' M. Masseron wondered. 'That's
the mystery. And why this intermediate stage in the basement, in the
Rue Raynouard? Another mystery. And now we have Fakhi, Bournef
and Co. declaring that, this time, it was not sent away, that the gold is
here and that it can be found for the searching. We have searched the
house. There is still the garden. Let us look there.'

It was a beautiful old garden and had once formed part of the wide-
stretching estate where people were in the habit, at the end of the
eighteenth century, of going to drink the Passy waters. With a two-
hundred-yard frontage, it ran from the Rue Raynouard to the quay

of the river-side and led, by four successive terraces, to an expanse of lawn as old as the rest of the garden, fringed with thickets of ever-greens and shaded by groups of tall trees.

But the beauty of the garden lay chiefly in its four terraces and in the view which they afforded of the river, the low ground on the left bank and the distant hills. They were united by twenty sets of steps; and twenty paths climbed from the one to the other, paths cut between the buttressing walls and sometimes hidden in the floods of ivy that dashed from top to bottom.

Here and there a statue stood out, a broken column, or the frag-ments of a capital. The stone balcony that edged the upper terrace was still adorned with all its old terra-cotta vases. On this terrace also were the ruins of two little round temples where, in the old days, the springs bubbled to the surface. In front of the library windows was a circular basin, with in the center the figure of a child shooting a slender thread of water through the funnel of a shell. It was the overflow from this basin, forming a little stream, that trickled over the rocks against which Patrice had stumbled on the first evening.

'Ten acres to explore before we've done,' said M. Masseron to himself.

He employed upon this work, in addition to Belval's cripples, a dozen of his own detectives. It was not a difficult business and was bound to lead to some definite result. As M. Masseron never ceased saying, eighteen hundred bags cannot remain invisible. An excavation leaves traces. You want a hole to go in and out by. But neither the grass of the lawns nor the sand of the paths showed any signs of earth recently disturbed. The ivy? The buttressing-walls? The terraces? Everything was inspected, but in vain. Here and there, in cutting up the ground, old conduit pipes were found, running towards the Seine, and remains of aqueducts that had once served to carry off the Passy waters. But there was no such thing as a cave, an underground chamber, a brick arch or anything that looked like a hiding-place.

Patrice and Coralie watched the progress of the search. And yet, though they fully realized its importance and though, on the other hand, they were still feeling the strain of the recent dramatic hours, in reality they were engrossed only in the inexplicable problem of their fate; and their conversation nearly always turned upon the mystery of the past.

Coralie's mother was the daughter of a French consul at Salonica, where she married a very rich man of a certain age, called Count Odolavitch, the head of an ancient Servian family. He died a year after Coralie was born. The widow and child were at that time in France, at this same house in the Rue Raynouard, which Count Odolavitch had purchased through a young Egyptian called Essarès, his secretary and factotum.

Coralie here spent three years of her childhood. Then she suddenly lost her mother and was left alone in the world. Essarès took her to Salonica, to a surviving sister of her grandfather the consul, a woman many years younger than her brother. This lady took charge of Coralie. Unfortunately, she fell under Essarès' influence, signed papers and made her little grand-niece sign papers, until the child's whole fortune, administered by the Egyptian, gradually disappeared.

At last, when she was about seventeen, Coralie became the victim of an adventure which left the most hideous memory in her mind and which had a fatal effect on her life. She was kidnapped one morning by a band of Turks on the plains of Salonica and spent a fortnight in the palace of the governor of the province, exposed to his desires. Essarès released her. But the release was brought about in so fantastic a fashion that Coralie must have often wondered afterwards whether the Turk and the Egyptian were not in collusion.

At any rate, sick in body and depressed in spirits, fearing a fresh assault upon her liberty and yielding to her aunt's wishes, a month later she married this Essarès, who had already been paying her his addresses and who now definitely assumed in her eyes the figure of a deliverer. It was a hopeless union, the horror of which became manifest to her on the very day on which it was cemented. Coralie was the wife of a man whom she hated and whose love only grew with the hatred and contempt which she showed for it.

Before the end of the year they came and took up their residence at the house in the Rue Raynouard. Essarès, who had long ago established and was at that time managing the Salonica branch of the Franco-Oriental Bank, bought up almost all the shares of the bank itself, acquired the building in the Rue Lafayette for the head office, became one of the financial magnates of Paris and received the title of bey in Egypt.

This was the story which Coralie told Patrice one day in the beautiful garden at Passy; and, in this unhappy past which they explored together and compared with Patrice Belval's own, neither he nor Coralie was able to discover a single point that was common to both. The two of them had lived in different parts of the world. Not one name evoked the same recollection in their minds. There was not a detail that enabled them to understand why each should possess a piece of the same amethyst bead nor why their joint images should be contained in the same medallion-pendant or stuck in the pages of the same album.

'Failing everything else,' said Patrice, 'we can explain that the pendant found in the hand of Essarès Bey was snatched by him from the unknown friend who was watching over us and whom he murdered. But what about the album, which he wore in a pocket sewn inside his vest?'

Neither attempted to answer the question. Then Patrice asked: 'Tell me about Siméon.'

'Siméon has always lived here.'

'Even in your mother's time?'

'No, it was one or two years after my mother's death and after I went to Salonica that Essarès put him to look after this property and keep it in good condition.'

'Was he Essarès' secretary?'

'I never knew what his exact functions were. But he was not Essarès' secretary, nor his confidant either. They never talked together intimately. He came to see us two or three times at Salonica. I remember one of his visits. I was quite a child and I heard him speaking to Essarès in a very angry tone, apparently threatening him.'

'With what?'

'I don't know. I know nothing at all about Siméon. He kept himself very much to himself and was nearly always in the garden, smoking his pipe, dreaming, tending the trees and flowers, sometimes with the assistance of two or three gardeners whom he would send for.'

'How did he behave to you?'

'Here again I can't give any definite impression. We never talked; and his occupations very seldom brought him into contact with me. Nevertheless I sometimes thought that his eyes used to seek me, through their yellow spectacles, with a certain persistency and perhaps even a certain interest. Moreover, lately, he liked going with me to the hospital; and he would then, either there or on the way, show himself more attentive, more eager to please . . . so much so that I have been wondering this last day or two . . . '

She hesitated for a moment, undecided whether to speak, and then continued: 'Yes, it's a very vague notion . . . but, all the same . . . Look here, there's one thing I forgot to tell you. Do you know why I joined the hospital in the Champs-Élysées, the hospital where you were lying wounded and ill? It was because Siméon took me there. He knew that I wanted to become a nurse and he suggested this hospital . . . And then, if you think, later on, the photograph in the pendant, the one showing you in uniform and me as a nurse, can only have been taken at the hospital. Well, of the people here, in this house, no one except Siméon ever went there . . . You will also remember that he used to come to Salonica, where he saw me as a child and afterwards as a girl, and that there also he may have taken the snapshots in the album. So that, if we allow that he had some correspondent who on his side followed your footsteps in life, it would not be impossible to believe that the unknown friend whom you assume to have intervened between us, the one who sent you the key of the garden . . . '

'Was old Siméon?' Patrice interrupted. 'The theory won't hold water.'

'Why not?'

'Because this friend is dead. The man who, as you say, sought to intervene between us, who sent me the key of the garden, who called me to the telephone to tell me the truth, that man was murdered. There is not the least doubt about it. I heard the cries of a man who is being killed, dying cries, the cries which a man utters when at the moment of death.'

'You can never be sure.'

'I am, absolutely. There is no shadow of doubt in my mind. The man whom I call our unknown friend died before finishing his work; he died murdered, whereas Siméon is alive. Besides,' continued Patrice, 'this man had a different voice from Siméon, a voice which I had never heard before and which I shall never hear again.'

Coralie was convinced and did not insist.

They were seated on one of the benches in the garden, enjoying the bright April sunshine. The buds of the chestnut-trees shone at the tips of the branches. The heavy scent of the wall-flowers rose from the borders; and their brown and yellow blossoms, like a cluster of bees and wasps pressed close together, swayed to the light breeze.

Suddenly Patrice felt a thrill. Coralie had placed her hand on his, with engaging friendliness; and, when he turned to look at her, he saw that she was in tears.

'What's the matter, Little Mother Coralie?'

Coralie's head bent down and her cheek touched the officer's shoulder. He dared not move. She was treating him as a protecting elder brother; and he shrank from showing any warmth of affection that might annoy her.

'What is it, dear?' he repeated. 'What's the matter?'

'Oh, it is so strange!' she murmured. 'Look, Patrice, look at those flowers.'

They were on the third terrace, commanding a view of the fourth; and this, the lowest of the terraces, was adorned not with borders of wall-flowers but with beds in which were mingled all manner of spring flowers; tulips, silvery alyssums, hyacinths, with a great round plot of pansies in the middle.

'Look over there,' she said, pointing to this plot with her out-stretched arm. 'Do you see? . . . Letters . . . '

Patrice looked and gradually perceived that the clumps of pansies were so arranged as to form on the ground some letters that stood out among the other flowers. It did not appear at the first glance. It took a certain time to see; but, once seen, the letters grouped themselves of their own accord, forming three words set down in a single line.

Patrice and Coralie

'Ah,' he said, in a low voice, 'I understand what you mean!'

It gave them a thrill of inexpressible excitement to read their two names, which a friendly hand had, so to speak, sown; their two names united in pansy-flowers. It was inexpressibly exciting too that he and she should always find themselves thus linked together, linked together by events, linked together by their portraits, linked together by an unseen force of will, linked together now by the struggling effort of little flowers that spring up, waken into life and blossom in predetermined order.

Coralie, sitting up, said: 'It's Siméon who attends to the garden.'

'Yes,' he said, wavering slightly. 'But surely that does not affect my opinion. Our unknown friend is dead, but Siméon may have known him. Siméon perhaps was acting with him in certain matters and must know a good deal. Oh, if he could only put us on the right road!'

An hour later, as the sun was sinking on the horizon, they climbed the terraces. On reaching the top they saw M. Masseron beckoning to them.

'I have something curious to show you,' he said, 'something I have found which will interest both you, madame, and you, captain, particularly.'

He led them to the very end of the terrace, outside the occupied part of the house next to the library. Two detectives were standing mattock in hand. In the course of their searching, M. Masseron explained, they had begun by removing the ivy from the low wall adorned with terra-cotta vases. Thereupon M. Masseron's attention was attracted by the fact that this wall was covered, for a length of some yards, by a layer of plaster which appeared to be more recent in date than the stone.

'What did it mean?' said M. Masseron. 'I had to presuppose some motive. I therefore had this layer of plaster demolished; and underneath it I found a second layer, not so thick as the first and mingled with the rough stone. Come closer . . . or, rather, no, stand back a little way: you can see better like that.'

The second layer really served only to keep in place some small white pebbles, which constituted a sort of mosaic set in black pebbles and formed a series of large, written letters, spelling three words. And these three words once again were:

Patrice and Coralie

'What do you say to that?' asked M. Masseron. 'Observe that the inscription goes several years back, at least ten years, when we consider the condition of the ivy clinging to this part of the wall.'

'At least ten years,' Patrice repeated, when he was once more alone with Coralie. 'Ten years ago was when you were not married, when you were still at Salonica and when nobody used to come to this garden . . . nobody except Siméon and such people as he chose to admit. And among these,' he concluded, 'was our unknown friend who is now dead. And Siméon knows the truth, Coralie.'

They saw old Siméon, late that afternoon, as they had seen him constantly since the tragedy, wandering in the garden or along the passages of the house, restless and distraught, with his comforter always wound round his head and his spectacles on his nose, stammering words which no one could understand. At night, his neighbor, one of the maimed soldiers, would often hear him humming to himself.

Patrice twice tried to make him speak. He shook his head and did not answer, or else laughed like an idiot.

The problem was becoming complicated; and nothing pointed to a possible solution. Who was it that, since their childhood, had promised them to each other as a pair betrothed long beforehand by an inflexible ordinance? Who was it that arranged the pansy-bed last autumn, when they did not know each other? And who was it that had written their two names, ten years ago, in white pebbles, within the thickness of a wall?

These were haunting questions for two young people in whom love had awakened quite spontaneously and who suddenly saw stretching behind them a long past common to them both. Each step that they took in the garden seemed to them a pilgrimage amid forgotten memories; and, at every turn in a path, they were prepared to discover some new proof of the bond that linked them together unknown to themselves.

As a matter of fact, during those few days, they saw their initials interlaced twice on the trunk of a tree, once on the back of a bench. And twice again their names appeared inscribed on old walls and concealed behind a layer of plaster overhung with ivy.

On these two occasions their names were accompanied by two separate dates.

Patrice and Coralie, 1904
Patrice and Coralie, 1907

'Eleven years ago and eight years ago,' said the officer. 'And always our two names: Patrice and Coralie.'

Their hands met and clasped each other. The great mystery of their past brought them as closely together as did the great love which filled them and of which they refrained from speaking.

In spite of themselves, however, they sought out solitude; and it was in this way that, a fortnight after the murder of Essarès Bey, as they passed the little door opening on the lane, they decided to go out by it and to stroll down to the river bank. No one saw them, for both the approach to the door and the path leading to it were hidden by a screen of tall bushes; and M. Masseron and his men were exploring the old green-houses, which stood at the other side of the garden, and the old furnace and chimney which had been used for signaling.

But, when he was outside, Patrice stopped. Almost in front of him, in the opposite wall, was an exactly similar door. He called Coralie's attention to it, but she said: 'There is nothing astonishing about that. This wall is the boundary of another garden which at one time belonged to the one we have just left.'

'But who lives there?'

'Nobody. The little house which overlooks it and which comes before mine, in the Rue Raynouard, is always shut up.'

'Same door, same key, perhaps,' Patrice murmured, half to himself.

He inserted in the lock the rusty key, which had reached him by messenger. The lock responded.

'Well,' he said, 'the series of miracles is continuing. Will this one be in our favor?'

The vegetation had been allowed to run riot in the narrow strip of ground that faced them. However, in the middle of the exuberant grass, a well-trodden path, which looked as if it were often used, started from the door in the wall and rose obliquely to the single terrace, on which stood a dilapidated lodge with closed shutters. It was built on one floor, but was surmounted by a small lantern-shaped belvedere. It had its own entrance in the Rue Raynouard, from which it was separated by a yard and a very high wall. This entrance seemed to be barricaded with boards and posts nailed together.

They walked round the house and were surprised by the sight that awaited them on the right-hand side. The foliage had been trained into rectangular cloisters, carefully kept, with regular arcades cut in yew- and box-hedges. A miniature garden was laid out in this space, the very home of silence and tranquillity. Here also were wall-flowers and pansies and hyacinths. And four paths, coming from four corners of the cloisters, met round a central space, where stood the five columns of a small, open temple, rudely constructed of pebbles and unmortared building-stones.

Under the dome of this little temple was a tombstone and, in front of it, an old wooden praying-chair, from the bars of which hung, on the left, an ivory crucifix and, on the right, a rosary composed of amethyst beads in a gold filigree setting.

'Coralie, Coralie,' whispered Patrice, in a voice trembling with emotion, 'who can be buried here?'

They went nearer. There were bead wreaths laid in rows on the tombstone. They counted nineteen, each bearing the date of one of the last nineteen years. Pushing them aside, they read the following inscription in gilt letters worn and soiled by the rain.

HERE LIE
PATRICE AND CORALIE,
BOTH OF WHOM WERE MURDERED
ON THE 14TH OF APRIL, 1895.
REVENGE TO ME: I WILL REPAY.

Chapter 10
The Red Cord

Coralie, feeling her legs give way beneath her, had flung herself on the prie-dieu and there knelt praying fervently and wildly. She could not tell on whose behalf, for the repose of what unknown soul her prayers were offered; but her whole being was afire with fever and exaltation and the very action of praying seemed able to assuage her.

'What was your mother's name, Coralie?' Patrice whispered.

'Louise,' she replied.

'And my father's name was Armand. It cannot be either of them, therefore; and yet . . . '

Patrice also was displaying the greatest agitation. Stooping down, he examined the nineteen wreaths, renewed his inspection of the tombstone and said: 'All the same, Coralie, the coincidence is really too extraordinary. My father died in 1895.'

'And my mother died in that year too,' she said, 'though I do not know the exact date.'

'We shall find out, Coralie,' he declared. 'These things can all be verified. But meanwhile one truth becomes clear. The man who used to interlace the names of Patrice and Coralie was not thinking only of us and was not considering only the future. Perhaps he thought even more of the past, of that Coralie and Patrice whom he knew to have suffered a violent death and whom he had undertaken to avenge. Come away, Coralie. No one must suspect that we have been here.'

They went down the path and through the two doors on the lane. They were not seen coming in. Patrice at once brought Coralie indoors, urged Ya-Bon and his comrades to increase their vigilance and left the house.

He came back in the evening only to go out again early the next day; and it was not until the day after, at three o'clock in the afternoon, that he asked to be shown up to Coralie.

'Have you found out?' she asked him at once.

'I have found out a great many things which do not dispel the darkness of the present. I am almost tempted to say that they increase it. They do, however, throw a very vivid light on the past.'

'Do they explain what we saw two days ago?' she asked, anxiously.

'Listen to me, Coralie.'

He sat down opposite her and said: 'I shall not tell you all the steps that I have taken. I will merely sum up the result of those which led to some result. I went, first of all, to the Mayor of Passy's office and from there to the Servian Legation.'

'Then you persist in assuming that it was my mother?'

'Yes. I took a copy of her death-certificate, Coralie. Your mother died on the fourteenth of April, 1895.'

'Oh!' she said. 'That is the date on the tomb!'

'The very date.'

'But the name? Coralie? My father used to call her Louise.'

'Your mother's name was Louise Coralie Countess Odolavitch.'

'Oh, my mother!' she murmured. 'My poor darling mother! Then it was she who was murdered. It was for her that I was praying over the way?'

'For her, Coralie, and for my father. I discovered his full name at the mayor's office in the Rue Drouot. My father was Armand Patrice Belval. He died on the fourteenth of April, 1895.'

Patrice was right in saying that a singular light had been thrown upon the past. He had now positively established that the inscription on the tombstone related to his father and Coralie's mother, both of whom were murdered on the same day. But by whom and for what reason, in consequence of what tragedies? This was what Coralie asked him to tell her.

'I cannot answer your questions yet,' he replied. 'But I addressed another to myself, one more easily solved; and that I did solve. This also makes us certain of an essential point. I wanted to know to whom the lodge belonged. The outside, in the Rue Raynouard, affords no clue. You have seen the wall and the door of the yard: they show nothing in particular. But the number of the property was sufficient for my purpose. I went to the local receiver and learnt that the taxes were paid by a notary in the Avenue de l'Opéra. I called on this notary, who told me . . .'

He stopped for a moment and then said: 'The lodge was bought twenty-one years ago by my father. Two years later my father died; and the lodge, which of course formed part of his estate, was put up for sale by the present notary's predecessor and bought by one Siméon Diodokis, a Greek subject.'

'It's he!' cried Coralie. 'Siméon's name is Diodokis.'

'Well, Siméon Diodokis,' Patrice continued, 'was a friend of my father's, because my father appointed him the sole executor of his will and because it was Siméon Diodokis who, through the notary in question and a London solicitor, paid my school-fees and, when I attained my majority, made over to me the sum of two hundred thousand francs, the balance of my inheritance.'

They maintained a long silence. Many things were becoming manifest, but indistinctly, as yet, and shaded, like things seen in the evening mist. And one thing stood in sharper outline than the rest, for Patrice murmured: 'Your mother and my father loved each other, Coralie.'

The thought united them more closely and affected them profoundly. Their love was the counterpart of another love, bruised by trials, like theirs, but still more tragic and ending in bloodshed and death.

'Your mother and my father loved each other,' he repeated. 'I should say they must have belonged to that class of rather enthusiastic lovers whose passion indulges in charming little childish ways, for they had a trick of calling each other, when alone, by names which nobody else used to them; and they selected their second Christian names, which were also yours and mine. One day your mother dropped her amethyst rosary. The largest of the beads broke in two pieces. My father had one of the pieces mounted as a trinket which he hung on his watch-chain. Both were widowed. You were two years old and I was eight. In order to devote himself altogether to the woman he loved, my father sent me to England and bought the lodge in which your mother, who lived in the big house next door, used to go and see him, crossing the lane and using the same key for both doors. It was no doubt in this lodge, or in the garden round it, that they were murdered. We shall find that out, because there must be visible proofs of the murder, proofs which Siméon Diodokis discovered, since he was not afraid to say so in the inscription on the tombstone.'

'And who was the murderer?' Coralie asked, under her breath.

'You suspect it, Coralie, as I do. The hated name comes to your mind, even though we have no grounds for speaking with certainty.'

'Essarès!' she cried, in anguish.

'Most probably.'

She hid her face in her hands.

'No, no, it is impossible. It is impossible that I should have been the wife of the man who killed my mother.'

'You bore his name, but you were never his wife. You told him so the evening before his death, in my presence. Let us say nothing that we are unable to say positively; but all the same let us remember that he was your evil genius. Remember also that Siméon, my father's friend and executor, the man who bought the lovers' lodge, the man who swore upon their tomb to avenge them: remember that Siméon, a few months after your mother's death, persuaded Essarès to engage him as caretaker of the estate, became his secretary and gradually made his way into Essarès' life. His only object must have been to carry out a plan of revenge.'

'There has been no revenge.'

'What do we know about it? Do we know how Essarès met his death? Certainly it was not Siméon who killed him, as Siméon was at the hospital. But he may have caused him to be killed. And revenge has a thousand ways of manifesting itself. Lastly, Siméon was most likely obeying instructions that came from my father. There is little doubt that he wanted first to achieve an aim which my father and your mother had at heart: the union of our destinies, Coralie. And it was this aim that ruled his life. It was he evidently who placed among the knick-knacks which I collected as a child this amethyst of which the other half formed a bead in your rosary. It was he who collected our photographs. He lastly was our unknown friend and protector, the one who sent me the key, accompanied by a letter which I never received, unfortunately.'

'Then, Patrice, you no longer believe that he is dead, this unknown friend, or that you heard his dying cries?'

'I cannot say. Siméon was not necessarily acting alone. He may have had a confidant, an assistant in the work which he undertook. Perhaps it was this other man who died at nineteen minutes past seven. I cannot say. Everything that happened on that ill-fated morning remains involved in the deepest mystery. The only conviction that we are able to hold is that for twenty years Siméon Diodokis has worked unobtrusively and patiently on our behalf, doing his utmost to defeat the murderer, and that Siméon Diodokis is alive. Alive, but mad!' Patrice added. 'So that we can neither thank him nor question him about the grim story which he knows or about the dangers that threaten you.'

* * *

Patrice resolved once more to make the attempt, though he felt sure of a fresh disappointment. Siméon had a bedroom, next to that occupied by two of the wounded soldiers, in the wing which formerly contained the servants' quarters. Here Patrice found him.

He was sitting half-asleep in a chair turned towards the garden. His pipe was in his mouth; he had allowed it to go out. The room was small, sparsely furnished, but clean and light. Hidden from view, the best part of the old man's life was spent here. M. Masseron had often visited the room, in Siméon's absence, and so had Patrice, each from his own point of view.

The only discovery worthy of note consisted of a crude diagram in pencil, on the white wall-paper behind a chest of drawers: three lines intersecting to form a large equilateral triangle. In the middle of this geometrical figure were three words clumsily inscribed in adhesive gold-leaf.

The Golden Triangle

There was nothing more, not another clue of any kind, to further M. Masseron's search.

Patrice walked straight up to the old man and tapped him on the shoulder.

'Siméon!' he said.

The other lifted his yellow spectacles to him, and Patrice felt a sudden wish to snatch away this glass obstacle which concealed the old fellow's eyes and prevented him from looking into his soul and his distant memories. Siméon began to laugh foolishly.

'So this,' thought Patrice, 'is my friend and my father's friend. He loved my father, respected his wishes, was faithful to his memory, raised a tomb to him, prayed on it and swore to avenge him. And now his mind has gone.'

Patrice felt that speech was useless. But, though the sound of his voice roused no echo in that wandering brain, it was possible that the eyes were susceptible to a reminder. He wrote on a clean sheet of paper the words that Siméon had gazed upon so often.

Patrice and Coralie
14 April, 1895

The old man looked, shook his head and repeated his melancholy, foolish chuckle.

The officer added a new line.

Armand Belval

The old man displayed the same torpor. Patrice continued the test. He wrote down the names of Essarès Bey and Colonel Fakhi. He drew a triangle. The old man failed to understand and went on chuckling.

But suddenly his laughter lost some of its childishness. Patrice had written the name of Bournef, the accomplice, and this time the old secretary appeared to be stirred by a recollection. He tried to get up, fell back in his chair, then rose to his feet again and took his hat from a peg on the wall.

He left his room and, followed by Patrice, marched out of the house and turned to the left, in the direction of Auteuil. He moved like a man in a trance who is hypnotized into walking without knowing where he is going. He led the way along the Rue de Boulainvilliers, crossed the Seine and turned down the Quai de Grenelle with an unhesitating step. Then, when he reached the boulevard, he stopped, putting out his arm, made a sign to Patrice to do likewise. A kiosk hid them from view. He put his head round it. Patrice followed his example.

Opposite, at the corner of the boulevard and a side-street, was a café, with a portion of the pavement in front of it marked out by dwarf shrubs in tubs. Behind these tubs four men sat drinking. Three of them had their backs turned to Patrice. He saw the only one that faced him, and he at once recognized Bournef.

By this time Siméon was some distance away, like a man whose part is played and who leaves it to others to complete the work. Patrice looked round, caught sight of a post-office and went in briskly. He knew that M. Masseron was at the Rue Raynouard. He telephoned and told him where Bournef was. M. Masseron replied that he would come at once.

Since the murder of Essarès Bey, M. Masseron's enquiry had made no progress in so far as Colonel Fakhi's four accomplices were concerned. True, they discovered the man Grégoire's sanctuary and the bedrooms with the wall-cupboards; but the whole place was empty. The accomplices had disappeared.

'Old Siméon,' said Patrice to himself, 'was acquainted with their habits. He must have known that they were accustomed to meet at this café on a certain day of the week, at a fixed hour, and he suddenly remembered it all at the sight of Bournef's name.'

A few minutes later M. Masseron alighted from his car with his men. The business did not take long. The open front of the café was surrounded. The accomplices offered no resistance. M. Masseron sent three of them under a strong guard to the Dépôt and hustled Bournef into a private room.

'Come along,' he said to Patrice. 'We'll question him.'

'Mme Essarès is alone at the house,' Patrice objected.

'Alone? No. There are all your soldier-men.'

'Yes, but I would rather go back, if you don't mind. It's the first time that I've left her and I'm justified in feeling anxious.'

'It's only a matter of a few minutes,' M. Masseron insisted. 'One should always take advantage of the fluster caused by the arrest.'

Patrice followed him, but they soon saw that Bournef was not one of those men who are easily put out. He simply shrugged his shoulders at their threats.

'It is no use, sir,' he said, 'to try and frighten me. I risk nothing. Shot, do you say? Nonsense! You don't shoot people in France for the least thing; and we are all four subjects of a neutral country. Tried? Sentenced? Imprisoned? Never! You forget that you have kept everything dark so far; and, when you hushed up the murder of Mustapha, of Fakhi and of Essarès, it was not done with the object of reviving the case for no valid reason. No, sir, I am quite easy. The internment-camp is the worst that can await me.'

'Then you refuse to answer?' said M. Masseron.

'Not a bit of it! I accept internment. But there are twenty different ways of treating a man in these camps, and I should like to earn your favor and, in so doing, make sure of reasonable comfort till the end of the war. But first of all, what do you know?'

'Pretty well everything.'

'That's a pity: it decreases my value. Do you know about Essarès' last night?'

'Yes, with the bargain of the four millions. What's become of the money?'

Bournef made a furious gesture.

'Taken from us! Stolen! It was a trap!'

'Who took it?'

'One Grégoire.'

'Who was he?'

'His familiar, as we have since learnt. We discovered that this Grégoire was no other than a fellow who used to serve as his chauffeur on occasion.'

'And who therefore helped him to convey the bags of gold from the bank to his house.'

'Yes. And we also think, we know . . . Look here, you may as well call it a certainty. Grégoire . . . is a woman.'

'A woman!'

'Exactly. His mistress. We have several proofs of it. But she's a trustworthy, capable woman, strong as a man and afraid of nothing.'

'Do you know her address?'

'No.'

'As to the gold: have you no clue to its whereabouts, no suspicion?'

'No. The gold is in the garden or in the house in the Rue Raynouard. We saw it being taken in every day for a week. It has not been taken out since. We kept watch every night. The bags are there.'

'No clue either to Essarès' murderer?'

'No, none.'

'Are you quite sure?'

'Why should I tell a lie?'

'Suppose it was yourself? Or one of your friends?'

'We thought that you would suspect us. Fortunately, we happen to have an alibi.'

'Easy to prove?'

'Impossible to upset.'

'We'll look into it. So you have nothing more to reveal?'

'No. But I have an idea . . . or rather a question which you will answer or not, as you please. Who betrayed us? Your reply may throw some useful light, for one person only knew of our weekly meetings here from four to five o'clock, one person only, Essarès Bey; and he himself often came here to confer with us. Essarès is dead. Then who gave us away?'

'Old Siméon.'

Bournef started with astonishment.

'What! Siméon? Siméon Diodokis?'

'Yes. Siméon Diodokis, Essarès Bey's secretary.'

'He? Oh, I'll make him pay for this, the blackguard! But no, it's impossible.'

'What makes you say that it's impossible?"

'Why, because . . . '

He stopped and thought for some time, no doubt to convince himself that there was no harm in speaking. Then he finished his sentence: 'Because old Siméon was on our side.'

'What's that you say?' exclaimed Patrice, whose turn it was to be surprised.

'I say and I swear that Siméon Diodokis was on our side. He was our man. It was he who kept us informed of Essarès Bey's shady tricks. It was he who rang us up at nine o'clock in the evening to tell us that Essarès had lit the furnace of the old hothouses and that the signal of the sparks was going to work. It was he who opened the door to us, pretending to resist, of course, and allowed us to tie him up in the porter's lodge. It was he, lastly, who paid and dismissed the men-servants.'

'But why? Why this treachery? For the sake of money?'

'No, from hatred. He bore Essarès Bey a hatred that often gave us the shudders.'

'What prompted it?'

'I don't know. Siméon keeps his own counsel. But it dated a long way back.'

'Did he know where the gold was hidden?' asked M. Masseron.

'No. And it was not for want of hunting to find out. He never knew how the bags got out the cellar, which was only a temporary hiding-place.'

'And yet they used to leave the grounds. If so, how are we to know that the same thing didn't happen this time?'

'This time we were keeping watch the whole way round outside, a thing which Siméon could not do by himself.'

Patrice now put the question: 'Can you tell us nothing more about him?'

'No, I can't. Wait, though; there was one rather curious thing. On the afternoon of the great day, I received a letter in which Siméon gave me certain particulars. In the same envelope was another letter, which had evidently got there by some incredible mistake, for it appeared to be highly important.'

'What did it say?' asked Patrice, anxiously.

'It was all about a key.'

'Don't you remember the details?'

'Here is the letter. I kept it in order to give it back to him and warn him what he had done. Here, it's certainly his writing . . . '

Patrice took the sheet of notepaper; and the first thing that he saw was his own name. The letter was addressed to him, as he anticipated.

Patrice,
You will this evening receive a key. The key opens two doors midway down a lane leading to the river: one, on the right,

is that of the garden of the woman you love; the other, on the left, that of a garden where I want you to meet me at nine o'clock in the morning on the 14th of April. She will be there also. You shall learn who I am and the object which I intend to attain. You shall both hear things about the past that will bring you still closer together.

From now until the 14th the struggle which begins tonight will be a terrible one. If anything happens to me, it is certain that the woman you love will run the greatest dangers. Watch over her, Patrice; do not leave her for an instant unprotected. But I do not intend to let anything happen to me; and you shall both know the happiness which I have been preparing for you so long.

My best love to you.

'It's not signed,' said Bournef, 'but, I repeat, it's in Siméon's hand-writing. As for the lady, she is obviously Mme Essarès.'

'But what danger can she be running?' exclaimed Patrice, uneasily. 'Essarès is dead, so there is nothing to fear.'

'I wouldn't say that. He would take some killing.'

'Whom can he have instructed to avenge him? Who would continue his work?'

'I can't say, but I should take no risks.'

Patrice waited to hear no more. He thrust the letter into M. Masseron's hand and made his escape.

'Rue Raynouard, fast as you can,' he said, springing into a taxi.

He was eager to reach his destination. The dangers of which old Siméon spoke seemed suddenly to hang over Coralie's head. Already the enemy, taking advantage of Patrice's absence, might be attacking his beloved. And who could defend her?

'If anything happens to me,' Siméon had said.

And the supposition was partly realized, since he had lost his wits.

'Come, come,' muttered Patrice, 'this is sheer idiocy . . . I am fancying things . . . There is no reason . . .'

But his mental anguish increased every minute. He reminded himself that old Siméon was still in full possession of his faculties at the time when he wrote that letter and gave the advice which it contained. He reminded himself that old Siméon had purposely informed him that the key opened the door of Coralie's garden, so that he, Patrice, might keep an effective watch by coming to her in case of need.

He saw Siméon some way ahead of him. It was growing late, and the old fellow was going home. Patrice passed him just outside the porter's lodge and heard him humming to himself.

'Any news?' Patrice asked the soldier on duty.

'No, sir.'

'Where's Little Mother Coralie?'

'She had a walk in the garden and went upstairs half an hour ago.'

'Ya-Bon?'

'Ya-Bon went up with Little Mother Coralie. He should be at her door.'

Patrice climbed the stairs, feeling a good deal calmer. But, when he came to the first floor, he was astonished to find that the electric light was not on. He turned on the switch. Then he saw, at the end of the passage, Ya-Bon on his knees outside Coralie's room, with his head leaning against the wall. The door was open.

'What are you doing there?' he shouted, running up.

Ya-Bon made no reply. Patrice saw that there was blood on the shoulder of his jacket. At that moment the Senegalese sank to the floor.

'Damn it! He's wounded! Dead perhaps.'

He leapt over the body and rushed into the room, switching on the light at once.

Coralie was lying at full length on a sofa. Round her neck was the terrible little red-silk cord. And yet Patrice did not experience that awful, numbing despair which we feel in the presence of irretrievable misfortunes. It seemed to him that Coralie's face had not the pallor of death.

He found that she was in fact breathing.

'She's not dead. She's not dead,' said Patrice to himself. 'And she's not going to die, I'm sure of it . . . nor Ya-Bon either . . . They've failed this time.'

He loosened the cords. In a few seconds Coralie heaved a deep breath and recovered consciousness. A smile lit up her eyes at the sight of him. But, suddenly remembering, she threw her arms, still so weak, around him.

'Oh, Patrice,' she said, in a trembling voice, 'I'm frightened . . . frightened for you!'

'What are you frightened of, Coralie? Who is the scoundrel?'

'I didn't see him . . . He put out the light, caught me by the throat and whispered, "You first . . . Tonight it will be your lover's turn!" . . . Oh, Patrice, I'm frightened for you! . . .'

Chapter 11

On the Brink

Patrice at once made up his mind what to do. He lifted Coralie to her bed and asked her not to move or call out. Then he made sure that Ya-Bon was not seriously wounded. Lastly, he rang violently, sounding all the bells that communicated with the posts which he had placed in different parts of the house.

The men came hurrying up.

'You're a pack of nincompoops,' he said. 'Someone's been here. Little Mother Coralie and Ya-Bon have had a narrow escape from being killed.'

They began to protest loudly.

'Silence!' he commanded. 'You deserve a good hiding, every one of you. I'll forgive you on one condition, which is that, all this evening and all tonight, you speak of Little Mother Coralie as though she were dead.'

'But whom are we to speak to, sir?' one of them objected. 'There's nobody here.'

'Yes, there is, you silly fool, since Little Mother Coralie and Ya-Bon have been attacked. Unless it was yourselves who did it! . . . It wasn't? Very well then . . . And let me have no more nonsense. It's not a question of speaking to others, but of talking among yourselves . . . and of thinking, even, without speaking. There are people listening to you, spying on you, people who hear what you say and who guess what you don't say. So, until tomorrow, Little Mother Coralie will not leave her room. You shall keep watch over her by turns. Those who are not watching will go to bed immediately after dinner. No moving about the house, do you understand? Absolute silence and quiet.'

'And old Siméon, sir?'

'Lock him up in his room. He's dangerous because he's mad. They may have taken advantage of his madness to make him open the door to them. Lock him up!'

Patrice's plan was a simple one. As the enemy, believing Coralie to be on the point of death, had revealed to her his intention, which was to kill Patrice as well, it was necessary that he should think himself free to act, with nobody to suspect his schemes or to be on his guard against him. He would enter upon the struggle and would then be caught in a trap.

Pending this struggle, for which he longed with all his might, Patrice saw to Ya-Bon's wound, which proved to be only slight, and questioned him and Coralie. Their answers tallied at all points. Coralie, feeling a little tired, was lying down reading. Ya-Bon remained in the passage, outside the open door, squatting on the floor, Arab-fashion. Neither of them heard anything suspicious. And suddenly Ya-Bon saw a shadow between himself and the light in the passage. This light, which came from an electric lamp, was put out at just about the same time as the light in the bed-room. Ya-Bon, already half-erect, felt a violent blow in the back of the neck and lost consciousness. Coralie tried to escape by the door of her boudoir, was unable to open it, began to cry out and was at once seized and thrown down. All this had happened within the space of a few seconds.

The only hint that Patrice succeeded in obtaining was that the man came not from the staircase but from the servants' wing. This had a smaller staircase of its own, communicating with the kitchen through a pantry by which the tradesmen entered from the Rue Raynouard. The door leading to the street was locked. But some-one might easily possess a key.

After dinner Patrice went in to see Coralie for a moment and then, at nine o'clock, retired to his bedroom, which was situated a little lower down, on the same side. It had been used, in Essarès Bey's lifetime, as a smoking-room.

As the attack from which he expected such good results was not likely to take place before the middle of the night, Patrice sat down at a roll-top desk standing against the wall and took out the diary in which he had begun his detailed record of recent events. He wrote on for half an hour or forty minutes and was about to close the book when he seemed to hear a vague rustle, which he would certainly not have noticed if his nerves had not been stretched to their utmost state of tension. And he remembered the day when he and Coralie had once before been shot at. This time, however, the window was not open nor even ajar.

He therefore went on writing without turning his head or doing anything to suggest that his attention had been aroused; and he set down, almost unconsciously, the actual phases of his anxiety.

'He is here. He is watching me. I wonder what he means to do. I doubt if he will smash a pane of glass and fire a bullet at me. He has tried that method before and found it uncertain and a failure. No, his plan is thought out, I expect, in a different and more intelligent fashion. He is more likely to wait for me to go to bed, when he can watch me sleeping and effect his entrance by some means which I can't guess.

'Meanwhile, it's extraordinarily exhilarating to know that his eyes are upon me. He hates me; and his hatred is coming nearer and nearer to mine, like one sword feeling its way towards another before clashing. He is watching me as a wild animal, lurking in the dark, watches its prey and selects the spot on which to fasten its fangs. But no, I am certain that it's he who is the prey, doomed beforehand to defeat and destruction. He is preparing his knife or his red-silk cord. And it's these two hands of mine that will finish the battle. They are strong and powerful and are already enjoying their victory. They will be victorious.'

*   *   *

Patrice shut down the desk, lit a cigarette and smoked it quietly, as his habit was before going to bed. Then he undressed, folded his clothes carefully over the back of a chair, wound up his watch, got into bed and switched off the light.

'At last,' he said to himself, 'I shall know the truth. I shall know who this man is. Some friend of Essarès', continuing his work? But why this hatred of Coralie? Is he in love with her, as he is trying to finish me off too? I shall know . . . I shall soon know . . . '

An hour passed, however, and another hour, during which nothing happened on the side of the window. A single creaking came from somewhere beside the desk. But this no doubt was one of those sounds of creaking furniture which we often hear in the silence of the night.

Patrice began to lose the buoyant hope that had sustained him so far. He perceived that his elaborate sham regarding Coralie's death was a poor thing after all and that a man of his enemy's stamp might well refuse to be taken in by it. Feeling rather put out, he was on the point of going to sleep, when he heard the same creaking sound at the same spot.

The need to do something made him jump out of bed. He turned on the light. Everything seemed to be as he had left it. There was no trace of a strange presence.

'Well,' said Patrice, 'one thing's certain: I'm no good. The enemy must have smelt a rat and guessed the trap I laid for him. Let's go to sleep. There will be nothing happening tonight.'

There was in fact no alarm.

Next morning, on examining the window, he observed that a stone ledge ran above the ground-floor all along the garden front of the house, wide enough for a man to walk upon by holding on to the balconies and rain-pipes. He inspected all the rooms to which the ledge gave access. None of them was old Siméon's room.

'He hasn't stirred out, I suppose?' he asked the two soldiers posted on guard.

'Don't think so, sir. In any case, we haven't unlocked the door.'

Patrice went in and, paying no attention to the old fellow, who was still sucking at his cold pipe, he searched the room, having it at the back of his mind that the enemy might take refuge there. He found nobody. But what he did discover, in a press in the wall, was a number of things which he had not seen on the occasion of his investigations in M. Masseron's company. These consisted of a rope-ladder, a coil of lead pipes, apparently gas-pipes, and a small soldering-lamp.

'This all seems devilish odd,' he said to himself. 'How did the things get in here? Did Siméon collect them without any definite object, mechanically? Or am I to assume that Siméon is merely an instrument of the enemy's? He used to know the enemy before he lost his reason; and he may be under his influence at present.'

Siméon was sitting at the window, with his back to the room. Patrice went up to him and gave a start. In his hands the old man held a funeral-wreath made of black and white beads. It bore a date, '14 April, 1915', and made the twentieth, the one which Siméon was preparing to lay on the grave of his dead friends.

'He will lay it there,' said Patrice, aloud. 'His instinct as an avenging friend, which has guided his steps through life, continues in spite of his insanity. He will lay it on the grave. That's so, Siméon, isn't it: you will take it there tomorrow? For tomorrow is the fourteenth of April, the sacred anniversary . . .'

He leant over the incomprehensible being who held the key to all the plots and counterplots, to all the treachery and benevolence that constituted the inextricable drama. Siméon thought that Patrice wanted to take the wreath from him and pressed it to his chest with a startled gesture.

'Don't be afraid,' said Patrice. 'You can keep it. Tomorrow, Siméon, tomorrow, Coralie and I will be faithful to the appointment which you gave us. And tomorrow perhaps the memory of the horrible past will unseal your brain.'

The day seemed long to Patrice, who was eager for something that would provide a glimmer in the surrounding darkness. And now this glimmer seemed about to be kindled by the arrival of this twentieth anniversary of the fourteenth of April.

At a late hour in the afternoon M. Masseron called at the Rue Raynouard.

'Look what I've just received,' he said to Patrice. 'It's rather curious: an anonymous letter in a disguised hand. Listen.

Sir, be warned. They're going away. Take care. Tomorrow evening the 1800 bags will be on their way out of the country.

A FRIEND OF FRANCE

'And tomorrow is the fourteenth of April,' said Patrice, at once connecting the two trains of thought in his mind.

'Yes. What makes you say that?'

'Nothing . . . Something that just occurred to me . . .'

He was nearly telling M. Masseron all the facts associated with the fourteenth of April and all those concerning the strange personality of old Siméon. If he did not speak, it was for obscure reasons, perhaps because he wished to work out this part of the case alone, perhaps also because of a sort of shyness which prevented him from admitting M. Masseron into all the secrets of the past. He said nothing about it, therefore, and asked: 'What do you think of the letter?'

'Upon my word, I don't know what to think. It may be a warning with something to back it, or it may be a trick to make us adopt one course of conduct rather than another. I'll talk about it to Bournef.'

'Nothing fresh on his side?'

'No; and I don't expect anything in particular. The alibi which he has submitted is genuine. His friends and he are so many supers. Their parts are played.'

The coincidence of dates was all that stuck in Patrice's mind. The two roads which M. Masseron and he were following suddenly met on this day so long since marked out by fate. The past and the present were about to unite. The catastrophe was at hand. The fourteenth of April was the day on which the gold was to disappear for good and also the day on which an unknown voice had summoned Patrice and

CHAPTER ELEVEN: ON THE BRINK

Coralie to the same tryst which his father and her mother had kept
twenty years ago.

And the next day was the fourteenth of April.

*   *   *

At nine o'clock in the morning Patrice asked after old Siméon.

'Gone out, sir. You had countermanded your orders.'

Patrice entered the room and looked for the wreath. It was not
there. Moreover, the three things in the cupboard, the rope-ladder,
the coil of lead and the glazier's lamp, were not there either.

'Did Siméon take anything with him?'

'Yes, sir, a wreath.'

'Nothing else?'

'No, sir.'

The window was open. Patrice came to the conclusion that the
things had gone by this way, thus confirming his theory that the old
fellow was an unconscious confederate.

Shortly before ten o'clock Coralie joined him in the garden. Patrice had told her the latest events. She looked pale and anxious.

They went round the lawns and, without being seen, reached the
clumps of dwarf shrubs which hid the door on the lane. Patrice
opened the door. As he started to open the other his hand hesitated.
He felt sorry that he had not told M. Masseron and that he and
Coralie were performing by themselves a pilgrimage which certain
signs warned him to be dangerous. He shook off the obsession,
however. He had two revolvers with him. What had he to fear?

'You're coming in, aren't you, Coralie?'

'Yes,' she said.

'I somehow thought you seemed undecided, anxious . . .'

'It's quite true,' said Coralie. 'I feel a sort of hollowness.'

'Why? Are you afraid?'

'No. Or rather yes. I'm not afraid for today, but in some way for
the past. I think of my poor mother, who went through this door,
as I am doing, one April morning. She was perfectly happy, she
was going to meet her love . . . And then I feel as if I wanted to
hold her back and cry, "Don't go on . . . Death is lying in wait for
you . . . Don't go on . . ." And it's I who hear those words of terror,
they ring in my ears; it's I who hear them and I dare not go on.
I'm afraid.'

'Let's go back, Coralie.'

She only took his arm.

'No,' she said, in a firm voice. 'We'll walk on. I want to pray. It will do me good.'

Boldly she stepped along the little slanting path which her mother had followed and climbed the slope amid the tangled weeds and the straggling branches. They passed the lodge on their left and reached the leafy cloisters where each had a parent lying buried. And at once, at the first glance, they saw that the twentieth wreath was there.

'Siméon has come,' said Patrice. 'An all-powerful instinct obliged him to come. He must be somewhere near.'

While Coralie knelt down beside the tombstone, he hunted around the cloisters and went as far as the middle of the garden. There was nothing left but to go to the lodge, and this was evidently a dread act which they put off performing, if not from fear, at least from the reverent awe which checks a man on entering a place of death and crime.

It was Coralie once again who gave the signal for action.

'Come,' she said.

Patrice did not know how they would make their way into the lodge, for all its doors and windows had appeared to them to be shut. But, as they approached, they saw that the back-door opening on the yard was wide open, and they at once thought that Siméon was waiting for them inside.

It was exactly ten o'clock when they crossed the threshold of the lodge. A little hall led to a kitchen on one side and a bedroom on the other. The principal room must be that opposite. The door stood ajar.

'That's where it must have happened . . . long ago,' said Coralie, in a frightened whisper.

'Yes,' said Patrice, 'we shall find Siméon there. But, if your courage fails you, Coralie, we had better give it up.'

An unquestioning force of will supported her. Nothing now would have induced her to stop. She walked on.

Though large, the room gave an impression of coziness, owing to the way in which it was furnished. The sofas, armchairs, carpet and hangings all tended to add to its comfort; and its appearance might well have remained unchanged since the tragic death of the two who used to occupy it. This appearance was rather that of a studio, because of a skylight which filled the middle of the high ceiling, where the belvedere was. The light came from here. There were two other windows, but these were hidden by curtains.

'Siméon is not here,' said Patrice.

Coralie did not reply. She was examining the things around her with an emotion which was reflected in every feature. There were books, all of them going back to the last century. Some of them were signed 'Coralie' in pencil on their blue or yellow wrappers. There were pieces of unfinished needlework, an embroidery-frame, a piece of tapestry with a needle hanging to it by a thread of wool. And there were also books signed 'Patrice' and a box of cigars and a blotting-pad and an inkstand and penholders. And there were two small framed photographs, those of two children, Patrice and Coralie. And thus the life of long ago went on, not only the life of two lovers who loved each other with a violent and fleeting passion, but of two beings who dwell together in the calm assurance of a long existence spent in common.

'Oh, my darling, darling mother!' Coralie whispered.

Her emotion increased with each new memory. She leant trembling on Patrice's shoulder.

'Let's go,' he said.

'Yes, dear, yes, we had better. We will come back again . . . We will come back to them . . . We will revive the life of love that was cut short by their death. Let us go for today; I have no strength left.'

But they had taken only a few steps when they stopped dismayed.

The door was closed.

Their eyes met, filled with uneasiness.

'We didn't close it, did we?' he asked.

'No,' she said, 'we didn't close it.'

He went to open it and perceived that it had neither handle nor lock.

It was a single door, of massive wood that looked hard and substantial. It might well have been made of one piece, taken from the very heart of an oak. There was no paint or varnish on it. Here and there were scratches, as if someone had been rapping at it with a tool. And then . . . and then, on the right, were these few words in pencil.

Patrice and Coralie, 14 April, 1895
God will avenge us

Below this was a cross and, below the cross, another date, but in a different and more recent handwriting.

14 April, 1915

'This is terrible, this is terrible,' said Patrice. 'Today's date! Who can have written that? It has only just been written. Oh, it's terrible! . . . Come, come, after all, we can't . . . '

He rushed to one of the windows, tore back the curtain that veiled it and pulled upon the casement. A cry escaped him. The window was walled up, walled up with building-stones that filled the space between the glass and the shutters.

He ran to the other window and found the same obstacle.

There were two doors, leading probably to the bedroom on the right and to a room next to the kitchen on the left. He opened them quickly. Both doors were walled up.

He ran in every direction, during the first moment of terror, and then hurled himself against the first of the three doors and tried to break it down. It did not move. It might have been an immovable block.

Then, once again, they looked at each other with eyes of fear; and the same terrible thought came over them both. The thing that had happened before was being repeated! The tragedy was being played a second time. After the mother and the father, it was the turn of the daughter and the son. Like the lovers of yesteryear, those of today were prisoners. The enemy held them in his powerful grip; and they would doubtless soon know how their parents had died by seeing how they themselves would die . . . 14 April, 1895 . . . 14 April, 1915 . . .

Chapter 12

In the Abyss

'No, no, no!' cried Patrice. 'I won't stand this!'

He flung himself against the windows and doors, took up an iron dog from the fender and banged it against the wooden doors and the stone walls. Barren efforts! They were the same which his father had made before him; and they could only result in the same mockery of impotent scratches on the wood and the stone.

'Oh, Coralie, Coralie!' he cried in his despair. 'It's I who have brought you to this! What an abyss I've dragged you into! It was madness to try to fight this out by myself! I ought to have called in those who understand, who are accustomed to it! . . . No, I was going to be so clever! . . . Forgive me, Coralie.'

She had sunk into a chair. He, almost on his knees beside her, threw his arms around her, imploring her pardon.

She smiled, to calm him.

'Come, dear,' she said, gently, 'don't lose courage. Perhaps we are mistaken . . . After all, there's nothing to show that it is not all an accident.'

'The date!' he said. 'The date of this year, of this day, written in another hand! It was your mother and my father who wrote the first . . . but this one, Coralie, this one proves premeditation, and an implacable determination to do away with us.'

She shuddered. Still she persisted in trying to comfort him.

'It may be. But yet it is not so bad as all that. We have enemies, but we have friends also. They will look for us.'

'They will look for us, but how can they ever find us, Coralie? We took steps to prevent them from guessing where we were going; and not one of them knows this house.'

'Old Siméon does.'

'Siméon came and placed his wreath, but someone else came with him, someone who rules him and who has perhaps already got rid of him, now that Siméon has played his part.'

'And what then, Patrice?'

He felt that she was overcome and began to be ashamed of his own weakness.

'Well,' he said, mastering himself, 'we must just wait. After all, the attack may not materialize. The fact of our being locked in does not mean that we are lost. And, even so, we shall make a fight for it, shall we not? You need not think that I am at the end of my strength or my resources. Let us wait, Coralie, and act.'

The main thing was to find out whether there was any entrance to the house which could allow of an unforeseen attack. After an hour's search they took up the carpet and found tiles which showed nothing unusual. There was certainly nothing except the door, and, as they could not prevent this from being opened, since it opened outwards, they heaped up most of the furniture in front of it, thus forming a barricade which would protect them against a surprise.

Then Patrice cocked his two revolvers and placed them beside him, in full sight.

'This will make us easy in our minds,' he said. 'Any enemy who appears is a dead man.'

But the memory of the past bore down upon them with all its awful weight. All their words and all their actions others before them had spoken and performed, under similar conditions, with the same thoughts and the same forebodings. Patrice's father must have prepared his weapons. Coralie's mother must have folded her hands and prayed. Together they had barricaded the door and together sounded the walls and taken up the carpet. What an anguish was this, doubled as it was by a like anguish!

To dispel the horror of the idea, they turned the pages of the books, works of fiction and others, which their parents had read. On certain pages, at the end of a chapter or volume, were lines constituting notes which Patrice's father and Coralie's mother used to write each other.

Darling Patrice,
I ran in this morning to recreate our life of yesterday and to dream of our life this afternoon. As you will arrive before me, you will read these lines. You will read that I love you . . .

And, in another book.

My own Coralie,
You have this minute gone; I shall not see you until tomorrow and I do not want to leave this haven where our love has tasted such delights without once more telling you . . . '

They looked through most of the books in this way, finding, however, instead of the clues for which they hoped, nothing but expressions of love and affection. And they spent more than two hours waiting and dreading what might happen.

'There will be nothing,' said Patrice. 'And perhaps that is the most awful part of it, for, if nothing occurs, it will mean that we are doomed not to leave this room. And, in that case . . . '

Patrice did not finish the sentence. Coralie understood. And together they received a vision of the death by starvation that seemed to threaten them. But Patrice exclaimed: 'No, no, we have not that to fear. No. For people of our age to die of hunger takes several days, three or four days or more. And we shall be rescued before then.'

'How?' asked Coralie.

'How? Why, by our soldiers, by Ya-Bon, by M. Masseron! They will be uneasy if we do not come home tonight.'

'You yourself said, Patrice, that they cannot know where we are.'

'They'll find out. It's quite simple. There is only the lane between the two gardens. Besides, everything we do is set down in my diary, which is in the desk in my room. Ya-Bon knows of its existence. He is bound to speak of it to M. Masseron. And then . . . and then there is Siméon. What will have become of him? Surely they will notice his movements? And won't he give a warning of some kind?'

But words were powerless to comfort them. If they were not to die of hunger, then the enemy must have contrived another form of torture. Their inability to do anything kept them on the rack. Patrice began his investigations again. A curious accident turned them in a new direction. On opening one of the books through which they had not yet looked, a book published in 1895, Patrice saw two pages turned down together. He separated them and read a letter addressed to him by his father.

Patrice, my dear Son,
If ever chance places this note before your eyes, it will prove that I have met with a violent death which has prevented my destroying it. In that case, Patrice, look for the truth concerning my death on the wall of the studio, between the two windows. I shall perhaps have time to write it down.

The two victims had therefore at that time foreseen the tragic fate in store for them; and Patrice's father and Coralie's mother knew the danger which they ran in coming to the lodge. It remained to be seen whether Patrice's father had been able to carry out his intention.

Between the two windows, as all around the room, was a wainscoting of varnished wood, topped at a height of six feet by a cornice. Above the cornice was the plain plastered wall. Patrice and Coralie had already observed, without paying particular attention to it, that the wainscoting seemed to have been renewed in this part, because the varnish of the boards did not have the same uniform color. Using one of the iron dogs as a chisel, Patrice broke down the cornice and lifted the first board. It broke easily. Under this plank, on the plaster of the wall, were lines of writing.

'It's the same method,' he said, 'as that which old Siméon has since employed. First write on the walls, then cover it up with wood or plaster.'

He broke off the top of the other boards and in this way brought several complete lines into view, hurried lines, written in pencil and slightly worn by time. Patrice deciphered them with the greatest emotion. His father had written them at a moment when death was stalking at hand. A few hours later he had ceased to live. They were the evidence of his death-agony and perhaps too an imprecation against the enemy who was killing him and the woman he loved.

Patrice read, in an undertone:

I am writing this in order that the scoundrel's plot may not be achieved to the end and in order to ensure his punishment. Coralie and I are no doubt going to perish, but at least we shall not die without revealing the cause of our death.

A few days ago, he said to Coralie, 'You spurn my love, you load me with your hatred. So be it. But I shall kill you both, your lover and you, in such a manner that I can never be accused of the death, which will look like suicide. Everything is ready. Beware, Coralie.'

Everything was, in fact, ready. He did not know me, but he must have known that Coralie used to meet somebody here daily; and it was in this lodge that he prepared our tomb.

What manner of death ours will be we do not know. Lack of food, no doubt. It is four hours since we were imprisoned. The door closed upon us, a heavy door which he must have placed there last night. All the other openings, doors and windows alike, are stopped up with blocks of stone laid and cemented since our last meeting. Escape is impossible. What is to become of us?

The uncovered portion stopped here. Patrice said: 'You see, Coralie, they went through the same horrors as ourselves. They too dreaded starvation. They too passed through long hours of waiting, when inaction is so painful; and it was more or less to distract their thoughts that they wrote those lines.'

He went on, after examining the spot: 'They counted, most likely, on what happened, that the man who was killing them would not read this document. Look, one long curtain was hung over these two windows and the wall between them, one curtain, as is proved by the single rod covering the whole distance. After our parents' death no one thought of drawing it, and the truth remained concealed until the day when Siméon discovered it and, by way of precaution, hid it again under a wooden panel and hung up two curtains in the place of one. In this way everything seemed normal.'

Patrice set to work again. A few more lines made their appearance.

Oh, if I were the only one to suffer, the only one to die! But the horror of it all is that I am dragging my dear Coralie with me. She fainted and is lying down now, prostrate by the fears which she tries so hard to overcome. My poor darling! I seem already to see the pallor of death on her sweet face. Forgive me, dearest, forgive me!

Patrice and Coralie exchanged glances. Here were the same sentiments which they themselves felt, the same scruples, the same delicacy, the same effacement of self in the presence of the other's grief.

'He loved your mother,' Patrice murmured, 'as I love you. I also am not afraid of death. I have faced it too often, with a smile! But you, Coralie, you, for whose sake I would undergo any sort of torture . . . !'

He began to walk up and down, once more yielding to his anger.

'I shall save you, Coralie, I swear it. And what a delight it will then be to take our revenge! He shall have the same fate which he was devising for us. Do you understand, Coralie? He shall die here, here in this room. Oh, how my hatred will spur me to bring that about!'

He tore down more pieces of boarding, in the hope of learning something that might be useful to him, since the struggle was being renewed under exactly similar conditions. But the sentences that followed, like those which Patrice had just uttered, were oaths of vengeance.

Coralie, he shall be punished, if not by us, then by the hand of God. No, his infernal scheme will not succeed. No, it will never be believed that we had recourse to suicide to relieve ourselves of an existence that was built up of happiness and joy.

No, his crime will be known. Hour by hour I shall here set down the undeniable proofs . . .

'Words, words!' cried Patrice, in a tone of exasperation. 'Words of vengeance and sorrow, but never a fact to guide us. Father, will you tell us nothing to save your Coralie's daughter? If your Coralie succumbed, let mine escape the disaster, thanks to your aid, father! Help me! Counsel me!'

But the father answered the son with nothing but more words of challenge and despair.

Who can rescue us? We are walled up in this tomb, buried alive and condemned to torture without being able to defend ourselves. My revolver lies there, upon the table. What is the use of it? The enemy does not attack us. He has time on his side, unrelenting time which kills of its own strength, by the mere fact that it is time. Who can rescue us? Who will save my darling Coralie?

The position was terrible, and they felt all its tragic horror. It seemed to them as though they were already dead, once they were enduring the same trial endured by others and that they were still enduring it under the same conditions. There was nothing to enable them to escape any of the phases through which the other two, his father and her mother, had passed. The similarity between their own and their parents' fate was so striking that they seemed to be suffering two deaths, and the second agony was now commencing.

Coralie gave way and began to cry. Moved by her tears, Patrice attacked the wainscoting with new fury, but its boards, strengthened by cross-laths, resisted his efforts.

At last he read.

What is happening? We had an impression that someone was walking outside, in the garden. Yes, when we put our ears to the stone wall built in the embrasure of the window, we thought we heard footsteps. Is it possible? Oh, if it only were! It would mean the struggle, at last. Anything rather than the maddening silence and endless uncertainty!

That's it! . . . That's it! . . . The sound is becoming more distinct . . . It is a different sound, like that which you make when you dig the ground with a pick-axe. Someone is digging the ground, not in front of the house, but on the right, near the kitchen . . .

Patrice redoubled his efforts. Coralie came and helped him. This time he felt that a corner of the veil was being lifted. The writing went on.

Another hour, with alternate spells of sound and silence: the same sound of digging and the same silence which suggests work that is being continued.

And then someone entered the hall, one person; he, evidently. We recognized his step . . . He walks without attempting to deaden it . . . Then he went to the kitchen, where he worked the same way as before, with a pick-axe, but on the stones this time. We also heard the noise of a pane of glass breaking.

And now he has gone outside again and there is a new sort of sound, against the house, a sound that seems to travel up the house as though the wretch had to climb to a height in order to carry out his plan . . .

Patrice stopped reading and looked at Coralie. Both of them were listening.

'Hark!' he said, in a low voice.

'Yes, yes,' she answered, 'I hear . . . Steps outside the house . . . in the garden . . .'

They went to one of the windows, where they had left the casement open behind the wall of building-stones, and listened. There was really someone walking; and the knowledge that the enemy was approaching gave them the same sense of relief that their parents had experienced.

Someone walked thrice round the house. But they did not, like their parents, recognize the sound of the footsteps. They were those of a stranger, or else steps that had changed their tread. Then, for a few minutes, they heard nothing more. And suddenly another sound arose; and, though in their innermost selves they were expecting it, they were nevertheless stupefied at hearing it. And Patrice, in a hollow voice, laying stress upon each syllable, uttered the sentence which his father had written twenty years before.

'It's the sound which you make when you dig the ground with a pick-axe.'

Yes, it must be that. Someone was digging the ground, not in front of the house, but on the right, near the kitchen.

And so the abominable miracle of the revived tragedy was continuing. Here again the former act was repeated, a simple enough act in itself, but one which became sinister because it was one of those which had already been performed and because it was announcing and preparing the death once before announced and prepared.

An hour passed. The work went on, paused and went on again. It was like the sound of a spade at work in a courtyard, when the grave-digger is in no hurry and takes a rest and then resumes his work.

Patrice and Coralie stood listening side by side, their eyes in each other's eyes, their hands in each other's hands.

'He's stopping,' whispered Patrice.

'Yes,' said Coralie; 'only I think . . . '

'Yes, Coralie, there's someone in the hall . . . Oh, we need not trouble to listen! We have only to remember. There: "He goes to the kitchen and digs as he did just now, but on the stones this time." . . . And then . . . and then . . . oh, Coralie, the same sound of broken glass!'

It was memories mingling with the gruesome reality. The present and the past formed but one. They foresaw events at the very instant when these took place.

The enemy went outside again; and, forthwith, the sound seemed 'to travel up the house as though the wretch had to climb to a height in order to carry out his plans.'

And then . . . and then what would happen next? They no longer thought of consulting the inscription on the wall, or perhaps they did not dare. Their attention was concentrated on the invisible and sometimes imperceptible deeds that were being accomplished against them outside, an uninterrupted stealthy effort, a mysterious twenty-year-old plan whereof each slightest detail was settled as by clockwork!

The enemy entered the house and they heard a rustling at the bottom of the door, a rustling of soft things apparently being heaped or pushed against the wood. Next came other vague noises in the two adjoining rooms, against the walled doors, and similar noises out-side, between the stones of the windows and the open shutters. And then they heard someone on the roof.

They raised their eyes. This time they felt certain that the last act was at hand, or at least one of the scenes of the last act. The roof to them was the framed skylight which occupied the center of the ceiling and admitted the only daylight that entered the room. And still the same agonizing question rose to their minds: what was going to happen? Would the enemy show his face outside the skylight and reveal himself at last?

This work on the roof continued for a considerable time. Footsteps shook the zinc sheets that covered it, moving between the right-hand side of the house and the edge of the skylight. And suddenly this skylight, or rather a part of it, a square containing four panes, was lifted, a very little way, by a hand which inserted a stick to keep it open.

And the enemy again walked across the roof and went down the side of the house.

They were almost disappointed and felt such a craving to know the truth that Patrice once more fell to breaking the boards of the wainscoting, removing the last pieces, which covered the end of the inscription. And what they read made them live the last few minutes all over again. The enemy's return, the rustle against the walls and the walled windows, the noise on the roof, the opening of the skylight, the method of supporting it: all this had happened in the same order and, so to speak, within the same limit of time. Patrice's father and Coralie's mother had undergone the same impressions. Destiny seemed bent on following the same paths and making the same movements in seeking the same object.

And the writing went on.

He is going up again, he is going up again . . . There's his footsteps on the roof . . . He is near the skylight . . . Will he look through? . . . Shall we see his hated face? . . .

'He is going up again, he is going up again,' gasped Coralie, nestling against Patrice.

The enemy's footsteps were pounding over the zinc.

'Yes,' said Patrice, 'he is going up as before, without departing from the procedure followed by the other. Only we do not know whose face will appear to us. Our parents knew their enemy.'

She shuddered at her image of the man who had killed her mother; and she asked: 'It was he, was it not?'

'Yes, it was he. There is his name, written by my father.'

Patrice had almost entirely uncovered the inscription. Bending low, he pointed with his finger.

'Look. Read the name: Essarès. You can see it down there: it was one of the last words my father wrote.'

And Coralie read.

The skylight rose higher, a hand lifted it and we saw . . . we saw, laughing as he looked down on us – oh, the scoundrel –

Essarès! . . . Essarès! . . . And then he passed something through the opening, something that came down, that unrolled itself in the middle of the room, over our heads: a ladder, a rope-ladder.

We did not understand. It was swinging in front of us. And then, in the end, I saw a sheet of paper rolled round the bottom rung and pinned to it. On the paper, in Essarès' handwriting, are the words, 'Send Coralie up by herself. Her life shall be saved. I give her ten minutes to accept. If not . . . '

'Ah,' said Patrice, rising from his stooping posture, 'will this also be repeated? What about the ladder, the rope-ladder, which I found in old Siméon's cupboard?'

Coralie kept her eyes fixed on the skylight, for the footsteps were moving around it. Then they stopped. Patrice and Coralie had not a doubt that the moment had come and that they also were about to see their enemy. And Patrice said huskily, in a choking voice: 'Who will it be? There are three men who could have played this sinister part as it was played before. Two are dead, Essarès and my father. And Siméon, the third, is mad. Is it he, in his madness, who has set the machine working again? But how are we to imagine that he could have done it with such precision? No, no, it is the other one, the one who directs him and who till now has remained in the background.'

He felt Coralie's fingers clutching his arm.

'Hush,' she said, 'here he is!'

'No, no.'

'Yes, I'm sure of it.'

Her imagination had foretold what was preparing; and in fact, as once before, the skylight was raised higher. A hand lifted it. And suddenly they saw a head slipping under the open framework.

It was the head of old Siméon.

'The madman!' Patrice whispered, in dismay. 'The madman!'

'But perhaps he isn't mad,' she said. 'He can't be mad.'

She could not check the trembling that shook her.

The man overhead looked down upon them, hidden behind his spectacles, which allowed no expression of satisfied hatred or joy to show on his impassive features.

'Coralie,' said Patrice, in a low voice, 'do what I say . . . Come . . . '

He pushed her gently along, as though he were supporting her and leading her to a chair. In reality he had but one thought, to reach the table on which he had placed his revolvers, take one of them and fire.

Siméon remained motionless, like some evil genius come to unloose the tempest . . . Coralie could not rid herself of that glance which weighted upon her.

'No,' she murmured, resisting Patrice, as though she feared that his intention would precipitate the dreaded catastrophe, 'no, you mustn't . . . '

But Patrice, displaying greater determination, was near his object. One more effort and his hand would hold the revolver.

He quickly made up his mind, took rapid aim and fired a shot.

The head disappeared from sight.

'Oh,' said Coralie, 'you were wrong, Patrice! He will take his revenge on us . . . '

'No, perhaps not,' said Patrice, still holding his revolver. 'I may very well have hit him. The bullet struck the frame of the skylight. But it may have glanced off, in which case . . . '

They waited hand in hand, with a gleam of hope, which did not last long, however.

The noise on the roof began again. And then, as before – and this they really had the impression of not seeing for the first time – as before, something passed through the opening, something that came down, that unrolled itself in the middle of the room, a ladder, a rope-ladder, the very one which Patrice had seen in old Siméon's cupboard.

As before, they looked at it; and they knew so well that everything was being done over again, that the facts were inexorably, pitilessly linked together, they were so certain of it that their eyes at once sought the sheet of paper which must inevitably be pinned to the bottom rung.

It was there, forming a little scroll, dry and discolored and torn at the edges. It was the sheet of twenty years ago, written by Essarès and now serving, as before, to convey the same temptation and the same threat.

'Send Coralie up by herself. Her life shall be saved. I give her ten minutes to accept. If not . . . '

Chapter 13
The Nails in the Coffin

'If not . . . '

Patrice repeated the words mechanically, several times over, while their formidable significance became apparent to both him and Coralie. The words meant that, if Coralie did not obey and did not deliver herself to the enemy, if she did not flee from prison to go with the man who held the keys of the prison, the alternative was death.

At that moment neither of them was thinking what end was in store for them nor even of that death itself. They thought only of the command to separate which the enemy had issued against them. One was to go and the other to die.

Coralie was promised her life if she would sacrifice Patrice. But what was the price of the promise? And what would be the form of the sacrifice demanded?

There was a long silence, full of uncertainty and anguish between the two lovers. They were coming to grips with something; and the drama was no longer taking place absolutely outside them, without their playing any other part than that of helpless victims. It was being enacted within themselves; and they had the power to alter its ending. It was a terrible problem. It had already been set to the earlier Coralie; and she had solved it as a lover would, for she was dead. And now it was being set again.

Patrice read the inscription; and the rapidly scrawled words became less distinct.

I have begged and entreated Coralie . . . She flung herself on her knees before me. She wants to die with me . . .

Patrice looked at Coralie. He had read the words in a very low voice; and she had not heard them. Then, in a burst of passion, he drew her eagerly to him and exclaimed: 'You must go, Coralie! You can understand that my not saying so at once was not due to hesitation. No, only . . . I was thinking of that man's offer . . . and I am frightened for your sake . . . What he asks, Coralie, is terrible. His reason for promising to save your life is that he loves you. And so you understand . . . But still, Coralie, you must obey . . . you must go on living . . . Go! It is no use waiting for the ten minutes to pass. He might change his mind and condemn you to death as well. No, Coralie, you must go, you must go at once!'

'I shall stay,' she replied, simply.

He gave a start.

'But this is madness! Why make a useless sacrifice? Are you afraid of what might happen if you obeyed him?'

'No.'

'Then go.'

'I shall stay.'

'But why? Why this obstinacy? It can do no good. Then why stay?'

'Because I love you, Patrice.'

He stood dumbfounded. He knew that she loved him and he had already told her so. But that she loved him to the extent of preferring to die in his company, this was an unexpected, exquisite and at the same time terrible delight.

'Ah,' he said, 'you love me, Coralie! You love me!'

'I love you, my own Patrice.'

She put her arms around his neck; and he felt that hers was an embrace too strong to be sundered. Nevertheless, he was resolved to save her; and he refused to yield.

'If you love me,' he said, 'you must obey me and save your life. Believe me, it is a hundred times more painful for me to die with you than to die alone. If I know that you are free and alive, death will be sweet to me.'

She did not listen and continued her confession, happy in making it, happy in uttering words which she had kept to herself so long: 'I have loved you, Patrice, from the first day I saw you. I knew it without your telling me; and my only reason for not telling you earlier was that I was waiting for a solemn occasion, for a time when it would be a glory to tell you so, while I looked into the depths of your eyes and offered myself to you entirely. As I have had to speak on the brink of the grave, listen to me and do not force upon me a separation which would be worse than death.'

'No, no,' he said, striving to release himself, 'it is your duty to go.'

He made another effort and caught hold of her hands.

'It is your duty to go,' he whispered, 'and, when you are free, to do all that you can to save me.'

'What are you saying, Patrice?'

'Yes,' he repeated, 'to save me. There is no reason why you should not escape from that scoundrel's clutches, report him, seek assistance, warn our friends. You can call out, you can play some trick . . . '

She looked at him with so sad a smile and such a doubting expression that he stopped speaking.

'You are trying to mislead me, my poor darling,' she said, 'but you are no more taken in by what you say than I am. No, Patrice, you well know that, if I surrender myself to that man, he will reduce me to silence or imprison me in some hiding-place, bound hand and foot, until you have drawn your last breath.'

'You really think that?'

'Just as you do, Patrice. Just as you are sure of what will happen afterwards.'

'Well, what will happen?'

'Ah, Patrice, if that man saves my life, it will not be out of generosity. Don't you see what his plan is, his abominable plan, once I am his prisoner? And don't you also see what my only means of escape will be? Therefore, Patrice, if I am to die in a few hours, why not die now, in your arms . . . at the same time as yourself, with my lips to yours? Is that dying? Is it not rather living, in one instant, the most wonderful of lives?'

He resisted her embrace. He knew that the first kiss of her proffered lips would deprive him of all his power of will.

'This is terrible,' he muttered. 'How can you expect me to accept your sacrifice, you, so young, with years of happiness before you?'

'Years of mourning and despair, if you are gone.'

'You must live, Coralie. I entreat you to, with all my soul.'

'I cannot live without you, Patrice. You are my only happiness. I have no reason for existence except to love you. You have taught me to love. I love you!'

Oh, those heavenly words! For the second time they rang between the four walls of that room. The same words, spoken by the daughter, which the mother had spoken with the same passion and the same glad acceptance of her fate! The same words made twice holy by the recollection of death past and the thought of death to come!

Coralie uttered them without alarm. All her fears seemed to disappear in her love; and it was love alone that shook her voice and dimmed the brightness of her eyes.

Patrice contemplated her with a rapt look. He too was beginning to think that minutes such as these were worth dying for. Nevertheless, he made a last effort.

'And if I ordered you to go, Coralie?'

'That is to say,' she murmured, 'if you ordered me to go to that man and surrender myself to him? Is that what you wish, Patrice?'

The thought was too much for him.

'Oh, the horror of it! That man . . . that man . . . you, my Coralie, so stainless and undefiled! . . . '

Neither he nor she pictured the man in the exact image of Siméon. To both of them, notwithstanding the hideous vision perceived above, the enemy retained a mysterious character. It was perhaps Siméon. It was perhaps another, of whom Siméon was but the instrument. Assuredly it was the enemy, the evil genius crouching above their heads, preparing their death-throes while he pursued Coralie with his foul desire.

Patrice asked one more question.

'Did you ever notice that Siméon sought your company?'

'No, never. If anything, he rather avoided me.'

'Then it's because he's mad . . . '

'I don't think he is mad: he is revenging himself.'

'Impossible. He was my father's friend. All his life long he worked to bring us together: surely he would not kill us deliberately?'

'I don't know, Patrice, I don't understand . . . '

They discussed it no further. It was of no importance whether their death was caused by this one or that one. It was death itself that they had to fight, without troubling who had set it loose against them. And what could they do to ward it off?

'You agree, do you not?' asked Coralie, in a low voice.

He made no answer.

'I shall not go,' she went on, 'but I want you to be of one mind with me. I entreat you. It tortures me to think that you are suffering more than I do. You must let me bear my share. Tell me that you agree.'

'Yes,' he said, 'I agree.'

'My own Patrice! Now give me your two hands, look right into my eyes and smile.'

Mad with love and longing they plunged themselves for an instant into a sort of ecstasy. Then she asked: 'What is it, Patrice? You seem distraught again.'

He gave a hoarse cry.

'Look! . . . Look . . . '

This time he was certain of what he had seen. The ladder was going up. The ten minutes were over.

He rushed forward and caught hold of one of the rungs. The ladder no longer moved.

He did not know exactly what he intended to do. The ladder afforded Coralie's only chance of safety. Could he abandon that hope and resign himself to the inevitable?

One or two minutes passed. The ladder must have been hooked fast again, for Patrice felt a firm resistance up above.

Coralie was entreating him: 'Patrice,' she asked, 'Patrice, what are you hoping for?'

He looked around and above him, as though seeking an idea, and he seemed also to look inside himself, as though he were seeking that idea amid all the memories which he had accumulated at the moment when his father also held the ladder, in a last effort of will. And suddenly, throwing up his leg, he placed his left foot on the fifth rung of the ladder and began to raise himself by the uprights.

It was an absurd attempt to scale the ladder, to reach the skylight, to lay hold of the enemy and thus save himself and Coralie. If his father had failed before him, how could he hope to succeed?

It was all over in less than three seconds. The ladder was at once unfastened from the hook that kept it hanging from the skylight; and Patrice and the ladder came to the ground together. At the same time a strident laugh rang out above, followed the next moment by the sound of the skylight closing.

Patrice picked himself up in a fury, hurled insults at the enemy and, as his rage increased, fired two revolver shots, which broke two of the panes. He next attacked the doors and windows, banging at them with the iron dog which he had taken from the fender. He hit the walls, he hit the floor, he shook his fist at the invisible enemy who was mocking him. But suddenly, after a few blows struck at space, he was compelled to stop. Something like a thick veil had glided overhead. They were in the dark.

He understood what had happened. The enemy had lowered a shutter upon the skylight, covering it entirely.

'Patrice! Patrice!' cried Coralie, maddened by the blotting out of the light and losing all her strength of mind. 'Patrice! Where are you, Patrice? Oh, I'm frightened! Where are you?'

They began to grope for each other, like blind people, and nothing that had gone before seemed to them more horrible than to be lost in this pitiless blackness.

'Patrice! Oh, Patrice! Where are you?'

Their hands touched, Coralie's poor little frozen fingers and Patrice's hands that burned with fever, and they pressed each other and twined together and clutched each other as though to assure themselves that they were still living.

'Oh, don't leave me, Patrice!' Coralie implored.

'I am here,' he replied. 'Have no fear: they can't separate us.'

'You are right,' she panted, 'they can't separate us. We are in our grave.'

The word was so terrible and Coralie uttered it so mournfully that a reaction overtook Patrice.

'No! What are you talking about?' he exclaimed. 'We must not despair. There is hope of safety until the last moment.'

Releasing one of his hands, he took aim with his revolver. A few faint rays trickled through the chinks around the skylight. He fired three times. They heard the crack of the wood-work and the chuckle of the enemy. But the shutter must have been lined with metal, for no split appeared.

Besides, the chinks were forthwith stopped up; and they became aware that the enemy was engaged in the same work that he had performed around the doors and windows. It was obviously very thorough and took a long time in the doing. Next came another work, completing the first. The enemy was nailing the shutter to the frame of the skylight.

It was an awful sound! Swift and light as were the taps of the hammer, they seemed to drive deep into the brain of those who heard them. It was their coffin that was being nailed down, their great coffin with a lid hermetically sealed that now bore heavy upon them. There was no hope left, not a possible chance of escape. Each tap of the hammer strengthened their dark prison, making yet more impregnable the walls that stood between them and the outer world and bade defiance to the most resolute assault.

'Patrice,' stammered Coralie, 'I'm frightened ... That tapping hurts me so!' ...

She sank back in his arms. Patrice felt tears coursing down her cheeks.

Meanwhile the work overhead was being completed. They underwent the terrible experience which condemned men must feel on the morning of their last day, when from their cells they hear the preparations: the engine of death that is being set up, or the electric batteries that are being tested. They hear men striving to have everything ready, so that not one propitious chance may remain and so that destiny may be fulfilled. Death had entered the enemy's service and was working hand in hand with him. He was death itself, acting, contriving and fighting against those whom he had resolved to destroy.

'Don't leave me,' sobbed Coralie, 'don't leave me! . . . '

'Only for a second or two,' he said. 'We must be avenged later.'

'What is the use, Patrice? What can it matter to us?'

He had a box containing a few matches. Lighting them one after the other, he led Coralie to the panel with the inscription.

'What are you going to do?' she asked.

'I will not have our death put down to suicide. I want to do what our parents did before us and to prepare for the future. Someone will read what I am going to write and will avenge us.'

He took a pencil from his pocket and bent down. There was a free space, right at the bottom of the panel. He wrote.

Patrice Belval and Coralie, his betrothed, die the same death, murdered by Siméon Diodokis, 14 April, 1915.

But, as he finished writing, he noticed a few words of the former inscription which he had not yet read, because they were placed outside it, so to speak, and did not appear to form part of it.

'One more match,' he said. 'Did you see? There are some words there, the last, no doubt, that my father wrote.'

She struck a match. By the flickering light they made out a certain number of misshapen letters, obviously written in a hurry and forming two words.

Asphyxiated . . . Oxide . . .

The match went out. They rose in silence. Asphyxiated! They understood. That was how their parents had perished and how they themselves would perish. But they did not yet fully realize how the thing would happen. The lack of air would never be great enough to suffocate them in this large room, which contained enough to last them for many days.

'Unless,' muttered Patrice, 'unless the quality of the air can be impaired and therefore . . . '

He stopped. Then he went on: 'Yes, that's it. I remember.'

He told Coralie what he suspected, or rather what conformed so well with the reality as to leave no room for doubt. He had seen in old Siméon's cupboard not only the rope-ladder which the mad-man had brought with him, but also a coil of lead pipes. And now

Siméon's behavior from the moment when they were locked in, his movements to and fro around the lodge, the care with which he had stopped up every crevice, his labors along the wall and on the roof: all this was explained in the most definite fashion. Old Siméon had simply fitted to a gas-meter, probably in the kitchen, the pipe which he had next laid along the wall and on the roof. This therefore was the way in which they were about to die, as their parents had died before them, stifled by ordinary gas.

Panic-stricken, they began to run aimlessly about the room, holding hands, while their disordered brains, bereft of thought or will, seemed like tiny things shaken by the fiercest gale. Coralie uttered incoherent words. Patrice, while imploring her to keep calm, was himself carried away by the storm and powerless to resist the terrible agony of the darkness wherein death lay waiting. At such times a man tries to flee, to escape the icy breath that is already chilling his marrow. He must flee, but where? Which way? The walls are insurmountable and the darkness is even harder than the walls.

They stopped, exhausted. A low hiss was heard somewhere in the room, the faint hiss that issues from a badly-closed gas-jet. They listened and perceived that it came from above. The torture was beginning.

'It will last half an hour, or an hour at most,' Patrice whispered.

Coralie had recovered her self-consciousness: 'We shall be brave,' she said.

'Oh, if I were alone! But you, you, my poor Coralie!'

'It is painless,' she murmured.

'You are bound to suffer, you, so weak!'

'One suffers less, the weaker one is. Besides, I know that we shan't suffer, Patrice.'

She suddenly appeared so placid that he on his side was filled with a great peace. Seated on a sofa, their fingers still entwined, they silently steeped themselves in the mighty calm which comes when we think that events have run their course. This calm is resignation, submission to superior forces. Natures such as theirs cease to rebel when destiny has manifested its orders and when nothing remains but acquiescence and prayer.

She put her arm round Patrice's neck.

'I am your bride in the eyes of God,' she said. 'May He receive us as He would receive a husband and wife.'

Her gentle resignation brought tears to his eyes. She dried them with her kisses, and, of her own seeking, offered him her lips.

They sat wrapped in an infinite silence. They perceived the first smell of gas descending around them, but they felt no fear.

'Everything will happen as it did before, Coralie,' whispered Patrice, 'down to the very last second. Your mother and my father, who loved each other as we do, also died in each other's arms, with their lips joined together. They had decided to unite us and they have united us.'

'Our grave will be near theirs,' she murmured.

Little by little their ideas became confused and they began to think much as a man sees through a rising mist. They had had nothing to eat; and hunger now added its discomfort to the vertigo in which their minds were imperceptibly sinking. As it increased, their uneasiness and anxiety left them, to be followed by a sense of ecstasy, then lassitude, extinction, repose. The dread of the coming annihilation faded out of their thoughts.

Coralie, the first to be affected, began to utter delirious words which astonished Patrice at first.

'Dearest, there are flowers falling, roses all around us. How delightful!'

Presently he himself grew conscious of the same blissful exaltation, expressing itself in tenderness and joyful emotion. With no sort of dismay he felt her gradually yielding in his arms and abandoning herself; and he had the impression that he was following her down a measureless abyss, all bathed with light, where they floated, he and she, descending slowly and without effort towards a happy valley.

Minutes or perhaps hours passed. They were still descending, he supporting her by the waist, she with her head thrown back a little way, her eyes closed and a smile upon her lips. He remembered pictures showing gods thus gliding through the blue of heaven; and, drunk with pure, radiant light and air, he continued to circle above the happy valley.

But, as he approached it, he felt himself grow weary. Coralie weighed heavily on his bent arm. The descent increased in speed. The waves of light turned to darkness. A thick cloud came, followed by others that formed a whirl of gloom.

And suddenly, worn out, his forehead bathed in sweat and his body shaking with fever, he pitched forward into a great black pit . . .

Chapter 14
A Strange Character

It was not yet exactly death. In his present condition of agony, what lingered of Patrice's consciousness mingled, as in a nightmare, the life which he knew with the imaginary world in which he now found himself, the world which was that of death.

In this world Coralie no longer existed; and her loss distracted him with grief. But he seemed to hear and see somebody whose presence was revealed by a shadow passing before his closed eyelids. This somebody he pictured to himself, though without reason, under the aspect of Siméon, who came to verify the death of his victims, began by carrying Coralie away, then came back to Patrice and carried him away also and laid him down somewhere. And all this was so well-defined that Patrice wondered whether he had not woke up.

Next hours passed . . . or seconds. In the end Patrice had a feeling that he was falling asleep, but as a man sleeps in hell, suffering the moral and physical tortures of the damned. He was back at the bottom of the black pit, which he was making desperate efforts to leave, like a man who has fallen into the sea and is trying to reach the surface. In this way, with the greatest difficulty, he passed through one waste of water after another, the weight of which stifled him. He had to scale them, gripping with his hands and feet to things that slipped, to rope-ladders which, possessing no points of support, gave way beneath him.

Meanwhile the darkness became less intense. A little muffled daylight mingled with it. Patrice felt less greatly oppressed. He half-opened his eyes, drew a breath or two and, looking round, beheld a sight that surprised him, the embrasure of an open door, near which he was lying in the air, on a sofa. Beside him he saw Coralie, on another sofa. She moved restlessly and seemed to be in great discomfort.

'She is climbing out of the black pit,' he thought to himself. 'Like me, she is struggling. My poor Coralie!'

There was a small table between them, with two glasses of water on it. Parched with thirst, he took one of them in his hand. But he dared not drink.

At that moment someone came through the open door, which Patrice perceived to be the door of the lodge; and he observed that it was not old Siméon, as he had thought, but a stranger whom he had never seen before.

'I am not asleep,' he said to himself. 'I am sure that I am not asleep and that this stranger is a friend.'

And he tried to say it aloud, to make certainty doubly sure. But he had not the strength.

The stranger, however, came up to him and, in a gentle voice, said: 'Don't tire yourself, captain. You're all right now. Allow me. Have some water.'

The stranger handed him one of the two glasses; Patrice emptied it at a draught, without any feeling of distrust, and was glad to see Coralie also drinking.

'Yes, I'm all right now,' he said. 'Heavens, how good it is to be alive! Coralie is really alive, isn't she?'

He did not hear the answer and dropped into a welcome sleep.

When he woke up, the crisis was over, though he still felt a buzzing in his head and a difficulty in drawing a deep breath. He stood up, however, and realized that all these sensations were not fanciful, that he was really outside the door of the lodge and that Coralie had drunk the glass of water and was peacefully sleeping.

'How good it is to be alive!' he repeated.

He now felt a need for action, but dared not go into the lodge, notwithstanding the open door. He moved away from it, skirting the cloisters containing the graves, and then, with no exact object, for he did not yet grasp the reason of his own actions, did not understand what had happened to him and was simply walking at random, he came back towards the lodge, on the other front, the one over-looking the garden.

Suddenly he stopped. A few yards from the house, at the foot of a tree standing beside the slanting path, a man lay back in a wicker long-chair, with his face in the shade and his legs in the sun. He was sleeping, with his head fallen forward and an open book upon his knees.

Then and not till then did Patrice clearly understand that he and Coralie had escaped being killed, that they were both really alive and that they owed their safety to this man whose sleep suggested a state of absolute security and satisfied conscience.

Patrice studied the stranger's appearance. He was slim of figure, but broad-shouldered, with a sallow complexion, a slight mustache on his lips and hair beginning to turn gray at the temples. His age was probably fifty at most. The cut of his clothes pointed to dandyism. Patrice leant forward and read the title of the book: *The Memoirs of Benjamin Franklin*. He also read the initials inside a hat lying on the grass: 'L. P.'

'It was he who saved me,' said Patrice to himself, 'I recognize him. He carried us both out of the studio and looked after us. But how was the miracle brought about? Who sent him?'

He tapped him on the shoulder. The man was on his feet at once, his face lit up with a smile.

'Pardon me, captain, but my life is so much taken up that, when I have a few minutes to myself, I use them for sleeping, wherever I may be . . . like Napoleon, eh? Well, I don't object to the comparison . . . But enough about myself. How are you feeling now? And madame – 'Little Mother Coralie' – is she better? I saw no use in waking you, after I had opened the doors and taken you outside. I had done what was necessary and felt quite easy. You were both breathing. So I left the rest to the good pure air.'

He broke off, at the sight of Patrice's disconcerted attitude; and his smile made way for a merry laugh.

'Oh, I was forgetting: you don't know me! Of course, it's true, the letter I sent you was intercepted. Let me introduce myself. Don Luis Perenna,[*] a member of an old Spanish family, genuine patent of nobility, papers all in order . . . But I can see that all this tells you nothing,' he went on, laughing still more gaily. 'No doubt Ya-Bon described me differently when he wrote my name on that street-wall, one evening a fortnight ago. Aha, you're beginning to understand! . . . Yes, I'm the man you sent for to help you. Shall I mention the name, just bluntly? Well, here goes, captain! . . . Arsène Lupin, at your service.'

Patrice was stupefied. He had utterly forgotten Ya-Bon's proposal and the unthinking permission which he had given him to call in the famous adventurer. And here was Arsène Lupin standing in front of him, Arsène Lupin, who, by a sheer effort of will that resembled an incredible miracle, had dragged him and Coralie out of their hermetically-sealed coffin.

He held out his hand and said: 'Thank you!'

[*] *The Teeth of the Tiger*. By Maurice Leblanc. Translated by Alexander Teixeira de Mattos. 'Luis Perenna' is one of several anagrams of 'Arsène Lupin'

'Tut!' said Don Luis, playfully. 'No thanks! Just a good hand-shake, that's all. And I'm a man you can shake hands with, captain, believe me. I may have a few peccadilloes on my conscience, but on the other hand I have committed a certain number of good actions which should win me the esteem of decent folk . . . beginning with my own. And so . . . '

He interrupted himself again, seemed to reflect and, taking Patrice by a button of his jacket, said: 'Don't move. We are being watched.'

'By whom?'

'Someone on the quay, right at the end of the garden. The wall is not high. There's a grating on the top of it. They're looking through the bars and trying to see us.'

'How do you know? You have your back turned to the quay; and then there are the trees.'

'Listen.'

'I don't hear anything out of the way.'

'Yes, the sound of an engine . . . the engine of a stopping car. Now what would a car want to stop here for, on the quay, opposite a wall with no house near it?'

'Then who do you think it is?'

'Why, old Siméon, of course!'

'Old Siméon!'

'Certainly. He's looking to see whether I've really saved the two of you.'

'Then he's not mad?'

'Mad? No more mad than you or I!'

'And yet . . . '

'What you mean is that Siméon used to protect you; that his object was to bring you two together; that he sent you the key of the garden-door; and so on and so on.'

'Do you know all that?'

'Well, of course! If not, how could I have rescued you?'

'But,' said Patrice, anxiously, 'suppose the scoundrel returns to the attack. Ought we not to take some precautions? Let's go back to the lodge: Coralie is all alone.'

'There's no danger.'

'Why?'

'Because I'm here.'

Patrice was more astounded than ever.

'Then Siméon knows you?' he asked. 'He knows that you are here?'

'Yes, thanks to a letter which I wrote you under cover to Ya-Bon and which he intercepted. I told you that I was coming; and he hurried to get to work. Only, as my habit is on these occasions, I hastened on my arrival by a few hours, so that I caught him in the act.'

'At that moment you did not know he was the enemy; you knew nothing?'

'Nothing at all.'

'Was it this morning?'

'No, this afternoon, at a quarter to two.'

Patrice took out his watch.

'And it's now four. So in two hours . . . '

'Not that. I've been here an hour.'

'Did you find out from Ya-Bon?'

'Do you think I've no better use for my time? Ya-Bon simply told me that you were not there, which was enough to astonish me.'

'After that?'

'I looked to see where you were.'

'How?'

'I first searched your room and, doing so in my own thorough fashion, ended by discovering that there was a crack at the back of your roll-top desk and that this crack faced a hole in the wall of the next room. I was able therefore to pull out the book in which you kept your diary and acquaint myself with what was going on. This, moreover, was how Siméon became aware of your least intentions. This was how he knew of your plan to come here, on a pilgrimage, on the fourteenth of April. This was how, last night, seeing you write, he preferred, before attacking you, to know what you were writing. Knowing it and learning, from your own words, that you were on your guard, he refrained. You see how simple it all is. If M. Masseron had grown uneasy at your absence, he would have been just as successful. Only he would have been successful tomorrow.'

'That is to say, too late.'

'Yes, too late. This really isn't his business, however, nor that of the police. So I would rather that they didn't meddle with it. I asked your wounded soldiers to keep silent about anything that may strike them as queer. Therefore, if M. Masseron comes today, he will think that everything is in order. Well, having satisfied my mind in this respect and possessing the necessary information from your diary, I took Ya-Bon with me and walked across the lane and into the garden.'

'Was the door open?'

'No, but Siméon happened to be coming out at that moment. Bad luck for him, wasn't it? I took advantage of it boldly. I put my hand on the latch and we went in, without his daring to protest. He certainly knew who I was.'

'But you didn't know at that time that he was the enemy?'

'I didn't know? And what about your diary?'

'I had no notion . . .'

'But, captain, every page is an indictment of the man. There's not an incident in which he did not take part, not a crime which he did not prepare.'

'In that case you should have collared him.'

'And if I had? What good would it have done me? Should I have compelled him to speak? No, I shall hold him tightest by leaving him his liberty. That will give him rope, you know. You see already he's prowling round the house instead of clearing out. Besides, I had something better to do: I had first to rescue you two . . . if there was still time. Ya-Bon and I therefore rushed to the door of the lodge. It was open; but the other, the door of the studio, was locked and bolted. I drew the bolts; and to force the lock was, for me, child's play. Then the smell of gas was enough to tell me what had happened. Siméon must have fitted an old meter to some outside pipe, probably the one which supplied the lamps on the lane, and he was suffocating you. All that remained for us to do was to fetch the two of you out and give you the usual treatment: rubbing, artificial respiration and so on. You were saved.'

'I suppose he removed all his murderous appliances?' asked Patrice.

'No, he evidently contemplated coming back and putting everything to rights, so that his share in the business could not be proved, so too that people might believe in your suicide, a mysterious suicide, death without apparent cause; in short, the same tragedy that happened with your father and Little Mother Coralie's mother.'

'Then you know? . . .'

'Why, haven't I eyes to read with? What about the inscription on the wall, your father's revelations? I know as much as you do, captain . . . and perhaps a bit more.'

'More?'

'Well, of course! Habit, you know, experience! Plenty of problems, unintelligible to others, seem to me the simplest and clearest that can be. Therefore . . .'

Don Luis hesitated whether to go on.

'No,' he said, 'it's better that I shouldn't speak. The mystery will be dispelled gradually. Let us wait. For the moment . . . '

He again stopped, this time to listen.

'There, he must have seen you. And now that he knows what he wants to, he's going away.'

Patrice grew excited.

'He's going away! You really ought to have collared him. Shall we ever find him again, the scoundrel? Shall we ever be able to take our revenge?'

Don Luis smiled.

'There you go, calling him a scoundrel, the man who watched over you for twenty years, who brought you and Little Mother Coralie together, who was your benefactor!'

'Oh, I don't know! All this is so bewildering! I can't help hating him . . . The idea of his getting away maddens me . . . I should like to torture him and yet . . . '

He yielded to a feeling of despair and took his head between his two hands.

Don Luis comforted him: 'Have no fear,' he said. 'He was never nearer his downfall than at the present moment. I hold him in my hand as I hold this leaf.'

'But how?'

'The man who's driving him belongs to me.'

'What's that? What do you mean?'

'I mean that I put one of my men on the driver's seat of a taxi, with instructions to hang about at the bottom of the lane, and that Siméon did not fail to take the taxi in question.'

'That is to say, you suppose so,' Patrice corrected him, feeling more and more astounded.

'I recognized the sound of the engine at the bottom of the garden when I told you.'

'And are you sure of your man?'

'Certain.'

'What's the use? Siméon can drive far out of Paris, stab the man in the back . . . and then when shall we get to know?'

'Do you imagine that people can get out of Paris and go running about the high-roads without a special permit? No, if Siméon leaves Paris he will have to drive to some railway station or other and we shall know of it twenty minutes after. And then we'll be off.'

'How?'

'By motor.'

'Then you have a pass?'

'Yes, valid for the whole of France.'

'You don't mean it!'

'I do; and a genuine pass at that! Made out in the name of Don Luis Perenna, signed by the minister of the interior and counter-signed . . . '

'By whom?'

'By the President of the Republic.'

Patrice felt his bewilderment change all at once into violent excite-ment. Hitherto, in the terrible adventure in which he was engaged, he had undergone the enemy's implacable will and had known little besides defeat and the horrors of ever-threatening death. But now a more powerful will suddenly arose in his favor. And everything was abruptly altered. Fate seemed to be changing its course, like a ship which an unexpected fair wind brings back into harbor.

'Upon my word, captain,' said Don Luis, 'I thought you were going to cry like Little Mother Coralie. Your nerves are overstrung. And I dare say you're hungry. We must find you something to eat. Come along.'

He led him slowly towards the lodge and, speaking in a rather serious voice: 'I must ask you,' he said, 'to be absolutely discreet in this whole matter. With the exception of a few old friends and of Ya-Bon, whom I met in Africa, where he saved my life, no one in France knows me by my real name. I call myself Don Luis Perenna. In Morocco, where I was soldiering, I had occasion to do a service to the very gracious sovereign of a neighboring neutral nation, who, though obliged to conceal his true feelings, is ardently on our side. He sent for me; and, in return, I asked him to give me my credentials and to obtain a pass for me. Officially, therefore, I am on a secret mission, which expires in two days. In two days I shall go back . . . to whence I came, to a place where, during the war, I am serving France in my fashion: not a bad one, believe me, as people will see one day.'

They came to the settee on which Coralie lay sleeping. Don Luis laid his hand on Patrice's arm.

'One word more, captain. I swore to myself and I gave my word of honor to him who trusted me that, while I was on this mission, my time should be devoted exclusively to defending the interests of my country to the best of my power. I must warn you, therefore, that, notwithstanding all my sympathy for you, I shall not be able to prolong my stay for a single minute after I have discovered the eighteen hundred bags of gold. They were the one and only reason why I came in answer to Ya-Bon's appeal. When the bags of gold are in our possession, that is to say, tomorrow evening at latest, I shall go away. However, the two quests are joined. The clearing up of the one will mean the end of the other. And now enough of words. Introduce me to Little Mother Coralie and let's get to work! Make no mystery with her, captain,' he added, laughing. 'Tell her my real name. I have nothing to fear: Arsène Lupin has every woman on his side.'

* * *

Forty minutes later Coralie was back in her room, well cared for and well watched. Patrice had taken a substantial meal, while Don Luis walked up and down the terrace smoking cigarettes.

'Finished, captain? Then we'll make a start.'

He looked at his watch.

'Half-past five. We have more than an hour of daylight left. That'll be enough.'

'Enough? You surely don't pretend that you will achieve your aim in an hour?'

'My definite aim, no, but the aim which I am setting myself at the moment, yes . . . and even earlier. An hour? What for? To do what? Why, you'll be a good deal wiser in a few minutes!'

Don Luis asked to be taken to the cellar under the library; where Essarès Bey used to keep the bags of gold until the time had come to send them off.

'Was it through this ventilator that the bags were let down?'

'Yes.'

'Is there no other outlet?'

'None except the staircase leading to the library and the other ventilator.'

'Opening on the terrace?'

'Yes.'

'Then that's clear. The bags used to come in by the first and go out by the second.'

'But . . .'

'There's no but about it, captain: how else would you have it happen? You see, the mistake people always make is to go looking for difficulties where there are none.'

They returned to the terrace. Don Luis took up his position near the ventilator and inspected the ground immediately around. It did not take long. Four yards away, outside the windows of the library, was the basin with the statue of a child spouting a jet of water through a shell.

Don Luis went up, examined the basin and, leaning forwards, reached the little statue, which he turned upon its axis from right to left. At the same time the pedestal described a quarter of a circle.

'That's it,' he said, drawing himself up again.

'What?'

'The basin will empty itself.'

He was right. The water sank very quickly and the bottom of the fountain appeared.

Don Luis stepped into it and squatted on his haunches. The inner wall was lined with a marble mosaic composing a wide red-and-white fretwork pattern. In the middle of one of the frets was a ring, which Don Luis lifted and pulled. All that portion of the wall which formed the pattern yielded to his effort and came down, leaving an opening of about twelve inches by ten.

'That's where the bags of gold went,' said Don Luis. 'It was the second stage. They were despatched in the same manner, on a hook sliding along a wire. Look, here is the wire, in this groove at the top.'

'By Jove!' cried Captain Belval. 'But you've unraveled this in a masterly fashion! What about the wire? Can't we follow it?'

'No, but it will serve our purpose if we know where it finishes. I say, captain, go to the end of the garden, by the wall, taking a line at right angles to the house. When you get there, cut off a branch of a tree, rather high up. Oh, I was forgetting! I shall have to go out by the lane. Have you the key of the door? Give it me, please.'

Patrice handed him the key and then went down to the wall beside the quay.

'A little farther to the right,' Don Luis instructed him. 'A little more still. That's better. Now wait.'

He left the garden by the lane, reached the quay and called out from the other side of the wall: 'Are you there, captain?'

'Yes.'

'Fix your branch so that I can see it from here. Capital.'

Patrice now joined Don Luis, who was crossing the road. All the way down the Seine are wharves, built on the bank of the river and used for loading and unloading vessels. Barges put in alongside, discharge their cargoes, take in fresh ones and often lie moored one next to the other. At the spot where Don Luis and Patrice descended by a flight of steps there was a series of yards, one of which, the one which they reached first, appeared to be abandoned, no doubt since the war. It contained, amid a quantity of useless materials, several heaps of bricks and building-stones, a hut with broken windows and the lower part of a steam-crane. A placard swinging from a post bore the inscription:

BERTHOU
WHARFINGER & BUILDER

Don Luis walked along the foot of the embankment, ten or twelve feet high, above which the quay was suspended like a terrace. Half of it was occupied by a heap of sand; and they saw in the wall the bars of an iron grating, the lower half of which was hidden by the sand-heap shored up with planks.

Don Luis cleared the grating and said, jestingly: 'Have you noticed that the doors are never locked in this adventure? Let's hope that it's the same with this one.'

His theory was confirmed, somewhat to his own surprise, and they entered one of those recesses where workmen put away their tools.

'So far, nothing out of the common,' said Don Luis, switching on an electric torch. 'Buckets, pick-axes, wheelbarrows, a ladder . . . Ah! Ah! Just as I expected: rails, a complete set of light rails! . . . Lend me a hand, captain. Let's clear out the back. Good, that's done it.'

Level with the ground and opposite the grating was a rectangular opening exactly similar to the one in the basin. The wire was visible above, with a number of hooks hanging from it.

'So this is where the bags arrived,' Don Luis explained. 'They dropped, so to speak, into one of the two little trollies which you see over there, in the corner. The rails were laid across the bank, of course at night; and the trollies were pushed to a barge into which they tipped their contents.'

'So that . . . ?'

'So that the French gold went this way . . . anywhere you like . . . somewhere abroad.'

'And you think that the last eighteen hundred bags have also been despatched?'

'I fear so.'

'Then we are too late?'

Don Luis reflected for a while without answering. Patrice, though disappointed by a development which he had not foreseen, remained amazed at the extraordinary skill with which his companion, in so short a time, had succeeded in unraveling a portion of the tangled skein.

'It's an absolute miracle,' he said, at last. 'How on earth did you do it?'

Without a word, Don Luis took from his pocket the book which Patrice had seen lying on his knees, *The Memoirs of Benjamin Franklin*, and motioned to him to read some lines which he indicated with his finger. They were written towards the end of the reign of Louis XVI and ran.

> We go daily to the village of Passy adjoining my home, where you take the waters in a beautiful garden. Streams and waterfalls pour down on all sides, this way and that, in artfully leveled beds. I am known to like skilful mechanism, so I have been shown the basin where the waters of all the rivulets meet and mingle. There stands a little marble figure in the midst; and the weight of water is strong enough to turn it a quarter circle to the left and then pour down straight to the Seine by a conduit, which opens in the ground of the basin.

Patrice closed the book; and Don Luis went on to explain: 'Things have changed since, no doubt thanks to the energies of Essarès Bey. The water escapes some other way now; and the aqueduct was used to drain off the gold. Besides, the bed of the river has narrowed. Quays have been built, with a system of canals underneath them. You see, captain, all this was easy enough to discover, once I had the book to tell me. *Doctus cum libro.*'

'Yes, but, even so, you had to read the book.'

'A pure accident. I unearthed it in Siméon's room and put it in my pocket, because I was curious to know why he was reading it.'

'Why, that's just how he must have discovered Essarès Bey's secret!' cried Patrice. 'He didn't know the secret. He found the book among his employer's papers and got up his facts that way. What do you think? Don't you agree? You seem not to share my opinion. Have you some other view?'

Don Luis did not reply. He stood looking at the river. Beside the wharves, at a slight distance from the yard, a barge lay moored, with apparently no one on her. But a slender thread of smoke now began to rise from a pipe that stood out above the deck.

'Let's go and have a look at her,' he said.

The barge was lettered.

LA NONCHALANTE   BEAUNE

They had to cross the space between the barge and the wharf and to step over a number of ropes and empty barrels covering the flat portions of the deck. A companion-way brought them to a sort of cabin, which did duty as a stateroom and a kitchen in one. Here they found a powerful-looking man, with broad shoulders, curly black hair and a clean-shaven face. His only clothes were a blouse and a pair of dirty, patched canvas trousers.

Don Luis offered him a twenty-franc note. The man took it eagerly.

'Just tell me something, mate. Have you seen a barge lately, lying at Berthou's Wharf?'

'Yes, a motor-barge. She left two days ago.'

'What was her name?'

'The *Belle Hélène*. The people on board, two men and a woman, were foreigners talking I don't know what lingo . . . We didn't speak to one another.'

'But Berthou's Wharf has stopped work, hasn't it?'

'Yes, the owner's joined the army . . . and the foremen as well. We've all got to, haven't we? I'm expecting to be called up myself . . . though I've got a weak heart.'

'But, if the yard's stopped work, what was the boat doing here?'

'I don't know. They worked the whole of one night, however. They had laid rails along the quay. I heard the trollies; and they were loading up. What with I don't know. And then, early in the morning, they unmoored.'

'Where did they go?'

'Down stream, Mantes way.'

'Thanks, mate. That's what I wanted to know.'

Ten minutes later, when they reached the house, Patrice and Don Luis found the driver of the cab which Siméon Diodokis had taken after meeting Don Luis. As Don Luis expected, Siméon had told the man to go to a railway-station, the Gare Saint-Lazare, and there bought his ticket.

'Where to?'

'To Mantes!'

'There's no mistake about it,' said Patrice. 'The information conveyed to M. Masseron that the gold had been sent away; the speed with which the work was carried out, at night, mechanically, by the people belonging to the boat; their alien nationality; the direction which they took: it all agrees. The probability is that, between the cellar into which the gold was shot and the place where it finished its journey, there was some spot where it used to remain concealed . . . unless the eighteen hundred bags can have awaited their despatch, slung one behind the other, along the wire. But that doesn't matter much. The great thing is to know that the *Belle Hélène*, hiding somewhere in the outskirts, lay waiting for the favorable opportunity. In the old days Essarès Bey, by way of precaution, used to send her a signal with the aid of that shower of sparks which I saw. This time old Siméon, who is continuing Essarès' work, no doubt on his own account, gave the crew notice; and the bags of gold are on their way to Rouen and Le Havre, where some steamer will take them over and carry them . . . eastwards. After all, forty or fifty tons, hidden in the hold under a layer of coal, is nothing. What do you say? That's it, isn't it? I feel positive about it . . . Then we have Mantes, to which he took his ticket and for which the *Belle Hélène* is bound. Could anything be clearer? Mantes, where he'll pick up his cargo of gold and go on board in some seafaring disguise, unknown and unseen . . . Loot and looter disappearing together. It's as clear as daylight. Don't you agree?'

Once again Don Luis did not answer. However, he must have acquiesced in Patrice's theories, for, after a minute, he declared: 'Very well. I'll go to Mantes.' And, turning to the chauffeur, 'Hurry off to the garage,' he said, 'and come back in the six-cylinder. I want to be at Mantes in less than an hour. You, captain . . . '

'I shall come with you.'

'And who will look after . . . ?'

'Coralie? She's in no danger! Who can attack her now? Siméon has failed in his attempt and is thinking only of saving his own skin . . . and his bags of gold.'

'You insist, do you?'

'Absolutely.'

'I don't know that you're wise. However, that's your affair. Let's go. By the way, though, one precaution.' He raised his voice. 'Ya-Bon!'

The Senegalese came hastening up. While Ya-Bon felt for Patrice all the affection of a faithful dog, he seemed to profess towards Don Luis something more nearly approaching religious devotion. The adventurer's slightest action roused him to ecstasy. He never stopped laughing in the great chief's presence.

'Ya-Bon, are you all right now? Is your wound healed? You don't feel tired? Good. In that case, come with me.'

He led him to the quay, a short distance away from Berthou's Wharf.

'At nine o'clock this evening,' he said, 'you're to be on guard here, on this bench. Bring your food and drink with you; and keep a particular look-out for anything that happens over there, down stream. Perhaps nothing will happen at all; but never mind: you're not to move until I come back . . . unless . . . unless something does happen, in which case you will act accordingly.'

He paused and then continued: 'Above all, Ya-Bon, beware of Siméon. It was he who gave you that wound. If you catch sight of him, leap at his throat and bring him here. But mind you don't kill him! No nonsense now. I don't want you to hand me over a corpse, but a live man. Do you understand, Ya-Bon?'

Patrice began to feel uneasy.

'Do you fear anything from that side?' he asked. 'Look here, it's out of the question, as Siméon has gone . . . '

'Captain,' said Don Luis, 'when a good general goes in pursuit of the enemy, that does not prevent him from consolidating his hold on the conquered ground and leaving garrisons in the fortresses. Berthou's Wharf is evidently one of our adversary's rallying-points. I'm keeping it under observation.'

Don Luis also took serious precautions with regard to Coralie. She was very much overstrained and needed rest and attention. They put her into the car and, after making a dash at full speed towards the center of Paris, so as to throw any spies off the scent, took her to the home on the Boulevard Maillot, where Patrice handed her over to the matron and recommended her to the doctor's care. The staff received strict orders to admit no strangers to see her. She was to answer no letter, unless the letter was signed 'Captain Patrice'.

At nine o'clock, the car sped down the Saint-Germain and Mantes road. Sitting inside with Don Luis, Patrice felt all the enthusiasm of victory and indulged freely in theories, every one of which possessed for him the value of an unimpeachable certainty. A few doubts lingered in his mind, however, points which remained obscure and on which he would have been glad to have Don Luis's opinion.

'There are two things,' he said, 'which I simply cannot understand. In the first place, who was the man murdered by Essarès, at nineteen minutes past seven in the morning, on the fourth of April? I heard his dying cries. Who was killed? And what became of the body?'

Don Luis was silent; and Patrice went on: 'The second point is stranger still. I mean Siméon's behavior. Here's a man who devotes his whole life to a single object, that of revenging his friend Belval's murder and at the same time ensuring my happiness and Coralie's. This is his one aim in life; and nothing can make him swerve from his obsession. And then, on the day when his enemy, Essarès Bey, is put out of the way, suddenly he turns round completely and persecutes Coralie and me, going to the length of using against us the horrible contrivance which Essarès Bey had employed so successfully against our parents! You really must admit that it's an amazing change! Can it be the thought of the gold that has hypnotized him? Are his crimes to be explained by the huge treasure placed at his disposal on the day when he discovered the secret? Has a decent man transformed himself into a bandit to satisfy a sudden instinct? What do you think?'

Don Luis persisted in his silence. Patrice, who expected to see every riddle solved by the famous adventurer in a twinkling, felt peevish and surprised. He made a last attempt.

'And the golden triangle? Another mystery! For, after all, there's not a trace of a triangle in anything we've seen! Where is this golden triangle? Have you any idea what it means?'

Don Luis allowed a moment to pass and then said: 'Captain, I have the most thorough liking for you and I take the liveliest interest in all that concerns you, but I confess that there is one problem which excludes all others and one object towards which all my efforts are now directed. That is the pursuit of the gold of which we have been robbed; and I don't want this gold to escape us. I have succeeded on your side, but not yet on the other. You are both of you safe and sound, but I haven't the eighteen hundred bags; and I want them, I want them.'

'You'll have them, since we know where they are.'

'I shall have them,' said Don Luis, 'when they lie spread before my eyes. Until then, I can tell you nothing.'

At Mantes the enquiries did not take long. They almost immediately had the satisfaction of learning that a traveler, whose description corresponded with old Siméon's, had gone to the Hôtel des Trois Empereurs and was now asleep in a room on the third floor.

Don Luis took a ground-floor room, while Patrice, who would have attracted the enemy's attention more easily, because of his lame leg, went to the Grand Hôtel.

He woke late the next morning. Don Luis rang him up and told him that Siméon, after calling at the post-office, had gone down to the river and then to the station, where he met a fashionably-dressed woman, with her face hidden by a thick veil, and brought her back to the hotel. The two were lunching together in the room on the third floor.

At four o'clock Don Luis rang up again, to ask Patrice to join him at once in a little café at the end of the town, facing the Seine. Here Patrice saw Siméon on the quay. He was walking with his hands behind his back, like a man strolling without any definite object.

'Comforter, spectacles, the same get-up as usual,' said Patrice. 'Not a thing about him changed. Watch him. He's putting on an air of indifference, but you can bet that his eyes are looking up stream, in the direction from which the *Belle Hélène* is coming.'

'Yes, yes,' said Don Luis. 'Here's the lady.'

'Oh, that's the one, is it?' said Patrice. 'I've met her two or three times already in the street.'

A dust-cloak outlined her figure and shoulders, which were wide and rather well-developed. A veil fell around the brim of her felt hat. She gave Siméon a telegram to read. Then they talked for a moment, seemed to be taking their bearings, passed by the café and stopped a little lower down. Here Siméon wrote a few words on a sheet of note-paper and handed it to his companion. She left him and went back into the town. Siméon resumed his walk by the riverside.

'You must stay here, captain,' said Don Luis.

'But the enemy doesn't seem to be on his guard,' protested Patrice. 'He's not turning round.'

'It's better to be prudent, captain. What a pity that we can't have a look at what Siméon wrote down!'

'I might . . . '

'Go after the lady? No, no, captain. Without wishing to offend you, you're not quite cut out for it. I'm not sure that even I . . . '

And he walked away.

Patrice waited. A few boats moved up or down the river. Mechanically, he glanced at their names. And suddenly, half an hour after Don Luis had left him, he heard the clearly-marked rhythm, the pulsation of one of those powerful motors which, for a few years past, have been fitted to certain barges.

At the bend of the river a barge appeared. As she passed in front of him, he distinctly and with no little excitement read the name of the *Belle Hélène*!

She was gliding along at a fair pace, to the accompaniment of a regular, throbbing beat. She was big and broad in the beam, heavy and pretty deep in the water, though she appeared to carry no cargo. Patrice saw two watermen on board, sitting and smoking carelessly. A dinghy floated behind at the end of a painter.

The barge went on and passed out of sight at the turn. Patrice waited another hour before Don Luis came back.

'Well?' he asked. 'Have you seen her?'

'Yes, they let go the dinghy, a mile and a half from here, and put in for Siméon.'

'Then he's gone with them?'

'Yes.'

'Without suspecting anything?'

'You're asking me too much, captain!'

'Never mind! We've won! We shall catch them up in the car, pass them and, at Vernon or somewhere, inform the military and civil authorities, so that they may proceed to arrest the men and seize the boat.'

'We shall inform nobody, captain. We shall proceed to carry out these little operations ourselves.'

'What do you mean? Surely . . . '

The two looked at each other. Patrice had been unable to dissemble the thought that occurred to his mind. Don Luis showed no resentment.

'You're afraid that I shall run away with the three hundred millions? By jingo, it's a largish parcel to hide in one's jacket-pocket!'

'Still,' said Patrice, 'may I ask what you intend to do?'

'You may, captain, but allow me to postpone my reply until we've really won. For the moment, we must first find the barge again.'

They went to the Hôtel des Trois Empereurs and drove off in the car towards Vernon. This time they were both silent.

The road joined the river a few miles lower down, at the bottom of the steep hill which begins at Rosny. Just as they reached Rosny the *Belle Hélène* was entering the long loop which curves out to La Roche-Guyon, turns back and joins the high-road again at Bonnières. She would need at least three hours to cover the distance, whereas the car, climbing the hill and keeping straight ahead, arrived at Bonnières in fifteen minutes.

They drove through the village. There was an inn a little way beyond it, on the right. Don Luis made his chauffeur stop here.

'If we are not back by twelve tonight,' he said, 'go home to Paris. Will you come with me, captain?'

Patrice followed him towards the right, whence a small road led them to the river-bank. They followed this for a quarter of an hour. At last Don Luis found what he appeared to be seeking, a boat fastened to a stake, not far from a villa with closed shutters. Don Luis unhooked the chain.

It was about seven o'clock in the evening. Night was falling fast, but a brilliant moonlight lit the landscape.

'First of all,' said Don Luis, 'a word of explanation. We're going to wait for the barge. She'll come in sight on the stroke of ten and find us lying across stream. I shall order her to heave to; and there's no doubt that, when they see your uniform by the light of the moon or of my electric lamp, they will obey. Then we shall go on board.'

'Suppose they refuse?'

'If they refuse, we shall board her by force. There are three of them and two of us. So . . . '

'And then?'

'And then? Well, there's every reason to believe that the two men forming the crew are only extra hands, employed by Siméon, but ignorant of his actions and knowing nothing of the nature of the cargo. Once we have reduced Siméon to helplessness and paid them handsomely, they'll take the barge wherever I tell them. But, mind you – and this is what I was coming to – I mean to do with the barge exactly as I please. I shall hand over the cargo as and when I think fit. It's my booty, my prize. No one is entitled to it but myself.'

The officer drew himself up.

'Oh, I can't agree to that, you know!'

'Very well, then give me your word of honor that you'll keep a secret which doesn't belong to you. After which, we'll say good-night

and go our own ways. I'll do the boarding alone and you can go back
to your own business. Observe, however, that I am not insisting on an
immediate reply. You have plenty of time to reflect and to take the
decision which your interest, honor and conscience may dictate to
you. For my part, excuse me, but you know my weakness: when
circumstances give me a little spare time, I take advantage of it to go to
sleep. *Carpe somnum*, as the poet says. Good-night, captain.'

And, without another word, Don Luis wrapped himself in his
great-coat, sprang into the boat and lay down.

Patrice had had to make a violent effort to restrain his anger. Don
Luis's calm, ironic tone and well-bred, bantering voice got on his
nerves all the more because he felt the influence of that strange man
and fully recognized that he was incapable of acting without his
assistance. Besides, he could not forget that Don Luis had saved his
life and Coralie's.

The hours slipped by. The adventurer slumbered peacefully in the
cool night air. Patrice hesitated what to do, seeking for some plan of
conduct which would enable him to get at Siméon and rid himself of
that implacable adversary and at the same time to prevent Don Luis
from laying hands on the enormous treasure. He was dismayed at the
thought of being his accomplice. And yet, when the first throbs of
the motor were heard in the distance and when Don Luis awoke,
Patrice was by his side, ready for action.

They did not exchange a word. A village-clock struck ten. The
Belle Hélène was coming towards them.

Patrice felt his excitement increase. The *Belle Hélène* meant Siméon's
capture, the recovery of the millions, Coralie out of danger, the end
of that most hideous nightmare and the total extinction of Essarès'
handiwork. The engine was throbbing nearer and nearer. Its loud and
regular beat sounded wide over the motionless Seine. Don Luis had
taken the sculls and was pulling hard for the middle of the river.
And suddenly they saw in the distance a black mass looming up in the
white moonlight. Twelve or fifteen more minutes passed and the *Belle
Hélène* was before them.

'Shall I lend you a hand?' whispered Patrice. 'It looks as if you had
the current against you and as if you had a difficulty in getting along.'

'Not the least difficulty,' said Don Luis; and he began to hum a
tune.

'But . . .'

Patrice was stupefied. The boat had turned in its own length and
was making for the bank.

'But, I say, I say,' he said, 'what's this? Are you going back? Are you giving up? . . . I don't understand . . . You're surely not afraid because they're three to our two?'

Don Luis leapt on shore at a bound and stretched out his hand to him. Patrice pushed it aside, growling: 'Will you explain what it all means?'

'Take too long,' replied Don Luis. 'Just one question, though. You know that book I found in old Siméon's room, *The Memoirs of Benjamin Franklin*: did you see it when you were making your search?'

'Look here, it seems to me we have other things to . . . '

'It's an urgent question, captain.'

'Well, no, it wasn't there.'

'Then that's it,' said Don Luis. 'We've been done brown, or rather, to be accurate, I have. Let's be off, captain, as fast as we can.'

Patrice was still in the boat. He pushed off abruptly and caught up the scull, muttering: 'As I live, I believe the beggar's getting at me!'

He was ten yards from shore when he cried: 'If you're afraid, I'll go alone. Don't want any help.'

'Right you are, captain!' replied Don Luis. 'I'll expect you presently at the inn.'

* * *

Patrice encountered no difficulties in his undertaking. At the first order, which he shouted in a tone of command, the *Belle Hélène* stopped; and he was able to board her peacefully. The two bargees were men of a certain age, natives of the Basque coast. He introduced himself as a representative of the military authorities; and they showed him over their craft. He found neither old Siméon nor the very smallest bag of gold. The hold was almost empty.

The questions and answers did not take long.

'Where are you going?'

'To Rouen. We've been requisitioned by the government for transport of supplies.'

'But you picked up somebody on the way.'

'Yes, at Mantes.'

'His name, please?'

'Siméon Diodokis.'

'Where's he got to?'

'He made us put him down a little after, to take the train.'

'What did he want?'

'To pay us.'

'For what?'

'For a shipload we took at Paris two days ago.'

'Bags?'

'Yes.'

'What of?'

'Don't know. We were well paid and asked no questions.'

'And what's become of the load?'

'We transhipped it last night to a small steamer that came alongside of us below Passy.'

'What's the steamer's name?'

'The *Chamois*. Crew of six.'

'Where is she now?'

'Ahead of us. She was going fast. She must be at Rouen by this time. Siméon Diodokis is on his way to join her.'

'How long have you known Siméon Diodokis?'

'It's the first time we saw him. But we knew that he was in M. Essarès' service.'

'Oh, so you've worked for M. Essarès?'

'Yes, often . . . Same job and same trip.'

'He called you by means of a signal, didn't he?'

'Yes, he used to light an old factory-chimney.'

'Was it always bags?'

'Yes. We didn't know what was inside. He was a good payer.'

Patrice asked no more questions. He hurriedly got into his boat, pulled back to shore and found Don Luis seated with a comfortable supper in front of him.

'Quick!' he said. 'The cargo is on board a steamer, the *Chamois*. We can catch her up between Rouen and Le Havre.'

Don Luis rose and handed the officer a white-paper packet.

'Here's a few sandwiches for you, captain,' he said. 'We've an arduous night before us. I'm very sorry that you didn't get a sleep, as I did. Let's be off, and this time I shall drive. We'll knock some pace out of her! Come and sit beside me, captain.'

They both stepped into the car; the chauffeur took his seat behind them. But they had hardly started when Patrice exclaimed: 'Hi! What are you up to? Not this way! We're going back to Mantes or Paris!'

'That's what I mean to do,' said Luis, with a chuckle.

'Eh, what? Paris?'

'Well, of course!'

'Oh, look here, this is a bit too thick! Didn't I tell you that the two bargees . . . ?'

'Those bargees of yours are humbugs.'

'They declared that the cargo . . .'

'Cargo? No go!'

'But the *Chamois* . . .'

'*Chamois*? Sham was! I tell you once more, we're done, captain, done brown! Old Siméon is a wonderful old hand! He's a match worth meeting. He gives you a run for your money. He laid a trap in which I've been fairly caught. It's a magnificent joke, but there's moderation in all things. We've been fooled enough to last us the rest of our lives. Let's be serious now.'

'But . . .'

'Aren't you satisfied yet, captain? After the *Belle Hélène* do you want to attack the *Chamois*? As you please. You can get out at Mantes: Only, I warn you, Siméon is in Paris, with three or four hours' start of us.'

Patrice gave a shudder. Siméon in Paris! In Paris, where Coralie was alone and unprotected! He made no further protest; and Don Luis ran on: 'Oh, the rascal! How well he played his hand! *The Memoirs of Benjamin Franklin* were a master stroke. Knowing of my arrival, he said to himself, "Arsène Lupin is a dangerous fellow, capable of disentangling the affair and putting both me and the bags of gold in his pocket. To get rid of him, there's only one thing to be done: I must act in such a way as to make him rush along the real track at so fast a rate of speed that he does not perceive the moment when the real track becomes a false track." That was clever of him, wasn't it? And so we have the Franklin book, held out as a bait; the page opening of itself, at the right place; my inevitable easy discovery of the conduit system; the clue of Ariadne most obligingly offered. I follow up the clue like a trusting child, led by Siméon's own hand, from the cellar down to Berthou's Wharf. So far all's well. But, from that moment, take care! There's nobody at Berthou's Wharf. On the other hand, there's a barge alongside, which means a chance of making enquiries, which means the certainty that I shall make enquiries. And I make enquiries. And, having made enquiries, I am done for.'

'But then that man . . . ?'

'Yes, yes, yes, an accomplice of Siméon's, whom Siméon, knowing that he would be followed to the Gare Saint-Lazare, instructs in this way to direct me to Mantes for the second time. At Mantes the comedy continues. The *Belle Hélène* passes, with her double freight, Siméon and the bags of gold. We go running after the *Belle Hélène*. Of course, on the *Belle Hélène* there's nothing: no Siméon, no bags of gold. "Run after the *Chamois*. We've transhipped it all on the *Chamois*." We run after the *Chamois*, to Rouen, to Le Havre, to the end of the world; and of course our pursuit is fruitless, for the *Chamois* does not exist. But we are convinced that she does exist and that she has escaped our search. And by this time the trick is played. The millions are gone, Siméon has disappeared and there is only one thing left for us to do, which is to resign ourselves and abandon our quest. You understand, we're to abandon our quest: that's the fellow's object. And he would have succeeded if . . . '

The car was traveling at full speed. From time to time Don Luis would stop her dead with extraordinary skill. Post of territorials. Pass to be produced. Then a leap onward and once more the breakneck pace.

'If what?' asked Patrice, half-convinced. 'Which was the clue that put you on the track?'

'The presence of that woman at Mantes. It was a vague clue at first. But suddenly I remembered that, in the first barge, the *Nonchalante*, the person who gave us information – do you recollect? – well, that this person somehow gave me the queer impression, I can't tell you why, that I might be talking to a woman in disguise. The impression occurred to me once more. I made a mental comparison with the woman at Mantes . . . And then . . . and then it was like a flash of light . . . '

Don Luis paused to think and, in a lower voice, continued: 'But who the devil can this woman be?'

There was a brief silence, after which Patrice said, from instinct rather than reason: 'Grégoire, I suppose.'

'Eh? What's that? Grégoire?'

'Yes. Yes, Grégoire is a woman.'

'What are you talking about?'

'Well, obviously. Don't you remember? The accomplice told me so, on the day when I had them arrested outside the café.'

'Why, your diary doesn't say a word about it!'

'Oh, that's true! . . . I forgot to put down that detail.'

'A detail! He calls it a detail! Why, it's of the greatest importance, captain! If I had known, I should have guessed that that bargee was no other than Grégoire and we should not have wasted a whole night. Hang it all, captain, you really are the limit!'

But all this was unable to affect his good-humor. While Patrice, overcome with presentiments, grew gloomier and gloomier, Don Luis began to sing victory in his turn.

'Thank goodness! The battle is becoming serious! Really, it was too easy before; and that was why I was sulking, I, Lupin! Do you imagine things go like that in real life? Does everything fit in so accurately? Benjamin Franklin, the uninterrupted conduit for the gold, the series of clues that reveal themselves of their own accord, the man and the bags meeting at Mantes, the *Belle Hélène*: no, it all worried me. The cat was being choked with cream! And then the gold escaping in a barge! All very well in times of peace, but not in war-time, in the face of the regulations: passes, patrol-boats, inspections and I don't know what... How could a fellow like Siméon risk a trip of that kind? No, I had my suspicions; and that was why, captain, I made Ya-Bon mount guard, on the off chance, outside Berthou's Wharf. It was just an idea that occurred to me. The whole of this adventure seemed to center round the wharf. Well, was I right or not? Is M. Lupin no longer able to follow a scent? Captain, I repeat, I shall go back tomorrow evening. Besides, as I told you, I've got to. Whether I win or lose, I'm going. But we shall win. Everything will be cleared up. There will be no more mysteries, not even the mystery of the golden triangle ... Oh, I don't say that I shall bring you a beautiful triangle of eighteen-carat gold! We mustn't allow ourselves to be fascinated by words. It may be a geometrical arrangement of the bags of gold, a triangular pile ... or else a hole in the ground dug in that shape. No matter, we shall have it! And the bags of gold shall be ours! And Patrice and Coralie shall appear before monsieur le maire and receive my blessing and live happily ever after!'

They reached the gates of Paris. Patrice was becoming more and more anxious.

'Then you think the danger's over?'

'Oh, I don't say that! The play isn't finished. After the great scene of the third act, which we will call the scene of the oxide of carbon, there will certainly be a fourth act and perhaps a fifth. The enemy has not laid down his arms, by any means.'

They were skirting the quays.

'Let's get down,' said Don Luis.

He gave a faint whistle and repeated it three times.

'No answer,' he said. 'Ya-Bon's not there. The battle has begun.'

'But Coralie ...'

'What are you afraid of for her? Siméon doesn't know her address.'

There was nobody on Berthou's Wharf and nobody on the quay below. But by the light of the moon they saw the other barge, the *Nonchalante*.

'Let's go on board,' said Don Luis. 'I wonder if the lady known as Grégoire makes a practise of living here? Has she come back, believing us on our way to Le Havre? I hope so. In any case, Ya-Bon must have been there and no doubt left something behind to act as a signal. Will you come, captain?'

'Right you are. It's a queer thing, though: I feel frightened!'

'What of?' asked Don Luis, who was plucky enough himself to understand this presentiment.

'Of what we shall see.'

'My dear sir, there may be nothing there!'

Each of them switched on his pocket-lamp and felt the handle of his revolver. They crossed the plank between the shore and the boat. A few steps downwards brought them to the cabin. The door was locked.

'Hi, mate! Open this, will you?'

There was no reply. They now set about breaking it down, which was no easy matter, for it was massive and quite unlike an ordinary cabin-door.

At last it gave way.

'By Jingo!' said Don Luis, who was the first to go in. 'I didn't expect this!'

'What?'

'Look. The woman whom they called Grégoire. She seems to be dead.'

She was lying back on a little iron bedstead, with her man's blouse open at the top and her chest uncovered. Her face still bore an expression of extreme terror. The disordered appearance of the cabin suggested that a furious struggle had taken place.

'I was right. Here, by her side, are the clothes she wore at Mantes. But what's the matter, captain?'

Patrice had stifled a cry.

'There ... opposite ... under the window ... '

It was a little window overlooking the river. The panes were broken.

'Well?' asked Don Luis. 'What? Yes, I believe someone's been thrown out that way.'

'The veil ... that blue veil,' stammered Patrice, 'is her nurse's veil ... Coralie's ... '

Don Luis grew vexed: 'Nonsense! Impossible! Nobody knew her address.'

'Still ... '

'Still what? You haven't written to her? You haven't telegraphed to her?'

'Yes . . . I telegraphed to her . . . from Mantes.'

'What's that? Oh, but look here. This is madness! You don't mean that you really telegraphed?'

'Yes, I do.'

'You telegraphed from the post-office at Mantes?'

'Yes.'

'And was there anyone in the post-office?'

'Yes, a woman.'

'What woman? The one who lies here, murdered?'

'Yes.'

'But she didn't read what you wrote?'

'No, but I wrote the telegram twice over.'

'And you threw the first draft anywhere, on the floor, so that anyone who came along . . . Oh, really, captain, you must confess . . . !'

But Patrice was running towards the car and was already out of ear-shot.

Half an hour after, he returned with two telegrams which he had found on Coralie's table. The first, the one which he had sent, said.

ALL WELL. BE EASY AND STAY INDOORS. FONDEST LOVE.

CAPTAIN PATRICE

The second, which had evidently been despatched by Siméon, ran as follows.

EVENTS TAKING SERIOUS TURN. PLANS CHANGED. COMING BACK. EXPECT YOU NINE O'CLOCK THIS EVENING AT THE SMALL DOOR OF YOUR GARDEN.

CAPTAIN PATRICE

This second telegram was delivered to Coralie at eight o'clock; and she had left the home immediately afterwards.

Chapter 16
The Fourth Act

'Captain,' said Don Luis, 'you've scored two fine blunders. The first was your not telling me that Grégoire was a woman. The second . . . '

But Don Luis saw that the officer was too much dejected for him to care about completing his charge. He put his hand on Patrice Belval's shoulder.

'Come,' he said, 'don't upset yourself. The position's not as bad as you think.'

'Coralie jumped out of the window to escape that man,' Patrice muttered.

'Your Coralie is alive,' said Don Luis, shrugging his shoulders. 'In Siméon's hands, but alive.'

'Why, what do you know about it? Anyway, if she's in that monster's hands, might she not as well be dead? Doesn't it mean all the horrors of death? Where's the difference?'

'It means a danger of death, but it means life if we come in time; and we shall.'

'Have you a clue?'

'Do you imagine that I have sat twiddling my thumbs and that an old hand like myself hasn't had time in half an hour to unravel the mysteries which this cabin presents?'

'Then let's go,' cried Patrice, already eager for the fray. 'Let's have at the enemy.'

'Not yet,' said Don Luis, who was still hunting around him. 'Listen to me. I'll tell you what I know, captain, and I'll tell it you straight out, without trying to dazzle you by a parade of reasoning and without even telling you of the tiny trifles that serve me as proofs. The bare facts, that's all. Well, then . . . '

'Yes?'

'Little Mother Coralie kept the appointment at nine o'clock. Siméon was there with his female accomplice. Between them they bound and gagged her and brought her here. Observe that, in their eyes, it was a safe spot for the job, because they knew for certain that you and I had not discovered the trap. Nevertheless, we may assume that it was a provisional base of operations, adopted for part of the night only, and that Siméon reckoned on leaving Little Mother Coralie in the hands of his accomplice and setting out in search of a definite place of confinement, a permanent prison. But luckily – and I'm rather proud of this – Ya-Bon was on the spot. Ya-Bon was watching on his bench, in the dark. He must have seen them cross the embankment and no doubt recognized Siméon's walk in the distance. We'll take it that he gave chase at once, jumped on to the deck of the barge and arrived here at the same time as the enemy, before they had time to lock themselves in. Four people in this narrow space, in pitch darkness, must have meant a frightful upheaval. I know my Ya-Bon. He's terrible at such times. Unfortunately, it was not Siméon whom he caught by the neck with that merciless hand of his, but . . . the woman. Siméon took advantage of this. He had not let go of Little Mother Coralie. He picked her up in his arms and went up the companionway, flung her on the deck and then came back to lock the door on the two as they struggled.'

'Do you think so? Do you think it was Ya-Bon and not Siméon who killed the woman?'

'I'm sure of it. If there were no other proof, there is this particular fracture of the wind-pipe, which is Ya-Bon's special mark. What I do not understand is why, when he had settled his adversary, Ya-Bon didn't break down the door with a push of his shoulder and go after Siméon. I presume that he was wounded and that he had not the strength to make the necessary effort. I presume also that the woman did not die at once and that she spoke, saying things against Siméon, who had abandoned her instead of defending her. This much is certain, that Ya-Bon broke the window-panes . . .'

'To jump into the Seine, wounded as he was, with his one arm?' said Patrice.

'Not at all. There's a ledge running along the window. He could set his feet on it and get off that way.'

'Very well. But he was quite ten or twenty minutes behind Siméon?'

'That didn't matter, if the woman had time, before dying, to tell him where Siméon was taking refuge.'

'How can we get to know?'

'I've been trying to find out all the time that we've been chatting . . . and I've just discovered the way.'

'Here?'

'This minute; and I expected no less from Ya-Bon. The woman told him of a place in the cabin – look, that open drawer, probably – in which there was a visiting-card with an address on it. Ya-Bon took it and, in order to let me know, pinned the card to the curtain over there. I had seen it already; but it was only this moment that I noticed the pin that fixed it, a gold pin with which I myself fastened the Morocco Cross to Ya-Bon's breast.'

'What is the address?'

'Amédée Vacherot, 18, Rue Guimard. The Rue Guimard is close to this, which makes me quite sure of the road they took.'

The two men at once went away, leaving the woman's dead body behind. As Don Luis said, the police must make what they could of it.

As they crossed Berthou's Wharf they glanced at the recess and Don Luis remarked: 'There's a ladder missing. We must remember that detail. Siméon has been in there. He's beginning to make blunders too.'

The car took them to the Rue Guimard, a small street in Passy. No. 18 was a large house let out in flats, of fairly ancient construction. It was two o'clock in the morning when they rang.

A long time elapsed before the door opened; and, as they passed through the carriage-entrance, the porter put his head out of his lodge.

'Who's there?' he asked.

'We want to see M. Amédée Vacherot on urgent business.'

'That's myself.'

'You?'

'Yes, I, the porter. But by what right . . . ?'

'Orders of the prefect of police,' said Don Luis, displaying a badge.

They entered the lodge. Amédée Vacherot was a little, respectable-looking old man, with white whiskers. He might have been a beadle.

'Answer my questions plainly,' Don Luis ordered, in a rough voice, 'and don't try to prevaricate. We are looking for a man called Siméon Diodokis.'

The porter took fright at once.

'To do him harm?' he exclaimed. 'If it's to do him harm, it's no use asking me any questions. I would rather die by slow tortures than injure that kind M. Siméon.'

Don Luis assumed a gentler tone.

'Do him harm? On the contrary, we are looking for him to do him a service, to save him from a great danger.'

'A great danger?' cried M. Vacherot. 'Oh, I'm not at all surprised! I never saw him in such a state of excitement.'

'Then he's been here?'

'Yes, since midnight.'

'Is he here now?'

'No, he went away again.'

Patrice made a despairing gesture and asked: 'Perhaps he left someone behind?'

'No, but he intended to bring someone.'

'A lady?'

M. Vacherot hesitated.

'We know,' Don Luis resumed, 'that Siméon Diodokis was trying to find a place of safety in which to shelter a lady for whom he entertained the deepest respect.'

'Can you tell me the lady's name?' asked the porter, still on his guard.

'Certainly, Mme Essarès, the widow of the banker to whom Siméon used to act as secretary. Mme Essarès is a victim of persecution; he is defending her against her enemies; and, as we ourselves want to help the two of them and to take this criminal business in hand, we must insist that you . . . '

'Oh, well!' said M. Vacherot, now fully reassured. 'I have known Siméon Diodokis for ever so many years. He was very good to me at the time when I was working for an undertaker; he lent me money; he got me my present job; and he used often to come and sit in my lodge and talk about heaps of things . . . '

'Such as relations with Essarès Bey?' asked Don Luis, carelessly. 'Or his plans concerning Patrice Belval?'

'Heaps of things,' said the porter, after a further hesitation. 'He is one of the best of men, does a lot of good and used to employ me in distributing his local charity. And just now again he was risking his life for Mme Essarès.'

'One more word. Had you seen him since Essarès Bey's death?'

'No, it was the first time. He arrived a little before one o'clock. He was out of breath and spoke in a low voice, listening to the sounds of the street outside: "I've been followed," said he; "I've been followed. I could swear it." "By whom?" said I. "You don't know him," said he. "He has only one hand, but he wrings your neck for you." And then he stopped. And then he began again, in a whisper, so that I could hardly hear: "Listen to me, you're coming with me. We're going to fetch a lady, Mme Essarès. They want to kill her. I've hidden her all right, but she's fainted: we shall have to carry her . . . Or no, I'll go alone. I'll manage. But I want to know, is my room still free?" I must tell you, he has a little lodging here, since the day when he too had to hide himself. He used to come to it sometimes and he kept it on in case he might want it, for it's a detached lodging, away from the other tenants.'

'What did he do after that?' asked Patrice, anxiously.

'After that, he went away.'

'But why isn't he back yet?'

'I admit that it's alarming. Perhaps the man who was following him has attacked him. Or perhaps something has happened to the lady.'

'What do you mean, something happened to the lady?'

'I'm afraid something may have. When he first showed me the way we should have to go to fetch her, he said, "Quick, we must hurry. To save her life, I had to put her in a hole. That's all very well for two or three hours. But, if she's left longer, she will suffocate. The want of air . . . " '

Patrice had leapt upon the old man. He was beside himself, maddened at the thought that Coralie, ill and worn-out as she was, might be at the point of death in some unknown place, a prey to terror and suffering.

'You shall speak,' he cried, 'and this very minute! You shall tell us where she is! Oh, don't imagine that you can fool us any longer! Where is she? You know! He told you!'

He was shaking M. Vacherot by the shoulders and hurling his rage into the old man's face with unspeakable violence.

Don Luis, on the other hand, stood chuckling.

'Splendid, captain,' he said, 'splendid! My best compliments! You're making real progress since I joined forces with you. M. Vacherot will go through fire and water for us now.'

'Well, you see if I don't make the fellow speak,' shouted Patrice.

'It's no use, sir,' declared the porter, very firmly and calmly. 'You have deceived me. You are enemies of M. Siméon's. I shall not say another word that can give you any information.'

'You refuse to speak, do you? You refuse to speak?'

In his exasperation Patrice drew his revolver and aimed it at the man.

'I'm going to count three. If, by that time, you don't make up your mind to speak, you shall see the sort of man that Captain Belval is!'

The porter gave a start.

'Captain Belval, did you say? Are you Captain Belval?'

'Ah, old fellow, that seems to give you food for thought!'

'Are you Captain Belval? Patrice Belval?'

'At your service; and, if in two seconds from this you haven't told me . . .'

'Patrice Belval! And you are M. Siméon's enemy? And you want to . . . ?'

'I want to do him up like the cur he is, your blackguard of a Siméon . . . and you, his accomplice, with him. A nice pair of rascals! . . . Well, have you made up your mind?'

'Unhappy man!' gasped the porter. 'Unhappy man! You don't know what you're doing. Kill M. Siméon! You? You? Why, you're the last man who could commit a crime like that!'

'What about it? Speak, will you, you old numskull!'

'You, kill M. Siméon? You, Patrice? You, Captain Belval? You?'

'And why not? Speak, damn it! Why not?'

'You are his son.'

All Patrice's fury, all his anguish at the thought that Coralie was in Siméon's power or else lying in some pit, all his agonized grief, all his alarm: all this gave way, for a moment, to a terrible fit of merriment, which revealed itself in a long burst of laughter.

'Siméon's son! What the devil are you talking about? Oh, this beats everything! Upon my word, you're full of ideas, when you're trying to save him! You old ruffian! Of course, it's most convenient: don't kill that man, he's your father. He my father, that putrid Siméon! Siméon Diodokis, Patrice Belval's father! Oh, it's enough to make a chap split his sides!'

Don Luis had listened in silence. He made a sign to Patrice.

'Will you allow me to clear up this business, captain? It won't take me more than a few minutes; and that certainly won't delay us.' And, without waiting for the officer's reply, he turned to the old man and said slowly, 'Let's have this out, M. Vacherot. It's of the highest importance. The great thing is to speak plainly and not to lose yourself in superfluous words. Besides, you have said too much not to finish your revelation. Siméon Diodokis is not your benefactor's real name, is it?'

'No, that's so.'

'He is Armand Belval; and the woman who loved him used to call him Patrice?'

'Yes, his son's name.'

'Nevertheless, this Armand Belval was a victim of the same murderous attempt as the woman he loved, who was Coralie Essarès' mother?'

'Yes, but Coralie Essarès' mother died; and he did not.'

'That was on the fourteenth of April, 1895.'

'The fourteenth of April, 1895.'

Patrice caught hold of Don Luis's arm.

'Come,' he spluttered, 'Coralie's at death's door. The monster has buried her. That's the only thing that matters.'

'Then you don't believe that monster to be your father?' asked Don Luis.

'You're mad!'

'For all that, captain, you're trembling! . . . '

'I dare say, I dare say, but it's because of Coralie . . . I can't even hear what the man's saying! . . . Oh, it's a nightmare, every word of it! Make him stop! Make him shut up! Why didn't I wring his neck?'

He sank into a chair, with his elbows on the table and his head in his hands. It was really a horrible moment; and no catastrophe would have overwhelmed a man more utterly.

Don Luis looked at him with feeling and then turned to the porter.

'Explain yourself, M. Vacherot,' he said. 'As briefly as possible, won't you? No details. We can go into them later. We were saying, on the fourteenth of April, 1895 . . . '

'On the fourteenth of April, 1895, a solicitor's clerk, accompanied by the commissary of police, came to my governor's, close by here, and ordered two coffins for immediate delivery. The whole shop got to work. At ten o'clock in the evening, the governor, one of my mates and I went to the Rue Raynouard, to a sort of pavilion or lodge, standing in a garden.'

'I know. Go on.'

'There were two bodies. We wrapped them in winding-sheets and put them into the coffins. At eleven o'clock my governor and my fellow-workmen went away and left me alone with a sister of mercy. There was nothing more to do except to nail the coffins down. Well, just then, the nun, who had been watching and praying, fell asleep and something happened . . . oh, an awful thing! It made my hair stand on end, sir. I shall never forget it as long as I live. My knees gave way beneath me, I shook with fright . . . Sir, the man's body had moved. The man was alive!'

'Then you didn't know of the murder at that time?' asked Don Luis. 'You hadn't heard of the attempt?'

'No, we were told that they had both suffocated themselves with gas . . . It was many hours before the man recovered consciousness entirely. He was in some way poisoned.'

'But why didn't you inform the nun?'

'I couldn't say. I was simply stunned. I looked at the man as he slowly came back to life and ended by opening his eyes. His first words were, "She's dead, I suppose?" And then at once he said, "Not a word about all this. Let them think me dead: that will be better." And I can't tell you why, but I consented. The miracle had deprived me of all power of will. I obeyed like a child . . . He ended by getting up. He leant over the other coffin, drew aside the sheet and kissed the dead woman's face over and over again, whispering, "I will avenge you. All my life shall be devoted to avenging you and also, as you wished, to uniting our children. If I don't kill myself, it will be for Patrice and Coralie's sake. Goodbye." Then he told me to help him. Between us, we lifted the woman out of the coffin and carried it into the little bedroom next door. Then we went into the garden, took some big stones and put them into the coffins where the two bodies had been. When this was done, I nailed the coffins down, woke the good sister and went away. The man had locked himself into the bedroom with the dead woman. Next morning the under-taker's men came and fetched away the two coffins.'

Patrice had unclasped his hands and thrust his distorted features between Don Luis and the porter. Fixing his haggard eyes upon the latter, he asked, struggling with his words: 'But the graves? The inscription saying that the remains of both lie there, near the lodge where the murder was committed? The cemetery?'

'Armand Belval wished it so. At that time I was living in a garret in this house. I took a lodging for him where he came and lived by stealth, under the name of Siméon Diodokis, since Armand Belval was dead, and where he stayed for several months without going out. Then, in his new name and through me, he bought his lodge. And, bit by bit, we dug the graves. Coralie's and his. His because, I repeat, he wished it so. Patrice and Coralie were both dead. It seemed to him, in this way, that he was not leaving her. Perhaps also, I confess, despair had upset his balance a little, just a very little, only in what concerned his memory of the woman who died on the fourteenth of April, 1895, and his devotion for her. He wrote her name and his own everywhere: on the grave and also on the walls, on the trees and in the very borders of the flower-beds. They were Coralie Essarès' name and yours . . . And for this, for all that had to do with his revenge upon the murderer and with his son and with the dead woman's daughter, oh, for these matters he had all his wits about him, believe me, sir!'

Patrice stretched his clutching hands and his distraught face towards the porter: 'Proofs, proofs, proofs!' he insisted, in a stifled voice. 'Give me proofs at once! There's someone dying at this moment by that scoundrel's criminal intentions, there's a woman at the point of death. Give me proofs!'

'You need have no fear,' said M. Vacherot. 'My friend has only one thought, that of saving the woman, not killing her . . .'

'He lured her and me into the lodge to kill us, as our parents were killed before us.'

'He is trying only to unite you.'

'Yes, in death.'

'No, in life. You are his dearly-loved son. He always spoke of you with pride.'

'He is a ruffian, a monster!' shouted the officer.

'He is the very best man living, sir, and he is your father.'

Patrice started, stung by the insult.

'Proofs,' he roared, 'proofs! I forbid you to speak another word until you have proved the truth in a manner admitting of no doubt.'

Without moving from his seat, the old man put out his arm towards an old mahogany escritoire, lowered the lid and, pressing a spring, pulled out one of the drawers. Then he held out a bundle of papers.

'You know your father's handwriting, don't you, captain?' he said. 'You must have kept letters from him, since the time when you were at school in England. Well, read the letters which he wrote to me. You will see your name repeated a hundred times, the name of his son; and you will see the name of the Coralie whom he meant you to marry. Your whole life – your studies, your journeys, your work – is described in these letters. And you will also find your photographs, which he had taken by various correspondents, and photographs of Coralie, whom he had visited at Salonica. And you will see above all his hatred for Essarès Bey, whose secretary he had become, and his plans of revenge, his patience, his tenacity. And you will also see his despair when he heard of the marriage between Essarès and Coralie and, immediately afterwards, his joy at the thought that his revenge would be more cruel when he succeeded in uniting his son Patrice with Essarès' wife.'

As the old fellow spoke, he placed the letters one by one under the eyes of Patrice, who had at once recognized his father's hand and sat greedily devouring sentences in which his own name was constantly repeated. M. Vacherot watched him.

'Have you any more doubts, captain?' he asked, at last.

The officer again pressed his clenched fists to his temples.

'I saw his face,' he said, 'above the skylight, in the lodge into which he had locked us . . . It was gloating over our death, it was a face mad with hatred . . . He hated us even more than Essarès did . . . '

'A mistake! Pure imagination!' the old man protested.

'Or madness,' muttered Patrice.

Then he struck the table violently, in a fit of revulsion.

'It's not true, it's not true!' he exclaimed. 'That man is not my father. What, a scoundrel like that! . . . '

He took a few steps round the little room and, stopping in front of Don Luis, jerked out: 'Let's go. Else I shall go mad too. It's a nightmare, there's no other word for it, a nightmare in which things turn upside down until the brain itself capsizes. Let's go. Coralie is in danger. That's the only thing that matters.'

The old man shook his head: 'I'm very much afraid . . . '

'What are *you* afraid of?' bellowed the officer.

'I'm afraid that my poor friend has been caught up by the person who was following him . . . and then how can he have saved Mme Essarès? The poor thing was hardly able to breathe, he told me.'

Hanging on to Don Luis's arm, Patrice staggered out of the porter's lodge like a drunken man.

'She's done for, she must be!' he cried.

'Not at all,' said Don Luis. 'Siméon is as feverishly active as yourself. He is nearing the catastrophe. He is quaking with fear and not in a condition to weigh his words. Believe me, your Coralie is in no immediate danger. We have some hours before us.'

'But Ya-Bon? Suppose Ya-Bon has laid hands upon him?'

'I gave Ya-Bon orders not to kill him. Therefore, whatever happens, Siméon is alive. That's the great thing. So long as Siméon is alive, there is nothing to fear. He won't let your Coralie die.'

'Why not, seeing that he hates her? Why not? What is there in that man's heart? He devotes all his existence to a work of love on our behalf; and, from one minute to the next, that love turns to execration.'

He pressed Don Luis's arm and, in a hollow voice, asked: 'Do you believe that he is my father?'

'Siméon Diodokis is your father, captain,' replied Don Luis.

'Ah, don't, don't! It's too horrible! God, but we are in the valley of the shadow!'

'On the contrary,' said Don Luis, 'the shadow is lifting slightly; and I confess that our talk with M. Vacherot has given me a little light.'

'Do you mean it?'

But, in Patrice Belval's fevered brain, one idea jostled another. He suddenly stopped.

'Siméon may have gone back to the porter's lodge! ... And we shan't be there! ... Perhaps he will bring Coralie back!'

'No,' Don Luis declared, 'he would have done that before now, if it could be done. No, it's for us to go to him.'

'But where?'

'Well, of course, where all the fighting has been ... where the gold lies. All the enemy's operations are centered in that gold; and you may be sure that, even in retreat, he can't get away from it. Besides, we know that he is not far from Berthou's Wharf.'

Patrice allowed himself to be led along without a word. But suddenly Don Luis cried: 'Did you hear?'

'Yes, a shot.'

At that moment they were on the point of turning into the Rue Raynouard. The height of the houses prevented them from perceiving the exact spot from which the shot had been fired, but it came approximately from the Essarès house or the immediate precincts. Patrice was filled with alarm.

'Can it be Ya-Bon?'

'I'm afraid so,' said Don Luis, 'and, as Ya-Bon wouldn't fire, someone must have fired a shot at him ... Oh, by Jove, if my poor Ya-Bon were to be killed ... !'

'And suppose it was at her, at Coralie?' whispered Patrice.

Don Luis began to laugh.

'Oh, my dear captain, I'm almost sorry that I ever mixed myself up in this business! You were much cleverer before I came and a good deal clearer-sighted. Why the devil should Siméon attack your Coralie, considering that she's already in his power?'

They hurried their steps. As they passed the Essarès house they saw that everything was quiet and they went on until they came to the lane, down which they turned.

Patrice had the key, but the little door which opened on to the garden of the lodge was bolted inside.

'Aha!' said Don Luis. 'That shows that we're warm. Meet me on the quay, captain. I shall run down to Berthou's Wharf to have a look round.'

During the past few minutes a pale dawn had begun to mingle with the shades of night. The embankment was still deserted, however.

Don Luis observed nothing in particular at Berthou's Wharf; but, when he returned to the quay above, Patrice showed him a ladder lying right at the end of the pavement which skirted the garden of the lodge; and Don Luis recognized the ladder as the one whose absence he had noticed from the recess in the yard. With that quick vision which was one of his greatest assets, he at once furnished the explanation.

'As Siméon had the key of the garden, it was obviously Ya-Bon who used the ladder to make his way in. Therefore he saw Siméon take refuge there on returning from his visit to old Vacherot and after coming to fetch Coralie. Now the question is, did Siméon succeed in fetching Little Mother Coralie, or did he run away before fetching her? That I can't say. But, in any case . . . '

Bending low down, he examined the pavement and continued: 'In any case, what is certain is that Ya-Bon knows the hiding-place where the bags of gold are stacked and that it is there most likely that your Coralie was and perhaps still is, worse luck, if the enemy, giving his first thought to his personal safety, has not had time to remove her.'

'Are you sure?'

'Look here, captain, Ya-Bon always carries a piece of chalk in his pocket. As he doesn't know how to write, except just the letters forming my name, he has drawn these two straight lines which, with the line of the wall, make a triangle . . . the golden triangle.'

Don Luis drew himself up.

'The clue is rather meager. But Ya-Bon looks upon me as a wizard. He never doubted that I should manage to find this spot and that those three lines would be enough for me. Poor Ya-Bon!'

'But,' objected Patrice, 'all this, according to you, took place before our return to Paris, between twelve and one o'clock, therefore.'

'Yes.'

'Then what about the shot which we have just heard, four or five hours later?'

'As to that I'm not so positive. We may assume that Siméon squatted somewhere in the dark. Possibly at the first break of day, feeling easier and hearing nothing of Ya-Bon, he risked taking a step or two. Then Ya-Bon, keeping watch in silence, would have leaped upon him.'

'So you think . . . '

'I think that there was a struggle, that Ya-Bon was wounded and that Siméon . . . '

'That Siméon escaped?'

'Or else was killed. However, we shall know all about it in a few minutes.'

He set the ladder against the railing at the top of the wall. Patrice climbed over with Don Luis's assistance. Then, stepping over the railing in his turn, Don Luis drew up the ladder, threw it into the garden and made a careful examination. Finally, they turned their steps, through the tall grasses and bushy shrubs, towards the lodge.

The daylight was increasing rapidly and the outlines of everything were becoming clearer. The two men walked round the lodge, Don Luis leading the way. When he came in sight of the yard, on the street side, he turned and said: 'I was right.'

And he ran forward.

Outside the hall-door lay the bodies of the two adversaries, clutching each other in a confused heap. Ya-Bon had a horrible wound in the head, from which the blood was flowing all over his face. With his right hand he held Siméon by the throat.

Don Luis at once perceived that Ya-Bon was dead and Siméon Diodokis alive.

Chapter 17

Siméon Gives Battle

It took them some time to loosen Ya-Bon's grip. Even in death the Senegalese did not let go his prey; and his fingers, hard as iron and armed with nails piercing as a tiger's claws, dug into the neck of the enemy, who lay gurgling, deprived of consciousness and strength.

Don Luis caught sight of Siméon's revolver on the cobbles of the yard.

'It was lucky for you, you old ruffian,' he said, in a low voice, 'that Ya-Bon did not have time to squeeze the breath out of you before you fired that shot. But I wouldn't chortle overmuch, if I were you. He might perhaps have spared you, whereas, now that Ya-Bon's dead, you can write to your family and book your seat below. *De profundis*, Diodokis!' And, giving way to his grief, he added, 'Poor Ya-Bon! He saved me from a horrible death one day in Africa . . . and today he dies by my orders, so to speak. My poor Ya-Bon!'

Assisted by Patrice, he carried the negro's corpse into the little bedroom next to the studio.

'We'll inform the police this evening, captain, when the drama is finished. For the moment, it's a matter of avenging him and the others.'

He thereupon applied himself to making a minute inspection of the scene of the struggle, after which he went back to Ya-Bon and then to Siméon, whose clothes and shoes he examined closely.

Patrice was face to face with his terrible enemy, whom he had propped against the wall of the lodge and was contemplating in silence, with a fixed stare of hatred. Siméon! Siméon Diodokis, the execrable demon who, two days before, had hatched the terrible plot and, bending over the skylight, had laughed as he watched their awful agony! Siméon Diodokis, who, like a wild beast, had hidden Coralie in some hole, so that he might go back and torture her at his ease!

He seemed to be in pain and to breathe with great difficulty. His wind-pipe had no doubt been injured by Ya-Bon's clutch. His yellow spectacles had fallen off during the fight. A pair of thick, grizzled eyebrows lowered about his heavy lids.

'Search him, captain,' said Don Luis.

But, as Patrice seemed to shrink from the task, he himself felt in Siméon's jacket and produced a pocket-book, which he handed to the officer.

It contained first of all a registration-card, in the name of Siméon Diodokis, Greek subject, with his photograph gummed to it. The photograph was a recent one, taken with the spectacles, the comforter and the long hair, and bore a police-stamp dated December, 1914. There was a collection of business documents, invoices and memoranda, addressed to Siméon as Essarès Bey's secretary, and, among these papers, a letter from Amédée Vacherot, running as follows.

Dear M. Siméon,
I have succeeded. A young friend of mine has taken a snapshot of Mme Essarès and Patrice at the hospital, at a moment when they were talking together. I am so glad to be able to gratify you. But when will you tell your dear son the truth? How delighted he will be when he hears it!

At the foot of the letter were a few words in Siméon's hand, a sort of personal note.

Once more I solemnly pledge myself not to reveal anything to my dearly-beloved son until Coralie, my bride, is avenged and until Patrice and Coralie Essarès are free to love each other and to marry.

'That's your father's writing, is it not?' asked Don Luis.

'Yes,' said Patrice, in bewilderment. 'And it is also the writing of the letters which he addressed to his friend Vacherot. Oh, it's too hideous to be true! What a man! What a scoundrel!'

Siméon moved. His eyes opened and closed repeatedly. Then, coming to himself entirely, he looked at Patrice, who at once, in a stifled voice, asked: 'Where's Coralie?'

And, as Siméon, still dazed, seemed not to understand and sat gazing at him stupidly, he repeated, in a harsher tone: 'Where's Coralie? What have you done with her? Where have you put her? She must be dying!'

Siméon was gradually recovering life and consciousness. He mumbled: 'Patrice . . . Patrice . . .'

He looked around him, saw Don Luis, no doubt remembered his fight to the death with Ya-Bon and closed his eyes again. But Patrice's rage increased.

'Will you attend?' he shouted. 'I won't wait any longer! It'll cost you your life if you don't answer!'

The man's eyes opened again, red-rimmed, bloodshot eyes. He pointed to his throat to indicate his difficulty in speaking. At last, with a visible effort, he repeated: 'Patrice! Is it you? . . . I have been waiting for this moment so long! . . . And now we are meeting as enemies! . . . '

'As mortal enemies,' said Patrice, with emphasis. 'Death stands between us: Ya-Bon's death, Coralie's perhaps . . . Where is she? You must speak, or . . . '

'Patrice, is it really you?' the man repeated, in a whisper.

The familiarity exasperated the officer. He caught his adversary by the lapel of his jacket and shook him. But Siméon had seen the pocket-book which he held in his other hand and, without resisting Patrice's roughness, whined: 'You wouldn't hurt me, Patrice. You must have found some letters; and you now know the link that binds us together. Oh, how happy I should have been . . . !'

Patrice had released his hold and stood staring at him in horror. Sinking his voice in his turn, he said: 'Don't dare to speak of that: I won't, I won't believe it!'

'It's the truth, Patrice.'

'You lie! You lie!' cried the officer, unable to restrain himself any longer, while his grief distorted his face out of all recognition.

'Ah, I see you have guessed it! Then I need not explain . . . '

'You lie! You're just a common scoundrel! . . . If what you say is true, why did you plot against Coralie and me? Why did you try to murder the two of us?'

'I was mad, Patrice. Yes, I go mad at times. All these tragedies have turned my head. My own Coralie's death . . . and then my life in Essarès' shadow . . . and then . . . and then, above all, the gold! . . . Did I really try to kill you both? I no longer remember. Or at least I remember a dream I had: it happened in the lodge, didn't it, as before? Oh, madness! What a torture! I'm like a man in the galleys. I have to do things against my will! . . . Then it was in the lodge, was it, as before? And in the same manner? With the same implements? . . . Yes, in my dream, I went through all my agony over again . . . and that of my darling . . . But, instead of being tortured, I was the torturer . . . What a torment!'

He spoke low, inside himself, with hesitations and intervals and an unspeakable air of suffering. Don Luis kept his eyes fixed on him, as though trying to discover what he was aiming at. And Siméon continued: 'My poor Patrice! . . . I was so fond of you! . . . And now you are my worst enemy! . . . How indeed could it be otherwise? . . . How could you forget? . . . Oh, why didn't they lock me up after Essarès' death? It was then that I felt my brain going . . . '

'So it was you who killed him?' asked Patrice.

'No, no, that's just it: somebody else robbed me of my revenge.'

'Who?'

'I don't know . . . The whole business is incomprehensible to me . . . Don't speak of it . . . It all pains me . . . I have suffered so since Coralie's death!'

'Coralie!' exclaimed Patrice.

'Yes, the woman I loved . . . As for little Coralie, I've suffered also on her account . . . She ought not to have married Essarès.'

'Where is she?' asked Patrice, in agony.

'I can't tell you.'

'Oh,' cried Patrice, shaking with rage, 'you mean she's dead!'

'No, she's alive, I swear it.'

'Then where is she? That's the only thing that matters. All the rest belongs to the past. But this thing, a woman's life, Coralie's life . . . '

'Listen.'

Siméon stopped and gave a glance at Don Luis.

'Tell him to go away,' he said.

Don Luis laughed: 'Of course! Little Mother Coralie is hidden in the same place as the bags of gold. To save her means surrendering the bags of gold.'

'Well?' said Patrice, in an almost aggressive tone.

'Well, captain,' replied Don Luis, not without a certain touch of banter in his voice, 'if this honorable gentleman suggested that you should release him on parole so that he might go and fetch your Coralie, I don't suppose you'd accept?'

'No.'

'You haven't the least confidence in him, have you? And you're right. The honorable gentleman, mad though he may be, gave such proofs of mental superiority and balance, when he sent us trundling down the road to Mantes, that it would be dangerous to attach the least credit to his promises. The consequence is . . . '

'Well?'

'This, captain, that the honorable gentleman means to propose a bargain to you, which may be couched thus: "You can have Coralie, but I'll keep the gold." '

'And then?'

'And then? It would be a capital notion, if you were alone with the honorable gentleman. The bargain would soon be concluded. But I'm here . . . by Jupiter!'

Patrice had drawn himself up. He stepped towards Don Luis and said, in a voice which became openly hostile: 'I presume that you won't raise any opposition. It's a matter of a woman's life.'

'No doubt. But, on the other hand, it's a matter of three hundred million francs.'

'Then you refuse?'

'Refuse? I should think so!'

'You refuse when that woman is at her last gasp? You would rather she died? . . . Look here, you seem to forget that this is my affair, that . . . that . . . '

The two men were standing close together. Don Luis retained that chaffing calmness, that air of knowing more than he chose to say, which irritated Patrice. At heart Patrice, while yielding to Don Luis's mastery, resented it and felt a certain embarrassment at accepting the services of a man with whose past he was so well acquainted.

'Then you actually refuse?' he rapped out, clenching his fists.

'Yes,' said Don Luis, preserving his coolness. 'Yes, Captain Belval, I refuse this bargain, which I consider absurd. Why, it's the confidence-trick! By Jingo! Three hundred millions! Give up a windfall like that? Never. But I haven't the least objection to leaving you alone with the honorable gentleman. That's what he wants, isn't it?'

'Yes.'

'Well, talk it over between yourselves. Sign the compact. The honorable gentleman, who, for his part, has every confidence in his son, will tell you the whereabouts of the hiding-place; and you shall release your Coralie.'

'And you? What about you?' snarled Patrice, angrily.

'I? I'm going to complete my little enquiry into the present and the past by revisiting the room where you nearly met your death. See you later, captain. And, whatever you do, insist on guarantees.'

Switching on his pocket-lamp, Don Luis entered the lodge and walked straight to the studio. Patrice saw the electric rays playing on the panels between the walled-up windows. He went back to where Siméon sat.

'Now then,' he said, in a voice of authority. 'Be quick about it.'

'Are you sure he's not listening?'

'Quite sure.'

'Be careful with him, Patrice. He means to take the gold and keep it.'

'Don't waste time,' said Patrice, impatiently. 'Get to Coralie.'

'I've told you Coralie was alive.'

'She was alive when you left her; but since then . . . '

'Yes, since then . . . '

'Since then, what? You seem to have your doubts.'

'It was last night, five or six hours ago, and I am afraid . . . '

Patrice felt a cold shudder run down his back. He would have given anything for a decisive word; and at the same time he was almost strangling the old man to punish him. He mastered himself, however.

'Don't let's waste time,' he repeated. 'Tell me where to go.'

'No, we'll go together.'

'You haven't the strength.'

'Yes, yes, I can manage . . . it's not far. Only, only, listen to me . . . '

The old man seemed utterly exhausted. From time to time his breathing was interrupted, as though Ya-Bon's hand were still clutching him by the throat, and he sank into a heap, moaning.

Patrice stooped over him.

'I'm listening,' he said. 'But, for God's sake, hurry!'

'All right,' said Siméon. 'All right. She'll be free in a few minutes. But on one condition, just one . . . Patrice, you must swear to me on Coralie's head that you will not touch the gold and that no one shall know . . . '

'I swear it on her head.'

'You swear it, yes; but the other one, your damned companion, he'll follow us, he'll see.'

'No, he won't.'

'Yes, he will, unless you consent . . . '

'To what? Oh, in Heaven's name, speak!'

'I'll tell you. Listen. But remember, we must go to Coralie's assistance . . . and that quickly . . . otherwise . . . '

Patrice hesitated, bending one leg, almost on his knees.

'Then come, do!' he said, modifying his tone. 'Please come, because Coralie . . . '

'Yes, but that man . . . '

'Oh, Coralie first!'

'What do you mean? Suppose he sees us? Suppose he takes the gold from us?'

'What does that matter!'

'Oh, don't say that, Patrice! . . . The gold! That's the one thing! Since that gold has been mine, my life is changed. The past no longer counts . . . nor does hatred . . . nor love . . . There's only the gold, the bags of gold . . . I'd rather die . . . and let Coralie die . . . and see the whole world disappear . . . '

'But, look here, what is it you want? What is it you demand?'

Patrice had taken the two arms of this man who was his father and whom he had never detested with greater vehemence. He was imploring him with all the strength of his being. He would have shed tears had he thought that the old man would allow himself to be moved by tears.

'What is it?'

'I'll tell you. Listen. He's there, isn't he?'

'Yes.'

'In the studio?'

'Yes.'

'In that case . . . he mustn't come out . . . '

'How do you mean?'

'No, he must stay there until we've done.'

'But . . . '

'It's quite easy. Listen carefully. You've only to make a movement, to shut the door on him. The lock has been forced, but there are the two bolts; and those will do. Do you consent?'

Patrice rebelled.

'But you're mad! I consent, I? . . . Why, the man saved my life! . . . He saved Coralie!'

'But he's doing for her now. Think a moment: if he were not there, if he were not interfering, Coralie would be free. Do you accept?'

'No.'

'Why not? Do you know what that man is? A highway robber . . . a wretch who has only one thought, to get hold of the millions. And you have scruples! Come, it's absurd, isn't it? . . . Do you accept?'

'No and again no!'

'Then so much the worse for Coralie . . . Oh, yes, I see you don't realize the position exactly! It's time you did, Patrice. Perhaps it's even too late.'

'Oh, don't say that!'

'Yes, yes, you must learn the facts and take your share of the responsibility. When that damned negro was chasing me, I got rid of Coralie as best I could, intending to release her in an hour or two. And then . . . and then you know what happened . . . It was eleven o'clock at night . . . nearly eight hours ago . . . So work it out for yourself . . . '

Patrice wrung his hands. Never had he imagined that a man could be tortured to such a degree. And Siméon continued, unrelentingly.

'She can't breathe, on my soul she can't! . . . Perhaps just a very little air reaches her, but that is all . . . Then again I can't tell that all that covers and protects her hasn't given way. If it has, she's suffocating . . . while you stand here arguing . . . Look here, can it matter to you to lock up that man for ten minutes? . . . Only ten minutes, you know. And you still hesitate! Then it's you who are killing her, Patrice. Think . . . buried alive!'

Patrice drew himself up. His resolve was taken. At that moment he would have shrunk from no act, however painful. And what Siméon asked was so little.

'What do you want me to do?' he asked. 'Give your orders.'

'You know what I want,' said the other. 'It's quite simple. Go to the door, bolt it and come back again.'

The officer entered the lodge with a firm step and walked through the hall. The light was dancing up and down at the far end of the studio.

Without a word, without a moment's hesitation, he slammed the door, shot both the bolts and hastened back. He felt relieved. The action was a base one, but he never doubted that he had fulfilled an imperative duty.

'That's it,' he said, 'Let's hurry.'

'Help me up,' said the old man. 'I can't manage by myself.'

Patrice took him under the armpits and lifted him to his feet. But he had to support him, for the old man's legs were swaying beneath him.

'Oh, curse it!' blurted Siméon. 'That blasted nigger has done for me. I'm suffocating too, I can't walk.'

Patrice almost carried him, while Siméon, in the last stage of weakness, stammered: 'This way . . . Now straight ahead . . . '

They passed the corner of the lodge and turned their steps towards the graves.

'You're quite sure you fastened the door?' the old man continued. 'Yes, I heard it slam. Oh, he's a terrible fellow, that! You have to be on your guard with him! But you swore not to say anything, didn't you? Swear it again, by your mother's memory . . . no, better, swear it by Coralie . . . May she die on the spot if you betray your oath!'

He stopped. A spasm prevented his going any further until he had drawn a little air into his lungs. Nevertheless he went on talking.

'I needn't worry, need I? Besides, you don't care about gold. That being so, why should you speak? Never mind, swear that you will be silent. Or, look here, give me your word of honor. That's best. Your word, eh?'

Patrice was still holding him round the waist. It was a terrible, long agony for the officer, this slow crawl and this sort of embrace which he was compelled to adopt in order to effect Coralie's release. As he felt the contact of the detested man's body, he was more inclined to squeeze the life out of it. And yet a vile phrase kept recurring deep down within him: 'I am his son, I am his son . . . '

'It's here,' said the old man.

'Here? But these are the graves.'

'Coralie's grave and mine. It's what we were making for.'

He turned round in alarm.

'I say, the footprints! You'll get rid of them on the way back, won't you? For he would find our tracks otherwise and he would know that this is the place . . . '

'Let's hurry . . . So Coralie is here? Down there? Buried? Oh, how horrible!'

It seemed to Patrice as if each minute that passed meant more than an hour's delay and as if Coralie's safety might be jeopardized by a moment's hesitation or a single false step.

He took every oath that was demanded of him. He swore upon Coralie's head. He pledged his word of honor. At that moment there was not an action which he would not have been ready to perform.

Siméon knelt down on the grass, under the little temple, pointing with his finger.

'It's there,' he repeated. 'Underneath that.'

'Under the tombstone?'

'Yes.'

'Then the stone lifts?' asked Patrice, anxiously. 'I can't lift it by myself. It can't be done. It would take three men to lift that.'

'No,' said the old man, 'the stone swings on a pivot. You'll manage quite easily. All you have to do is to pull at one end . . . this one, on the right.'

Patrice came and caught hold of the great stone slab, with its inscription, 'Here lie Patrice and Coralie,' and pulled.

The stone rose at the first endeavor, as if a counterweight had forced the other end down.

'Wait,' said the old man. 'We must hold it in position, or it will fall down again. You'll find an iron bar at the bottom of the second step.'

There were three steps running into a small cavity, barely large enough to contain a man stooping. Patrice saw the iron bar and, propping up the stone with his shoulder, took the bar and set it up.

'Good,' said Siméon. 'That will keep it steady. What you must now do is to lie down in the hollow. This was where my coffin was to have been and where I often used to come and lie beside my dear Coralie. I would remain for hours, flat on the ground, speaking to her . . . We both talked . . . Yes, I assure you, we used to talk . . . Oh, Patrice! . . . '

Patrice had bent his tall figure in the narrow space where he was hardly able to move.

'What am I to do?' he asked.

'Don't you hear your Coralie? There's only a partition-wall between you: a few bricks hidden under a thin layer of earth. And a door. The other vault, Coralie's, is behind it. And behind that there's a third, with the bags of gold.'

The old man was bending over and directing the search as he knelt on the grass.

'The door's on the left. Farther than that. Can't you find it? That's odd. You mustn't be too slow about it, though. Ah, have you got it now? No? Oh, if I could only go down too! But there's not room for more than one.'

There was a brief silence. Then he began again: 'Stretch a bit farther. Good. Can you move?'

'Yes,' said Patrice.

'Then go on moving, my lad!' cried the old man, with a yell of laughter.

And, stepping back briskly, he snatched away the iron bar. The enormous block of stone came down heavily, slowly, because of the counterweight, but with irresistible force.

Though floundering in the newly-turned earth, Patrice tried to rise, at the sight of his danger. Siméon had taken up the iron bar and now struck him a blow on the head with it. Patrice gave a cry and moved no more. The stone covered him up. The whole incident had lasted but a few seconds.

Siméon did not lose an instant. He knew that Patrice, wounded as he was bound to be and weakened by the posture to which he was condemned, was incapable of making the necessary effort to lift the lid of his tomb. On that side, therefore, there was no danger.

He went back to the lodge and, though he walked with some difficulty, he had no doubt exaggerated his injuries, for he did not stop until he reached the door. He even scorned to obliterate his footprints and went straight ahead.

On entering the hall he listened. Don Luis was tapping against the walls and the partition inside the studio and the bedroom.

'Capital!' said Siméon, with a grin. 'His turn now.'

It did not take long. He walked to the kitchen on the right, opened the door of the meter and, turning the key, released the gas, thus beginning again with Don Luis what he had failed to achieve with Patrice and Coralie.

Not till then did he yield to the immense weariness with which he was overcome and allow himself to lie back in a chair for two or three minutes.

His most terrible enemy also was now out of the way. But it was still necessary for him to act and ensure his personal safety. He walked round the lodge, looked for his yellow spectacles and put them on, went through the garden, opened the door and closed it behind him. Then he turned down the lane to the quay.

Once more stopping, in front of the parapet above Berthou's Wharf, he seemed to hesitate what to do. But the sight of people passing, carmen, market-gardeners and others, put an end to his indecision. He hailed a taxi and drove to the Rue Guimard.

His friend Vacherot was standing at the door of his lodge.

'Oh, is that you, M. Siméon?' cried the porter. 'But what a state you're in!'

'Hush, no names!' he whispered, entering the lodge. 'Has anyone seen me?'

'No. It's only half-past seven and the house is hardly awake. But, Lord forgive us, what have the scoundrels done to you? You look as if you had no breath left in your body!'

'Yes, that nigger who came after me . . . '

'But the others?'

'What others?'

'The two who were here? Patrice?'

'Eh? Has Patrice been?' asked Siméon, still speaking in a whisper.

'Yes, last night, after you left.'

'And you told him?'

'That he was your son.'

'Then that,' mumbled the old man, 'is why he did not seem surprised at what I said.'

'Where are they now?'

'With Coralie. I was able to save her. I've handed her over to them. But it's not a question of her. Quick, I must see a doctor; there's no time to lose.'

'We have one in the house.'

'No, that's no use. Have you a telephone-directory?'

'Here you are.'

'Turn up Dr Géradec.'

'What? You can't mean that?'

'Why not? He has a private hospital quite close, on the Boulevard de Montmorency, with no other house near it.'

'That's so, but haven't you heard? There are all sorts of rumors about him afloat: something to do with passports and forged certificates.'

'Never mind that.'

M. Vacherot hunted out the number in the directory and rang up the exchange. The line was engaged; and he wrote down the number on the margin of a newspaper. Then he telephoned again. The answer was that the doctor had gone out and would be back at ten.

'It's just as well,' said Siméon. 'I'm not feeling strong enough yet. Say that I'll call at ten o'clock.'

'Shall I give your name as Siméon?'

'No, my real name, Armand Belval. Say it's urgent, say it's a surgical case.'

The porter did so and hung up the instrument, with a moan: 'Oh, my poor M. Siméon! A man like you, so good and kind to everybody! Tell me what happened?'

'Don't worry about that. Is my place ready?'

'To be sure it is.'

'Take me there without anyone seeing us.'

'As usual.'

'Be quick. Put your revolver in your pocket. What about your lodge? Can you leave it?'

'Five minutes won't hurt.'

The lodge opened at the back on a small courtyard, which communicated with a long corridor. At the end of this passage was another yard, in which stood a little house consisting of a ground-floor and an attic.

They went in. There was an entrance-hall followed by three rooms, leading one into the other. Only the second room was furnished. The third had a door opening straight on a street that ran parallel with the Rue Guimard.

They stopped in the second room.

'Did you shut the hall-door after you?'

'Yes, M. Siméon.'

'No one saw us come in, I suppose?'

'Not a soul.'

'No one suspects that you're here?'

'No.'

'Give me your revolver.'

'Here it is.'

'Do you think, if I fired it off, anyone would hear?'

'No, certainly not. Who is there to hear? But . . . '

'But what?'

'You're surely not going to fire?'

'Yes, I am.'

'At yourself, M. Siméon, at yourself? Are you going to kill yourself?'

'Don't be an ass.'

'Well, who then?'

'You, of course!' chuckled Siméon.

Pressing the trigger, he blew out the luckless man's brains. His victim fell in a heap, stone dead. Siméon flung aside the revolver and remained impassive, a little undecided as to his next step. He opened out his fingers, one by one, up to six, apparently counting the six persons of whom he had got rid in a few hours: Grégoire, Coralie, Ya-Bon, Patrice, Don Luis, old Vacherot!

His mouth gave a grin of satisfaction. One more endeavor; and his flight and safety were assured.

For the moment he was incapable of making the endeavor. His head whirled. His arms struck out at space. He fell into a faint, with a gurgle in his throat, his chest crushed under an unbearable weight.

But, at a quarter to ten, with an effort of will, he picked himself up and, mastering himself and disregarding the pain, he went out by the other door of the house.

At ten o'clock, after twice changing his taxi, he arrived at the Boulevard Montmorency, just at the moment when Dr Géradec was alighting from his car and mounting the steps of the handsome villa in which his private hospital had been installed since the beginning of the war.

Chapter 18
Siméon's Last Victim

Dr Géradec's hospital had several annexes, each of which served a specific purpose, grouped around it in a fine garden. The villa itself was used for the big operations. The doctor had his consulting-room here also; and it was to this room that Siméon Diodokis was first shown. But, after answering a few questions put to him by a male nurse, Siméon was taken to another room in a separate wing.

Here he was received by the doctor, a man of about sixty, still young in his movements, clean-shaven and wearing a glass screwed into his right eye, which contracted his features into a constant grimace. He was wrapped from the shoulders to the feet in a large white operating-apron.

Siméon explained his case with great difficulty, for he could hardly speak. A footpad had attacked him the night before, taken him by the throat and robbed him, leaving him half-dead in the road.

'You have had time to send for a doctor since,' said Dr Géradec, fixing him with a glance.

Siméon did not reply; and the doctor added: 'However, it's nothing much. The fact that you are alive shows that there's no fracture. It reduces itself therefore to a contraction of the larynx, which we shall easily get rid of by tubing.'

He gave his assistant some instructions. A long aluminum tube was inserted in the patient's wind-pipe. The doctor, who had absented himself meanwhile, returned and, after removing the tube, examined the patient, who was already beginning to breathe with greater ease.

'That's over,' said Dr Géradec, 'and much quicker than I expected. There was evidently in your case an inhibition which caused the throat to shrink. Go home now; and, when you've had a rest, you'll forget all about it.'

Siméon asked what the fee was and paid it. But, as the doctor was seeing him to the door, he stopped and, without further preface, said: 'I am a friend of Mme Albonin's.'

The doctor did not seem to understand what he meant.

'Perhaps you don't recognize the name,' Siméon insisted. 'When I tell you, however, that it conceals the identity of Mme Mosgranem, I have no doubt that we shall be able to arrange something.'

'What about?' asked the doctor, while his face displayed still greater astonishment.

'Come, doctor, there's no need to be on your guard. We are alone. You have sound-proof, double doors. Sit down and let's talk.'

He took a chair. The doctor sat down opposite him, looking more and more surprised. And Siméon proceeded with his statement: 'I am a Greek subject. Greece is a neutral, indeed, I may say, a friendly country; and I can easily obtain a passport and leave France. But, for personal reasons, I want the passport made out not in my own name but in some other, which you and I will decide upon together and which will enable me, with your assistance, to go away without any danger.'

The doctor rose to his feet indignantly.

Siméon persisted: 'Oh, please don't be theatrical! It's a question of price, is it not? My mind is made up. How much do you want?'

The doctor pointed to the door.

Siméon raised no protest. He put on his hat. But, on reaching the door, he said: 'Twenty thousand francs? Is that enough?'

'Do you want me to ring?' asked the doctor, 'and have you turned out?'

Siméon laughed and quietly, with a pause after each figure.

'Thirty thousand?' he asked. 'Forty? . . . Fifty? . . . Oh, I see, we're playing a great game, we want a round sum . . . All right. Only, you know, everything must be included in the price we settle. You must not only fix me up a passport so genuine that it can't be disputed, but you must guarantee me the means of leaving France, as you did for Mme Mosgranem, on terms not half so handsome, by Jove! However, I'm not haggling. I need your assistance. Is it a bargain? A hundred thousand francs?'

Dr Géradec bolted the door, came back, sat down at his desk and said, simply: 'We'll talk about it.'

'I repeat the question,' said Siméon, coming closer. 'Are we agreed at a hundred thousand?'

'We are agreed,' said the doctor, 'unless any complications appear later.'

'What do you mean?'

'I mean that the figure of a hundred thousand francs forms a suitable basis for discussion, that's all.'

Siméon hesitated a second. The man struck him as rather greedy. However, he sat down once more; and the doctor at once resumed the conversation.

'Your real name, please.'

'You mustn't ask me that. I tell you, there are reasons . . . '

'Then it will be two hundred thousand francs.'

'Eh?' said Siméon, with a start. 'I say, that's a bit steep! I never heard of such a price.'

'You're not obliged to accept,' replied Géradec, calmly. 'We are discussing a bargain. You are free to do as you please.'

'But, look here, once you agree to fix me up a false passport, what can it matter to you whether you know my name or not?'

'It matters a great deal. I run an infinitely greater risk in assisting the escape – for that's the only word – of a spy than I do in assisting the escape of a respectable man.'

'I'm not a spy.'

'How do I know? Look here, you come to me to propose a shady transaction. You conceal your name and your identity; and you're in such a hurry to disappear from sight that you're prepared to pay me a hundred thousand francs to help you. And, in the face of that, you lay claim to being a respectable man! Come, come! It's absurd! A respectable man does not behave like a burglar or a murderer.'

Old Siméon did not wince. He slowly wiped his forehead with his handkerchief. He was evidently thinking that Géradec was a hardy antagonist and that he would perhaps have done better not to go to him. But, after all, the contract was a conditional one. There would always be time enough to break it off.

'I say, I say!' he said, with an attempt at a laugh. 'You are using big words!'

'They're only words,' said the doctor. 'I am stating no hypothesis. I am content to sum up the position and to justify my demands.'

'You're quite right.'

'Then we're agreed?'

'Yes. Perhaps, however – and this is the last observation I propose to make – you might let me off more cheaply, considering that I'm a friend of Mme Mosgranem's.'

'What do you suggest by that?' asked the doctor.

'Mme Mosgranem herself told me that you charged her nothing.'

'That's true, I charged her nothing,' replied the doctor, with a fatuous smile, 'but perhaps she presented me with a good deal. Mme

Mosgranem was one of those attractive women whose favors command their own price.'

There was a silence. Old Siméon seemed to feel more and more uncomfortable in his interlocutor's presence. At last the doctor sighed.

'Poor Mme Mosgranem!'

'What makes you speak like that?' asked Siméon.

'What! Haven't you heard?'

'I have had no letters from her since she left.'

'I see. I had one last night; and I was greatly surprised to learn that she was back in France.'

'In France! Mme Mosgranem!'

'Yes. And she even gave me an appointment for this morning, a very strange appointment.'

'Where?' asked Siméon, with visible concern.

'You'll never guess. On a barge, yes, called the *Nonchalante*, moored at the Quai de Passy, alongside Berthou's Wharf.'

'Is it possible?' said Siméon.

'It's as I tell you. And do you know how the letter was signed? It was signed Grégoire.'

'Grégoire? A man's name?' muttered the old man, almost with a groan.

'Yes, a man's name. Look, I have the letter on me. She tells me that she is leading a very dangerous life, that she distrusts the man with whom her fortunes are bound up and that she would like to ask my advice.'

'Then . . . then you went?'

'Yes, I was there this morning, while you were ringing up here. Unfortunately . . .'

'Well?'

'I arrived too late. Grégoire, or rather Mme Mosgranem, was dead. She had been strangled.'

'So you know nothing more than that?' asked Siméon, who seemed unable to get his words out.

'Nothing more about what?'

'About the man whom she mentioned.'

'Yes, I do, for she told me his name in the letter. He's a Greek, who calls himself Siméon Diodokis. She even gave me a description of him. I haven't read it very carefully.'

He unfolded the letter and ran his eyes down the second page, mumbling: 'A broken-down old man . . . Passes himself off as mad . . . Always goes about in a comforter and a pair of large yellow spectacles . . . '

Dr Géradec ceased reading and looked at Siméon with an air of amazement. Both of them sat for a moment without speaking. Then the doctor said: 'You are Siméon Diodokis.'

The other did not protest. All these incidents were so strangely and, at the same time, so naturally interlinked as to persuade him that lying was useless.

'This alters the situation,' declared the doctor. 'The time for trifling is past. It's a most serious and terribly dangerous matter for me, I can tell you! You'll have to make it a million.'

'Oh, no!' cried Siméon, excitedly. 'Certainly not! Besides, I never touched Mme Mosgranem. I was myself attacked by the man who strangled her, the same man – a negro called Ya-Bon – who caught me up and took me by the throat.'

'Ya-Bon? Did you say Ya-Bon?'

'Yes, a one-armed Senegalese.'

'And did you two fight?'

'Yes.'

'And did you kill him?'

'Well . . . '

The doctor shrugged his shoulders with a smile.

'Listen, sir, to a curious coincidence. When I left the barge, I met half-a-dozen wounded soldiers. They spoke to me and said that they were looking for a comrade, this very Ya-Bon, and also for their captain, Captain Belval, and a friend of this officer's and a lady, the lady they were staying with. All these people had disappeared; and they accused a certain person . . . wait, they told me his name . . . Oh, but this is more and more curious! The man's name was Siméon Diodokis. It was you they accused! . . . Isn't it odd? But, on the other hand, you must confess that all this constitutes fresh facts and therefore . . . '

There was a pause. Then the doctor formulated his demand in plain tones.

'I shall want two millions.'

This time Siméon remained impassive. He felt that he was in the man's clutches, like a mouse clawed by a cat. The doctor was playing with him, letting him go and catching him again, without giving him the least hope of escaping from this grim sport.

'This is blackmail,' he said, quietly.

The doctor nodded.

'There's no other word for it,' he admitted. 'It's blackmail. More-over, it's a case of blackmail in which I have not the excuse of creating the opportunity that gives me my advantage. A wonderful chance comes within reach of my hand. I grab at it, as you would do in my place. What else is possible? I have had a few differences, which you know of, with the police. We've signed a peace, the police and I. But my professional position has been so much injured that I cannot afford to reject with scorn what you so kindly bring me.'

'Suppose I refuse to submit?'

'Then I shall telephone to the headquarters of police, with whom I stand in great favor at present, as I am able to do them a good turn now and again.'

Siméon glanced at the window and at the door. The doctor had his hand on the receiver of the telephone. There was no way out of it.

'Very well,' he declared. 'After all, it's better so. You know me; and I know you. We can come to terms.'

'On the basis suggested?'

'Yes. Tell me your plan.'

'No, it's not worth while. I have my methods; and there's no object in revealing them beforehand. The point is to secure your escape and to put an end to your present danger. I'll answer for all that.'

'What guarantee have I . . . ?'

'You will pay me half the money now and the other half when the business is done. There remains the matter of the passport, a second-ary matter for me. Still, we shall have to make one out. In what name is it to be?'

'Any name you like.'

The doctor took a sheet of paper and wrote down the description, looking at Siméon between the phrases and muttering: 'Gray hair . . . Clean-shaven . . . Yellow spectacles . . . '

Then he stopped and asked: 'But how do I know that I shall be paid the money? That's essential, you know. I want bank-notes, real ones.'

'You shall have them.'

'Where are they?'

'In a hiding-place that can't be got at.'

'Tell me where.'

'I have no objection. Even if I give you a clue to the general position, you'll never find it.'

'Well, go on.'

'Grégoire had the money in her keeping, four million francs. It's on board the barge. We'll go there together and I'll count you out the first million.'

'You say those millions are on board the barge?'

'Yes.'

'And there are four of those millions?'

'Yes.'

'I won't accept any of them in payment.'

'Why not? You must be mad!'

'Why not? Because you can't pay a man with what already belongs to him.'

'What's that you're saying?' cried Siméon, in dismay.

'Those four millions belong to me, so you can't offer them to me.'

Siméon shrugged his shoulders.

'You're talking nonsense. For the money to belong to you, it must first be in your possession.'

'Certainly.'

'And is it?'

'It is.'

'Explain yourself, explain yourself at once!' snarled Siméon, beside himself with anger and alarm.

'I will explain myself. The hiding-place that couldn't be got at consisted of four old books, back numbers of Bottin's directory for Paris and the provinces, each in two volumes. The four volumes were hollow inside, as though they had been scooped out; and there was a million francs in each of them.'

'You lie! You lie!'

'They were on a shelf, in a little lumber-room next the cabin.'

'Well, what then?'

'What then? They're here.'

'Here?'

'Yes, here, on that bookshelf, in front of your nose. So, in the circumstances, you see, as I am already the lawful owner, I can't accept . . . '

'You thief! You thief!' shouted Siméon, shaking with rage and clenching his fist. 'You're nothing but a thief; and I'll make you disgorge. Oh, you dirty thief!'

Dr Géradec smiled very calmly and raised his hand in protest.

'This is strong language and quite unjustified! quite unjustified! Let me remind you that Mme Mosgranem honored me with her affection. One day, or rather one morning, after a moment of expansiveness, "My dear friend," she said – she used to call me her dear friend – "my dear friend, when I die" – she was given to those gloomy forebodings – "when I die, I bequeath to you the contents of my home!" Her home, at that moment, was the barge. Do you suggest that I should insult her memory by refusing to obey so sacred a wish?'

Old Siméon was not listening. An infernal thought was awakening in him; and he turned to the doctor with a movement of affrighted attention.

'We are wasting precious time, my dear sir,' said the doctor. 'What have you decided to do?'

He was playing with the sheet of paper on which he had written the particulars required for the passport. Siméon came up to him without a word. At last the old man whispered: 'Give me that sheet of paper . . . I want to see . . . '

He took the paper out of the doctor's hand, ran his eyes down it and suddenly leapt backwards.

'What name have you put? What name have you put? What right have you to give me that name? Why did you do it?'

'You told me to put any name I pleased, you know.'

'But why this one? Why this one?'

'Can it be your own?'

The old man started with terror and, bending lower and lower over the doctor, said, in a trembling voice: 'One man alone, one man alone was capable of guessing . . . '

There was a long pause. Then the doctor gave a little chuckle.

'I know that only one man was capable of it. So let's take it that I'm the man.'

'One man alone,' continued the other, while his breath once again seemed to fail him, 'one man alone could find the hiding-place of the four millions in a few seconds.'

The doctor did not answer. He smiled; and his features gradually relaxed.

In a sort of terror-stricken tone Siméon hissed out: 'Arsène Lupin! . . . Arsène Lupin! . . . '

'You've hit it in one,' exclaimed the doctor, rising.

He dropped his eye-glass, took from his pocket a little pot of grease, smeared his face with it, washed it off in a basin in a recess and reappeared with a clear skin, a smiling, bantering face and an easy carriage.

'Arsène Lupin!' repeated Siméon, petrified. 'Arsène Lupin! I'm in for it!'

'Up to the neck, you old fool! And what a silly fool you must be! Why, you know me by reputation, you feel for me the intense and wholesome awe with which a decent man of my stamp is bound to inspire an old rascal like you . . . and you go and imagine that I should be ass enough to let myself be bottled up in that lethal chamber of yours! Mind you, at that very moment I could have taken you by the hair of the head and gone straight on to the great scene in the fifth act, which we are now playing. Only my fifth act would have been a bit short, you see; and I'm a born actor-manager. As it is, observe how well the interest is sustained! And what fun it was seeing the thought of it take birth in your old Turkish noddle! And what a lark to go into the studio, fasten my electric lamp to a bit of string, make poor, dear Patrice believe that I was there and go out and hear Patrice denying me three times and carefully bolting the door on . . . what? My electric lamp! That was all first-class work, don't you think? What do you say to it? I can feel that you're speechless with admiration . . . And, ten minutes after, when you came back, the same scene in the wings and with the same success. Of course, you old Siméon, I was banging at the walled-up door, between the studio and the bedroom on the left. Only I wasn't in the studio: I was in the bedroom; and you went away quietly, like a good kind landlord. As for me, I had no need to hurry. I was as certain as that twice two is four that you would go to your friend M. Amédée Vacherot, the porter. And here, I may say, old Siméon, you committed a nice piece of imprudence, which got me out of my difficulty. No one in the porter's lodge: that couldn't be helped; but what I did find was a telephone-number on a scrap of newspaper. I did not hesitate for a moment. I rang up the number, coolly: "Monsieur, it was I who telephoned to you just now. Only I've got your number, but not your address." Back came the answer: "Dr Géradec, Boulevard de Montmorency." Then I understood. Dr Géradec? You would want your throat tubed for a bit, then the all-essential passport; and I came off here, without troubling about your poor friend M. Vacherot, whom you murdered in some corner or other to escape a possible give-away on his side. And I saw Dr Géradec, a charming man, whose worries have made him very wise and submissive and who . . . lent me his place for the morning. I had still two hours before me. I went to the barge, took the millions, cleared up a few odds and ends and here I am!'

He came and stood in front of the old man.

'Well, are you ready?' he asked.

Siméon, who seemed absorbed in thought, gave a start.

'Ready for what?' said Don Luis, replying to his unspoken question. 'Why, for the great journey, of course! Your passport is in
order. Your ticket's taken: Paris to Hell, single. Non-stop hearse.
Sleeping-coffin. Step in, sir!'

The old man, tottering on his legs, made an effort and stammered:
'And Patrice?'

'What about him?'

'I offer you his life in exchange for my own.'

Don Luis folded his arms across his chest.

'Well, of all the cheek! Patrice is a friend; and you think me
capable of abandoning him like that? Do you see me, Lupin, making
more or less witty jokes upon your imminent death while my friend
Patrice is in danger? Old Siméon, you're getting played out. It's time
you went and rested in a better world.'

He lifted a hanging, opened a door and called out: 'Well, captain,
how are you getting on? Ah, I see you've recovered consciousness!
Are you surprised to see me? No, no thanks, but please come in here.
Our old Siméon's asking for you.'

Then, turning to the old man, he said: 'Here's your son, you
unnatural father!'

Patrice entered the room with his head bandaged, for the blow
which Siméon had struck him and the weight of the tombstone had
opened his old wounds. He was very pale and seemed to be in great
pain.

At the sight of Siméon Diodokis he gave signs of terrible anger. He
controlled himself, however. The two men stood facing each other,
without stirring, and Don Luis, rubbing his hands, said, in an undertone: 'What a scene! What a splendid scene! Isn't it well-arranged?
The father and the son! The murderer and his victim! Listen to
the orchestra! . . . A slight tremolo . . . What are they going to do?
Will the son kill his father or the father kill his son? A thrilling
moment . . . And the mighty silence! Only the call of the blood is
heard . . . and in what terms! Now we're off! The call of the blood
has sounded; and they are going to throw themselves into each
other's arms, the better to strangle the life out of each other!'

Patrice had taken two steps forward; and the movement suggested
by Don Luis was about to be performed. Already the officer's arms
were flung wide for the fight. But suddenly Siméon, weakened by

pain and dominated by a stronger will than his own, let himself go and implored his adversary.

'Patrice!' he entreated. 'Patrice! What are you thinking of doing?'

Stretching out his hands, he threw himself upon the other's pity; and Patrice, arrested in his onrush, stood perplexed, staring at the man to whom he was bound by so mysterious and strange a tie.

'Coralie,' he said, without lowering his hands, 'Coralie . . . tell me where she is and I'll spare your life.'

The old man started. His evil nature was stimulated by the remembrance of Coralie; and he recovered a part of his energy at the possibility of wrong-doing. He gave a cruel laugh.

'No, no,' he answered. 'Coralie in one scale and I in the other? I'd rather die. Besides, Coralie's hiding-place is where the gold is. No, never! I may just as well die.'

'Kill him then, captain,' said Don Luis, intervening. 'Kill him, since he prefers it.'

Once more the thought of immediate murder and revenge sent the red blood rushing to the officer's face. But the same hesitation unnerved him.

'No, no,' he said, in a low voice, 'I can't do it.'

'Why not?' Don Luis insisted. 'It's so easy. Come along! Wring his neck, like a chicken's, and have done with it!'

'I can't.'

'But why? Do you dislike the thought of strangling him? Does it repel you? And yet, if it were a Boche, on the battlefield . . .'

'Yes . . . but this man . . .'

'Is it your hands that refuse? The idea of taking hold of the flesh and squeezing? . . . Here, captain, take my revolver and blow out his brains.'

Patrice accepted the weapon eagerly and aimed it at old Siméon. The silence was appalling. Old Siméon's eyes had closed and drops of sweat were streaming down his livid cheeks.

At last the officer lowered his arm.

'I can't do it,' he said.

'Nonsense,' said Don Luis. 'Get on with the work.'

'No . . . No . . .'

'But, in Heaven's name, why not?'

'I can't.'

'You can't? Shall I tell you the reason? You are thinking of that man as if he were your father.'

'Perhaps it's that,' said the officer, speaking very low. 'There's a chance of it, you know.'

'What does it matter, if he's a beast and a blackguard?'

'No, no, I haven't the right. Let him die by all means, but not by my hand. I haven't the right.'

'You have the right.'

'No, it would be abominable! It would be monstrous!'

Don Luis went up to him and, tapping him on the shoulder, said, gravely: 'You surely don't believe that I should stand here, urging you to kill that man, if he were your father?'

Patrice looked at him wildly.

'Do you know something? Do you know something for certain? Oh, for Heaven's sake . . . !'

Don Luis continued: 'Do you believe that I would even encourage you to hate him, if he were your father?'

'Oh!' exclaimed Patrice. 'Do you mean that he's not my father?'

'Of course he's not!' cried Don Luis, with irresistible conviction and increasing eagerness. 'Your father indeed! Why, look at him! Look at that scoundrelly head. Every sort of vice and violence is written on the brute's face. Throughout this adventure, from the first day to the last, there was not a crime committed but was his handiwork: not one, do you follow me? There were not two criminals, as we thought, not Essarès, to begin the hellish business, and old Siméon, to finish it. There was only one criminal, one, do you understand, Patrice? Before killing Coralie and Ya-Bon and Vacherot the porter and the woman who was his own accomplice, he killed others! He killed one other in particular, one whose flesh and blood you are, the man whose dying cries you heard over the telephone, the man who called you Patrice and who only lived for you! He killed that man; and that man was your father, Patrice; he was Armand Belval! Now do you understand?'

Patrice did not understand. Don Luis's words fell uncomprehended; not one of them lit up the darkness of Patrice's brain. However, one thought insistently possessed him; and he stammered: '*That* was my father? I heard his voice, you say? Then it was *he* who called to me?'

'Yes, Patrice, your father.'

'And the man who killed him . . . ?'

'Was this one,' said Don Luis, pointing to Siméon.

The old man remained motionless, wild-eyed, like a felon awaiting sentence of death. Patrice, quivering with rage, stared at him fixedly: 'Who are you? Who are you?' he asked. And, turning to Don Luis, 'Tell me his name, I beseech you. I want to know his name, before I destroy him.'

'His name? Haven't you guessed it yet? Why, from the very first day, I took it for granted! After all, it was the only possible theory.'

'But what theory? What was it you took for granted?' cried Patrice, impatiently.

'Do you really want to know?'

'Oh, please! I'm longing to kill him, but I must first know his name.'

'Well, then . . . '

There was a long silence between the two men, as they stood close together, looking into each other's eyes. Then Lupin let fall these four syllables: 'Essarès Bey.'

Patrice felt a shock that ran through him from head to foot. Not for a second did he try to understand by what prodigy this revelation came to be merely an expression of the truth. He instantly accepted this truth, as though it were undeniable and proved by the most evident facts. The man was Essarès Bey and had killed his father. He had killed him, so to speak, twice over: first years ago, in the lodge in the garden, taking from him all the light of life and any reason for living; and again the other day, in the library, when Armand Belval had telephoned to his son.

This time Patrice was determined to do the deed. His eyes expressed an indomitable resolution. His father's murderer, Coralie's murderer, must die then and there. His duty was clear and precise. The terrible Essarès was doomed to die by the hand of the son and the bridegroom.

'Say your prayers,' said Patrice, coldly. 'In ten seconds you will be a dead man.'

He counted out the seconds and, at the tenth, was about to fire, when his enemy, in an access of mad energy proving that, under the outward appearance of old Siméon, there was hidden a man still young and vigorous, shouted with a violence so extraordinary that it made Patrice hesitate.

'Very well, kill me! . . . Yes, let it be finished! . . . I am beaten: I accept defeat. But it is a victory all the same, because Coralie is dead and my gold is saved! . . . I shall die, but nobody shall have either one or the other, the woman whom I love or the gold that was my life. Ah, Patrice, Patrice, the woman whom we both loved to distraction is no longer alive . . . or else she is dying without a possibility of saving her now. If I cannot have her, you shall not have her either, Patrice. My revenge has done its work. Coralie is lost!'

He had recovered a fierce energy and was shouting and stammering at the same time. Patrice stood opposite him, holding him covered with the revolver, ready to act, but still waiting to hear the terrible words that tortured him.

'She is lost, Patrice!' Siméon continued, raising his voice still louder. 'Lost! There's nothing to be done! And you will not find even her body in the bowels of the earth, where I buried her with the bags of gold. Under the tombstone? No, not such a fool! No, Patrice, you will never find her. The gold is stifling her. She's dead! Coralie is dead! Oh, the delight of throwing that in your face! The anguish you must be feeling! Coralie is dead! Coralie is dead!'

'Don't shout so, you'll wake her,' said Don Luis, calmly.

The brief sentence was followed by a sort of stupor which paralyzed the two adversaries. Patrice's arms dropped to his sides. Siméon turned giddy and sank into a chair. Both of them, knowing the things of which Don Luis was capable, knew what he meant.

But Patrice wanted something more than a vague sentence that might just as easily be taken as a jest. He wanted a certainty.

'Wake her?' he asked, in a broken voice.

'Well, of course!' said Don Luis. 'When you shout too loud, you wake people up.'

'Then she's alive?'

'You can't wake the dead, whatever people may say. You can only wake the living.'

'Coralie is alive! Coralie is alive!' Patrice repeated, in a sort of rapture that transfigured his features. 'Can it be possible? But then she must be here! Oh, I beg of you, say you're in earnest, give me your word! . . . Or no, it's not true, is it? I can't believe it . . . you must be joking . . .'

'Let me answer you, captain, as I answered that wretch just now. You are admitting that it is possible for me to abandon my work before completing it. How little you know me! What I undertake to do I do. It's one of my habits and a good one at that. That's why I cling to it. Now watch me.'

He turned to one side of the room. Opposite the hanging that covered the door by which Patrice had entered was a second curtain, concealing another door. He lifted the curtain.

'No, no, she's not there,' said Patrice, in an almost inaudible voice. 'I dare not believe it. The disappointment would be too great. Swear to me . . .'

'I swear nothing, captain. You have only to open your eyes. By Jove, for a French officer, you're cutting a pretty figure! Why, you're as white as a sheet! Of course it's she! It's Little Mother Coralie! Look, she's in bed asleep, with two nurses to watch her. But there's no danger; she's not wounded. A bit of a temperature, that's all, and extreme weakness. Poor Little Mother Coralie! I never could have imagined her in such a state of exhaustion and coma.'

Patrice had stepped forward, brimming over with joy. Don Luis stopped him.

'That will do, captain. Don't go any nearer. I brought her here, instead of taking her home, because I thought a change of scene and atmosphere essential. But she must have no excitement. She's had her share of that; and you might spoil everything by showing yourself.'

'You're right,' said Patrice. 'But are you quite sure . . . ?'

'That she's alive?' asked Don Luis, laughing. 'She's as much alive as you or I and quite ready to give you the happiness you deserve and to change her name to Mme Patrice Belval. You must have just a little patience, that's all. And there is yet one obstacle to overcome, captain, for remember she's a married woman!'

He closed the door and led Patrice back to Essarès Bey.

'There's the obstacle, captain. Is your mind made up now? This wretch still stands between you and your Coralie.'

Essarès had not even glanced into the next room, as though he knew that there could be no doubt about Don Luis's word. He sat shivering in his chair, cowering, weak and helpless.

'You don't seem comfortable,' said Don Luis. 'What's worrying you? You're frightened, perhaps? What for? I promise you that we will do nothing except by mutual consent and until we are all of the same opinion. That ought to cheer you up. We'll be your judges, the three of us, here and now. Captain Patrice Belval, Arsène Lupin and old Siméon will form the court. Let the trial begin. Does anyone wish to speak in defense of the prisoner at the bar, Essarès Bey? No one. The prisoner at the bar is sentenced to death. Extenuating circumstances? No notice of appeal? No. Commutation of sentence? No. Reprieve? No. Immediate execution? Yes. You see, there's no delay. What about the means of death? A revolver-shot? That will do. It's clean, quick work. Captain Belval, your bird. The gun's loaded. Here you are.'

Patrice did not move. He stood gazing at the foul brute who had done him so many injuries. His whole being seethed with hatred. Nevertheless, he replied: 'I will not kill that man.'

'I agree, captain. Your scruples do you honor. You have not the right to kill a man whom you know to be the husband of the woman you love. It is not for you to remove the obstacle. Besides, you hate taking life. So do I. This animal is too filthy for words. And so, my good man, there's no one left but yourself to help us out of this delicate position.'

Don Luis ceased speaking for a moment and leant over Essarès. Had the wretched man heard? Was he even alive? He looked as if he were in a faint, deprived of consciousness.

Don Luis shook him by the shoulder.

'The gold,' moaned Essarès, 'the bags of gold . . . '

'Oh, you're thinking of that, you old scoundrel, are you? You're still interested? The bags of gold are in my pocket . . . if a pocket can contain eighteen hundred bags of gold.'

'The hiding-place?'

'Your hiding-place? It doesn't exist, so far as I'm concerned. I needn't prove it to you, need I, since Coralie's here? As Coralie was buried among the bags of gold, you can draw your own conclusion. So you're nicely done. The woman you wanted is free and, what is worse still, free by the side of the man whom she adores and whom she will never leave. And, on the other hand, your treasure is discovered. So it's all finished, eh? We are agreed? Come, here's the toy that will release you.'

He handed him the revolver. Essarès took it mechanically and pointed it at Don Luis; but his arm lacked the strength to take aim and fell by his side.

'Capital!' said Don Luis. 'We understand each other; and the action which you are about to perform will atone for your evil life, you old blackguard. When a man's last hope is dispelled, there's nothing for it but death. That's the final refuge.'

He took hold of the other's hand and, bending Essarès' nerveless fingers round the revolver, forced him to point it towards his own face.

'Come,' said he, 'just a little pluck. What you've resolved to do is a very good thing. As Captain Belval and I refuse to disgrace ourselves by killing you, you've decided to do the job yourself. We are touched; and we congratulate you. But you must behave with courage. No resistance, come! That's right, that's much more like it. Once more, my compliments. It's very smart, your manner of getting out of it. You perceive that there's no room for you on earth, that you're standing in the way of Patrice and Coralie and that the best thing you can do is to retire. And you're jolly well right! No love and no gold! No gold, Siméon! The beautiful shiny coins which you coveted, with which you would have managed to secure a nice, comfortable existence, all fled, vanished! You may just as well vanish yourself, what?'

Whether because he felt himself to be helpless or because he really understood that Don Luis was right and that his life was no longer worth living, Siméon offered hardly any resistance. The revolver rose to his forehead. The barrel touched his temple.

At the touch of the cold steel he gave a moan: 'Mercy!'

'No, no, no!' said Don Luis. 'You mustn't show yourself any mercy. And I won't help you either. Perhaps, if you hadn't killed my poor Ya-Bon, we might have put our heads together and sought for another ending. But, honestly, you inspire me with no more pity than you feel for yourself. You want to die and you are right. I won't prevent you. Besides, your passport is made out; you've got your ticket in your pocket. They are expecting you down below. And, you know, you need have no fear of being bored. Have you ever seen a picture of Hell? Everyone has a huge stone over his tomb; and everyone is lifting the stone and supporting it with his back, in order to escape the flames bursting forth beneath him. You see, there's plenty of fun. Well, your grave is reserved. Bath's ready, sir!'

Slowly and patiently he had succeeded in slipping the wretched man's fore-finger under the handle, so as to bring it against the trigger. Essarès was letting himself go. He was little more than a limp rag. Death had already cast its shadow upon him.

'Mind you,' said Don Luis, 'you're perfectly free. You can pull the trigger if you feel like it. It's not my business. I'm not here to compel you to commit suicide, but only to advise you and to lend you a hand.'

He had in fact let go the fore-finger and was holding only the arm. But he was bearing upon Essarès with all his extraordinary power of will, the will to seek destruction, the will to seek annihilation, an indomitable will which Essarès was unable to resist. Every second death sank a little deeper into that invertebrate body, breaking up instinct, obscuring thought and bringing an immense craving for rest and inaction.

'You see how easy it is. The intoxication is flying to your brain. It's an almost voluptuous feeling, isn't it? What a riddance! To cease living! To cease suffering! To cease thinking of that gold which you no longer possess and can never possess again, of that woman who belongs to another and offers him her lips and all her entrancing self! . . . You couldn't live, could you, with that thought on you? Then come on! . . . '

Seized with cowardice, the wretch was yielding by slow degrees. He found himself face to face with one of those crushing forces, one of nature's forces, powerful as fate, which a man must needs accept. His head turned giddy and swam. He was descending into the abyss.

'Come along now, show yourself a man. Don't forget either that you are dead already. Remember, you can't appear in this world again without falling into the hands of the police. And, of course, I'm there to inform them in case of need. That means prison and the scaffold. The scaffold, my poor fellow, the icy dawn, the knife . . . '

It was over. Essarès was sinking into the depths of darkness. Everything whirled around him. Don Luis's will penetrated him and annihilated his own.

For one moment he turned to Patrice and tried to implore his aid. But Patrice persisted in his impassive attitude. Standing with his arms folded, he gazed with eyes devoid of pity upon his father's murderer. The punishment was well-deserved. Fate must be allowed to take its course. Patrice did not interfere.

And Don Luis continued, unrelentingly and without intermission: 'Come along, come along! . . . It's a mere nothing and it means eternal rest! . . . How good it feels, already! To forget! To cease fighting! . . . Think of the gold which you have lost . . . Three hundred millions gone for ever! . . . And Coralie lost as well. Mother and daughter: you can't have either. In that case, life is nothing but a snare and a delusion. You may as well leave it. Come, one little effort, one little movement . . . '

That little movement the miscreant made. Hardly knowing what he did, he pulled the trigger. The shot rang through the room; and Essarès fell forward, with his knees on the floor. Don Luis had to spring to one side to escape being splashed by the blood that trickled from the man's shattered head.

'By Jove!' he cried. 'The blood of vermin like that would have brought me ill-luck. And, Lord, what crawling vermin it is! . . . Upon my word, I believe that this makes one more good action I've done in my life and that this suicide entitles me to a little seat in Paradise. What say you, captain?'

Chapter 19

Fiat Lux!

On the evening of the same day, Patrice was pacing up and down the Quai de Passy. It was nearly six o'clock. From time to time, a tram-car passed, or some motor-lorry. There were very few people about on foot. Patrice had the pavement almost to himself.

He had not seen Don Luis Perenna since the morning, had merely received a line in which Don Luis asked him to have Ya-Bon's body moved into the Essarès house and afterwards to meet him on the quay above Berthou's Wharf. The time appointed for the meeting was near at hand and Patrice was looking forward to this interview in which the truth would be revealed to him at last. He partly guessed the truth, but no little darkness and any number of unsolved problems remained. The tragedy was played out. The curtain had fallen on the villain's death. All was well: there was nothing more to fear, no more pitfalls in store for them. The formidable enemy was laid low. But Patrice's anxiety was intense as he waited for the moment when light would be cast freely and fully upon the tragedy.

'A few words,' he said to himself, 'a few words from that incredible person known as Arsène Lupin, will clear up the mystery. It will not take him long. He will be gone in an hour. Will he take the secret of the gold with him, I wonder? Will he solve the secret of the golden triangle for me? And how will he keep the gold for himself? How will he take it away?'

A motor-car arrived from the direction of the Trocadéro. It slowed down and stopped beside the pavement. It must be Don Luis, thought Patrice. But, to his great surprise, he recognized M. Masseron, who opened the door and came towards him with outstretched hand.

'Well, captain, how are you? I'm punctual for the appointment, am I not? But, I say, have you been wounded in the head again?'

'Yes, an accident of no importance,' replied Patrice. 'But what appointment are you speaking of?'

'Why, the one you gave me, of course!'

'I gave you no appointment.'

'Oh, I say!' said M. Masseron. 'What does this mean? Why, here's the note they brought me at the police-office: "Captain Belval's compliments to M. Masseron. The problem of the golden triangle is solved. The eighteen hundred bags are at his disposal. Will he please come to the Quai de Passy, at six o'clock, with full powers from the government to accept the conditions of delivery. It would be well if he brought with him twenty powerful detectives, of whom half should be posted a hundred yards on one side of Essarès' property and the other half on the other." There you are. Is it clear?'

'Perfectly clear,' said Patrice, 'but I never sent you that note.'

'Who sent it then?'

'An extraordinary man who deciphered all those problems like so many children's riddles and who certainly will be here himself to bring you the solution.'

'What's his name?'

'I shan't say.'

'Oh, I don't know about that! Secrets are hard to keep in war-time.'

'Very easy, on the contrary, sir,' said a voice behind M. Masseron. 'All you need do is to make up your mind to it.'

M. Masseron and Patrice turned round and saw a gentleman dressed in a long, black overcoat, cut like a frock-coat, and a tall collar which gave him a look of an English clergyman.

'This is the friend I was speaking of,' said Patrice, though he had some difficulty in recognizing Don Luis. 'He twice saved my life and also that of the lady whom I am going to marry. I will answer for him in every respect.'

M. Masseron bowed; and Don Luis at once began, speaking with a slight accent: 'Sir, your time is valuable and so is mine, for I am leaving Paris tonight and France tomorrow. My explanation therefore will be brief. I will pass over the drama itself, of which you have followed the main vicissitudes so far. It came to an end this morning. Captain Belval will tell you all about it. I will merely add that our poor Ya-Bon is dead and that you will find three other bodies: that of Grégoire, whose real name was Mme Mosgranem, in the barge over there; that of one Vacherot, a hall-porter, in some corner of a block of flats at 18, Rue Guimard; and lastly the body of Siméon Diodokis, in Dr Géradec's private hospital on the Boulevard de Montmorency.'

'Old Siméon?' asked M. Masseron in great surprise.

'Old Siméon has killed himself. Captain Belval will give you every possible information about that person and his real identity; and I think you will agree with me that this business will have to be hushed up. But, as I said, we will pass over all this. There remains the question of the gold, which, if I am not mistaken, interests you more than anything else. Have you brought your men?'

'Yes, I have. But why? The hiding-place, even after you have told me where it is, will be what it was before, undiscovered by those who do not know it.'

'Certainly; but, as the number of those who do know it increases, the secret may slip out. In any case that is one of my two conditions.'

'As you see, it is accepted. What is the other?'

'A more serious condition, sir, so serious indeed that, whatever powers may have been conferred upon you, I doubt whether they will be sufficient.'

'Let me hear; then we shall see.'

'Very well.'

And Don Luis, speaking in a phlegmatic tone, as though he were telling the most unimportant story, calmly set forth his incredible proposal.

'Two months ago, sir, thanks to my connection with the Near East and to my influence in certain Ottoman circles, I persuaded the clique which rules Turkey today to accept the idea of a separate peace. It was simply a question of a few hundred millions for distribution. I had the offer transmitted to the Allies, who rejected it, certainly not for financial reasons, but for reasons of policy, which it is not for me to judge. But I am not content to suffer this little diplomatic check. I failed in my first negotiation; I do not mean to fail in the second. That is why I am taking my precautions.'

He paused and then resumed, while his voice took on a rather more serious tone: 'At this moment, in April, 1915, as you are well aware, conferences are in progress between the Allies and the last of the great European powers that has remained neutral. These conferences are going to succeed; and they will succeed because the future of that power demands it and because the whole nation is uplifted with enthusiasm. Among the questions raised is one which forms the object of a certain divergency of opinion. I mean the question of money. This foreign power is asking us for a loan of three hundred million francs in gold, while making it quite clear that a refusal on our part would in no way affect a decision which is already irrevocably taken. Well, I have three hundred millions in gold; I have them at my command; and I desire to place them at the disposal of our new allies. This is my second and, in reality, my only condition.'

M. Masseron seemed utterly taken aback.

'But, my dear sir,' he said, 'these are matters quite outside our province; they must be examined and decided by others, not by us.'

'Everyone has the right to dispose of his money as he pleases.'

M. Masseron made a gesture of distress.

'Come, sir, think a moment. You yourself said that this power was only putting forward the question as a secondary one.'

'Yes, but the mere fact that it is being discussed will delay the conclusion of the agreement for a few days.'

'Well, a few days will make no difference, surely?'

'Sir, a few hours *will* make a difference.'

'But why?'

'For a reason which you do not know and which nobody knows . . . except myself and a few people some fifteen hundred miles away.'

'What reason?'

'The Russians have no munitions left.'

M. Masseron shrugged his shoulders impatiently. What had all this to do with the matter?

'The Russians have no munitions left,' repeated Don Luis. 'Now there is a tremendous battle being fought over there, a battle which will be decided not many hours hence. The Russian front will be broken and the Russian troops will retreat and retreat . . . Heaven knows when they'll stop retreating! Of course, this assured, this inevitable contingency will have no influence on the wishes of the great power of which we are talking. Nevertheless, that nation has in its midst a very considerable party on the side of neutrality, a party which is held in check, but none the less violent for that. Think what a weapon you will place in its hands by postponing the agreement! Think of the difficulties which you are making for rulers preparing to go to war! It would be an unpardonable mistake, from which I wish to save my country. That is why I have laid down this condition.'

M. Masseron seemed quite discomforted. Waving his hands and shaking his head, he mumbled: 'It's impossible. Such a condition as that will never be accepted. It will take time, it will need discussion . . . '

A hand was laid on his arm by someone who had come up a moment before and who had listened to Don Luis's little speech. Its owner had alighted from a car which was waiting some way off; and, to Patrice's great astonishment, his presence had aroused no opposition on the part of either M. Masseron or Don Luis Perenna. He was a man well-advanced in years, with a powerful, lined face.

'My dear Masseron,' he said, 'it seems to me that you are not looking at the question from the right point of view.'

'That's what I think, monsieur le président,' said Don Luis.

'Ah, do you know me, sir?'

'M. Valenglay, I believe? I had the honor of calling on you some years ago, sir, when you were president of the council.'

'Yes, I thought I remembered . . . though I can't say exactly . . . '

'Please don't tax your memory, sir. The past does not concern us. What matters is that you should be of my opinion.'

'I don't know that I am of your opinion. But I consider that this makes no difference. And that is what I was telling you, my dear Masseron. It's not a question of knowing whether you ought to discuss this gentleman's conditions. It's a question of accepting them or refusing them without discussion. There's no bargain to be driven in the circumstances. A bargain presupposes that each party has something to offer. Now we have no offer to make, whereas this gentleman comes with his offer in his hand and says, "Would you like three hundred million francs in gold? In that case you must do so-and-so with it. If that doesn't suit you, good-evening." That's the position, isn't it, Masseron?'

'Yes, monsieur le président.'

'Well, can you dispense with our friend here? Can you, without his assistance, find the place where the gold is hidden? Observe that he makes things very easy for you by bringing you to the place and almost pointing out the exact spot to you. Is that enough? Have you any hope of discovering the secret which you have been seeking for weeks and months?'

M. Masseron was very frank in his reply.

'No, Monsieur le Président,' he said, plainly and without hesitation.

'Well, then . . . '

And, turning to Don Luis: 'And you, sir,' Valenglay asked, 'is it your last word?'

'My last word.'

'If we refuse . . . good-evening?'

'You have stated the case precisely, monsieur le président.'

'And, if we accept, will the gold be handed over at once?'

'At once.'

'We accept.'

And, after a slight pause, he repeated: 'We accept. The ambassador shall receive his instructions this evening.'

'Do you give me your word, sir?'

'I give you my word.'

'In that case, we are agreed.'

'We are agreed. Now then! . . . '

All these sentences were uttered rapidly. Not five minutes had elapsed since the former prime minister had appeared upon the scene. Nothing remained to do but for Don Luis to keep his promise.

It was a solemn moment. The four men were standing close together, like acquaintances who have met in the course of a walk and who stop for a minute to exchange their news. Valenglay, leaning with one arm on the parapet overlooking the lower quay, had his face turned to the river and kept raising and lowering his cane above the sand-heap. Patrice and M. Masseron stood silent, with faces a little set.

Don Luis gave a laugh: 'Don't be too sure, monsieur le président,' he said, 'that I shall make the gold rise from the ground with a magic wand or show you a cave in which the bags lie stacked. I always thought those words, "the golden triangle", misleading, because they suggest something mysterious and fabulous. Now according to me it was simply a question of the space containing the gold, which space would have the shape of a triangle. The golden triangle, that's it: bags of gold arranged in a triangle, a triangular site. The reality is much simpler, therefore; and you will perhaps be disappointed.'

'I shan't be,' said Valenglay, 'if you put me with my face towards the eighteen hundred bags of gold.'

'You're that now, sir.'

'What do you mean?'

'Exactly what I say. Short of touching the bags of gold, it would be difficult to be nearer to them than you are.'

For all his self-control, Valenglay could not conceal his surprise.

'You are not suggesting, I suppose, that I am walking on gold and that we have only to lift up the flags of the pavement or to break down this parapet?'

'That would be removing obstacles, sir, whereas there is no obstacle between you and what you are seeking.'

'No obstacle!'

'None, monsieur le président, for you have only to make the least little movement in order to touch the bags.'

'The least little movement!' said Valenglay, mechanically repeating Don Luis's words.

'I call a little movement what one can make without an effort, almost without stirring, such as dipping one's stick into a sheet of water, for instance, or . . . '

'Or what?'

'Well, or a heap of sand.'

Valenglay remained silent and impassive, with at most a slight shiver passing across his shoulders. He did not make the suggested movement. He had no need to make it. He understood.

The others also did not speak a word, struck dumb by the simplicity of the amazing truth which had suddenly flashed upon them like lightning. And, amid this silence, unbroken by protest or sign of incredulity, Don Luis went on quietly talking.

'If you had the least doubt, monsieur le président – and I see that you have not – you would dig your cane, no great distance, twenty inches at most, into the sand beneath you. You would then encounter a resistance which would compel you to stop. That is the bags of gold. There ought to be eighteen hundred of them; and, as you see, they do not make an enormous heap. A kilogram of gold represents three thousand one hundred francs. Therefore, according to my calculation, a bag containing approximately fifty kilograms, or one hundred and fifty-five thousand francs done up in rouleaus of a thousand francs, is not a very large bag. Piled one against the other and one on top of the other, the bags represent a bulk of about fifteen cubic yards, no more. If you shape the mass roughly like a triangular pyramid you will have a base each of whose sides would be three yards long at most, or three yards and a half allowing for the space lost between the rouleaus of coins. The height will be that of the wall, nearly. Cover the whole with a layer of sand and you have the heap which lies before your eyes . . .'

Don Luis paused once more before continuing: 'And which has been there for months, monsieur le président, safe from discovery not only by those who were looking for it, but also by accident on the part of a casual passer-by. Just think, a heap of sand! Who would dream of digging a hole in it to see what is going on inside? The dogs sniff at it, the children play beside it and make mudpies, an occasional tramp lies down against it and takes a snooze. The rain softens it, the sun hardens it, the snow whitens it all over; but all this happens on the surface, in the part that shows. Inside reigns impenetrable mystery, darkness unexplored. There is not a hiding-place in the world to equal the inside of a sand heap exposed to view in a public place. The man who thought of using it to hide three hundred millions of gold, monsieur le président, knew what he was about.'

The late prime minister had listened to Don Luis's explanation without interrupting him. When Don Luis had finished, Valenglay nodded his head once or twice and said: 'He did indeed. But there is one man who is cleverer still.'

'I don't believe it.'

'Yes, there's the man who guessed that the heap of sand concealed the three hundred million francs. That man is a master, before whom we must all bow.'

Flattered by the compliment, Don Luis raised his hat. Valenglay gave him his hand.

'I can think of no reward worthy of the service which you have done the country.'

'I ask for no reward,' said Don Luis.

'I dare say, sir, but I should wish you at least to be thanked by voices that carry more weight than mine.'

'Is it really necessary, monsieur le président?'

'I consider it essential. May I also confess that I am curious to learn how you discovered the secret? I should be glad, therefore, if you would call at my department in an hour's time.'

'I am very sorry, sir, but I shall be gone in fifteen minutes.'

'No, no, you can't go like this,' said Valenglay, with authority.

'Why not, sir?'

'Well, because we don't know your name or anything about you.'

'That makes so little difference!'

'In peace-time, perhaps. But, in war-time, it won't do at all.'

'Surely, monsieur le président, you will make an exception in my case?'

'An exception, indeed? What next?'

'Suppose it's the reward which I ask, will you refuse me then?'

'It's the only one which we are obliged to refuse you. However, you won't ask for it. A good citizen like yourself understands the constraints to which everybody is bound to submit. My dear Masseron, arrange it with this gentleman. At the department in an hour from now. Goodbye till then, sir. I shall expect you.'

And, after a very civil bow, he walked away to his car, twirling his stick gaily and escorted by M. Masseron.

'Well, on my soul!' chuckled Don Luis. 'There's a character for you! In the twinkling of an eye, he accepts three hundred millions in gold, signs an epoch-making treaty and orders the arrest of Arsène Lupin!'

'What do you mean?' cried Patrice, startled out of his life. 'Your arrest?'

'Well, he orders me to appear before him, to produce my papers and the devil knows what.'

'But that's monstrous!'

'It's the law of the land, my dear captain. We must bow to it.'

'But . . .'

'Captain, believe me when I say that a few little worries of this sort deprive me of none of the whole-hearted satisfaction which I feel at rendering this great service to my country. I wanted, during the war, to do something for France and to make the most of the time which I was able to devote to her during my stay. I've done it. And then I have another reward: the four millions. For I think highly enough of your Coralie to believe her incapable of wishing to touch this money . . . which is really her property.'

'I'll go bail for her over that.'

'Thank you. And you may be sure that the gift will be well employed. So everything is settled. I have still a few minutes to give you. Let us turn them to good account. M. Masseron is collecting his men by now. To simplify their task and avoid a scandal, we'll go down to the lower quay, by the sand-heap. It'll be easier for him to collar me there.'

'I accept your few minutes,' said Patrice, as they went down the steps. 'But first of all I want to apologize . . .'

'For what? For behaving a little treacherously and locking me into the studio of the lodge? You couldn't help yourself: you were trying to assist your Coralie. For thinking me capable of keeping the treasure on the day when I discovered it? You couldn't help that either: how could you imagine that Arsène Lupin would despise three hundred million francs?'

'Very well, no apologies,' said Patrice, laughing. 'But all my thanks.'

'For what? For saving your life and saving Coralie's? Don't thank me. It's a hobby of mine, saving people.'

Patrice took Don Luis's hand and pressed it firmly. Then, in a chaffing tone which hid his emotion, he said: 'Then I won't thank you. I won't tell you that you rid me of a hideous nightmare by letting me know that I was not that monster's son and by unveiling his real identity. I will not tell you either that I am a happy man now that life is opening radiantly before me, with Coralie free to love me. No, we won't talk of it. But shall I confess to you that my happiness is still a little – what shall I say? – a little dim, a little timid? I no longer feel any doubt; but in spite of all, I don't quite understand the truth, and, until I do understand it, the truth will cause me some anxiety. So tell me . . . explain to me . . . I want to know . . .'

'And yet the truth is so obvious!' cried Don Luis. 'The most complex truths are always so simple! Look here, don't you understand anything? Just think of the way in which the problem is set. For sixteen or eighteen years, Siméon Diodokis behaves like a perfect friend, devoted to the pitch of self-denial, in short, like a father. He has not a thought, outside that of his revenge, but to secure your happiness and Coralie's. He wants to bring you together. He collects your photographs. He follows the whole course of your life. He almost gets into touch with you. He sends you the key of the garden and prepares a meeting. Then, suddenly, a complete change takes place. He becomes your inveterate enemy and thinks of nothing but killing the pair of you. What is there that separates those two states of mind? One fact, that's all, or rather one date, the night of the third of April and the tragedy that takes place that night and the following day at Essarès' house. Until that date, you were Siméon Diodokis' son. After that date, you were Siméon Diodokis' greatest enemy. Does that suggest nothing to you? It's really curious. As for me, all my discoveries are due to this general view of the case which I took from the beginning.'

Patrice shook his head without replying. He did not understand. The riddle retained a part of its unfathomable secret.

'Sit down there,' said Don Luis, 'on our famous sand-heap, and listen to me. It won't take me ten minutes.'

They were on Berthou's Wharf. The light was beginning to wane and the outlines on the opposite bank of the river were becoming indistinct. The barge rocked lazily at the edge of the quay.

Don Luis expressed himself in the following terms.

'On the evening when, from the inner gallery of the library, you witnessed the tragedy at Essarès' house, you saw before your eyes two men bound by their accomplices: Essarès Bey and Siméon Diodokis. They are both dead. One of them was your father. Let us speak first of the other. Essarès Bey's position was a critical one that evening. After draining our gold currency on behalf of an eastern power, he was trying to filch the remainder of the millions of francs collected. The *Belle Hélène*, summoned by the rain of sparks, was lying moored alongside Berthou's Wharf. The gold was to be shifted at night from the sand-bags to the motor-barge. All was going well, when the accomplices, warned by Siméon, broke in. Thereupon we have the blackmailing-scene, Colonel Fakhi's death and so on, with Essarès learning at one and the same time that his accomplices knew of his schemes and his plan to pilfer the gold and also that Colonel

Fakhi had informed the police about him. He was cornered. What could he do? Run away? But, in war-time, running away is almost impossible. Besides, running away meant giving up the gold and likewise giving up Coralie, which would never have done. So there was only one thing, to disappear from sight. To disappear from sight and yet to remain there, on the battlefield, near the gold and near Coralie. Night came; and he employed it in carrying out his plan. So much for Essarès. We now come to Siméon Diodokis.'

Don Luis stopped to take breath. Patrice had been listening eagerly, as though each word had brought its share of light into the oppressive darkness.

'The man who was known as old Siméon,' continued Don Luis, 'that is to say, your father, Armand Belval, a former victim, together with Coralie's mother, of Essarès Bey, had also reached a turning-point of his career. He was nearly achieving his object. He had betrayed and delivered his enemy, Essarès, into the hands of Colonel Fakhi and the accomplices. He had succeeded in bringing you and Coralie together. He had sent you the key of the lodge. He was justified in hoping that, in a few days more, everything would end according to his wishes. But, next morning, on waking, certain indic-ations unknown to me revealed to him a threatening danger; and he no doubt foresaw the plan which Essarès was engaged in elaborating. And he too put himself the same question: What was he to do? What was there for him to do? He must warn you, warn you without delay, telephone to you at once. For time was pressing, the danger was becoming definite. Essarès was watching and hunting down the man whom he had chosen as his victim for the second time. You can picture Siméon possibly feeling himself pursued and locking himself into the library. You can picture him wondering whether he would ever be able to telephone to you and whether you would be there. He asks for you. He calls out to you. Essarès hammers away at the door. And your father, gasping for breath, shouts, "Is that you, Patrice? Have you the key? . . . And the letter? . . . No? . . . But this is terrible! Then you don't know" . . . And then a hoarse cry, which you hear at your end of the wire, and incoherent noises, the sound of an altercation. And then the lips gluing themselves to the instrument and stammering words at random: "Patrice, the amethyst pendant . . . Patrice, I should so much have liked . . . Patrice, Coralie!" Then a loud scream . . . cries that grow weaker and weaker . . . silence, and that is all. Your father is dead, murdered. This time, Essarès Bey, who had failed before, in the lodge, took his revenge on his old rival.'

'Oh, my unhappy father!' murmured Patrice, in great distress.

'Yes, it was he. That was at nineteen minutes past seven in the morning, as you noted. A few minutes later, eager to know and understand, you yourself rang up; and it was Essarès who replied, with your father's dead body at his feet.'

'Oh, the scoundrel! So that this body, which we did not find and were not able to find . . . '

'Was simply made up by Essarès, made up, disfigured, transformed into his own likeness. That, captain, is how – and the whole mystery lies in this – Siméon Diodokis, dead, became Essarès Bey, while Essarès Bey, transformed into Siméon Diodokis, played the part of Siméon Diodokis.'

'Yes,' said Patrice, 'I see, I understand.'

'As to the relations existing between the two men,' continued Don Luis, 'I am not certain. Essarès may or may not have known before that old Siméon was none other than his former rival, the lover of Coralie's mother, the man in short who had escaped death. He may or may not have known that Siméon was your father. These are points which will never be decided and which, moreover, do not matter. What I do take for granted is that this new murder was not improvised on the spot. I firmly believe that Essarès, having noticed certain similarities in height and figure, had made every preparation to take Siméon's place if circumstances obliged him to disappear. And it was easily done. Siméon Diodokis wore a wig and no beard. Essarès, on the contrary, was bald-headed and had a beard. He shaved himself, smashed Siméon's face against the grate, mingled the hairs of his own beard with the bleeding mass, dressed the body in his clothes, took his victim's clothes for himself, put on the wig, the spectacles and the comforter. The transformation was complete.'

Patrice thought for a moment. Then he raised an objection: 'Yes, that's what happened at nineteen minutes past seven. But something else happened at twenty-three minutes past twelve.'

'No, nothing at all.'

'But that clock, which stopped at twenty-three minutes past twelve?'

'I tell you, nothing happened at all. Only, he had to put people off the scent. He had above all to avoid the inevitable accusation that would have been brought against the new Siméon.'

'What accusation?'

'What accusation? Why, that he had killed Essarès Bey, of course! A dead body is discovered in the morning. Who has committed the murder? Suspicion would at once have fallen on Siméon. He would have been questioned and arrested. And Essarès would have been found under Siméon's mask. No, he needed liberty and facilities to move about as he pleased. To achieve this, he kept the murder concealed all the morning and arranged so that no one set foot in the library. He went three times and knocked at his wife's door, so that she should say that Essarès Bey was still alive during the morning. Then, when she went out, he raised his voice and ordered Siméon, in other words himself, to see her to the hospital in the Champs-Élysées. And in this way Mme Essarès thought that she was leaving her husband behind her alive and that she was escorted by old Siméon, whereas actually she was leaving old Siméon's corpse in an empty part of the house and was escorted by her husband. Then what happened? What the rascal had planned. At one o'clock, the police, acting on the information laid by Colonel Fakhi, arrived and found themselves in the presence of a corpse. Whose corpse? There was not a shadow of hesitation on that point. The maids recognized their master; and, when Mme Essarès returned, it was her husband whom she saw lying in front of the fireplace at which he had been tortured the night before. Old Siméon, that is to say, Essarès himself, helped to establish the identification. You yourself were taken in. The trick was played.'

'Yes,' said Patrice, nodding his head, 'that is how things must have gone. They all fit in.'

'The trick was played,' Don Luis repeated, 'and nobody could make out how it was done. Was there not this further proof, the letter written in Essarès' own hand and found on his desk? The letter was dated at twelve o'clock on the fourth of April, addressed to his wife, and told her that he was going away. Better still, the trick was so successfully played that the very clues which ought to have revealed the truth merely concealed it. For instance, your father used to carry a tiny album of photographs in a pocket stitched inside his under-vest. Essarès did not notice it and did not remove the vest from the body. Well, when they found the album, they at once accepted that most unlikely hypothesis: Essarès Bey carrying on his person an album filled with photographs of his wife and Captain Belval! In the same way, when they found in the dead man's hand an amethyst pendant containing your two latest photographs and when they also found a crumpled paper with something on it about the golden triangle, they at once admitted that Essarès Bey had stolen the pendant and the document and was holding them in his hand when he died! So absolutely certain were they all that it was Essarès Bey who had been murdered, that his dead body lay before their eyes and that they must not trouble about the question any longer. And in this way the new Siméon was master of the situation. Essarès Bey is dead, long live Siméon!'

Don Luis indulged in a hearty laugh. The adventure struck him as really amusing.

'Then and there,' he went on, 'Essarès, behind his impenetrable mask, set to work. That very day he listened to your conversation with Coralie and, overcome with fury at seeing you bend over her, fired a shot from his revolver. But, when this new attempt failed, he ran away and played an elaborate comedy near the little door in the garden, crying murder, tossing the key over the wall to lay a false scent and falling to the ground half dead, as though he had been strangled by the enemy who was supposed to have fired the shot. The comedy ended with a skilful assumption of madness.'

'But what was the object of this madness?'

'What was the object? Why, to make people leave him alone and keep them from questioning him or suspecting him. Once he was looked upon as mad, he could remain silent and unobserved. Otherwise, Mme Essarès would have recognized his voice at the first words he spoke, however cleverly he might have altered his tone. From this time onward, he is mad. He is an irresponsible being. He goes about as he pleases. He is a madman! And his madness is so thoroughly admitted that he leads you, so to speak, by the hand to his former accomplices and causes you to have them arrested, without asking yourself for an instant if this madman is not acting with the clearest possible sense of his own interest. He's a madman, a poor, harmless madman, one of those unfortunates with whom nobody dreams of interfering. Henceforth, he has only his last two adversaries to fight: Coralie and you. And this is an easy matter for him. I presume that he got hold of a diary kept by your father. At any rate, he knows every day of the one which you keep. From this he learns the whole story of the graves; and he knows that, on the fourteenth of April, Coralie and you are both going on a pilgrimage to those graves. Besides, he plans to make you go there, for his plot is laid. He prepares against the son and the daughter, against the Patrice and Coralie of today, the attempt which he once prepared against the father and the mother. The attempt succeeds at the start. It would have succeeded to the end, but for an idea that occurred to our poor Ya-Bon, thanks to which a new adversary, in the person of myself, entered the lists...
But I need hardly go on. You know the rest as well as I do; and, like

myself, you can judge in all his glory the inhuman villain who, in the space of those twenty-four hours, allowed his accomplice Grégoire to be strangled, buried your Coralie under the sand-heap, killed Ya-Bon, locked me in the lodge, or thought he did, buried you alive in the grave dug by your father and made away with Vacherot, the porter. And now, Captain Belval, do you think that I ought to have prevented him from committing suicide, this pretty gentleman who, in the last resort, was trying to pass himself off as your father?'

'You were right,' said Patrice. 'You have been right all through, from start to finish. I see it all now, as a whole and in every detail. Only one point remains: the golden triangle. How did you find out the truth? What was it that brought you to this sand-heap and enabled you to save Coralie from the most awful death?'

'Oh, that part was even simpler,' replied Don Luis, 'and the light came almost without my knowing it! I'll tell it you in a few words. But let us move away first. M. Masseron and his men are becoming a little troublesome.'

The detectives were distributed at the two entrances to Berthou's Wharf. M. Masseron was giving them his instructions. He was obviously speaking to them of Don Luis and preparing to accost him.

'Let's get on the barge,' said Don Luis. 'I've left some important papers there.'

Patrice followed him. Opposite the cabin containing Grégoire's body was another cabin, reached by the same companion-way. It was furnished with a table and a chair.

'Here, captain,' said Don Luis, taking a letter from the drawer of the table and settling it, 'is a letter which I will ask you to . . . but don't let us waste words. I shall hardly have time to satisfy your curiosity. Our friends are coming nearer. Well, we were saying, the golden triangle . . . '

He listened to what was happening outside with an attention whose real meaning Patrice was soon to understand. And, continuing to give ear, he resumed.

'The golden triangle? There are problems which we solve more or less by accident, without trying. We are guided to a right solution by external events, among which we choose unconsciously, feeling our way in the dark, examining this one, thrusting aside that one and suddenly beholding the object aimed at . . . Well, this morning, after taking you to the tombs and burying you under the stone, Essarès Bey came back to me. Believing me to be locked into the studio, he had the pretty thought to turn on the gas-meter and then went off to the quay above Berthou's Wharf. Here he hesitated; and his hesitation provided me with a precious clue. He was certainly then thinking of releasing Coralie. People passed and he went away. Knowing where he was going, I returned to your assistance, told your friends at Essarès' house and asked them to look after you. Then I came back here. Indeed, the whole course of events obliged me to come back. It was unlikely that the bags of gold were inside the conduit; and, as the *Belle Hélène* had not taken them off, they must be beyond the garden, outside the conduit and therefore somewhere near here. I explored the barge we are now on, not so much with the object of looking for the bags as with the hope of finding some unexpected piece of inform-ation and also, I confess, the four millions in Grégoire's possession. Well, when I start exploring a place where I fail to find what I want, I always remember that capital story of Edgar Allan Poe's, *The Purloined Letter*. Do you recollect? The stolen diplomatic document which was known to be hidden in a certain room. The police invest-igate every nook and corner of the room and take up all the boards of the floor, without results. But Dupin arrives and almost immediately goes to a card-rack dangling from a little brass knob on the wall and containing a solitary soiled and crumpled letter. This is the document of which he was in search. Well, I instinctively adopted the same process. I looked where no one would dream of looking, in places which do not constitute a hiding-place because it would really be too easy to discover. This gave me the idea of turning the pages of four old directories standing in a row on that shelf. The four millions were there. And I knew all that I wanted to know.'

'About what?'

'About Essarès' temperament, his habits, the extent of his attain-ments, his notion of a good hiding-place. We had plunged on the expectation of meeting with difficulties; we ought to have looked at the outside, to have looked at the surface of things. I was assisted by two further clues. I had noticed that the uprights of the ladder which Ya-Bon must have taken from here had a few grains of sand on them. Lastly, I remembered that Ya-Bon had drawn a triangle on the pavement with a piece of chalk and that this triangle had only two sides, the third side being formed by the foot of the wall. Why this detail? Why not a third line in chalk? . . . To make a long story short, I lit a cigarette, sat down upstairs, on the deck of the barge, and, looking round me, said to myself, "Lupin, my son, five minutes and no more." When I say, "Lupin, my son", I simply can't resist myself. By the time I had smoked a quarter of the cigarette, I was there.'

'You had found out?'

'I had found out. I can't say which of the factors at my disposal kindled the spark. No doubt it was all of them together. It's a rather complicated psychological operation, you know, like a chemical experiment. The correct idea is formed suddenly by mysterious reactions and combinations among the elements in which it existed in a potential stage. And then I was carrying within myself an intuitive principle, a very special incentive which obliged me, which inevitably compelled me, to discover the hiding-place: Little Mother Coralie was there! I knew for certain that failure on my part, prolonged weakness or hesitation would mean her destruction. There was a woman there, within a radius of a dozen yards or so. I had to find out and I found out. The spark was kindled. The elements combined. And I made straight for the sand-heap. I at once saw the marks of footsteps and, almost at the top, the signs of a slight stamping. I started digging. You can imagine my excitement when I first touched one of the bags. But I had no time for excitement. I shifted a few bags. Coralie was there, unconscious, hardly protected from the sand which was slowly stifling her, trickling through, stopping up her eyes, suffocating her. I needn't tell you more, need I? The wharf was deserted, as usual. I got her out. I hailed a taxi. I first took her home. Then I turned my attention to Essarès, to Vacherot the porter; and, when I had discovered our enemy's plans, I went and made my arrangements with Dr Géradec. Lastly, I had you moved to the private hospital on the Boulevard de Montmorency and gave orders for Coralie to be taken there too. And there you are, captain! All done in three hours. When the doctor's car brought me back to the hospital, Essarès arrived at the same time, to have his injuries seen to. I had him safe.'

Don Luis ceased speaking. There were no words necessary between the two men. One had done the other the greatest services which a man has it in his power to render; and the other knew that these were services for which no thanks are adequate. And he also knew that he would never have an opportunity to prove his gratitude. Don Luis was in a manner above those proofs, owing to the mere fact that they were impossible. There was no service to be rendered to a man like him, disposing of his resources and performing miracles with the same ease with which we perform the trivial actions of everyday life.

Patrice once again pressed his hand warmly, without a word. Don Luis accepted the homage of this silent emotion and said: 'If ever people talk of Arsène Lupin before you, captain, say a good word for him, won't you? He deserves it.' And he added, with a laugh,

'It's funny, but, as I get on in life, I find myself caring about my reputation. The devil was old, the devil a monk would be!'

He pricked up his ears and, after a moment, said: 'Captain, it is time for us to part. Present my respects to Little Mother Coralie. I shall not have known her, so to speak, and she will not know me. It is better so. Goodbye, captain.'

'Then we are taking leave of each other?'

'Yes, I hear M. Masseron. Go to him, will you, and have the kindness to bring him here?'

Patrice hesitated. Why was Don Luis sending him to meet M. Masseron? Was it so that he, Patrice, might intervene in his favor?

The idea appealed to him; and he ran up the companion-way.

Then a thing happened which Patrice was destined never to understand, something very quick and quite inexplicable. It was as though a long and gloomy adventure were to finish suddenly with melodramatic unexpectedness.

Patrice met M. Masseron on the deck of the barge.

'Is your friend here?' asked the magistrate.

'Yes. But one word first: you don't mean to . . . ?'

'Have no fear. We shall do him no harm, on the contrary.'

The answer was so definite that the officer could find nothing more to say. M. Masseron went down first, with Patrice following him.

'Hullo!' said Patrice. 'I left the cabin-door open!'

He pushed the door. It opened. But Don Luis was no longer in the cabin.

Immediate enquiries showed that no one had seen him go, neither the men remaining on the wharf nor those who had already crossed the gangway.

'When you have time to examine this barge thoroughly,' said Patrice, 'I've no doubt you will find it pretty nicely faked.'

'So your friend has probably escaped through some trap-door and swum away?' asked M. Masseron, who seemed greatly annoyed.

'I expect so,' said Patrice, laughing. 'Unless he's gone off on a submarine!'

'A submarine in the Seine?'

'Why not? I don't believe that there's any limit to my friend's resourcefulness and determination.'

But what completely dumbfounded M. Masseron was the discovery, on the table, of a letter directed to himself, the letter which Don Luis had placed there at the beginning of his interview with Patrice.

'Then he knew that I should come here? He foresaw, even before we met, that I should ask him to fulfil certain formalities?'

The letter ran as follows.

Sir,

Forgive my departure and believe that I, on my side, quite understand the reason that brings you here. My position is not in fact regular; and you are entitled to ask me for an explanation. I will give you that explanation some day or other. You will then see that, if I serve France in a manner of my own, that manner is not a bad one and that my country will owe me some gratitude for the immense services, if I may venture to use the word, which I have done her during this war. On the day of our interview, I should like you to thank me, sir. You will then – for I know your secret ambition – be prefect of police. Perhaps I shall even be able personally to forward a nomination which I consider well-deserved. I will exert myself in that direction without delay.

I have the honor to be, etc.

M. Masseron remained silent for a time.

'A strange character!' he said, at last. 'Had he been willing, we should have given him great things to do. That was what I was instructed to tell him.'

'You may be sure, sir,' said Patrice, 'that the things which he is actually doing are greater still.' And he added, 'A strange character, as you say. And stranger still, more powerful and more extraordinary than you can imagine. If each of the allied nations had had three or four men of his stamp at its disposal, the war would have been over in six months.'

'I quite agree,' said M. Masseron. 'Only those men are usually solitary, intractable people, who act solely upon their own judgment and refuse to accept any authority. I'll tell you what: they're something like that famous adventurer who, a few years ago, compelled the Kaiser to visit him in prison and obtain his release . . . and afterwards, owing to a disappointment in love, threw himself into the sea from the cliffs at Capri.'

'Who was that?'

'Oh, you know the fellow's name as well as I do! . . . Lupin, that's it: Arsène Lupin.'

THE END

THE EIGHT STROKES
OF THE CLOCK

AUTHOR'S NOTE

These adventures were told to me in the old days by
Arsène Lupin, as though they had happened to a friend of
his, named Prince Rénine. As for me, considering the way
in which they were conducted, the actions, the behaviour
and the very character of the hero, I find it very difficult
not to identify the two friends as one and the same person.
Arsène Lupin is gifted with a powerful imagination and is
quite capable of attributing to himself adventures which
are not his at all and of disowning those which are really
his. The reader will judge for himself.

M. L.

On the Top of the Tower

Hortense Daniel pushed her window ajar and whispered: 'Are you there, Rossigny?'

'I am here,' replied a voice from the shrubbery at the front of the house.

Leaning forward, she saw a rather fat man looking up at her out of a gross red face with its cheeks and chin set in unpleasantly fair whiskers.

'Well?' he asked.

'Well, I had a great argument with my uncle and aunt last night. They absolutely refuse to sign the document of which my lawyer sent them the draft, or to restore the dowry squandered by my husband.'

'But your uncle is responsible by the terms of the marriage-settlement.'

'No matter. He refuses.'

'Well, what do you propose to do?'

'Are you still determined to run away with me?' she asked, with a laugh.

'More so than ever.'

'Your intentions are strictly honourable, remember!'

'Just as you please. You know that I am madly in love with you.'

'Unfortunately I am not madly in love with you!'

'Then what made you choose me?'

'Chance. I was bored. I was growing tired of my humdrum existence. So I'm ready to run risks . . . Here's my luggage: catch!'

She let down from the window a couple of large leather kit-bags. Rossigny caught them in his arms.

'The die is cast,' she whispered. 'Go and wait for me with your car at the If cross-roads. I shall come on horseback.'

'Hang it, I can't run off with your horse!'

'He will go home by himself.'

'Capital! . . . Oh, by the way . . . '

'What is it?'

'Who is this Prince Rénine, who's been here the last three days and whom nobody seems to know?'

'I don't know much about him. My uncle met him at a friend's shoot and asked him here to stay.'

'You seem to have made a great impression on him. You went for a long ride with him yesterday. He's a man I don't care for.'

'In two hours I shall have left the house in your company. The scandal will cool him off . . . Well, we've talked long enough. We have no time to lose.'

For a few minutes she stood watching the fat man bending under the weight of her traps as he moved away in the shelter of an empty avenue. Then she closed the window.

Outside, in the park, the huntsmen's horns were sounding the reveille. The hounds burst into frantic baying. It was the opening day of the hunt that morning at the Château de la Marèze, where, every year, in the first week in September, the Comte d'Aigleroche, a mighty hunter before the Lord, and his countess were accustomed to invite a few personal friends and the neighbouring landowners.

Hortense slowly finished dressing, put on a riding-habit, which revealed the lines of her supple figure, and a wide-brimmed felt hat, which encircled her lovely face and auburn hair, and sat down to her writing-desk, at which she wrote to her uncle, M. d'Aigleroche, a farewell letter to be delivered to him that evening. It was a difficult letter to word; and, after beginning it several times, she ended by giving up the idea.

'I will write to him later,' she said to herself, 'when his anger has cooled down.'

And she went downstairs to the dining-room.

Enormous logs were blazing in the hearth of the lofty room. The walls were hung with trophies of rifles and shotguns. The guests were flocking in from every side, shaking hands with the Comte d'Aigleroche, one of those typical country squires, heavily and power-fully built, who lives only for hunting and shooting. He was standing before the fire, with a large glass of old brandy in his hand, drinking the health of each new arrival.

Hortense kissed him absently.

'What, uncle! You who are usually so sober!'

'Pooh!' he said. 'A man may surely indulge himself a little once a year! . . .'

'Aunt will give you a scolding!'

'Your aunt has one of her sick headaches and is not coming down. Besides,' he added, gruffly, 'it is not her business . . . and still less is it yours, my dear child.'

Prince Rénine came up to Hortense. He was a young man, very smartly dressed, with a narrow and rather pale face, whose eyes held by turns the gentlest and the harshest, the most friendly and the most satirical expression. He bowed to her, kissed her hand and said: 'May I remind you of your kind promise, dear madame?'

'My promise?'

'Yes, we agreed that we should repeat our delightful excursion of yesterday and try to go over that old boarded-up place the look of which made us so curious. It seems to be known as the Domaine de Halingre.'

She answered a little curtly.

'I'm extremely sorry, monsieur, but it would be rather far and I'm feeling a little done up. I shall go for a canter in the park and come indoors again.'

There was a pause. Then Serge Rénine said, smiling, with his eyes fixed on hers and in a voice which she alone could hear.

'I am sure that you'll keep your promise and that you'll let me come with you. It would be better.'

'For whom? For you, you mean?'

'For you, too, I assure you.'

She coloured slightly, but did not reply, shook hands with a few people around her and left the room.

A groom was holding the horse at the foot of the steps. She mounted and set off towards the woods beyond the park.

It was a cool, still morning. Through the leaves, which barely quivered, the sky showed crystalline blue. Hortense rode at a walk down winding avenues which in half an hour brought her to a country-side of ravines and bluffs intersected by the high-road.

She stopped. There was not a sound. Rossigny must have stopped his engine and concealed the car in the thickets around the If cross-roads.

She was five hundred yards at most from that circular space. After hesitating for a few seconds, she dismounted, tied her horse care-lessly, so that he could release himself by the least effort and return to the house, shrouded her face in the long brown veil that hung over her shoulders and walked on.

As she expected, she saw Rossigny directly she reached the first turn in the road. He ran up to her and drew her into the coppice!

'Quick, quick! Oh, I was so afraid that you would be late . . . or even change your mind! And here you are! It seems too good to be true!'

She smiled.

'You appear to be quite happy to do an idiotic thing!'

'I should think I *am* happy! And so will you be, I swear you will! Your life will be one long fairy-tale. You shall have every luxury, and all the money you can wish for.'

'I want neither money nor luxuries.'

'What then?'

'Happiness.'

'You can safely leave your happiness to me.'

She replied, jestingly: 'I rather doubt the quality of the happiness which you would give me.'

'Wait! You'll see! You'll see!'

They had reached the motor. Rossigny, still stammering expressions of delight, started the engine. Hortense stepped in and wrapped herself in a wide cloak. The car followed the narrow, grassy path which led back to the cross-roads and Rossigny was accelerating the speed, when he was suddenly forced to pull up. A shot had rung out from the neighbouring wood, on the right. The car was swerving from side to side.

'A front tire burst,' shouted Rossigny, leaping to the ground.

'Not a bit of it!' cried Hortense. 'Somebody fired!'

'Impossible, my dear! Don't be so absurd!'

At that moment, two slight shocks were felt and two more reports were heard, one after the other, some way off and still in the wood.

Rossigny snarled: 'The back tires burst now . . . both of them . . . But who, in the devil's name, can the ruffian be? . . . Just let me get hold of him, that's all! . . . '

He clambered up the road-side slope. There was no one there. Moreover, the leaves of the coppice blocked the view.

'Damn it! Damn it!' he swore. 'You were right: somebody was firing at the car! Oh, this is a bit thick! We shall be held up for hours! Three tires to mend! . . . But what are you doing, dear girl?'

Hortense herself had alighted from the car. She ran to him, greatly excited.

'I'm going.'

'But why?'

'I want to know. Someone fired. I want to know who it was.'

'Don't let us separate, please!'

'Do you think I'm going to wait here for you for hours?'

'What about your running away? . . . All our plans . . . ?'

'We'll discuss that tomorrow. Go back to the house. Take back my things with you . . . And goodbye for the present.'

She hurried, left him, had the good luck to find her horse and set off at a gallop in a direction leading away from La Marèze.

There was not the least doubt in her mind that the three shots had been fired by Prince Rénine.

'It was he,' she muttered, angrily, 'it was he. No one else would be capable of such behaviour.'

Besides, he had warned her, in his smiling, masterful way, that he would expect her.

She was weeping with rage and humiliation. At that moment, had she found herself face to face with Prince Rénine, she could have struck him with her riding-whip.

Before her was the rugged and picturesque stretch of country which lies between the Orne and the Sarthe, above Alençon, and which is known as Little Switzerland. Steep hills compelled her frequently to moderate her pace, the more so as she had to cover some six miles before reaching her destination. But, though the speed at which she rode became less headlong, though her physical effort gradually slackened, she nevertheless persisted in her indignation against Prince Rénine. She bore him a grudge not only for the unspeakable action of which he had been guilty, but also for his behaviour to her during the last three days, his persistent attentions, his assurance, his air of excessive politeness.

She was nearly there. In the bottom of a valley, an old park-wall, full of cracks and covered with moss and weeds, revealed the ball-turret of a château and a few windows with closed shutters. This was the Domaine de Halingre.

She followed the wall and turned a corner. In the middle of the crescent-shaped space before which lay the entrance-gates, Serge Rénine stood waiting beside his horse.

She sprang to the ground, and, as he stepped forward, hat in hand, thanking her for coming, she cried: 'One word, monsieur, to begin with. Something quite inexplicable happened just now. Three shots were fired at a motor-car in which I was sitting. Did you fire those shots?'

'Yes.'

She seemed dumbfounded.

'Then you confess it?'

'You have asked a question, madame, and I have answered it.'

'But how dared you? What gave you the right?'

'I was not exercising a right, madame; I was performing a duty!'

'Indeed! And what duty, pray?'

'The duty of protecting you against a man who is trying to profit by your troubles.'

'I forbid you to speak like that. I am responsible for my own actions, and I decided upon them in perfect liberty.'

'Madame, I overheard your conversation with M. Rossigny this morning and it did not appear to me that you were accompanying him with a light heart. I admit the ruthlessness and bad taste of my interference and I apologise for it humbly; but I risked being taken for a ruffian in order to give you a few hours for reflection.'

'I have reflected fully, monsieur. When I have once made up my mind to a thing, I do not change it.'

'Yes, madame, you do, sometimes. If not, why are you here instead of there?'

Hortense was confused for a moment. All her anger had subsided. She looked at Rénine with the surprise which one experiences when confronted with certain persons who are unlike their fellows, more capable of performing unusual actions, more generous and disinterested. She realised perfectly that he was acting without any ulterior motive or calculation, that he was, as he had said, merely fulfilling his duty as a gentleman to a woman who has taken the wrong turning.

Speaking very gently, he said: 'I know very little about you, madame, but enough to make me wish to be of use to you. You are twenty-six years old and have lost both your parents. Seven years ago, you became the wife of the Comte d'Aigleroche's nephew by marriage, who proved to be of unsound mind, half insane indeed, and had to be confined. This made it impossible for you to obtain a divorce and compelled you, since your dowry had been squandered, to live with your uncle and at his expense. It's a depressing environment. The count and countess do not agree. Years ago, the count was deserted by his first wife, who ran away with the countess's first husband. The abandoned husband and wife decided out of spite to unite their fortunes, but found nothing but disappointment and ill-will in this second marriage. And you suffer the consequences. They lead a monotonous, narrow, lonely life for eleven months or more out of the year. One day, you met M. Rossigny, who fell in love with you and suggested an elopement. You did not care for him. But you were bored, your youth was being wasted, you longed for the unexpected, for adventure . . . in a word, you accepted with the very definite intention of keeping your admirer at arm's length, but also with the rather ingenuous hope that the scandal would force your uncle's hand and make him account for his trusteeship and assure you of an independent existence. That is how you stand. At present you have to choose between placing yourself in M. Rossigny's hands . . . or trusting yourself to me.'

She raised her eyes to his. What did he mean? What was the purport of this offer which he made so seriously, like a friend who asks nothing but to prove his devotion?

After a moment's silence, he took the two horses by the bridle and tied them up. Then he examined the heavy gates, each of which was strengthened by two planks nailed cross-wise. An electoral poster, dated twenty years earlier, showed that no one had entered the domain since that time.

Rénine tore up one of the iron posts which supported a railing that ran round the crescent and used it as a lever. The rotten planks gave way. One of them uncovered the lock, which he attacked with a big knife, containing a number of blades and implements. A minute later, the gate opened on a waste of bracken which led up to a long, dilapidated building, with a turret at each corner and a sort of a belvedere, built on a taller tower, in the middle.

The Prince turned to Hortense.

'You are in no hurry,' he said. 'You will form your decision this evening; and, if M. Rossigny succeeds in persuading you for the second time, I give you my word of honour that I shall not cross your path. Until then, grant me the privilege of your company. We made up our minds yesterday to inspect the château. Let us do so. Will you? It is as good a way as any of passing the time and I have a notion that it will not be uninteresting.'

He had a way of talking which compelled obedience. He seemed to be commanding and entreating at the same time. Hortense did not even seek to shake off the enervation into which her will was slowly sinking. She followed him to a half-demolished flight of steps at the top of which was a door likewise strengthened by planks nailed in the form of a cross.

Rénine went to work in the same way as before. They entered a spacious hall paved with white and black flagstones, furnished with old sideboards and choir-stalls and adorned with a carved escutcheon which displayed the remains of armorial bearings, representing an eagle standing on a block of stone, all half-hidden behind a veil of cobwebs which hung down over a pair of folding-doors.

'The door of the drawing-room, evidently,' said Rénine.

He found this more difficult to open; and it was only by repeatedly charging it with his shoulder that he was able to move one of the doors.

Hortense had not spoken a word. She watched not without surprise this series of forcible entries, which were accomplished with a really masterly skill. He guessed her thoughts and, turning round, said in a serious voice: 'It's child's-play to me. I was a locksmith once.'

She seized his arm and whispered: 'Listen!'

'To what?' he asked.

She increased the pressure of her hand, to demand silence. The next moment, he murmured: 'It's really very strange.'

'Listen, listen!' Hortense repeated, in bewilderment. 'Can it be possible?'

They heard, not far from where they were standing, a sharp sound, the sound of a light tap recurring at regular intervals; and they had only to listen attentively to recognise the ticking of a clock. Yes, it was this and nothing else that broke the profound silence of the dark room; it was indeed the deliberate ticking, rhythmical as the beat of a metronome, produced by a heavy brass pendulum. That was it! And nothing could be more impressive than the measured pulsation of this trivial mechanism, which by some miracle, some inexplicable phenomenon, had continued to live in the heart of the dead château.

'And yet,' stammered Hortense, without daring to raise her voice, 'no one has entered the house?'

'No one.'

'And it is quite impossible for that clock to have kept going for twenty years without being wound up?'

'Quite impossible.'

'Then . . . ?'

Serge Rénine opened the three windows and threw back the shutters.

He and Hortense were in a drawing-room, as he had thought; and the room showed not the least sign of disorder. The chairs were in their places. Not a piece of furniture was missing. The people who had lived there and who had made it the most individual room in their house had gone away leaving everything just as it was, the books which they used to read, the knick-knacks on the tables and consoles.

Rénine examined the old grandfather's clock, contained in its tall carved case which showed the disk of the pendulum through an oval pane of glass. He opened the door of the clock. The weights hanging from the cords were at their lowest point.

At that moment there was a click. The clock struck eight with a serious note which Hortense was never to forget.

'How extraordinary!' she said.

'Extraordinary indeed,' said he, 'for the works are exceedingly simple and would hardly keep going for a week.'

'And do you see nothing out of the common?'

'No, nothing . . . or, at least . . . '

He stooped and, from the back of the case, drew a metal tube which was concealed by the weights. Holding it up to the light: 'A telescope,' he said, thoughtfully. 'Why did they hide it? . . . And they left it drawn out to its full length . . . That's odd . . . What does it mean?'

The clock, as is sometimes usual, began to strike a second time, sounding eight strokes. Rénine closed the case and continued his inspection without putting his telescope down. A wide arch led from the drawing-room to a smaller apartment, a sort of smoking-room. This also was furnished, but contained a glass case for guns of which the rack was empty. Hanging on a panel near by was a calendar with the date of the 5th of September.

'Oh,' cried Hortense, in astonishment, 'the same date as today! . . . They tore off the leaves until the 5th of September . . . And this is the anniversary! What an astonishing coincidence!'

'Astonishing,' he echoed. 'It's the anniversary of their departure . . . twenty years ago today.'

'You must admit,' she said, 'that all this is incomprehensible.'

'Yes, of course . . . but, all the same . . . perhaps not.'

'Have you any idea?'

He waited a few seconds before replying.

'What puzzles me is this telescope hidden, dropped in that corner, at the last moment. I wonder what it was used for . . . From the ground-floor windows you see nothing but the trees in the garden . . . and the same, I expect, from all the windows . . . We are in a valley, without the least open horizon . . . To use the telescope, one would have to go up to the top of the house . . . Shall we go up?'

She did not hesitate. The mystery surrounding the whole adventure excited her curiosity so keenly that she could think of nothing but accompanying Rénine and assisting him in his investigations.

They went upstairs accordingly, and, on the second floor, came to a landing where they found the spiral staircase leading to the belvedere.

At the top of this was a platform in the open air, but surrounded by a parapet over six feet high.

'There must have been battlements which have been filled in since,' observed Prince Rénine. 'Look here, there were loop-holes at one time. They may have been blocked.'

'In any case,' she said, 'the telescope was of no use up here either and we may as well go down again.'

'I don't agree,' he said. 'Logic tells us that there must have been some gap through which the country could be seen and this was the spot where the telescope was used.'

He hoisted himself by his wrists to the top of the parapet and then saw that this point of vantage commanded the whole of the valley, including the park, with its tall trees marking the horizon; and, beyond, a depression in a wood surmounting a hill, at a distance of some seven or eight hundred yards, stood another tower, squat and in ruins, covered with ivy from top to bottom.

Rénine resumed his inspection. He seemed to consider that the key to the problem lay in the use to which the telescope was put and that the problem would be solved if only they could discover this use.

He studied the loop-holes one after the other. One of them, or rather the place which it had occupied, attracted his attention above the rest. In the middle of the layer of plaster, which had served to block it, there was a hollow filled with earth in which plants had grown. He pulled out the plants and removed the earth, thus clearing the mouth of a hole some five inches in diameter, which completely penetrated the wall. On bending forward, Rénine perceived that this deep and narrow opening inevitably carried the eye, above the dense tops of the trees and through the depression in the hill, to the ivy-clad tower.

At the bottom of this channel, in a sort of groove which ran through it like a gutter, the telescope fitted so exactly that it was quite impossible to shift it, however little, either to the right or to the left.

Rénine, after wiping the outside of the lenses, while taking care not to disturb the lie of the instrument by a hair's breadth, put his eye to the small end.

He remained for thirty or forty seconds, gazing attentively and silently. Then he drew himself up and said, in a husky voice: 'It's terrible . . . it's really terrible.'

'What is?' she asked, anxiously.

'Look.'

She bent down but the image was not clear to her and the telescope had to be focused to suit her sight. The next moment she shuddered and said: 'It's two scarecrows, isn't it, both stuck up on the top? But why?'

'Look again,' he said. 'Look more carefully under the hats . . . the faces . . .'

'Oh!' she cried, turning faint with horror, 'how awful!'

The field of the telescope, like the circular picture shown by a magic lantern, presented this spectacle: the platform of a broken tower, the walls of which were higher in the more distant part and formed as it were a back-drop, over which surged waves of ivy. In front, amid a cluster of bushes, were two human beings, a man and a woman, leaning back against a heap of fallen stones.

But the words man and woman could hardly be applied to these two forms, these two sinister puppets, which, it is true, wore clothes and hats – or rather shreds of clothes and remnants of hats – but had lost their eyes, their cheeks, their chins, every particle of flesh, until they were actually and positively nothing more than two skeletons.

'Two skeletons,' stammered Hortense. 'Two skeletons with clothes on. Who carried them up there?'

'Nobody.'

'But still . . .'

'That man and that woman must have died at the top of the tower, years and years ago . . . and their flesh rotted under their clothes and the ravens ate them.'

'But it's hideous, hideous!' cried Hortense, pale as death, her face drawn with horror.

* * *

Half an hour later, Hortense Daniel and Rénine left the Château de Halingre. Before their departure, they had gone as far as the ivy-grown tower, the remains of an old donjon-keep more than half demolished. The inside was empty. There seemed to have been a way of climbing to the top, at a comparatively recent period, by means of wooden stairs and ladders which now lay broken and scattered over the ground. The tower backed against the wall which marked the end of the park.

A curious fact, which surprised Hortense, was that Prince Rénine had neglected to pursue a more minute enquiry, as though the matter had lost all interest for him. He did not even speak of it any longer; and, in the inn at which they stopped and took a light meal in the nearest village, it was she who asked the landlord about the abandoned château. But she learnt nothing from him, for the man was new to the district and could give her no particulars. He did not even know the name of the owner.

They turned their horses' heads towards La Marèze. Again and again Hortense recalled the squalid sight which had met their eyes. But Rénine, who was in a lively mood and full of attentions to his companion, seemed utterly indifferent to those questions.

'But, after all,' she exclaimed, impatiently, 'we can't leave the matter there! It calls for a solution.'

'As you say,' he replied, 'a solution is called for. M. Rossigny has to know where he stands and you have to decide what to do about him.'

She shrugged her shoulders: 'He's of no importance for the moment. The thing today . . . '

'Is what?'

'Is to know what those two dead bodies are.'

'Still, Rossigny . . . '

'Rossigny can wait. But I can't. You have shown me a mystery which is now the only thing that matters. What do you intend to do?'

'To do?'

'Yes. There are two bodies . . . You'll inform the police, I suppose.'

'Gracious goodness!' he exclaimed, laughing. 'What for?'

'Well, there's a riddle that has to be cleared up at all costs, a terrible tragedy.'

'We don't need anyone to do that.'

'What! Do you mean to say that you understand it?'

'Almost as plainly as though I had read it in a book, told in full detail, with explanatory illustrations. It's all so simple!'

She looked at him askance, wondering if he was making fun of her. But he seemed quite serious.

'Well?' she asked, quivering with curiosity.

The light was beginning to wane. They had trotted at a good pace; and the hunt was returning as they neared La Marèze.

'Well,' he said, 'we shall get the rest of our information from people living round about . . . from your uncle, for instance; and you will see how logically all the facts fit in. When you hold the first link of a chain, you are bound, whether you like it or not, to reach the last. It's the greatest fun in the world.'

Once in the house, they separated. On going to her room, Hortense found her luggage and a furious letter from Rossigny in which he bade her goodbye and announced his departure.

Then Rénine knocked at her door.

'Your uncle is in the library,' he said. 'Will you go down with me? I've sent word that I am coming.'

She went with him. He added: 'One word more. This morning, when I thwarted your plans and begged you to trust me, I naturally undertook an obligation towards you which I mean to fulfill without delay. I want to give you a positive proof of this.'

She laughed.

'The only obligation which you took upon yourself was to satisfy my curiosity.'

'It shall be satisfied,' he assured her, gravely, 'and more fully than you can possibly imagine.'

M. d'Aigleroche was alone. He was smoking his pipe and drinking sherry. He offered a glass to Rénine, who refused.

'Well, Hortense!' he said, in a rather thick voice. 'You know that it's pretty dull here, except in these September days. You must make the most of them. Have you had a pleasant ride with Rénine?'

'That's just what I wanted to talk about, my dear sir,' interrupted the prince.

'You must excuse me, but I have to go to the station in ten minutes, to meet a friend of my wife's.'

'Oh, ten minutes will be ample!'

'Just the time to smoke a cigarette?'

'No longer.'

He took a cigarette from the case which M. d'Aigleroche handed to him, lit it and said: 'I must tell you that our ride happened to take us to an old domain which you are sure to know, the Domaine de Halingre.'

'Certainly I know it. But it has been closed, boarded up for twenty-five years or so. You weren't able to get in, I suppose?'

'Yes, we were.'

'Really? Was it interesting?'

'Extremely. We discovered the strangest things.'

'What things?' asked the count, looking at his watch.

Rénine described what they had seen.

'On a tower some way from the house there were two dead bodies, two skeletons rather . . . a man and a woman still wearing the clothes which they had on when they were murdered.'

'Come, come, now! Murdered?'

'Yes; and that is what we have come to trouble you about. The tragedy must date back to some twenty years ago. Was nothing known of it at the time?'

'Certainly not,' declared the count. 'I never heard of any such crime or disappearance.'

'Oh, really!' said Rénine, looking a little disappointed. 'I hoped to obtain a few particulars.'

'I'm sorry.'

'In that case, I apologise.'

He consulted Hortense with a glance and moved towards the door. But on second thought: 'Could you not at least, my dear sir, bring me into touch with some persons in the neighbourhood, some members of your family, who might know more about it?'

'Of my family? And why?'

'Because the Domaine de Halingre used to belong and no doubt still belongs to the d'Aigleroches. The arms are an eagle on a heap of stones, on a rock. This at once suggested the connection.'

This time the count appeared surprised. He pushed back his decanter and his glass of sherry and said: 'What's this you're telling me? I had no idea that we had any such neighbours.'

Rénine shook his head and smiled.

'I should be more inclined to believe, sir, that you were not very eager to admit any relationship between yourself . . . and the unknown owner of the property.'

'Then he's not a respectable man?'

'The man, to put it plainly, is a murderer.'

'What do you mean?'

The count had risen from his chair. Hortense, greatly excited, said: 'Are you really sure that there has been a murder and that the murder was done by someone belonging to the house?'

'Quite sure.'

'But why are you so certain?'

'Because I know who the two victims were and what caused them to be killed.'

Prince Rénine was making none but positive statements and his method suggested the belief that he supported by the strongest proofs.

M. d'Aigleroche strode up and down the room, with his hands behind his back. He ended by saying: 'I always had an instinctive feeling that something had happened, but I never tried to find out . . . Now, as a matter of fact, twenty years ago, a relation of mine, a distant cousin, used to live at the Domaine de Halingre. I hoped, because of the name I bear, that this story, which, as I say, I never knew but suspected, would remain hidden for ever.'

'So this cousin killed somebody?'

'Yes, he was obliged to.'

Rénine shook his head.

'I am sorry to have to amend that phrase, my dear sir. The truth, on the contrary, is that your cousin took his victims' lives in cold blood and in a cowardly manner. I never heard of a crime more deliberately and craftily planned.'

'What is it that you know?'

The moment had come for Rénine to explain himself, a solemn and anguish-stricken moment, the full gravity of which Hortense understood, though she had not yet divined any part of the tragedy which the prince unfolded step by step.'

'It's a very simple story,' he said. 'There is every reason to believe that M. d'Aigleroche was married and that there was another couple living in the neighbourhood with whom the owner of the Domaine de Halingre was on friendly terms. What happened one day, which of these four persons first disturbed the relations between the two households, I am unable to say. But a likely version, which at once occurs to the mind, is that your cousin's wife, Madame d'Aigleroche, was in the habit of meeting the other husband in the ivy-covered tower, which had a door opening outside the estate. On discovering the intrigue, your cousin d'Aigleroche resolved to be revenged, but in such a manner that there should be no scandal and that no one even should ever know that the guilty pair had been killed. Now he had ascertained – as I did just now – that there was a part of the house, the belvedere, from which you can see, over the trees and the undulations of the park, the tower standing eight hundred yards away, and that this was the only place that overlooked the top of the tower. He therefore pierced a hole in the parapet, through one of the former loopholes, and from there, by using a telescope which fitted exactly in the grove which he had hollowed out, he watched the meetings of the two lovers. And it was from there, also, that, after carefully taking all his measurements, and calculating all his distances, on a Sunday, the 5th of September, when the house was empty, he killed them with two shots.'

The truth was becoming apparent. The light of day was breaking. The count muttered: 'Yes, that's what must have happened. I expect that my cousin d'Aigleroche . . .'

'The murderer,' Rénine continued, 'stopped up the loophole neatly with a clod of earth. No one would ever know that two dead bodies were decaying on the top of that tower which was never visited and of which he took the precaution to demolish the wooden stairs. Nothing therefore remained for him to do but to explain the disappearance of his wife and his friend. This presented no difficulty. He accused them of having eloped together.'

Hortense gave a start. Suddenly, as though the last sentence were a complete and to her an absolutely unexpected revelation, she understood what Rénine was trying to convey.

'What do you mean?' she asked.

'I mean that M. d'Aigleroche accused his wife and his friend of eloping together.'

'No, no!' she cried. 'I can't allow that! . . . You are speaking of a cousin of my uncle's? Why mix up the two stories?'

'Why mix up this story with another which took place at that time?' said the prince. 'But I am not mixing them up, my dear madame; there is only one story and I am telling it as it happened.'

Hortense turned to her uncle. He sat silent, with his arms folded; and his head remained in the shadow cast by the lamp-shade. Why had he not protested?

Rénine repeated in a firm tone: 'There is only one story. On the evening of that very day, the 5th of September at eight o'clock, M. d'Aigleroche, doubtless alleging as his reason that he was going in pursuit of the runaway couple, left his house after boarding up the entrance. He went away, leaving all the rooms as they were and removing only the firearms from their glass case. At the last minute, he had a presentiment, which has been justified today, that the discovery of the telescope which had played so great a part in the preparation of his crime might serve as a clue to an enquiry; and he threw it into the clock-case, where, as luck would have it, it interrupted the swing of the pendulum. This unreflecting action, one of those which every criminal inevitably commits, was to betray him twenty years later. Just now, the blows which I struck to force the door of the drawing-room released the pendulum. The clock was set going, struck eight o'clock . . . and I possessed the clue of thread which was to lead me through the labyrinth.'

'Proofs!' stammered Hortense. 'Proofs!'

'Proofs?' replied Rénine, in a loud voice. 'Why, there are any number of proofs; and you know them as well as I do. Who could have killed at that distance of eight hundred yards, except an expert shot, an ardent sportsman? You agree, M. d'Aigleroche, do you not? . . . Proofs? Why was nothing removed from the house, nothing except the guns, those guns which an ardent sportsman cannot afford to leave behind – you agree, M. d'Aigleroche – those guns which we find here, hanging in trophies on the walls! . . . Proofs? What about that date, the 5th of September, which was the date of the crime and which has left such a horrible memory in the criminal's mind that every year at this time – at this time alone – he surrounds himself with distractions and that every year, on this same 5th of September, he forgets his habits of temperance? Well, today is the 5th of September . . . Proofs? Why, if there weren't any others, would that not be enough for you?'

And Rénine, flinging out his arm, pointed to the Comte d'Aigleroche, who, terrified by this evocation of the past, had sunk huddled into a chair and was hiding his head in his hands.

Hortense did not attempt to argue with him. She had never liked her uncle, or rather her husband's uncle. She now accepted the accusation laid against him.

Sixty seconds passed. Then M. d'Aigleroche walked up to them and said: 'Whether the story be true or not, you can't call a husband a criminal for avenging his honour and killing his faithless wife.'

'No,' replied Rénine, 'but I have told only the first version of the story. There is another which is infinitely more serious . . . and more probable, one to which a more thorough investigation would be sure to lead.'

'What do you mean?'

'I mean this. It may not be a matter of a husband taking the law into his own hands, as I charitably supposed. It may be a matter of a ruined man who covets his friend's money and his friend's wife and who, with this object in view, to secure his freedom, to get rid of his friend and of his own wife, draws them into a trap, suggests to them that they should visit that lonely tower and kills them by shooting them from a distance safely under cover.'

'No, no,' the count protested. 'No, all that is untrue.'

'I don't say it isn't. I am basing my accusation on proofs, but also on intuitions and arguments which up to now have been extremely accurate. All the same, I admit that the second version may be incorrect. But, if so, why feel any remorse? One does not feel remorse for punishing guilty people.'

'One does for taking life. It is a crushing burden to bear.'

'Was it to give himself greater strength to bear this burden that M. d'Aigleroche afterwards married his victim's widow? For that, sir, is the crux of the question. What was the motive of that marriage? Was M. d'Aigleroche penniless? Was the woman he was taking as his second wife rich? Or were they both in love with each other and did M. d'Aigleroche plan with her to kill his first wife and the husband of his second wife? These are problems to which I do not know the answer. They have no interest for the moment; but the police, with all the means at their disposal, would have no great difficulty in elucidating them.'

M. d'Aigleroche staggered and had to steady himself against the back of a chair. Livid in the face, he spluttered: 'Are you going to inform the police?'

'No, no,' said Rénine. 'To begin with, there is the statute of limitations. Then there are twenty years of remorse and dread, a memory which will pursue the criminal to his dying hour, accompanied no doubt by domestic discord, hatred, a daily hell . . . and, in the end, the necessity of returning to the tower and removing the traces of the two murders, the frightful punishment of climbing that tower, of touching those skeletons, of undressing them and burying them. That will be enough. We will not ask for more. We will not give it to the public to batten on and create a scandal which would recoil upon M. d'Aigleroche's niece. No, let us leave this disgraceful business alone.'

The count resumed his seat at the table, with his hands clutching his forehead, and asked: 'Then why . . . ?'

'Why do I interfere?' said Rénine. 'What you mean is that I must have had some object in speaking. That is so. There must indeed be a penalty, however slight, and our interview must lead to some practical result. But have no fear: M. d'Aigleroche will be let off lightly.'

The contest was ended. The count felt that he had only a small formality to fulfil, a sacrifice to accept; and, recovering some of his self-assurance, he said, in an almost sarcastic tone: 'What's your price?'

Rénine burst out laughing.

'Splendid! You see the position. Only, you make a mistake in drawing me into the business. I'm working for the glory of the thing.'

'In that case?'

'You will be called upon at most to make restitution.'

'Restitution?'

Rénine leant over the table and said: 'In one of those drawers is a deed awaiting your signature. It is a draft agreement between you and your niece Hortense Daniel, relating to her private fortune, which fortune was squandered and for which you are responsible. Sign the deed.'

M. d'Aigleroche gave a start.

'Do you know the amount?'

'I don't wish to know it.'

'And if I refuse? . . . '

'I shall ask to see the Comtesse d'Aigleroche.'

Without further hesitation, the count opened a drawer, produced a document on stamped paper and quickly signed it.

'Here you are,' he said, 'and I hope . . . '

'You hope, as I do, that you and I may never have any future dealings? I'm convinced of it. I shall leave this evening; your niece, no doubt, tomorrow. Goodbye.'

* * *

In the drawing-room, which was still empty, while the guests at the house were dressing for dinner, Rénine handed the deed to Hortense. She seemed dazed by all that she had heard; and the thing that bewildered her even more than the relentless light shed upon her uncle's past was the miraculous insight and amazing lucidity displayed by this man: the man who for some hours had controlled events and conjured up before her eyes the actual scenes of a tragedy which no one had beheld.

'Are you satisfied with me?' he asked.

She gave him both her hands.

'You have saved me from Rossigny. You have given me back my freedom and my independence. I thank you from the bottom of my heart.'

'Oh, that's not what I am asking you to say!' he answered. 'My first and main object was to amuse you. Your life seemed so humdrum and lacking in the unexpected. Has it been so today?'

'How can you ask such a question? I have had the strangest and most stirring experiences.'

'That is life,' he said. 'When one knows how to use one's eyes. Adventure exists everywhere, in the meanest hovel, under the mask of the wisest of men. Everywhere, if you are only willing, you will find an excuse for excitement, for doing good, for saving a victim, for ending an injustice.'

Impressed by his power and authority, she murmured: 'Who are you exactly?'

'An adventurer. Nothing more. A lover of adventures. Life is not worth living except in moments of adventure, the adventures of others or personal adventures. Today's has upset you because it affected the innermost depths of your being. But those of others are no less stimulating. Would you like to make the experiment?'

'How?'

'Become the companion of my adventures. If anyone calls on me for help, help him with me. If chance or instinct puts me on the track of a crime or the trace of a sorrow, let us both set out together. Do you consent?'

'Yes,' she said, 'but . . .'

She hesitated, as though trying to guess Rénine's secret intentions.

'But,' he said, expressing her thoughts for her, with a smile, 'you are a trifle sceptical. What you are saying to yourself is, "How far does that lover of adventures want to make me go? It is quite obvious that I attract him; and sooner or later he would not be sorry to receive payment for his services." You are quite right. We must have a formal contract.'

'Very formal,' said Hortense, preferring to give a jesting tone to the conversation. 'Let me hear your proposals.'

He reflected for a moment and continued: 'Well, we'll say this. The clock at Halingre gave eight strokes this afternoon, the day of the first adventure. Will you accept its decree and agree to carry out seven more of these delightful enterprises with me, during a period, for instance, of three months? And shall we say that, at the eighth, you will be pledged to grant me . . .'

'What?'

He deferred his answer.

'Observe that you will always be at liberty to leave me on the road if I do not succeed in interesting you. But, if you accompany me to the end, if you allow me to begin and complete the eighth enterprise with you, in three months, on the 5th of December, at the very moment when the eighth stroke of that clock sounds – and it will sound, you may be sure of that, for the old brass pendulum will not stop swinging again – you will be pledged to grant me . . .'

'What?' she repeated, a little unnerved by waiting.

He was silent. He looked at the beautiful lips which he had meant to claim as his reward. He felt perfectly certain that Hortense had understood and he thought it unnecessary to speak more plainly.

'The mere delight of seeing you will be enough to satisfy me. It is not for me but for you to impose conditions. Name them: what do you demand?'

She was grateful for his respect and said, laughingly: 'What do I demand?'

'Yes.'

'Can I demand anything I like, however difficult and impossible?'

'Everything is easy and everything is possible to the man who is bent on winning you.'

Then she said: 'I demand that you shall restore to me a small, antique clasp, made of a cornelian set in a silver mount. It came to me from my mother and everyone knew that it used to bring her happiness and me too. Since the day when it vanished from my jewel-case, I have had nothing but unhappiness. Restore it to me, my good genius.'

'When was the clasp stolen?'

She answered gaily: 'Seven years ago . . . or eight . . . or nine; I don't know exactly . . . I don't know where . . . I don't know how . . . I know nothing about it . . . '

'I will find it,' Rénine declared, 'and you shall be happy.'

Thw Water-Bottle

Four days after she had settled down in Paris, Hortense Daniel agreed to meet Prince Rénine in the Bois. It was a glorious morning and they sat down on the terrace of the Restaurant Impérial, a little to one side.

Hortense, feeling glad to be alive, was in a playful mood, full of attractive grace. Rénine, lest he should startle her, refrained from alluding to the compact into which they had entered at his suggestion. She told him how she had left La Marèze and said that she had not heard of Rossigny.

'I have,' said Rénine. 'I've heard of him.'

'Oh?'

'Yes, he sent me a challenge. We fought a duel this morning. Rossigny got a scratch in the shoulder. That finished the duel. Let's talk of something else.'

There was no further mention of Rossigny. Rénine at once expounded to Hortense the plan of two enterprises which he had in view and in which he offered, with no great enthusiasm, to let her share.

'The finest adventure,' he declared, 'is that which we do not foresee. It comes unexpectedly, unannounced; and no one, save the initiated, realizes that an opportunity to act and to expend one's energies is close at hand. It has to be seized at once. A moment's hesitation may mean that we are too late. We are warned by a special sense, like that of a sleuth-hound which distinguishes the right scent from all the others that cross it.'

The terrace was beginning to fill up around them. At the next table sat a young man reading a newspaper. They were able to see his insignificant profile and his long, dark moustache. From behind them, through an open window of the restaurant, came the distant strains of a band; in one of the rooms a few couples were dancing.

As Rénine was paying for the refreshments, the young man with the long moustache stifled a cry and, in a choking voice, called one of the waiters.

'What do I owe you? . . . No change? Oh, good Lord, hurry up!'

Rénine, without a moment's hesitation, had picked up the paper. After casting a swift glance down the page, he read, under his breath.

Maître Dourdens, the counsel for the defence in the trial of Jacques Aubrieux, has been received at the Élysée. We are informed that the President of the Republic has refused to reprieve the condemned man and that the execution will take place tomorrow morning.

After crossing the terrace, the young man found himself faced, at the entrance to the garden, by a lady and gentleman who blocked his way; and the latter said: 'Excuse me, sir, but I noticed your agitation. It's about Jacques Aubrieux, isn't it?'

'Yes, yes, Jacques Aubrieux,' the young man stammered. 'Jacques, the friend of my childhood. I'm hurrying to see his wife. She must be beside herself with grief.'

'Can I offer you my assistance? I am Prince Rénine. This lady and I would be happy to call on Madame Aubrieux and to place our services at her disposal.'

The young man, upset by the news which he had read, seemed not to understand. He introduced himself awkwardly.

'My name is Dutreuil, Gaston Dutreuil.'

Rénine beckoned to his chauffeur, who was waiting at some little distance, and pushed Gaston Dutreuil into the car, asking: 'What address? Where does Madame Aubrieux live?'

'23 *bis*, Avenue du Roule.'

After helping Hortense in, Rénine repeated the address to the chauffeur and, as soon as they drove off, tried to question Gaston Dutreuil.

'I know very little of the case,' he said. 'Tell it to me as briefly as you can. Jacques Aubrieux killed one of his near relations, didn't he?'

'He is innocent, sir,' replied the young man, who seemed incapable of giving the least explanation. 'Innocent, I swear it. I've been Jacques's friend for twenty years . . . He is innocent . . . and it would be monstrous . . . '

There was nothing to be got out of him. Besides, it was only a short drive. They entered Neuilly through the Porte des Sablons and, two minutes later, stopped before a long, narrow passage between high walls which led them to a small, one-storeyed house.

Gaston Dutreuil rang.

'Madame is in the drawing-room, with her mother,' said the maid who opened the door.

'I'll go in to the ladies,' he said, taking Rénine and Hortense with him.

It was a fair-sized, prettily-furnished room, which, in ordinary times, must have been used also as a study. Two women sat weeping, one of whom, elderly and grey-haired, came up to Gaston Dutreuil. He explained the reason for Rénine's presence and she at once cried, amid her sobs: 'My daughter's husband is innocent, sir. Jacques? A better man never lived. He was so good-hearted! Murder his cousin? But he worshipped his cousin! I swear that he's not guilty, sir! And they are going to commit the infamy of putting him to death? Oh, sir, it will kill my daughter!'

Rénine realized that all these people had been living for months under the obsession of that innocence and in the certainty that an innocent man could never be executed. The news of the execution, which was now inevitable, was driving them mad.

He went up to a poor creature bent in two whose face, a quite young face, framed in pretty, flaxen hair, was convulsed with desperate grief. Hortense, who had already taken a seat beside her, gently drew her head against her shoulder. Rénine said to her: 'Madame, I do not know what I can do for you. But I give you my word of honour that, if anyone in this world can be of use to you, it is myself. I therefore implore you to answer my questions as though the clear and definite wording of your replies were able to alter the aspect of things and as though you wished to make me share your opinion of Jacques Aubrieux. For he is innocent, is he not?'

'Oh, sir, indeed he is!' she exclaimed; and the woman's whole soul was in the words.

'You are certain of it. But you were unable to communicate your certainty to the court. Well, you must now compel me to share it. I am not asking you to go into details and to live again through the hideous torment which you have suffered, but merely to answer certain questions. Will you do this?'

'I will.'

Rénine's influence over her was complete. With a few sentences Rénine had succeeded in subduing her and inspiring her with the will to obey. And once more Hortense realized all the man's power, authority and persuasion.

'What was your husband?' he asked, after begging the mother and Gaston Dutreuil to preserve absolute silence.

'An insurance-broker.'

'Lucky in business?'

'Until last year, yes.'

'So there have been financial difficulties during the past few months?'

'Yes.'

'And the murder was committed when?'

'Last March, on a Sunday.'

'Who was the victim?'

'A distant cousin, M. Guillaume, who lived at Suresnes.'

'What was the sum stolen?'

'Sixty thousand-franc notes, which this cousin had received the day before, in payment of a long-outstanding debt.'

'Did your husband know that?'

'Yes. His cousin told him of it on the Sunday, in the course of a conversation on the telephone, and Jacques insisted that his cousin ought not to keep so large a sum in the house and that he ought to pay it into a bank next day.'

'Was this in the morning?'

'At one o'clock in the afternoon. Jacques was to have gone to M. Guillaume on his motor-cycle. But he felt tired and told him that he would not go out. So he remained here all day.'

'Alone?'

'Yes. The two servants were out. I went to the Cinéma des Ternes with my mother and our friend Dutreuil. In the evening, we learnt that M. Guillaume had been murdered. Next morning, Jacques was arrested.'

'On what evidence?'

The poor creature hesitated to reply: the evidence of guilt had evidently been overwhelming. Then, obeying a sign from Rénine, she answered without a pause: 'The murderer went to Suresnes on a motorcycle and the tracks discovered were those of my husband's machine. They found a handkerchief with my husband's initials; and the revolver which was used belonged to him. Lastly, one of our neighbours maintains that he saw my husband go out on his bicycle at three o'clock and another that he saw him come in at half-past four. The murder was committed at four o'clock.'

'And what does Jacques Aubrieux say in his defence?'

'He declares that he slept all the afternoon. During that time, someone came who managed to unlock the cycle-shed and take the motor-cycle to go to Suresnes. As for the handkerchief and the revolver, they were in the tool-bag. There would be nothing surprising in the murderer's using them.'

'It seems a plausible explanation.'

'Yes, but the prosecution raised two objections. In the first place, nobody, absolutely nobody, knew that my husband was going to stay at home all day, because, on the contrary, it was his habit to go out on his motor-cycle every Sunday afternoon.'

'And the second objection?'

She flushed and murmured: 'The murderer went to the pantry at M. Guillaume's and drank half a bottle of wine straight out of the bottle, which shows my husband's fingerprints.'

It seemed as though her strength was exhausted and as though, at the same time, the unconscious hope which Rénine's intervention had awakened in her had suddenly vanished before the accumulation of adverse facts. Again she collapsed, withdrawn into a sort of silent meditation from which Hortense's affectionate attentions were unable to distract her.

The mother stammered: 'He's not guilty, is he, sir? And they can't punish an innocent man. They haven't the right to kill my daughter. Oh dear, oh dear, what have we done to be tortured like this? My poor little Madeleine!'

'She will kill herself,' said Dutreuil, in a scared voice. 'She will never be able to endure the idea that they are guillotining Jacques. She will kill herself presently . . . this very night . . .'

Rénine was striding up and down the room.

'You can do nothing for her, can you?' asked Hortense.

'It's half-past eleven now,' he replied, in an anxious tone, 'and it's to happen tomorrow morning.'

'Do you think he's guilty?'

'I don't know . . . I don't know . . . The poor woman's conviction is too impressive to be neglected. When two people have lived together for years, they can hardly be mistaken about each other to that degree. And yet . . .'

He stretched himself out on a sofa and lit a cigarette. He smoked three in succession, without a word from anyone to interrupt his train of thought. From time to time he looked at his watch. Every minute was of such importance!

At last he went back to Madeleine Aubrieux, took her hands and said, very gently: 'You must not kill yourself. There is hope left until the last minute has come; and I promise you that, for my part, I will not be disheartened until that last minute. But I need your calmness and your confidence.'

'I will be calm,' she said, with a pitiable air.

'And confident?'

'And confident.'

'Well, wait for me. I shall be back in two hours from now. Will you come with us, M. Dutreuil?'

As they were stepping into his car, he asked the young man: 'Do you know any small, unfrequented restaurant, not too far inside Paris?'

'There's the Brasserie Lutetia, on the ground-floor of the house in which I live, on the Place des Ternes.'

'Capital. That will be very handy.'

They scarcely spoke on the way. Rénine, however, said to Gaston Dutreuil: 'So far as I remember, the numbers of the notes are known, aren't they?'

'Yes. M. Guillaume had entered the sixty numbers in his pocket-book.'

Rénine muttered, a moment later: 'That's where the whole problem lies. Where are the notes? If we could lay our hands on them, we should know everything.'

At the Brasserie Lutetia there was a telephone in the private room where he asked to have lunch served. When the waiter had left him alone with Hortense and Dutreuil, he took down the receiver with a resolute air.

'Hullo! . . . Prefecture of police, please . . . Hullo! Hullo! . . . Is that the Prefecture of police? Please put me on to the criminal investigation department. I have a very important communication to make. You can say it's Prince Rénine.'

Holding the receiver in his hand, he turned to Gaston Dutreuil.

'I can ask someone to come here, I suppose? We shall be quite undisturbed?'

'Quite.'

He listened again.

'The secretary to the head of the criminal investigation department? Oh, excellent! Mr Secretary, I have on several occasions been in communication with M. Dudouis and have given him information which has been of great use to him. He is sure to remember Prince Rénine. I may be able today to show him where the sixty thousand-franc notes are hidden which Aubrieux the murderer stole from his cousin. If he's interested in the proposal, beg him to send an inspector to the Brasserie Lutetia, Place des Ternes. I shall be there with a lady and M. Dutreuil, Aubrieux's friend. Good day, Mr Secretary.'

When Rénine hung up the instrument, he saw the amazed faces of Hortense and of Gaston Dutreuil confronting him.

Hortense whispered: 'Then you know? You've discovered . . . ?'

'Nothing,' he said, laughing.

'Well?'

'Well, I'm acting as though I knew. It's not a bad method. Let's have some lunch, shall we?'

The clock marked a quarter to one.

'The man from the prefecture will be here,' he said, 'in twenty minutes at latest.'

'And if no one comes?' Hortense objected.

'That would surprise me. Of course, if I had sent a message to M. Dudouis saying, "Aubrieux is innocent", I should have failed to make any impression. It's not the least use, on the eve of an execution, to attempt to convince the gentry of the police or of the law that a man condemned to death is innocent. No. From henceforth Jacques Aubrieux belongs to the executioner. But the prospect of securing the sixty bank-notes is a windfall worth taking a little trouble over. Just think: that was the weak point in the indictment, those sixty notes which they were unable to trace.'

'But, as you know nothing of their whereabouts . . . '

'My dear girl – I hope you don't mind my calling you so? – my dear girl, when a man can't explain this or that physical phenomenon, he adopts some sort of theory which explains the various manifestations of the phenomenon and says that everything happened as though the theory were correct. That's what I am doing.'

'That amounts to saying that you are going upon a supposition?'

Rénine did not reply. Not until some time later, when lunch was over, did he say: 'Obviously I am going upon a supposition. If I had several days before me, I should take the trouble of first verifying my theory, which is based upon intuition quite as much as upon a few scattered facts. But I have only two hours; and I am embarking on the unknown path as though I were certain that it would lead me to the truth.'

'And suppose you are wrong?'

'I have no choice. Besides, it is too late. There's a knock. Oh, one word more! Whatever I may say, don't contradict me. Nor you, M. Dutreuil.'

He opened the door. A thin man, with a red imperial, entered.

'Prince Rénine?'

'Yes, sir. You, of course, are from M. Dudouis?'

'Yes.'

And the newcomer gave his name.

'Chief-inspector Morisseau.'

'I am obliged to you for coming so promptly, Mr Chief-inspector,' said Prince Rénine, 'and I hope that M. Dudouis will not regret having placed you at my disposal.'

'At your entire disposal, in addition to two inspectors whom I have left in the square outside and who have been in the case, with me, from the first.'

'I shall not detain you for any length of time,' said Rénine, 'and I will not even ask you to sit down. We have only a few minutes in which to settle everything. You know what it's all about?'

'The sixty thousand-franc notes stolen from M. Guillaume. I have the numbers here.'

Rénine ran his eyes down the slip of paper which the chief-inspector handed him and said: 'That's right. The two lists agree.'

Inspector Morisseau seemed greatly excited.

'The chief attaches the greatest importance to your discovery. So you will be able to show me? . . . '

Rénine was silent for a moment and then declared: 'Mr Chief-inspector, a personal investigation – and a most exhaustive investigation it was, as I will explain to you presently – has revealed the fact that, on his return from Suresnes, the murderer, after replacing the motor-cycle in the shed in the Avenue du Roule, ran to the Ternes and entered this house.'

'This house?'

'Yes.'

'But what did he come here for?'

'To hide the proceeds of his theft, the sixty bank-notes.'

'How do you mean? Where?'

'In a flat of which he had the key, on the fifth floor.'

Gaston Dutreuil exclaimed, in amazement: 'But there's only one flat on the fifth floor and that's the one I live in!'

'Exactly; and, as you were at the cinema with Madame Aubrieux and her mother, advantage was taken of your absence . . . '

'Impossible! No one has the key except myself.'

'One can get in without a key.'

'But I have seen no marks of any kind.'

Morisseau intervened.

'Come, let us understand one another. You say the bank-notes were hidden in M. Dutreuil's flat?'

'Yes.'

'Then, as Jacques Aubrieux was arrested the next morning, the notes ought to be there still?'

'That's my opinion.'

Gaston Dutreuil could not help laughing.

'But that's absurd! I should have found them!'

'Did you look for them?'

'No. But I should have come across them at any moment. The place isn't big enough to swing a cat in. Would you care to see it?'

'However small it may be, it's large enough to hold sixty bits of paper.'

'Of course, everything is possible,' said Dutreuil. 'Still, I must repeat that nobody, to my knowledge, has been to my rooms; that there is only one key; that I am my own housekeeper; and that I can't quite understand . . . '

Hortense too could not understand. With her eyes fixed on Prince Rénine's, she was trying to read his innermost thoughts. What game was he playing? Was it her duty to support his statements? She ended by saying: 'Mr Chief-inspector, since Prince Rénine maintains that the notes have been put away upstairs, wouldn't the simplest thing be to go and look? M. Dutreuil will take us up, won't you?'

'This minute,' said the young man. 'As you say, that will be simplest.'

They all four climbed the five storeys of the house and, after Dutreuil had opened the door, entered a tiny set of chambers consisting of a sitting-room, bedroom, kitchen and bathroom, all arranged with fastidious neatness. It was easy to see that every chair in the sitting-room occupied a definite place. The pipes had a rack to themselves; so had the matches. Three walking-sticks, arranged according to their length, hung from three nails. On a little table before the window a hat-box, filled with tissue-paper, awaited the felt hat which Dutreuil carefully placed in it. He laid his gloves beside it, on the lid.

He did all this with sedate and mechanical movements, like a man who loves to see things in the places which he has chosen for them. Indeed, no sooner did Rénine shift something than Dutreuil made a slight gesture of protest, took out his hat again, stuck it on his head, opened the window and rested his elbows on the sill, with his back turned to the room, as though he were unable to bear the sight of such vandalism.

'You're positive, are you not?' the inspector asked Rénine.

'Yes, yes, I'm positive that the sixty notes were brought here after the murder.'

'Let's look for them.'

This was easy and soon done. In half an hour, not a corner remained unexplored, not a knick-knack unlifted.

'Nothing,' said Inspector Morisseau. 'Shall we continue?'

'No,' replied Rénine, 'The notes are no longer here.'

'What do you mean?'

'I mean that they have been removed.'

'By whom? Can't you make a more definite accusation?'

Rénine did not reply. But Gaston Dutreuil wheeled round. He was choking and spluttered.

'Mr Inspector, would you like *me* to make the accusation more definite, as conveyed by this gentleman's remarks? It all means that there's a dishonest man here, that the notes hidden by the murderer were discovered and stolen by that dishonest man and deposited in another and safer place. That is your idea, sir, is it not? And you accuse me of committing this theft don't you?'

He came forward, drumming his chest with his fists: 'Me! Me! I found the notes, did I, and kept them for myself? You dare to suggest that!'

Rénine still made no reply. Dutreuil flew into a rage and, taking Inspector Morisseau aside, exclaimed: 'Mr Inspector, I strongly protest against all this farce and against the part which you are unconsciously playing in it. Before your arrival, Prince Rénine told this lady and myself that he knew nothing, that he was venturing into this affair at random and that he was following the first road that offered, trusting to luck. Do you deny it, sir?'

Rénine did not open his lips.

'Answer me, will you? Explain yourself; for, really, you are putting forward the most improbable facts without any proof whatever. It's easy enough to say that I stole the notes. And how were you to know that they were here at all? Who brought them here? Why should the murderer choose this flat to hide them in? It's all so stupid, so illogical and absurd! . . . Give us your proofs, sir . . . one single proof!'

Inspector Morisseau seemed perplexed. He questioned Rénine with a glance. Rénine said: 'Since you want specific details, we will get them from Madame Aubrieux herself. She's on the telephone. Let's go downstairs. We shall know all about it in a minute.'

Dutreuil shrugged his shoulders.

'As you please; but what a waste of time!'

He seemed greatly irritated. His long wait at the window, under a blazing sun, had thrown him into a sweat. He went to his bedroom and returned with a bottle of water, of which he took a few sips, afterwards placing the bottle on the window-sill.

'Come along,' he said.

Prince Rénine chuckled.

'You seem to be in a hurry to leave the place.'

'I'm in a hurry to show you up,' retorted Dutreuil, slamming the door.

They went downstairs to the private room containing the telephone. The room was empty. Rénine asked Gaston Dutreuil for the Aubrieux's number, took down the instrument and was put through.

The maid who came to the telephone answered that Madame Aubrieux had fainted, after giving way to an access of despair, and that she was now asleep.

'Fetch her mother, please. Prince Rénine speaking. It's urgent.'

He handed the second receiver to Morisseau. For that matter, the voices were so distinct that Dutreuil and Hortense were able to hear every word exchanged.

'Is that you, madame?'

'Yes. Prince Rénine, I believe?'

'Prince Rénine.'

'Oh, sir, what news have you for me? Is there any hope?' asked the old lady, in a tone of entreaty.

'The enquiry is proceeding very satisfactorily,' said Rénine, 'and you may hope for the best. For the moment, I want you to give me some very important particulars. On the day of the murder, did Gaston Dutreuil come to your house?'

'Yes, he came to fetch my daughter and myself, after lunch.'

'Did he know at the time that M. Guillaume had sixty thousand francs at his place?'

'Yes, I told him.'

'And that Jacques Aubrieux was not feeling very well and was proposing not to take his usual cycle-ride but to stay at home and sleep?'

'Yes.'

'You are sure?'

'Absolutely certain.'

'And you all three went to the cinema together?'

'Yes.'

'And you were all sitting together?'

'Oh, no! There was no room. He took a seat farther away.'

'A seat where you could see him?'

'No.'

'But he came to you during the interval?'

'No, we did not see him until we were going out.'

'There is no doubt of that?'

'None at all.'

'Very well, madame. I will tell you the result of my efforts in an hour's time. But above all, don't wake up Madame Aubrieux.'

'And suppose she wakes of her own accord?'

'Reassure her and give her confidence. Everything is going well, very well indeed.'

He hung up the receiver and turned to Dutreuil, laughing.

'Ha, ha, my boy! Things are beginning to look clearer. What do you say?'

It was difficult to tell what these words meant or what conclusions Rénine had drawn from his conversation. The silence was painful and oppressive.

'Mr Chief-Inspector, you have some of your men outside, haven't you?'

'Two detective-sergeants.'

'It's important that they should be there. Please also ask the manager not to disturb us on any account.'

And, when Morisseau returned, Rénine closed the door, took his stand in front of Dutreuil and, speaking in a good-humoured but emphatic tone, said: 'It amounts to this, young man, that the ladies saw nothing of you between three and five o'clock on that Sunday. That's rather a curious detail.'

'A perfectly natural detail,' Dutreuil retorted, 'and one, moreover, which proves nothing at all.'

'It proves, young man, that you had a good two hours at your disposal.'

'Obviously. Two hours which I spent at the cinema.'

'Or somewhere else.'

Dutreuil looked at him.

'Somewhere else?'

'Yes. As you were free, you had plenty of time to go wherever you liked . . . to Suresnes, for instance.'

'Oh!' said the young man, jesting in his turn. 'Suresnes is a long way off!'

'It's quite close! Hadn't you your friend Jacques Aubrieux's motor-cycle?'

A fresh pause followed these words. Dutreuil had knitted his brows as though he were trying to understand. At last he was heard to whisper: 'So that is what he was trying to lead up to! . . . The brute! . . . '

Rénine brought down his hand on Dutreuil's shoulder.

'No more talk! Facts! Gaston Dutreuil, you are the only person who on that day knew two essential things: first, that Cousin Guill-aume had sixty thousand francs in his house; secondly, that Jacques Aubrieux was not going out. You at once saw your chance. The motor-cycle was available. You slipped out during the performance. You went to Suresnes. You killed Cousin Guillaume. You took the sixty bank-notes and left them at your rooms. And at five o'clock you went back to fetch the ladies.'

Dutreuil had listened with an expression at once mocking and flurried, casting an occasional glance at Inspector Morisseau as though to enlist him as a witness.

'The man's mad,' it seemed to say. 'It's no use being angry with him.'

When Rénine had finished, he began to laugh.

'Very funny! . . . A capital joke! . . . So it was I whom the neigh-bours saw going and returning on the motor-cycle?'

'It was you disguised in Jacques Aubrieux's clothes.'

'And it was my finger-prints that were found on the bottle in M. Guillaume's pantry?'

'The bottle had been opened by Jacques Aubrieux at lunch, in his own house, and it was you who took it with you to serve as evidence.'

'Funnier and funnier!' cried Dutreuil, who had the air of being frankly amused. 'Then I contrived the whole affair so that Jacques Aubrieux might be accused of the crime?'

'It was the safest means of not being accused yourself.'

'Yes, but Jacques is a friend whom I have known from childhood.'

'You're in love with his wife.'

The young man gave a sudden, infuriated start.

'You dare! . . . What! You dare make such an infamous suggestion?'

'I have proof of it.'

'That's a lie! I have always respected Madeleine Aubrieux and revered her . . . '

'Apparently. But you're in love with her. You desire her. Don't contradict me. I have abundant proof of it.'

'That's a lie, I tell you! You have only known me a few hours!'

'Come, come! I've been quietly watching you for days, waiting for the moment to pounce upon you.'

He took the young man by the shoulders and shook him.

'Come, Dutreuil, confess! I hold all the proofs in my hand. I have witnesses whom we shall meet presently at the criminal investigation department. Confess, can't you? In spite of everything, you're tortured by remorse. Remember your dismay, at the restaurant, when you had seen the newspaper. What? Jacques Aubrieux condemned to die? That's more than you bargained for! Penal servitude would have suited your book; but the scaffold! . . . Jacques Aubrieux executed tomorrow, an innocent man! . . . Confess, won't you? Confess to save your own skin! Own up!'

Bending over the other, he was trying with all his might to extort a confession from him. But Dutreuil drew himself up and coldly, with a sort of scorn in his voice, said: 'Sir, you are a madman. Not a word that you have said has any sense in it. All your accusations are false. What about the bank-notes? Did you find them at my place as you said you would?'

Rénine, exasperated, clenched his fist in his face.

'Oh, you swine, I'll dish you yet, I swear I will!'

He drew the inspector aside.

'Well, what do you say to it? An arrant rogue, isn't he?'

The inspector nodded his head.

'It may be . . . But, all the same . . . so far there's no real evidence.'

'Wait, M. Morisseau,' said Rénine. 'Wait until we've had our interview with M. Dudouis. For we shall see M. Dudouis at the prefecture, shall we not?'

'Yes, he'll be there at three o'clock.'

'Well, you'll be convinced, Mr Inspector! I tell you here and now that you will be convinced.'

Rénine was chuckling like a man who feels certain of the course of events. Hortense, who was standing near him and was able to speak to him without being heard by the others, asked, in a low voice: 'You've got him, haven't you?'

He nodded his head in assent.

'Got him? I should think I have! All the same, I'm no farther forward than I was at the beginning.'

'But this is awful! And your proofs?'

'Not the shadow of a proof . . . I was hoping to trip him up. But he's kept his feet, the rascal!'

'Still, you're certain it's he?'

'It can't be anyone else. I had an intuition at the very outset; and I've not taken my eyes off him since. I have seen his anxiety increasing as my investigations seemed to centre on him and concern him more closely. Now I know.'

'And he's in love with Madame Aubrieux?'

'In logic, he's bound to be. But so far we have only hypothetical suppositions, or rather certainties which are personal to myself. We shall never intercept the guillotine with those. Ah, if we could only find the bank-notes! Given the bank-notes, M. Dudouis would act. Without them, he will laugh in my face.'

'What then?' murmured Hortense, in anguished accents.

He did not reply. He walked up and down the room, assuming an air of gaiety and rubbing his hands. All was going so well! It was really a treat to take up a case which, so to speak, worked itself out automatically.

'Suppose we went on to the prefecture, M. Morisseau? The chief must be there by now. And, having gone so far, we may as well finish. Will M. Dutreuil come with us?'

'Why not?' said Dutreuil, arrogantly.

But, just as Rénine was opening the door, there was a noise in the passage and the manager ran up, waving his arms.

'Is M. Dutreuil still here? . . . M. Dutreuil, your flat is on fire! . . . A man outside told us. He saw it from the square.'

The young man's eyes lit up. For perhaps half a second his mouth was twisted by a smile which Rénine noticed.

'Oh, you ruffian!' he cried. 'You've given yourself away, my beauty! It was you who set fire to the place upstairs; and now the notes are burning.'

He blocked his exit.

'Let me pass,' shouted Dutreuil. 'There's a fire and no one can get in, because no one else has a key. Here it is. Let me pass, damn it!'

Rénine snatched the key from his hand and, holding him by the collar of his coat.

'Don't you move, my fine fellow! The game's up! You precious blackguard! M. Morisseau, will you give orders to the sergeant not to let him out of his sight and to blow out his brains if he tries to get away? Sergeant, we rely on you! Put a bullet into him, if necessary! . . .'

He hurried up the stairs, followed by Hortense and the chief inspector, who was protesting rather peevishly.

'But, I say, look here, it wasn't he who set the place on fire! How do you make out that he set it on fire, seeing that he never left us?'

'Why, he set it on fire beforehand, to be sure!'

'How? I ask you, how?'

'How do I know? But a fire doesn't break out like that, for no reason at all, at the very moment when a man wants to burn compromising papers.'

They heard a commotion upstairs. It was the waiters of the restaurant trying to burst the door open. An acrid smell filled the well of the stair-case.

Rénine reached the top floor.

'By your leave, friends. I have the key.'

He inserted it in the lock and opened the door.

He was met by a gust of smoke so dense that one might well have supposed the whole floor to be ablaze. Rénine at once saw that the fire had gone out of its own accord, for lack of fuel, and that there were no more flames.

'M. Morisseau, you won't let anyone come in with us, will you? An intruder might spoil everything. Bolt the door, that will be best.'

He stepped into the front room, where the fire had obviously had its chief centre. The furniture, the walls and the ceiling, though blackened by the smoke, had not been touched. As a matter of fact, the fire was confined to a blaze of papers which was still burning in the middle of the room, in front of the window.

Rénine struck his forehead.

'What a fool I am! What an unspeakable ass!'

'Why?' asked the inspector.

'The hat-box, of course! The cardboard hat-box which was standing on the table. That's where he hid the notes. They were there all through our search.'

'Impossible!'

'Why, yes, we always overlook that particular hiding-place, the one just under our eyes, within reach of our hands! How could one imagine that a thief would leave sixty thousand francs in an open cardboard box, in which he places his hat when he comes in, with an absent-minded air? That's just the one place we don't look in . . . Well played, M. Dutreuil!'

The inspector, who remained incredulous, repeated: 'No, no, impossible! We were with him and he could not have started the fire himself.'

'Everything was prepared beforehand on the supposition that there might be an alarm . . . The hat-box . . . the tissue paper . . . the bank-notes: they must all have been steeped in some inflammable liquid. He must have thrown a match, a chemical preparation or what not into it, as we were leaving.'

'But we should have seen him, hang it all! And then is it credible that a man who has committed a murder for the sake of sixty thousand francs should do away with the money in this way? If the hiding-place was such a good one – and it was, because we never discovered it – why this useless destruction?'

'He got frightened, M. Morisseau. Remember that his head is at stake and he knows it. Anything rather than the guillotine; and they – the bank-notes – were the only proof which we had against him. How could he have left them where they were?'

Morisseau was flabbergasted: 'What! The only proof?'

'Why, obviously!'

'But your witnesses? Your evidence? All that you were going to tell the chief?'

'Mere bluff.'

'Well, upon my word,' growled the bewildered inspector, 'you're a cool customer!'

'Would you have taken action without my bluff?'

'No.'

'Then what more do you want?'

Rénine stooped to stir the ashes. But there was nothing left, not even those remnants of stiff paper which still retain their shape.

'Nothing,' he said. 'It's queer, all the same! How the deuce did he manage to set the thing alight?'

He stood up, looking attentively about him. Hortense had a feeling that he was making his supreme effort and that, after this last struggle in the dark, he would either have devised his plan of victory or admit that he was beaten.

Faltering with anxiety, she asked: 'It's all up, isn't it?'

'No, no,' he said, thoughtfully, 'it's not all up. It was, a few seconds ago. But now there is a gleam of light . . . and one that gives me hope.'

'God grant that it may be justified!'

'We must go slowly,' he said. 'It is only an attempt, but a fine, a very fine attempt; and it may succeed.'

He was silent for a moment; then, with an amused smile and a click of the tongue, he said: 'An infernally clever fellow, that Dutreuil! His trick of burning the notes: what a fertile imagination! And what coolness! A pretty dance the beggar has led me! He's a master!'

He fetched a broom from the kitchen and swept a part of the ashes into the next room, returning with a hat-box of the same size and appearance as the one which had been burnt. After crumpling the tissue paper with which it was filled, he placed the hat-box on the little table and set fire to it with a match.

It burst into flames, which he extinguished when they had consumed half the cardboard and nearly all the paper. Then he took from an inner pocket of his waistcoat a bundle of bank-notes and selected six, which he burnt almost completely, arranging the remains and hiding the rest of the notes at the bottom of the box, among the ashes and the blackened bits of paper.

'M. Morisseau,' he said, when he had done, 'I am asking for your assistance for the last time. Go and fetch Dutreuil. Tell him just this: "You are unmasked. The notes did not catch fire. Come with me." And bring him up here.'

Despite his hesitation and his fear of exceeding his instructions from the head of the detective service, the chief-inspector was powerless to throw off the ascendancy which Rénine had acquired over him. He left the room.

Rénine turned to Hortense.

'Do you understand my plan of battle?'

'Yes,' she said, 'but it's a dangerous experiment. Do you think that Dutreuil will fall into the trap?'

'Everything depends on the state of his nerves and the degree of demoralization to which he is reduced. A surprise attack may very well do for him.'

'Nevertheless, suppose he recognizes by some sign that the box has been changed?'

'Oh, of course, he has a few chances in his favour! The fellow is much more cunning than I thought and quite capable of wriggling out of the trap. On the other hand, however, how uneasy he must be! How the blood must be buzzing in his ears and obscuring his sight! No, I don't think that he will avoid the trap . . . He will give in . . . He will give in . . . '

They exchanged no more words. Rénine did not move. Hortense was stirred to the very depths of her being. The life of an innocent man hung trembling in the balance. An error of judgment, a little bad luck . . . and, twelve hours later, Jacques Aubrieux would be put to death. And together with a horrible anguish she experienced, in spite of all, a feeling of eager curiosity. What was Prince Rénine going to do? What would be the outcome of the experiment on which he was venturing? What resistance would Gaston Dutreuil offer? She lived through one of those minutes of super-human tension in which life becomes intensified until it reaches its utmost value.

They heard footsteps on the stairs, the footsteps of men in a hurry. The sound drew nearer. They were reaching the top floor.

Hortense looked at her companion. He had stood up and was listening, his features already transfigured by action. The footsteps were now echoing in the passage. Then, suddenly, he ran to the door and cried: 'Quick! Let's make an end of it!'

Two or three detectives and a couple of waiters entered. He caught hold of Dutreuil in the midst of the detectives and pulled him by the arm, gaily exclaiming: 'Well done, old man! That trick of yours with the table and the water-bottle was really splendid! A masterpiece, on my word! Only, it didn't come off!'

'What do you mean? What's the matter?' mumbled Gaston Dutreuil, staggering.

'What I say: the fire burnt only half the tissue-paper and the hat-box; and, though some of the bank-notes were destroyed, like the tissue-paper, the others are there, at the bottom . . . You understand? The long-sought notes, the great proof of the murder: they're there, where you hid them . . . As chance would have it, they've escaped burning . . . Here, look: there are the numbers; you can check them . . . Oh, you're done for, done for, my beauty!'

The young man drew himself up stiffly. His eyelids quivered. He did not accept Rénine's invitation to look; he examined neither the hat-box nor the bank-notes. From the first moment, without taking the time to reflect and before his instinct could warn him, he believed what he was told and collapsed heavily into a chair, weeping.

The surprise attack, to use Rénine's expression, had succeeded. On seeing all his plans baffled and the enemy master of his secrets, the wretched man had neither the strength nor the perspicacity necessary to defend himself. He threw up the sponge.

Rénine gave him no time to breathe.

'Capital! You're saving your head; and that's all, my good youth! Write down your confession and get it off your chest. Here's a fountain-pen . . . The luck has been against you, I admit. It was devilishly well thought out, your trick of the last moment. You had the bank-notes which were in your way and which you wanted to destroy. Nothing simpler. You take a big, round-bellied water-bottle and stand it on the window-sill. It acts as a burning-glass, concentrating the rays of the sun on the cardboard and tissue-paper, all nicely prepared. Ten minutes later, it bursts into flames. A splendid idea! And, like all great discoveries, it came quite by chance, what? It reminds one of Newton's apple . . . One day, the sun, passing through the water in that bottle, must have set fire to a scrap of cotton or the head of a match; and, as you had the sun at your disposal just now, you said to yourself, "Now's the time," and stood the bottle in the right position. My congratulations, Gaston! . . . Look, here's a sheet of paper. Write down: "It was I who murdered M. Guillaume." Write, I tell you!'

Leaning over the young man, with all his implacable force of will he compelled him to write, guiding his hand and dictating the sentences. Dutreuil, exhausted, at the end of his strength, wrote as he was told.

'Here's the confession, Mr Chief-inspector,' said Rénine. 'You will be good enough to take it to M. Dudouis. These gentlemen,' turning to the waiters, from the restaurant, 'will, I am sure, consent to serve as witnesses.'

And, seeing that Dutreuil, overwhelmed by what had happened, did not move, he gave him a shake.

'Hi, you, look alive! Now that you've been fool enough to confess, make an end of the job, my gentle idiot!'

The other watched him, standing in front of him.

'Obviously,' Rénine continued, 'you're only a simpleton. The hat-box was fairly burnt to ashes: so were the notes. That hat-box, my dear fellow, is a different one; and those notes belong to me. I even burnt six of them to make you swallow the stunt. And you couldn't make out what had happened. What an owl you must be! To furnish me with evidence at the last moment, when I hadn't a single proof of my own! And such evidence! A written confession! Written before witnesses! . . . Look here, my man, if they do cut off your head – as I sincerely hope they will – upon my word, you'll have jolly well deserved it! Goodbye, Dutreuil!'

* * *

Downstairs, in the street, Rénine asked Hortense Daniel to take the car, go to Madeleine Aubrieux and tell her what had happened.

'And you?' asked Hortense.

'I have a lot to do . . . urgent appointments . . . '

'And you deny yourself the pleasure of bringing the good news?'

'It's one of the pleasures that pall upon one. The only pleasure that never flags is that of the fight itself. Afterwards, things cease to be interesting.'

She took his hand and for a moment held it in both her own. She would have liked to express all her admiration to that strange man, who seemed to do good as a sort of game and who did it with something like genius. But she was unable to speak. All these rapid incidents had upset her. Emotion constricted her throat and brought the tears to her eyes.

Rénine bowed his head, saying: 'Thank you. I have my reward.'

The Case of Jean Louis

'Monsieur,' continued the young girl, addressing Serge Rénine, 'it was while I was spending the Easter holidays at Nice with my father that I made the acquaintance of Jean Louis d'Imbleval . . . '

Rénine interrupted her.

'Excuse me, mademoiselle, but just now you spoke of this young man as Jean Louis Vaurois.'

'That's his name also,' she said.

'Has he two names then?'

'I don't know . . . I don't know anything about it,' she said, with some embarrassment, 'and that is why, by Hortense's advice, I came to ask for your help.'

This conversation was taking place in Rénine's flat on the Boulevard Haussmann, to which Hortense had brought her friend Geneviève Aymard, a slender, pretty little creature with a face overshadowed by an expression of the greatest melancholy.

'Rénine will be successful, take my word for it, Geneviève. You will, Rénine, won't you?'

'Please tell me the rest of the story, mademoiselle,' he said.

Geneviève continued.

'I was already engaged at the time to a man whom I loathe and detest. My father was trying to force me to marry him and is still trying to do so. Jean Louis and I felt the keenest sympathy for each other, a sympathy that soon developed into a profound and passionate affection which, I can assure you, was equally sincere on both sides. On my return to Paris, Jean Louis, who lives in the country with his mother and his aunt, took rooms in our part of the town; and, as I am allowed to go out by myself, we used to see each other daily. I need not tell you that we were engaged to be married. I told my father so. And this is what he said: "I don't particularly like the fellow. But, whether it's he or another, what I want is that you should get married. So let him come and ask for your hand. If not, you must do as I say." In the middle of June, Jean Louis went home to arrange matters with his mother and aunt. I received some passionate letters; and then just these few words.

> There are too many obstacles in the way of our happiness. I give up. I am mad with despair. I love you more than ever. Goodbye and forgive me.

'Since then, I have received nothing: no reply to my letters and telegrams.'

'Perhaps he has fallen in love with somebody else?' asked Rénine. 'Or there may be some old connection which he is unable to shake off.'

Geneviève shook her head.

'Monsieur, believe me, if our engagement had been broken off for an ordinary reason, I should not have allowed Hortense to trouble you. But it is something quite different, I am absolutely convinced. There's a mystery in Jean Louis's life, or rather an endless number of mysteries which hamper and pursue him. I never saw such distress in a human face; and, from the first moment of our meeting, I was conscious in him of a grief and melancholy which have always persisted, even at times when he was giving himself to our love with the greatest confidence.'

'But your impression must have been confirmed by minor details, by things which happened to strike you as peculiar?'

'I don't quite know what to say.'

'These two names, for instance?'

'Yes, there was certainly that.'

'By what name did he introduce himself to you?'

'Jean Louis d'Imbleval.'

'But Jean Louis Vaurois?'

'That's what my father calls him.'

'Why?'

'Because that was how he was introduced to my father, at Nice, by a gentleman who knew him. Besides, he carries visiting-cards which describe him under either name.'

'Have you never questioned him on this point?'

'Yes, I have, twice. The first time, he said that his aunt's name was Vaurois and his mother's d'Imbleval.'

'And the second time?'

'He told me the contrary: he spoke of his mother as Vaurois and of his aunt as d'Imbleval. I pointed this out. He coloured up and I thought it better not to question him any further.'

'Does he live far from Paris?'

'Right down in Brittany: at the Manoir d'Elseven, five miles from Carhaix.'

Rénine rose and asked the girl, seriously: 'Are you quite certain that he loves you, mademoiselle?'

'I am certain of it and I know too that he represents all my life and all my happiness. He alone can save me. If he can't, then I shall be married in a week's time to a man whom I hate. I have promised my father; and the banns have been published.'

'We shall leave for Carhaix, Madame Daniel and I, this evening,' said Rénine.

That evening he and Hortense took the train for Brittany. They reached Carhaix at ten o'clock in the morning; and, after lunch, at half past twelve o'clock they stepped into a car borrowed from a leading resident of the district.

* * *

'You're looking a little pale, my dear,' said Rénine, with a laugh, as they alighted by the gate of the garden at Elseven.

'I'm very fond of Geneviève,' she said. 'She's the only friend I have. And I'm feeling frightened.'

He called her attention to the fact that the central gate was flanked by two wickets bearing the names of Madame d'Imbleval and Madame Vaurois respectively. Each of these wickets opened on a narrow path which ran among the shrubberies of box and aucuba to the left and right of the main avenue. The avenue itself led to an old manor-house, long, low and picturesque, but provided with two clumsily-built, ugly wings, each in a different style of architecture and each forming the destination of one of the side-paths. Madame d'Imbleval evidently lived on the left and Madame Vaurois on the right.

Hortense and Rénine listened. Shrill, hasty voices were disputing inside the house. The sound came through one of the windows of the ground-floor, which was level with the garden and covered throughout its length with red creepers and white roses.

'We can't go any farther,' said Hortense. 'It would be indiscreet.'

'All the more reason,' whispered Rénine. 'Look here: if we walk straight ahead, we shan't be seen by the people who are quarrelling.'

The sounds of conflict were by no means abating; and, when they reached the window next to the front-door, through the roses and creepers they could both see and hear two old ladies shrieking at the tops of their voices and shaking their fists at each other.

The women were standing in the foreground, in a large dining-room where the table was not yet cleared; and at the farther side of the table sat a young man, doubtless Jean Louis himself, smoking his pipe and reading a newspaper, without appearing to trouble about the two old harridans.

One of these, a thin, tall woman, was wearing a purple silk dress; and her hair was dressed in a mass of curls much too yellow for the ravaged face around which they tumbled. The other, who was still thinner, but quite short, was bustling round the room in a cotton dressing-gown and displayed a red, painted face blazing with anger.

'A baggage, that's what you are!' she yelped. 'The wickedest woman in the world and a thief into the bargain!'

'I, a thief!' screamed the other.

'What about that business with the ducks at ten francs apiece: don't you call that thieving?'

'Hold your tongue, you low creature! Who stole the fifty-franc note from my dressing-table? Lord, that I should have to live with such a wretch!'

The other started with fury at the outrage and, addressing the young man, cried: 'Jean, are you going to sit there and let me be insulted by your hussy of a d'Imbleval?'

And the tall one retorted, furiously: 'Hussy! Do you hear that, Louis? Look at her, your Vaurois! She's got the airs of a super-annuated barmaid! Make her stop, can't you?'

Suddenly Jean Louis banged his fist upon the table, making the plates and dishes jump, and shouted: 'Be quiet, both of you, you old lunatics!'

They turned upon him at once and loaded him with abuse.

'Coward! . . . Hypocrite! . . . Liar! . . . A pretty sort of son you are! . . . The son of a slut and not much better yourself! . . . '

The insults rained down upon him. He stopped his ears with his fingers and writhed as he sat at table like a man who has lost all patience and has need to restrain himself lest he should fall upon his enemy.

Rénine whispered: 'Now's the time to go in.'

'In among all those infuriated people?' protested Hortense.

'Exactly. We shall see them better with their masks off.'

And, with a determined step, he walked to the door, opened it and entered the room, followed by Hortense.

His advent gave rise to a feeling of stupefaction. The two women stopped yelling, but were still scarlet in the face and trembling with rage. Jean Louis, who was very pale, stood up.

Profiting by the general confusion, Rénine said briskly: 'Allow me to introduce myself. I am Prince Rénine. This is Madame Daniel. We are friends of Mlle Geneviève Aymard and we have come in her name. I have a letter from her addressed to you, monsieur.'

Jean Louis, already disconcerted by the newcomers' arrival, lost countenance entirely on hearing the name of Geneviève. Without quite knowing what he was saying and with the intention of responding to Rénine's courteous behaviour, he tried in his turn to introduce the two ladies and let fall the astounding words: 'My mother, Madame d'Imbleval; my mother, Madame Vaurois.'

For some time no one spoke. Rénine bowed. Hortense did not know with whom she should shake hands, with Madame d'Imbleval, the mother, or with Madame Vaurois, the mother. But what happened was that Madame d'Imbleval and Madame Vaurois both at the same time attempted to snatch the letter which Rénine was holding out to Jean Louis, while both at the same time mumbled: 'Mlle Aymard! . . . She has had the coolness . . . she has had the audacity . . . !'

Then Jean Louis, recovering his self-possession, laid hold of his mother d'Imbleval and pushed her out of the room by a door on the left and next of his mother Vaurois and pushed her out of the room by a door on the right. Then, returning to his two visitors, he opened the envelope and read, in an undertone.

I am to be married in a week, Jean Louis. Come to my rescue, I beseech you. My friend Hortense and Prince Rénine will help you to overcome the obstacles that baffle you. Trust them. I love you.

GENEVIÈVE

He was a rather dull-looking young man, whose very swarthy, lean and bony face certainly bore the expression of melancholy and distress described by Geneviève. Indeed, the marks of suffering were visible in all his harassed features, as well as in his sad and anxious eyes.

He repeated Geneviève's name over and over again, while looking about him with a distracted air. He seemed to be seeking a course of conduct.

He seemed on the point of offering an explanation but could find nothing to say. The sudden intervention had taken him at a disadvantage, like an unforeseen attack which he did not know how to meet.

Rénine felt that the adversary would capitulate at the first summons. The man had been fighting so desperately during the last few months and had suffered so severely in the retirement and obstinate silence in which he had taken refuge that he was not thinking of defending himself. Moreover, how could he do so, now that they had forced their way into the privacy of his odious existence?

'Take my word for it, monsieur,' declared Rénine, 'that it is in your best interests to confide in us. We are Geneviève Aymard's friends. Do not hesitate to speak.'

'I can hardly hesitate,' he said, 'after what you have just heard. This is the life I lead, monsieur. I will tell you the whole secret, so that you may tell it to Geneviève. She will then understand why I have not gone back to her . . . and why I have not the right to do so.'

He pushed a chair forward for Hortense. The two men sat down, and, without any need of further persuasion, rather as though he himself felt a certain relief in unburdening himself, he said: 'You must not be surprised, monsieur, if I tell my story with a certain flippancy, for, as a matter of fact, it is a frankly comical story and cannot fail to make you laugh. Fate often amuses itself by playing these imbecile tricks, these monstrous farces which seem as though they must have been invented by the brain of a madman or a drunkard. Judge for yourself. Twenty-seven years ago, the Manoir d'Elseven, which at that time consisted only of the main building, was occupied by an old doctor who, to increase his modest means, used to receive one or two paying guests. In this way, Madame d'Imbleval spent the summer here one year and Madame Vaurois the following summer. Now these two ladies did not know each other. One of them was married to a Breton of a merchant-vessel and the other to a commercial traveller from the Vendée.

'It so happened that they lost their husbands at the same time, at a period when each of them was expecting a baby. And, as they both lived in the country, at places some distance from any town, they wrote to the old doctor that they intended to come to his house for their confinement . . . He agreed. They arrived almost on the same day, in the autumn. Two small bedrooms were prepared for them, behind the room in which we are sitting. The doctor had engaged a nurse, who slept in this very room. Everything was perfectly satisfactory. The ladies were putting the finishing touches to their baby-clothes and were getting on together splendidly. They were determined that their children should be boys and had chosen the names of Jean and Louis respectively . . . One evening the doctor was called out to a case and drove off in his gig with the man-servant, saying that he would not be back till next day. In her master's absence, a little girl who served as maid-of-all-work ran out to keep company

with her sweetheart. These accidents destiny turned to account
with diabolical malignity. At about midnight, Madame d'Imbleval was
seized with the first pains. The nurse, Mlle Boussignol, had had some
training as a midwife and did not lose her head. But, an hour later,
Madame Vaurois's turn came; and the tragedy, or I might rather say
the tragi-comedy, was enacted amid the screams and moans of the two
patients and the bewildered agitation of the nurse running from one
to the other, bewailing her fate, opening the window to call out for the
doctor or falling on her knees to implore the aid of Providence . . .
Madame Vaurois was the first to bring a son into the world. Mlle
Boussignol hurriedly carried him in here, washed and tended him and
laid him in the cradle prepared for him . . . But Madame d'Imbleval
was screaming with pain; and the nurse had to attend to her while the
newborn child was yelling like a stuck pig and the terrified mother,
unable to stir from her bed, fainted . . . Add to this all the wretchedness of darkness and disorder, the only lamp, without any oil, for the
servant had neglected to fill it, the candles burning out, the moaning
of the wind, the screeching of the owls, and you will understand that
Mlle Boussignol was scared out of her wits. However, at five o'clock in
the morning, after many tragic incidents, she came in here with the
d'Imbleval baby, likewise a boy, washed and tended him, laid him in
his cradle and went off to help Madame Vaurois, who had come to
herself and was crying out, while Madame d'Imbleval had fainted in
her turn. And, when Mlle Boussignol, having settled the two mothers,
but half-crazed with fatigue, her brain in a whirl, returned to the new-
born children, she realized with horror that she had wrapped them in
similar binders, thrust their feet into similar woolen socks and laid
them both, side by side, *in the same cradle*, so that it was impossible to
tell Louis d'Imbleval from Jean Vaurois! . . . To make matters worse,
when she lifted one of them out of the cradle, she found that his hands
were cold as ice and that he had ceased to breathe. He was dead. What
was his name and what the survivor's? . . . Three hours later, the
doctor found the two women in a condition of frenzied delirium,
while the nurse was dragging herself from one bed to the other,
entreating the two mothers to forgive her. She held me out first
to one, then to the other, to receive their caresses – for I was the
surviving child – and they first kissed me and then pushed me away;
for, after all, who was I? The son of the widowed Madame d'Imbleval
and the late merchant-captain or the son of the widowed Madame
Vaurois and the late commercial traveller? There was not a clue by
which they could tell . . . The doctor begged each of the two mothers

to sacrifice her rights, at least from the legal point of view, so that I might be called either Louis d'Imbleval or Jean Vaurois. They refused absolutely. "Why Jean Vaurois, if he's a d'Imbleval?" protested the one. "Why Louis d'Imbleval, if he's a Vaurois?" retorted the other. And I was registered under the name of Jean Louis, the son of an unknown father and mother.'

Prince Rénine had listened in silence. But Hortense, as the story approached its conclusion, had given way to a hilarity which she could no longer restrain and suddenly, in spite of all her efforts, she burst into a fit of the wildest laughter.

'Forgive me,' she said, her eyes filled with tears, 'do forgive me; it's too much for my nerves . . .'

'Don't apologize, madame,' said the young man, gently, in a voice free from resentment. 'I warned you that my story was laughable; I, better than anyone, know how absurd, how nonsensical it is. Yes, the whole thing is perfectly grotesque. But believe me when I tell you that it was no fun in reality. It seems a humorous situation and it remains humorous by the force of circumstances; but it is also horrible. You can see that for yourself, can't you? The two mothers, neither of whom was certain of being a mother, but neither of whom was certain that she was not one, both clung to Jean Louis. He might be a stranger; on the other hand, he might be their own flesh and blood. They loved him to excess and fought for him furiously. And, above all, they both came to hate each other with a deadly hatred. Differing completely in character and education and obliged to live together because neither was willing to forego the advantage of her possible maternity, they lived the life of irreconcilable enemies who can never lay their weapons aside . . . I grew up in the midst of this hatred and had it instilled into me by both of them. When my childish heart, hungering for affection, inclined me to one of them, the other would seek to inspire me with loathing and contempt for her. In this manor-house, which they bought on the old doctor's death and to which they added the two wings, I was the involuntary torturer and their daily victim. Tormented as a child, and, as a young man, leading the most hideous of lives, I doubt if anyone on earth ever suffered more than I did.'

'You ought to have left them!' exclaimed Hortense, who had stopped laughing.

'One can't leave one's mother; and one of those two women was my mother. And a woman can't abandon her son; and each of them was entitled to believe that I was her son. We were all three chained together like convicts, with chains of sorrow, compassion, doubt and also of hope that the truth might one day become apparent. And here we still are, all three, insulting one another and blaming one another for our wasted lives. Oh, what a hell! And there was no escaping it. I tried often enough . . . but in vain. The broken bonds became tied again. Only this summer, under the stimulus of my love for Geneviève, I tried to free myself and did my utmost to persuade the two women whom I call mother. And then . . . and then! I was up against their complaints, their immediate hatred of the wife, of the stranger, whom I was proposing to force upon them . . . I gave way. What sort of a life would Geneviève have had here, between Madame d'Imbleval and Madame Vaurois? I had no right to victimize her.'

Jean Louis, who had been gradually becoming excited, uttered these last words in a firm voice, as though he would have wished his conduct to be ascribed to conscientious motives and a sense of duty. In reality, as Rénine and Hortense clearly saw, his was an unusually weak nature, incapable of reacting against a ridiculous position from which he had suffered ever since he was a child and which he had come to look upon as final and irremediable. He endured it as a man bears a cross which he has no right to cast aside; and at the same time he was ashamed of it. He had never spoken of it to Geneviève, from dread of ridicule; and afterwards, on returning to his prison, he had remained there out of habit and weakness.

He sat down to a writing-table and quickly wrote a letter which he handed to Rénine.

'Would you be kind enough to give this note to Mlle Aymard and beg her once more to forgive me?'

Rénine did not move and, when the other pressed the letter upon him, he took it and tore it up.

'What does this mean?' asked the young man.

'It means that I will not charge myself with any message.'

'Why?'

'Because you are coming with us.'

'I?'

'Yes. You will see Mlle Aymard tomorrow and ask for her hand in marriage.'

Jean Louis looked at Rénine with a rather disdainful air, as though he were thinking: 'Here's a man who has not understood a word of what I've been explaining to him.'

But Hortense went up to Rénine.

'Why do you say that?'

'Because it will be as I say.'

'But you must have your reasons?'

'One only; but it will be enough, provided this gentleman is so kind as to help me in my enquiries.'

'Enquiries? With what object?' asked the young man.

'With the object of proving that your story is not quite accurate.'

Jean Louis took umbrage at this.

'I must ask you to believe, monsieur, that I have not said a word which is not the exact truth.'

'I expressed myself badly,' said Rénine, with great kindliness. 'Certainly you have not said a word that does not agree with what you believe to be the exact truth. But the truth is not, cannot be what you believe it to be.'

The young man folded his arms.

'In any case, monsieur, it seems likely that I should know the truth better than you do.'

'Why better? What happened on that tragic night can obviously be known to you only at secondhand. You have no proofs. Neither have Madame d'Imbleval and Madame Vaurois.'

'No proofs of what?' exclaimed Jean Louis, losing patience.

'No proofs of the confusion that took place.'

'What! Why, it's an absolute certainty! The two children were laid in the same cradle, with no marks to distinguish one from the other; and the nurse was unable to tell . . . '

'At least, that's her version of it,' interrupted Rénine.

'What's that? Her version? But you're accusing the woman.'

'I'm accusing her of nothing.'

'Yes, you are: you're accusing her of lying. And why should she lie? She had no interest in doing so; and her tears and despair are so much evidence of her good faith. For, after all, the two mothers were there . . . they saw the woman weeping . . . they questioned her . . . And then, I repeat, what interest had she . . . ?'

Jean Louis was greatly excited. Close beside him, Madame d'Imbleval and Madame Vaurois, who had no doubt been listening behind the doors and who had stealthily entered the room, stood stammering, in amazement.

'No, no . . . it's impossible . . . We've questioned her over and over again. Why should she tell a lie? . . . '

'Speak, monsieur, speak,' Jean Louis enjoined. 'Explain yourself. Give your reasons for trying to cast doubt upon an absolute truth!'

'Because that truth is inadmissible,' declared Rénine, raising his voice and growing excited in turn to the point of punctuating his remarks by thumping the table. 'No, things don't happen like that. No, fate does not display those refinements of cruelty, and chance is not added to chance with such reckless extravagance! It was already an unprecedented chance that, on the very night on which the doctor, his man-servant and his maid were out of the house, the two ladies should be seized with labour-pains at the same hour and should bring two sons into the world at the same time. Don't let us add a still more exceptional event! Enough of the uncanny! Enough of lamps that go out and candles that refuse to burn! No and again no, it is not admissable that a midwife should become confused in the essential details of her trade. However bewildered she may be by the unforeseen nature of the circumstances, a remnant of instinct is still on the alert, so that there is a place prepared for each child and each is kept distinct from the other. The first child is here, the second is there. Even if they are lying side by side, one is on the left and the other on the right. Even if they are wrapped in the same kind of binders, some little detail differs, a trifle which is recorded by the memory and which is inevitably recalled to the mind without any need of reflection. Confusion? I refuse to believe in it. Impossible to tell one from the other? It isn't true. In the world of fiction, yes, one can imagine all sorts of fantastic accidents and heap contradiction on contradiction. But, in the world of reality, at the very heart of reality, there is always a fixed point, a solid nucleus, about which the facts group themselves in accordance with a logical order. I therefore declare most positively that Nurse Boussignol could not have mixed up the two children.'

All this he said decisively, as though he had been present during the night in question; and so great was his power of persuasion that from the very first he shook the certainty of those who for more than a quarter of a century had never doubted.

The two women and their son pressed round him and questioned him with breathless anxiety.

'Then you think that she may know . . . that she may be able to tell us . . . ?'

He corrected himself.

'I don't say yes and I don't say no. All I say is that there was something in her behaviour during those hours that does not tally with her statements and with reality. All the vast and intolerable mystery that has weighed down upon you three arises not from a momentary lack of attention but from something of which we do not know, but of which she does. That is what I maintain; and that is what happened.'

Jean Louis said, in a husky voice: 'She is alive . . . She lives at Carhaix . . . We can send for her . . . '

Hortense at once proposed: 'Would you like me to go for her? I will take the motor and bring her back with me. Where does she live?'

'In the middle of the town, at a little draper's shop. The chauffeur will show you. Mlle Boussignol: everybody knows her . . . '

'And, whatever you do,' added Rénine, 'don't warn her in any way. If she's uneasy, so much the better. But don't let her know what we want with her.'

Twenty minutes passed in absolute silence. Rénine paced the room, in which the fine old furniture, the handsome tapestries, the well-bound books and pretty knick-knacks denoted a love of art and a seeking after style in Jean Louis. This room was really his. In the adjoining apartments on either side, through the open doors, Rénine was able to note the bad taste of the two mothers.

He went up to Jean Louis and, in a low voice, asked: 'Are they well off?'

'Yes.'

'And you?'

'They settled the manor-house upon me, with all the land around it, which makes me quite independent.'

'Have they any relations?'

'Sisters, both of them.'

'With whom they could go to live?'

'Yes; and they have sometimes thought of doing so. But there can't be any question of that. Once more, I assure you . . . '

Meantime the car had returned. The two women jumped up hurriedly, ready to speak.

'Leave it to me,' said Rénine, 'and don't be surprised by anything that I say. It's not a matter of asking her questions but of frightening her, of flurrying her . . . The sudden attack,' he added between his teeth.

The car drove round the lawn and drew up outside the windows. Hortense sprang out and helped an old woman to alight, dressed in a fluted linen cap, a black velvet bodice and a heavy gathered skirt.

The old woman entered in a great state of alarm. She had a pointed face, like a weasel's, with a prominent mouth full of protruding teeth.

'What's the matter, Madame d'Imbleval?' she asked, timidly step-ping into the room from which the doctor had once driven her. 'Good day to you, Madame Vaurois.'

The ladies did not reply. Rénine came forward and said, sternly: 'Mlle Boussignol, I have been sent by the Paris police to throw light upon a tragedy which took place here twenty-seven years ago. I have just secured evidence that you have distorted the truth and that, as the result of your false declarations, the birth-certificate of one of the children born in the course of that night is inaccurate. Now false declarations in matters of birth-certificates are mis-demeanours punishable by law. I shall therefore be obliged to take you to Paris to be interrogated . . . unless you are prepared here and now to confess everything that might repair the consequences of your offence.'

The old maid was shaking in every limb. Her teeth were chatter-ing. She was evidently incapable of opposing the least resistance to Rénine.

'Are you ready to confess everything?' he asked.

'Yes,' she panted.

'Without delay? I have to catch a train. The business must be settled immediately. If you show the least hesitation, I take you with me. Have you made up your mind to speak?'

'Yes.'

He pointed to Jean Louis.

'Whose son is this gentleman? Madame d'Imbleval's?'

'No.'

'Madame Vaurois's, therefore?'

'No.'

A stupefied silence welcomed the two replies.

'Explain yourself,' Rénine commanded, looking at his watch.

Then Madame Boussignol fell on her knees and said, in so low and dull a voice that they had to bend over her in order to catch the sense of what she was mumbling.

'Someone came in the evening . . . a gentleman with a new-born baby wrapped in blankets, which he wanted the doctor to look after. As the doctor wasn't there, he waited all night and it was he who did it all.'

'Did what?' asked Rénine. 'What did he do? What happened?'

'Well, what happened was that it was not one child but the two of them that died: Madame d'Imbleval's and Madame Vaurois's too, both in convulsions. Then the gentleman, seeing this, said, "This shows me where my duty lies. I must seize this opportunity of making sure that my own boy shall be happy and well cared for. Put him in the place of one of the dead children." He offered me a big sum of money, saying that this one payment would save him the expense of providing for his child every month; and I accepted. Only, I did not know in whose place to put him and whether to say that the boy was Louis d'Imbleval or Jean Vaurois. The gentleman thought a moment and said neither. Then he explained to me what I was to do and what I was to say after he had gone. And, while I was dressing his boy in vest and binders the same as one of the dead children, he wrapped the other in the blankets he had brought with him and went out into the night.'

Mlle Boussignol bent her head and wept. After a moment, Rénine said: 'Your deposition agrees with the result of my investigations.'

'Can I go?'

'Yes.'

'And is it over, as far as I'm concerned? They won't be talking about this all over the district?'

'No. Oh, just one more question: do you know the man's name?'

'No. He didn't tell me his name.'

'Have you ever seen him since?'

'Never.'

'Have you anything more to say?'

'No.'

'Are you prepared to sign the written text of your confession?'

'Yes.'

'Very well. I shall send for you in a week or two. Till then, not a word to anybody.'

He saw her to the door and closed it after her. When he returned, Jean Louis was between the two old ladies and all three were holding hands. The bond of hatred and wretchedness which had bound them had suddenly snapped; and this rupture, without requiring them to reflect upon the matter, filled them with a gentle tranquillity of which they were hardly conscious, but which made them serious and thoughtful.

'Let's rush things,' said Rénine to Hortense. 'This is the decisive moment of the battle. We must get Jean Louis on board.'

Hortense seemed preoccupied. She whispered: 'Why did you let the woman go? Were you satisfied with her statement?'

'I don't need to be satisfied. She told us what happened. What more do you want?'

'Nothing . . . I don't know . . . '

'We'll talk about it later, my dear. For the moment, I repeat, we must get Jean Louis on board. And immediately . . . Otherwise . . . '

He turned to the young man.

'You agree with me, don't you, that, things being as they are, it is best for you and Madame Vaurois and Madame d'Imbleval to separate for a time? That will enable you all to see matters more clearly and to decide in perfect freedom what is to be done. Come with us, monsieur. The most pressing thing is to save Geneviève Aymard, your *fiancée*.'

Jean Louis stood perplexed and undecided. Rénine turned to the two women.

'That is your opinion too, I am sure, ladies?'

They nodded.

'You see, monsieur,' he said to Jean Louis, 'we are all agreed. In great crises, there is nothing like separation . . . a few days' respite. Quickly now, monsieur.'

And, without giving him time to hesitate, he drove him towards his bedroom to pack up.

Half an hour later, Jean Louis left the manor-house with his new friends.

* * *

'And he won't go back until he's married,' said Rénine to Hortense, as they were waiting at Carhaix station, to which the car had taken them, while Jean Louis was attending to his luggage. 'Everything's for the best. Are you satisfied?'

'Yes, Geneviève will be glad,' she replied, absently.

When they had taken their seats in the train, Rénine and she repaired to the dining-car. Rénine, who had asked Hortense several questions to which she had replied only in monosyllables, protested: 'What's the matter with you, my child? You look worried!'

'I? Not at all!'

'Yes, yes, I know you. Now, no secrets, no mysteries!'

She smiled.

'Well, since you insist on knowing if I am satisfied, I am bound to admit that of course I am . . . as regards my friend Geneviève, but that, in another respect – from the point of view of the adventure – I have an uncomfortable sort of feeling . . . '

'To speak frankly, I haven't "staggered" you this time?'

'Not very much.'

'I seem to you to have played a secondary part. For, after all, what have I done? We arrived. We listened to Jean Louis's tale of woe. I had a midwife fetched. And that was all.'

'Exactly. I want to know if that *was* all; and I'm not quite sure. To tell you the truth, our other adventures left behind them an impression which was – how shall I put it? – more definite, clearer.'

'And this one strikes you as obscure?'

'Obscure, yes, and incomplete.'

'But in what way?'

'I don't know. Perhaps it has something to do with that woman's confession. Yes, very likely that is it. It was all so unexpected and so short.'

'Well, of course, I cut it short, as you can readily imagine!' said Rénine, laughing. 'We didn't want too many explanations.'

'What do you mean?'

'Why, if she had given her explanations with too much detail, we should have ended by doubting what she was telling us.'

'By doubting it?'

'Well, hang it all, the story is a trifle far-fetched! That fellow arriving at night, with a live baby in his pocket, and going away with a dead one: the thing hardly holds water. But you see, my dear, I hadn't much time to coach the unfortunate woman in her part.'

Hortense stared at him in amazement.

'What on earth do you mean?'

'Well, you know how dull-witted these countrywomen are. And she and I had no time to spare. So we worked out a little scene in a hurry . . . and she really didn't act it so badly. It was all in the right key: terror, *tremolo*, tears . . . '

'Is it possible?' murmured Hortense. 'Is it possible? You had seen her beforehand?'

'I had to, of course.'

'But when?'

'This morning, when we arrived. While you were titivating yourself at the hotel at Carhaix, I was running round to see what inform-ation I could pick up. As you may imagine, everybody in the district knows the d'Imbleval-Vaurois story. I was at once directed to the former midwife, Mlle Boussignol. With Mlle Boussignol it did not take long. Three minutes to settle a new version of what had happened and ten thousand francs to induce her to repeat that . . . more or less credible . . . version to the people at the manor-house.'

'A quite incredible version!'

'Not so bad as all that, my child, seeing that you believed it . . . and the others too. And that was the essential thing. What I had to do was to demolish at one blow a truth which had been twenty-seven years in existence and which was all the more firmly established because it was founded on actual facts. That was why I went for it with all my might and attacked it by sheer force of eloquence. Impossible to identify the children? I deny it. Inevitable confusion? It's not true. "You're all three," I say, "the victims of something which I don't know but which it is your duty to clear up!" "That's easily done," says Jean Louis, whose conviction is at once shaken. "Let's send for Mlle Boussignol." "Right! Let's send for her." Whereupon Mlle Boussignol arrives and mumbles out the little speech which I have taught her. Sensation! General stupefaction . . . of which I take advantage to carry off our young man!'

Hortense shook her head.

'But they'll get over it, all three of them, on thinking!'

'Never! Never! They will have their doubts, perhaps. But they will never consent to feel certain! They will never agree to think! Use your imagination! Here are three people whom I have rescued from the hell in which they have been floundering for a quarter of a century. Do you think they're going back to it? Here are three people who, from weakness or a false sense of duty, had not the courage to escape. Do you think that they won't cling like grim death to the liberty which I'm giving them? Nonsense! Why, they would have swallowed a hoax twice as difficult to digest as that which Mlle Boussignol dished up for them! After all, my version was no more absurd than the truth. On the contrary. And they swallowed it whole! Look at this: before we left, I heard Madame d'Imbleval and Madame Vaurois speak of an immediate removal. They were already becoming quite affectionate at the thought of seeing the last of each other.'

'But what about Jean Louis?'

'Jean Louis? Why, he was fed up with his two mothers! By Jingo, one can't do with two mothers in a life-time! What a situation! And when one has the luck to be able to choose between having two mothers or none at all, why, bless me, one doesn't hesitate! And, besides, Jean Louis is in love with Geneviève.' He laughed. 'And he loves her well enough, I hope and trust, not to inflict two mothers-in-law upon her! Come, you may be easy in your mind. Your friend's happiness is assured; and that is all you asked for. All that matters is the object which we achieve and not the more or less peculiar nature of the methods which we employ. And, if some adventures are wound up and some mysteries elucidated by looking for and finding cigarette-ends, or incendiary water-bottles and blazing hat-boxes as on our last expedition, others call for psychology and for purely psychological solutions. I have spoken. And I charge you to be silent.'

'Silent?'

'Yes, there's a man and woman sitting behind us who seem to be saying something uncommonly interesting.'

'But they're talking in whispers.'

'Just so. When people talk in whispers, it's always about something shady.'

He lit a cigarette and sat back in his chair. Hortense listened, but in vain. As for him, he was emitting little slow puffs of smoke.

Fifteen minutes later, the train stopped and the man and woman got out.

'Pity,' said Rénine, 'that I don't know their names or where they're going. But I know where to find them. My dear, we have a new adventure before us.'

Hortense protested.

'Oh, no, please, not yet! . . . Give me a little rest! . . . And oughtn't we to think of Geneviève?'

He seemed greatly surprised.

'Why, all that's over and done with! Do you mean to say you want to waste any more time over that old story? Well, I for my part confess that I've lost all interest in the man with the two mammas.'

And this was said in such a comical tone and with such diverting sincerity that Hortense was once more seized with a fit of giggling. Laughter alone was able to relax her exasperated nerves and to distract her from so many contradictory emotions.

4

The Tell-Tale Film

'Do look at the man who's playing the butler,' said Serge Rénine.

'What is there peculiar about him?' asked Hortense.

They were sitting in the balcony at a picture-palace, to which Hortense had asked to be taken so that she might see on the screen the daughter of a lady, now dead, who used to give her piano-lessons. Rose Andrée, a lovely girl with lissom movements and a smiling face, was that evening figuring in a new film, *The Happy Princess*, which she lit up with her high spirits and her warm, glowing beauty.

Rénine made no direct reply, but, during a pause in the performance, continued: 'I sometimes console myself for an indifferent film by watching the subordinate characters. It seems to me that those poor devils, who are made to rehearse certain scenes ten or twenty times over, must often be thinking of other things than their parts at the time of the final exposure. And it's great fun noting those little moments of distraction which reveal something of their temperament, of their instinct self. As, for instance, in the case of that butler: look!'

The screen now showed a luxuriously served table. The Happy Princess sat at the head, surrounded by all her suitors. Half-a-dozen footmen moved about the room, under the orders of the butler, a big fellow with a dull, coarse face, a common appearance and a pair of enormous eyebrows which met across his forehead in a single line.

'He looks a brute,' said Hortense, 'but what do you see in him that's peculiar?'

'Just note how he gazes at the princess and tell me if he doesn't stare at her oftener than he ought to.'

'I really haven't noticed anything, so far,' said Hortense.

'Why, of course he does!' Serge Rénine declared. 'It is quite obvious that in actual life he entertains for Rose Andrée personal feelings which are quite out of place in a nameless servant. It is possible that, in real life, no one has any idea of such a thing; but, on the screen, when he is not watching himself, or when he thinks that the actors at rehearsal cannot see him, his secret escapes him. Look . . . '

The man was standing still. It was the end of dinner. The princess was drinking a glass of champagne and he was gloating over her with his glittering eyes half-hidden behind their heavy lids.

Twice again they surprised in his face those strange expressions to which Rénine ascribed an emotional meaning which Hortense refused to see.

'It's just his way of looking at people,' she said.

The first part of the film ended. There were two parts, divided by an *entr'acte*. The notice on the programme stated that a year had elapsed and that the Happy Princess was living in a pretty Norman cottage, all hung with creepers, together with her husband, a poor musician.

The princess was still happy, as was evident on the screen, still as attractive as ever and still besieged by the greatest variety of suitors. Nobles and commoners, peasants and financiers, men of all kinds fell swooning at her feet; and prominent among them was a sort of boorish solitary, a shaggy, half-wild woodcutter, whom she met whenever she went out for a walk. Armed with his axe, a formidable, crafty being, he prowled around the cottage; and the spectators felt with a sense of dismay that a peril was hanging over the Happy Princess' head.

'Look at that!' whispered Rénine. 'Do you realise who the man of the woods is?'

'No.'

'Simply the butler. The same actor is doubling the two parts.'

In fact, notwithstanding the new figure which he cut, the butler's movements and postures were apparent under the heavy gait and rounded shoulders of the woodcutter, even as under the unkempt beard and long, thick hair the once clean-shaven face was visible with the cruel expression and the bushy line of the eyebrows.

The princess, in the background, was seen to emerge from the thatched cottage. The man hid himself behind a clump of trees. From time to time, the screen displayed, on an enormously enlarged scale, his fiercely rolling eyes or his murderous hands with their huge thumbs.

'The man frightens me,' said Hortense. 'He is really terrifying.'

'Because he's acting on his own account,' said Rénine. 'You must understand that, in the space of three or four months that appears to separate the dates at which the two films were made, his passion has made progress; and to him it is not the princess who is coming but Rose Andrée.'

The man crouched low. The victim approached, gaily and unsuspectingly. She passed, heard a sound, stopped and looked about her with a smiling air which became attentive, then uneasy, and then more and more anxious. The woodcutter had pushed aside the branches and was coming through the copse.

They were now standing face to face. He opened his arms as though to seize her. She tried to scream, to call out for help; but the arms closed around her before she could offer the slightest resistance. Then he threw her over his shoulder and began to run.

'Are you satisfied?' whispered Rénine. 'Do you think that this fourth-rate actor would have had all that strength and energy if it had been any other woman than Rose Andrée?'

Meanwhile the woodcutter was crossing the skirt of a forest and plunging through great trees and masses of rocks. After setting the princess down, he cleared the entrance to a cave which the daylight entered by a slanting crevice.

A succession of views displayed the husband's despair, the search and the discovery of some small branches which had been broken by the princess and which showed the path that had been taken. Then came the final scene, with the terrible struggle between the man and the woman when the woman, vanquished and exhausted, is flung to the ground, the sudden arrival of the husband and the shot that puts an end to the brute's life . . .

*　　*　　*

'Well,' said Rénine, when they had left the picture-palace – and he spoke with a certain gravity – 'I maintain that the daughter of your old piano-teacher has been in danger ever since the day when that last scene was filmed. I maintain that this scene represents not so much an assault by the man of the woods on the Happy Princess as a violent and frantic attack by an actor on the woman he desires. Certainly it all happened within the bounds prescribed by the part and nobody saw anything in it – nobody except perhaps Rose Andrée herself – but I, for my part, have detected flashes of passion which leave not a doubt in my mind. I have seen glances that betrayed the wish and even the intention to commit murder. I have seen clenched hands, ready to strangle, in short, a score of details which prove to me that, at that time, the man's instinct was urging him to kill the woman who could never be his.'

'And it all amounts to what?'

'We must protect Rose Andrée if she is still in danger and if it is not too late.'

'And to do this?'

'We must get hold of further information.'

'From whom?'

'From the World's Cinema Company, which made the film. I will go to them tomorrow morning. Will you wait for me in your flat about lunch-time?'

At heart, Hortense was still sceptical. All these manifestations of passion, of which she denied neither the ardour nor the ferocity, seemed to her to be the rational behaviour of a good actor. She had seen nothing of the terrible tragedy which Rénine contended that he had divined; and she wondered whether he was not erring through an excess of imagination.

'Well,' she asked, next day, not without a touch of irony, 'how far have you got? Have you made a good bag? Anything mysterious? Anything thrilling?'

'Pretty good.'

'Oh, really? And your so-called lover . . .'

'Is one Dalbrèque, originally a scene-painter, who played the butler in the first part of the film and the man of the woods in the second and was so much appreciated that they engaged him for a new film. Consequently, he has been acting lately. He was acting near Paris. But, on the morning of Friday the 18th of September, he broke into the garage of the World's Cinema Company and made off with a magnificent car and forty thousand francs in money. Information was lodged with the police; and on the Sunday the car was found a little way outside Dreux. And up to now the enquiry has revealed two things, which will appear in the papers tomorrow: first, Dalbrèque is alleged to have committed a murder which created a great stir last year, the murder of Bourguet, the jeweller; secondly, on the day after his two robberies, Dalbrèque was driving through Le Havre in a motor-car with two men who helped him to carry off, in broad daylight and in a crowded street, a lady whose identity has not yet been discovered.'

'Rose Andrée?' asked Hortense, uneasily.

'I have just been to Rose Andrée's: the World's Cinema Company gave me her address. Rose Andrée spent this summer travelling and then stayed for a fortnight in the Seine-inférieure, where she has a small place of her own, the actual cottage in *The Happy Princess*. On receiving an invitation from America to do a film there, she came back to Paris, registered her luggage at the Gare Saint-Lazare and left on Friday the 18th of September, intending to sleep at Le Havre and take Saturday's boat.'

'Friday the 18th,' muttered Hortense, 'the same day on which that man . . .'

'And it was on the Saturday that a woman was carried off by him at Le Havre. I looked in at the Compagnie Transatlantique and a brief investigation showed that Rose Andrée had booked a cabin but that the cabin remained unoccupied. The passenger did not turn up.'

'This is frightful. She has been carried off. You were right.'

'I fear so.'

'What have you decided to do?'

'Adolphe, my chauffeur, is outside with the car. Let us go to Le Havre. Up to the present, Rose Andrée's disappearance does not seem to have become known. Before it does and before the police identify the woman carried off by Dalbrèque with the woman who did not turn up to claim her cabin, we will get on Rose Andrée's track.'

There was not much said on the journey. At four o'clock Hortense and Rénine reached Rouen. But here Rénine changed his road.

'Adolphe, take the left bank of the Seine.'

He unfolded a motoring-map on his knees and, tracing the route with his finger, showed Hortense that, if you draw a line from Le Havre, or rather from Quillebeuf, where the road crosses the Seine, to Dreux, where the stolen car was found, this line passes through Routot, a market-town lying west of the forest of Brotonne.

'Now it was in the forest of Brotonne,' he continued, 'according to what I heard, that the second part of *The Happy Princess* was filmed. And the question that arises is this: having got hold of Rose Andrée, would it not occur to Dalbrèque, when passing near the forest on the Saturday night, to hide his prey there, while his two accomplices went on to Dreux and from there returned to Paris? The cave was quite near. Was he not bound to go to it? How should he do otherwise? Wasn't it while running to this cave, a few months ago, that he held in his arms, against his breast, within reach of his lips, the woman whom he loved and whom he has now conquered? By every rule of fate and logic, the adventure is being repeated all over again . . . but this time in reality. Rose Andrée is a captive. There is no hope of rescue. The forest is vast and lonely. That night, or on one of the following nights, Rose Andrée must surrender . . . or die.'

Hortense gave a shudder.

'We shall be too late. Besides, you don't suppose that he's keeping her a prisoner?'

'Certainly not. The place I have in mind is at a cross-roads and is not a safe retreat. But we may discover some clue or other.'

The shades of night were falling from the tall trees when they entered the ancient forest of Brotonne, full of Roman remains and mediaeval relics. Rénine knew the forest well and remembered that near a famous oak, known as the Wine-cask, there was a cave which must be the cave of the Happy Princess. He found it easily, switched on his electric torch, rummaged in the dark corners and brought Hortense back to the entrance.

'There's nothing inside,' he said, 'but here is the evidence which I was looking for. Dalbrèque was obsessed by the recollection of the film, but so was Rose Andrée. The Happy Princess had broken off the tips of the branches on the way through the forest. Rose Andrée has managed to break off some to the right of this opening, in the hope that she would be discovered as on the first occasion.'

'Yes,' said Hortense, 'it's a proof that she has been here; but the proof is three weeks old. Since that time . . . '

'Since that time, she is either dead and buried under a heap of leaves or else alive in some hole even lonelier than this.'

'If so, where is he?'

Rénine pricked up his ears. Repeated blows of the axe were sounding from some distance, no doubt coming from a part of the forest that was being cleared.

'He?' said Rénine, 'I wonder whether he may not have continued to behave under the influence of the film and whether the man of the woods in *The Happy Princess* has not quite naturally resumed his calling. For how is the man to live, to obtain his food, without attracting attention? He will have found a job.'

'We can't make sure of that.'

'We might, by questioning the woodcutters whom we can hear.'

The car took them by a forest-road to another cross-roads where they entered on foot a track which was deeply rutted by waggon-wheels. The sound of axes ceased. After walking for a quarter of an hour, they met a dozen men who, having finished work for the day, were returning to the villages near by.

'Will this path take us to Routot?' ask Rénine, in order to open a conversation with them.

'No, you're turning your backs on it,' said one of the men, gruffly. And he went on, accompanied by his mates.

Hortense and Rénine stood rooted to the spot. They had recognized the butler. His cheeks and chin were shaved, but his upper lip was covered by a black moustache, evidently dyed. The eyebrows no longer met and were reduced to normal dimensions.

* * *

Thus, in less than twenty hours, acting on the vague hints supplied by the bearing of a film-actor, Serge Rénine had touched the very heart of the tragedy by means of purely psychological arguments.

'Rose Andrée is alive,' he said. 'Otherwise Dalbrèque would have left the country. The poor thing must be imprisoned and bound up; and he takes her some food at night.'

'We will save her, won't we?'

'Certainly, by keeping a watch on him and, if necessary, but in the last resort, compelling him by force to give up his secret.'

They followed the woodcutter at a distance and, on the pretext that the car needed overhauling, engaged rooms in the principal inn at Routot.

Attached to the inn was a small café from which they were separated by the entrance to the yard and above which were two rooms, reached by a wooden outer staircase, at one side. Dalbrèque occupied one of these rooms and Rénine took the other for his chauffeur.

Next morning he learnt from Adolphe that Dalbrèque, on the previous evening, after all the lights were out, had carried down a bicycle from his room and mounted it and had not returned until shortly before sunrise.

The bicycle tracks led Rénine to the uninhabited Château des Landes, five miles from the village. They disappeared in a rocky path which ran beside the park down to the Seine, opposite the Jumièges peninsula.

Next night, he took up his position there. At eleven o'clock, Dalbrèque climbed a bank, scrambled over a wire fence, hid his bicycle under the branches and moved away. It seemed impossible to follow him in the pitchy darkness, on a mossy soil that muffled the sound of footsteps. Rénine did not make the attempt; but, at daybreak, he came with his chauffeur and hunted through the park all the morning. Though the park, which covered the side of a hill and was bounded below by the river, was not very large, he found no clue which gave him any reason to suppose that Rose Andrée was imprisoned there.

He therefore went back to the village, with the firm intention of taking action that evening and employing force.

'This state of things cannot go on,' he said to Hortense. 'I must rescue Rose Andrée at all costs and save her from that ruffian's clutches. He must be made to speak. He must. Otherwise there's a danger that we may be too late.'

That day was Sunday; and Dalbrèque did not go to work. He did not leave his room except for lunch and went upstairs again immediately afterwards. But at three o'clock Rénine and Hortense, who were keeping a watch on him from the inn, saw him come down the wooden staircase, with his bicycle on his shoulder. Leaning it against the bottom step, he inflated the tires and fastened to the handle-bar a rather bulky object wrapped in a newspaper.

'By Jove!' muttered Rénine.

'What's the matter?'

In front of the café was a small terrace bordered on the right and left by spindle-trees planted in boxes, which were connected by a paling. Behind the shrubs, sitting on a bank but stooping forward so that they could see Dalbrèque through the branches, were four men.

'Police!' said Rénine. 'What bad luck! If those fellows take a hand, they will spoil everything.'

'Why? On the contrary, I should have thought . . . '

'Yes, they will. They will put Dalbrèque out of the way . . . and then? Will that give us Rose Andrée?'

Dalbrèque had finished his preparations. Just as he was mounting his bicycle, the detectives rose in a body, ready to make a dash for him. But Dalbrèque, though quite unconscious of their presence, changed his mind and went back to his room as though he had forgotten something.

'Now's the time!' said Rénine. 'I'm going to risk it. But it's a difficult situation and I've no great hopes.'

He went out into the yard and, at a moment when the detectives were not looking, ran up the staircase, as was only natural if he wished to give an order to his chauffeur. But he had no sooner reached the rustic balcony at the back of the house, which gave admission to the two bedrooms than he stopped. Dalbrèque's door was open. Rénine walked in.

Dalbrèque stepped back, at once assuming the defensive.

'What do you want? Who said you could . . . '

'Silence!' whispered Rénine, with an imperious gesture. 'It's all up with you!'

'What are you talking about?' growled the man, angrily.

'Lean out of your window. There are four men below on the watch for you to leave, four detectives.'

Dalbrèque leant over the terrace and muttered an oath.

'On the watch for me?' he said, turning round. 'What do I care?'

'They have a warrant.'

He folded his arms.

'Shut up with your piffle! A warrant! What's that to me?'

'Listen,' said Rénine, 'and let us waste no time. It's urgent. Your name's Dalbrèque, or, at least, that's the name under which you acted in *The Happy Princess* and under which the police are looking for you as being the murderer of Bourguet the jeweller, the man who stole a motor-car and forty thousand francs from the World's Cinema Company and the man who abducted a woman at Le Havre. All this is known and proved . . . and here's the upshot. Four men downstairs. Myself here, my chauffeur in the next room. You're done for. Do you want me to save you?'

Dalbrèque gave his adversary a long look.

'Who are you?'

'A friend of Rose Andrée's,' said Rénine.

The other started and, to some extent dropping his mask, retorted: 'What are your conditions?'

'Rose Andrée, whom you have abducted and tormented, is dying in some hole or corner. Where is she?'

A strange thing occurred and impressed Rénine. Dalbrèque's face, usually so common, was lit up by a smile that made it almost attractive. But this was only a flashing vision: the man immediately resumed his hard and impassive expression.

'And suppose I refuse to speak?' he said.

'So much the worse for you. It means your arrest.'

'I dare say; but it means the death of Rose Andrée. Who will release her?'

'You. You will speak now, or in an hour, or two hours hence at least. You will never have the heart to keep silent and let her die.'

Dalbrèque shrugged his shoulders. Then, raising his hand, he said: 'I swear on my life that, if they arrest me, not a word will leave my lips.'

'What then?'

'Then save me. We will meet this evening at the entrance to the Parc des Landes and say what we have to say.'

'Why not at once?'

'I have spoken.'

'Will you be there?'

'I shall be there.'

Rénine reflected. There was something in all this that he failed to grasp. In any case, the frightful danger that threatened Rose Andrée dominated the whole situation; and Rénine was not the man to despise this threat and to persist out of vanity in a perilous course. Rose Andrée's life came before everything.

He struck several blows on the wall of the next bedroom and called his chauffeur.

'Adolphe, is the car ready?'

'Yes, sir.'

'Set her going and pull her up in front of the terrace outside the café, right against the boxes so as to block the exit. As for you,' he continued, addressing Dalbrèque, 'you're to jump on your machine and, instead of making off along the road, cross the yard. At the end of the yard is a passage leading into a lane. There you will be free. But no hesitation and no blundering . . . else you'll get yourself nabbed. Good luck to you.'

He waited till the car was drawn up in accordance with his instructions and, when he reached it, he began to question his chauffeur, in order to attract the detectives' attention.

One of them, however, having cast a glance through the spindle-trees, caught sight of Dalbrèque just as he reached the bottom of the staircase. He gave the alarm and darted forward, followed by his comrades, but had to run round the car and bumped into the chauffeur, which gave Dalbrèque time to mount his bicycle and cross the yard unimpeded. He thus had some seconds' start. Unfortunately for him as he was about to enter the passage at the back, a troop of boys and girls appeared, returning from vespers. On hearing the shouts of the detectives, they spread their arms in front of the fugitive, who gave two or three lurches and ended by falling.

Cries of triumph were raised.

'Lay hold of him! Stop him!' roared the detectives as they rushed forward.

Rénine, seeing that the game was up, ran after the others and called out: 'Stop him!'

He came up with them just as Dalbrèque, after regaining his feet, knocked one of the policemen down and levelled his revolver. Rénine snatched it out of his hands. But the two other detectives, startled, had also produced their weapons. They fired. Dalbrèque, hit in the leg and the chest, pitched forward and fell.

'Thank you, sir,' said the inspector to Rénine introducing himself. 'We owe a lot to you.'

'It seems to me that you've done for the fellow,' said Rénine. 'Who is he?'

'One Dalbrèque, a scoundrel for whom we were looking.'

Rénine was beside himself. Hortense had joined him by this time; and he growled: 'The silly fools! Now they've killed him!'

'Oh, it isn't possible!'

'We shall see. But, whether he's dead or alive, it's death to Rose Andrée. How are we to trace her? And what chance have we of finding the place – some inaccessible retreat – where the poor thing is dying of misery and starvation?'

The detectives and peasants had moved away, bearing Dalbrèque with them on an improvised stretcher. Rénine, who had at first followed them, in order to find out what was going to happen, changed his mind and was now standing with his eyes fixed on the ground. The fall of the bicycle had unfastened the parcel which Dalbrèque had tied to the handle-bar; and the newspaper had burst, revealing its contents, a tin saucepan, rusty, dented, battered and useless.

'What's the meaning of this?' he muttered. 'What was the idea? . . . '

He picked it up examined it. Then he gave a grin and a click of the tongue and chuckled, slowly: 'Don't move an eyelash, my dear. Let all these people clear off. All this is no business of ours, is it? The troubles of police don't concern us. We are two motorists travelling for our pleasure and collecting old saucepans if we feel so inclined.'

He called his chauffeur: 'Adolphe, take us to the Parc des Landes by a roundabout road.'

Half an hour later they reached the sunken track and began to scramble down it on foot beside the wooded slopes. The Seine, which was very low at this time of day, was lapping against a little jetty near which lay a worm-eaten, mouldering boat, full of puddles of water.

Rénine stepped into the boat and at once began to bale out the puddles with his saucepan. He then drew the boat alongside of the jetty, helped Hortense in and used the one oar which he shipped in a gap in the stern to work her into midstream.

'I believe I'm there!' he said, with a laugh. 'The worst that can happen to us is to get our feet wet, for our craft leaks a trifle. But haven't we a saucepan? Oh, blessings on that useful utensil! Almost as soon as I set eyes upon it, I remembered that people use those articles to bale out the bottoms of leaky boats. Why, there was bound to be a boat in the Landes woods! How was it I never thought of that? But of course Dalbrèque made use of her to cross the Seine! And, as she made water, he brought a saucepan.'

'Then Rose Andrée . . . ?' asked Hortense.

'Is a prisoner on the other bank, on the Jumièges peninsula. You see the famous abbey from here.'

They ran aground on a beach of big pebbles covered with slime.

'And it can't be very far away,' he added. 'Dalbrèque did not spend the whole night running about.'

A tow-path followed the deserted bank. Another path led away from it. They chose the second and, passing between orchards enclosed by hedges, came to a landscape that seemed strangely familiar to them. Where had they seen that pool before, with the willows overhanging it? And where had they seen that abandoned hovel?

Suddenly both of them stopped with one accord.

'Oh!' said Hortense. 'I can hardly believe my eyes!'

Opposite them was the white gate of a large orchard, at the back of which, among groups of old, gnarled apple-trees, appeared a cottage with blue shutters, the cottage of the Happy Princess.

'Of course!' cried Rénine. 'And I ought to have known it, considering that the film showed both this cottage and the forest close by. And isn't everything happening exactly as in *The Happy Princess*? Isn't Dalbrèque dominated by the memory of it? The house, which is certainly the one in which Rose Andrée spent the summer, was empty. He has shut her up there.'

'But the house, you told me, was in the Seine-inférieure.'

'Well, so are we! To the left of the river, the Eure and the forest of Brotonne; to the right, the Seine-inférieure. But between them is the obstacle of the river, which is why I didn't connect the two. A hundred and fifty yards of water form a more effective division than dozens of miles.'

The gate was locked. They got through the hedge a little lower down and walked towards the house, which was screened on one side by an old wall shaggy with ivy and roofed with thatch.

'It seems as if there was somebody there,' said Hortense. 'Didn't I hear the sound of a window?'

'Listen.'

Someone struck a few chords on a piano. Then a voice arose, a woman's voice softly and solemnly singing a ballad that thrilled with restrained passion. The woman's whole soul seemed to breathe itself into the melodious notes.

They walked on. The wall concealed them from view, but they saw a sitting-room furnished with bright wall-paper and a blue Roman carpet. The throbbing voice ceased. The piano ended with a last chord; and the singer rose and appeared framed in the window.

'Rose Andrée!' whispered Hortense.

'Well!' said Rénine, admitting his astonishment. 'This is the last thing that I expected! Rose Andrée! Rose Andrée at liberty! And singing Massenet in the sitting room of her cottage!'

'What does it all mean? Do you understand?'

'Yes, but it has taken me long enough! But how could we have guessed . . . ?'

Although they had never seen her except on the screen, they had not the least doubt that this was she. It was really Rose Andrée, or rather, the Happy Princess, whom they had admired a few days before, amidst the furniture of that very sitting-room or on the threshold of that very cottage. She was wearing the same dress; her hair was done in the same way; she had on the same bangles and necklaces as in *The Happy Princess*; and her lovely face, with its rosy cheeks and laughing eyes, bore the same look of joy and serenity.

Some sound must have caught her ear, for she leant over towards a clump of shrubs beside the cottage and whispered into the silent garden: 'Georges . . . Georges . . . Is that you, my darling?'

Receiving no reply, she drew herself up and stood smiling at the happy thoughts that seemed to flood her being.

But a door opened at the back of the room and an old peasant woman entered with a tray laden with bread, butter and milk.

'Here, Rose, my pretty one, I've brought you your supper. Milk fresh from the cow . . . '

And, putting down the tray, she continued: 'Aren't you afraid, Rose, of the chill of the night air? Perhaps you're expecting your sweetheart?'

'I haven't a sweetheart, my dear old Catherine.'

'What next!' said the old woman, laughing. 'Only this morning there were footprints under the window that didn't look at all proper!'

'A burglar's footprints perhaps, Catherine.'

'Well, I don't say they weren't, Rose dear, especially as in your calling you have a lot of people round you whom it's well to be careful of. For instance, your friend Dalbrèque, eh? Nice goings on his are! You saw the paper yesterday. A fellow who has robbed and murdered people and carried off a woman at Le Havre . . . !'

Hortense and Rénine would have much liked to know what Rose Andrée thought of the revelations, but she had turned her back to them and was sitting at her supper; and the window was now closed, so that they could neither hear her reply nor see the expression of her features.

They waited for a moment. Hortense was listening with an anxious face. But Rénine began to laugh.

'Very funny, really funny! And such an unexpected ending! And we who were hunting for her in some cave or damp cellar, a horrible tomb where the poor thing was dying of hunger! It's a fact, she knew the terrors of that first night of captivity; and I maintain that, on that first night, she was flung, half-dead, into the cave. Only, there you are: the next morning she was alive! One night was enough to tame the little rogue and to make Dalbrèque as handsome as Prince Charming in her eyes! For see the difference. On the films or in novels, the Happy Princesses resist or commit suicide. But in real life . . . oh, woman, woman!'

'Yes,' said Hortense, 'but the man she loves is almost certainly dead.'

'And a good thing too! It would be the best solution. What would be the outcome of this criminal love for a thief and murderer?'

A few minutes passed. Then, amid the peaceful silence of the waning day, mingled with the first shadows of the twilight, they again heard the grating of the window, which was cautiously opened. Rose Andrée leant over the garden and waited, with her eyes turned to the wall, as though she saw something there.

Presently, Rénine shook the ivy-branches.

'Ah!' she said. 'This time I know you're there! Yes, the ivy's moving. Georges, Georges darling, why do you keep me waiting? Catherine has gone. I am all alone . . .'

She had knelt down and was distractedly stretching out her shapely arms covered with bangles which clashed with a metallic sound.

'Georges! . . . Georges! . . .'

Her every movement, the thrill of her voice, her whole being expressed desire and love. Hortense, deeply touched, could not help saying: 'How the poor thing loves him! If she but knew . . .'

'Ah!' cried the girl. 'You've spoken. You're there, and you want me to come to you, don't you? Here I am, Georges! . . .'

She climbed over the window-ledge and began to run, while Rénine went round the wall and advanced to meet her.

She stopped short in front of him and stood choking at the sight of this man and woman whom she did not know and who were stepping out of the very shadow from which her beloved appeared to her each night.

Rénine bowed, gave his name and introduced his companion.

'Madame Hortense Daniel, a pupil and friend of your mother's.'

Still motionless with stupefaction, her features drawn, she stammered: 'You know who I am? . . . And you were there just now? . . . You heard what I was saying . . . ?'

Rénine, without hesitating or pausing in his speech, said: 'You are Rose Andrée, the Happy Princess. We saw you on the films the other evening; and circumstances led us to set out in search of you . . . to Le Havre, where you were abducted on the day when you were to have left for America, and to the forest of Brotonne, where you were imprisoned.'

She protested eagerly, with a forced laugh: 'What is all this? I have not been to Le Havre. I came straight here. Abducted? Imprisoned? What nonsense!'

'Yes, imprisoned, in the same cave as the Happy Princess; and you broke off some branches to the right of the cave.'

'But how absurd! Who would have abducted me? I have no enemy.'

'There is a man in love with you: the one whom you were expecting just now.'

'Yes, my lover,' she said, proudly. 'Have I not the right to receive whom I like?'

'You have the right; you are a free agent. But the man who comes to see you every evening is wanted by the police. His name is Georges Dalbrèque. He killed Bourguet the jeweller.'

The accusation made her start with indignation and she exclaimed: 'It's a lie! An infamous fabrication of the newspapers! Georges was in Paris on the night of the murder. He can prove it.'

'He stole a motor car and forty thousand francs in notes.'

She retorted vehemently: 'The motor-car was taken back by his friends and the notes will be restored. He never touched them. My leaving for America had made him lose his head.'

'Very well. I am quite willing to believe everything that you say. But the police may show less faith in these statements and less indulgence.'

She became suddenly uneasy and faltered: 'The police . . . There's nothing to fear from them . . . They won't know . . . '

'Where to find him? I succeeded, at all events. He's working as a woodcutter, in the forest of Brotonne.'

'Yes, but . . . you . . . that was an accident . . . whereas the police . . . '

The words left her lips with the greatest difficulty. Her voice was trembling. And suddenly she rushed at Rénine, stammering: 'He is arrested? . . . I am sure of it! . . . And you have come to tell me . . . Arrested! Wounded! Dead perhaps? . . . Oh, please, please! . . . '

She had no strength left. All her pride, all the certainty of her great love gave way to an immense despair and she sobbed out.

'No, he's not dead, is he? No, I feel that he's not dead. Oh, sir, how unjust it all is! He's the gentlest man, the best that ever lived. He has changed my whole life. Everything is different since I began to love him. And I love him so! I love him! I want to go to him. Take me to him. I want them to arrest me too. I love him . . . I could not live without him . . . '

An impulse of sympathy made Hortense put her arms around the girl's neck and say warmly: 'Yes, come. He is not dead, I am sure, only wounded; and Prince Rénine will save him. You will, won't you, Rénine? . . . Come. Make up a story for your servant: say that you're going somewhere by train and that she is not to tell anybody. Be quick. Put on a wrap. We will save him, I swear we will.'

Rose Andrée went indoors and returned almost at once, disguised beyond recognition in a long cloak and a veil that shrouded her face; and they all took the road back to Routot. At the inn, Rose Andrée passed as a friend whom they had been to fetch in the neighbourhood and were taking to Paris with them. Rénine ran out to make enquiries and came back to the two women.

'It's all right. Dalbrèque is alive. They have put him to bed in a private room at the mayor's offices. He has a broken leg and a rather high temperature; but all the same they expect to move him to Rouen tomorrow and they have telephoned there for a motor-car.'

'And then?' asked Rose Andrée, anxiously.

Rénine smiled.

'Why, then we shall leave at daybreak. We shall take up our positions in a sunken road, rifle in hand, attack the motor-coach and carry off Georges!'

'Oh, don't laugh!' she said, plaintively. 'I am so unhappy!'

But the adventure seemed to amuse Rénine; and, when he was alone with Hortense, he exclaimed: 'You see what comes of preferring dishonour to death! But hang it all, who could have expected this? It isn't a bit the way in which things happen in the pictures! Once the man of the woods had carried off his victim and considering that for three weeks there was no one to defend her, how could we imagine – we who had been proceeding all along under the influence of the pictures – that in the space of a few hours the victim would become a princess in love? Confound that Georges! I now understand the sly, humorous look which I surprised on his mobile features! He remembered, Georges did, and he didn't care a hang for me! Oh, he tricked me nicely! And you, my dear, he tricked you too! And it was all the influence of the film. They show us, at the cinema, a brute beast, a sort of long-haired, ape-faced savage. What can a man like that be in real life? A brute, inevitably, don't you agree? Well, he's nothing of the kind; he's a Don Juan! The humbug!'

'You will save him, won't you?' said Hortense, in a beseeching tone.

'Are you very anxious that I should?'

'Very.'

'In that case, promise to give me your hand to kiss.'

'You can have both hands, Rénine, and gladly.'

The night was uneventful. Rénine had given orders for the two ladies to be waked at an early hour. When they came down, the motor was leaving the yard and pulling up in front of the inn. It was raining; and Adolphe, the chauffeur, had fixed up the long, low hood and packed the luggage inside.

Rénine called for his bill. They all three took a cup of coffee. But, just as they were leaving the room, one of the inspector's men came rushing in.

'Have you seen him?' he asked. 'Isn't he here?'

The inspector himself arrived at a run, greatly excited.

'The prisoner has escaped! He ran back through the inn! He can't be far away!'

A dozen rustics appeared like a whirlwind. They ransacked the lofts, the stables, the sheds. They scattered over the neighbourhood. But the search led to no discovery.

'Oh, hang it all!' said Rénine, who had taken his part in the hunt. 'How can it have happened?'

'How do I know?' spluttered the inspector in despair. 'I left my three men watching in the next room. I found them this morning fast asleep, stupefied by some narcotic which had been mixed with their wine! And the Dalbrèque bird had flown!'

'Which way?'

'Through the window. There were evidently accomplices, with ropes and a ladder. And, as Dalbrèque had a broken leg, they carried him off on the stretcher itself.'

'They left no traces?'

'No traces of footsteps, true. The rain has messed everything up. But they went through the yard, because the stretcher's there.'

'You'll find him, Mr Inspector, there's no doubt of that. In any case, you may be sure that you won't have any trouble over the affair. I shall be in Paris this evening and shall go straight to the prefecture, where I have influential friends.'

Rénine went back to the two women in the coffee-room and Hortense at once said: 'It was you who carried him off, wasn't it? Please put Rose Andrée's mind at rest. She is so terrified!'

He gave Rose Andrée his arm and led her to the car. She was staggering and very pale; and she said, in a faint voice: 'Are we going? And he: is he safe? Won't they catch him again?'

Looking deep into her eyes, he said: 'Swear to me, Rose Andrée, that in two months, when he is well and when I have proved his innocence, swear that you will go away with him to America.'

'I swear.'

'And that, once there, you will marry him.'

'I swear.'

He spoke a few words in her ear.

'Ah!' she said. 'May Heaven bless you for it!'

Hortense took her seat in front, with Rénine, who sat at the wheel. The inspector, hat in hand, fussed around the car until it moved off.

They drove through the forest, crossed the Seine at La Mailleraie and struck into the Havre-Rouen road.

'Take off your glove and give me your hand to kiss,' Rénine ordered. 'You promised that you would.'

'Oh!' said Hortense. 'But it was to be when Dalbrèque was saved.'

'He is saved.'

'Not yet. The police are after him. They may catch him again. He will not be really saved until he is with Rose Andrée.'

'He is with Rose Andrée,' he declared.

'What do you mean?'

'Turn round.'

She did so.

In the shadow of the hood, right at the back, behind the chauffeur, Rose Andrée was kneeling beside a man lying on the seat.

'Oh,' stammered Hortense, 'it's incredible! Then it was you who hid him last night? And he was there, in front of the inn, when the inspector was seeing us off?'

'Lord, yes! He was there, under the cushions and rugs!'

'It's incredible!' she repeated, utterly bewildered. 'It's incredible! How were you able to manage it all?'

'I wanted to kiss your hand,' he said.

She removed her glove, as he bade her, and raised her hand to his lips.

The car was speeding between the peaceful Seine and the white cliffs that border it. They sat silent for a long while. Then he said: 'I had a talk with Dalbrèque last night. He's a fine fellow and is ready to do anything for Rose Andrée. He's right. A man must do anything for the woman he loves. He must devote himself to her, offer her all that is beautiful in this world: joy and happiness . . . and, if she should be bored, stirring adventures to distract her, to excite her and to make her smile . . . or even weep.'

Hortense shivered; and her eyes were not quite free from tears. For the first time he was alluding to the sentimental adventure that bound them by a tie which as yet was frail, but which became stronger and more enduring with each of the ventures on which they entered together, pursuing them feverishly and anxiously to their close. Already she felt powerless and uneasy with this extraordinary man, who subjected events to his will and seemed to play with the destinies of those whom he fought or protected. He filled her with dread and at the same time he attracted her. She thought of him sometimes as her master, sometimes as an enemy against whom she must defend herself, but oftenest as a perturbing friend, full of charm and fascination . . .

Thérèse and Germaine

The weather was so mild that autumn that, on the 12th of October, in the morning, several families still lingering in their villas at Étretat had gone down to the beach. The sea, lying between the cliffs and the clouds on the horizon, might have suggested a mountain-lake slumbering in the hollow of the enclosing rocks, were it not for that crispness in the air and those pale, soft and indefinite colours in the sky which give a special charm to certain days in Normandy.

'It's delicious,' murmured Hortense. But the next moment she added: 'All the same, we did not come here to enjoy the spectacle of nature or to wonder whether that huge stone Needle on our left was really at one time the home of Arsène Lupin.'

'We came here,' said Prince Rénine, 'because of the conversation which I overheard, a fortnight ago, in a dining-car, between a man and a woman.'

'A conversation of which I was unable to catch a single word.'

'If those two people could have guessed for an instant that it was possible to hear a single word of what they were saying, they would not have spoken, for their conversation was one of extraordinary gravity and importance. But I have very sharp ears; and though I could not follow every sentence, I insist that we may be certain of two things. First, that man and woman, who are brother and sister, have an appointment at a quarter to twelve this morning, the 12th of October, at the spot known as the Trois Mathildes, with a third person, who is married and who wishes at all costs to recover his or her liberty. Secondly, this appointment, at which they will come to a final agreement, is to be followed this evening by a walk along the cliffs, when the third person will bring with him or her the man or woman, I can't definitely say which, whom they want to get rid of. That is the gist of the whole thing. Now, as I know a spot called the Trois Mathildes some way above Étretat and as this is not an everyday name, we came down yesterday to thwart the plan of these objectionable persons.'

'What plan?' asked Hortense. 'For, after all, it's only your assumption that there's to be a victim and that the victim is to be flung off the top of the cliffs. You yourself told me that you heard no allusion to a possible murder.'

'That is so. But I heard some very plain words relating to the marriage of the brother or the sister with the wife or the husband of the third person, which implies the need for a crime.'

They were sitting on the terrace of the casino, facing the stairs which run down to the beach. They therefore overlooked the few privately-owned cabins on the shingle, where a party of four men were playing bridge, while a group of ladies sat talking and knitting.

A short distance away and nearer to the sea was another cabin, standing by itself and closed.

Half-a-dozen bare-legged children were paddling in the water.

'No,' said Hortense, 'all this autumnal sweetness and charm fails to attract me. I have so much faith in all your theories that I can't help thinking, in spite of everything, of this dreadful problem. Which of those people yonder is threatened? Death has already selected its victim. Who is it? Is it that young, fair-haired woman, rocking herself and laughing? Is it that tall man over there, smoking his cigar? And which of them has the thought of murder hidden in his heart? All the people we see are quietly enjoying themselves. Yet death is prowling among them.'

'Capital!' said Rénine. 'You too are becoming enthusiastic. What did I tell you? The whole of life's an adventure; and nothing but adventure is worth while. At the first breath of coming events, there you are, quivering in every nerve. You share in all the tragedies stirring around you; and the feeling of mystery awakens in the depths of your being. See, how closely you are observing that couple who have just arrived. You never can tell: that may be the gentleman who proposes to do away with his wife? Or perhaps the lady contemplates making away with her husband?'

'The d'Ormevals? Never! A perfectly happy couple! Yesterday, at the hotel, I had a long talk with the wife. And you yourself . . . '

'Oh, I played a round of golf with Jacques d'Ormeval, who rather fancies himself as an athlete, and I played at dolls with their two charming little girls!'

The d'Ormevals came up and exchanged a few words with them. Madame d'Ormeval said that her two daughters had gone back to Paris that morning with their governess. Her husband, a great tall fellow with a yellow beard, carrying his blazer over his arm and puffing out his chest under a cellular shirt, complained of the heat.

'Have you the key of the cabin, Thérèse?' he asked his wife, when they had left Rénine and Hortense and stopped at the top of the stairs, a few yards away.

'Here it is,' said the wife. 'Are you going to read your papers?'

'Yes. Unless we go for a stroll? . . . '

'I had rather wait till the afternoon: do you mind? I have a lot of letters to write this morning.'

'Very well. We'll go on the cliff.'

Hortense and Rénine exchanged a glance of surprise. Was this suggestion accidental? Or had they before them, contrary to their expectations, the very couple of whom they were in search?

Hortense tried to laugh.

'My heart is thumping,' she said. 'Nevertheless, I absolutely refuse to believe in anything so improbable. "My husband and I have never had the slightest quarrel," she said to me. No, it's quite clear that those two get on admirably.'

'We shall see presently, at the Trois Mathildes, if one of them comes to meet the brother and sister.'

M. d'Ormeval had gone down the stairs, while his wife stood leaning on the balustrade of the terrace. She had a beautiful, slender, supple figure. Her clear-cut profile was emphasized by a rather too prominent chin when at rest; and, when it was not smiling, the face gave an expression of sadness and suffering.

'Have you lost something, Jacques?' she called out to her husband, who was stooping over the shingle.

'Yes, the key,' he said. 'It slipped out of my hand.'

She went down to him and began to look also. For two or three minutes, as they sheered off to the right and remained close to the bottom of the under-cliff, they were invisible to Hortense and Rénine. Their voices were covered by the noise of a dispute which had arisen among the bridge-players.

They reappeared almost simultaneously. Madame d'Ormeval slowly climbed a few steps of the stairs and then stopped and turned her face towards the sea. Her husband had thrown his blazer over his shoulders and was making for the isolated cabin. As he passed the bridge-players, they asked him for a decision, pointing to their cards spread out upon the table. But, with a wave of the hand, he refused to give an opinion and walked on, covered the thirty yards which divided them from the cabin, opened the door and went in.

Thérèse d'Ormeval came back to the terrace and remained for ten minutes sitting on a bench. Then she came out through the casino.

Hortense, on leaning forward, saw her entering one of the chalets annexed to the Hôtel Hauville and, a moment later, caught sight of her again on the balcony.

'Eleven o'clock,' said Rénine. 'Whoever it is, he or she, or one of the card-players, or one of their wives, it won't be long before someone goes to the appointed place.'

Nevertheless, twenty minutes passed and twenty-five; and no one stirred.

'Perhaps Madame d'Ormeval has gone.' Hortense suggested, anxiously. 'She is no longer on her balcony.'

'If she is at the Trois Mathildes,' said Rénine, 'we will go and catch her there.'

He was rising to his feet, when a fresh discussion broke out among the bridge-players and one of them exclaimed: 'Let's put it to d'Ormeval.'

'Very well,' said his adversary. 'I'll accept his decision . . . if he consents to act as umpire. He was rather huffy just now.'

They called out: 'D'Ormeval! D'Ormeval!'

They then saw that d'Ormeval must have shut the door behind him, which kept him in the half dark, the cabin being one of the sort that has no window.

'He's asleep,' cried one. 'Let's wake him up.'

All four went to the cabin, began by calling to him and, on receiving no answer, thumped on the door.

'Hi! D'Ormeval! Are you asleep?'

On the terrace Serge Rénine suddenly leapt to his feet with so uneasy an air that Hortense was astonished. He muttered: 'If only it's not too late!'

And, when Hortense asked him what he meant, he tore down the steps and started running to the cabin. He reached it just as the bridge-players were trying to break in the door.

'Stop!' he ordered. 'Things must be done in the regular fashion.'

'What things?' they asked.

He examined the Venetian shutters at the top of each of the folding-doors and, on finding that one of the upper slats was partly broken, hung on as best he could to the roof of the cabin and cast a glance inside. Then he said to the four men: 'I was right in thinking that, if M. d'Ormeval did not reply, he must have been prevented by some serious cause. There is every reason to believe that M. d'Ormeval is wounded . . . or dead.'

'Dead!' they cried. 'What do you mean? He has only just left us.'

Rénine took out his knife, prised open the lock and pulled back the two doors.

There were shouts of dismay. M. d'Ormeval was lying flat on his face, clutching his jacket and his newspaper in his hands. Blood was flowing from his back and staining his shirt.

'Oh!' said someone. 'He has killed himself!'

'How can he have killed himself?' said Rénine. 'The wound is right in the middle of the back, at a place which the hand can't reach. And, besides, there's not a knife in the cabin.'

The others protested.

'If so, he has been murdered. But that's impossible! There has been nobody here. We should have seen, if there had been. Nobody could have passed us without our seeing . . . '

The other men, all the ladies and the children paddling in the sea had come running up. Rénine allowed no one to enter the cabin, except a doctor who was present. But the doctor could only say that M. d'Ormeval was dead, stabbed with a dagger.

At that moment, the mayor and the policeman arrived, together with some people of the village. After the usual enquiries, they carried away the body.

A few persons went on ahead to break the news to Thérèse d'Ormeval, who was once more to be seen on her balcony.

*   *   *

And so the tragedy had taken place without any clue to explain how a man, protected by a closed door with an uninjured lock, could have been murdered in the space of a few minutes and in front of twenty witnesses, one might almost say, twenty spectators. No one had entered the cabin. No one had come out of it. As for the dagger with which M. d'Ormeval had been stabbed between the shoulders, it could not be traced. And all this would have suggested the idea of a trick of sleight-of-hand performed by a clever conjuror, had it not concerned a terrible murder, committed under the most mysterious conditions.

Hortense was unable to follow, as Rénine would have liked, the small party who were making for Madame d'Ormeval; she was para-lyzed with excitement and incapable of moving. It was the first time that her adventures with Rénine had taken her into the very heart of the action and that, instead of noting the consequences of a murder, or assisting in the pursuit of the criminals, she found herself con-fronted with the murder itself.

It left her trembling all over; and she stammered: 'How horrible! . . . The poor fellow! . . . Ah, Rénine, you couldn't save him this time! . . . And that's what upsets me more than anything, that we could and should have saved him, since we knew of the plot . . . '

Rénine made her sniff at a bottle of salts; and when she had quite recovered her composure, he said, while observing her attentively.

'So you think that there is some connection between the murder and the plot which we were trying to frustrate?'

'Certainly,' said she, astonished at the question.

'Then, as that plot was hatched by a husband against his wife or by a wife against her husband, you admit that Madame d'Ormeval . . . ?'

'Oh, no, impossible!' she said. 'To begin with, Madame d'Ormeval did not leave her rooms . . . and then I shall never believe that pretty woman capable . . . No, no, of course there was something else . . . '

'What else?'

'I don't know . . . You may have misunderstood what the brother and sister were saying to each other . . . You see, the murder has been committed under quite different conditions . . . at another hour and another place . . . '

'And therefore,' concluded Rénine, 'the two cases are not in any way related?'

'Oh,' she said, 'there's no making it out! It's all so strange!'

Rénine became a little satirical.

'My pupil is doing me no credit today,' he said. 'Why, here is a perfectly simple story, unfolded before your eyes. You have seen it reeled off like a scene in the cinema; and it all remains as obscure to you as though you were hearing of an affair that happened in a cave a hundred miles away!'

Hortense was confounded.

'What are you saying? Do you mean that you have understood it? What clues have you to go by?'

Rénine looked at his watch.

'I have not understood everything,' he said. 'The murder itself, the mere brutal murder, yes. But the essential thing, that is to say, the psychology of the crime: I've no clue to that. Only, it is twelve o'clock. The brother and sister, seeing no one come to the appointment at the Trois Mathildes, will go down to the beach. Don't you think that we shall learn something then of the accomplice whom I accuse them of having and of the connection between the two cases?'

They reached the esplanade in front of the Hauville chalets, with the capstans by which the fishermen haul up their boats to the beach.

A number of inquisitive persons were standing outside the door of one of the chalets. Two coastguards, posted at the door, prevented them from entering.

The mayor shouldered his way eagerly through the crowd. He was back from the post-office, where he had been telephoning to Le Havre, to the office of the procurator-general, and had been told that the public prosecutor and an examining-magistrate would come on to Étretat in the course of the afternoon.

'That leaves us plenty of time for lunch,' said Rénine. 'The tragedy will not be enacted before two or three o'clock. And I have an idea that it will be sensational.'

They hurried nevertheless. Hortense, overwrought by fatigue and her desire to know what was happening, continually questioned Rénine, who replied evasively, with his eyes turned to the esplanade, which they could see through the windows of the coffee-room.

'Are you watching for those two?' asked Hortense.

'Yes, the brother and sister.'

'Are you sure that they will venture? . . . '

'Look out! Here they come!'

He went out quickly.

Where the main street opened on the sea-front, a lady and gentleman were advancing with hesitating steps, as though unfamiliar with the place. The brother was a puny little man, with a sallow complexion. He was wearing a motoring-cap. The sister too was short, but rather stout, and was wrapped in a large cloak. She struck them as a woman of a certain age, but still good-looking under the thin veil that covered her face.

They saw the groups of bystanders and drew nearer. Their gait betrayed uneasiness and hesitation.

The sister asked a question of a seaman. At the first words of his answer, which no doubt conveyed the news of d'Ormeval's death, she uttered a cry and tried to force her way through the crowd. The brother, learning in his turn what had happened, made great play with his elbows and shouted to the coast-guards: 'I'm a friend of d'Ormeval's! . . . Here's my card! Frédéric Astaing . . . My sister, Germaine Astaing, knows Madame d'Ormeval intimately! . . . They were expecting us . . . We had an appointment! . . . '

They were allowed to pass. Rénine, who had slipped behind them, followed them in without a word, accompanied by Hortense.

The d'Ormevals had four bedrooms and a sitting-room on the second floor. The sister rushed into one of the rooms and threw herself on her knees beside the bed on which the corpse lay stretched. Thérèse d'Ormeval was in the sitting-room and was sobbing in the midst of a small company of silent persons. The brother sat down beside her, eagerly seized her hands and said, in a trembling voice: 'My poor friend! . . . My poor friend! . . . '

Rénine and Hortense gazed at the pair of them: and Hortense whispered: 'And she's supposed to have killed him for that? Impossible!'

'Nevertheless,' observed Rénine, 'they are acquaintances; and we know that Astaing and his sister were also acquainted with a third person who was their accomplice. So that . . . '

'It's impossible!' Hortense repeated.

And, in spite of all presumption, she felt so much attracted by Thérèse that, when Frédéric Astaing stood up, she proceeded straightway to sit down beside her and consoled her in a gentle voice. The unhappy woman's tears distressed her profoundly.

Rénine, on the other hand, applied himself from the outset to watching the brother and sister, as though this were the only thing that mattered, and did not take his eyes off Frédéric Astaing, who, with an air of indifference, began to make a minute inspection of the premises, examining the sitting-room, going into all the bedrooms, mingling with the various groups of persons present and asking questions about the manner in which the murder had been committed. Twice his sister came up and spoke to him. Then he went back to Madame d'Ormeval and again sat down beside her, full of earnest sympathy. Lastly, in the lobby, he had a long conversation with his sister, after which they parted, like people who have come to a perfect understanding. Frédéric then left. These manoeuvers had lasted quite thirty or forty minutes.

It was at this moment that the motor-car containing the examining-magistrate and the public prosecutor pulled up outside the chalets. Rénine, who did not expect them until later, said to Hortense: 'We must be quick. On no account leave Madame d'Ormeval.'

Word was sent up to the persons whose evidence might be of any service that they were to go to the beach, where the magistrate was beginning a preliminary investigation. He would call on Madame d'Ormeval afterwards. Accordingly, all who were present left the chalet. No one remained behind except the two guards and Germaine Astaing.

Germaine knelt down for the last time beside the dead man and, bending low, with her face in her hands, prayed for a long time.

Then she rose and was opening the door on the landing, when Rénine came forward.

'I should like a few words with you, madame.'

She seemed surprised and replied: 'What is it, monsieur? I am listening.'

'Not here.'

'Where then, monsieur?'

'Next door, in the sitting-room.'

'No,' she said, sharply.

'Why not? Though you did not even shake hands with her, I presume that Madame d'Ormeval is your friend?'

He gave her no time to reflect, drew her into the next room, closed the door and, at once pouncing upon Madame d'Ormeval, who was trying to go out and return to her own room, said: 'No, madame, listen, I implore you. Madame Astaing's presence need not drive you away. We have very serious matters to discuss, without losing a minute.'

The two women, standing face to face, were looking at each other with the same expression of implacable hatred, in which might be read the same confusion of spirit and the same restrained anger. Hortense, who believed them to be friends and who might, up to a certain point, have believed them to be accomplices, foresaw with terror the hostile encounter which she felt to be inevitable. She compelled Madame d'Ormeval to resume her seat, while Rénine took up his position in the middle of the room and spoke in resolute tones.

'Chance, which has placed me in possession of part of the truth, will enable me to save you both, if you are willing to assist me with a frank explanation that will give me the particulars which I still need. Each of you knows the danger in which she stands, because each of you is conscious in her heart of the evil for which she is responsible. But you are carried away by hatred; and it is for me to see clearly and to act. The examining-magistrate will be here in half-an-hour. By that time, you must have come to an agreement.'

They both started, as though offended by such a word.

'Yes, an agreement,' he repeated, in a more imperious tone. 'Whether you like it or not, you will come to an agreement. You are not the only ones to be considered. There are your two little daughters, Madame d'Ormeval. Since circumstances have set me in their path, I am intervening in their defence and for their safety. A blunder, a word too much; and they are ruined. That must not happen.'

At the mention of her children, Madame d'Ormeval broke down and sobbed. Germaine Astaing shrugged her shoulders and made a movement towards the door. Rénine once more blocked the way.

'Where are you going?'

'I have been summoned by the examining-magistrate.'

'No, you have not.'

'Yes, I have. Just as all those have been who have any evidence to give.'

'You were not on the spot. You know nothing of what happened. Nobody knows anything of the murder.'

'I know who committed it.'

'That's impossible.'

'It was Thérèse d'Ormeval.'

The accusation was hurled forth in an outburst of rage and with a fiercely threatening gesture.

'You wretched creature!' exclaimed Madame d'Ormeval, rushing at her. 'Go! Leave the room! Oh, what a wretch the woman is!'

Hortense was trying to restrain her, but Rénine whispered: 'Let them be. It's what I wanted . . . to pitch them one against the other and so to let in the day-light.'

Madame Astaing had made a convulsive effort to ward off the insult with a jest; and she sniggered: 'A wretched creature? Why? Because I have accused you?'

'Why? For every reason! You're a wretched creature! You hear what I say, Germaine: you're a wretch!'

Thérèse d'Ormeval was repeating the insult as though it afforded her some relief. Her anger was abating. Very likely also she no longer had the strength to keep up the struggle; and it was Madame Astaing who returned to the attack, with her fists clenched and her face distorted and suddenly aged by fully twenty years.

'You! You dare to insult me, you! You after the murder you have committed! You dare to lift up your head when the man whom you killed is lying in there on his death-bed! Ah, if one of us is a wretched creature, it's you, Thérèse, and you know it! You have killed your husband! You have killed your husband!'

She leapt forward, in the excitement of the terrible words which she was uttering; and her finger-nails were almost touching her friend's face.

'Oh, don't tell me you didn't kill him!' she cried. 'Don't say that: I won't let you. Don't say it. The dagger is there, in your bag. My brother felt it, while he was talking to you; and his hand came out with stains of blood upon it: your husband's blood, Thérèse. And then, even if I had not discovered anything, do you think that I should not have guessed, in the first few minutes? Why, I knew the truth at once, Thérèse! When a sailor down there answered, "M. d'Ormeval? He has been murdered," I said to myself then and there, "It's she, it's Thérèse, she killed him." '

Thérèse did not reply. She had abandoned her attitude of protest. Hortense, who was watching her with anguish, thought that she could perceive in her the despondency of those who know them-selves to be lost. Her cheeks had fallen in and she wore such an expression of despair that Hortense, moved to compassion, implored her to defend herself.

'Please, please, explain things. When the murder was committed, you were here, on the balcony . . . But then the dagger . . . how did you come to have it . . . ? How do you explain it? . . . '

'Explanations!' sneered Germaine Astaing. 'How could she poss-ibly explain? What do outward appearances matter? What does it matter what anyone saw or did not see? The proof is the thing that tells . . . The dagger is there, in your bag, Thérèse: that's a fact . . . Yes, yes, it was you who did it! You killed him! You killed him in the end! . . . Ah, how often I've told my brother, "She will kill him yet!" Frédéric used to try to defend you. He always had a weakness for you. But in his innermost heart he foresaw what would happen . . . And now the horrible thing has been done. A stab in the back! Coward! Coward! . . . And you would have me say nothing? Why, I didn't hesitate a moment! Nor did Frédéric. We looked for proofs at once . . . And I've denounced you of my own free will, perfectly well aware of what I was doing . . . And it's over, Thérèse. You're done for. Nothing can save you now. The dagger is in that bag which you are clutching in your hand. The magistrate is coming; and the dagger will be found, stained with the blood of your husband. So will your pocket-book. They're both there. And they will be found . . . '

Her rage had incensed her so vehemently that she was unable to continue and stood with her hand outstretched and her chin twitch-ing with nervous tremors.

Rénine gently took hold of Madame d'Ormeval's bag. She clung to it, but he insisted and said: 'Please allow me, madame. Your friend Germaine is right. The examining-magistrate will be here presently; and the fact that the dagger and the pocket-book are in your possession will lead to your immediate arrest. This must not happen. Please allow me.'

His insinuating voice diminished Thérèse d'Ormeval's resistance. She released her fingers, one by one. He took the bag, opened it, produced a little dagger with an ebony handle and a grey leather pocket-book and quietly slipped the two into the inside pocket of his jacket.

Germaine Astaing gazed at him in amazement: 'You're mad, monsieur! What right have you . . . ?'

'These things must not be left lying about. I shan't worry now. The magistrate will never look for them in my pocket.'

'But I shall denounce you to the police,' she exclaimed, indignantly. 'They shall be told!'

'No, no,' he said, laughing, 'you won't say anything! The police have nothing to do with this. The quarrel between you must be settled in private. What an idea, to go dragging the police into every incident of one's life!'

Madame Astaing was choking with fury.

'But you have no right to talk like this, monsieur! Who are you, after all? A friend of that woman's?'

'Since you have been attacking her, yes.'

'But I'm only attacking her because she's guilty. For you can't deny it: she has killed her husband.'

'I don't deny it,' said Rénine, calmly. 'We are all agreed on that point. Jacques d'Ormeval was killed by his wife. But, I repeat, the police must not know the truth.'

'They shall know it through me, monsieur, I swear they shall. That woman must be punished: she has committed murder.'

Rénine went up to her and, touching her on the shoulder: 'You asked me just now by what right I was interfering. And you yourself, madame?'

'I was a friend of Jacques d'Ormeval.'

'Only a friend?'

She was a little taken aback, but at once pulled herself together and replied: 'I was his friend and it is my duty to avenge his death.'

'Nevertheless, you will remain silent, as he did.'

'He did not know, when he died.'

'That's where you are wrong. He could have accused his wife, if he had wished. He had ample time to accuse her; and he said nothing.'

'Why?'

'Because of his children.'

Madame Astaing was not appeased; and her attitude displayed the same longing for revenge and the same detestation. But she was influenced by Rénine in spite of herself. In the small, closed room, where there was such a clash of hatred, he was gradually becoming the master; and Germaine Astaing understood that it was against him that she had to struggle, while Madame d'Ormeval felt all the comfort of that unexpected support which was offering itself on the brink of the abyss.

'Thank you, monsieur,' she said. 'As you have seen all this so clearly, you also know that it was for my children's sake that I did not give myself up. But for that . . . I am so tired . . . !'

And so the scene was changing and things assuming a different aspect. Thanks to a few words let fall in the midst of the dispute, the culprit was lifting her head and taking heart, whereas her accuser was hesitating and seemed to be uneasy. And it also came about that the accuser dared not say anything further and that the culprit was nearing the moment at which the need is felt of breaking silence and of speaking, quite naturally, words that are at once a confession and a relief.

'The time, I think, has come,' said Rénine to Thérèse, with the same unvarying gentleness, 'when you can and ought to explain yourself.'

She was again weeping, lying huddled in a chair. She too revealed a face aged and ravaged by sorrow; and, in a very low voice, with no display of anger, she spoke, in short, broken sentences.

'She has been his mistress for the last four years . . . I can't tell you how I suffered . . . She herself told me of it . . . out of sheer wickedness . . . Her loathing for me was even greater than her love for Jacques . . . and every day I had some fresh injury to bear . . . She would ring me up to tell me of her appointments with my husband . . . she hoped to make me suffer so much I should end by killing myself . . . I did think of it sometimes, but I held out, for the children's sake . . . Jacques was weakening. She wanted him to get a divorce . . . and little by little he began to consent . . . dominated by her and by her brother, who is slyer than she is, but quite as dangerous . . . I felt all this . . . Jacques was becoming harsh to me . . . He had not the courage to leave me, but I was the obstacle and he bore me a grudge . . . Heavens, the tortures I suffered! . . . '

'You should have given him his liberty,' cried Germaine Astaing. 'A woman doesn't kill her husband for wanting a divorce.'

Thérèse shook her head and answered: 'I did not kill him because he wanted a divorce. If he had really wanted it, he would have left me; and what could I have done? But your plans had changed, Germaine;

divorce was not enough for you; and it was something else that you would have obtained from him, another, much more serious thing which you and your brother had insisted on . . . and to which he had consented . . . out of cowardice . . . in spite of himself . . . '

'What do you mean?' spluttered Germaine. 'What other thing?'

'My death.'

'You lie!' cried Madame Astaing.

Thérèse did not raise her voice. She made not a movement of aversion or indignation and simply repeated: 'My death, Germaine. I have read your latest letters, six letters from you which he was foolish enough to leave about in his pocket-book and which I read last night, six letters in which the terrible word is not set down, but in which it appears between every line. I trembled as I read it! That Jacques should come to this! . . . Nevertheless the idea of stabbing him did not occur to me for a second. A woman like myself, Germaine, does not readily commit murder . . . If I lost my head, it was after that . . . and it was your fault . . . '

She turned her eyes to Rénine as if to ask him if there was no danger in her speaking and revealing the truth.

'Don't be afraid,' he said. 'I will be answerable for everything.'

She drew her hand across her forehead. The horrible scene was being reenacted within her and was torturing her. Germaine Astaing did not move, but stood with folded arms and anxious eyes, while Hortense Daniel sat distractedly awaiting the confession of the crime and the explanation of the unfathomable mystery.

'It was after that and it was through your fault Germaine . . . I had put back the pocket-book in the drawer where it was hidden; and I said nothing to Jacques this morning . . . I did not want to tell him what I knew . . . It was too horrible . . . All the same, I had to act quickly; your letters announced your secret arrival today . . . I thought at first of running away, of taking the train . . . I had mechanically picked up that dagger, to defend myself . . . But when Jacques and I went down to the beach, I was resigned . . . Yes, I had accepted death: "I will die," I thought, "and put an end to all this nightmare!" . . . Only, for the children's sake, I was anxious that my death should look like an accident and that Jacques should have no part in it. That was why your plan of a walk on the cliff suited me . . . A fall from the top of a cliff seems quite natural . . . Jacques therefore left me to go to his cabin, from which he was to join you later at the Trois Mathildes. On the way, below the terrace, he dropped the key of the cabin. I went down and began to

look for it with him . . . And it happened then . . . through your
fault . . . yes, Germaine, through your fault . . . Jacques's pocket-
book had slipped from his jacket, without his noticing it, and,
together with the pocket-book, a photograph which I recognized at
once: a photograph, taken this year, of myself and my two children.
I picked it up . . . and I saw . . . You know what I saw, Germaine.
Instead of my face, the face in the photograph was *yours*! . . . You
had put in your likeness, Germaine, and blotted me out! It was
your face! One of your arms was round my elder daughter's neck;
and the younger was sitting on your knees . . . It was you, Germaine, the wife of my husband, the future mother of my children,
you, who were going to bring them up . . . you, you! . . . Then I lost
my head. I had the dagger . . . Jacques was stooping . . . I stabbed
him . . . '

Every word of her confession was strictly true. Those who listened
to her felt this profoundly; and nothing could have given Hortense
and Rénine a keener impression of tragedy.

She had fallen back into her chair, utterly exhausted. Nevertheless,
she went on speaking unintelligible words; and it was only gradually
by leaning over her, that they were able to make out.

'I thought that there would be an outcry and that I should be
arrested. But no. It happened in such a way and under such conditions that no one had seen anything. Further, Jacques had drawn
himself up at the same time as myself; and he actually did not fall.
No, he did not fall! I had stabbed him; and he remained standing! I
saw him from the terrace, to which I had returned. He had hung
his jacket over his shoulders, evidently to hide his wound, and he
moved away without staggering . . . or staggering so little that I
alone was able to perceive it. He even spoke to some friends who
were playing cards. Then he went to his cabin and disappeared . . .
In a few moments, I came back indoors. I was persuaded that all
of this was only a bad dream . . . that I had not killed him . . . or that
at the worst the wound was a slight one. Jacques would come
out again. I was certain of it . . . I watched from my balcony . . .
If I had thought for a moment that he needed assistance, I should
have flown to him . . . But truly I didn't know . . . I didn't guess . . .
People speak of presentiments: there are no such things. I was
perfectly calm, just as one is after a nightmare of which the memory
is fading away . . . No, I swear to you, I knew nothing . . . until the
moment . . . '

She interrupted herself, stifled by sobs.

Rénine finished her sentence for her,

'Until the moment when they came and told you, I suppose?'

Thérèse stammered: 'Yes. It was not till then that I was conscious of what I had done . . . and I felt that I was going mad and that I should cry out to all those people, "Why, it was I who did it! Don't search! Here is the dagger . . . I am the culprit!" Yes, I was going to say that, when suddenly I caught sight of my poor Jacques . . . They were carrying him along . . . His face was very peaceful, very gentle . . . And, in his presence, I understood my duty, as he had understood his . . . He had kept silent, for the sake of the children. I would be silent too. We were both guilty of the murder of which he was the victim; and we must both do all we could to prevent the crime from recoiling upon them . . . He had seen this clearly in his dying agony. He had had the amazing courage to keep his feet, to answer the people who spoke to him and to lock himself up to die. He had done this, wiping out all his faults with a single action, and in so doing had granted me his forgiveness, because he was not accusing me . . . and was ordering me to hold my peace . . . and to defend myself . . . against everybody . . . especially against you, Germaine.'

She uttered these last words more firmly. At first wholly over-whelmed by the unconscious act which she had committed in killing her husband, she had recovered her strength a little in thinking of what she had done and in defending herself with such energy. Faced by the intriguing woman whose hatred had driven both of them to death and crime, she clenched her fists, ready for the struggle, all quivering with resolution.

Germaine Astaing did not flinch. She had listened without a word, with a relentless expression which grew harder and harder as Thérèse's confessions became precise. No emotion seemed to soften her and no remorse to penetrate her being. At most, towards the end, her thin lips shaped themselves into a faint smile. She was holding her prey in her clutches.

Slowly, with her eyes raised to a mirror, she adjusted her hat and powdered her face. Then she walked to the door.

Thérèse darted forward.

'Where are you going?'

'Where I choose.'

'To see the examining-magistrate?'

'Very likely.'

'You shan't pass!'

'As you please. I'll wait for him here.'

'And you'll tell him what?'

'Why, all that you've said, of course, all that you've been silly enough to say. How could he doubt the story? You have explained it all to me so fully.'

Thérèse took her by the shoulders.

'Yes, but I'll explain other things to him at the same time, Germaine, things that concern you. If I'm ruined, so shall you be.'

'You can't touch me.'

'I can expose you, show your letters.'

'What letters?'

'Those in which my death was decided on.'

'Lies, Thérèse! You know that famous plot exists only in your imagination. Neither Jacques nor I wished for your death.'

'You did, at any rate. Your letters condemn you.'

'Lies! They were the letters of a friend to a friend.'

'Letters of a mistress to her paramour.'

'Prove it.'

'They are there, in Jacques's pocket-book.'

'No, they're not.'

'What's that you say?'

'I say that those letters belonged to me. I've taken them back, or rather my brother has.'

'You've stolen them, you wretch! And you shall give them back again,' cried Thérèse, shaking her.

'I haven't them. My brother kept them. He has gone.'

Thérèse staggered and stretched out her hands to Rénine with an expression of despair. Rénine said: 'What she says is true. I watched the brother's proceedings while he was feeling in your bag. He took out the pocket-book, looked through it with his sister, came and put it back again and went off with the letters.'

Rénine paused and added, 'Or, at least, with five of them.'

The two women moved closer to him. What did he intend to convey? If Frédéric Astaing had taken away only five letters, what had become of the sixth?

'I suppose,' said Rénine, 'that, when the pocket-book fell on the shingle, that sixth letter slipped out at the same time as the photograph and that M. d'Ormeval must have picked it up, for I found it in the pocket of his blazer, which had been hung up near the bed. Here it is. It's signed Germaine Astaing and it is quite enough to prove the writer's intentions and the murderous counsels which she was pressing upon her lover.'

Madame Astaing had turned grey in the face and was so much disconcerted that she did not try to defend herself. Rénine continued, addressing his remarks to her: 'To my mind, madame, you are responsible for all that happened. Penniless, no doubt, and at the end of your resources, you tried to profit by the passion with which you inspired M. d'Ormeval in order to make him marry you, in spite of all the obstacles, and to lay your hands upon his fortune. I have proofs of this greed for money and these abominable calculations and can supply them if need be. A few minutes after I had felt in the pocket of that jacket, you did the same. I had removed the sixth letter, but had left a slip of paper which you looked for eagerly and which also must have dropped out of the pocket-book. It was an uncrossed cheque for a hundred thousand francs, drawn by M. d'Ormeval in your brother's name . . . just a little wedding-present . . . what we might call pin-money. Acting on your instructions, your brother dashed off by motor to Le Havre to reach the bank before four o'clock. I may as well tell you that he will not have cashed the cheque, for I had a telephone-message sent to the bank to announce the murder of M. d'Ormeval, which stops all payments. The upshot of all this is that the police, if you persist in your schemes of revenge, will have in their hands all the proofs that are wanted against you and your brother. I might add, as an edifying piece of evidence, the story of the conversation which I overheard between your brother and yourself in a dining-car on the railway between Brest and Paris, a fortnight ago. But I feel sure that you will not drive me to adopt these extreme measures and that we understand each other. Isn't that so?'

Natures like Madame Astaing's, which are violent and headstrong so long as a fight is possible and while a gleam of hope remains, are easily swayed in defeat. Germaine was too intelligent not to grasp the fact that the least attempt at resistance would be shattered by such an adversary as this. She was in his hands. She could but yield.

She therefore did not indulge in any play-acting, nor in any demonstration such as threats, outbursts of fury or hysterics. She bowed.

'We are agreed,' she said. 'What are your terms?'

'Go away. If ever you are called upon for your evidence, say that you know nothing.'

She walked away. At the door, she hesitated and then, between her teeth, said: 'The cheque.'

Rénine looked at Madame d'Ormeval, who declared: 'Let her keep it. I would not touch that money.'

* * *

When Rénine had given Thérèse d'Ormeval precise instructions as to how she was to behave at the enquiry and to answer the questions put to her, he left the chalet, accompanied by Hortense Daniel.

On the beach below, the magistrate and the public prosecutor were continuing their investigations, taking measurements, examining the witnesses and generally laying their heads together.

'When I think,' said Hortense, 'that you have the dagger and M. d'Ormeval's pocket-book on you!'

'And it strikes you as awfully dangerous, I suppose?' he said, laughing. 'It strikes *me* as awfully comic.'

'Aren't you afraid?'

'Of what?'

'That they may suspect something?'

'Lord, they won't suspect a thing! We shall tell those good people what we saw and our evidence will only increase their perplexity, for we saw nothing at all. For prudence sake we will stay a day or two, to see which way the wind is blowing. But it's quite settled: they will never be able to make head or tail of the matter.'

'Nevertheless, *you* guessed the secret and from the first. Why?'

'Because, instead of seeking difficulties where none exist, as people generally do, I always put the question as it should be put; and the solution comes quite naturally. A man goes to his cabin and locks himself in. Half an hour later, he is found inside, dead. No one has gone in. What has happened? To my mind there is only one answer. There is no need to think about it. As the murder was not committed in the cabin, it must have been committed beforehand and the man was already mortally wounded when he entered his cabin. And forthwith the truth in this particular case appeared to me. Madame d'Ormeval, who was to have been killed this evening, forestalled her murderers and while her husband was stooping to the ground, in a moment of frenzy stabbed him in the back. There was nothing left to do but look for the reasons that prompted her action. When I knew them, I took her part unreservedly. That's the whole story.'

The day was beginning to wane. The blue of the sky was becoming darker and the sea, even more peaceful than before.

'What are you thinking of?' asked Rénine, after a moment.

'I am thinking,' she said, 'that if I too were the victim of some machination, I should trust you whatever happened, trust you through and against all. I know, as certainly as I know that I exist, that you would save me, whatever the obstacles might be. There is no limit to the power of your will.'

He said, very softly: 'There is no limit to my wish to please you.'

The Lady with the Hatchet

One of the most incomprehensible incidents that preceded the great war was certainly the one which was known as the episode of the lady with the hatchet. The solution of the mystery was unknown and would never have been known, had not circumstances in the cruellest fashion obliged Prince Rénine – or should I say, Arsène Lupin? – to take up the matter and had I not been able today to tell the true story from the details supplied by him.

Let me recite the facts. In a space of eighteen months, five women disappeared, five women of different stations in life, all between twenty and thirty years of age and living in Paris or the Paris district.

I will give their names: Madame Ladoue, the wife of a doctor; Mlle Ardant, the daughter of a banker; Mlle Covereau, a washer-woman of Courbevoie; Mlle Honorine Vernisset, a dressmaker; and Madame Grollinger, an artist. These five women disappeared without the possibility of discovering a single particular to explain why they had left their homes, why they did not return to them, who had enticed them away, and where and how they were detained.

Each of these women, a week after her departure, was found somewhere or other in the western outskirts of Paris; and each time it was a dead body that was found, the dead body of a woman who had been killed by a blow on the head from a hatchet. And each time, not far from the woman, who was firmly bound, her face covered with blood and her body emaciated by lack of food, the marks of carriage-wheels proved that the corpse had been driven to the spot.

The five murders were so much alike that there was only a single investigation, embracing all the five enquiries and, for that matter, leading to no result. A woman disappeared; a week later, to a day, her body was discovered; and that was all. The bonds that fastened her were similar in each case; so were the tracks left by the wheels; so were the blows of the hatchet, all of which were struck vertically at the top and right in the middle of the forehead.

The motive of the crime? The five women had been completely stripped of their jewels, purses and other objects of value. But the robberies might well have been attributed to marauders or any passers-by, since the bodies were lying in deserted spots. Were the authorities to believe in the execution of a plan of revenge or of a plan intended to do away with the series of persons mutually connected, persons, for instance, likely to benefit by a future inheritance? Here again the same obscurity prevailed. Theories were built up, only to be demolished forthwith by an examination of the facts. Trails were followed and at once abandoned.

And suddenly there was a sensation. A woman engaged in sweeping the roads picked up on the pavement a little note-book which she brought to the local police-station. The leaves of this note-book were all blank, excepting one, on which was written a list of the murdered women, with their names set down in order of date and accompanied by three figures: Ladoue, 132; Vernisset, 118; and so on.

Certainly no importance would have been attached to these entries, which anybody might have written, since everyone was acquainted with the sinister list. But, instead of five names, it included six! Yes, below the words 'Grollinger, 128,' there appeared 'Williamson, 114.' Did this indicate a sixth murder?

The obviously English origin of the name limited the field of the investigations, which did not in fact take long. It was ascertained that, a fortnight ago, a Miss Hermione Williamson, a governess in a family at Auteuil, had left her place to go back to England and that, since then, her sisters, though she had written to tell them that she was coming over, had heard no more of her.

A fresh enquiry was instituted. A postman found the body in the Meudon woods. Miss Williamson's skull was split down the middle.

I need not describe the public excitement at this stage nor the shudder of horror which passed through the crowd when it read this list, written without a doubt in the murderer's own hand. What could be more frightful than such a record, kept up to date like a careful tradesman's ledger?

'On such a day, I killed so-and-so; on such a day so-and-so!'

And the sum total was six dead bodies.

Against all expectation, the experts in handwriting had no difficulty in agreeing and unanimously declared that the writing was 'that of a woman, an educated woman, possessing artistic tastes, imagination and an extremely sensitive nature.' The 'lady with the hatchet', as the journalists christened her, was decidedly no ordinary person; and scores of newspaper-articles made a special study of her case, exposing her mental condition and losing themselves in far-fetched explanations.

Nevertheless it was the writer of one of these articles, a young journalist whose chance discovery made him the centre of public attention, who supplied the one element of truth and shed upon the darkness the only ray of light that was to penetrate it. In casting about for the meaning of the figures which followed the six names, he had come to ask himself whether those figures did not simply represent the number of the days separating one crime from the next. All that he had to do was to check the dates. He at once found that his theory was correct. Mlle Vernisset had been carried off one hundred and thirty-two days after Madame Ladoue; Mlle Covereau one hundred and eighteen days after Honorine Vernisset; and so on.

There was therefore no room for doubt; and the police had no choice but to accept a solution which so precisely fitted the circumstances: the figures corresponded with the intervals. There was no mistake in the records of the lady with the hatchet.

But then one deduction became inevitable. Miss Williamson, the latest victim, had been carried off on the 26th of June last, and her name was followed by the figures 114: was it not to be presumed that a fresh crime would be committed a hundred and fourteen days later, that is to say, on the 18th of October? Was it not probable that the horrible business would be repeated in accordance with the murderer's secret intentions? Were they not bound to pursue to its logical conclusion the argument which ascribed to the figures – to all the figures, to the last as well as to the others – their value as eventual dates?

Now it was precisely this deduction which was drawn and was being weighed and discussed during the few days that preceded the 18th of October, when logic demanded the performance of yet another act of the abominable tragedy. And it was only natural that, on the morning of that day, Prince Rénine and Hortense, when making an appointment by telephone for the evening, should allude to the newspaper-articles which they had both been reading.

'Look out!' said Rénine, laughing. 'If you meet the lady with the hatchet, take the other side of the road!'

'And, if the good lady carries me off, what am I to do?'

'Strew your path with little white pebbles and say, until the very moment when the hatchet flashes in the air, "I have nothing to fear;

he will save me.' *He* is myself . . . and I kiss your hands. Till this evening, my dear.'

That afternoon, Rénine had an appointment with Rose Andrée and Dalbrèque to arrange for their departure for the States.*

Before four and seven o'clock, he bought the different editions of the evening papers. None of them reported an abduction.

At nine o'clock he went to the Gymnase, where he had taken a private box.

At half-past nine, as Hortense had not arrived, he rang her up, though without thought of anxiety. The maid replied that Madame Daniel had not come in yet.

Seized with a sudden fear, Rénine hurried to the furnished flat which Hortense was occupying for the time being, near the Parc Monceau, and questioned the maid, whom he had engaged for her and who was completely devoted to him. The woman said that her mistress had gone out at two o'clock, with a stamped letter in her hand, saying that she was going to the post and that she would come back to dress. This was the last that had been seen of her.

'To whom was the letter addressed?'

'To you, sir. I saw the writing on the envelope: Prince Serge Rénine.'

He waited until midnight, but in vain. Hortense did not return; nor did she return next day.

'Not a word to anyone,' said Rénine to the maid. 'Say that your mistress is in the country and that you are going to join her.'

For his own part, he had not a doubt: Hortense's disappearance was explained by the very fact of the date, the 18th of October. She was the seventh victim of the lady with the hatchet.

* * *

'The abduction,' said Rénine to himself, 'precedes the blow of the hatchet by a week. I have, therefore, at the present moment, seven full days before me. Let us say six, to avoid any surprise. This is Saturday: Hortense must be set free by mid-day on Friday; and, to make sure of this, I must know her hiding-place by nine o'clock on Thursday evening at latest.'

Rénine wrote, 'THURSDAY EVENING, NINE O'CLOCK,' in big letters, on a card which he nailed above the mantelpiece in his study. Then at midday on Saturday, the day after the disappearance, he locked himself into the study, after telling his man not to disturb him except for meals and letters.

*See 'The Tell-tale Film'.

He spent four days there, almost without moving. He had immediately sent for a set of all the leading newspapers which had spoken in detail of the first six crimes. When he had read and re-read them, he closed the shutters, drew the curtains and lay down on the sofa in the dark, with the door bolted, thinking.

By Tuesday evening he was no further advanced than on the Saturday. The darkness was as dense as ever. He had not discovered the smallest clue for his guidance, nor could he see the slightest reason to hope.

At times, notwithstanding his immense power of self-control and his unlimited confidence in the resources at his disposal, at times he would quake with anguish. Would he arrive in time? There was no reason why he should see more clearly during the last few days than during those which had already elapsed. And this meant that Hortense Daniel would inevitably be murdered.

The thought tortured him. He was attached to Hortense by a much stronger and deeper feeling than the appearance of the relations between them would have led an onlooker to believe. The curiosity at the beginning, the first desire, the impulse to protect Hortense, to distract her, to inspire her with a relish for existence: all this had simply turned to love. Neither of them was aware of it, because they barely saw each other save at critical times when they were occupied with the adventures of others and not with their own. But, at the first onslaught of danger, Rénine realized the place which Hortense had taken in his life and he was in despair at knowing her to be a prisoner and a martyr and at being unable to save her.

He spent a feverish, agitated night, turning the case over and over from every point of view. The Wednesday morning was also a terrible time for him. He was losing ground. Giving up his hermit-like seclusion, he threw open the windows and paced to and fro through his rooms, ran out into the street and came in again, as though fleeing before the thought that obsessed him.

'Hortense is suffering . . . Hortense is in the depths . . . She sees the hatchet . . . She is calling to me . . . She is entreating me . . . And I can do nothing . . . '

It was at five o'clock in the afternoon that, on examining the list of the six names, he received that little inward shock which is a sort of signal of the truth that is being sought for. A light shot through his mind. It was not, to be sure, that brilliant light in which every detail is made plain, but it was enough to tell him in which direction to move.

His plan of campaign was formed at once. He sent Adolphe, his chauffeur, to the principal newspapers, with a few lines which were to appear in type among the next morning's advertisements. Adolphe was also told to go to the laundry at Courbevoie, where Mlle Covereau, the second of the six victims, had been employed.

On the Thursday, Rénine did not stir out of doors. In the afternoon, he received several letters in reply to his advertisement. Then two telegrams arrived. Lastly, at three o'clock, there came a pneumatic letter, bearing the Trocadéro postmark, which seemed to be what he was expecting.

He turned up a directory, noted an address – 'M. de Lourtier-Vaneau, retired colonial governor, 47 *bis*, Avenue Kléber' – and ran down to his car.

'Adolphe, 47 *bis*, Avenue Kléber.'

*   *   *

He was shown into a large study furnished with magnificent bookcases containing old volumes in costly bindings. M. de Lourtier-Vaneau was a man still in the prime of life, wearing a slightly grizzled beard and, by his affable manners and genuine distinction, commanding confidence and liking.

'M. de Lourtier,' said Rénine, 'I have ventured to call on your excellency because I read in last year's newspapers that you used to know one of the victims of the lady with the hatchet, Honorine Vernisset.'

'Why, of course we knew her!' cried M. de Lourtier. 'My wife used to employ her as a dressmaker by the day. Poor girl!'

'M. de Lourtier, a lady of my acquaintance has disappeared as the other six victims disappeared.

'What!' exclaimed M. de Lourtier, with a start. 'But I have followed the newspapers carefully. There was nothing on the 18th of October.'

'Yes, a woman of whom I am very fond, Madame Hortense Daniel, was abducted on the 17th of October.'

'And this is the 22nd!'

'Yes; and the murder will be committed on the 24th.'

'Horrible! Horrible! It must be prevented at all costs . . . '

'And I shall perhaps succeed in preventing it, with your excellency's assistance.'

'But have you been to the police?'

'No. We are faced by mysteries which are, so to speak, absolute and compact, which offer no gap through which the keenest eyes can see and which it is useless to hope to clear up by ordinary methods, such as inspection of the scenes of the crimes, police enquiries, searching for finger-prints and so on. As none of those proceedings served any good purpose in the previous cases, it would be waste of time to resort to them in a seventh, similar case. An enemy who displays such skill and subtlety would not leave behind her any of those clumsy traces which are the first things that a professional detective seizes upon.'

'Then what have you done?'

'Before taking any action, I have reflected. I gave four days to thinking the matter over.'

M. de Lourtier-Vaneau examined his visitor closely and, with a touch of irony, asked: 'And the result of your meditations . . . ?'

'To begin with,' said Rénine, refusing to be put out of countenance, 'I have submitted all these cases to a comprehensive survey, which hitherto no one else had done. This enabled me to discover their general meaning, to put aside all the tangle of embarrassing theories and, since no one was able to agree as to the motives of all this filthy business, to attribute it to the only class of persons capable of it.'

'That is to say?'

'Lunatics, your excellency.'

M. de Lourtier-Vaneau started.

'Lunatics? What an idea!'

'M. de Lourtier, the woman known as the lady with the hatchet is a madwoman.'

'But she would be locked up!'

'We don't know that she's not. We don't know that she is not one of those half-mad people, apparently harmless, who are watched so slightly that they have full scope to indulge their little manias, their wild-beast instincts. Nothing could be more treacherous than these creatures. Nothing could be more crafty, more patient, more persistent, more dangerous and at the same time more absurd and more logical, more slovenly and more methodical. All these epithets, M. de Lourtier, may be applied to the doings of the lady with the hatchet. The obsession of an idea and the continual repetition of an act are characteristics of the maniac. I do not yet know the idea by which the lady with the hatchet is obsessed but I do know the act that results from it; and it is always the same. The victim is bound with precisely similar ropes. She is killed after the same number of days. She is struck by an identical blow, with the same instrument, in the same place, the middle of the forehead, producing an absolutely vertical wound. An ordinary murderer displays some variety. His trembling hand swerves aside and strikes awry. The lady with the hatchet does not tremble. It is as though she had taken measurements; and the edge of her weapon does not swerve by a hair's breadth. Need I give you any further proofs or examine all the other details with you? Surely not. You now possess the key to the riddle; and you know as I do that only a lunatic can behave in this way, stupidly, savagely, mechanically, like a striking clock or the blade of the guillotine . . . '

M. de Lourtier-Vaneau nodded his head.

'Yes, that is so. One can see the whole affair from that angle . . . and I am beginning to believe that this is how one ought to see it. But, if we admit that this madwoman has the sort of mathematical logic which governed the murders of the six victims, I see no connection between the victims themselves. She struck at random. Why this victim rather than that?'

'Ah,' said Rénine. 'Your excellency is asking me a question which I asked myself from the first moment, the question which sums up the whole problem and which cost me so much trouble to solve! Why Hortense Daniel rather than another? Among two millions of women who might have been selected, why Hortense? Why little Vernisset? Why Miss Williamson? If the affair is such as I conceived it, as a whole, that is to say, based upon the blind and fantastic logic of a madwoman, a choice was inevitably exercised. Now in what did that choice consist? What was the quality, or the defect, or the sign needed to induce the lady with the hatchet to strike? In a word, if she chose – and she must have chosen – what directed her choice?'

'Have you found the answer?'

Rénine paused and replied: 'Yes, your excellency, I have. And I could have found it at the very outset, since all that I had to do was to make a careful examination of the list of victims. But these flashes of truth are never kindled save in a brain overstimulated by effort and reflection. I stared at the list twenty times over, before that little detail took a definite shape.'

'I don't follow you,' said M. de Lourtier-Vaneau.

'M. de Lourtier, it may be noted that, if a number of persons are brought together in any transaction, or crime, or public scandal or what not, they are almost invariably described in the same way. On this occasion, the newspapers never mentioned anything more than their surnames in speaking of Madame Ladoue, Mlle Ardent or Mlle Covereau. On the other hand, Mlle Vernisset and Miss Williamson were always described by their Christian names as well: Honorine and Hermione. If the same thing had been done in the case of all the six victims, there would have been no mystery.'

'Why not?'

'Because we should at once have realized the relation existing between the six unfortunate women, as I myself suddenly realized it on comparing those two Christian names with that of Hortense Daniel. You understand now, don't you? You see the three Christian names before your eyes . . . '

M. de Lourtier-Vaneau seemed to be perturbed. Turning a little pale, he said: 'What do you mean? What do you mean?'

'I mean,' continued Rénine, in a clear voice, sounding each syllable separately, 'I mean that you see before your eyes three Christian names which all three begin with the same initial and which all three, by a remarkable coincidence, consist of the same number of letters, as you may prove. If you enquire at the Courbevoie laundry, where Mlle Covereau used to work, you will find that her name was Hilairie. Here again we have the same initial and the same number of letters. There is no need to seek any farther. We are sure, are we not, that the Christian names of all the victims offer the same peculiarities? And this gives us, with absolute certainty, the key to the problem which was set us. It explains the madwoman's choice. We now know the connection between the unfortunate victims. There can be no mistake about it. It's that and nothing else. And how this method of choosing confirms my theory! What proof of madness! Why kill these women rather than any others? Because their names begin with an H and consist of eight letters! You understand me, M. de Lourtier, do you not? The number of letters is eight. The initial letter is the eighth letter of the alphabet; and the word *huit*, eight, begins with an H. Always the letter H. *And the implement used to commit the crime was a hatchet.* Is your excellency prepared to tell me that the lady with the hatchet is not a madwoman?'

Rénine interrupted himself and went up to M. de Lourtier-Vaneau.

'What's the matter, your excellency? Are you unwell?'

'No, no,' said M. de Lourtier, with the perspiration streaming down his forehead. 'No . . . but all this story is so upsetting! Only think, I knew one of the victims! And then . . . '

Rénine took a water-bottle and tumbler from a small table, filled the glass and handed it to M. de Lourtier, who sipped a few mouthfuls from it and then, pulling himself together, continued, in a voice which he strove to make firmer than it had been: 'Very well. We'll admit your supposition. Even so, it is necessary that it should lead to tangible results. What have you done?'

'This morning I published in all the newspapers an advertisement worded as follows: "Excellent cook seeks situation. Write before 5 p.m. to Herminie, Boulevard Haussmann, etc." You continue to follow me, don't you, M. de Lourtier? Christian names beginning with an H and consisting of eight letters are extremely rare and are all rather out of date: Herminie, Hilairie, Hermione. Well, these Christian names, for reasons which I do not understand, are essential to the madwoman. She cannot do without them. To find women bearing one of these Christian names and for this purpose only she summons up all her remaining powers of reason, discernment, reflection and intelligence. She hunts about. She asks questions. She lies in wait. She reads newspapers which she hardly understands, but in which certain details, certain capital letters catch her eye. And consequently I did not doubt for a second that this name of Herminie, printed in large type, would attract her attention and that she would be caught today in the trap of my advertisement.'

'Did she write?' asked M. de Lourtier-Vaneau, anxiously.

'Several ladies,' Rénine continued, 'wrote the letters which are usual in such cases, to offer a home to the so-called Herminie. But I received an express letter which struck me as interesting.'

'From whom?'

'Read it, M. de Lourtier.'

M. de Lourtier-Vaneau snatched the sheet from Rénine's hands and cast a glance at the signature. His first movement was one of surprise, as though he had expected something different. Then he gave a long, loud laugh of something like joy and relief.

'Why do you laugh, M. de Lourtier? You seem pleased.'

'Pleased, no. But this letter is signed by my wife.'

'And you were afraid of finding something else?'

'Oh no! But since it's my wife . . . '

He did not finish his sentence and said to Rénine: 'Come this way.'

He led him through a passage to a little drawing-room where a fair-haired lady, with a happy and tender expression on her comely face, was sitting in the midst of three children and helping them with their lessons.

She rose. M. de Lourtier briefly presented his visitor and asked his wife: 'Suzanne, is this express message from you?'

'To Mlle Herminie, Boulevard Haussmann? Yes,' she said, 'I sent it. As you know, our parlour-maid's leaving and I'm looking out for a new one.'

Rénine interrupted her.

'Excuse me, madame. Just one question: where did you get the woman's address?'

She flushed. Her husband insisted.

'Tell us, Suzanne. Who gave you the address?'

'I was rung up.'

'By whom?'

She hesitated and then said: 'Your old nurse.'

'Félicienne?'

'Yes.'

M. de Lourtier cut short the conversation and, without permitting Rénine to ask any more questions, took him back to the study.

'You see, monsieur, that pneumatic letter came from a quite natural source. Félicienne, my old nurse, who lives not far from Paris on an allowance which I make her, read your advertisement and told Madame de Lourtier of it. For, after all,' he added laughing, 'I don't suppose that you suspect my wife of being the lady with the hatchet.'

'No.'

'Then the incident is closed . . . at least on my side. I have done what I could, I have listened to your arguments and I am very sorry that I can be of no more use to you . . .'

He drank another glass of water and sat down. His face was distorted. Rénine looked at him for a few seconds, as a man will look at a failing adversary who has only to receive the knock-out blow, and, sitting down beside him, suddenly gripped his arm.

'Your excellency, if you do not speak, Hortense Daniel will be the seventh victim.'

'I have nothing to say, monsieur! What do you think I know?'

'The truth! My explanations have made it plain to you. Your distress, your terror are positive proofs.'

'But, after all, monsieur, if I knew, why should I be silent?'

'For fear of scandal. There is in your life, so a profound intuition assures me, something that you are constrained to hide. The truth about this monstrous tragedy, which suddenly flashed upon you, this truth, if it were known, would spell dishonour to you, disgrace . . . and you are shrinking from your duty.'

M. de Lourtier did not reply. Rénine leant over him and, looking him in the eyes, whispered: 'There will be no scandal. I shall be the only person in the world to know what has happened. And I am as much interested as yourself in not attracting attention, because I love Hortense Daniel and do not wish her name to be mixed up in your horrible story.'

They remained face to face during a long interval. Rénine's expression was harsh and unyielding. M. de Lourtier felt that nothing would bend him if the necessary words remained unspoken; but he could not bring himself to utter them.

'You are mistaken,' he said. 'You think you have seen things that don't exist.'

Rénine received a sudden and terrifying conviction that, if this man took refuge in a stolid silence, there was no hope for Hortense Daniel; and he was so much infuriated by the thought that the key to the riddle lay there, within reach of his hand, that he clutched M. de Lourtier by the throat and forced him backwards.

'I'll have no more lies! A woman's life is at stake! Speak . . . and speak at once! If not . . . !'

M. de Lourtier had no strength left in him. All resistance was impossible. It was not that Rénine's attack alarmed him, or that he was yielding to this act of violence, but he felt crushed by that indomitable will, which seemed to admit no obstacle, and he stammered: 'You are right. It is my duty to tell everything, whatever comes of it.'

'Nothing will come of it, I pledge my word, on condition that you save Hortense Daniel. A moment's hesitation may undo us all. Speak. No details, but the actual facts.'

'Madame de Lourtier is not my wife. The only woman who has the right to bear my name is one whom I married when I was a young colonial official. She was a rather eccentric woman, of feeble mentality and incredibly subject to impulses that amounted to monomania. We had two children, twins, whom she worshipped and in whose company she would no doubt have recovered her mental balance and moral health, when, by a stupid accident – a passing carriage – they were killed before her eyes. The poor thing went mad . . . with the silent, secretive madness which you imagined. Some time afterwards, when I was appointed to an Algerian station, I brought her to France and put her in the charge of a worthy creature who had nursed me and brought me up. Two years later, I made the acquaintance of the woman who was to become the joy of my life. You saw her just now. She is the mother of my children and she passes as my wife. Are we to sacrifice her? Is our whole existence to be shipwrecked in horror and must our name be coupled with this tragedy of madness and blood?'

Rénine thought for a moment and asked: 'What is the other one's name?'

'Hermance.'

'Hermance! Still that initial . . . still those eight letters!'

'That was what made me realize everything just now,' said M. de Lourtier. 'When you compared the different names, I at once reflected that my unhappy wife was called Hermance and that she was mad . . . and all the proofs leapt to my mind.'

'But, though we understand the selection of the victims, how are we to explain the murders? What are the symptoms of her madness? Does she suffer at all?'

'She does not suffer very much at present. But she has suffered in the past, the most terrible suffering that you can imagine: since the moment when her two children were run over before her eyes, night and day she had the horrible spectacle of their death before her eyes, without a moment's interruption, for she never slept for a single second. Think of the torture of it! To see her children dying through all the hours of the long day and all the hours of the interminable night!'

'Nevertheless,' Rénine objected, 'it is not to drive away that picture that she commits murder?'

'Yes, possibly,' said M. de Lourtier, thoughtfully, 'to drive it away by sleep.'

'I don't understand.'

'You don't understand, because we are talking of a madwoman . . . and because all that happens in that disordered brain is necessarily incoherent and abnormal?'

'Obviously. But, all the same, is your supposition based on facts that justify it?'

'Yes, on facts which I had, in a way, overlooked but which today assume their true significance. The first of these facts dates a few years back, to a morning when my old nurse for the first time found Hermance fast asleep. Now she was holding her hands clutched around a puppy which she had strangled. And the same thing was repeated on three other occasions.'

'And she slept?'

'Yes, each time she slept a sleep which lasted for several nights.'

'And what conclusion did you draw?'

'I concluded that the relaxation of the nerves provoked by taking life exhausted her and predisposed her for sleep.'

Rénine shuddered.

'That's it! There's not a doubt of it! The taking life, the effort of killing makes her sleep. And she began with women what had served her so well with animals. All her madness has become concentrated on that one point: she kills them to rob them of their sleep! She wanted sleep; and she steals the sleep of others! That's it, isn't it? For the past two years, she has been sleeping?'

'For the past two years, she has been sleeping,' stammered M. de Lourtier.

Rénine gripped him by the shoulder.

'And it never occurred to you that her madness might go farther, that she would stop at nothing to win the blessing of sleep! Let us make haste, monsieur! All this is horrible!'

They were both making for the door, when M. de Lourtier hesitated. The telephone-bell was ringing.

'It's from there,' he said.

'From there?'

'Yes, my old nurse gives me the news at the same time every day.'

He unhooked the receivers and handed one to Rénine, who whispered in his ear the questions which he was to put.

'Is that you, Félicienne? How is she?'

'Not so bad, sir.'

'Is she sleeping well?'

'Not very well, lately. Last night, indeed, she never closed her eyes. So she's very gloomy just now.'

'What is she doing at the moment?'

'She is in her room.'

'Go to her, Félicienne, and don't leave her.'

'I can't. She's locked herself in.'

'You must, Félicienne. Break open the door. I'm coming straight on . . . Hullo! Hullo! . . . Oh, damnation, they've cut us off!'

Without a word, the two men left the flat and ran down to the avenue. Rénine hustled M. de Lourtier into the car.

'What address?'

'Ville d'Avray.'

'Of course! In the very center of her operations . . . like a spider in the middle of her web! Oh, the shame of it!'

He was profoundly agitated. He saw the whole adventure in its monstrous reality.

'Yes, she kills them to steal their sleep, as she used to kill the animals. It is the same obsession, but complicated by a whole array of utterly incomprehensible practices and superstitions. She evidently fancies that the similarity of the Christian names to her own is indispensable and that she will not sleep unless her victim is an Hortense or an Honorine. It's a madwoman's argument; its logic escapes us and we know nothing of its origin; but we can't get away from it. She has to hunt and has to find. And she finds and carries off her prey beforehand and watches over it for the appointed number of days, until the moment when, crazily, through the hole which she digs with a hatchet in the middle of the skull, she absorbs the sleep which stupefies her and grants her oblivion for a given period. And here again we see absurdity and madness. Why does she fix that period at so many days? Why should one victim ensure her a hundred and twenty days of sleep and another a hundred and twenty-five? What insanity! The calculation is mysterious and of course mad; but the fact remains that, at the end of a hundred or a hundred and twenty-five days, as the case may be, a fresh victim is sacrificed; and there have been six already and the seventh is awaiting her turn. Ah, monsieur, what a terrible responsibility for you! Such a monster as that! She should never have been allowed out of sight!'

M. de Lourtier-Vaneau made no protest. His air of dejection, his pallor, his trembling hands, all proved his remorse and his despair: 'She deceived me,' he murmured. 'She was outwardly so quiet, so docile! And, after all, she's in a lunatic asylum.'

'Then how can she . . . ?'

'The asylum,' explained M. de Lourtier, 'is made up of a number of separate buildings scattered over extensive grounds. The sort of cottage in which Hermance lives stands quite apart. There is first a room occupied by Félicienne, then Hermance's bedroom and two separate rooms, one of which has its windows overlooking the open country. I suppose it is there that she locks up her victims.'

'But the carriage that conveys the dead bodies?'

'The stables of the asylum are quite close to the cottage. There's a horse and carriage there for station work. Hermance no doubt gets up at night, harnesses the horse and slips the body through the window.'

'And the nurse who watches her?'

'Félicienne is very old and rather deaf.'

'But by day she sees her mistress moving to and fro, doing this and that. Must we not admit a certain complicity?'

'Never! Félicienne herself has been deceived by Hermance's hypocrisy.'

'All the same, it was she who telephoned to Madame de Lourtier first, about that advertisement . . . '

'Very naturally. Hermance, who talks now and then, who argues, who buries herself in the newspapers, which she does not understand, as you were saying just now, but reads through them attentively, must have seen the advertisement and, having heard that we were looking for a servant, must have asked Félicienne to ring me up.'

'Yes . . . yes . . . that is what I felt,' said Rénine, slowly. 'She marks down her victims . . . With Hortense dead, she would have known, once she had used up her allowance of sleep, where to find an eighth victim . . . But how did she entice the unfortunate women? How did she entice Hortense?'

The car was rushing along, but not fast enough to please Rénine, who rated the chauffeur.

'Push her along, Adolphe, can't you? . . . We're losing time, my man.'

Suddenly the fear of arriving too late began to torture him. The logic of the insane is subject to sudden changes of mood, to any perilous idea that may enter the mind. The madwoman might easily mistake the date and hasten the catastrophe, like a clock out of order which strikes an hour too soon.

On the other hand, as her sleep was once more disturbed, might she not be tempted to take action without waiting for the appointed moment? Was this not the reason why she had locked herself into her room? Heavens, what agonies her prisoner must be suffering! What shudders of terror at the executioner's least movement!

'Faster, Adolphe, or I'll take the wheel myself! Faster, hang it.'

At last they reached Ville d'Avray. There was a steep, sloping road on the right and walls interrupted by a long railing.

'Drive round the grounds, Adolphe. We mustn't give warning of our presence, must we, M. de Lourtier? Where is the cottage?'

'Just opposite,' said M. de Lourtier-Vaneau.

They got out a little farther on. Rénine began to run along a bank at the side of an ill-kept sunken road. It was almost dark. M. de Lourtier said: 'Here, this building standing a little way back . . . Look at that window on the ground-floor. It belongs to one of the separate rooms . . . and that is obviously how she slips out.'

'But the window seems to be barred.'

'Yes; and that is why no one suspected anything. But she must have found some way to get through.'

The ground-floor was built over deep cellars. Rénine quickly clambered up, finding a foothold on a projecting ledge of stone.

Sure enough, one of the bars was missing.

He pressed his face to the window-pane and looked in.

The room was dark inside. Nevertheless he was able to distinguish at the back a woman seated beside another woman, who was lying on a mattress. The woman seated was holding her forehead in her hands and gazing at the woman who was lying down.

'It's she,' whispered M. de Lourtier, who had also climbed the wall. 'The other one is bound.'

Rénine took from his pocket a glazier's diamond and cut out one of the panes without making enough noise to arouse the madwoman's attention. He next slid his hand to the window-fastening and turned it softly, while with his left hand he levelled a revolver.

'You're not going to fire, surely!' M. de Lourtier-Vaneau entreated.

'If I must, I shall.'

Rénine pushed open the window gently. But there was an obstacle of which he was not aware, a chair which toppled over and fell.

He leapt into the room and threw away his revolver in order to seize the madwoman. But she did not wait for him. She rushed to the door, opened it and fled, with a hoarse cry.

M. de Lourtier made as though to run after her.

'What's the use?' said Rénine, kneeling down, 'Let's save the victim first.'

He was instantly reassured: Hortense was alive.

The first thing that he did was to cut the cords and remove the gag that was stifling her. Attracted by the noise, the old nurse had hastened to the room with a lamp, which Rénine took from her, casting its light on Hortense.

He was astounded: though livid and exhausted, with emaciated features and eyes blazing with fever, Hortense was trying to smile. She whispered: 'I was expecting you . . . I did not despair for a moment . . . I was sure of you . . . '

She fainted.

An hour later, after much useless searching around the cottage, they found the madwoman locked into a large cupboard in the loft. She had hanged herself.

* * *

Hortense refused to stay another night. Besides, it was better that the cottage should be empty when the old nurse announced the madwoman's suicide. Rénine gave Félicienne minute directions as to what she should do and say; and then, assisted by the chauffeur and M. de Lourtier, carried Hortense to the car and brought her home.

She was soon convalescent. Two days later, Rénine carefully questioned her and asked her how she had come to know the madwoman.

'It was very simple,' she said. 'My husband, who is not quite sane, as I have told you, is being looked after at Ville d'Avray; and I sometimes go to see him, without telling anybody, I admit. That was how I came to speak to that poor madwoman and how, the other day, she made signs that she wanted me to visit her. We were alone. I went into the cottage. She threw herself upon me and overpowered me before I had time to cry for help. I thought it was a jest; and so it was, wasn't it: a madwoman's jest? She was quite gentle with me . . . All the same, she let me starve. But I was so sure of you!'

'And weren't you frightened?'

'Of starving? No. Besides, she gave me some food, now and then, when the fancy took her . . . And then I was sure of you!'

'Yes, but there was something else: that other peril . . . '

'What other peril?' she asked, ingenuously.

Rénine gave a start. He suddenly understood – it seemed strange at first, though it was quite natural – that Hortense had not for a moment suspected and did not yet suspect the terrible danger which she had run. Her mind had not connected with her own adventure the murders committed by the lady with the hatchet.

He thought that it would always be time enough to tell her the truth. For that matter, a few days later her husband, who had been locked up for years, died in the asylum at Ville d'Avray, and Hortense, who had been recommended by her doctor a short period of rest and solitude, went to stay with a relation living near the village of Bassicourt, in the centre of France.

Footprints in the Snow

To Prince Serge Rénine
Boulevard Haussmann
Paris

La Roncière
near Bassicourt
14 November

MY DEAR FRIEND –

You must be thinking me very ungrateful. I have been here three weeks; and you have had not one letter from me! Not a word of thanks! And yet I ended by realizing from what terrible death you saved me and understanding the secret of that terrible business! But indeed, indeed I couldn't help it! I was in such a state of prostration after it all! I needed rest and solitude so badly! Was I to stay in Paris? Was I to continue my expeditions with you? No, no, no! I had had enough adventures! Other people's are very interesting, I admit. But when one is oneself the victim and barely escapes with one's life? . . . Oh, my dear friend, how horrible it was! Shall I ever forget it? . . .

Here, at la Roncière, I enjoy the greatest peace. My old spinster cousin Ermelin pets and coddles me like an invalid. I am getting back my colour and am very well, physically . . . so much so, in fact, that I no longer ever think of interesting myself in other people's business. Never again! For instance (I am only telling you this because you are incorrigible, as inquisitive as any old charwoman, and always ready to busy yourself with things that don't concern you), yesterday I was present at a rather curious meeting. Antoinette had taken me to the inn at Bassicourt, where we were having tea in the public room, among the peasants (it was market-day), when the arrival of three people, two men and a woman, caused a sudden pause in the conversation.

One of the men was a fat farmer in a long blouse, with a jovial, red face, framed in white whiskers. The other was younger, was dressed in corduroy and had lean, yellow, cross-grained features. Each of them carried a gun slung over his shoulder. Between them was a short, slender young woman, in a brown cloak and a fur cap, whose rather thin and extremely pale face was surprisingly delicate and distinguished-looking.

'Father, son and daughter-in-law,' whispered my cousin.

'What! Can that charming creature be the wife of that clodhopper?'

'And the daughter-in-law of Baron de Gorne.'

'Is the old fellow over there a baron?'

'Yes, descended from a very ancient, noble family which used to own the château in the old days. He has always lived like a peasant: a great hunter, a great drinker, a great litigant, always at law with somebody, now very nearly ruined. His son Mathias was more ambitious and less attached to the soil and studied for the bar. Then he went to America. Next, the lack of money brought him back to the village, whereupon he fell in love with a young girl in the nearest town. The poor girl consented, no one knows why, to marry him; and for five years past she has been leading the life of a hermit, or rather of a prisoner, in a little manor-house close by, the Manoir-au-Puits, the Well Manor.'

'With the father and the son?' I asked.

'No, the father lives at the far end of the village, on a lonely farm.'

'And is Master Mathias jealous?'

'A perfect tiger!'

'Without reason?'

'Without reason, for Natalie de Gorne is the straightest woman in the world and it is not her fault if a handsome young man has been hanging around the manor-house for the past few months. However, the de Gornes can't get over it.'

'What, the father neither?'

'The handsome young man is the last descendant of the people who bought the château long ago. This explains old de Gorne's hatred. Jérôme Vignal – I know him and am very fond of him – is a good-looking fellow and very well off; and he has sworn to run off with Natalie de Gorne. It's the old man who says so, whenever he has had a drop too much. There, listen!'

The old chap was sitting among a group of men who were amusing themselves by making him drink and plying him with

questions. He was already a little bit 'on' and was holding forth
with a tone of indignation and a mocking smile which formed the
most comic contrast.

'He's wasting his time, I tell you, the coxcomb! It's no manner
of use his poaching round our way and making sheep's-eyes at
the wench . . . The coverts are watched! If he comes too near, it
means a bullet, eh, Mathias?'

He gripped his daughter-in-law's hand.

'And then the little wench knows how to defend herself too,'
he chuckled. 'Eh, you don't want any admirers, do you Natalie?'

The young wife blushed, in her confusion at being addressed
in these terms, while her husband growled: 'You'd do better to
hold your tongue, father. There are things one doesn't talk about
in public.'

'Things that affect one's honour are best settled in public,'
retorted the old one. 'Where I'm concerned, the honour of the
de Gornes comes before everything; and that fine spark, with his
Paris airs, shan't . . .'

He stopped short. Before him stood a man who had just come
in and who seemed to be waiting for him to finish his sentence.
The newcomer was a tall, powerfully-built young fellow, in
riding-kit, with a hunting-crop in his hand. His strong and
rather stern face was lighted up by a pair of fine eyes in which
shone an ironical smile.

'Jérôme Vignal,' whispered my cousin.

The young man seemed not at all embarrassed. On seeing
Natalie, he made a low bow; and, when Mathias de Gorne took a
step forward, he eyed him from head to foot, as though to say:
'Well, what about it?'

And his attitude was so haughty and contemptuous that the de
Gornes unslung their guns and took them in both hands, like
sportsmen about to shoot. The son's expression was very fierce.

Jérôme was quite unmoved by the threat. After a few seconds,
turning to the inn-keeper, he remarked: 'Oh, I say! I came to see
old Vasseur. But his shop is shut. Would you mind giving him
the holster of my revolver? It wants a stitch or two.'

He handed the holster to the inn-keeper and added, laughing:
'I'm keeping the revolver, in case I need it. You never can tell!'

Then, still very calmly, he took a cigarette from a silver case, lit
it and walked out. We saw him through the window vaulting on
his horse and riding off at a slow trot.

Old de Gorne tossed off a glass of brandy, swearing most horribly.

His son clapped his hand to the old man's mouth and forced him to sit down. Natalie de Gorne was weeping beside them . . .

That's my story, dear friend. As you see, it's not tremendously interesting and does not deserve your attention. There's no mystery in it and no part for you to play. Indeed, I particularly insist that you should not seek a pretext for any untimely inter-ference. Of course, I should be glad to see the poor thing pro-tected: she appears to be a perfect martyr. But, as I said before, let us leave other people to get out of their own troubles and go no farther with our little experiments . . .

* * *

Rénine finished reading the letter, read it over again and ended by saying: 'That's it. Everything's right as right can be. She doesn't want to continue our little experiments, because this would make the seventh and because she's afraid of the eighth, which under the terms of our agreement has a very particular significance. She doesn't want to . . . and she does want to . . . without seeming to want to.'

* * *

He rubbed his hands. The letter was an invaluable witness to the influence which he had gradually, gently and patiently gained over Hortense Daniel. It betrayed a rather complex feeling, composed of admiration, unbounded confidence, uneasiness at times, fear and almost terror, but also love: he was convinced of that. His com-panion in adventures which she shared with a good fellowship that excluded any awkwardness between them, she had suddenly taken fright; and a sort of modesty, mingled with a certain coquetry, was impelling her to hold back.

That very evening, Sunday, Rénine took the train.

And, at break of day, after covering by diligence, on a road white with snow, the five miles between the little town of Pompignat, where he alighted, and the village of Bassicourt, he learnt that his journey might prove of some use: three shots had been heard during the night in the direction of the Manoir-au-Puits.

'Three shots, sergeant. I heard them as plainly as I see you standing before me,' said a peasant whom the gendarmes were questioning in the parlour of the inn which Rénine had entered.

'So did I,' said the waiter. 'Three shots. It may have been twelve o'clock at night. The snow, which had been falling since nine, had stopped . . . and the shots sounded across the fields, one after the other: bang, bang, bang.'

Five more peasants gave their evidence. The sergeant and his men had heard nothing, because the police-station backed on the fields. But a farm-labourer and a woman arrived, who said that they were in Mathias de Gorne's service, that they had been away for two days because of the intervening Sunday and that they had come straight from the manor-house, where they were unable to obtain admission.

'The gate of the grounds is locked, sergeant,' said the man. 'It's the first time I've known this to happen. M. Mathias comes out to open it himself, every morning at the stroke of six, winter and summer. Well, it's past eight now. I called and shouted. Nobody answered. So we came on here.'

'You might have enquired at old M. de Gorne's,' said the sergeant. 'He lives on the high-road.'

'On my word, so I might! I never thought of that.'

'We'd better go there now,' the sergeant decided. Two of his men went with him, as well as the peasants and a locksmith whose services were called into requisition. Rénine joined the party.

Soon, at the end of the village, they reached old de Gorne's farmyard, which Rénine recognized by Hortense's description of its position.

The old fellow was harnessing his horse and trap. When they told him what had happened, he burst out laughing.

'Three shots? Bang, bang, bang? Why, my dear sergeant, there are only two barrels to Mathias' gun!'

'What about the locked gate?'

'It means that the lad's asleep, that's all. Last night, he came and cracked a bottle with me . . . perhaps two . . . or even three; and he'll be sleeping it off, I expect . . . he and Natalie.'

He climbed on to the box of his trap – an old cart with a patched tilt – and cracked his whip.

'Goodbye, gentlemen all. Those three shots of yours won't stop me from going to market at Pompignat, as I do every Monday. I've a couple of calves under the tilt; and they're just fit for the butcher. Good-day to you!'

The others walked on. Rénine went up to the sergeant and gave him his name.

'I'm a friend of Mlle Ermelin, of La Roncière; and, as it's too early
to call on her yet, I shall be glad if you'll allow me to go round by the
manor with you. Mlle Ermelin knows Madame de Gorne; and it will
be a satisfaction to me to relieve her mind, for there's nothing wrong
at the manor-house, I hope?'

'If there is,' replied the sergeant, 'we shall read all about it as
plainly as on a map, because of the snow.'

He was a likeable young man and seemed smart and intelligent.
From the very first he had shown great acuteness in observing the
tracks which Mathias had left behind him, the evening before, on
returning home, tracks which soon became confused with the footprints made in going and coming by the farm-labourer and the
woman. Meanwhile they came to the walls of a property of which the
locksmith readily opened the gate.

From here onward, a single trail appeared upon the spotless
snow, that of Mathias; and it was easy to perceive that the son must
have shared largely in the father's libations, as the line of footprints
described sudden curves which made it swerve right up to the trees
of the avenue.

Two hundred yards farther stood the dilapidated two-storeyed
building of the Manoir-au-Puits. The principal door was open.

'Let's go in,' said the sergeant.

And, the moment he had crossed the threshold, he muttered:
'Oho! Old de Gorne made a mistake in not coming. They've been
fighting in here.'

The big room was in disorder. Two shattered chairs, the over-
turned table and much broken glass and china bore witness to the
violence of the struggle. The tall clock, lying on the ground, had
stopped at twenty past eleven.

With the farm-girl showing them the way, they ran up to the first
floor. Neither Mathias nor his wife was there. But the door of their
bedroom had been broken down with a hammer which they discovered under the bed.

Rénine and the sergeant went downstairs again. The living-room
had a passage communicating with the kitchen, which lay at the
back of the house and opened on a small yard fenced off from the
orchard. At the end of this enclosure was a well near which one was
bound to pass.

Now, from the door of the kitchen to the well, the snow, which was
not very thick, had been pressed down to this side and that, as though
a body had been dragged over it. And all around the well were tangled

traces of trampling feet, showing that the struggle must have been resumed at this spot. The sergeant again discovered Mathias' footprints, together with others which were shapelier and lighter.

These latter went straight into the orchard, by themselves. And, thirty yards on, near the footprints, a revolver was picked up and recognized by one of the peasants as resembling that which Jérôme Vignal had produced in the inn two days before.

The sergeant examined the cylinder. Three of the seven bullets had been fired.

And so the tragedy was little by little reconstructed in its main outlines; and the sergeant, who had ordered everybody to stand aside and not to step on the site of the footprints, came back to the well, leant over, put a few questions to the farm-girl and, going up to Rénine, whispered: 'It all seems fairly clear to me.'

Rénine took his arm.

'Let's speak out plainly, sergeant. I understand the business pretty well, for, as I told you, I know Mlle Ermelin, who is a friend of Jérôme Vignal's and also knows Madame de Gorne. Do you suppose . . . ?'

'I don't want to suppose anything. I simply declare that someone came there last night . . . '

'By which way? The only tracks of a person coming towards the manor are those of M. de Gorne.'

'That's because the other person arrived before the snowfall, that is to say, before nine o'clock.'

'Then he must have hidden in a corner of the living-room and waited for the return of M. de Gorne, who came after the snow?'

'Just so. As soon as Mathias came in, the man went for him. There was a fight. Mathias made his escape through the kitchen. The man ran after him to the well and fired three revolver-shots.'

'And where's the body?'

'Down the well.'

Rénine protested.

'Oh, I say! Aren't you taking a lot for granted?'

'Why, sir, the snow's there, to tell the story; and the snow plainly says that, after the struggle, after the three shots, one man alone walked away and left the farm, one man only, and his footprints are not those of Mathias de Gorne. Then where can Mathias de Gorne be?'

'But the well . . . can be dragged?'

'No. The well is practically bottomless. It is known all over the district and gives its name to the manor.'

'So you really believe . . . ?'

'I repeat what I said. Before the snowfall, a single arrival, Mathias, and a single departure, the stranger.'

'And Madame de Gorne? Was she too killed and thrown down the well like her husband?'

'No, carried off.'

'Carried off?'

'Remember that her bedroom was broken down with a hammer.'

'Come, come, sergeant! You yourself declare that there was only one departure, the stranger's.'

'Stoop down. Look at the man's footprints. See how they sink into the snow, until they actually touch the ground. Those are the footprints of a man, laden with a heavy burden. The stranger was carrying Madame de Gorne on his shoulder.'

'Then there's an outlet this way?'

'Yes, a little door of which Mathias de Gorne always had the key on him. The man must have taken it from him.'

'A way out into the open fields?'

'Yes, a road which joins the departmental highway three quarters of a mile from here . . . And do you know where?'

'Where?'

'At the corner of the château.'

'Jérôme Vignal's château?'

'By Jove, this is beginning to look serious! If the trail leads to the château and stops there, we shall know where we stand.'

The trail did continue to the château, as they were able to perceive after following it across the undulating fields, on which the snow lay heaped in places. The approach to the main gates had been swept, but they saw that another trail, formed by the two wheels of a vehicle, was running in the opposite direction to the village.

The sergeant rang the bell. The porter, who had also been sweeping the drive, came to the gates, with a broom in his hand. In answer to a question, the man said that M. Vignal had gone away that morning before anyone else was up and that he himself had harnessed the horse to the trap.

'In that case,' said Rénine, when they had moved away, 'all we have to do is to follow the tracks of the wheels.'

'That will be no use,' said the sergeant. 'They have taken the railway.'

'At Pompignat station, where I came from? But they would have passed through the village.'

'They have gone just the other way, because it leads to the town, where the express trains stop. The procurator-general has an office in the town. I'll telephone; and, as there's no train before eleven o'clock, all that they need do is to keep a watch at the station.'

'I think you're doing the right thing, sergeant,' said Rénine, 'and I congratulate you on the way in which you have carried out your investigation.'

They parted. Rénine went back to the inn in the village and sent a note to Hortense Daniel by hand.

MY VERY DEAREST FRIEND,

I seemed to gather from your letter that, touched as always by anything that concerns the heart, you were anxious to protect the love-affair of Jérôme and Natalie. Now there is every reason to suppose that these two, without consulting their fair protectress, have run away, after throwing Mathias de Gorne down a well.

Forgive me for not coming to see you. The whole thing is extremely obscure; and, if I were with you, I should not have the detachment of mind which is needed to think the case over.

It was then half-past ten. Rénine went for a walk into the country, with his hands clasped behind his back and without vouchsafing a glance at the exquisite spectacle of the white meadows. He came back for lunch, still absorbed in his thoughts and indifferent to the talk of the customers of the inn, who on all sides were discussing recent events.

He went up to his room and had been asleep some time when he was awakened by a tapping at the door. He got up and opened it.

'Is it you? . . . Is it you?' he whispered.

Hortense and he stood gazing at each other for some seconds in silence, holding each other's hands, as though nothing, no irrelevant thought and no utterance, must be allowed to interfere with the joy of their meeting. Then he asked: 'Was I right in coming?'

'Yes,' she said, gently, 'I expected you.'

'Perhaps it would have been better if you had sent for me sooner, instead of waiting . . . Events did not wait, you see, and I don't quite know what's to become of Jérôme Vignal and Natalie de Gorne.'

'What, haven't you heard?' she said, quickly. 'They've been arrested. They were going to travel by the express.'

'Arrested? No.' Rénine objected. 'People are not arrested like that. They have to be questioned first.'

'That's what's being done now. The authorities are making a search.'

'Where?'

'At the château. And, as they are innocent . . . For they are innocent, aren't they? You don't admit that they are guilty, any more than I do?'

He replied: 'I admit nothing, I can admit nothing, my dear. Nevertheless, I am bound to say that everything is against them . . . except one fact, which is that everything is too much against them. It is not normal for so many proofs to be heaped up one on top of the other and for the man who commits a murder to tell his story so frankly. Apart from this, there's nothing but mystery and discrepancy.'

'Well?'

'Well, I am greatly puzzled.'

'But you have a plan?'

'None at all, so far. Ah, if I could see him, Jérôme Vignal, and her, Natalie de Gorne, and hear them and know what they are saying in their own defence! But you can understand that I shan't be permitted either to ask them any questions or to be present at their examination. Besides, it must be finished by this time.'

'It's finished at the château,' she said, 'but it's going to be continued at the manor-house.'

'Are they taking them to the manor-house?' he asked eagerly.

'Yes . . . at least, judging by what was said to the chauffeur of one of the procurator's two cars.'

'Oh, in that case,' exclaimed Rénine, 'the thing's done! The manor-house! Why, we shall be in the front row of the stalls! We shall see and hear everything; and, as a word, a tone of the voice, a quiver of the eyelids will be enough to give me the tiny clue I need, we may entertain some hope. Come along.'

He took her by the direct route which he had followed that morning, leading to the gate which the locksmith had opened. The gendarmes on duty at the manor-house had made a passage through the snow, beside the line of footprints and around the house. Chance enabled Rénine and Hortense to approach unseen and through a side-window to enter a corridor near a back-staircase. A few steps up was a little chamber which received its only light through a sort of bull's-eye, from the large room on the ground-floor. Rénine, during the morning visit, had noticed the bull's-eye, which was covered on the inside with a piece of cloth. He removed the cloth and cut out one of the panes.

A few minutes later, a sound of voices rose from the other side of the house, no doubt near the well. The sound grew more distinct. A number of people flocked into the house. Some of them went upstairs to the first floor, while the sergeant arrived with a young man of whom Rénine and Hortense were able to distinguish only the tall figure.

'Jérôme Vignal,' said she.

'Yes,' said Rénine. 'They are examining Madame de Gorne first, upstairs, in her bedroom.'

A quarter of an hour passed. Then the persons on the first floor came downstairs and went in. They were the procurator's deputy, his clerk, a commissary of police and two detectives.

Madame de Gorne was shown in and the deputy asked Jérôme Vignal to step forward.

Jérôme Vignal's face was certainly that of the strong man whom Hortense had depicted in her letter. He displayed no uneasiness, but rather decision and a resolute will. Natalie, who was short and very slight, with a feverish light in her eyes, nevertheless produced the same impression of quiet confidence.

The deputy, who was examining the disordered furniture and the traces of the struggle, invited her to sit down and said to Jérôme: 'Monsieur, I have not asked you many questions so far. This is a summary enquiry which I am conducting in your presence and which will be continued later by the examining-magistrate; and I wished above all to explain to you the very serious reasons for which I asked you to interrupt your journey and to come back here with Madame de Gorne. You are now in a position to refute the truly distressing charges that are hanging over you. I therefore ask you to tell me the exact truth.'

'Mr Deputy,' replied Jérôme, 'the charges in question trouble me very little. The truth for which you are asking will defeat all the lies which chance has accumulated against me. It is this.'

He reflected for an instant and then, in clear, frank tones, said: 'I love Madame de Gorne. The first time I met her, I conceived the greatest sympathy and admiration for her. But my affection has always been directed by the sole thought of her happiness. I love her, but I respect her even more. Madame de Gorne must have told you and I tell you again that she and I exchanged our first few words last night.'

He continued, in a lower voice: 'I respect her the more inasmuch as she is exceedingly unhappy. All the world knows that every minute of her life was a martyrdom. Her husband persecuted her with ferocious hatred and frantic jealousy. Ask the servants. They will tell you of the long suffering of Natalie de Gorne, of the blows which she received and the insults which she had to endure. I tried to stop this torture by resorting to the rights of appeal which the merest stranger may claim when unhappiness and injustice pass a certain limit. I went three times to old de Gorne and begged him to interfere; but I found in him an almost equal hatred towards his daughter-in-law, the hatred which many people feel for anything beautiful and noble. At last I resolved on direct action and last night I took a step with regard to Mathias de Gorne which was . . . a little unusual, I admit, but which seemed likely to succeed, considering the man's character. I swear, Mr Deputy, that I had no other intention than to talk to Mathias de Gorne. Knowing certain particulars of his life which enabled me to bring effective pressure to bear upon him, I wished to make use of this advantage in order to achieve my purpose. If things turned out differently, I am not wholly to blame . . . So I went there a little before nine o'clock. The servants, I knew, were out. He opened the door himself. He was alone.'

'Monsieur,' said the deputy, interrupting him, 'you are saying something – as Madame de Gorne, for that matter, did just now – which is manifestly opposed to the truth. Mathias de Gorne did not come home last night until eleven o'clock. We have two definite proofs of this: his father's evidence and the prints of his feet in the snow, which fell from a quarter past nine o'clock to eleven.'

'Mr Deputy,' Jérôme Vignal declared, without heeding the bad effect which his obstinacy was producing, 'I am relating things as they were and not as they may be interpreted. But to continue. That clock marked ten minutes to nine when I entered this room. M. de Gorne, believing that he was about to be attacked, had taken down his gun. I placed my revolver on the table, out of reach of my hand, and sat down: "I want to speak to you, monsieur," I said. "Please listen to me." He did not stir and did not utter a single syllable. So I spoke. And straightway, crudely, without any previous explanations which might have softened the bluntness of my proposal, I spoke the few words which I had prepared beforehand: "I have spent some months, monsieur," I said, "in making careful enquiries into your financial position. You have mortgaged every foot of your land. You have signed bills which will shortly be falling due and which it will be absolutely impossible for you to honour. You have nothing to hope for from your father, whose own affairs are in a very bad condition. So you are ruined. I have come to save you." . . . He watched me, still without speaking, and sat down, which I took to mean that my suggestion was not entirely displeasing. Then I took a sheaf of bank-notes from my pocket, placed it before him and continued: "Here is sixty thousand francs, monsieur. I will buy the Manoir-au-Puits, its lands and dependencies and take over the mortgages. The sum named is exactly twice what they are worth." . . . I saw his eyes glittering. He asked my conditions. "Only one," I said, "that you go to America." . . . Mr Deputy, we sat discussing for two hours. It was not that my offer roused his indignation – I should not have risked it if I had not known with whom I was dealing – but he wanted more and haggled greedily, though he refrained from mentioning the name of Madame de Gorne, to whom I myself had not once alluded. We might have been two men engaged in a dispute and seeking an agreement on common ground, whereas it was the happiness and the whole destiny of a woman that were at stake. At last, weary of the discussion, I accepted a compromise and we came to terms, which I resolved to make definite then and there. Two letters were exchanged between us: one in which he made the Manoir-au-Puits over to me for the sum which I had paid him; and one, which he pocketed immediately, by which I was to send him as much more in America on the day on which the decree of divorce was pronounced . . . So the affair was settled. I am sure that at that moment he was accepting in good faith. He looked upon me less as an enemy and a rival than as a man who was doing him a service. He even went so far as to give me the key of the little door which opens on the fields, so that I might go home by the short cut. Unfortunately, while I was picking up my cap and greatcoat, I made the mistake of leaving on the table the letter of sale which he had signed. In a moment, Mathias de Gorne had seen the advantage which he could take of my slip: he could keep his property, keep his wife . . . and keep the money. Quick as lightning, he tucked away the paper, hit me over the head with the butt-end of his gun, threw the gun on the floor and seized me by the throat with both hands. He had reckoned without his host. I was the stronger of the two; and after a sharp but short struggle, I mastered him and tied him up with a cord which I found lying in a corner . . . Mr Deputy, if my enemy's resolve was sudden, mine was no less so. Since, when all was said, he had accepted the bargain, I would force him to keep it, at least in so far as I was interested. A very few steps brought me to the first floor . . . I had not a doubt that Madame de Gorne was there and had heard the sound of our discussion. Switching on the light of my pocket-torch, I looked into three bedrooms. The fourth was locked. I knocked at the door. There was no reply. But this was one of the moments in which a man allows no obstacle to stand in his way. I had seen a hammer in one of the rooms. I picked it up and smashed in the door . . . Yes, Natalie was lying there, on the floor, in a dead faint. I took her in my arms, carried her downstairs and went through the kitchen. On seeing the snow outside, I at once realized that my footprints would be easily traced. But what did it matter? Was there any reason why I should put Mathias de Gorne off the scent? Not at all. With the sixty thousand francs in his possession, as well as the paper in which I undertook to pay him a like sum on the day of his divorce, to say nothing of his house and land, he would go away, leaving Natalie de Gorne to me. Nothing was changed between us, except one thing: instead of awaiting his good pleasure, I had at once seized the precious pledge which I coveted. What I feared, therefore, was not so much any subsequent attack on the part of Mathias de Gorne, but rather the indignant reproaches of his wife. What would she say when she realized that she was a prisoner in my hands? . . . The reasons why I escaped reproach Madame de Gorne has, I believe, had the frankness to tell you. Love calls forth love. That night, in my house, broken by emotion, she confessed her feeling for me. She loved me as I loved her. Our destinies were henceforth mingled. She and I set out at five o'clock this morning . . . not foreseeing for an instant that we were amenable to the law.'

Jérôme Vignal's story was finished. He had told it straight off the reel, like a story learnt by heart and incapable of revision in any detail.

There was a brief pause, during which Hortense whispered: 'It all sounds quite possible and, in any case, very logical.'

'There are the objections to come,' said Rénine. 'Wait till you hear them. They are very serious. There's one in particular . . . '

The deputy-procurator stated it at once.

'And what became of M. de Gorne in all this?'

'Mathias de Gorne?' asked Jérôme.

'Yes. You have related, with an accent of great sincerity, a series of facts which I am quite willing to admit. Unfortunately, you have forgotten a point of the first importance: what became of Mathias de

Gorne? You tied him up here, in this room. Well, this morning he was gone.'

'Of course, Mr Deputy, Mathias de Gorne accepted the bargain in the end and went away.'

'By what road?'

'No doubt by the road that leads to his father's house.'

'Where are his footprints? The expanse of snow is an impartial witness. After your fight with him, we see you, on the snow, moving away. Why don't we see him? He came and did not go away again. Where is he? There is not a trace of him . . . or rather . . . '

The deputy lowered his voice.

'Or rather, yes, there are some traces on the way to the well and around the well . . . traces which prove that the last struggle of all took place there . . . And after that there is nothing . . . not a thing . . . '

Jérôme shrugged his shoulders.

'You have already mentioned this, Mr Deputy, and it implies a charge of homicide against me. I have nothing to say to it.'

'Have you anything to say to the fact that your revolver was picked up within fifteen yards of the well?'

'No.'

'Or to the strange coincidence between the three shots heard in the night and the three cartridges missing from your revolver?'

'No, Mr Deputy, there was not, as you believe, a last struggle by the well, because I left M. de Gorne tied up, in this room, and because I also left my revolver here. On the other hand, if shots were heard, they were not fired by me.'

'A casual coincidence, therefore?'

'That's a matter for the police to explain. My only duty is to tell the truth and you are not entitled to ask more of me.'

'And if that truth conflicts with the facts observed?'

'It means that the facts are wrong, Mr Deputy.'

'As you please. But, until the day when the police are able to make them agree with your statements, you will understand that I am obliged to keep you under arrest.'

'And Madame de Gorne?' asked Jérôme, greatly distressed.

The deputy did not reply. He exchanged a few words with the commissary of police and then, beckoning to a detective, ordered him to bring up one of the two motor-cars. Then he turned to Natalie.

'Madame, you have heard M. Vignal's evidence. It agrees word for word with your own. M. Vignal declares in particular that you had fainted when he carried you away. But did you remain unconscious all the way?'

It seemed as though Jérôme's composure had increased Madame de Gorne's assurance. She replied: 'I did not come to, monsieur, until I was at the château.'

'It's most extraordinary. Didn't you hear the three shots which were heard by almost everyone in the village?'

'I did not.'

'And did you see nothing of what happened beside the well?'

'Nothing did happen. M. Vignal has told you so.'

'Then what has become of your husband?'

'I don't know.'

'Come, madame, you really must assist the officers of the law and at least tell us what you think. Do you believe that there may have been an accident and that possibly M. de Gorne, who had been to see his father and had more to drink than usual, lost his balance and fell into the well?'

'When my husband came back from seeing his father, he was not in the least intoxicated.'

'His father, however, has stated that he was. His father and he had drunk two or three bottles of wine.'

'His father is not telling the truth.'

'But the snow tells the truth, madame,' said the deputy, irritably. 'And the line of his footprints wavers from side to side.'

'My husband came in at half-past-eight, monsieur, before the snow had begun to fall.'

The deputy struck the table with his fist.

'But, really, madame, you're going right against the evidence! . . . That sheet of snow cannot speak false! . . . I may accept your denial of matters that cannot be verified. But these footprints in the snow . . . in the snow . . . '

He controlled himself.

The motor-car drew up outside the windows. Forming a sudden resolve, he said to Natalie: 'You will be good enough to hold yourself at the disposal of the authorities, madame, and to remain here, in the manor-house . . . '

And he made a sign to the sergeant to remove Jérôme Vignal in the car.

The game was lost for the two lovers. Barely united, they had to separate and to fight, far away from each other, against the most grievous accusations.

Jérôme took a step towards Natalie. They exchanged a long, sorrowful look. Then he bowed to her and walked to the door, in the wake of the sergeant of gendarmes.

'Halt!' cried a voice. 'Sergeant, right about . . . turn! . . . Jérôme Vignal, stay where you are!'

The ruffled deputy raised his head, as did the other people present. The voice came from the ceiling. The bulls-eye window had opened and Rénine, leaning through it, was waving his arms.

'I wish to be heard! . . . I have several remarks to make . . . especially in respect of the zigzag footprints! . . . It all lies in that! . . . Mathias had not been drinking! . . . '

He had turned round and put his two legs through the opening, saying to Hortense, who tried to prevent him.

'Don't move . . . No one will disturb you.'

And, releasing his hold, he dropped into the room.

The deputy appeared dumbfounded.

'But, really, monsieur, who are you? Where do you come from?'

Rénine brushed the dust from his clothes and replied: 'Excuse me, Mr Deputy. I ought to have come the same way as everybody else. But I was in a hurry. Besides, if I had come in by the door instead of falling from the ceiling, my words would not have made the same impression.'

The infuriated deputy advanced to meet him.

'Who are you?'

'Prince Rénine. I was with the sergeant this morning when he was pursuing his investigations, wasn't I, sergeant? Since then I have been hunting about for information. That's why, wishing to be present at the hearing, I found a corner in a little private room . . . '

'You were there? You had the audacity? . . . '

'One must needs be audacious, when the truth's at stake. If I had not been there, I should not have discovered just the one little clue which I missed. I should not have known that Mathias de Gorne was not the least bit drunk. Now that's the key to the riddle. When we know that, we know the solution.'

The deputy found himself in a rather ridiculous position. Since he had failed to take the necessary precautions to ensure the secrecy of his enquiry, it was difficult for him to take any steps against this interloper. He growled: 'Let's have done with this. What are you asking?'

'A few minutes of your kind attention.'

'And with what object?'

'To establish the innocence of M. Vignal and Madame de Gorne.'

He was wearing that calm air, that sort of indifferent look which was peculiar to him in moments of actions when the crisis of the drama depended solely upon himself. Hortense felt a thrill pass through her and at once became full of confidence.

'They're saved,' she thought, with sudden emotion. 'I asked him to protect that young creature; and he is saving her from prison and despair.'

Jérôme and Natalie must have experienced the same impression of sudden hope, for they had drawn nearer to each other, as though this stranger, descended from the clouds, had already given them the right to clasp hands.

The deputy shrugged his shoulders.

'The prosecution will have every means, when the time comes, of establishing their innocence for itself. You will be called.'

'It would be better to establish it here and now. Any delay might lead to grievous consequences.'

'I happen to be in a hurry.'

'Two or three minutes will do.'

'Two or three minutes to explain a case like this!'

'No longer, I assure you.'

'Are you as certain of it as all that?'

'I am now. I have been thinking hard since this morning.'

The deputy realized that this was one of those gentry who stick to you like a leech and that there was nothing for it but to submit. In a rather bantering tone, he asked: 'Does your thinking enable you to tell us the exact spot where M. Mathias de Gorne is at this moment?'

Rénine took out his watch and answered: 'In Paris, Mr Deputy.'

'In Paris? Alive then?'

'Alive and, what is more, in the pink of health.'

'I am delighted to hear it. But then what's the meaning of the footprints around the well and the presence of that revolver and those three shots?'

'Simply camouflage.'

'Oh, really? Camouflage contrived by whom?'

'By Mathias de Gorne himself.'

'That's curious! And with what object?'

'With the object of passing himself off for dead and of arranging subsequent matters in such a way that M. Vignal was bound to be accused of the death, the murder.'

'An ingenious theory,' the deputy agreed, still in a satirical tone. 'What do you think of it, M. Vignal?'

'It is a theory which flashed through my own mind. Mr Deputy,' replied Jérôme. 'It is quite likely that, after our struggle and after I had gone, Mathias de Gorne conceived a new plan by which, this time, his hatred would be fully gratified. He both loved and detested his wife. He held me in the greatest loathing. This must be his revenge.'

'His revenge would cost him dear, considering that, according to your statement, Mathias de Gorne was to receive a second sum of sixty thousand francs from you.'

'He would receive that sum in another quarter, Mr Deputy. My examination of the financial position of the de Gorne family revealed to me the fact that the father and son had taken out a life-insurance policy in each other's favour. With the son dead, or passing for dead, the father would receive the insurance-money and indemnify his son.'

'You mean to say,' asked the deputy, with a smile, 'that in all this camouflage, as you call it, M. de Gorne the elder would act as his son's accomplice?'

Rénine took up the challenge.

'Just so, Mr Deputy. The father and son are accomplices.

'Then we shall find the son at the father's?'

'You would have found him there last night.'

'What became of him?'

'He took the train at Pompignat.'

'That's a mere supposition.'

'No, a certainty.'

'A moral certainty, perhaps, but you'll admit there's not the slightest proof.'

The deputy did not wait for a reply. He considered that he had displayed an excessive goodwill and that patience has its limits and he put an end to the interview.

'Not the slightest proof,' he repeated, taking up his hat. 'And, above all, . . . above all, there's nothing in what you've said that can contradict in the very least the evidence of that relentless witness, the snow. To go to his father, Mathias de Gorne must have left this house. Which way did he go?'

'Hang it all, M. Vignal told you: by the road which leads from here to his father's!'

'There are no tracks in the snow.'

'Yes, there are.'

'But they show him coming here and not going away from here.'

'It's the same thing.'

'What?'

'Of course it is. There's more than one way of walking. One doesn't always go ahead by following one's nose.'

'In what other way can one go ahead?'

'By walking backwards, Mr Deputy.'

These few words, spoken very simply, but in a clear tone which gave full value to every syllable, produced a profound silence. Those present at once grasped their extreme significance and, by adapting it to the actual happenings, perceived in a flash the impenetrable truth, which suddenly appeared to be the most natural thing in the world.

Rénine continued his argument. Stepping backwards in the direction of the window, he said: 'If I want to get to that window, I can of course walk straight up to it; but I can just as easily turn my back to it and walk that way. In either case I reach my goal.'

And he at once proceeded in a vigorous tone: 'Here's the gist of it all. At half-past eight, before the snow fell, M. de Gorne comes home from his father's house. M. Vignal arrives twenty minutes later. There is a long discussion and a struggle, taking up three hours in all. It is then, after M. Vignal has carried off Madame de Gorne and made his escape, that Mathias de Gorne, foaming at the mouth, wild with rage, but suddenly seeing his chance of taking the most terrible revenge, hits upon the ingenious idea of using against his enemy the very snowfall upon whose evidence you are now relying. He therefore plans his own murder, or rather the appearance of his murder and of his fall to the bottom of the well and makes off backwards, step by step, thus recording his arrival instead of his departure on the white page.'

The deputy sneered no longer. This eccentric intruder suddenly appeared to him in the light of a person worthy of attention, whom it would not do to make fun of. He asked: 'And how could he have left his father's house?'

'In a trap, quite simply.'

'Who drove it?'

'The father. This morning the sergeant and I saw the trap and spoke to the father, who was going to market as usual. The son was hidden under the tilt. He took the train at Pompignat and is in Paris by now.'

Rénine's explanation, as promised, had taken hardly five minutes. He had based it solely on logic and the probabilities of the case. And yet not a jot was left of the distressing mystery in which they were floundering. The darkness was dispelled. The whole truth appeared.

Madame de Gorne wept for joy and Jérôme Vignal thanked the good genius who was changing the course of events with a stroke of his magic wand.

'Shall we examine those footprints together, Mr Deputy?' asked Rénine. 'Do you mind? The mistake which the sergeant and I made this morning was to investigate only the footprints left by the alleged murderer and to neglect Mathias de Gorne's. Why indeed should they have attracted our attention? Yet it was precisely there that the crux of the whole affair was to be found.'

They stepped into the orchard and went to the well. It did not need a long examination to observe that many of the footprints were awkward, hesitating, too deeply sunk at the heel and toe and differing from one another in the angle at which the feet were turned.

'This clumsiness was unavoidable,' said Rénine. 'Mathias de Gorne would have needed a regular apprenticeship before his backward progress could have equalled his ordinary gait; and both his father and he must have been aware of this, at least as regards the zigzags which you see here since old de Gorne went out of his way to tell the sergeant that his son had had too much drink.' And he added 'Indeed it was the detection of this falsehood that suddenly enlightened me. When Madame de Gorne stated that her husband was not drunk, I thought of the footprints and guessed the truth.'

The deputy frankly accepted his part in the matter and began to laugh.

'There's nothing left for it but to send detectives after the bogus corpse.'

'On what grounds, Mr Deputy?' asked Rénine. 'Mathias de Gorne has committed no offence against the law. There's nothing criminal in trampling the soil around a well, in shifting the position of a revolver that doesn't belong to you, in firing three shots or in walking backwards to one's father's house. What can we ask of him? The sixty thousand francs? I presume that this is not M. Vignal's intention and that he does not mean to bring a charge against him?'

'Certainly not,' said Jérôme.

'Well, what then? The insurance-policy in favour of the survivor? But there would be no misdemeanour unless the father claimed payment. And I should be greatly surprised if he did . . . Hullo, here the old chap is! You'll soon know all about it.'

Old de Gorne was coming along, gesticulating as he walked. His easy-going features were screwed up to express sorrow and anger.

'Where's my son?' he cried. 'It seems the brute's killed him! . . . My poor Mathias dead! Oh, that scoundrel of a Vignal!'

And he shook his fist at Jérôme.

The deputy said, bluntly: 'A word with you, M. de Gorne. Do you intend to claim your rights under a certain insurance-policy?'

'Well, what do *you* think?' said the old man, off his guard.

'The fact is . . . your son's not dead. People are even saying that you were a partner in his little schemes and that you stuffed him under the tilt of your trap and drove him to the station.'

The old fellow spat on the ground, stretched out his hand as though he were going to take a solemn oath, stood for an instant without moving and then, suddenly, changing his mind and his tactics with ingenuous cynicism, he relaxed his features, assumed a conciliatory attitude and burst out laughing.

'That blackguard Mathias! So he tried to pass himself off as dead? What a rascal! And he reckoned on me to collect the insurance-money and send it to him? As if I should be capable of such a low, dirty trick! . . . You don't know me, my boy!'

And, without waiting for more, shaking with merriment like a jolly old fellow amused by a funny story, he took his departure, not forgetting, however, to set his great hob-nail boots on each of the compromising footprints which his son had left behind him.

* * *

Later, when Rénine went back to the manor to let Hortense out, he found that she had disappeared.

He called and asked for her at her cousin Ermelin's. Hortense sent down word asking him to excuse her: she was feeling a little tired and was lying down.

'Capital!' thought Rénine. 'Capital! She avoids me, therefore she loves me. The end is not far off.'

At the Sign of Mercury

To Madame Daniel
La Roncière
near Bassicourt

Paris 30 November

My dear Friend –
There has been no letter from you for a fortnight; so I don't expect
now to receive one for that troublesome date of the 5th of December, which we fixed as the last day of our partnership. I rather wish
it would come, because you will then be released from a contract
which no longer seems to give you pleasure. To me the seven
battles which we fought and won together were a time of endless
delight and enthusiasm. I was living beside you. I was conscious of
all the good which that more active and stirring existence was
doing you. My happiness was so great that I dared not speak of it
to you or let you see anything of my secret feelings except my
desire to please you and my passionate devotion. Today you have
had enough of your brother in arms. Your will shall be law.

But, though I bow to your decree, may I remind I you what it
was that I always believed our final adventure would be? May I
repeat your words, not one of which I have forgotten?

'I demand,' you said, 'that you shall restore to me a small,
antique clasp, made of a cornelian set in a filigree mount. It came
to me from my mother; and everyone knew that it used to bring
her happiness and me too. Since the day when it vanished from
my jewel-case, I have had nothing but unhappiness. Restore it to
me, my good genius.'

And, when I asked you when the clasp had disappeared, you
answered, with a laugh: 'Seven years ago . . . or eight . . . or nine:
I don't know exactly . . . I don't know when . . . I don't know
how . . . I know nothing about it . . . '

You were challenging me, were you not, and you set me that
condition because it was one which I could not fulfil? Nevertheless,

I promised and I should like to keep my promise. What I have tried to do, in order to place life before you in a more favourable light, would seem purposeless, if your confidence feels the lack of this talisman to which you attach so great a value. We must not laugh at these little superstitions. They are often the mainspring of our best actions.

Dear friend, if you had helped me, I should have achieved yet one more victory. Alone and hard pushed by the proximity of the date, I have failed, not however without placing things on such a footing that the undertaking, if you care to follow it up, has the greatest chance of success.

And you will follow it up, won't you? We have entered into a mutual agreement which we are bound to honour. It behooves us, within a fixed time, to inscribe in the book of our common life eight good stories, to which we shall have brought energy, logic, perseverance, some subtlety and occasionally a little heroism. This is the eighth of them. It is for you to act so that it may be written in its proper place on the 5th of December, before the clock strikes eight in the evening.

And, on that day, you will act as I shall now tell you.

First of all – and above all, my dear, do not complain that my instructions are fanciful: each of them is an indispensable condition of success – first of all, cut in your cousin's garden three slender lengths of rush. Plait them together and bind up the two ends so as to make a rude switch, like a child's whiplash.

When you get to Paris, buy a long necklace of jet beads, cut into facets, and shorten it so that it consists of seventy-five beads, of almost equal size.

Under your winter cloak, wear a blue woollen gown. On your head, a toque with red leaves on it. Round your neck, a feather boa. No gloves. No rings.

In the afternoon, take a cab along the left bank of the river to the church of Saint-Étienne-du-Mont. At four o'clock exactly, there will be, near the holy-water basin, just inside the church, an old woman dressed in black, saying her prayers on a silver rosary. She will offer you holy water. Give her your necklace. She will count the beads and hand it back to you. After this, you will walk behind her, you will cross an arm of the Seine and she will lead you, down a lonely street in the Île Saint-Louis, to a house which you will enter by yourself.

On the ground-floor of this house, you will find a youngish man with a very pasty complexion. Take off your cloak and then say to him: 'I have come to fetch my clasp.'

Do not be astonished by his agitation or dismay. Keep calm in his presence. If he questions you, if he wants to know your reason for applying to him or what impels you to make that request, give him no explanation. Your replies must be confined to these brief formulas: 'I have come to fetch what belongs to me. I don't know you, I don't know your name; but I am obliged to come to you like this. I must have my clasp returned to me. I must.'

I honestly believe that, if you have the firmness not to swerve from that attitude, whatever farce the man may play, you will be completely successful. But the contest must be a short one and the issue will depend solely on your confidence in yourself and your certainty of success. It will be a sort of match in which you must defeat your opponent in the first round. If you remain impassive, you will win. If you show hesitation or uneasiness, you can do nothing against him. He will escape you and regain the upper hand after a first moment of distress; and the game will be lost in a few minutes. There is no midway house between victory or . . . defeat.

In the latter event, you would be obliged – I beg you to pardon me for saying so – again to accept my collaboration. I offer it you in advance, my dear, and without any conditions, while stating quite plainly that all that I have been able to do for you and all that I may yet do gives me no other right than that of thanking you and devoting myself more than ever to the woman who represents my joy, my whole life.

* * *

Hortense, after reading the letter, folded it up and put it away at the back of a drawer, saying, in a resolute voice: 'I shan't go.'

To begin with, although she had formerly attached some slight importance to this trinket, which she had regarded as a mascot, she felt very little interest in it now that the period of her trials was apparently at an end. She could not forget that figure eight, which was the serial number of the next adventure. To launch herself upon it meant taking up the interrupted chain, going back to Rénine and giving him a pledge which, with his powers of suggestion, he would know how to turn to account.

Two days before the 5th of December, she was still in the same frame of mind. So she was on the morning of the 4th; but suddenly, without even having to contend against preliminary subterfuges, she ran out into the garden, cut three lengths of rush, plaited them as she used to do in her childhood and at twelve o'clock had herself driven to the station. She was uplifted by an eager curiosity. She was unable to resist all the amusing and novel sensations which the adventure, proposed by Rénine, promised her. It was really too tempting. The jet necklace, the toque with the autumn leaves, the old woman with the silver rosary: how could she resist their mysterious appeal and how could she refuse this opportunity of showing Rénine what she was capable of doing?

'And then, after all,' she said to herself, laughing, 'he's summoning me to Paris. Now eight o'clock is dangerous to me at a spot three hundred miles from Paris, in that old deserted Château de Halingre, but nowhere else. The only clock that can strike the threatening hour is down there, under lock and key, a prisoner!'

She reached Paris that evening. On the morning of the 5th she went out and bought a jet necklace, which she reduced to seventy-five beads, put on a blue gown and a toque with red leaves and, at four o'clock precisely, entered the church of Saint-Étienne-du-Mont.

Her heart was throbbing violently. This time she was alone; and how acutely she now felt the strength of that support which, from unreflecting fear rather than any reasonable motive, she had thrust aside! She looked around her, almost hoping to see him. But there was no one there . . . no one except an old lady in black, standing beside the holy water basin.

Hortense went up to her. The old lady, who held a silver rosary in her hands, offered her holy water and then began to count the beads of the necklace which Hortense gave her.

She whispered: 'Seventy-five. That's right. Come.'

Without another word, she toddled along under the light of the street-lamps, crossed the Pont des Tournelles to the Île Saint-Louis and went down an empty street leading to a cross-roads, where she stopped in front of an old house with wrought-iron balconies.

'Go in,' she said.

And the old lady went away.

* * *

Hortense now saw a prosperous-looking shop which occupied almost the whole of the ground-floor and whose windows, blazing with electric light, displayed a huddled array of old furniture and anti-quities. She stood there for a few seconds, gazing at it absently. A sign-board bore the words 'The Mercury', together with the name of the owner of the shop, 'Pancaldi'. Higher up, on a projecting cornice which ran on a level with the first floor, a small niche sheltered a terra-cotta Mercury poised on one foot, with wings to his sandals and the caduceus in his hand, who, as Hortense noted, was leaning a little too far forward in the ardour of his flight and ought logically to have lost his balance and taken a header into the street.

'Now!' she said, under her breath.

She turned the handle of the door and walked in.

Despite the ringing of the bells actuated by the opening door, no one came to meet her. The shop seemed to be empty. However, at the extreme end there was a room at the back of the shop and after that another, both crammed with furniture and knick-knacks, many of which looked very valuable. Hortense followed a narrow gangway which twisted and turned between two walls built up of cupboards, cabinets and console-tables, went up two steps and found herself in the last room of all.

A man was sitting at a writing-desk and looking through some account-books. Without turning his head, he said: 'I am at your service, madam . . . Please look round you . . . '

This room contained nothing but articles of a special character which gave it the appearance of some alchemist's laboratory in the middle ages: stuffed owls, skeletons, skulls, copper alembics, astrolabes, and all around, hanging on the walls, amulets of every description, mainly hands of ivory or coral with two fingers point-ing to ward off ill-luck.

'Are you wanting anything in particular, madam?' asked M. Pan-caldi, closing his desk and rising from his chair.

'It's the man,' thought Hortense.

He had in fact an uncommonly pasty complexion. A little forked beard, flecked with grey, lengthened his face, which was surmounted by a bald, pallid forehead, beneath which gleamed a pair of small, prominent, restless, shifty eyes.

Hortense, who had not removed her veil or cloak, replied: 'I want a clasp.'

'They're in this show-case,' he said, leading the way to the con-necting room.

Hortense glanced over the glass case and said: 'No, no, . . . I don't see what I'm looking for. I don't want just any clasp, but a clasp which I lost out of a jewel-case some years ago and which I have to look for here.'

She was astounded to see the commotion displayed on his features. His eyes became haggard.

'Here? . . . I don't think you are in the least likely . . . What sort of clasp is it? . . . '

'A cornelian, mounted in gold filigree . . . of the 1830 period.'

'I don't understand,' he stammered. 'Why do you come to me?'

She now removed her veil and laid aside her cloak.

He stepped back, as though terrified by the sight of her, and whispered: 'The blue gown! . . . The toque! . . . And – can I believe my eyes? – the jet necklace! . . . '

It was perhaps the whip-lash formed of three rushes that excited him most violently. He pointed his finger at it, began to stagger where he stood and ended by beating the air with his arms, like a drowning man, and fainting away in a chair.

Hortense did not move.

'Whatever farce he may play,' Rénine had written, 'have the courage to remain impassive.'

Perhaps he was not playing a farce. Nevertheless she forced herself to be calm and indifferent.

This lasted for a minute or two, after which M. Pancaldi recovered from his swoon, wiped away the perspiration streaming down his forehead and, striving to control himself, resumed, in a trembling voice: 'Why do you apply to me?'

'Because the clasp is in your possession.'

'Who told you that?' he said, without denying the accusation. 'How do you know?'

'I know because it is so. Nobody has told me anything. I came here positive that I should find my clasp and with the immovable determination to take it away with me.'

'But do you know me? Do you know my name?'

'I don't know you. I did not know your name before I read it over your shop. To me you are simply the man who is going to give me back what belongs to me.'

He was greatly agitated. He kept on walking to and fro in a small empty space surrounded by a circle of piled-up furniture, at which he hit out idiotically, at the risk of bringing it down.

Hortense felt that she had the whip hand of him; and, profiting by his confusion, she said, suddenly, in a commanding and threatening tone: 'Where is the thing? You must give it back to me. I insist upon it.'

Pancaldi gave way to a moment of despair. He folded his hands and mumbled a few words of entreaty. Then, defeated and suddenly resigned, he said, more distinctly: 'You insist? . . . '

'I do. You must give it to me.'

'Yes, yes, I must . . . I agree.'

'Speak!' she ordered, more harshly still.

'Speak, no, but write: I will write my secret . . . And that will be the end of me.'

He turned to his desk and feverishly wrote a few lines on a sheet of paper, which he put into an envelope and sealed it.

'See,' he said, 'here's my secret . . . It was my whole life . . . '

And, so saying, he suddenly pressed against his temple a revolver which he had produced from under a pile of papers and fired.

With a quick movement, Hortense struck up his arm. The bullet struck the mirror of a cheval-glass. But Pancaldi collapsed and began to groan, as though he were wounded.

Hortense made a great effort not to lose her composure.

'Rénine warned me,' she reflected. 'The man's a play-actor. He has kept the envelope. He has kept his revolver, I won't be taken in by him.'

Nevertheless, she realized that, despite his apparent calmness, the attempt at suicide and the revolver-shot had completely unnerved her. All her energies were dispersed, like the sticks of a bundle whose string has been cut; and she had a painful impression that the man, who was grovelling at her feet, was in reality slowly getting the better of her.

She sat down, exhausted. As Rénine had foretold, the duel had not lasted longer than a few minutes but it was she who had succumbed, thanks to her feminine nerves and at the very moment when she felt entitled to believe that she had won.

The man Pancaldi was fully aware of this; and, without troubling to invent a transition, he ceased his jeremiads, leapt to his feet, cut a sort of agile caper before Hortense' eyes and cried, in a jeering tone: 'Now we are going to have a little chat; but it would be a nuisance to be at the mercy of the first passing customer, wouldn't it?'

He ran to the street-door, opened it and pulled down the iron shutter which closed the shop. Then, still hopping and skipping, he came back to Hortense.

'Oof! I really thought I was done for! One more effort, madam, and you would have pulled it off. But then I'm such a simple chap! It seemed to me that you had come from the back of beyond, as an emissary of Providence, to call me to account; and, like a fool, I was about to give the thing back . . . Ah, Mlle Hortense – let me call you so: I used to know you by that name – Mlle Hortense, what you lack, to use a vulgar expression, is gut.'

He sat down beside her and, with a malicious look, said, savagely: 'The time has come to speak out. Who contrived this business? Not you; eh? It's not in your style. Then who? . . . I have always been honest in my life, scrupulously honest . . . except once . . . in the matter of that clasp. And, whereas I thought the story was buried and forgotten, here it is suddenly raked up again. Why? That's what I want to know.'

Hortense was no longer even attempting to fight. He was bringing to bear upon her all his virile strength, all his spite, all his fears, all the threats expressed in his furious gestures and on his features, which were both ridiculous and evil.

'Speak, I want to know. If I have a secret foe, let me defend myself against him! Who is he? Who sent you here? Who urged you to take action? Is it a rival incensed by my good luck, who wants in his turn to benefit by the clasp? Speak, can't you, damn it all . . . or, I swear by Heaven, I'll make you! . . . '

She had an idea that he was reaching out for his revolver and stepped back, holding her arms before her, in the hope of escaping.

They thus struggled against each other; and Hortense, who was becoming more and more frightened, not so much of the attack as of her assailant's distorted face, was beginning to scream, when Pancaldi suddenly stood motionless, with his arms before him, his fingers outstretched and his eyes staring above Hortense's head.

'Who's there? How did you get in?' he asked, in a stifled voice.

Hortense did not even need to turn round to feel assured that Rénine was coming to her assistance and that it was his inexplicable appearance that was causing the dealer such dismay. As a matter of fact, a slender figure stole through a heap of easy chairs and sofas: and Rénine came forward with a tranquil step.

'Who are you?' repeated Pancaldi. 'Where do you come from?'

'From up there,' he said, very amiably, pointing to the ceiling.

'From up there?'

'Yes, from the first floor. I have been the tenant of the floor above this for the past three months. I heard a noise just now. Someone was calling out for help. So I came down.'

'But how did you get in here?'

'By the staircase.'

'What staircase?'

'The iron staircase, at the end of the shop. The man who owned it before you had a flat on my floor and used to go up and down by that hidden staircase. You had the door shut off. I opened it.'

'But by what right, sir? It amounts to breaking in.'

'Breaking in is allowed, when there's a fellow-creature to be rescued.'

'Once more, who are you?'

'Prince Rénine . . . and a friend of this lady's,' said Rénine, bending over Hortense and kissing her hand.

Pancaldi seemed to be choking, and mumbled: 'Oh, I understand! . . . You instigated the plot . . . it was you who sent the lady . . . '

'It was, M. Pancaldi, it was!'

'And what are your intentions?'

'My intentions are irreproachable. No violence. Simply a little interview. When that is over, you will hand over what I in my turn have come to fetch.'

'What?'

'The clasp.'

'That, never!' shouted the dealer.

'Don't say no. It's a foregone conclusion.'

'No power on earth, sir, can compel me to do such a thing!'

'Shall we send for your wife? Madame Pancaldi will perhaps realize the position better than you do.'

The idea of no longer being alone with this unexpected adversary seemed to appeal to Pancaldi. There was a bell on the table beside him. He struck it three times.

'Capital!' exclaimed Rénine 'You see, my dear, M. Pancaldi is becoming quite amiable. Not a trace left of the devil broken loose who was going for you just now. No, M. Pancaldi only has to find himself dealing with a man to recover his qualities of courtesy and kindness. A perfect sheep! Which does not mean that things will go quite of themselves. Far from it! There's no more obstinate animal than a sheep . . . '

Right at the end of the shop, between the dealer's writing-desk and the winding staircase, a curtain was raised, admitting a woman who was holding a door open. She might have been thirty years of age. Very simply dressed, she looked, with the apron on her, more like a cook than like the mistress of a household. But she had an attractive face and a pleasing figure.

Hortense, who had followed Rénine, was surprised to recognize her as a maid whom she had had in her service when a girl.

'What! Is that you, Lucienne? Are you Madame Pancaldi?'

The newcomer looked at her, recognized her also and seemed embarrassed. Rénine said to her: 'Your husband and I need your assistance, Madame Pancaldi, to settle a rather complicated matter, a matter in which you played an important part . . . '

She came forward without a word, obviously ill at ease, asking her husband, who did not take his eyes off her.

'What is it? . . . What do they want with me? . . . What is he referring to?'

'It's about the clasp!' Pancaldi whispered, under his breath.

These few words were enough to make Madame Pancaldi realize to the full the seriousness of her position. And she did not try to keep her countenance or to retort with futile protests. She sank into a chair, sighing.

'Oh, that's it! . . . I understand . . . Mlle Hortense has found the track . . . Oh, it's all up with us!'

There was a moment's respite. The struggle between the adversaries had hardly begun, before the husband and wife adopted the attitude of defeated persons whose only hope lay in the victor's clemency. Staring motionless before her, Madame Pancaldi began to cry. Rénine bent over her and said: 'Do you mind if we go over the case from the beginning? We shall then see things more clearly; and I am sure that our interview will lead to a perfectly natural solution . . . This is how things happened: nine years ago, when you were lady's maid to Mlle Hortense in the country, you made the acquaintance of M. Pancaldi, who soon became your lover. You were both of you Corsicans, in other words, you came from a country where superstitions are very strong and where questions of good and bad luck, the evil eye, and spells and charms exert a profound influence over the lives of one and all. Now it was said that your young mistress's clasp had always brought luck to its owners. That was why, in a weak moment prompted by M. Pancaldi, you stole the clasp. Six months afterwards, you became Madame Pancaldi . . . That is your whole story, is it not, told in a few sentences? The whole story of two people who would have remained honest members of society, if they had been able to resist that casual temptation? . . . I need not tell you how you both succeeded in life and how, possessing the talisman, believing its powers and trusting in yourselves, you rose to the first rank of antiquarians. Today, well-off, owning this shop, 'The Mercury', you attribute the success of your undertakings to that clasp. To lose it would to your eyes spell bankruptcy and

poverty. Your whole life has been centred upon it. It is your fetish. It
is the little household god who watches over you and guides your
steps. It is there, somewhere, hidden in this jungle; and no one of
course would ever have suspected anything – for I repeat, you are
decent people, but for this one lapse – if an accident had not led me to
look into your affairs.'

Rénine paused and continued: 'That was two months ago, two
months of minute investigations, which presented no difficulty to me,
because, having discovered your trail, I hired the flat overhead and
was able to use that staircase . . . but, all the same, two months wasted
to a certain extent because I have not yet succeeded. And Heaven
knows how I have ransacked this shop of yours! There is not a piece of
furniture that I have left unsearched, not a plank in the floor that I
have not inspected. All to no purpose. Yes, there was one thing, an
incidental discovery. In a secret recess in your writing-table, Pancaldi,
I turned up a little account-book in which you have set down your
remorse, your uneasiness, your fear of punishment and your dread of
God's wrath . . . It was highly imprudent of you, Pancaldi! People
don't write such confessions! And, above all, they don't leave them
lying about! Be this as it may, I read them and I noted one passage,
which struck me as particularly important and was of use to me in
preparing my plan of campaign: Should she come to me, the woman
whom I robbed, should she come to me as I saw her in her garden,
while Lucienne was taking the clasp; should she appear to me wearing
the blue gown and the toque of red leaves, with the jet necklace and
the whip of three plaited rushes which she was carrying that day;
should she appear to me thus and say: "I have come to claim my
property," then I shall understand that her conduct is inspired from
on high and that I must obey the decree of Providence.' That is what
is written in your book, Pancaldi, and it explains the conduct of the
lady whom you call Mlle Hortense. Acting on my instructions and in
accordance with the setting thought out by yourself, she came to
you, from the back of beyond, to use your own expression. A little
more self-possession on her part; and you know that she would have
won the day. Unfortunately, you are a wonderful actor; your sham
suicide put her out; and you understood that this was not a decree of
Providence, but simply an offensive on the part of your former victim.
I had no choice, therefore, but to intervene. Here I am . . . And now
let's finish the business. Pancaldi, that clasp!'

'No,' said the dealer, who seemed to recover all his energy at the
very thought of restoring the clasp.

'And you, Madame Pancaldi.'

'I don't know where it is,' the wife declared.

'Very well. Then let us come to deeds. Madame Pancaldi, you have a son of seven whom you love with all your heart. This is Thursday and, as on every Thursday, your little boy is to come home alone from his aunt's. Two of my friends are posted on the road by which he returns and, in the absence of instructions to the contrary, will kidnap him as he passes.'

Madame Pancaldi lost her head at once.

'My son! Oh, please, please . . . not that! . . . I swear that I know nothing. My husband would never consent to confide in me.'

Rénine continued: 'Next point. This evening, I shall lodge an information with the public prosecutor. Evidence: the confessions in the account-book. Consequences: action by the police, search of the premises and the rest.'

Pancaldi was silent. The others had a feeling that all these threats did not affect him and that, protected by his fetish, he believed himself to be invulnerable. But his wife fell on her knees at Rénine's feet and stammered: 'No, no . . . I entreat you! . . . It would mean going to prison and I don't want to go! . . . And then my son! . . . Oh, I entreat you! . . . '

Hortense, seized with compassion, took Rénine to one side.

'Poor woman! Let me intercede for her.'

'Set your mind at rest,' he said. 'Nothing is going to happen to her son.'

'But your two friends?'

'Sheer bluff.'

'Your application to the public prosecutor?'

'A mere threat.'

'Then what are you trying to do?'

'To frighten them out of their wits, in the hope of making them drop a remark, a word, which will tell us what we want to know. We've tried every other means. This is the last; and it is a method which, I find, nearly always succeeds. Remember our adventures.'

'But if the word which you expect to hear is not spoken?'

'It must be spoken,' said Rénine, in a low voice. 'We must finish the matter. The hour is at hand.'

His eyes met hers; and she blushed crimson at the thought that the hour to which he was alluding was the eighth and that he had no other object than to finish the matter before that eighth hour struck.

'So you see, on the one hand, what you are risking,' he said to the Pancaldi pair. 'The disappearance of your child . . . and prison: prison for certain, since there is the book with its confessions. And now, on the other hand, here's my offer: twenty thousand francs if you hand over the clasp immediately, this minute. Remember, it isn't worth three louis.'

No reply. Madame Pancaldi was crying.

Rénine resumed, pausing between each proposal.

'I'll double my offer . . . I'll treble it . . . Hang it all, Pancaldi, you're unreasonable! . . . I suppose you want me to make it a round sum? All right: a hundred thousand francs.'

He held out his hand as if there was no doubt that they would give him the clasp.

Madame Pancaldi was the first to yield and did so with a sudden outburst of rage against her husband.

'Well, confess, can't you? . . . Speak up! . . . Where have you hidden it? . . . Look here, you aren't going to be obstinate, what? If you are, it means ruin . . . and poverty . . . And then there's our boy! . . . Speak out, do!'

Hortense whispered: 'Rénine, this is madness; the clasp has no value . . .'

'Never fear,' said Rénine, 'he's not going to accept . . . But look at him . . . How excited he is! Exactly what I wanted . . . Ah, this, you know, is really exciting! . . . To make people lose their heads! To rob them of all control over what they are thinking and saying! . . . And, in the midst of this confusion, in the storm that tosses them to and fro, to catch sight of the tiny spark which will flash forth somewhere or other! . . . Look at him! Look at the fellow! A hundred thousand francs for a valueless pebble . . . if not, prison: it's enough to turn any man's head!'

Pancaldi, in fact, was grey in the face; his lips were trembling and a drop of saliva was trickling from their corners. It was easy to guess the seething turmoil of his whole being, shaken by conflicting emotions, by the clash between greed and fear. Suddenly he burst out; and it was obvious that his words were pouring forth at random, without his knowing in the least what he was saying.

'A hundred thousand francs! Two hundred thousand! Five hundred thousand! A million! Two! A fig for your millions! What's the use of millions? One loses them. They disappear . . . They go . . . There's only one thing that counts: luck. It's on your side or else against you. And luck has been on my side these last nine years. It has never betrayed me; and you expect me to betray it? Why? Out of fear? Prison? My son? Bosh! . . . No harm will come to me so long as I compel luck to work on my behalf. It's my servant, it's my friend. It clings to the clasp. How? How can I tell? It's the cornelian, no doubt . . . There are magic stones, which hold happiness, as others hold fire, or sulphur, or gold . . . '

Rénine kept his eyes fixed upon him, watching for the least word, the least modulation of the voice. The curiosity-dealer was now laughing, with a nervous laugh, while resuming the self-control of a man who feels sure of himself: and he walked up to Rénine with jerky movements that revealed an increasing resolution.

'Millions? My dear sir, I wouldn't have them as a gift. The little bit of stone which I possess is worth much more than that. And the proof of it lies in all the pains which you are at to take it from me. Aha! Months devoted to looking for it, as you yourself confess! Months in which you turned everything topsy-turvy, while I, who suspected nothing, did not even defend myself! Why should I? The little thing defended itself all alone . . . It does not want to be discovered and it shan't be . . . It likes being here . . . It presides over a good, honest business that satisfies it . . . Pancaldi's luck! Why, it's known to all the neighbourhood, among all the dealers! I proclaim it from the house-tops: "I'm a lucky man!" I even made so bold as to take the god of luck, Mercury, as my patron! He too protects me. See, I've got Mercuries all over my shop! Look up there, on that shelf, a whole row of stat- uettes, like the one over the front-door, proofs signed by a great sculptor who went smash and sold them to me . . . Would you like one, my dear sir? It will bring you luck too. Take your pick! A present from Pancaldi, to make up to you for your defeat! Does that suit you?'

He put a stool against the wall, under the shelf, took down a statuette and plumped it into Rénine's arms. And, laughing heartily, growing more and more excited as his enemy seemed to yield ground and to fall back before his spirited attack, he explained: 'Well done! He accepts! And the fact that he accepts shows that we are all agreed! Madame Pancaldi, don't distress yourself. Your son's coming back and nobody's going to prison! Goodbye, Mlle Hortense! Good-day, sir! Hope to see you again! If you want to speak to me at any time, just give three thumps on the ceiling. Goodbye . . . don't forget your present . . . and may Mercury be kind to you! Goodbye, my dear Prince! Goodbye, Mlle Hortense! . . . '

He hustled them to the iron staircase, gripped each of them by the arm in turn and pushed them up to the little door hidden at the top of the stairs.

And the strange thing was that Rénine made no protest. He did not attempt to resist. He allowed himself to be led along like a naughty child that is taken up to bed.

Less than five minutes had elapsed between the moment when he made his offer to Pancaldi and the moment when Pancaldi turned him out of the shop with a statuette in his arms.

* * *

The dining-room and drawing-room of the flat which Rénine had taken on the first floor looked out upon the street. The table in the dining-room was laid for two.

'Forgive me, won't you?' said Rénine, as he opened the door of the drawing-room for Hortense. 'I thought that, whatever happened, I should most likely see you this evening and that we might as well dine together. Don't refuse me this kindness, which will be the last favour granted in our last adventure.'

Hortense did not refuse him. The manner in which the battle had ended was so different from everything that she had seen hitherto that she felt disconcerted. At any rate, why should she refuse, seeing that the terms of the contract had not been fulfilled?

Rénine left the room to give an order to his manservant. Two minutes later, he came back for Hortense. It was then a little past seven.

There were flowers on the table; and the statue of Mercury, Pancaldi's present, stood overtopping them.

'May the god of luck preside over our repast,' said Rénine.

He was full of animation and expressed his great delight at having her sitting opposite him.

'Yes,' he exclaimed, 'I had to resort to powerful means and attract you by the bait of the most fabulous enterprises. You must confess that my letter was jolly smart! The three rushes, the blue gown; simply irresistible! And, when I had thrown in a few puzzles of my own invention, such as the seventy-five beads of the necklace and the old woman with the silver rosary, I knew that you were bound to succumb to the temptation. Don't be angry with me. I wanted to see you and I wanted it to be today. You have come and I thank you.'

He next told her how he had got on the track of the stolen trinket.

'You hoped, didn't you, in laying down that condition, that I shouldn't be able to fulfil it? You made a mistake, my dear. The test, at least at the beginning, was easy enough, because it was based upon an undoubted fact: the talismanic character attributed to the clasp. I had only to hunt about and see whether among the people around you, among your servants, there was ever anyone upon whom that character may have exercised some attraction. Now, on the list of persons which I succeeded in drawing up. I at once noticed the name of Mlle Lucienne, as coming from Corsica. This was my starting-point. The rest was a mere concatenation of events.'

Hortense stared at him in amazement. How was it that he was accepting his defeat with such a careless air and even talking in a tone of triumph, whereas really he had been soundly beaten by Pancaldi and even made to look just a trifle ridiculous?

She could not help letting him feel this; and the fashion in which she did so betrayed a certain disappointment, a certain humiliation.

'Everything is a concatenation of events: very well. But the chain is broken, because, when all is said, though you know the thief, you did not succeed in laying hands upon the stolen clasp.'

The reproach was obvious. Rénine had not accustomed her to failure. And furthermore she was irritated to see how heedlessly he was accepting a blow which, after all, entailed the ruin of any hopes that he might have entertained.

He did not reply. He had filled their two glasses with champagne and was slowly emptying his own, with his eyes fixed on the statuette of Mercury. He turned it about on its pedestal and examined it with the eye of a delighted connoisseur.

'What a beautiful thing is a harmonious line! Colour does not uplift me so much as outline, proportion, symmetry and all the wonderful properties of form. Look at this little statue. Pancaldi's right: it's the work of a great artist. The legs are both slender and muscular; the whole figure gives an impression of buoyancy and speed. It is very well done. There's only one fault, a very slight one: perhaps you've not noticed it?'

'Yes, I have,' said Hortense. 'It struck me the moment I saw the sign, outside. You mean, don't you, a certain lack of balance? The god is leaning over too far on the leg that carries him. He looks as though he were going to pitch forward.'

'That's very clever of you,' said Rénine. 'The fault is almost imperceptible and it needs a trained eye to see it. Really, however, as a matter of logic, the weight of the body ought to have its way and, in accordance with natural laws, the little god ought to take a header.'

After a pause he continued.

'I noticed that flaw on the first day. How was it that I did not draw an inference at once? I was shocked because the artist had sinned against an aesthetic law, whereas I ought to have been shocked because he had overlooked a physical law. As though art and nature were not blended together! And as though the laws of gravity could be disturbed without some fundamental reason!'

'What do you mean?' asked Hortense, puzzled by these reflections, which seemed so far removed from their secret thoughts. 'What do you mean?'

'Oh, nothing!' he said. 'I am only surprised that I didn't understand sooner why Mercury did not plump forward, as he should have done.'

'And what is the reason?'

'The reason? I imagine that Pancaldi, when pulling the statuette about to make it serve his purpose, must have disturbed its balance, but that this balance was restored by something which holds the little god back and which makes up for his really too dangerous posture.'

'Something, you say?'

'Yes, a counterweight.'

Hortense gave a start. She too was beginning to see a little light. She murmured: 'A counterweight? . . . Are you thinking that it might be . . . in the pedestal?'

'Why not?'

'Is that possible? But, if so, how did Pancaldi come to give you this statuette?'

'He never gave me *this* one,' Rénine declared. 'I took this one myself.'

'But where? And when?'

'Just now, while you were in the drawing-room. I got out of that window, which is just over the signboard and beside the niche containing the little god. And I exchanged the two, that is to say, I took the statue which was outside and put the one which Pancaldi gave me in its place.'

'But doesn't that one lean forward?'

'No, no more than the others do, on the shelf in his shop. But Pancaldi is not an artist. A lack of equilibrium does not impress him; he will see nothing wrong; and he will continue to think himself favoured by luck, which is another way of saying that luck will continue to favour him. Meanwhile, here's the statuette, the one used for the sign. Am I to break the pedestal and take your clasp out of the leaden sheath, soldered to the back of the pedestal, which keeps Mercury steady?'

'No, no, there's no need for that,' Hortense hurriedly murmured.

Rénine's intuition, his subtlety, the skill with which he had managed the whole business: to her, for the moment, all these things remained in the background. But she suddenly remembered that the eighth adventure was completed, that Rénine had surmounted every obstacle, that the test had turned to his advantage and that the extreme limit of time fixed for the last of the adventures was not yet reached.

He had the cruelty to call attention to the fact.

'A quarter to eight,' he said.

An oppressive silence fell between them. Both felt its discomfort to such a degree that they hesitated to make the least movement. In order to break it, Rénine jested: 'That worthy M. Pancaldi, how good it was of him to tell me what I wished to know! I knew, however, that by exasperating him, I should end by picking up the missing clue in what he said. It was just as though one were to hand someone a flint and steel and suggest to him that he was to use it. In the end, the spark is obtained. In my case, what produced the spark was the unconscious but inevitable comparison which he drew between the cornelian clasp, the element of luck, and Mercury, the god of luck. That was enough. I understood that this association of ideas arose from his having actually associated the two factors of luck by embodying one in the other, or, to speak more plainly, by hiding the trinket in the statuette. And I at once remembered the Mercury outside the door and its defective poise . . . '

Rénine suddenly interrupted himself. It seemed to him that all his remarks were falling on deaf ears. Hortense had put her hand to her forehead and, thus veiling her eyes, sat motionless and remote.

She was indeed not listening. The end of this particular adventure and the manner in which Rénine had acted on this occasion no longer interested her. What she was thinking of was the complex series of adventures amid which she had been living for the past three months and the wonderful behaviour of the man who had offered her his devotion. She saw, as in a magic picture, the fabulous deeds performed by him, all the good that he had done, the lives saved, the sorrows assuaged, the order restored wherever his masterly will had been brought to bear. Nothing was impossible to him. What he undertook to do he did. Every aim that he set before him was attained in advance. And all this without excessive effort, with the calmness of one who knows his own strength and knows that nothing can resist it.

Then what could she do against him? Why should she defend herself and how? If he demanded that she should yield, would he not know how to make her do so and would this last adventure be any more difficult for him than the others? Supposing that she ran away: did the wide world contain a retreat in which she would be safe from his pursuit? From the first moment of their first meeting, the end was certain, since Rénine had decreed that it should be so.

However, she still cast about for weapons, for protection of some sort; and she said to herself that, though he had fulfilled the eight conditions and restored the cornelian clasp to her before the eighth hour had struck, she was nevertheless protected by the fact that this eighth hour was to strike on the clock of the Château de Halingre and not elsewhere. It was a formal compact. Rénine had said that day, gazing on the lips which he longed to kiss.

'The old brass pendulum will start swinging again; and when, on the fixed date, the clock once more strikes eight, then . . . '

She looked up. He was not moving either, but sat solemnly, patiently waiting.

She was on the point of saying, she was even preparing her words: 'You know, our agreement says it must be the Halingre clock. All the other conditions have been fulfilled . . . but not this one. So I am free, am I not? I am entitled not to keep my promise, which, moreover, I never made, but which in any case falls to the ground? . . . And I am perfectly free . . . released from any scruple of conscience? . . . '

She had not time to speak. At that precise moment, there was a click behind her, like that of a clock about to strike.

A first stroke sounded, then a second, then a third.

Hortense moaned. She had recognized the very sound of the old clock, the Halingre clock, which three months ago, by breaking in a supernatural manner the silence of the deserted château, had set both of them on the road of the eight adventures.

She counted the strokes. The clock struck eight.

'Ah!' she murmured, half swooning and hiding her face in her hands. 'The clock . . . the clock is here . . . the one from over there . . . I recognize its voice . . . '

She said no more. She felt that Rénine had his eyes fixed upon her and this sapped all her energies. Besides, had she been able to recover them, she would have been no better off nor sought to offer him the least resistance, for the reason that she did not wish to resist. All the adventures were over, but one remained to be undertaken, the anticipation of which wiped out the memory of all the rest. It was the adventure of love, the most delightful, the most bewildering, the most adorable of all adventures. She accepted fate's decree, rejoicing in all that might come, because she was in love. She smiled in spite of herself, as she reflected that happiness was again to enter her life at the very moment when her well-beloved was bringing her the cornelian clasp.

The clock struck the hour for the second time.

Hortense raised her eyes to Rénine. She struggled a few seconds longer. But she was like a charmed bird, incapable of any movement of revolt; and at the eighth stroke she fell upon his breast and offered him her lips . . .

THE END